*A Book Of*

# ADVANCED ACCOUNTING

**For Third Year B.Com.
As Per the New Revised Syllabus
Effective from June 2015**

**Dr. Suhas Mahajan**
B.A., M.Com., Ph.D. (Finance)
Associate Professor and Research Guide,
Ness Wadia Research Institute
Pune - 400001.

**Dr. Mahesh Kulkarni**
M.Com., M. Phil., L.L.B., D.T.L., Ph.D. (Management)
Associate Professor and Research Guide,
BYK College of Commerce
Nashik - 422101.

N1742

**Advanced Accounting (T.Y.B.Com.)**  ISBN 978-93-5164-542-9

Third Edition : April 2017
© : Authors




**Published By :**  CPT
**NIRALI PRAKASHAN**
Abhyudaya Pragati, 1312, Shivaji Nagar,
Off J.M. Road, PUNE – 411005
Tel - (020) 25512336/37/39, Fax - (020) 25511379
Email : niralipune@pragationline.com


## ☞ DISTRIBUTION CENTRES

### PUNE

Nirali Prakashan : 119, Budhwar Peth, Jogeshwari Mandir Lane, Pune 411002, Maharashtra
Tel : (020) 2445 2044, 66022708, Fax : (020) 2445 1538
Email : bookorder@pragationline.com, niralilocal@pragationline.com

Nirali Prakashan : S. No. 28/27, Dhyari, Near Pari Company, Pune 411041
Tel : (020) 24690204 Fax : (020) 24690316
Email : dhyari@pragationline.com, bookorder@pragationline.com

### MUMBAI

Nirali Prakashan : 385, S.V.P. Road, Rasdhara Co-op. Hsg. Society Ltd.,
Girgaum, Mumbai 400004, Maharashtra
Tel : (022) 2385 6339 / 2386 9976, Fax : (022) 2386 9976
Email : niralimumbai@pragationline.com

## ☞ DISTRIBUTION BRANCHES

### JALGAON

Nirali Prakashan : 34, V. V. Golani Market, Navi Peth, Jalgaon 425001,
Maharashtra, Tel : (0257) 222 0395, Mob : 94234 91860

### KOLHAPUR

Nirali Prakashan : New Mahadvar Road, Kedar Plaza, 1st Floor Opp. IDBI Bank
Kolhapur 416 012, Maharashtra. Mob : 9850046155

### NAGPUR

Pratibha Book Distributors : Above Maratha Mandir, Shop No. 3, First Floor,
Rani Jhanshi Square, Sitabuldi, Nagpur 440012, Maharashtra
Tel : (0712) 254 7129

### DELHI

Nirali Prakashan : 4593/21, Basement, Aggarwal Lane 15, Ansari Road, Daryaganj
Near Times of India Building, New Delhi  110002
Mob : 08505972553

### BENGALURU

Pragati Book House : House No. 1, Sanjeevappa Lane, Avenue Road Cross,
Opp. Rice Church, Bengaluru – 560002.
Tel : (080) 64513344, 64513355,Mob : 9880582331, 9845021552
Email:bharatsavla@yahoo.com

### CHENNAI

Pragati Books : 9/1, Montieth Road, Behind Taas Mahal, Egmore,
Chennai 600008 Tamil Nadu, Tel : (044) 6518 3535,
Mob : 94440 01782 / 98450 21552 / 98805 82331,
Email : bharatsavla@yahoo.com



niralipune@pragationline.com | www.pragationline.com

Also find us on f www.facebook.com/niralibooks

# Preface ...

There are a number of books on the subject of **Advanced Accounting** available in the learners market but they do not meet the basic requirements of T.Y.B.Com. students. This book is written as per the revised syllabus prescribed for T.Y.B.Com. students from June, 2015. We do hope that this book will definitely help to meet the growing requirements of the students of Accounting from the Faculty of Commerce and Management. This book adopts a modern and novel approach towards the study of Advanced Accounting in view with the specific requirements of the readers and practitioners of this subject.

All the topics included in the syllabus are explained in simple but apt language. Equal stress is also given for necessary accounting theory and wide variety of practical problems. We have taken appropriate care to incorporate basic accounting concepts, accounting standards and tabular representation of classified financial statements. Proper emphasis is also given on charts and graphs to simplify the accounting theories and practices. This book has been designed to serve as a self sufficient text for T.Y.B.Com. students. It will definitely add to our satisfaction if this book would be more useful as a guide for practicing accountants, professional managers, dynamic entrepreneurs and enthusiastic teachers of the subject concern.

We would sincerely like to thank the senior faculty members from various Colleges, Management Institutes and Accounting Association for guiding and constantly encouraging us in our enterprise and the student community who inspired us to write this book.

We are also very thankful to **Shri. Dineshbhai Furia** and **Shri. Jigneshbhai Furia**, **Malik Shaikh, Prasad Chintakindi** and the entire **staff** of **Nirali Prakashan**, Pune for their earnest help in bringing out this book with vigour and accuracy. We have taken maximum efforts to make the text error free. Nevertheless, we do not rule out the possibility of certain shortcomings or misprints still remaining; we will be grateful to the readers if such errors are being pointed out from time to time.

We must concede that this book would never have been written without the support, encouragement and inspiration of our family members, many, many thanks to them.

Any criticism or valuable suggestions for further improvement of this book will be gratefully acknowledged and highly appreciated.

**Dr. Suhas Mahajan**
**Dr. Mahesh Kulkarni**

# Syllabus ...

| Unit No. | Topic and Contents | Number of Lectures |
|---|---|---|
| | **Term I** | |
| 1. | **Accounting Standards and Financial Reporting (Introduction to IFRS)**<br><br>Brief Review of Indian Accounting Standard : AS-3, AS-7, AS-8, AS-12 and AS-15, AS-17 to AS-25 simple practical examples of application nature. | 12 |
| 2. | **Final Accounts of Banking Companies**<br><br>* Introduction of Banking Company - Legal Provisions - Non-Performing Assets (NPA) - Reserve Fund - Acceptance, Endorsements and Other Obligations - Bills for Collection - Rebate on Bills Discounted - Provision for Bad and Doubtful Debts - Preparation of Final Accounts in vertical form as per Banking Regulation Act 1949.<br><br>* Introduction to Core Banking System. | 12 |
| 3. | **Insurance Claim Accounts**<br><br>**A. Claim for Loss of Stock** - Introduction - Procedure for Calculation - Average Clause - Treatment of abnormal items of goods - Under and Overvaluation of Stock.<br><br>**B. Claim for Loss of Profit** - Introduction - Indemnity under policy - Some important terms - Procedure for ascertaining claims.<br><br>**C. Claim for Loss of Fixed Assets** - Introduction - Some important terms - Procedure for ascertaining claims. | 12 |
| 4. | **Final Accounts of Co-operative Societies**<br><br>(a) Co-operative Housing Societies<br><br>(b) Consumer Co-operative Societies<br><br>Meaning - Preparation of an Income and Expenditure Account and Balance Sheet from Receipt and Payment Account and also prepare Receipt and Payment Account from Income and Expenditure Account As per Maharashtra State Co-operative Societies Act. (As per revised Format). | 12 |
| | **Total** | 48 |

| | Term II | |
|---|---|---|
| 5. | **Computerised Accounting Practices**<br><br>A. VAT and VAT Report<br><br>B. Service Tax<br><br>C. Central Value Added Tax (Demonstration and Hands Experience)<br><br>D. Income Tax - Tax Deducted at Source (TDS)<br><br>Including Entries with the help of Accounting Software | 12 |
| 6. | **Branch Accounts**<br><br>Stock and Debtors System : Introduction - Types of Branches - Goods supplied at Cost and Invoice Price. | 12 |
| 7. | **Single Entry System**<br><br>Conversion of Single Entry into Double Entry : Introduction - Preparation of Cash Book - Total Debtor Account - Total Creditor Account - Final Accounts. | 12 |
| 8. | **Analysis of Financial Statements**<br><br>Ratio Analysis :- Meaning - Objectives - Nature of Ratio analysis Problems on Ratio Analysis restricted to the following Ratio only - *Gross Profit Ratio *Net Profit Ratio * Operating Ratio * Stock Turnover Ratio * Debtor Turnover Ratio * Current Ratio * Liquid Ratio Debt to Equity Ratio. | 12 |
| | **Total** | 48 |

*******

# Contents ...



***

# List of Figures, Graphs and Charts ...



***

$$\boxed{\textbf{Term - I}}$$

*Chapter* **1**

# ACCOUNTING STANDARDS AND FINANCIAL REPORTING (INTRODUCTION TO IFRS)

$$\boxed{\textbf{SYNOPSIS}}$$

1.1 Meaning, Objectives and Advantages
1.2 AS-3: Cash Flow Statements (1-4-1997)
1.3 AS-7: Construction Contracts (1-4-1991)
1.4 AS-8: Accounting for Research and Development (1-4-1991)
1.5 AS-12: Accounting for Government Grants (1-4-1994)
1.6 AS-15: Employee Benefits Revised (2005)
1.8 AS-17 : Segment Reporting (1-4-2001)
1.9 AS-18 : Related Party Disclosure (1-4-2001)
1.10 AS-19 : Leases (1-4-2001)
1.11 AS-20 : Earnings Per Share (1-4-2001)
1.12 AS-21 : Consolidated Financial Statements (1-4-2001)
1.13 AS-22 : Accounting for Taxes on Income (1-4-2001)
1.14 AS-23: Accounting for Investments in Associates in Consolidated Financial Statements (1-4-2002)
1.15 AS-24 : Discontinued Operations (8-2-2002)
1.16 AS-25 : Interim Financial Reporting (1-4-2002)
• Questions for Self-Study
• Practical Problems

**Accounting Standards :**

**Accounting** as a 'language of business' communicates the financial performance and position of an enterprise to various interested parties by means of financial statements which have to exhibit a 'true and fair' view of financial results and its state of affairs. Like any other language, accounting has its own complicated set of rules. The **basic conventions or rules used** in preparing financial statements had evolved over many years as a product of the collective experience of practicing accountants. As a result, a wide variety of accounting methods were used by different companies. It was, then, felt that there should be some **standardised set of rules** and **accounting principles** to reduce or eliminate confusing variations in the methods used to prepare financial statements. However, such **accounting rules** should have a reasonable degree of flexibility in view of specific circumstances of an enterprise and also in line with the changes in the economic environment, social needs, legal requirements and technological developments.

## 1.1 MEANING, OBJECTIVES AND ADVANTAGES

The use of the word '**Standard**' in accounting literature is of a recent origin. What is described as 'standard' today, used to be generally known as 'principles' a few years ago. The British introduced the term 'standards' in place of 'principles' when they set up their Accounting Standards Steering Committee at the end of 1969, and the Americans adopted the same term

(1.1)

('standard') in 1973, when the Accounting Principles Board was wound up and the Financial Accounting Standards Board was created. In India, this term has mainly become popular since the formation of **Accounting Standards Board (ASB)** in April 1977 by the Institute of Chartered Accountants of India. In order to suggest rules and criteria of accounting measurements several accounting standard setting bodies were established in developed and developing countries. The setting of accounting standards is a social decision. Standards place restrictions on behaviour and therefore they must be accepted by affected parties.

**Definitions :**

An **Accounting Standard** is a selected set of accounting policies or broad guidelines regarding the principles and methods to be chosen out of several alternatives. Standards conform to applicable laws, customs, usage and business environment. So there is no universal acceptable set of standards.

The term **'Accounting Standard'** may be defined as written statements issued from time to time by institutions of the accounting profession or institutions in which it has sufficient involvement and which are established expressly for this purpose. Such accounting institutions or bodies are currently found in many countries of the world, e.g., Accounting Standards Board (India), Financial Accounting Standards Board (USA), Accounting Standards Board (UK), Accounting Standards Committee (Canada), etc. At the international level, International Accounting Standards Committee (IASC) has been created "to formulate and publish, in the public interest, basic standards to be observed in the presentation of audited accounts and financial statements and to promote their worldwide acceptance and observance."

**A. C. Littleton,** in his book "Structure of Accounting Theory" defines "standard" as, "a **standard** is an agreed upon criteria of what is proper practice in a given situation; a basis for comparison and judgement; a point of departure when variation is justifiable by the circumstances and reported as such. Standards are not designed to confine practise within rigid limits but rather to serve as guideposts to truth, honesty and fair dealing. They are not accidental but intentional in origin; they are expected to be expressive of the deliberately chosen policies of the highest types of businessmen and the most experienced accountants; they direct a high but attainable level of performance, without precluding justifiable departures and variations in the procedures employed."

**R. I. Ticker, comments** in his article 'Corporate Responsibility, Institutional Governance and the Role of Accounting Standards, **Accounting Standards** deal mainly with financial measurements and disclosures used in producing a set of fairly presented financial statements. In this respect, accounting standards can be thought of as a system of measurement disclosure. They also draw the boundaries within which acceptable conduct lies in that and many other respects, they are similar in nature to laws. Accounting standards can thus be seen as a technical response to calls for better financial accounting and reporting; or as a reflection of a society's changing expectations of corporate behaviour and a vehicle in social and political monitoring and control of the enterprise.

**Bromwich** in his book, "The Economics of Accounting Standard Setting" observes, "**Accounting Standards** (are) uniform rules for financial reporting applicable either to all or to a certain class of entity promulgated by what is perceived of as predominantly an element of the accounting community specially created for this purpose. Standard setters can be seen as seeking to prescribe a preferred accounting treatment from the available set of methods for treating one or more accounting problems. Other policy statements by the profession will be referred to as recommendations."

In short, **Accounting Standards** are written documents, policy documents issued by expert accounting body or by Government or other regulatory body covering the aspects of recognition, measurement, treatment, presentation and disclosure of accounting transactions in the financial statement. Accounting Standards in India are issued by the Institute of Chartered Accountants of India (ICAI).

**Objectives :**

The main objective of **Accounting Standards** is to harmonise the diverse accounting policies and practices at present in use in India. However, harmonisation does not mean that accounting standards should become very rigid. Infact, harmonisation of accounting standards do permit flexibility to make the necessary adjustments to suit their purpose.

Objective of **Accounting Standards** is to standardise the diverse accounting policies and practices with a view to eliminate to the extent possible the non-comparability of financial statements and add reliability to the financial statements. The Institute of Chartered Accountants of India, recognising the need to harmonise the diverse accounting policies and practices, constituted an Accounting Standard Board (ASB) on 21st April, 1977.

**Compliance with Accounting Standards issued by ICAI :**

Sub-section (3A) to section 211 of Companies Act, 1956 requires that every Profit and Loss Account and Balance Sheet shall comply with the Accounting Standards. Accounting Standards mean the standard of accounting recommended by the ICAI and prescribed by the Central Government in consultation with the National Advisory Committee on Accounting Standards (NACAs) constituted under section 210A(1) of Companies Act, 1956.

**Auditor's Duties in relation to Accounting Standards :**

Auditors are duty bound while discharging their attest function to ensure that the Accounting Standards issued and made mandatory by the ICAI are implemented. Section 227(3) of Companies Act, 1956 requires the auditor to report whether in his opinion the Profit and Loss Account and Balance Sheet comply with the Accounting Standards referred in Section 211 (3C) of Companies Act, 1956. Auditor's duties in relation to Mandatory Accounting Standards are explained in the following Figure. 1.1.

**Auditor's Duties in relation to Mandatory Accounting Standards**

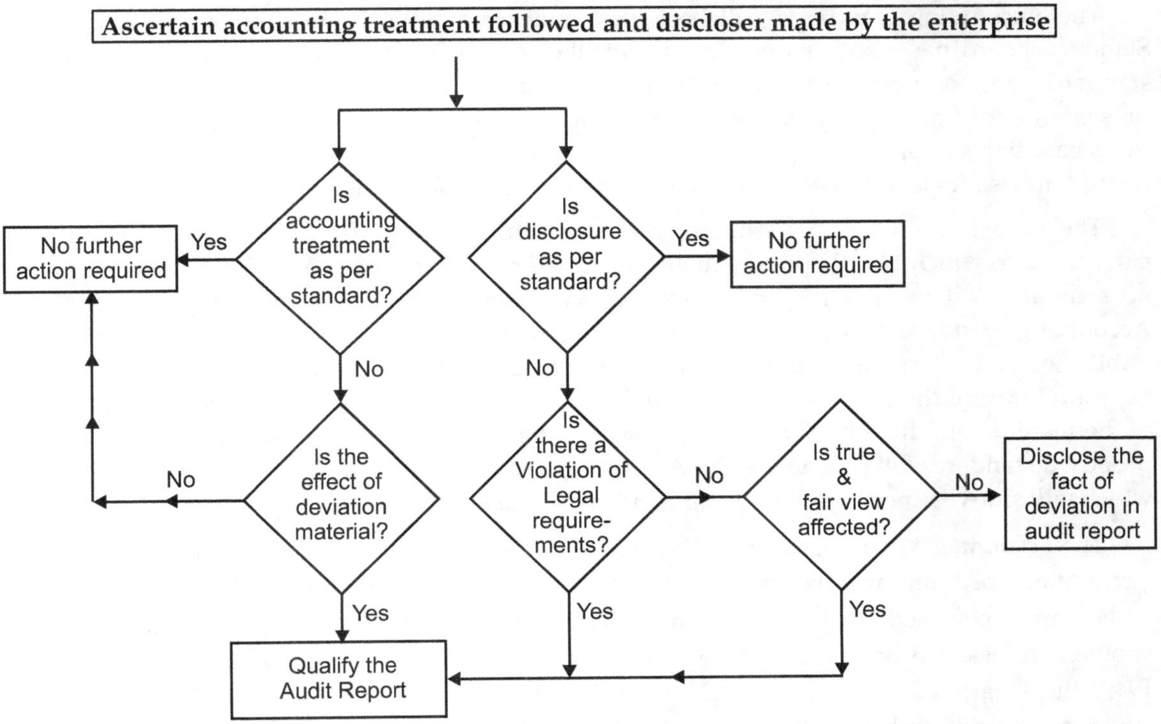


**Fig. 1.1 : Auditor's Duties in Relation to Mandatory Accounting Standards**

**Preface to the statements on "Accounting Standards" in India :**

Recognising the need to harmonise the diverse accounting policies and practises in India and keeping in view the international development in the field of accounting, the Institute of Chartered Accountants of India constituted the **Accounting Standard Board (ASB)** in April 1977. The Accounting Standard Board is entrusted with the following functions :

i)   To formulate accounting standards which may be established by the Council of ICAI in India. While formulating standards, the Accounting Standard Board is required to take into consideration the applicable laws, customs and usages and business environment; it is also required to give due consideration to International Accounting Standards issued by IASC and to integrate them, to the extent possible, in the light of the conditions and practises prevailing in India.

ii)  To propagate the Accounting Standards and persuade the concerned parties to adopt them in the preparation and presentation of financial statements.

iii) To issue guidance notes on the Accounting Standards and give clarifications on issues arising therefrom.

iv)  To review the Accounting Standards at periodical intervals.

The Institute is one of the members of the International Accounting Committee (IASC) and has agreed to support the objectives of IASC. While formulating the accounting standards, Accounting Standard Board will give due consideration to International Accounting Standards issued by IASC and try to integrate them, to the extent possible, in the light of the conditions and practises prevailing in India.

The Accounting Standards will be issued under the authority of the council. Accounting Standard Board has also been entrusted with the responsibility of propagating the accounting standards and of persuading the concerned parties to adopt them in the preparation and presentation of financial settlements. Accounting Standard Board will issue guidance quotes on the accounting standards and give clarifications on issues arising therefrom. Accounting Standard Board will also review the accounting standards at periodic intervals.

The date from which a particular standard will come to effect, as well as the class of enterprises to which it will apply, will also be specified by the Institute. Unless otherwise stated, no standard will have retrospective application. Normally before formulating the standards, Accounting Standard Board will hold discussions with the representatives of the Government, Public Sector Undertakings, Industry and other organisations, for ascertaining their views. An exposure draft of the proposed standard will be prepared and issued for comments by members of the Institute and the public at large. After considering the comments received, the draft of the proposed standard will be finalised by Accounting Standard Board and submitted to the Council which will study it, modify it if necessary and issue it under its own authority.

The accountancy profession in India consists of two main bodies, the Institute of Chartered Accountants of India and the Institute of Cost and Works Accountants of India. Both of these bodies are recognised by the Government. The Institute of Company Secretariats of India is another professional body, its members are generally employed as secretaries of companies. In 1949, the Chartered Accountants Act gave the Institute of Chartered Accountants statutory authority to guide and regulate the work of Chartered Accountants in the country.

The Accounting Standards Board set up in India in 1977, as stated earlier, has undertaken to formulate accounting standards and propagate them among the Indian industries. Although the company's financial reporting in India is influenced greatly by the Indian Companies Acts, the accounting standards established by Accounting Standard Board are likely to find favour among the Indian companies.

It is the responsibility of Accounting Standard Board to educate the Indian companies about the accounting standards, their role in improving financial accounting and reporting, and the procedure followed in developing such standards. The Accounting Standard Board needs to issue a Conceptual Framework on Financial Reporting, in the Indian context, to provide general guidance for solving accounting issues.

**Accounting Standard and Board's Report :**

Section 217 (2AA) (1) of Companies Act, 1956 states that a Director's responsibility statement should include that in the preparation of the annual accounts, the applicable Accounting Standards have been followed alongwith proper explanations relating to the material departure.

**Procedure for issuing Accounting Standards by the Institute of Chartered Accountants of India (ICAI) :**

Broadly, the following procedure will be adopted for formulating Accounting Standards :

Step 1   :   To determine the broad areas in which accounting standards need to be formulated and the priority in regard to the selection thereof.

Step 2   :   To hold a dialogue with the representatives of the Government, public sector undertakings, industry and other organisations for ascertaining their views.

Step 3   :   On the basis of the work of the study groups and the dialogue with the representatives, to prepare and issue the exposure of draft of the proposed standard for comments by members of the Institute and the public at large.

Step 4   :   To finalise the draft of the proposed standard after taking into consideration the comments received.

Step 5   :   To submit the final draft of the proposed standard to the Council of the Institute. This council of the Institute will consider the final draft of the proposed standard, and if found necessary, modify the same in consultation with Accounting Standard Board. The accounting standard on the relevant subject will then be issued under the authority of the Council.

**The draft of the proposed standard will include the following basic points :**

- A Statement of concepts and fundamental accounting principles relating to the Standard.
- Definitions of the terms used in the Standard.
- The manner in which the accounting principles have been applied for formulating the Standard.
- The presentation and disclosure requirements in complying with the standard.
- Class of enterprises to which the Standard will apply.
- Date from which the Standard will be effective.

The adoption and application of Accounting Standards ensures uniformity, comparability and qualitative improvement in the preparation and presentation of financial statements.

The Accounting Standards seek to describe the accounting principles, the valuation techniques and the methods of applying the accounting principles in the preparation and presentation of financial statements so that they may give a true and fair view. The ostensible purpose of the standard setting bodies is to promote the dissemination of timely and useful financial information to investors and certain other parties having an interest in companies financial performance.

**Advantages of Accounting Standards :**

At present, **Accounting Standards** are regarded as a major component in the framework of accounting and reporting practices. Standards exist to help the accounting practitioners to apply those accounting practices regarded as the most suitable for the circumstances covered. Further, they help individual companies and their managements to justify whatever practices they adopt when producing their financial statements. The advantages of establishing accounting standards manifest themselves in different ways, either because they are real effects of those standards, because people perceive certain effects, or because they expect certain effects to follow and modify their behaviour accordingly. The setting of accounting standards has the following advantages :

**i) Reduction in variations :**

Standards reduce to a reasonable extent or eliminate altogether confusing variations in the accounting treatments used to prepare financial statements.

**ii) Disclosure beyond that required by law :**

There are certain areas where important information is not statutorily required to be disclosed. Standards may call for disclosure beyond that required by law.

**iii) Facilitates comparison :**

The application of accounting standards would to a limited extent, facilitate comparison of financial statements of companies situated in different parts of the world and also of different companies situated in the same country. However, it should be noted in this respect that differences in the institutions, traditions and legal systems from one country to another country gives rise to differences in accounting standards practised in different countries.

**iv) Benefits to the Accountants and Auditors :**

Though individual accountant and chartered accountancy firm are concerned with their own reputation, the other accountants and firms misconduct would prove costly since all accountants belong to a class in the eyes of public. While members of a chartered accountancy firm can discipline their fellow partners, it is difficult to monitor the performance of other chartered accountants. For this purpose, the establishment of standard to which all chartered or certified accountants subscribe is useful. Thus, accounting standards are beneficial not only to the business enterprises but also to the accountants and auditors as well.

# BRIEF REVIEW OF INDIAN ACCOUNTING STANDARDS

## 1.2 AS – 3 : CASH FLOW STATEMENTS (1-4-1997)

**Introduction :**

This Standard deals with the financial statement which summarises for a given period the sources and applications of funds of an enterprise. This Standard supersedes Accounting Standard (AS) 3, 'Changes in Financial Position', issued in June 1981. The cash flows are to be classified into three categories, viz. operating activities, investing activities and financing activities.

**Meaning :**

Cash flow statement is an additional information to the user of financial statement. This statement exhibits the flow of incoming and outgoing cash. This statement assesses the ability of the enterprise to generate cash and to utilise the cash. This statement is one of the tools for assessing the liquidity and solvency of the enterprise.

**Applicability :**

This standard applies to the following enterprises :

- Which have a turnover of more than ₹ 50 crores in a preceeding financial year.
- Non-SMC.
- Borrowing more than 10 crores at any time during the accounting period.

**Features :**

Cash Flow Statement explains cash movement under the following three different heads, viz.

i)    Cash flow from **Operating Activities.**

ii)   Cash flow from **Investing Activities.**

iii)  Cash flow from **Financing Activities.**

Sum of these three types of cash flow reflects net increase or decrease of cash and cash equivalents.

- **Cash :**

It consists of cash in hand and demand deposits.

- **Cash Equivalent :**

It consists of short-term highly liquid investment having maturity less than three months, which can be readily converted into cash without decline in its value. In other words, these investments can be converted into cash without any risk.

**i)  Operating Activities :**

They are principal revenue producing activities of the enterprises other than investing and financial activities. Examples of cash flow from operating activities are as follows :

- Cash receipts from the sale of goods and the rendering of services;
- Cash receipts from royalties, fees, commissions and other revenue;
- Cash payments to suppliers for goods and services;
- Cash payments to and on behalf of the employees.

## ii) Investment Activities :

The activities of acquisition and disposal of long-term assets and other investments not included in cash equivalents are investing activities. They include making and collecting loans, acquiring and disposal of debt and equity instruments, property and fixed assets, etc. Examples of cash flow arising from investing activities are :

- Cash payments to acquire fixed assets (including intangibles). These payments include those relating to capitalisation, research and development costs and self-constructed fixed assets;

- Cash receipts from disposal of fixed assets (including intangibles). These payments to acquire shares, warrants or debt instruments of other enterprise and interests in joint ventures (other than payments for those instruments considered be cash equivalents and those held for dealing or trading, purpose);

- Cash receipts from disposal of shares, warrants or debt instruments of other enterprises and interests in joint ventures (other than receipts from those instruments considered to be cash equivalents and those held for dealing or trading purposes).

## iii) Financial Activities :

These are the activities which result in change in size and composition of owners capital and borrowing of the organisation. These include receipts from issuing shares, debentures, bonds, borrowing and payment of borrowing amount, loan, etc.

- Sale of shares.

- Buy back of shares.

- Redemption of preference shares.

- Issue/redemption of debentures.

- Long-term loan/payment thereof.

- Dividend/interest paid.

## Cash Flow from Operating Activities :

It can be derived either from direct method or indirect method :

- **Direct Method :**

In this method, gross receipts and gross payment of cash are disclosed.

- **Indirect Method :**

In this method, profit and loss account is adjusted for the effects of transaction of non-cash nature.

- **Interest :**

## Interest Received :

- From investment, it is in investment activities.

- From short-term investment classified as cash equivalents should be considered as cash inflows.

- On trade advances and operating receivables should be in operating activities.

**Interest Paid :**

- On loans or debts are in financing activities.

- On working capital loan and any other loan taken to finance operating activities are in operating activities.

- **Dividend :**

**Dividend Received :**

- For Financial Enterprises - in operating activities.

- For other than Financial Enterprises - in investing activities.
- *Dividend Paid* - Always classified as financing activities.

**Note :** Cash flow from interest and dividend should be separately disclosed.

**Cash Flow from foreign currency transactions :**

The effect of change in exchange rate in cash and cash equivalents held in foreign currency should be reported as a separate part of the reconciliation of cash and cash equivalents. Unrealised gains and losses arising from changes in foreign exchange rates are not cash flows.

**Extraordinary items :**

The cash flows associated with extraordinary items should be classified as arising from operating, investing or financing activities as appropriate and separately disclosed.

**Treatment of Tax :**

- Cash flow for tax payments or refund should be classified as cash flow from operating activities.

- If cash flow can be specifically identified as cash flow from investment or financing activities, appropriate classification should be made.

**Cash flow relating Investments in associates, subsidiaries and joint venture :**

Enterprises having investments in associates, subsidiaries and joint venture should report in the cash flow statement only cash flow between itself and the investee.

**Reporting cash - flow on net basis :**

In the following cases cash flow should be reported on the net basis (activity wise) :

- Cash receipts and payment on behalf of customers when the cash flows reflect the activities of the customer rather than those of the enterprise (e.g. acceptance and repayment of demand deposits by bank, funds held for customers by investment enterprise); and

- Cash receipts and payments for items in which the turnover is quick, the amounts are large, and the maturities are short (e.g., principal amount relating to credit card customers, the purchase or sale of investment other than short-term borrowing having maturity period of three months and less).

  **Cash flow relating to acquisition or disposal of subsidiaries :**

- Cash flow arising from acquisition and from disposal of subsidiaries or other business units should be presented separately and, classified as investing activities.

- Total purchase or total disposal should be disclosed separately.

- The position of the purchase or disposal consideration discharged by means of cash and cash equivalents should be disclosed.

  **Non-cash transactions :**

- Investing and financing transactions that do not involve the use of cash and cash equivalents should be excluded from a cash flow statement.

- Such transactions should be disclosed in the financial statements. Examples of non-cash transactions are :

    - Acquisition of assets by assuming directly related liabilities.
    - Acquisition of an enterprise by means of issue of shares.
    - Conversion of debt to equity.

  **Disclosure of cash and cash equivalents :**

- An enterprise should disclose the components of cash and cash equivalents and should present a reconciliation of the amount in the cash flow statement with the equivalent items reported in the balance sheet.

- An enterprise should disclose the amount of significant cash and cash equivalent balance held by the enterprises that are not available for use by it with explanation of the Management.

## PRACTICAL EXAMPLES

### Example 1

Andhra Bank received a gross ₹ 1,500 crores demand deposits from customers and customers withdrawn ₹ 1,300 crores of demand deposit during the financial year 2015-2016. How will you classify such receipts and payments in Cash Flow Statement of Bank and the manner of such presentation ?

### Answer

Operating activities, on net basis, ₹ 200 crores inflow.

### Example 2

Barua Ltd. paid an interim dividend of ₹ 1,00,000 during the financial year 2015-2016. Alongwith, they also paid ₹ 10,200 as corporate dividend tax. While preparing cash flow statement for 2015-2016, classified dividend paid as financing activities and corporate dividend Tax paid as cash-flow from operating activities. Do you agree with such treatment ? Answer your question in framework of AS-3.

### Answer

Payment of dividend and corporate dividend tax, both should be shown as financial activities.

### Example 3

Which of the following methods can be followed for preparation and presentation of cash flow statements by the listed companies ?

a)    Indirect method

b)    Direct method

c)    Both – a) and b) are permissible

d)    SEBI has prescribed the presentation format.

**Answer**

a)    Indirect Method.

**Example 4**

Which of the following cash flows are excluded from the cash flows that arise from financing activities ?

a)    Cash receipts from disposal of shares.

b)    Cash receipts from disposal of intangible assets.

c)    Cash payments for future contracts.

d)    All of the above.

**Answer**

**d)**    All of the above, cash flows are excluded.

**Example 5**

Exchange difference on cash or cash equivalent held at the end of the year is ?
a)    Operating activities cash flow.
b)    Financing activities cash flow.
c)    Investing activities cash flow.
d)    Reported as a separate part of reconciliation of cash and cash equivalent.

**Answer**

d)    Reported as a separate part of reconciliation of cash and cash equivalent.

**Example 6**

As per AS-3, what are the important features of Cash Flow Statements ?

**Answer**

Important features of cash flow statements (As per AS-3) are as follows :

i)    According to AS-3, cash flow statement deals with the provisions of information about the historical changes in cash and cash equivalents of an enterprise during the stated period from operating, investing and financing activities.

ii)    Cash flow from operating activities can be reported using either :

- the direct method, in which mostly the classes of gross cash receipts and gross cash payments are disclosed.

- the indirect method, in this net profit or loss is adjusted for the purpose of transactions of non-cash nature.

iii) According to para 42 of AS-3 (Revised), an enterprise must disclose the components of cash and cash equivalents and must present a reconciliation of amounts in its cash flow statement with the equivalent items reported in the balance sheet.

iv) When the cash flow statement is used alongwith the other financial statements, it provides information that enables the user to evaluate the changes in net assets of an enterprise. This statement also enhances the comparability of the operating performances.

v) For companies listed on stock exchanges, compliance of AS-3 is compulsory due to the listing agreement.

**Example 7**

From the following Trading and Profit and Loss Account for the year ended 31st March, 2016 of Comet Ltd., calculate Net Cash Flows from operating activities as per direct method.

**In the books of Comet Ltd.**

Dr.        **Trading and Profit and Loss Account for the year ended 31st March, 2016**        Cr.

| Particulars | ₹ | Particulars | ₹ |
|---|---|---|---|
| To Purchases | | By Sales : | |
| • Cash | 6,00,000 | • Cash | 9,00,000 |
| • Credit | 2,00,000 | • Credit | 1,00,000 |
| To Wages | 1,00,000 | | |
| To Gross Profit C/D | 1,00,000 | | |
| | **10,00,000** | | **10,00,000** |
| To Depreciation on Plant | 20,000 | By Gross Profit B/D | 1,00,000 |
| To Salaries | 50,000 | By Interest Received | 20,000 |
| To Loss on Sale of Plant | 5,000 | By Profit on Sale of long-term | 30,000 |
| To Net Profit C/D | 75,000 | investments | |
| | **1,50,000** | | **1,50,000** |

All credit sales and purchases were made during the last quarter of the financial year. Therefore, no cash was paid to creditors or collected from debtors during the year.

**Answer**

**In the books of Comet Ltd.**
**Statement showing Calculation of Net Cash Flows**
**from Operating Activities as per Direct Method**

| Particulars | | | ₹ | ₹ |
|---|---|---|---|---|
| | Cash Sales | | | 9,00,000 |
| **Add :** | Cash Received from Customers | | | (+)        – |
| | | | | 9,00,000 |
| **Less :** | • Cash Purchases | | 6,00,000 | |
| | • Cash paid to Suppliers | | – | |
| | • Cash Expenses i.e. i) Wages | 1,00,000 | | |
| | ii) Salaries | (+) 50,000 | (+) 1,50,000 | (–) 7,50,000 |
| ∴ | Net Cash Flows from Operating Activities | | | 1,50,000 |

---

**Example 8**

From the following comparative accounting information, calculate the amount of Net Cash Flows from Investing Activities of Dabur Ltd.

| Particulars | 2015 ₹ | 2016 ₹ |
|---|---|---|
| Plant and Machinery | 8,50,000 | 10,00,000 |
| Long Term Investments | 40,000 | 1,00,000 |
| Land at Cost | 2,00,000 | 1,00,000 |

**Additional information :**
- i) Depreciation charged on Plant and Machinery amounted to ₹ 50,000.
- ii) Plant and Machinery with a book value of ₹ 60,000 was sold for ₹ 40,000.
- iii) Land was sold at a profit of ₹ 60,000.
- iv) Investments were not sold at all during the year.

**Answer**

**In the books of Dabur Ltd**
**Statement showing Calculation of Net Cash Flows from Investing Activities**

| Particulars | ₹ | ₹ |
|---|---|---|
| Payment to acquire Plant and Machinery | (2,60,000) | |
| Receipts from sale of Plant and Machinery | 40,000 | |
| Payment to acquire Investments | (60,000) | |
| Receipts from sale of Land [₹ 1,00,000 + ₹ 60,000 (Profit)] | 1,60,000 | |
| ∴ Net Cash Flows from Investing Activities | | (1,20,000) |

**Working Notes :**

1) **Calculation of cash payment made for purchases of new plant and machinery :**

Dr.        **Plant and Machinery Account**        Cr.

| Date 2016 | Particulars | ₹ | Date 2016 | Particulars | ₹ |
|---|---|---|---|---|---|
| Jan. 1 | To Balance B/D | 8,50,000 | Dec. 31 | By Bank | 40,000 |
| Jan. 1 | To Bank* (New purchases i.e. Balancing Figure) | 2,60,000 | Dec. 31 | By Loss on Sale of Plant and Machinery | 20,000 |
| | | | Dec. 31 | By Depreciation | 50,000 |
| | | | Dec. 31 | By Balance C/D | 10,00,000 |
| | | 11,10,000 | | | 11,10,000 |

## 1.3 AS-7 : CONSTRUCTION CONTRACTS (1-4-1991)

**Introduction :**

This Standard deals with accounting for Construction Contracts in financial statements of contractors. The contracts may fall into the category of fixed price contracts or cost plus contracts. The accounting for such contracts may be followed either by the percentage of completion method or completed contract method.

**Objective :**

Accounting for long-term construction contracts involves a question as to when revenue should be recognised and how to measure the revenue in the books of the contractor. As the period of construction contract is long, work of construction starts in one year and is completed in another Year or after 4-5 years or so. Therefore, question arises how the profit or loss of construction contract by a contractor should be determined. There may be following two ways to determine profit or loss :

- **On Year-to-Year basis based on percentage of completion or**
- **On completion of the contract.**

Till the revision of this Accounting Standard both the methods were recommended. However, the revised standard has eliminated the existing option, by adopting only percentage of completion method for recognising the revenue. And this method justifies the accrual system of accounting which is fundamental accounting assumption.

The **percentage of completion method** is justified on the basis of accrual because under most long-term construction contracts both the customer and the contractor obtains enforceable rights, The customer has legal ownership claim to the contractor's work-in-progress and the contractor under most long-term contracts has a right to acquire the customer to make progress payment during the construction period. Substance of business activity is that the continuous sale occurs as the work progresses from the point of view of the contractor.

Therefore, primary objective of this accounting standard is the **allocation of 'contract revenue' and 'contract cost' to the accounting period** in which construction work is performed.

**Applicability :**

This Accounting Standard is applicable in accounting for construction contracts in contractor's financial statements. In other words, the accounting standard does not apply to customer i.e. Contractee.

Accounting Standard would not be applicable for the construction projects undertaken by the enterprise on its own account as a commercial venture in the nature of production activities, e.g. construction or developing housing projects on its own account and selling of these self-constructed residential units or commercial flats to the public etc.

**Meaning :**

As per AS-7, **Construction Contract** is a contract specifically negotiated for the Construction of an asset or combination of assets closely interrelated or interdependent, e.g., contract for construction of bridge, building, dam, road, pipeline etc. This accounting standard further mentions that the following are also included in Construction Contract :

- Contracts for rendering of services which are directly related to the construction of assets, e.g. service of architect, and
- Contract for destruction or restoration of assets and the restoration of the environment following the demolition of assets. e.g. if existing structure or building in a plot of land has to be demolished before a new building as per new design is constructed, the destruction of building is construction contract.

**Types of Construction Contract :**

Construction contracts are of the types viz.

i) Fixed price contracts, ii) Cost plus contracts and iii) Some construction contracts may be a mix of the both.

**i)   Fixed price contract :**

In these contracts, contractor agrees for fixed price of the contract or fixed rate per unit. However, in some cases the contract price is subject to escalation.

**ii)  Cost plus contract :**

In these contracts, contractor is reimbursed the cost as defined plus fixed percentage of fee or profit.

**iii) Combining and segmenting contracts :**

For accounting purpose usually requirement of this accounting standard is applied separately to each contract to calculate profit or loss from the contract but under some circumstances the profit or loss may be calculated in combination of two or more contracts or group of combined contracts. Basically, group of contracts may be combined for accounting purpose because in substance these contracts are part of a single project with an overall profit margin.

**Contract Options :**

A contract may provide for the construction of an additional asset at the option of the customer. Such construction of additional asset should be treated as a separate construction contract, if :

- Asset differs significantly as compared to original contract or
- Price of the additional asset is independent of original contract.

**Calculating the profit or loss of a Construction Contract :**

The profit or loss of construction contract is to be calculated as follows :

Profit or Loss of a Construction Contract = Contract Revenue Less Contract Cost.

**Contract Revenue :**

Usually, Contract Revenue consists of the following :

- Revenue or price agreed as per Contract.
- Revenue arising due to escalation clause.
- **Claims :** It is the amount that contractor's seek to collect from the customer as reimbursement of cost not included in contract price.
- Increase in revenue due to increase in units of output.
- Increase or decrease in revenue due to change or variation in scope of work to be performed.
- Incentive payments to the contractors.
- Decrease in contract revenue due to penalties.

**Measurement of Contract Revenue :**

As per para 31 of AS, the contract revenue and contract cost associated with the construction contract should recognise revenue and expenses, respectively, with reference to stage of completion of the contract activity on the reporting date.

Recognition of revenue and expenses by reference to the stage of completion of a contract is generally referred as the **Percentage of Completion Method.** Under this method, revenue is recognised as revenue in the statement of profit or loss in the accounting period in which the work is performed.

**Determination of Stage of Completion :**

Stage of Completion may be determined in a variety of ways as follows :

**Cost to Cost Method :**

The percentage of completion would be estimated by comparing total cost incurred to date with total cost expected for the entire contract :

$$\text{Percentage of Completion} = \frac{\text{Cost to date}}{\text{Cumulative cost incurred (+) Estimated cost to complete}} \times 100$$

$$\frac{\text{Current Revenue}}{\text{from Contract}} = \frac{\text{Contract}}{\text{Price}} \times \frac{\text{Percentage}}{\text{of completion}} \ (-) \ \frac{\text{Revenue}}{\text{previously recognised}}$$

Completion of physical proportion of the contract work.

**Exclusion from Contract Cost :**

While calculating the contract cost to date as mentioned in above formula, the following contract cost should be excluded :

- Contract cost that relates to future activity on the contract such as cost of materials that have been delivered to a contract site or set aside for use of a contract but not used and applied,
- Payment made to sub-contractors in advance of work performed under the sub-contract.

**Basic principles of recognition of revenue and expenses :**

Basic principles are as under :

- Revenue recognised in the period in which work is performed.
- Expenses recognised in the period in which the work to which expenses relate is performed.

**Conditions for recognising the contract revenue :**

Following conditions must be fulfilled for recognising the contract revenue :
- Total contract revenue can measured reliably.
- It is probable that economic benefits associated with contract will flow to the enterprise/ contractor.
- Total contract cost and cost up to stage of completion is measured reliably.
- Contract cost attributable to contract can in be clearly identified.

**Uncertainty in collection amounts to expenses :**

When an uncertainty arises about the collectability of an amount  already included in contract revenue and already recognised in profit and loss statements, it amounts to expense. This uncollectable amount of which recovery has ceased to be probable is recognised as an expense rather than as an adjustment to contract revenue.

**When outcome of contract cannot be estimated reliable :**

In those circumstances, the revenue should be recognised only to the extent of contract costs incurred of which recovery is probable, thus, no profit is recognised. However, contract cost recovery of which is not probable, is recognised as an expense resulting in loss. But when the uncertainties no longer exist and contract outcome can be reliably estimated, recognition should be done as per this accounting standard.

**Contract Costs :**

Generally, Contract Costs consist of the following :

**Specific costs to contract :**

These costs are as under :
- Site labour cost including supervision.
- Cost of material used in construction.
- Depreciation of plant and equipments used in the contract.
- Cost of moving plant, equipments and materials from contract site.
- Cost of hiring plant.
- Cost of design and technical assistance.
- Estimated cost of rectification and guarantee work including expected warranty cost.
- Claim from third parties.
- Pre-contract cost, if it is probable that contract will be obtained.

These costs should be reduced by incidental income if they are not included in contract revenue, material, disposal of plant and equipment at the end of contract.

**Costs attributable to contract :**

These costs are as under :
- Insurance.
- Cost of design and technical assistance that is not directly related to a specific contract.
- Construction overheads.

Costs specifically chargeable from customers under the terms of contract.

These costs are as under :
- Some general administration costs, for which reimbursement is specified.
- Development cost.
- Reimbursement of any other cost.

**Costs to be excluded :**

Following costs are excluded from contract cost unless specifically chargeable under the terms of contract :
- General administration cost.
- Selling cost.
- Research and development.
- Depreciation cost of idle plant and equipment.
- Cost incurred in securing the contract. Pre-contract cost - if it is not probable that contract will be obtained.

However, costs that relate directly to a contract and which are incurred in securing the contract if they can be separately identified and it is probable that contract will be obtained, such costs are also included in contract cost.

**Provision for Expected Losses :**

When it is probable that total contract cost will exceed total contract revenue, the expected losses should be recognised as an expense irrespective of,

- Whether or not work has commenced.
- Stage of completion of contract.
- The amount of profit on other contracts which are not treated as a single contract.

**Effect of change in estimate in construction contract :**

As the recognition of revenue and expenses in Construction Contract is based on reliable estimate, nevertheless the estimate is bound to vary from one accounting period to another accounting period of the construction contract; the effect of change in estimate of contract revenue or contract cost is accounted as change in accounting estimate as per AS-5.

As per para 21 of AS-5, the change in accounting estimates does not bring the adjustment within the definition of in extraordinary item, or 'prior period items'. Therefore, changed estimates are used to determine the amount of contract revenue and contract expenses recognised in the statement of profit and loss in the period in which the change is made and in subsequent periods.

**Disclosure by Contractor**

An enterprise i.e. contractor should disclose the following policy :

- The method used to determine the stage of completion of contract-in-progress.
- The method used to determine the contract revenue recognised in the period.

**Example of Accounting Policy :**

"Revenue from fixed price construction contract is recognised on the basis of percentage of completion method measured by reference to the percentage of labour hours incurred upto the reporting date to estimated total labour hours of each contract".

In addition to policy disclosure, following disclosures are also required to be made by the enterprise i.e. contractor :

- The amount of contract revenue recognised in the period.
- Contract cost incurred and recognised profit (less recognised losses) up to the reporting period.
- Advances received.
- Gross amount due to customer for contract work [(cost incurred + recognised profit) − (sum of recognised losses + progress billing)].

Gross amount due to customer for contract work.

[(Some of recognised losses + Progress billing) − (Cost incurred + Recognised profit)]

**'Turnover' and AS-7 :**

**Issue :**

AS-7, Construction Contracts (Revised 2002) deals, *inter alia*, with recognition in respect of construction contracts in the financial statements of contractors. It requires recognition of revenue by reference to stage of completion of contract (referred to as 'percentage of completion method'). This method results in reporting of revenue, which can be attributed to the proportion of work completed. Under this method, contract revenue is recognised as revenue in the statement of profit and loss in the accounting period in which the work is performed.

The issue is whether the revenue so recognised in the financial statements of contracts as per the requirements of AS-7 can be considered as 'Turnover'.

**Consensus :**

The amount of contract revenue recognised as revenue in the statement of profit and loss as per the requirements of AS-7 should be considered as 'Turnover'.

## PRACTICAL EXAMPLES

### Example 1

Calculate the **Contract Revenue** of Adarsh Builders from the following details :

(₹ in Crores)

| Particulars | Years | | |
|---|---|---|---|
| | I | II | III |
| • Initial Contract Revenue | 1,000 | 1,000 | 1,000 |
| • Revenue increase due to escalation in II^nd year | – | 200 | – |
| • Claims | – | – | 100 |
| • Incentive Payments | – | – | 150 |
| • Penalties | – | 50 | – |

**Answer**

**In the books of Adarsh Builders**
**Statement showing Calculation of Contract Revenue**

(₹ in Crores)

| Particulars | | Years | | |
|---|---|---|---|---|
| | | I | II | III |
| • Initial Contract Revenue | | 1,000 | 1,000 | 1,000 |
| • Increase in revenue due to escalation | | – | 200 | 200 |
| • Claims | | – | – | 100 |
| • Incentive | | – | – | 150 |
| • Penalties | (+) | – | (50) | (50) |
| ∴ Contract Revenue | | 1,000 | 1,150 | 1,400 |

### Example 2

What conditions must be met for the recognition of contracts revenue for claims ?

**Answer**

For claim revenue to be recognised, the following conditions must be met.
a) the contract must provide a legal basis for the claim.
b) additional costs were caused by unforeseen circumstances.
c) costs are identified.
d) evidence in support of the claims is objective and variable.

### Example 3

How many types of pricing arrangement are typical for long-term contracts ?

**Answer**

The types of pricing, arrangement are,
a) Fixed price
b) Cost plus
c) Mixed of fixed price and cost plus.

### Example 4

How is progress towards completion usually measured under the percentage of completion method ?

**Answer**

Progress towards completion is usually measured by the cost-to-cost method, by survey of work performed, completion of physical proportion of the contract work.

**Example 5**

Which of the following cost should be excluded from the cost of a construction or contract ?
a)   Site labour cost including supervision.
b)   Cost material used in construction.
c)   Depreciation of plant and equipments used in the contract.
d)   Cost incurred in securing the contract, pre-contract cost – if it is not probable that contract will be obtained.

**Answer**

d)   Cost incurred in securing the contract, pre-contract cost if it is not probable that contract will be obtained.

**Example 6**

Contract Revenue consists of –
a)   Revenue arising due to escalation clause.
b)   Decrease in contract revenue due to penalties.
c)   Claims that contractors seek to collect from the customer as reimbursement of cost not included in contract price.
d)   All of the above.

**Answer**

d)   All of the above.

**Eample 7**

Which of the following method is allowed under AS-7 (Revised) for the accounting of Construction Contracts ?
a)   Percentage completion method.
b)   Completed contract method.
c)   Both a) and b).
d)   None of the above.

**Answer**

a)   Percentage Completion Method.

**Example 8**

AS-7 (Revised) is to be applied in accounting construction contracts in the financial statements of the :
a)   Contractor
b)   Contractee
c)   Both (a) and (b)
d)   None of the above.

**Answer**

a)   Contractor.

**Example 9**

On 1st December, 2015 Bhojwani Construction Co. Ltd. undertook a contract to construct a building for ₹ 85,00,000. On 31st March, 2016 the company found that it had already spent ₹ 64,99,000 on the construction. Prudent estimate of the additional cost for completion was ₹ 32,01,000. What is the additional provision for foreseeable loss which must be made in the final accounts for the year ended 31st March, 2016 as per provision of the AS-7 on "Accounting for Construction Contracts" ?

**Answer**

As per para 35 of AS-7, when it is probable that total contract costs will exceed total contract revenue, the expected loss should be recognised as an expense immediately. Para 36 states that the amount of such a loss is determined irrespective of,

    i)    whether or not work has commenced on the contract; and

    ii)   the stage of completion of contract activity; and

    iii)  the amount of profits expected to arise on other contracts, which are not treated as a single construction contract.

Here, in the present case, the contract price is ₹ 85,00,000 whereas the costs incurred and costs to be incurred to complete the contract comes to ₹ 97,00,000 (₹ 64,99,000 + ₹ 32,01,000). Therefore, the probable loss is ₹ 12,00,000 (₹ 97,00,000 – ₹ 85,00,000). As per the requirement of the AS-7, the company should recognise the entire loss of ₹ 12,00,000 in the current accounting year.

**Example 10**

Chetna Builders Limited received a contract for ₹ 10,00,000 which required three years to complete and incurred a total cost of ₹ 8, 10,000. The following information is available in regard to the contract :

| Particulars | Year 1 ₹ | Year 2 ₹ | Year 3 ₹ |
|---|---|---|---|
| Costs incurred to date | 3,00,000 | 7,20,000 | 8,10,000 |
| Estimated costs to be incurred | 6,00,000 | 80,000 | – |
| Progress billing made | 2,00,000 | 7,40,000 | 6,00,000 |
| Cash received | 1,50,000 | 6,00,000 | 2,50,000 |

The company seeks your advice in the presentation of accounts keeping in view the requirements of AS-7.

**Answer**

**In the books of Chetna Builders**
**Statement showing calculation of Estimated Profit**

| Particulars | | Year 1 ₹ | Year 2 ₹ | Year 3 ₹ |
|---|---|---|---|---|
| Contract Price (A) | | 10,00,000 | 10,00,000 | 10,00,000 |
| Contract Cost | | | | |
|    •   incurred | | 3,00,000 | 7,20,000 | 8,10,000 |
|    •   to be incurred | (+) | 6,00,000 | 80,000 | – |
| ∴   Estimated Contract Cost (B) | (–) | 9,00,000 | 8,00,000 | 8,10,000 |
| Estimated Profit (A – B) | | 1,00,000 | 2,00,000 | 1,90,000 |

### Statement showing Calculation of Stage of Completion

| Year 1 | Year 2 | Year 3 |
|---|---|---|
| $\dfrac{₹\,3,00,000}{₹\,9,00,000} \times 100 = 33\,{}^1/_3\%$ | $\dfrac{₹\,7,20,000}{₹\,8,00,000} \times 100 = 90\%$ | $\dfrac{₹\,8,10,000}{₹\,8,10,000} \times 100 = 100\%$ |

### Statement showing Calculation of Revenue and Expenses Recognised in the Financial Statements

| Particulars | | | Year End ₹ | Recognised in Previous Year ₹ | Recognised in Current Year ₹ |
|---|---|---|---|---|---|
| **Year 1 :** | | | | | |
| | Revenue (33 ${}^1/_3$% of ₹ 10,00,000) | | 3,33,333 | – | 3,33,333 |
| **Less :** | Expenses (33 ${}^1/_3$% of ₹ 8,10,000) | (–) | 2,70,000 | – | 2,70,000 |
| | ∴ Profit | | 63,300 | – | 63,333 |
| **Year 2 :** | | | | | |
| | Revenue (90% of ₹ 10,00,000) | | 9,00,000 | 3,33,333 | 5,66,667 |
| **Less :** | Expenses (90% of ₹ 8,10,000) | (–) | 7,29,000 | 2,70,000 | 4,59,000 |
| | ∴ Profit | | 1,71,000 | 63,333 | 1,07,6667 |
| **Year 3 :** | | | | | |
| | Revenue (100% of ₹ 10,00,000) | | 10,00,000 | 9,00,000 | 1,00,000 |
| **Less :** | Expenses (100% of ₹ 8,10,000) | (–) | 8,10,000 | 7,29,000 | 81,000 |
| | ∴ Profit | | **1,90,000** | **1,71,000** | **19,000** |

## 1.4 AS-8 : ACCOUNTING FOR RESEARCH AND DEVELOPMENT (1-4-1991)

This Standard deals with the treatment of costs of research and development in financial statements. This standard, however, does not deal with the accounting implications of the following specialised activities :

i)     research and development activities conducted for others under a contract;

ii)     exploration for oil, gas and mineral deposits; and

iii)     research and development activities of enterprises at the construction stage.

Now, this standard is withdrawn and included in AS-26.

AS-26 : This standard deals with the accounting treatment for intangible assets that are not dealt with specifically in another Accounting Standard. An intangible asset is an indentifiable non-monetary asset, without physical substance, held for use in the production or supply of goods or services, for rental to other's or for administrative purposes. This standard has already been studied in S.Y.B.Com. in 'Corporate Accounting'.

## 1.5 AS-12 : ACCOUNTING FOR GOVERNMENT GRANTS (1-4-1994)

**Introduction :**

This Standard deals with the accounting for Government Grants. **Government Grants** are sometimes called by other names such as subsidies, cash incentives, duty drawbacks, etc. This standard does not deal with : i) the special problems arising in accounting for Government Grants in financial statements reflecting the effects of changing prices or in supplementary information of a similar nature; ii) Government Assistance other than in the form of Government Grants; and iii) Government participation in the ownership of the enterprise.

**Meaning :**

**Government Grants** are assistance by the Government in the form of cash or kind to an enterprise in return for past or future compliance with certain conditions. Government assistance, which cannot be valued reasonably, is excluded from Government Grants. Those transactions with Government, which cannot be distinguished from the normal trading transactions of the enterprise, are not considered as **Government Grants.**

- **Government Grants :**

Are sometimes called as subsidies, cash incentives, etc. Government means Government agencies and similar bodies, whether local, national or international. This statement does not deal with :

**i)  Government Assistance :**

Other than in the form of Government grants i.e., tax holiday in backward area, tax exemption in notified area.

**ii)  Government Participation :**

In the ownership of an enterprise i.e. investment by Government as equity.

**Recognition of Government Grants :**

Government Grants should be recognised when there is reasonable assurance that :

- the enterprise will comply with the conditions attached to them and
- grants will be received.

Only receipt of a grant is not a conclusive evidence that conditions attached to the grant have been or will be fulfilled.

**Kinds of Government Grants :**

Government Grants may be of two types : monetary or non-monetary.

**Non-monetary Government Grants :**

(Grants in form of assets such as Land, Plant and Machinery, etc.).

- If grants are given at concessional rate, then such assets are accounted for at their acquisition cost.
- If grants are given free of cost, then such assets are recorded at nominal value.

- **Monetary Government Grants :**

Grants related to depreciable fixed assets.

There are two accounting treatments :

- Grant is shown as a deduction from the gross value of the assets in arriving at this book value. When the grant equals to the cost of assets, the assets should be shown in the balance sheet at a nominal value.
- Grants are treated as deferred income. The deferred income is recognised in profit and loss account on a systematic and rational basis over the useful lives of assets. Such allocation to income is made over the periods and in proportions in which depreciation on related assets is charged.

**Grants related to Non-Depreciable Fixed Assets :**

- Grant is shown as deduction from the gross value of asset in arriving at its book value. When the grant equals to the cost of assets, the assets should be shown in balance sheet at a nominal value; or
- If the conditions attached to grants are fulfilled (i.e., grants received after fulfilment of the conditions attached to grants), grants are credited to capital reserve account;
- If a condition attached to grants is yet to be fulfilled :
  - Grants are credited to income over the same period over which the cost of meeting such conditions is charged to income.
  - Unapportioned deferred income is disclosed in the Balance Sheet as "Deferred Government Grants.

**Grants related to Revenue :**

- Grants should be recognised in Profit and Loss Account over the period necessary to match them with related costs which they are intended to compensate. Such grants should either be shown as "Other Income" or be deducted from the related expenses.

- If a grant is to be received as a compensation for expenses or losses already incurred or for the purpose of giving immediate financial support, then such grant should be recognised in the profit and loss account of the period in which it becomes receivable as extraordinary item (AS-5).

**Grants in nature of Promoter's Contribution :**

Grants should be credited to capital reserve and it should form a part of the shareholder's fund.

**Refund of Government Grants :**

Government grants become refundable because of non-fulfillment of the conditions attached to that grant. Refund of grants should be accounted for as under :

**Refund of Grants related to revenue :**

- The amount of refund should be adjusted against any unamortised "deferred Government Grants", if any.

- Remaining balance amount of refund should be to Profit and Loss Account as an extraordinary item.

**Refund of Grants related to specific assets :**

Following are the accounting treatments in different conditions :

- When the grant was received, it was deducted from gross value of assets.
    - Refundable amount should he recorded by increasing the book value of the asset.
    - Depreciation on the revised book value should be provided prospectively over the residual useful life of an asset.
- When the grant was received, it was treated as deferred income.
    - Refundable amount should be adjusted with unamortised deferred income.
- When the grant was received it was credited to capital reserves.
    - Refundable amount should be adjusted with the capital reserve.

**Contingency related to Government Grants :**

A contingency relating to Government Grants arising after the grant has been recognised, should be treated in accordance with accounting standard (AS-4).

**Disclosure :**

The following disclosures are appropriate :

- The accounting policy adopted for Government Grants including the methods of presentation in the financial statement.

- The nature and extent of Government Grants recognised in the financial statements including grants of non-monetary assets given at a concessional rate or free of cost.

## PRACTICAL EXAMPLES

### Example 1

How would you treat the following in accounts ?

a)   Subsidy received from the Central Govt. on installation of Anti-Pollution Equipment.

b)   Subsidy received from the Central Govt. for setting up a factory in a backward area.

c)   A 'better performance award' received from the Govt. of India for a plant on the condition that the award amount be spent for plant renovation within two years and unspent portion, if any, be refunded to the Govt. It is expected that renovation would involve 60% to capital expenditure and balance to revenue expenditure.

d)   The Co. acquired assets for ₹ 5,00,00,000 on which they received Govt. Grants of    10%.

e)   The Co. purchased special purpose machinery for ₹ 25,00,000. It received a Central Govt. Grant for 20% of the price. The machine has an effective life of ten years.

### Answer

a)   Amount to be deducted from the cost of Anti-Pollution Equipment.

b)   The amount to be credited to Capital Reserve.

c)   60% of award to be deducted from Capital Expenditure and balance from Revenue Expenditure.

d)   Amount to be deducted from Fixed Assets.

e)   ₹ 5,00,000 deducted from the Cost of Machinery.

### Example 2

Government Grant that becomes refundable should be treated as :

a)   Extraordinary items

b)   Prior period items

c)   Change in accounting estimates

d)   Change in accounting policy

### Answer

a)   Extraordinary items.

### Example 3

AS- 12 does not deal with :

a)   Special problems arising in accounting for Govt. Grants in financial statements reflecting the effects of changing prices or in supplementary information of a similar nature.

b)   Govt. assistance other than in form of Govt. grants.

c)   Govt. participation in the ownership of the enterprise.

d)   All of the above.

### Answer

d)   All of the above.

### Example 4

Govt. Grants should be recognised when :

a)   There is reasonable assurance that the enterprise will comply with the attached conditions.

b)   Such benefits have been earned by the enterprise and it is reasonably certain that the ultimate collection will be made.

c)   Both a) and b) are satisfied.

d)   As soon as grant is received

Answer

c)   Both a) and b) are satisfied.

Example 5

How will you treat the following ?

A Govt. Grant of ₹ 10,00,000 for a new factory has been approved and, although the funds have not been received, the project was completed during the financial year.

Answer

Govt. Grant is accounted for on accrual basis. It should, therefore, be recorded in the books as Govt. Grant Receivable.

Example 6

On 1-4-2015, Atlas Ltd.; Anand purchased machinery for ₹ 10,00,000 with an estimated life of 10 years and no residual value. A Govt. Grant of ₹ 1,50,000 was received relating to this asset one month after purchases. The company follows straight line method of depreciation and makes its accounts up to 31st March each year.

You are required to show the different accounting methods of treating the grant which are acceptable under AS-12 by showing the relevant :

a)   Balance Sheet figures at 31-03-2016.

b)   Profit and Loss Account figures at 31-03-2016.

Answer

Govt. Grants related to specific fixed assets should be treated as under :

To credit the amount of the grant to Profit and Loss Account on a systematic and rational basis over the useful life of the asset by either,

i)   reducing the cost of acquisition of the fixed asset by the amount of the grant; or

ii)  treating the amount of the grant as a deferred credit, a portion of which is transferred to Profit and Loss Account.

It should be noted that both the methods achieve the result of spreading the grant over the useful life of the asset: the grant either reduces the annual charge for depreciation [method i] or results in a credit annually to the Profit and Loss Account [method ii)].

**Method i) Reduce the cost of the acquisition of the fixed asset by the amount of the grant**

**In the books of Atlas Ltd.; Anand**

**Balance Sheet as on 31st March, 2016**

| Liabilities | ₹ | ₹ | Assets | ₹ | ₹ |
|---|---|---|---|---|---|
|  |  |  | Machinery at cost | 10,00,000 | 7,65,000 |
|  |  |  | **Less** : Govt. Grant        (−) | 1,50,000 |  |
|  |  |  |  | 8,50,000 |  |
|  |  |  | **Less** : Provision for Dep.    (−) | 85,000 |  |

| Dr. | Profit and Loss Account for the year ended 31st March 2016 | | | | Cr. |
|---|---|---|---|---|---|
| **Particulars** | ₹ | | **Particulars** | | ₹ |
| To Depreciation of Machinery | 85,000 | | | | |

**Method ii) Treat the grant as a deferred credit, a portion of which is transferred to Profit and Loss Account annually.**

**In the books of Atlas Ltd.; Anand**
**Balance Sheet as on 31ˢᵗ March, 2016**

| Liabilities | ₹ | ₹ | Assets | ₹ | ₹ |
|---|---|---|---|---|---|
| **Deferred Income :** | | | Machinery at cost | 10,00,000 | |
| Govt. Grant | 1,50,000 | | **Less :** Provision for Depreciation | 1,00,000 | *9,00,000 |
| **Less :** Transfer to Profit and | | | | | |
| Loss Account     (–) | 15,000 | *1,35,000 | | | |

* The net effect on net assets is ₹ 7,65,000 (₹ 9,00,000 – ₹ 1,35,000) as in the first method.

| Dr. | | Profit and Loss Account for the year ended 31ˢᵗ March 2016 | | Cr. |
|---|---|---|---|---|
| Particulars | ₹ | Particulars | | ₹ |
| To Depreciation on Machinery | **1,00,000 | By Government Grant | | **15,000 |

**   The net effect is ₹ 85,000 (₹ 1,00,000 – ₹ 15,000) as in the first method.

(**N.B.** : Govt. Grant is allocated to income over the periods and in proportion in which depreciation is charged i.e. 1/10ᵗʰ).

## 1.6 AS-15 : EMPLOYEE BENEFITS (REVISED-2005)

**Introduction :**

This Standard deals with accounting for retirement benefits in the financial statements of employers. For this purpose, the retirement benefits considered may be in the form of provident fund, superannuation or pension, gratuity, leave encashment benefits on retirement, post-retirement health and welfare scheme and any other retirement benefits.

AS-15 has been revised by the Institute of 'Chartered Accountants of India' and is applicable in respect of accounting periods commencing on or after 1ˢᵗ April, 2006. The scope of the accounting standard has been enlarged, to include accounting for short-term employee benefits and termination benefits. Further, the detailed principles for the retirement benefits have also been laid down.

**Applicability :**

AS-15 is made applicable to different types of enterprises as under :

**Level-1 Enterprises :** In its entirety.

**Other than Level-I Enterprises :**

a)   If average number of persons employed during the year is 50 or more :

The accounting standard is applicable to such enterprises except the provision relating to -

- Recognition and measurement of short-term accumulating cornpensated absences in respect of which employees are not entitled to cash payment for unused leave at the time of leaving the service.
- Discounting the amount payable after 12 months of Balance Sheet as regards defined contribution plans and termination benefits.
- Recognition, measurement and disclosure principles in respect of defined benefit plans and other long-term employee benefits plan. However such enterprises should provide and disclose the accrued liability in respect of defined benefit plan and other long-term employee benefit plan as per actuarial valuation based on projected unit credit method and discount rate based on yield on Government bonds.

b) If average number of persons employed during the year is less than 50 :

Such enterprises can determine and provide the liability and expense as regard defined benefit plans and long-term employee benefits by assuming that such benefits are payable to all employees at the end of the accounting year and therefore recognition, measurement and disclosure principles as laid down in this accounting standard in respect of defined benefit plan and long-term employee benefits will not apply to such enterprises.

**Meaning :**

**Employee Benefits** are all forms of consideration given by an enterprise directly to the employee or their spouses, children or other dependants, or to others such as trust, insurance companies in exchange of services rendered by the employees.

*Whether an enterprise is required to provide for employee benefits arising from informal practices :*

If the practice established by an employer as that of a consistent benefit granted either as part of union negotiations or otherwise that clearly established a pattern (e.g., a cost of living adjustment or fixed rupee increase), it could be concluded that an obligation exists and that those additional benefits should be included in the measurement of benefit obligation.

*Who is an Employee ?*

For the purpose of this standard employee includes whole time directors and management personnel. The standard is applicable to all forms of employer-employee relationships. There is no requirement for a formal employer-employee relationship. Several factors need to be considered to determine the nature of relationship.

Generally, **'Outsourcing Contract'** may not meet the definition of employer-employee relationship. However, such contracts need to be carefully examined to distinguish between a "contract of service" and a "contract for services". A **"Contract for Services"** implies a contract for rendering services, e.g. professional or technical services which is subject to limited direction and control whereas a 'contract of service' implies relationship of an employer and employee and the person is obliged to obey orders in the work to be performed and as to its mode and manner of performance.

**Types of Employee Benefits and Overview of their Accounting :**

This standard is applicable to following four types of employees' benefits :

| Sr. No. | Employee Benefits | Overview of Accounting |
|---|---|---|
| i) | **Short-term employee benefits,** such as wages, salaries and social security contributions, paid annual leave and paid sick leave, profit sharing and bonuses (if payable within 12 months and non-monetary benefits) (such as medical care, housing, cars, and free or subsidized goods or service) for current employees. | When an employee has rendered services in exchange for these benefits by debiting to expense. |
| ii) | **Post-employment benefits** such as pensions, other retirement benefits, post-employment life insurance and post-employment medical care. | Such benefits may be of defined contribution plans or defined benefit plans. If covered by defined contribution plans, contribution is recognised as an expense. Contribution due on the date of balance sheet is treated as liability and excess paid is treated as asset. |

| | | |
|---|---|---|
| | | Accounting for defined benefit plans is complex and will be discussed later in this chapter. |
| iii) | **Other long-term employee benefits,** including long-service leave or sabbatical leave, jubilee or other long-service benefits, long-term disability and, if they are payable 12 months or more after the end of the period, profit-sharing, bonuses and deferred compensation. | Legal and constructive obligation under the plan is calculated on actuarial valuation and is recognised as an expense and defined liability (Net of fair value of plan asset) in the balance sheet. |
| iv) | **Termination benefits** including Voluntary Retirement Benefits. | Termination benefits are recognised as an expense immediately. However, where enterprises incur expenditure on termination benefits on or before 31st March, 2009, it may choose to follow the accounting policy of deferring such expenditure over its pay-back period. |

**What Employee Benefits not covered ?**

Benefits in the form of employee share-based payment like stock option are not covered by this standard. Such payment is covered by the guidance note on accounting for employee share-based payments issued by the Institute of Chartered Accountants of India.

**Accounting for Short-term Employee Benefits :**

Short-term employee benefits include items such as,

- Wages, Salaries and social security contribution;
- Short-term compensated absences (such as paid annual leave) where the absences are expected to occur within 12 months after the end of period in which the employees render the related employee services;
- Profit-sharing and bonuses payable within 12 months after the end of the period in which the employees render the related services; and
- Non-monetary benefits (such as medical care, housing, cars and free or subsidies goods or services for current employees).

**Accounting for short-term employee benefits** as classified above is simple as there is no actuarial gain or loss to be recognised, as these are accounted for on undiscounted basis. Basic principles for accounting short-employee benefits are that the undiscounted amount of short-tern employee benefits should be recognised when the employee rendered service.

- It is recognised as an expense unless another Standard such as **AS-10 "Fixed Assets"** requires it to be included in the cost of assets.
- It is recognised as a liability if the amount of short-term benefits exceeds amount actually paid or spent.
- It is recognised as asset (pre/paid expenses) when the amount actually paid exceeds the amount of short-term benefits.

**Short-term Compensated Absences :**

These are of two types, accumulating and non-accumulating. **Accumulating compensated absences** can be carried forward if the current period's entitlement is not used in full. These may be of vesting and non-vesting types. Vesting compensated absence means entitlement of cash payment is not conditional on future employment. In case of vesting type of accumulating, compensated absent employees are entitled to a cash payment when they leave the enterprise. In case of non-vesting, obligation of cash payment does not arise.

Para 11 of AS-15 (revised, 2005) requires to recognise expected cost of accumulating compensated absences (both vesting and non-vesting) when the employee renders service that increases their entitlement to future compensated absences. An enterprise should recognise non-accumulating short compensating absences.

Cost of non-accumulating type of compensated absences is automatically computed if the employees are on the regular pay-roll. In case employees are not in the regular pay-roll, then cost should be computed during their absences in the period in which the absences occur.

Expected cost of accumulating compensated absences is the additional amount that the enterprise has to pay as a result of the unused entitlement that has accumulated at the balance sheet date.

*What is an appropriate measure of cost of compensated absences which can be carried forward for their availament or encashment in future period(s) ?*

When an employee avails the leave at future date the cost of leave would be the compensation and other benefits which the employee would be paid for the period of his absence. In some enterprises the amount payable to an employee on encashment would not be the same as the compensation and other benefits the employee would be paid in case the leave is availed. For instance, an enterprise could have a practise of paying only basic wage when leave is encashed whereas the employee would be entitled to basic wage, allowances and other benefits when the leave is availed. Such situation would require estimation of additional amount the enterprise expects to pay.

AS-15 also focuses on the following important points :
- Profit sharing and Bonus Plan.
- Post Employment Benefits.
- Defined Contribution Plans.
- Post Employment Benefits – Defined Benefit Plan.
- Other Long-term Employee Benefits.
- Announcement of ICAI.
- Termination Benefits.
- Recognition of Actuarial Gains and Losses.
- Accounting for Employee Share-based Payments.

## 1.8 AS-17 : SEGMENT REPORTING (1-4-2001)

**Introduction :**

This Standard applies to companies which have an annual turnover of ₹ 50 crores or more. This standard requires that the accounting information should be reported on segment basis. The segments may be based on products, services, geographical area, etc. It helps the user of financial statements to understand the performance of the enterprise segment-wise.

**Meaning :**

An enterprise deals in multiple products or services and operates in different geographical areas. Multiple products or services and its operations in different geographical areas are exposed to different risks and returns. Information about multiple products or services and its operation in different geographical areas is called **Segment Information.** Such information is used to assess the risk and return of multiple products or services and its operation in different geographical areas. Disclosure of such information is called **Segment Reporting.**

**Objectives :**

**Segment Reporting** helps users of financial statements in achieving the following **objectives** :

i)    to better understand the performance of the enterprise,

ii)    to better assess the risks and returns of the enterprises and

iii)    to make more informed judgements about the enterprises as a whole.

**Types of Segment :**

There are two types of Segments :

**i)    Business Segment :**

Segment is made on the basis of products or services, which are exposed to different risks and returns. A business segment is a component of an enterprise which satisfies the following conditions :

- It is a distinguishable component of an enterprise,
- It is engaged in providing an individual product or service or group of related products or services, and
- It is subject to risks and returns that are different from those of other business segments.

Factors that should be considered in determining whether products or services are related includes,

- The nature of products or services,
- The nature of the production processes,
- The methods used to distribute the products or provide the services; and
- If applicable, the nature of the regulatory environment, i.e. banking, insurance or public utilities.

**ii)  Geographical Segment :**

Segment is made on the basis of its operation in different geographical areas, which are exposed to different risks and returns. A geographical segment is a component of an enterprise, which satisfies the following conditions :

- It is a distinguishable component of an enterprise;
- It is engaged in providing products or services within a particular economic environment. The risks and returns of an enterprise are influenced both by the geographical location of its operations (where its products are produced or where its services rendering activities are based) and also by the location of its customer's (where its products are sold or services are rendered. The definition allows geographical segment to be based on either :
    - the location of production or service facilities and other assets of all enterprise; or
    - the location of its customers.

In the process of identifying the predominant source of risk and returns of the company, internal organisation and management structure of a company and system of internal reporting to Board of Directors and chief executive officer provides the best evidence of the predominant source of risks and returns of the company.

So, the reportable segment may be either a Business Segment or a Geographical Segment.

**Notable terms :**

**a)    Enterprise Revenue :**

**Enterprise Revenue** is a revenue from sales to external customers as reported in the statement of profit or loss.

**b) Segment Revenue :**

Segment Revenue is the aggregate of :

- the portion of enterprise revenue that is directly attributable to a segment,
- the relevant portion of enterprise revenue that can be allocated on a reasonable basis to a segment, and
- revenue from transactions with other segments of an enterprise.

**Segment Revenue** does not include :

i) Extraordinary items.

ii) Interest or dividend income including interest earned on advances or loans to other segments; and

iii) Gains on sales of investments or on extinguishments of debt.

However, segment revenue shall include items in ii) and iii) above if, two operations of the segment are primarily of a financial nature.

**c) Segment Expenses :**

**Segment Expense** is the aggregate of,

- The expenses resulting from the operating activities of a segment that is directly attributable to the segment,
- The relevant portion of enterprise expense that can be allocated on reasonable basis to the segment,
- Expenses relating to the transactions with other segments of the enterprise,
- Costs sometimes incurred at the enterprise level on behalf of a segment are part of segment expenses if :
  - they relate to the operating activities of the segment, and
  - they can be directly attributed or allocated to the segment on a reasonable basis.

**Segment Expense** does not include :

i) Extraordinary items.

ii) Interest expenses, including interest incurred on advances or loans from other segment, unless the operations of the segment are primarily of a financial nature;

iii) Losses on sales of investments or losses on extinguishments of debt unless the operations of the segment are primarily of a financial nature;

iv) Income-tax expense; and

v) General administrative expenses, head office expenses and other expenses that arise at the enterprise level and relate to the enterprise as a whole.

**d) Segment Result :**

**Segment Result** is segment revenue less segment expenses (it is segment profit or loss).

**e) Segment Assets :**

i) Segment Assets are those operating assets that are :

- Employed by a segment in its operating activities, and
- Directly attributable to the segment or can be allocated to the segment on a reasonable basis (i.e., Current Assets Tangible and Intangible Fixed Assets).

ii) If the segment result of a segment includes interest or dividend income, its segment assets include the related receivables, loans, investments or other interest or dividend generating assets.

iii) Segment assets do not include :

- Income-tax assets
- Assets used for general enterprise or head office purpose.

iv) Segment assets are determined after deducting related allowances/provisions that arc reported as direct offsets in the balance sheet of the enterprise e.g. fixed assets less depreciation provision or debtors less provision for doubtful debts.

v) Segment assets include,

- Operating assets shared by two or more segments if a reasonable basis for allocation exists,

- Goodwill that is directly attributable to a segment or that can be allocated to a segment on a reasonable basis.

vi) If segment assets have been revalued subsequent to acquisition, then they will be measured on the revalued amounts.

**f) Segment Liabilities :**

i) Segment Liabilities are,

- Operating liabilities,

- That result from the operating activities of a segment,

- That either is directly attributable to the segment or can be allocated to the segment on a reasonable basis (i.e. trade and other payables, accrued liabilities, customer advances, product warranty provisions, and other claims relating to the provision of goods and services).

ii) If the segment result of a segment includes interest expense, its segment liabilities include the related interest bearing liabilities.

iii) Segment liabilities do not include :

- Income-tax liabilities.

- Borrowing and other liabilities that are incurred for financing operating purposes.

iv) The liabilities of segments whose operations are not primarily of a financial nature do not include borrowings and similar liabilities because segment result represents an operating rather than a net of financing, profit or loss. Further, because debt is often issued at the head office level on an enterprise wide basis, it is often not possible to directly attribute, or reasonably allocate, the interest bearing liabilities to segments.

**Identification of Reportable Segments (Sub-Segments) :**

Reportable Segment is a business segment or a geographical segment identified on the basis of their definitions for which segment information is required to be disclosed by the statement.

Business segment or geographical segment which has been identified as reportable segment shall be further divided to include sub-segments based on the following conditions

- Segment Revenue from sales to external customers and internal transfer is 10% or more than total external and internal revenue of all segments.

or

- 10% or more of segment result.

  (Segment result means : if some segments are in loss then total loss of all loss-making segments or if some segments are in profit, total profit of all profit-making segments. Whichever is higher i.e. total profit or total loss figure in absolute terms).

or

- Segment asset is 10% or more than total assets of all segments.

- All the above three criteria must be applied first and –

  - Further, Management may at its discretion choose any segment as reportable segment even if such segment does not fulfil the criteria stated above.

  - Ensure whether at least 75% of total *external revenue* should be in the reportable segments.

  - If 75% of total external revenue is not in the reportable segments, then additional reportable segments should be identified ignoring 10% threshold limits until at least 75% of total external revenue is included in reportable segments.

(**Note** : Any segment, which was reportable segment in the previous year on the fulfilment of 10% threshold limit, should be reportable segment during current year even if 10% threshold limit in current year is not fulfilled.

Reportable Segments are classified in following two parts for the purpose of disclosure :

i)    Primacy Reportable Segment.

ii)   Secondary Reportable Segment.

**Basis of Classification :**

Following are the methods or conditions to identify the primary reportable segment or secondary reportable segments.

**Disclosure :**

The **disclosure requirements of primary segments** are as under :

- Revenue from external customers.

- Revenue from transactions with other segments.

- Segment result.

- Cost to acquire tangible and intangible fixed assets.

- Depreciation and amortisation expenses.

- Carrying amount of segment assets.

- Segment liabilities.

- Non-cash expenses other than depreciation and amortisation.

- Reconciliation of revenue, result, assets and liabilities.

**Disclosure of Segment Information (ASI-20) :**

**Issue :**

1.  Whether an enterprise, which has neither more than one business segment nor more than one geographical segment, is required to disclose segment information as per AS-17.

**Consensus :**

2.  In case, by applying the definitions of 'business segment' and 'geographical segment', contained in AS-17, it is concluded that there is neither more than one business segment nor more than one geographical segment, segment information as per AS-17 is not required to be disclosed. However, the fact that there is only one 'business segment' and 'geographical segment' should be disclosed by way of note.

## PRACTICAL EXAMPLES

### Example 1

Define a "Business Segment" and a 'Geographical Segment' as per AS-17.

### Answer

**i) Business Segment :**

A **business segment** is a notable part of an enterprise that is involved in providing an individual product or services or a group of related product or services and that is subject to risks and return which are totally different from those of other business segments. Points which must be considered in determining whether products or services are related include :

- nature of the products and services;
- the type or class of customers for the products or services;
- nature of the production processes;
- the method used to distribute the products or provide the services, and
- if allowed to use, the nature of the regulatory environment.

**ii) Geographical Segment :**

It is also one of the notable part of an enterprise, which is engaged in providing product or services within a particular economic environment and that is subject to risks and returns that are different from these components operating in other economic environments.

Point which must be considered in identifying geographical segments are :

- similarity of economic and political conditions.
- proximity of operations.
- exchange control regulations.
- relationship between operations in different geographical areas.
- special risks associated with an operation in a particular area.
- the underlying currency risks.

### Example 2

Atlas Ltd., had total turnover of ₹ 60 crores including interdivision transfer of 14 crores Whether Atlas Ltd. is liable to give segment reporting as per AS-17 ?

### Answer

**No.**

### Example 3

What are Segment Liabilities ?

### Answer

**Segment Liabilities** are those operating liabilities that result from the operating activities of a segment and that either are directly attributable or reasonably allocable to a segment. If the result of a segment includes interest expense (in the case of segments which are primarily of a financial nature), its segment liabilities include the related interest-bearing liabilities. Segment liabilities do not include income-tax liabilities. Liabilities that are jointly owned by two or more segments should be allocated to segments if, and only if, their related revenue impact also are allocated to those segments. Examples of segment liabilities include trade and other payables, accrued liabilities, customer advances, product warranty provisions, and other claims relating to the provisions of goods and services.

## Example 4

What is **'Segment Expense"** ?

## Answer

**Segment Expense** is one that is directly attributable and that can be allocated on a reasonable basis and includes transactions with other segments of the same enterprise. It excludes the following :

- Extraordinary items (defined under AS-5);

- Interest, including interest incurred on advances or loans from other segments, unless the operations of the segment are primarily of a financial nature;

- Losses on sale of investments or losses on extinguishment of debt unless the operations of the segment are primarily of a financial nature;

- Income tax expenses; and

- General administrative expenses; head office expenses and other expenses that arise at the enterprise level and relate to the enterprise as a whole. However, costs are sometimes incurred at the enterprise level on behalf of a segment. Such costs are segment expenses if they relate to segment operating activities and if they can be directly attributed or reasonably allocated to the segment.

## Example 5

Arvind Mills Ltd., Anand has three divisions A, B and C. Details of their turnover, results and net assets are given below.

**(in ₹ '000)**

| Division A | ₹ | Division B | ₹ | Division C | ₹ |
|---|---|---|---|---|---|
| • Sales to B | 3,050 | • Sales to C | 30 | • Export Sales to | |
| • Other Sales (Home) | 60 | • Export Order to | | America | 180 |
| Export Sales)    (+) | 4,090 | Europe    (+) | 200 | (+) | |
| ∴ Total | **7,200** | ∴ Total | **230** | ∴ Total | **180** |

| Particulars | Head Office | Divisions | | |
|---|---|---|---|---|
| | | A | B | C |
| | ₹ | ₹ | ₹ | ₹ |
| Operating Profit or (Loss) before Tax | – | 160 | 20 | (8) |
| Re-allocated Cost from Head Office | – | 48 | 24 | 24 |
| Interest Costs | – | 4 | 5 | 1 |
| Fixed Assets | 50 | 200 | 40 | 120 |
| Net Current Assets | 48 | 120 | 40 | 90 |
| Long-term Liabilities | 38 | 20 | 10 | 120 |

Prepare a Segmental Report for Arvind Mills Ltd., Anand.

**Answer**

### In the books of Arvind Mills Ltd., Anand
#### Segment Report
(in ₹ '000)

| | Particulars | A ₹ | B ₹ | C ₹ | Inter Segment Eliminations ₹ | Consolidated Total ₹ |
|---|---|---|---|---|---|---|
| i) | **Sales Revenue :** | | | | | |
| | • Domestic | 60 | – | – | – | 60 |
| | • Export | 4,090 | 200 | 180 | – | 4,470 |
| | • Inter-segment Sales (+) | 3,050 | 30 | – | 3,080 | – |
| | ∴ Total Sales Revenue | 7,200 | 230 | 180 | 3,080 | 4,530 |
| ii) | **Results :** | | | | | |
| | • Segment Result | 160 | 20 | (8) | – | 172 |
| | • Head Office Expenses | – | – | – | – | (96) |
| | • Operating Profit | | | | | 76 |
| | • Interest Costs | | | | | (10) |
| | • Profit Before Tax | | | | | 66 |
| iii) | **Other Information :** | | | | | |
| | • Fixed Assets | 200 | 40 | 120 | – | 360 |
| | • Net Current Assets | 120 | 40 | 90 | – | 250 |
| | • Unallocated Corporate Assets | – | – | – | – | 98 |
| | • Long-term Segment Liabilities | 20 | 10 | 120 | – | 150 |
| | • Unallocated Corporate Liabilities | – | – | – | – | 38 |

#### Statement showing Sales Revenue by Geographical Market
(₹ '000)

| Domestic Sales ₹ | Export Sales (Division A) ₹ | Export to Europe ₹ | Export to America ₹ | Consolidated Total ₹ |
|---|---|---|---|---|
| 60 | 4,090 | 200 | 180 | 4,530 |

## 1.9 AS-18 : RELATED PARTY DISCLOSURE (1-4-2001)

**Introduction :**

This Standard requires certain disclosures which must be made for transactions between the enterprise and the related parties. The standard reorganised related party as an enterprise which has a common control with reporting enterprise, associate or joint venture of reporting enterprise, individual having direct or indirect interest in the voting power of reporting enterprise, key management personnel, and enterprise over which any person having direct or indirect interest in voting power or key management personnel is able to exercise significance influence.

**Objectives :**

Sometimes, business transactions between related parties lose the features, and characters of the arms length transactions. Related party relationship affects the volume and decision of business of one enterprise for the benefit of the other enterprise. Hence, disclosure of related transaction is essential for proper understanding of financial performance and financial position of an enterprise.

**Related Party :**

A **related party** is essentially all party that controls or can significantly influence the management or operating policies of the company during the reporting period AS-18, only deals with the following related party relationship :

- Enterprises that directly or indirectly through one or more intermediaries, control, or are controlled by, or are under common control with the reporting enterprise (this includes holding companies, subsidiaries and fellow subsidiaries);
- Associates and joint ventures of the reporting enterprise and the investing party or venture in respect of which the reporting enterprise is an associate or a joint venture;
- Individuals owing, directly or indirectly, an interest in the voting power of the reporting enterprise that gives them control or significant influence over the enterprise and relatives of any such individual. "Relative" means the spouse, son, daughter, brother, sister, father and mother who may be expected to influence, or be influenced by that individual in his/her dealings with the reporting enterprise.
- Key management personnel and relatives of such personnel are those persons who have authority and responsibility for planning, directing and controlling the activities of the reporting enterprise;

Enterprise over which individual or key management personnel described as above is able to exercise significant influence. This includes enterprises owned by directors or major shareholders of the reporting enterprise.

**What should be disclosed ?**

According to this accounting standard, following facts should be disclosed :

- Related party relationship.
- Transactions between a reporting enterprise and its related parties.

**Classification of Related Party**

The concept and definition of related parties is based on the following basis :

**i)  Control Concept :**

One party has the ability to control the other party in the following ways :

- Control by ownership (directly or indirectly) more than 50% of voting Power of an enterprise.
- Control over composition of board of directors or other governing body.
- Control of substantial interest in the voting power and power to direct the financial or operating policies of the enterprise - for example associate and joint venture companies.

**ii)  Significant Influence :**

Significant influence can be exercised in many ways. e.g.

- By representation of the Board of directors
- Participation in policy-making process.
- Material inter-company transactions.
- Inter-change of managerial personnel.
- Dependence on technical information.

**Exceptions of Related Party :**

Following relationships will not be deemed as related party :

- Two companies have a director in common but director is not able to influence the mutual dealing between the companies.
- A single customer or supplier or franchiser or distributor or general agent with whom enterprises transactions are in significant volume.

- Providers of finance.
- Trade union.
- Government departments and agencies.
- State controlled enterprises as regards related party relationship with other State controlled enterprises.

**Related Party Transactions :**

It means a transfer of resource or obligations between related parties regardless of whether or not a price is charged. Examples of related party transactions are as under :

- Purchase or sales of goods (finished or unfinished).
- Purchase or sales of fixed assets.
- Rendering or receiving of services.
- Leasing or hire purchase arrangements.
- Transfer of research and development.
- License agreements.
- Finance (including loan and equity contributions).
- Guarantees and collaterals.
- Management contracts including for deputation of employees.

**Disclosure :**

For the purpose of disclosure related parties relationship can be categorised as under :

When the existence of relationship is due to the concept of the control even when there are no transactions between the related parties, still the following disclosure is needed :

- Name of the related party should be disclosed and
- Nature of the related party relationship should be disclosed.

When the existence of relationship is due to significant influence, then no disclosure is required if there are no transactions during the year between related parties.

There are related party transaction in which following details should be disclosed in both the cases whether relationship is of control or of influence :

- Name of the related party.
- Description of relationship.
- Description of the nature of transaction.
- Volume of the transactions either as an amount  or as an appropriate proportion.
- Any other element of the transactions, which is essential for understanding the financial statements.
- Amount or appropriate proportion of outstanding items and provision for doubtful debts.
- Amount written off or written back in the period in respect of debts due from related party.

This disclosure is not applicable in a case where providing such disclosures would conflict with the reporter's duties of confidentiality as specifically required.

Disclosure is a must for the related parties even if the transactions are arms length transactions or transactions are not influenced by the relationship suggested disclosures format is as follows :

**Suggested Disclosures Format :**

| | Transactions | Holding Company | Subsidiaries | Fellow Subsidiaries | Associates | Key Management Personnel | Relatives of Management Personnel | Total |
|---|---|---|---|---|---|---|---|---|
| i) | Purchase of goods | | | | | | | |
| ii) | Sale of goods | | | | | | | |
| iii) | Purchase of Fixed Assets | | | | | | | |
| iv) | Sale of Fixed Assets | | | | | | | |
| v) | Rendering of Services | | | | | | | |
| vi) | Receiving of Services | | | | | | | |
| vii) | Agency Arrangements | | | | | | | |
| viii) | Leasing or hire purchase Arrangements | | | | | | | |
| ix) | Licence Agreements | | | | | | | |
| x) | Finance (including loans and equity contributions in cash or in kind) | | | | | | | |
| xi) | Guarantees and collaterals | | | | | | | |
| xii) | Management contracts including for deputation of employees | | | | | | | |

**Meaning of similar nature or type of related party (AS-18) :**

**Issues :**

1) Para 23 of AS-18 requires certain disclosures in respect of transactions between related parties. Para 26 of AS-18, *inter alia*, provides that items of a similar nature may be disclosed in aggregate by type of related party. The issue is as to what is the meaning of related party for this purpose.

2) Para 27 of AS-18 provides that "Disclosure of details of Particular transactions with individual related parties would frequently be too voluminous to be easily understood. Accordingly, items of a similar nature may be disclosed in aggregate by type of related party. However, this is not done in such a way as to obscure the importance of significant transactions. Hence, purchases or sales of goods are not aggregated with purchases or sales of fixed assets. Nor a material related party transaction with an individual party is clubbed in an aggregated disclosure" (emphasis added). The issue is as to how the test of the materiality should be applied for this purpose.

**Consensus :**

3)    The type of related party for the purpose of aggregation of items of a similar nature should be construed to mean the related party relationships given in Para 3 of AS-18. The manner of disclosure required by Para 23 of AS-18, read with Para 26 thereof, in accordance with the above requirement is illustrated in suggested disclosure format as in para 18.7.

4)    Materiality primarily depends on the facts and circumstances of each case. In deciding whether an item or an aggregate of items is material, the nature and the size of the item(s) are evaluated together. Depending on the circumstances, either the nature or the size of the item could be the determining factor. As regards size, for the purpose of applying the test of materiality as per Para 27 of AS-18, ordinarily a related party transaction, the amount of which is in excess of 10% of the total related party transactions of the same type (such as purchase of goods), is considered material, unless on the basis of facts and circumstances of the case it can be concluded that even a transaction of less than 10% is material. As regards nature, ordinarily the related party transactions, which are not entered in the normal course of the business of the reporting enterprise, are considered material subject to the facts and circumstances of the case.

AS-18 also focus on the following points :
- State controlled enterprise.
- Significant difference among AS-18, IFRC/IAS and USGAAP.

## PRACTICAL EXAMPLES

### Example 1

Define Related Party Transactions under AS-18.

### Answer

**Related Party Transaction** is defined in AS-18 as, "transfer of resources or obligations between related parties, regardless of whether or not a price is charged".

As per the standard, related parties, are defined in the following words, "Parties are considered to be related if at any time during the reporting period one party has the ability to control the other party or exercise significant influence over the other party in making financial and/or operating decisions".

Some of the examples of related party are stated in para 24 which are as follows :

- Purchases or sales of good (finished or unfinished).
- Rendering or receiving of services.
- Purchases or sales of fixed assets.
- Agency arrangements.
- Transfer of research and development.
- Leasing or hire purchase arrangements.
- License agreements.
- Guarantees and collaterals etc.

### Example 2

**Answer the following :**

i)   Mr. Raj a relative of key management personnel received remuneration of ₹ 2,50,000 for his services in the company for the period from 1.4.2015 to 30.6.2015. On 1.7.2015 he left the service. Should the relative be identified at the closing date i.e. on 31.3.2016 for the purposes of AS-18 ?

ii)  Adwani Ltd, sold goods to its associate Co. for the I$^{st}$ quarter ending 30.6.2015. After that the related party relationship ceased to exist. However, goods were supplied to as were supplied to any other ordinary customer. Decide whether transactions of the entire year had to be disclosed as related party transaction.

### Answer

i)   As per para 10 of AS 18 on Related Party Disclosures, parties are considered to be related at any time during the reporting period. One party has the power to exercise significant influence over the other party or has the ability to control the other party in making financial and / or operating decisions. Hence, in this case, Mr. Raj, a relative of key management personnel should be identified as relative as at the closing data i.e. on 31$^{st}$ March, 2016.

ii)  According to para 13 of AS-18 on Related Party Disclosure transactions of Adwani Ltd. with its associate company for the first quarter ending on 30$^{th}$ June, 2015 only are required to be disclosed as related party transactions. The transactions for the period in which related party relationship did not exist need not be reported.

### Example 3

Which of the two transactions would be disclosed as related party transactions in Arihant Ltd. 2015-2016 financial statements ?
a)   Neither transaction only.
b)   ₹ 1,00,000 transaction only.
c)   ₹ 250,000 transaction only.
d)   Both the transactions.

### Answer

d)   Both the transactions.

### Example 4

Identify the related parties in respect of all enterprises mentioned under AS-18, if,
- X Ltd. holds 51% of Y Ltd.
- Y Ltd. holds 51% of Z Ltd.
- O Ltd. holds 49% of Z Ltd.

### Answer

X Ltd., Y Ltd. and Z Ltd. are related to each other. O Ltd. and Z Ltd. are also related to each other by virtue of associate relationship. However, neither X Ltd. nor Y Ltd. is related to O Ltd. and *vice-versa*.

### Example 5

A husband and wife are controlling 34% of voting power in Aishwarya Ltd. They are having a separate partnership firm, which supplies mainly the raw material to the Co. The management says that the above transaction need not be disclosed.

### Answer

The Co.'s contention would be acceptable if it is not a listed company. The Co. does not have an annual turnover exceeding ₹ 50 crores. However, if AS-18, applies then in accordance with Para 3 (c) & (e) of AS-18, Aishwarya Ltd. and the partnership firm are related parties and hence disclosure would be required irrespective of whether they are at arm's length or not.

### Example 6

X Ltd. has a full time director "A" who is also a director in Z Ltd.. A does not actively participate in the operating and financial decisions of Z Ltd. Do you think Z Ltd. will be a related party to X Ltd. ?

### Answer

As per para 3 of AS-18, among others, the following are considered related party relationships :
c)   individuals owning, directly or indirectly, an interest in the voting power of the reporting enterprise that gives them control or significant influence over the enterprise, and relatives of any such individual;
d)   key managerial personnel and relatives of such personnel;
e)   enterprises over which any person described in (c) or (d) is able to. exercise significant influence. This includes enterprises owned by directors or major shareholders of the reporting enterprise and enterprises that have a number of key management in common with the reporting enterprise.

Para 4 states that, among others, the following are deemed not to be related parties :

a)  two companies simply because they have a director in common, notwithstanding para 3 (d) or (e) above (unless the director is able to affect the policies of both companies in their mutual dealings).

Since A does not participate in the operating and financing decisions of Z Ltd., Z Ltd. is not a related party to X Ltd.

## 1.10 AS-19 : LEASES (1-4-2001)

**Introduction :**

This Standard deals with the accounting treatment of transactions related to lease agreements. For this purpose, the standard divides the agreements into operating and financing lease. A Finance lease is a lease that transfers substantially all the risks and rewards incident to ownership of an asset. An operating lease is a lease other than a financial lease.

**Objectives :**

**Lease** is an arrangement by which the lessor gives the right to use an asset for given period of time to the lessee on rent. It involves two parties, a **lessor** and a **lessee** and an **asset** which is to be leased. The **lessor** who owns the asset agrees to allow the lessee to use it for a specified period of time in return for periodic rent payments. The lease transaction derives its accounting complexity from a number of alternatives available to the parties involved. Lease can be structured to take tax benefit. It can he used to transfer ownership of the leased asset, and it ran also be used to transfer the risk of ownership.

In any event, substance of transactions dictate the accounting treatment. The lease transaction (finance lease) is probably the best example of accounting profession's substance over legal form.

If the transactions effectively transfer ownership to lessee, then substance of the transaction is that of a sale and should be recognised as such, even though transactions take form of a lease.

**Types of Lease :**

For the purpose of accounting, the lease is classified into two categories as i) Finance Lease and ii) Operating Lease.

**i)  Finance Lease :**

It is a lease which transfers substantially all the risks and rewards incidential to ownership of an asset to the lessee by the lessor but not the legal ownership. In following situations, the lease transactions are called **finance lease** :

- The lessee will get the ownership of leased asset at the end of the lease term.
- The lessee has an option to buy the leased asset at the end of term at a price which is lower than its expected fair value on the date on which option will be exercised.
- The lease term covers the major part of the life of asset.
- At the beginning of lease term, present value of minimum lease rental covers substantially the initial fair value of the leased asset,
- The asset given on lease to lessee is of specialised nature and can only be used by the lessee without major modification,

**ii)  Operating Lease :**

It is a lease which does not transfer substantially all the risks and rewards incidental to ownership.

Classification of lease is made at the inception of the lease; if at any time the lessee and lessor agree to change the provision of lease and it results in different category of lease, it will be treated as separate agreement.

**Applicability :**

The Accounting Standard is not applicable to following types of lease :

- Lease agreement to explore natural resources such as oil, gas, timber, metal and other mineral rights.
- Licensing agreements for motion picture film, video recording, plays, manuscripts, patents and other rights.
- Lease agreement to use land.

**Notable Terms :**

**a)  Guaranteed Residual Value :**

- **In respect of lessee :**

Such part of the residual value, which is guaranteed by or on be all of the lessee.

- **In respect of lessor :**

Such part of the residual value, which is guaranteed by or on behalf of the lessee or by an independent third party.

For the lessor the residual value guaranteed by the third party can accrue when the asset is leased to the third party after the first lease has expired and therefore it can be called the residual value guaranteed by the third party to the lessor.

**b)  Unguaranteed Residual Value :**

The difference between residual value of asset and its guaranteed residual value is unguaranteed residual value.

**c)  Gross Investment :**

Gross investment in lease is the sum of,

- Minimum lease payment (from the standpoint of lessor) and
- Any unguaranteed residual value accruing to the lessor.

**d)  Interest Rate Implicit in the Lease :**

When the lessor gives an asset on lease (particularly on finance lease), the total amount, which he receives over lease period by giving the asset on lease, includes the element of interest plus payment of principal amount of asset. The rate at which the interest amount is calculated can be simply called implicit rate of interest. In other words, it is implied interest rate at which the lease transaction is done. More accurately it can be expressed as under :

|  |  |  |
|---|---|---|
| It is the discount rate at Fair Value of Leased Asset (At the inception of lease) | = | Present value of [Minimum lease payment (In respect of lessor) (+) any unguaranteed residual value accruing to the lessor] |

**e)  Contingent Rent :**

Lease rent fixed on the basis of percentage of sales, amount of usage, price indices, market rate of interest is called contingent rent. In other words, lease rent is not fixed, but it is based on a factor other than time.

**f)  Minimum Lease payments [MLP] :**

- For Lessor        = Total lease rent to be paid by lessee over the lease terms (+) any guaranteed residual value (by or on behalf of a lessee)
- Contingent Rent = Cost for service and tax to be paid by and reimbursed to lessor (+) residual value guaranteed by third party.
- For Lessee        = Total lease rent to be paid by lessee over the lease terms (+) any guaranteed residual value (for lessee).

**g)  Hire Purchase Agreements :**

The definition of a 'lease' includes agreement or the hire of an asset, which contains a provision giving the hirer an option to acquire title to the asset upon the fulfilment of agreed conditions. These agreements are commonly known as **'hire purchase agreements'**.

**Accounting for Finance Lease in the books of Lessee :**

As it is already mentioned that legally the ownership of leased asset remains with lessor but risk and reward of leased asset is transferred to lessee. Therefore, the substance of transaction is that lessee becomes the owner, hence, the transaction is recorded by substance and not by its legal form.

- Leased asset as well as liability for lease should be recognised at the lower of –
- Fair value of the leased asset at the inception of lease or
- Present value of minimum lease payment from the lessee's point of view, whichever is lower.

- **Apportionment of Lease Payment** :

Each lease payment is apportioned between finance charge and principal amount. Principal amount is reduced from the outstanding liability. Finance charge is allocated over the lease term in such a manner that it would produce a constant rate of return on the remaining principal balance.

- The lessee in its books should charge depreciation on finance lease asset as per AS-6.
- Initial direct cost for finance lease is included in asset under lease.

**Accounting for Finance Lease, in the books of Lessor :**

The substance of finance lease is that lessor sells the leased assets to lessee.

- Therefore, the lessor should recognise the assets given under finance lease as receivable at an amount equal to net investment in the lease and corresponding credit to sale of asset.

$$\text{Net Investment} = \text{Gross Investment} (-) \text{Unearned finance income}$$

$$\text{Gross Investment} = (\text{Minimum lease payment from lessor point of view } (+) \text{ Unguaranteed residual value})$$

$$\text{Unearned Finance Income} = \text{Gross Investment} (-) \text{Present Value of Gross Investment}$$

**Recognition of Finance Income :**

The lessor should recognise the finance income based on a pattern reflecting constant periodic return on the net investment outstanding in respect of the finance lease. In simple words, interest/finance income will be recognised in proportion to outstanding balance receivable from lessee over lease period.

**Accounting for Operating Lease :**

In the books of Lessor :

- Record leased out asset as the fixed asset in the Balance Sheet.
- Charge depreciation as per AS-6.
- Recognise lease income in profit and loss account using straight line method. If any other method reflects more systematic allocation of earning derived from the diminishing value of leased out asset, that approach can be adopted.
- Other costs of operating lease should be recognised as expenses in the year in which they are incurred.
- Initial direct cost of the lease may be expensed immediately or deferred.

**Accounting for Operating Lease, in the Books of Lessee :**

Lease payment should be recognised as an expense in the profit and loss account on straight line basis over the lease term. If any other method is more representative of the time pattern of the user's benefit, that method can be used.

**Sale and Lease Back :**

A **sale and lease** back transaction involves the sale of an asset by vendor and leasing of the same asset back to the vendor.

**Accounting treatment of Sale and Lease Back**

**i)  If lease back is Finance Lease :**
- Any profit or loss of sale proceeds over the carrying amount should not be immediately recognised as profit or loss in the financial statements of a seller-lessee.
- It should be deferred and amortised over lease term in proportion to the depreciation of leased asset.

**ii)  If lease back is Operating Lease :**
- Any profit or loss arising out of sale transaction is recognised immediately, when sale price is equal to fair value.

**iii)  If sale price is below Fair Value :**
- Profit, i.e. carrying amount is less than sale value, recognise profit immediately.
- Loss, i.e. carrying amount is more than the sale value, recognise loss immediatey provided loss is not compensated by future lease payment.
- Loss – i.e. carrying amount is more than sale price, defer and amortise loss if loss is compensated by future lease payment.

**iv)  If sale price is above Fair Value :**
- If carrying amount is equal to fair value which will result in profit, amortise the profit over lease profit.
- If carrying amount is less than fair value which will result in profit, amortise and defer the profit equal to sale price less fair value and recognise balance profit immediately.
- If carrying amount is more than the fair value, it will result in loss equal to carrying amount less than fair value which should be recognised immediately. Profit equal to - selling price less fair value should be amortised.

**Disclosure :**

The following disclosures in financial statements of the lessee and lessor should be made as regards lease :

**i)  Disclosure in Operating Lease by Lessor :**
- General description of significant leasing arrangements.
- Accounting policy for initial direct payment.
- Future lease payments in aggregate classified as :
  a)  not later than one year;
  b)  later than one year but not later than five years;
  c)  later than five years;

**ii)  Disclosure in Operating Lease by the Lessee :**
- General description of significant leasing arrangements.
- Total of future minimum lease payments in following period.
  a)  not later than one year;
  b)  later than one year but not later than five years;
  c)  later than five years;
- Lease payments recognised in profit/loss Account for the period.

**iii)  Disclosure in Finance Lease by the Lessor :**
- General description of the significant leasing arrangement.
- Accounting policy for initial direct cost.
- Reconciliation of total gross investment in lease with present value of MLP receivable on Balance Sheet date.

- Minimum lease payment (MLP) receivable in following categories :
  a) not later than one year;
  b) later than one year but not later than five years;
  c) later than five years;

iv) **Disclosure in Finance Lease by the Lessee :**
- Asset under finance lease segregated from an asset owned.
- Reconciliation of total MLP with its present value on Balance Sheet date.
- MLP in following categories on Balance Sheet date :
  a) not later than one year;
  b) later than one year but not later five years;
  c) later than five years;

## PRACTICAL EXAMPLES

**Example 1**

What are the differences between Operating Leases and Financing Leases ?

**Answer**

Financial Lease substantially transfers all the risk and reward to ownership of an asset to the lessee, whereas in Operating Lease risk and reward is not transferred to the lessee.

**Example 2**

Describe the accounting treatment in the book of lessee where fair value of the property exceeds the present value of the property's minimum lease payment at the inception of the lease in finance lease.

**Answer**

When the fair value of the property exceeds the present value of the minimum lease payment at the inception of the lease the lessee records the assets under finance lease at present value of minimum lease payment.

**Example 3**

Describe the lessor's accounting for initial direct cost in an operating lease.

**Answer**

The lessor will amortise initial direct leasing costs over the lease term as the revenue is recognised for operating leases (usually straight-line). However, it may be expensed immediately if the situations are such.

**Example 4**

On 31.03.2016, Apollo Ltd. sold an equipment to Bajaj and simultaneously leased it back for twelve years. Prominent information at this date is as follows :

| | |
|---|---|
| Sales Price | ₹ 4,80,000 |
| Carrying Amount | ₹ 3,60,000 |
| Estimated remaining Economic Life | 15 yrs. |

For the financial year 2015-2016, how much should Apollo Ltd. report as deferred gain from the sale of equipment ?

**Answer**

₹ 1,20,000.

## Example 5

Gross investment in the finance lease is ₹ 5,00,000. Present value of minimum lease payments for the lessor is ₹ 3,00,000. Present value of unguaranteed residual value accruing to the lessor at the implicit rate of interest is ₹ 1,00,000. Unearned finance income will be,

a)   ₹ 2,00,000,

b)   ₹ 1,00,000,

c)   ₹ 4,00,000,

d)   None of the above.

## Answer

b)   ₹ 1,00,000.

## Example 6

Depreciation on leased assets is governed by :

a)   AS-6 (Revised),

b)   AS-10,

c)   AS-19,

d)   Income-Tax Act, 1961.

## Answer

a)   AS-6 (Revised).

## Example 7

In financial lease, as per AS-19 leased asset :

a)   is shown in the Balance Sheet of lessee

b)   is shown in the Balance Sheet of lessor

c)   not shown in the Balance Sheet of either

d)   disclosed as contingent asset by the lessee

## Answer

a)   is shown in the Balance Sheet of lessee.

## Example 8

What is "Sale and Lease-back transaction ?"

## Answer

**Sale and Leaseback Transactions :**

According to the AS-19 which is on 'Lease', a sale and lease back transaction includes the sale of an asset by the vendor and the leasing of the asset back to the vendor. The lease payments and the sale price are mostly interdependent as they are negotiated as a package. The accounting treatment of a sale and lease back transaction depends upon the type of lease considered.

If a sale and lease back transaction results in a finance lease, any excess or deficiency of sale proceeded over the carrying amount must be deferred and amortised over the lease term in proportion to the depreciation of the leased assets.

If sale and leaseback transaction results in a operating lease and it is at a fair value, then the profit or loss must be recognised immediately. If the sale price is below fair value any profit or loss should be recognised immediately, except, that if the loss is compensated by future lease payments at below market price, it must be deferred and amortised in proportion to the lease payments over the period for which the asset is expected to be used. If the sale price is above fair value, the excess over fair value must be deferred and amortised over the period.

Example 9

Camlin Ltd. wishes to obtain a machine tool costing ₹ 20,00,000 by way of lease. The effective life of the machine tool is twelve years but the company requires it only for the first five years. It enters into an agreement with Dabur Ltd. for a lease rental of ₹ 2,00,000 p.a.

The Finance Director of Camlin Ltd. is not sure about the treatment of these lease rentals and hence requests your assistance in proper disclosure of the same. For calculation purposes, the implicit rate of interest may be taken at 15%. Discount factors : 0.87, 0.76, 0.66, 0.57 and 0.50.

Answer

In this case, the lease is to be classified as an operating lease, because the asset is leased only for a part of its useful life. The estimated life of the lease is 12 years, whereas it has been leased out for only 5 years.

Para 23 states that lease payments under an operating lease should be recognised as an expense in the Statement of Profit and Loss on a straight line basis over the lease term unless another systematic basis is more representative of the time pattern of the user's benefit.

An operating lease gives the lessee only the use of the asset, while leaving the lessor with all substantial burdens and benefits of ownership. Therefore, an asset acquired under an operating lease is not shown in the Balance Sheet.

**Present Value of Minimum Lease Payments : Interest Rate – 15%**

| Year | | Amount of Lease Payments ₹ | Present Value of ₹ 1 ₹ | | Present Value of Lease Payments ₹ |
|---|---|---|---|---|---|
| 1 | | 2,00,000 | 1.00 | | 2,00,000 |
| 2 | | 2,00,000 | 0.87 | | 1,74,000 |
| 3 | | 2,00,000 | 0.76 | | 1,52,000 |
| 4 | | 2,00,000 | 0.66 | | 1,32,000 |
| 5 | (+) | 2,00,000 | 0.50 | (+) | 1,00,000 |
| | | 10,00,000 | | | 7,58,000 |

The following disclosure should be made :

The total of future minimum lease payments will be ₹ 2,00,000 and

i)   Not later than 1 year

ii)  Later than 1 year but not later than 5 years (₹ 7,58,000 – ₹ 2,00,000) will be ₹ 5,58,000.

Example 10

Essoo Ltd. purchased a machine for ₹ 42,000 and leased out to Forex Ltd. on 1.1.2012. The lease term is 4 years and the scrap value of the computer at the end of the lease term is 5% of the cost of the asset. The lease rental is payable in advance and is ₹ 24,500, ₹ 11,200, ₹ 5,600 and ₹ 3,150 respectively for these four years. The rate of depreciation is 25% p.a. The asset is to be taken over Forex Ltd. on termination of the lease.

You are required to calculate :

i) calculate the implicit rate in the lease; ii) prepare a statement showing the allocation between capital and interest charges of the lease rentals; and iii) pass Journal Entries in the books of both the parties.

Given, the present value of Rupee 1 :

| Year | 1 ₹ | 2 ₹ | 3 ₹ | 4 ₹ |
|---|---|---|---|---|
| 13% | 0.885 | 0.783 | 0.693 | 0.613 |
| 14% | 0.877 | 0.769 | 0.675 | 0.592 |
| 15% | 0.870 | 0.750 | 0.658 | 0.572 |

Answer

## Statement showing calculation of the present value of lease rentals at different discount rates

| Year | Lease Payments ₹ | Present Value Factor at 13% Re. | Present Value of Lease Payments ₹ | Present Value Factor of 14% Re. | Present Value Lease Payments ₹ | Present Value Factor of 15% Re. | Present Value Lease Payments ₹ |
|---|---|---|---|---|---|---|---|
| 2012 | 24,500 | 1 | 24,500 | 1 | 24,500 | 1 | 24,500 |
| 2013 | 11,200 | 0.885 | 9,912 | 0.877 | 9,822 | 0.870 | 9,744 |
| 2014 | 5,600 | 0.783 | 4,385 | 0.769 | 4,306 | 0.756 | 4,234 |
| 2015 (Op.) | 3,150 | 0.693 | 2,183 | 0.675 | 2,126 | 0.658 | 2,073 |
| 2015 (Cl.) | 2,100 (Scrap) | 0.613 | 1,287 | 0.592 | 1,243 | 0.572 | 1,201 |
| | 46,550 | | 42,267 | | 41,997 | | 41,752 |

Since the present value of lease payment at 14% discount rate is almost equal to the cost of the asset, 14% is the implicit rate of interest in the lease.

## Statement Showing the Schedule of Payments

| Year (A) | Opening Balance (B) | Interest @ 14% for the year [14% of (B)] (C) | Repayment of Capital (D) | Closing Balance [(B) – (D)] (E) ₹ |
|---|---|---|---|---|
| 1 | 42,000 | – | 24,500 | 17,500 |
| 2 | 17,500 | 2,450 | 8,750 | 8,750 |
| 3 | 8,750 | 1,225 | 4,375 | 4,375 |
| 4 | 4,375 | 613 | 2,537 | – |

## Journal Entries in the books of Lessor-Essoo Ltd.,

| Date | Particulars | L.F. | Debit Amount ₹ | Credit Amount ₹ |
|---|---|---|---|---|
| – | Machinery A/c | | 42,000 | |
| | To Bank A/c | | | 42,000 |
| | (Being the purchase of machinery for leasing) | | | |
| 1.1.2012 | Rent Receivable A/c                     Dr. | | 42,000 | |
| | To Machinery A/c | | | 42,000 |
| | (Being the leasing out of the machinery to the lessee) | | | |
| 1.1.2012 | Bank A/c                                      Dr. | | 24,500 | |
| | To Rent Receivable A/c | | | 24,500 |
| | (Being the first instalment received) | | | |
| 31.12. 2012 | Interest Receivable A/c                 Dr. | | 2,450 | |
| | To Interest A/c | | | 2,450 |
| | (Being the interest charged) | | | |
| 31.12. 2012 | Interest A/c                               Dr. | | 2,450 | |
| | To Profit and Loss A/c | | | 2,450 |
| | (Being interest credited to Profit and Loss Account) | | | |

| Date | Particulars | L.F. | Debit Amount ₹ | Credit Amount ₹ |
|---|---|---|---|---|
| 1.1.2013 | Bank A/c                                                    Dr. | | 11,200 | |
| | To Rent Receivable A/c | | | 8,750 |
| | To Interest Receivable A/c | | | 2,450 |
| | (Being the repayment of capital and interest charges received) | | | |
| 31.12.2013 | Interest Receivable A/c                          Dr. | | 1,225 | |
| | To Interest A/c | | | 1,225 |
| | (Being the interest charged) | | | |
| 31.12.2013 | Interest A/c                                              Dr. | | 1,225 | |
| | To Profit and Loss A/c | | | 1,225 |
| | (Being interest credited to Profit and Loss Account) | | | |
| 1.1.2014 | Bank A/c                                                    Dr. | | 5,600 | |
| | To Rent Receivable A/c | | | 4,379 |
| | To Interest Receivable A/c | | | 1,221 |
| | (Being the repayment of capital and interest charges received) | | | |
| 31.12.2014 | Interest Receivable A/c                          Dr. | | 613 | |
| | To Interest A/c | | | 613 |
| | (Being the interest charged) | | | |
| 31.12.2014 | Interest A/c                                              Dr. | | 613 | |
| | To Profit and Loss A/c | | | 613 |
| | (Being interest credit to Profit and Loss Account) | | | |
| 1.1.2015 | Bank A/c                                                    Dr. | | 3,150 | |
| | To Rent Receivable A/c | | | 2,537 |
| | To Interest Receivable A/c | | | 613 |
| | (Being the repayment of capital and interest charges received | | | |
| 31.12.2015 | Bank A/c                                                    Dr. | | 2,100 | |
| | To Profit on Sale of Asset A/c | | | 2,100 |
| | (Being the sale of the leased asset on the termination of the lease at its scrap value) | | | |

**Journal Entries in the books of Lessee-Forex Ltd.**

| Date | Particulars | L.F. | Debit Amount ₹ | Credit Amount ₹ |
|---|---|---|---|---|
| 1.1.2012 | Asset under Lease A/c                            Dr. | | 42,000 | |
| | To Lease Payable A/c | | | 42,000 |
| | (Being the acquisition of the asset under lease) | | | |
| 1.1.2012 | Lease Payable A/c                                  Dr. | | 24,500 | |
| | To Bank A/c | | | 24,500 |
| | (Being the first instalment paid) | | | |

| Date | Particulars | | L.F. | Debit Amount ₹ | Credit Amount ₹ |
|---|---|---|---|---|---|
| 31.12.2012 | Depreciation A/c | Dr. | | 10,500 | |
| | To Provision for Depreciation A/c | | | | 10,500 |
| | (Being the depreciation charged) | | | | |
| 31.12.2012 | Interest A/c | Dr. | | 2,450 | |
| | To Interest Payable A/c | | | | 2,450 |
| | (Being the interest payable) | | | | |
| 31.12.2012 | Profit and Loss A/c | Dr. | | 12,950 | |
| | To Depreciation A/c | | | | 10,500 |
| | To Interest A/c | | | | 2,450 |
| | (Being depreciation and interest charged to Profit and Loss Account) | | | | |
| 1.1.2013 | Lease Payable A/c | Dr. | | 8,780 | |
| | Interest Payable A/c | Dr. | | 2,450 | |
| | To Bank A/c | | | | 11,200 |
| | (Being the repayment of capital and interest) | | | | |
| 31.12.2013 | Depreciation A/c | Dr. | | 10,500 | |
| | To Provision for Depreciation A/c | | | | 10,500 |
| | (Being the depreciation charged) | | | | |
| 31.12.2013 | Interest A/c | Dr. | | 1,225 | |
| | To Interest Payable A/c | | | | 1,225 |
| | (Being the interest payable) | | | | |
| 31.12.2013 | Profit and Loss A/c | Dr. | | 11,725 | |
| | To Depreciation A/c | | | | 10,500 |
| | To Interest A/c | | | | 1,225 |
| | (Being depreciation and interest charged to Profit and Loss Account) | | | | |
| 1.1.2014 | Lease Payable A/c | Dr. | | 4,375 | |
| | Interest Payable A/c | Dr. | | 1,225 | |
| | To Bank A/c | | | | 5,600 |
| | (Being the repayment of capital and interest) | | | | |
| 31.12.2014 | Depreciation A/c | Dr. | | 10,500 | |
| | To Provision for Depreciation A/c | | | | 10,500 |
| | (Being the depreciation charged) | | | | |
| 31.12.2014 | Interest A/c | Dr. | | 613 | |
| | To Interest Payable | | | | 613 |
| | (Being the interest payable) | | | | |
| 31.12.2014 | Profit and Loss A/c | Dr. | | 11,113 | |
| | To Depreciation A/c | | | | 10,500 |
| | To Interest A/c | | | | 613 |
| | (Being depreciation and interest charged to Profit and Loss Account) | | | | |

| Date | Particulars | | L.F. | Debit Amount ₹ | Credit Amount ₹ |
|---|---|---|---|---|---|
| 1.1.2015 | Lease Payable A/c | Dr. | | 2,537 | |
| | Interest Payable | Dr. | | 613 | |
| | To Bank A/c | | | | 3,150 |
| | (Being the repayment of capital and interest) | | | | |
| 31.12.2015 | Machinery A/c | Dr. | | 2,100 | |
| | To Bank A/c | | | | 2,100 |
| | (Being the asset taken over the termination of the lease) | | | | |
| 31.12.2015 | Depreciation A/c | Dr. | | 10,500 | |
| | To Provision for Depreciation A/c | | | | 10,500 |
| | (Being the depreciation charged) | | | | |
| 31.12.2015 | Provision for Depreciation A/c | Dr. | | 42,000 | |
| | To Asset under Lease A/c | | | | 42,000 |
| | (Being the depreciation written-off) | | | | |

**Working Notes :**

**Calculation of Depreciation :**

i) Depreciation = ₹ 42,000/4 years = ₹ 10,500.

ii) At the end of the lease period year, balance of Provision for Depreciation Account is adjusted against the Asset Account.

## 1.11 AS-20 : EARNINGS PER SHARE (1.4.2001)

**Introduction :**

This Standard deals with the presentation and computation of Earning Per Share (EPS). This standard requires the earnings per share to be calculated on consolidated basis as well as for the parent (holding) company while presenting the financial statements of the parent company. The standard requires to compute and present basic as well as diluted earnings per share.

**Objective :**

Earning per-Share (EPS) is a financial ratio that gives the information regarding earning available to each equity share. It is very important financial ratio for assessing the state of market price of share. This accounting standard gives computational methodology for the determination and presentation of earning per share, which will improve the comparison of earnings per share. The statement is applicable to the enterprise whose equity shares or potential equity shares are listed in stock exchange. This standard is applicable to enterprises whose equity shares or potential equity shares are listed on a recognised stock exchange in India.

**Types of Earnings per Share :**

There are two types of earning per share (EPS), which are to be reported by an enterprise on the face of the statement of profit and loss, i) Basic earnings per share and ii) Diluted earnings per share.

**i) Basic Earnings per Share :**

Basic Earnings per Share is calculated as under :

$$\text{Basic Earnings per Share} = \frac{\text{Net Profit or Loss for the period attributable to equity shareholder}}{\text{Weighted average number of equity shares outstanding during the period}}$$

- **Calculation of Net Profit or Loss for the period attributable to Equity Shareholders :**
  - Calculate the net profit or loss for the period including prior period items and extraordinary items as per AS-5 and also deduct tax expense (Current Tax (+) Deferred Tax) unless the AS-5 requires otherwise.
  - Deduct the amount of preference dividend and any attributable tax on preference dividend from the figure calculated above. Dividend on non-cumulative preference share is deducted if dividend is provided. However, in case of cumulative preference share, dividend of current year is deducted even if not provided in accounts. Dividend paid during the current year in respect of previous periods is to be excluded.
- **Calculation of weighted average number of outstanding Equity Shares during the period :**

Weighted average outstanding equity shares should be computed adjusting for the change in equity shares, as per the following. However, if an enterprise has more than one class of equity shares, net profit or loss for that period is to be apportioned over the different classes of shares in accordance with their dividend rights.

| List of shares issued, which are to be adjusted | Weight to be considered from |
|---|---|
| • Equity shares issued in exchange of cash. | • Date of cash receivable. |
| • Equity shares against conversion of debt instrument. | • Date of conversion. |
| • Equity shares against interest or principal of any financial instrument. | • Date when interest ceases to accrue. |
| • Equity shares issued in exchange for the settlement of a liability of the enterprise. | • Date on which settlement becomes effective. |
| • Equity shares issued in consideration of acquisition of assets other than cash. | • Date on which acquisition is recognised. |
| • Equity shares issued against services rendered. | • When service is rendered. |
| • Partly paid up share. | • Partly paid up equity should be counted as fraction of equity shares in ratio of amount paid up to the total face value of the share. |
| • Right issue. | • Adjusted with Right factor. |
| • Equity shares issued as a consideration in amalgamation by way of, | |
|    – Merger | – Shares included in the calculation of weighted average from the beginning of the reporting period. |
|    – Purchase | – Included in the weighted average from the date of acquisition. |
|    – Bonus share | – Shares included in weighted average from the beginning of the reporting period (refer illustrations 1, 2 & 3). |

**Right Issue :**

**Right Issue** is generally made at a price lower than fair value of share. Therefore, a right issue usually includes a bonus element. Since right issue includes a bonus element, the number of equity shares to be used in calculating basic earnings per share for all periods prior to right issue is the number of equity shares outstanding prior to the issue multiplied by right factor which is calculated as under :

$$\text{Right Factor} = \frac{\text{Fair value per share immediately prior to right issue}}{\text{Theoretical ex-right fair value per share}}$$

**Theoretical Ex-right fair value :**

$$= \frac{\text{Aggregate fair value of share immediately prior to the exercise of the rights} \;(+)\; \text{Proceeds from exercise of the rights}}{\text{Number of shares outstanding immediately after the right issue}}$$

**ii)  Diluted Earning per Share :**

Diluted earning per share is calculated when there are potential equity shares in capital structure of the enterprise. A potential equity share is that financial instrument which entitles the holder the right of equity shares like convertible debentures, convertible preference shares, options, warrants, etc.

- **Diluted Earning per Share :**

$$= \frac{\text{Net profit attributable to equity shareholders (after adjustment for diluted earnings)}}{\text{Average number of weighted equity shares outstanding during the period (assuming the conversion of diluted potential equity shares)}}$$

**Diluted Potential Equity Shares :**

Potential equity shares are diluted if their conversion into equity shares reduces the earning per share. If their conversion does not decrease the EPS, rather it increases the EPS, then the potential equity shares are not to be considered dilutive.

**Diluted Earning :**

- Compute net profit or loss for the period attributable to existing equity shareholder.
- Add back dividend along with distribution tax on convertible preference shares previously deducted.
- Add back interest net of tax effect charged on convertible debenture or loans.

*Order in which potential equity share be considered* - Potential equity share should be ranked in order of dilutive effect. Dilutive effect is determined by dividing incremental net profit by incremental equity share arising out of conversion.

**Re-Statement :**

If the number of equity shares or potential equity shares outstanding is increased as a result of bonus issue, share split, consolidation of shares, the calculation of basic and diluted equity per share should be adjusted for all the periods presented.

If changes occur after the balance sheet date but before the approval of financial statements by the competent authority, the EPS calculation for these financial statements and any prior period financial Statements should be restated on the basis of new number of shares.

**Disclosure :**

- **Disclosure of numerator and reconciliation :** The amount used as numerator for calculating basic and diluted EPS and its reconciliation with net profit or loss for that period.
- **Disclosure of denominator and reconciliation :** Weighted average number of shares used as denominator lot calculating basic and diluted EPS and reconciliation of their denominators to each other.

**Basic and Diluted Earnings Per Share :**

Limited revision of AS-20 prescribes that if profit or loss includes extraordinary items as per AS-5, the enterprise may also present, with appropriate description on the face of the Statement of Profit or Loss :

i)   Basic earning per share computed on the basis of earnings excluding extraordinary items (net of tax expense).

ii)  Diluted earning per share computed on the basis of earnings excluding extraordinary items (net of tax expense).

**EPS to be disclosed in Part IV of the Schedule V1, (AS-12) :**

It has been clarified by the ICAI that earning per share to be disclosed in Part IV of Schedule VI to the Companies Act, 1956 should be in accordance with AS-20 whether its equity shares or potential equity shares are listed on a recognised stock exchange in India or not.

## PRACTICAL EXAMPLES

**Example 1**

Asia Ltd. had 1,800 equity shares outstanding as on 01.01.2015 fully paid of ₹ 10. On 31.10.2015 it issued 6 equity shares of ₹ 10 each, 5 paid. Calculate weighted number of equity shares as on 31.12.2015.

**Answer**

Calculation of weighted number of shares as per para 19 of AS-20. Assuming that partly paid up shares are entitled to participate in the dividend to the extent of amount paid, number of partly paid up shares would be taken as 300 for the purpose of computation of earning per share. Computation of weighted average would be as follows :

=   (1,800 shares × 12/12) (+) (300 shares × 2/12) = 1,850 shares.

**Example 2**

Net Profit for the current year - ₹ 1,00,00,000.

Number of Equity Shares outstanding - 50,00,000

Basic Earnings per share - ₹ 2.00.

Number of 12% Convertible Debentures of ₹ 100 each - 1,00,000.

Each Debenture is Convertible into 10 Equity Shares.

Interest expense for the current year - ₹ 12,00,000.

Tax relating to interest expense (30%) - ₹ 3,60,000.

Compute Diluted Earnings Per Share.

**Answer**

Adjusted net profit for the current year

        Net Profit      Interest            Tax

(₹ 1,00,00,000 + ₹ 12,00,000 − ₹ 3,60,000) = Rs 1,08,40,000).

Number of Equity Shares resulting from Conversion of Debentures = 1,00,000 12% Convertible Deb. × 10 Equity Shares = 10,00,000 Shares.

Number of Equity Shares used to compute diluted EPS : (50,00,000 shares + 10,00,000 shares) = 60,00,000 shares Diluted Earrings per share :

=   ₹ 1,08,40,000/60,00,000 shares

=   ₹ 1.81.

**Example 3**

Potential equity shares are anti-dilutive when their incremental earning per equity share would :
- a)  Decrease EPS from continuing ordinary activities.
- b)  Increase loss per share from continuing ordinary activities.
- c)  Both a) and b).
- d)  None of the above

**Answer**

d)  None of the above.

**Example 4**

Weight of Bonus Shares is calculated from,
- a)  the date when board of directors passes resolution for Bonus.
- b)  the date when the price of shares become ex-bonus in stock exchange.
- c)  first day of the accounting year.
- d)  when the bonus share get listed in stock exchange.

**Answer**

c)  First day of the accounting year.

**Example 5**

Information regarding basic and dilutive earnings per share is to be disclosed on the face of,
- a)  Profit and Loss Account.
- b)  Notes to the Account.
- c)  Balance Sheet.
- d)  Cash Statement.

**Answer**

a)  Profit and Loss Account

**Example 6**

In April, 2015, Barua Ltd. issued 1,20,000 equity shares of ₹ 100 each. ₹ 50 per share was called upon that date which was paid by all shareholders. The remaining ₹ 50 was called up on 1.9.2015. All shareholders paid the sum in September, 2015, except one shareholder having 24,000 shares. The net profit for the year ended 31.3.2016 was ₹ 2,64,000 after dividend on preference shares and dividend distribution tax of ₹ 64,000.

Compute a basic earnings per share for the year ended 3 1.3. 2016 as per AS-20.

**Answer**

$$\text{Basic Earning per Share (EPS)} = \frac{\text{Net Profit attributable to equity shareholders}}{\text{Weighted Average number of equity shares outstanding during the year}}$$

**Working Notes :**
**i)  Calculation of weighted average number of equity shares**

| Date | No. Equity Shares | Nominal value of shares ₹ | Amount paid ₹ |
|---|---|---|---|
| 1.4.2015 | 1,20,000 | 100 | 50 |
| 1.9.2015 | 96,000 | 100 | 100 |
| 1.9.2015 | 24,000 | 100 | 50 |

Para 19 of AS-20 on earning per share states that partly paid equity shares are treated as a fraction of equity shares to the extent that they were entitled to participate in dividends relative to a fully paid equity share during the reporting period, Assuming that the partly paid shares are entitled to participate in the dividends to the extent of amount paid, weighted average number of shares will be calculated as follows :

$$= \quad \text{Shares } 1,20,000 \times \frac{1}{2} \times \frac{5}{12} \qquad = \qquad 25,000 \text{ shares}$$

$$= \quad \text{Shares } 96,000 \times \frac{7}{12} \qquad = \qquad 56,000 \text{ shares}$$

$$= \quad \text{Shares } 24,000 \times \frac{1}{2} \times \frac{7}{12} \qquad = (+) \ \underline{7,000} \text{ shares}$$

$$\therefore \text{ Weighted Average Number of Equity Shares } = \qquad \underline{88,000} \text{ shares}$$

### Example 7

The following are the details of equity share capital of Cummins Ltd. for the year ended 31.12.2014 and 31.12.2015.

10,00,000 equity shares of ₹ 10 each fully paid on 1.1.2014.

Issue of bonus shares made on 1.6.2009 in the ratio of 1 : 1.

Net profit after tax : 31.12.2014 – ₹ 45,00,000; 31.12.2015 – ₹ 60,00,000.

You are required to compute basic earnings per share.

### Answer

**Statement Showing Weighted Average Shares Outstanding**

| Particulars | Date | Period Outstanding Years | Weighted Average Number of Shares |
|---|---|---|---|
| Fully paid equity shares | 1.1.2014 | 1 | 10,00,000 |
| Issue of bonus shares (1 : 1) | 1.6.2014 | 1 | (+) 10,00,000 |
| ∴ Weighted Average Shares Outstanding on 2014 and 2015 | | | **20,00,000*** |

* Since the bonus issue is an issue without consideration, the issue is treated as if it had occurred prior to the beginning of the year 2014, the earliest period reported.

**Statement Showing Computation of Basic Earnings per Share**

| Particulars | | 31.12.2014 | 31.12.2015 |
|---|---|---|---|
| Net Profit After Tax (A) | ₹ | = 45,00,000 | = 60,00,000 |
| Weighted Average Number of Equity Shares (as above) (B) | Shares | 20,00,000 | 20,00,000 |
| Basic Earnings Per Share (A/B) | ₹ | 2.25 | 3.00 |

### Example 8

On 1.1.2014, Dolphin Ltd. had 1,00,000 equity shares of ₹ 10 each fully paid. On 1.7.2015, it issued rights shares to the existing shareholders in the ratio of 1 : 1 at a price of ₹ 20 each. The closing market price of the shares prior to the issue was ₹ 35. The basic reported earnings per share for the year ended 31.12.2014 was ₹ 2.20. The net profit after tax for the year ended 31st December were : 2014 – ₹ 2,20,000; 2015 – ₹ 2,40,000.

You are required to compute the basic Earning per share.

**Answer**

**i) Computation of Theoretical Ex-Rights Price :**

$$= \frac{\text{Fair Value of all Outstanding Shares immediately prior to exercise of Rights} \ (+) \ \text{Total Received from Exercise}}{\text{Number of Shares Outstanding Prior to Exercise (+) Number of Shares Issued in the Exercise}}$$

$$= \frac{₹ \ (1,00,000 \text{ shares} \times ₹ \ 35) + (1,00,000 \text{ shares} \times ₹ \ 20)}{1,00,000 \text{ shares} + 1,00,000 \text{ shares}}$$

$$= ₹ \ 27.50$$

Therefore, the theoretical Ex-Rights Price is ₹ 27,50.

**ii) Computation of Adjustment Factor :**

$$= \frac{\text{Fair value per share prior to exercise of rights}}{\text{Theoretical ex-rights value per share}}$$

$$= \frac{₹ \ 35}{₹ \ 27.50}$$

$$= ₹ \ 1.27$$

Therefore, the adjustment factor is 1.27.

**iii) Computation of Earnings per Share :**

| Particulars | 31.12.2014 ₹ | 31.12.2009 ₹ |
|---|---|---|
| EPS for the year 2013-14 (as given) : | 2.20 | – |
| EPS for the year 2013-14 restated for rights issue | 1.73 | – |
| $= \dfrac{₹ \ 2,20,000}{(1,00,000 \text{ shares} \times ₹ \ 1.27)}$ | | |
| EPS for the year 2014-15 including effects of rights issue | – | 1.47 |
| $= \dfrac{₹ \ 2,40,000}{(1,00,000 \text{ shares} \times 1.27 \times 6/12) + (2,00,000 \text{ shares} \times 6/12)}$ | | |

## 1.12 AS-21 : CONSOLIDATED FINANCIAL STATEMENTS (1-4-2001)

**Introduction :**

This Standard deals with the preparation of **Consolidated Financial Statements** with an intention to provide information about the activities of a group (parent company and companies under its control referred to as subsidiary companies).

**Objective :**

The objective of this statement is to present financial statements of a parent and its subsidiary(ies) as a single economic entity. In other words, the holding company and its subsidiary(ies) are treated as one entity for the preparation of these Consolidated Financial Statements. Consolidated Profit or Loss Account and Consolidated Balance Sheet are prepared for disclosing the total profit or loss of the group and total assets and liabilities of the group. As per this accounting standard, the consolidated Balance Sheet if prepared should be prepared in the manner prescribed by this statement.

**Notable Terms :**

**a) Parent :**

A parent is an enterprise that has one or more subsidiaries.

**b) Subsidiary :**

A subsidiary is an enterprise that is controlled by another enterprise known as parent.

**c)  Control :**

Control can be exercised directly or indirectly (through a subsidiary) by purchasing more than 50% of the voting power of an enterprise or by controlling composition of board of directors or governing body. Generally, it is done by purchasing more than 50% of the equity shares (voting power) of an enterprise.

**Format of consolidated Financial Statements :**

These are prepared or presented in the same format as that followed by the parent for preparation of its separate financial statements.

**Application of other accounting standards in preparation of Consolidated financial statements :**

As per this accounting standards while preparing the consolidated financial statements, the other accounting standards shall apply in the same manner as they apply in preparing the separate financial statements.

**Accounting for investments made by parents in its subsidiary(ies) while preparing separate financial statements :**

A parent should account for the investment in subsidiary(ies) in accordance with AS-13, "Accounting for investment". As per Accounting Standard-13, the investment made by a parent in subsidiary(ies) should be recorded at cost.

**Consolidated Financial Statements are no substitute for separate financial statements :**

Consolidated Financial Statements are not the substitute for separate financial statements of a parent and its subsidiary(ies). In other words, a parent and its subsidiary(ies), shall prepare separate financial statements as per governing law. The consolidated financial statement made by a parent is in addition to the separate financial statements.

**Scope of Consolidated Financial Statement :**

A parent, which is required to prepare the **Consolidated Financial Statements**, should consolidate the financial statements of all its subsidiary(ies), whether domestic or foreign.

**Exceptions :**

Consolidated Financial Statements are not required to be prepared even if parent subsidiary(ies) relationship exists when :

- a parent acquires the control (investment in subsidiary), which is intended to be temporary as the investment (control) is to be disposed in the near future.
- the subsidiary operates under severe long-term restrictions and due to this its ability to transfer the funds to parent is significantly weakened.

Dissimilar activities of parent and its subsidiaries cannot be the ground for non-consolidation of financial statements.

**Consolidation Procedure :**

In preparing **Consolidated Financial Statements** the financial statements (Balance Sheet and Profit and Loss Account) of the parent and its subsidiaries should be combined or added on line by line basis by adding the like items of assets, like items of liabilities, like items of income and expense.

- The (Cost of Investment of parent in each subsidiary should be cancelled or eliminated with parent's portion of equity of each subsidiary on the date on which the investment was acquired in each subsidiary. Parents portion of equity means share of parent (holding), in equity share capital of subsidiary (+) share in reserve and surplus of the subsidiary on the date of acquisition of share. In other words, parent's portion of equity in each subsidiary(ies) on the date of acquisition is paid up share capital held by holding (+) Share of pre-acquisition profits.

- If cost of investment in a subsidiary exceeds the parent's (holding) portion of equity i.e. paid up capital held by the holding plus share of pre-acquisition profits on the date of consolidation, the excess is **Goodwill**, and such goodwill arising due to consolidation procedure should be shown as an asset in consolidated financial statement.

- When the cost of investment in subsidiary is less than the paid up equity capital held by holding (parent) plus share of pre-acquisition profits, the difference is credited **Capital Reserve** and this capital reserve is shown in consolidated financial statement under the head 'Reserves and Surplus'.

- **Minority Interest** should be calculated and shown in the consolidated financial statements separately under separate heads. Minority interest means the portion of net assets of subsidiary on the date of consolidation not controlled by the parent, itself or through its subsidiary. Minority interest = Paid up equity capital held by an outsider (outside the group) plus share of 'reserve and surplus' on the date of consolidation. Preference share capital not held by parent or group is also shown alongwith minority interest.

- While calculating minority interest, share of minority in net profit of consolidated subsidiaries for the reporting period should be calculated and charged against the consolidated profit: consequently balance profit after charging minority interest represents the parent (holding company) share in profit which will he shown under the head 'Reserves and Surplus' in consolidated Balance Sheet.

- Intra-Group Balances and transactions i.e. inter-company debtor or creditors, inter-company purchases or sales and resulting unrealised profit shall be eliminated in full.

**Unrealised Losses :**

Unrealised Losses from intra-group transactions should also be eliminated if recoverable amount is more than the cost of transactions, e.g., if X Ltd. (holding company), sells goods costing ₹ 5,00,000 to its subsidiary, Y Ltd. at ₹ 4,00,000 and on the date of consolidation. The goods are lying in stock of Y Ltd. The recoverable amount of stock is ₹ 5,50,000; as the recoverable amount is more than the cost of the transaction, the unrealised loss of ₹ 1,00,000 should be eliminated by adding to stock and adding to consolidated Profit and Loss Account in consolidated Balance Sheet.

It should be noted that if unrealised losses are on account of intra-group sale or purchase of assets, the recoverable amount shall have the meaning as described in accounting standard on **'Impairment of Assets"**.

**Consolidation when different reporting Date :**

Financial statement of parents and its subsidiary used for consolidation are generally of same date, however when reporting dates are different and it is not practical to prepare the financial statements of subsidiary of the same date, the different reporting date financial statement can be consolidated making adjustment for the effects of significant transactions that occur between those dates and parent financial statements provided difference is not more than six months. If parent and its subsidiaries are following different accounting policies, the consolidated financial statement should be prepared using uniform accounting policies, if it is not practicable, then the items in which different accounting policies have been followed should be disclosed.

**Disposal of investment in a subsidiary :**

The difference between the proceeds front the disposal of investments in a subsidiary and the carrying amount of its assets less liabilities as of the date of disposal is recognised in the consolidated statement of profit and loss as the profit or loss on the disposal of the investment in a subsidiary.

**Successive purchase of shares in a subsidiary by the parent :**

If all enterprise purchases two or more the investment of other enterprise and eventually obtains control of the other enterprise, the consolidated financial statement is prepared from the date on which holding subsidiary relationship is established. Further, in such cases goodwill or capital reserve on consolidation should be determined on a step by step basis, however if small investments are made over a period of time, then the date of latest major investment which resulted in control, should be considered as date of investment for all successive purchases and, accordingly calculation of goodwill/capital reserve should be made.

**Minority interest is in Negative :**

When minority interest comes in negative (minus), this should be adjusted against majority interest. In other words, negative minority interest will not be shown in consolidated Balance Sheet. If the subsidiary subsequently reports profits, all such profits should be allocated to majority interest until minority share of losses previously absorbed by the majority has been recovered.

**Arrears of Cumulative Preference Share of a subsidiary :**

If the subsidiary has arrears of cumulative preference shares which are held outside the group, then the holding company share of profits is calculated after charging the arrear of cumulative preference dividend of a subsidiary, whether declared or not.

**Disclosure :**

Following disclosure should be made in Consolidated Financial Statements :

- List of all subsidiaries.
- Proportion of ownership interest.
- Nature of relationship between parent and subsidiary whether direct control or control through subsidiaries.
- Name of the subsidiary of which reporting dates are different.
- The fact for different accounting policies applied for preparation of consolidated financial statements.
- If consolidation of particular subsidiary has not been made as per the grounds allowed in accounting standards the reason for not consolidating should be disclosed.

AS-21 also focusses on the following points :

- Interpretations issued by the ICAI.
- Transactional provisions.
- Significant differences among AS, IFRS/IAS and US GAAP.

## PRACTICAL EXAMPLES

**Example 1**

What are the exceptions to AS-21 ?

**Answer**

AS-21 does not deal with :

i) Methods of accounting for amalgamations and their effects on consolidation, including goodwill arising on amalgamation (see AS-14, Accounting for Amalgamations);

ii) Accounting for investments in associates (at present governed by AS-23, Accounting for Investments in Associates in Consolidated Financial Statements) and

iii) Accounting for investments in joint ventures (governed by AS-27, Financial Reporting of Interests in Joint Ventures).

### Example 2

If A is holding 60% in B and B is holding 60% in C, will C be consolidated in B and ultimately in A ?

### Answer

Consolidation is required when there is ownership of more than one-half of voting power directly or indirectly through subsidiaries. In this case though the effective ownership of, A is 36%, A is able to exercise more than one-half of the voting power in C through its majority holding in B. E.g., if a resolution is put to vote in C, A because of its control over B will be able to pass or veto that resolution. Hence, C will be consolidated in B, and consequently in A.

### Example 3

Parent Co. A owns 100% of subsidiary B and 49% of C. Subsidiary B in turn, owns 10% of C. Parent Co. A controls C through direct and indirect ownership and would therefore consolidate it.

### Answer

Parent Co. A owns 51% of subsidiary B, which in turn owns 51% of subsidiary C. Again parent Co. A controls subsidiary C and would consolidate it. On the other hand, if parent company A owned only 49% of B, control would not result. If company A does not control company B, company B's investment in company C is irrelevant to whether company A controls company C.

### Example 4

X Ltd. is Textile Manufacturing Co., it has purchased 75% equity shares of Y Ltd., which is a Software Company. X Ltd, did not consolidate the accounts of Y Ltd, on the pretext that subsidiary business is entirely different and it does not make sense to consolidate the subsidiary Y Ltd. accounts. Comment.

### Answer

Contention is not correct as per AS-21.

### Example 5

While consolidating the financial statement the Minority Interest was calculated as minus ₹ 50,000. The accountant wants to show it in assets side of consolidated Balance Sheet.
Comment.

### Answer

₹ 50,000 to be adjusted with Majority Interest.

## 1.13 AS-22 : ACCOUNTING FOR TAXES ON INCOME (1-4-2001)

**Introduction :**

This Standard deals with determination of the amount of **Tax Expenses** for the related revenues. The **tax expense** comprises current tax and deferred tax for the purpose of determining the net profit or loss for the period.

**Objective :**

AS-22, prescribes the accounting treatment for taxes on income. Traditionally, amount of tax payable was determined on the profit or loss computed as per income-tax laws. According to AS-22, tax on income is determined on the **principle of accrual** concept. According to this concept, tax should be accounted in the period in which corresponding revenue and expenses are accounted. In simple words, tax shall be accounted on accrual basis not on liability to pay basis.

**Scope :**
- Taxes on income include all domestic and foreign taxes, which are based on taxable income.
- Taxes on income exclude tax payable on distribution of dividends and other distribution made by an enterprise.

**Recognition and Measurement :**

**a)  Recognition :**

As per AS-22, the income-tax expense should be treated just like any other expenses on accrual basis irrespective of the timing of payment of tax. Tax Expenses for the period to be recognised consist of current tax and deferred tax.

**i)  Current Tax :**

**Current Tax** is the amount of income-tax determined to be payable (recoverable, in respect of the taxable income (tax loss) for a period.

**ii)  Deferred Tax :**

**Deferred Tax** is the tax effect of timing difference. Difference between the tax expenses (which is calculated on accrual basis) and current tax liability to be paid for a particular period as per the Income-Tax Act is called deferred tax (assets or liability). Therefore,

Tax Expenses = Current Tax (+) Deferred Tax

The difference between tax expenses and current tax arises only on account of timing difference and thus creates deferred tax, asset/ liability.

**b)  Measurement :**

**i)  Current Tax :**

Current Tax should be measured at the amount expected to be paid to (recovered from) taxation authorities using applicable tax rates and tax laws.

**ii)  Deferred Tax :**

Deferred Tax should be measured using the rates and tax laws that have been enacted or substantially enacted by the Balance Sheet date.

**Difference in Accounting Profit and Tax Profit :**

As we know that profit as shown in accounts differ with the profit (taxable) calculated as per Income-tax Act. The reasons of difference between two profits are of two types.

**Timing Difference :**

These differences originate in one period and are capable of reversal in one or more subsequent periods. Examples :
- Difference due to rate of depreciation.
- Difference due to method of depreciation.
- Expenses debited in the statement of profit and loss for accounting purpose but allowed for tax purpose in the subsequent year like section 43B of Income-tax Act, 1961.

**Deferred Tax :**

Deferred Tax is a tax effect of timing difference :

| | | | |
|---|---|---|---|
| a) | Accounting income is excess than tax income | Tax on accounting income is more whereas tax payable is less as per Income-tax law for the period. | Create deferred tax liability by crediting to deferred tax and debit to profit and loss account. |
| b) | Accounting income is less than tax income | Tax on accounting income is less whereas tax payable is more as per Income-tax law. | Create deferred tax asset by debiting deferred tax. |

| | | | |
|---|---|---|---|
| c) | There is income as per income-tax but loss as per accounts. | Tax on accounting loss is nil but there is liability to pay tax. | Create deferred tax assets by debiting deferred tax (subject to recoverability/ adjustments from future income). |
| d) | Accounting profit but loss as per income-tax law, however MAT is payable. | Tax on accounting profit but tax as per tax law Nil. Carry forward of loss allowed. | Create deferred tax liability for the difference. |

**A Deferred Tax Liability :**

It is recognised for temporary differences that will result in taxable amounts in future years. For example, a temporary difference is created between the depreciation as per the books of account and the depreciation claimed under the tax laws which, in the initial years, are higher than depreciation claimed as expenses in the financial statements. This would lead to a higher taxable income in future.

**A Deferred Tax Asset :**

It is recognised for temporary differences that will result in deductible amounts in future years and for carry forward. For example, a temporary difference is created between the reported amount and the tax basis of a liability for estimated expenses as for tax purpose, those estimated expenses are not deductible until a future year. Settlement of that liability will result in tax deduction in future years, and a deferred tax asset is recognised in the current year for the reduction in taxes payable in future years.

**Transitional Provision :**

When this accounting standard of taxes on income is first time applied, the amount of deferred tax asset or liability should be created in the same way had this accounting standard been in effect from the beginning. The corresponding debit or credit to the revenue reserves subject to the consideration of prudence in case of deferred tax assets.

**Prudence for Recognising Deferred Tax Asset :**

Deferred tax asset or liability should be measured for all timing differences. But deferred tax asset should be recognised and carried forward only to the extent it is reasonably certain that there will be sufficient future income to recover such deferred tax asset. In case, there is no future sufficient income, deferred tax asset should be recognised only to the extent such asset can be recovered by way of tax saving.

**Unabsorbed Depreciation and Carry Forward Losses :**

Since there is an eight time-limit for carry forward of business loss and unabsorbed depreciation in Indian tax law recognition of the deferred tax asset should be guided by the concept whether sufficient profit will be generated within the prescribed time period. To recognise deferred tax assets on this account there should be convincing evidence that sufficient taxable income will be available against which such deferred tax assets can be realised. In such circumstances, the nature of the evidence supporting its recognition is disclosed.

**Re-assessment of Unrecognised Deferred Tax Asset :**

Previously unrecognised deferred tax asset is re-assessed at every balance sheet date. If it becomes reasonably certain that such unrecognised deferred tax asset will be realised then unrecognised deferred tax asset is recognised now.

**Deferred Tax Asset and Liability :**

Should be accounted on the basis of tax rate applicable for the subsequent relevant year known at balance sheet date. When different tax rates apply to different levels of taxable income average rates should be used.

**Review of Deferred Tax Asset :**

The carrying amount of deferred tax assets should be reviewed at each balance sheet date. If it is evident that any portion of the deferred tax asset is not recoverable because of uncertainty of future income the deferred tax asset should be written down. Any such written down amount may be reversed in subsequent period to the extent that it becomes reasonably certain that sufficient future taxable income will be availably. Deferred tax assets and liabilities should not be discounted to their present value.

**Disclosure :**

- The break-up of deferred tax asset or liability should be disclosed.
- In case of deferred tax, asset arises out of unabsorbed depreciation or loss, evidence supporting recognition should be disclosed.
- Deferred tax asset or liability should be disclosed separately from current assets or liabilities. They should also be distinguished from advance tax/tax provision/tax refund due. As per the clarification issued by the ICAI, deferred tax liability should be shown after the head "Unsecured Loan" and deferred tax asset after the head "Investment" with a separate heading.
- Deferred tax asset and liability should be set off if permissible under the tax laws but to be shown separately if not permissible.
  AS-22 also focuses on the following points :
  i)   AS-22 and Income Tax Act.
  ii)  AS-22 and AS-28.
  iii) Significant difference among AS-22, IFRS/IAS-12 and USGAAP (SFAS-109).

**PRACTICAL EXAMPLES**

**Example 1**

Aditya Ltd. prepared the following reconciliation of its pre-tax financial statement income to taxable income for the financial year 2015-16. Reconciliation is given as follows :

| Particulars | ₹ |
|---|---|
| Pre-tax financial income | 1,60,000 |
| Non-taxable interest received on Government Bonds | (5,000) |
| Long-term loss accrual in excess of deductible amount | 10,000 |
| Depreciation in excess of financial statement account | (25,000) |
| ∴  Taxable Income | 1,40,000 |
| Tax rate is 35% | |

Compute: i) Current Tax, ii) Tax Expense and iii) Deferred Tax Asset/Liability.

**Answer**

i) ₹ 49,000, ii) ₹ 57,750, iii) Deferred Tax Liability ₹ 8,750.

**Example 2**

From the following details of Birla Ltd. for the year ended 31-03-2016, calculate the Deferred Tax Asset/ Liability as per AS-22.

| | ₹ |
|---|---|
| Accounting Profit | 5,00,000 |
| Book Profit as per MAT | 4,50,000 |
| Profit as per Income-Tax Act | 50,000 |
| Tax Rate | 30% |
| MAT Rate | 7.50% |

**Answer**

Tax as per accounting profit ........................... ₹ 5,00,000 × 30%     =     ₹ 1,50,000

Tax as per Income-tax profit ........................... ₹ 50,000 × 30%     =     ₹ 15,000

Tax as per MAT ........................................ ₹ 4,50,000 × 7.50%     =     ₹ 33,750

Tax Expense = Current Tax (+) Deferred Tax

₹ 1,50,000 = ₹ 15,000 (+) Deferred Tax

Therefore, Deferred Tax Liability as on 31-03-2002

= ₹ 1,50,000 (–) ₹ 15,000 = ₹ 1,35,000

Amount of tax to be debited in Profit and Loss Account for the year 31-03-2007

= Current Tax (+) Deferred Tax Liability (+) Excess of MAT over Current Tax

= ₹ 15,000 (+) ₹ 1,35,000 (+) ₹ 18,750

= ₹ 1,68,750.

**Example 3**

Justification for method of determining periodic deferred tax is based on the concept of,

a) Matching of periodic expense to periodic revenue.
b) Objectivity in calculation of periodic expense.
c) Recognition of assets and liabilities.
d) Consistency of tax expense measurements with actual tax planning strategy.

**Answer**

a) Matching of periodic expense to periodic revenue.

**EXample 4**

Castrol Ltd. reported income of ₹ 90,000 for the financial year 2015-16. Compute the provision for income-tax and deferred tax asset/liability. The following data are provided :

Rent deceived in Advance                                                          ₹ 16,000
Income from exempted Government Bonds                                              ₹ 20,000
Depreciation deducted for income-tax purpose in
excess of depreciation reported for accounting income                             ₹ 10,000
Income-tax Rate                                                                         35%

**Answer**

Current Tax ₹ 26,600, Deferred Tax Asset ₹ 2,100.

**Example 5**

Dalmiya Ltd. presents the following information for the year ending 31.3.2015 and 31.3.2016 from which you are required to calculate the Deferred Tax Asset/Liability and state how the same should be dealt with as per relevant accounting standard.

(₹ in Lakhs)

| Particulars | 31.3.2015 | 31.3.2016 |
|---|---|---|
| Depreciation | 4,010.10 | 4,023.54 |
| Unabsorbed carry forward Business Loss and Depreciation Allowance | 2,016.60 | 4,110.00 |
| Disallowance u/s. 43B of Income Tax Act, 1961 | 518.35 | 611.45 |
| Deferred Revenue Expenses | 4.88 | – |
| Provision for Doubtful Debts | 282.51 | 294.35 |

Dalmiya Ltd. had incurred a loss of ₹ 504 lakhs for the year ending 31.3.2016 before providing for current tax of ₹ 26 lakhs.

Answer

Applying income tax rate @ 35% (assumed), we calculate Deferred Tax Asset Liability as under :

(₹ in Lakhs)

| Deferred Tax Asset (A) : | | 31.3.2015 | 31.3.2016 |
|---|---|---|---|
| Unabsorbed carry forward Business Loss and Depreciation Allowance | | 705.81 | 1,438.50 |
| Disallowance u/s. 43B of Income Tax Act, 1961 | | 181.43 | 214.01 |
| Provision for Doubtful Debts | (+) | 98.99 | 103.02 |
| | | 986.23 | 1,755.53 |
| **Deferred Tax Liability (B) :** | | | |
| Deferred Revenue Expenses | | 1.71 | – |
| Net Deferred Tax Asset (A – B) | | 984.41 | 1,755.53 |

(₹ in Lakhs)

| | Balance Sheet as on | |
|---|---|---|
| Treatment in Financial Statements as per AS-22 | 31.3.2015 | 31.3.2016 |
| **Alternative I :** | | |
| Deferred Tax Asset | 986.12 | 1,755.53 |
| Deferred Tax Liability | 1.71 | NIL |
| **Alternative II :** | | |
| Net Deferred Tax Asset (+) | 984.41 | 1,755.53 |

**Notes :**

i)   Deferred tax asset is to be shown under the head 'Investments', whereas, deferred tax liability is to be shown under the head 'Unsecured loans'.

ii)  It is assumed that there is a virtual certainty that there would be sufficient taxable profits in future year(s) to set off carry forward losses.

Example 6

Eastern Ltd.'s accounting year ends on 31st March. The company made a loss of ₹ 2,00,000 for the year ending 31.3.2014. For the year ending 31.3.2015 and 31.3.2016, it made profits of ₹ 1,00,000 and ₹ 1,20,000 respectively. It is assumed that the loss of a year can be carried forward for eight years and tax rate is 40%. By the end of 31.3.2014, the company feels that there will be sufficient taxable income in the future years against which carry forward loss can be set off. There is no difference between taxable income and accounting income except that the carry forward loss is allowed in the years ending 2015 and 2016 for tax purposes.

Prepare a statement of profit and loss for the years ending 2014, 2015 and 2016.

Answer

**In the books of Eastern Ltd.**
**Statement Showing Profit and Loss for the year ended 31st March ...**

| Particulars | 2014 ₹ | 2015 ₹ | 2016 ₹ |
|---|---|---|---|
| Profit/(Loss) | (2,00,000) | 1,00,000 | 1,20,000 |
| Current Tax @ 40% | – | – | (8,000) |
| **Deferred Tax Asset** | | | |
| Tax effect on timing difference – | | | |
| • Originating during the year | 80,000 | – | – |
| • Reversing during the year | – | (40,000) | (40,000) |
| ∴ **Profit and Loss after Tax Effect** | **1,20,000** | **60,000** | **72,000** |

## 1.14  AS-23:  ACCOUNTING  FOR  INVESTMENTS  IN  ASSOCIATES  IN CONSOLIDATED FINANCIAL STATEMENTS (1-4-2002))

**Introduction :**

This Standard deals with the principles and procedures to be followed for recognising in the consolidated financial statements, the effect of the investments in associates on the financial position and operating results of a group.

**Objective :**

The accounting standard was formulated with the objective to set out the principles and procedures for recognising the investment in associates in the consolidated financial statements of the investor, so that the effect of investment in associates on the financial position of the group is indicated.

**Applicability :**

This accounting standard is applicable for investment in associates when the investor prepares consolidated financial statements. In other words, if the investor is not required to prepare consolidated financial statement, the accounting standard has no applicability.

AS-23 is not applicable in following cases :

- The investment is acquired and held exclusively with a view to its subsequent disposal in the near future.
- The associates operate under long-term restrictions that significantly impair its ability to transfer funds to the investor.
- When the investor has no significant influence in an associate or ceases to have the significant influence.
- When consolidated financial statement of investor is not made.

**What is an associate ?**

An associate is an enterprise in which the investor has significant influence and which is neither a subsidiary nor a joint venture of the investor. Significant influences mean the power to participate in the financial and operating decisions of the associate, but the investor does not control associates. Control means power to govern the financial and operating policies of an associate.

Significant influence is gained by share ownership, statute or agreement. If an investor holds directly or indirectly 20% or more of the voting power of associate, then it is assumed that investor has significant influence. However, in spite of holding 20% or more of the voting power of associate, the investor does not enjoy significant influence, then assumption of criteria of 20% or more of the voting power is null and void.

If investor holds directly or indirectly less than 20% of the voting power of the associate, it is presumed that investor does not have significant influence, unless such influence can be clearly demonstrated. The existence of the significant influence is identified by one or more of the following criteria :

- Representation in the board of directors.
- Participation in the policy-making body.
- Material transactions between investor and investee.
- Inter-change of managerial personnel.
- Provision of technical information.

It shall he noted that AS-23 is applicable only when investor has significant influence and not control, merely by purchasing 20% or more shares by the investor, the investee does not become an associate.

**Accounting for Investments in Associates :**

Investment in associate should be accounted for as per equity method in consolidated financial statement if the investor is required to prepare consolidated financial statement. From the date of cessation of significant influence, the investment in such associate should be accounted for as per AS-13 even if consolidated statements are prepared by the investor. The carrying amount of the investment at that date should be regarded as cost thereafter in the consolidated financial statement.

**Equity Method Accounting :**

The following procedure should be followed in the Equity Method of Accounting :

- The investment is initially recorded at cost.
- Identify only (not record the accounting entry for goodwill/capital reserve) any goodwill/capital reserve at the time of acquisition of investment.
- Goodwill/ Capital Reserve identified at the time of acquisition of investment should be included in the carrying amount investment in associate but should be disclosed separately.
- Carrying amount is increased/decreased to recognise the investor's share of the profits and losses of the associate after the date of acquisition.
- Distributions received from associate should be reduced from the carrying amount.
- Adjustment to the carrying amount should be made for alterations in the investor's proportionate interest in the associate arising from changes in the associate's equity that have not been included in the profit and loss account. Such as changes arising from revaluation of fixed assets and investment, from foreign exchange transaction etc.
- Unrealised profits and losses resulting front transactions between investor and the associate should be eliminated to the extent of the investor's interest in tile associate.
- Unrealised losses should not be eliminated. However, if the recoverable amount of transferred asset is more than the transfer cost of the asset the unrealised losses should also be eliminated.
- Investor share in associate's profits or losses should be computed after adjusting dividend on cumulative preference share whether or not dividend has been declared.

The meaning of the recoverable amount should be taken from AS-28.

**Carrying Amount of Investment in associate :**

If there is permanent decrease in the value of investment in associate, the carrying amount of investment in associate should be reduced by the amount of permanent reduction.

If investor's share of losses in associates equals or exceeds the carrying amount of investment, the investor discontinues recognising its share of further losses and investment is reported at nil value.

**Consolidated Financial Statements :**

Where an associate presents consolidated financial statements, the results and net assets to be taken into account are those reported in that associate's consolidated financial statements.

**Contingencies :**

In the Consolidated financial statement of investor following facts should be disclosed :

- Its share of the contingencies and capital commitments of an associate for which it is also contingently liable.
- Those contingencies that arise because the investor is severally liable for the liabilities of the associate.

**Disclosures :**

Investor should disclose in its consolidated financial statement the following :
- Description of associate including the proportion of ownership interest should be disclosed.
- Investment in associates accounted for using the equity method should be classified as long-term investments.
- Difference in reporting dates of financial statements of associates and of the investor should be disclosed.
- In case an associate uses accounting policies other than those adopted for the consolidated financial statements for transactions and events in similar circumstances and it is not practicable to make appropriate adjustments to the associate's financial statements, the fact should be disclosed along with a brief description of the differences in the accounting policies.

AS-23 also focuses on the following points :
- Interpretation issued by ICAI.
- Transactional provision.
- Significant difference among AS-23, IFRS/IAS-28 and USGAAP (APB-18).

## PRACTICAL EXAMPLES

**Example 1**

Axis Ltd acquired 25% of Bosch Ltd.'s share on 6th April, 2015; the price paid was ₹ 1,25,000. Bosch Ltd.'s shareholder equity on that day was as follows :

| Particulars | | ₹ |
|---|---|---|
| Share Capital | | 1,00,000 |
| **Add :** Retained Earnings | (+) | 20,000 |
| ∴ **Shareholders Equity** | | **1,20,000** |

Further, Axis Ltd. incurred a heavy loss of ₹ 8,00,000, for the financial year 2015-16. What will be the amount of investment to be shown in the consolidated Balance Sheet of Bosch Ltd. as on 31.03.2009 ?

**Answer**

Consolidated Balance Sheet – Investment – Nil.

**Example 2**

An investor owns 10,000 shares (30%) of Crompton Ltd. common stock for which it paid ₹ 2,50,000, ten years ago, On 1st October, 2014 the investor sold Crompton Ltd.'s 5,000 shares for ₹ 3,75,000. The balance in the investment in Crompton Ltd. account on 1-4-2014 is ₹ 6,00,000 in consolidated financial statement. Assuming that the investee had net income of ₹ 1,00,000 for 6 months upto 30th September, 2007.
- a) calculate the gain (loss) upon the sale of 5,000 shares in separate financial statement.
- b) calculate the carrying amount of investment in consolidated Balance Sheet of the investor.

   Further, Crompton Ltd. reported earning for the second half of financial year 2014-15 and for financial year 2015-16 respectively of ₹ 1,50,000 and ₹ 3,50,000 Crompton Ltd. paid dividends of ₹ 1,00,000 and ₹ 1,50,000 in the month of March of these years. On 2nd April 2015, the investor purchased 10,000 shares of Crompton Ltd. for ₹ 7,00,000 increasing its ownership to 45%.
- c) calculate the value of investment in consolidated Balance Sheet of the investor.

**Answer**

a) ₹ 2,50,000, b) ₹ 3,15,000, c) ₹ 11,05,000.

**Example 3**

Deccan Ltd., acquired 40% shares of Elecon Ltd., for ₹ 2,80,000 on 5th May, 2016. The shareholders' equity of Elecon Ltd. was as under :

| Particulars | | ₹ |
|---|---|---|
| | Equity Share Capital | 1,00,000 |
| **Add :** | Securities Premium | 3,00,000 |
| **Add :** | Profit and Loss Account    (+) | 1,00,000 |
| ∴ | **Shareholders Equity** | **5,00,000** |

For the year ended 31.3.2015, Elecon Ltd. reported a net profit after tax of ₹ 60,000 and paid dividend of ₹ 20,000. Calculate the amount at which the investment in Elecon Ltd. should be shown in the Consolidated Financial Statements of Deccan Ltd., assuming it has subsidiaries on 31.3.2015.

**Answer**

**In the books of Deccan Ltd.**
**Consolidated Financial Statements as on 31.3.2015**

| Liabilities | ₹ | Assets | ₹ |
|---|---|---|---|
| | | Investment in Associate (Goodwill ₹ 80,000*) | 2,96,000** |
| | | **Goodwill :** | |
| | | Cost of Investment | 2,80,000 |
| | | **Less :** 40% of Shareholders | |
| | | Equity of Elecon Ltd.    (−) | 2,00,000 |
| | | | 80,000 |
| | | ****Long-term Investment in Associate :** | |
| | | Investment at Cost | 2,80,000 |
| | | **Add :** Share of Profit (40% of | |
| | | ₹ 60,000)    (+) | 24,000 |
| | | | 3,04,000 |
| | | **Less :** Dividend received (40% of ₹ 20,000)    (−) | 8,000 |
| | | | 2,96,000 |

**Example 4**

Felcon Ltd. purchased 30% equity shares of Gemini Ltd. on 1.4.2014 at a cost of ₹ 10,00,000. The shareholders' equity of Gemini Ltd. on that date was as under :

| Particulars | | ₹ |
|---|---|---|
| | Equity Share Capital | 20,00,000 |
| **Add :** | Reserves and Surplus    (+) | 6,00,000 |
| ∴ | **Shareholders Equity** | **26,00,000** |

During the financial years 2014-15 and 2015-16, Gemini Ltd incurred losses of ₹ 20,00,000 and ₹ 30,00,000 respectively. You are required to show how the investment will be shown in the Consolidated Financial Statements of Felcon Ltd. as on 31.3.2015 and 31.3.2016.

Answer

**In the books of Felcon Ltd.**
**Consolidated Financial Statements as on 31.3.2015**

| Liabilities | ₹ | Assets | ₹ |
|---|---|---|---|
| | | Investment in Associate (Goodwill ₹ 2,20,000*) | 4,00,000** |
| | | | ₹ |
| | | **Goodwill :** | |
| | | Cost of Investment | 10,00,000 |
| | | **Less :** 30% of Shareholders of Gemini Ltd. | |
| | | (30% of ₹ 26,00,000)                   (–) | 7,80,000 |
| | | | **2,20,000** |
| | | ****Long-term Investment in Associate :** | ₹ |
| | | Investment at Cost | 10,00,000 |
| | | **Less :** Share of Loss | |
| | | (30% of ₹ 20,00,000)                   (–) | 6,00,000 |
| | | | **4,00,000** |

**Consolidated Financial Statements as on 31.3.2016**

| Liabilities | ₹ | Assets | ₹ |
|---|---|---|---|
| | | Investment in Associate | Nil* |
| | | ** Long-term Investment in Associate | ₹ |
| | | Investment at book value | |
| | |                                   4,00,000 | 4,00,000 |
| | | **Less :** Share of Loss | |
| | | (30% of ₹ 30,00,000)                   (–) | 9,00,000 |
| | | | **Nil** |

## 1.15 AS-24 : DISCONTINUED OPERATIONS (8-2-2002)

**Introduction :**

This Standard lays down the principles for reporting information about discontinued operations, with an objective to enhance the ability of users of financial statements to make projection of enterprises' cash flows, earnings generating capacity, and financial position by segregating information about discontinued operations from information about continuing operations.

**Objective :**

The objective of this statement is to establish principles for reporting information about discontinuing operations. This standard covers **"discontinuing operations"** rather than **"discontinued operations".** The focus of the disclosure of the information is on the operations which the enterprise plans to discontinue rather than disclosing about the operations which are already discontinued. However, the disclosure about discontinued operation is also covered by this standard.

Traditionally, the Profit and Loss Account provides the information about the overall profit of the enterprise; if the segment information as per AS-17 is provided, a user can get the information about business segment and geographical segments. However, whether these segments will be continued in future or not is not provided by AS-17. If the enterprise has some plans to discontinue the operation of particular segment, the user has to understand the information About the discontinuing operation distinctly from those of the continuing operation so that the user can make projections of an enterprise cash flows, earning generating capacity and financial position by segregating information about discontinuing operation from information about continuing operation.

**Meaning :**

As per paragraph 3 of the standard a **Discontinuing Operation** is a component of an enterprise :

- That the enterprise, pursuant to a single plan is,
  - Disposing of substantially in its entirety such as selling the component in a single transaction or by demerger or spin off of ownership of the component to the enterprise's shareholders or
  - Disposing of piecemeal, such as by selling off the components assets and setting its liabilities individually or
  - Terminating through abandonment and
  - That represents separate major line of business or geographical area of operation and
  - That can be distinguished operationally and for financial reporting purposes.

It is very clear from the above definition that **Discontinuing Operation** is relatively large component of an enterprise which is major line of business of geographical segment, this is distinguishable operationally or for financial reporting. Such component of business is being disposed on the basis of an overall plan in its entirety or in piecemeal. Discontinuance will be carried either through demerger or spin-off piecemeal, disposal of assets and settling of liabilities or by abandonment, e.g. Tata Ltd, has three major lines of business steel, tea and electrical appliances, it had decided to sell the steel division during the financial year 2015-2016. A sale agreement has been entered into on 30th November 2015 with Zensar Ltd. under which steel division shall be transferred to Zenzar Ltd. on 30th March, 2016. This is a case of disposing of substantially in its entirety. However, if resolution is passed for sale of various assets and to repay the various liabilities individually of steel division, accordingly the assets like land and buildings, plant and machinery are sold separately and various liabilities like those of creditors are paid individually, it is a case of **"disposing by piecemeal"**.

**Termination by Abandonment :**

An enterprise may terminate an operation by abandonment without substantial sale of assets, however, if scope of operation is changed, it is not a case of discontinuing operation as the operation is continuing although in altered manner; closure of product line may not necessarily signify discontinuing operation if the operation is continuing for a different product. It should be noted that any planned change in the product line may not be treated as **Discontinuing Operation.**

**Abrupt or Unplanned Changes :**

Further, any abrupt change or unplanned change in the product line is not discontinuing operation, e.g. Accounting Standard gives some examples which do not necessarily satisfy criteria of discontinuing operation but might be considered discontinuing operation in combination with other circumstances e.g.

- Gradual phasing out of product line of class of service,
- Discontinuing, even if abruptly, several products within an ongoing line of business.
- Shifting of some production or marketing activities for particular line of business from one location to another.
- Closing of facility to achieve productivity, improvements or other cost savings.
- Selling a subsidiary whose activities are similar to those of the parent or other subsidiaries - this is in relation to consolidated financial statements. In fact, it is a case of disposing of investments in subsidiary of subsidiaries,

**Initial Disclosure Event :**

Information about panned discontinuance must be disclosed in the first set of financial statement immediately after the 'initial disclosure event', initial disclosure event is the event out of these two and whichever occurs earlier –

- Entering into an agreement to sell substantially all the assets of the discontinuing operation.
- Approving and announcing of the discontinuance plan.

**Presentation and Disclosure :**

- **Initial Disclosure :**
  First disclosure after initial disclosure event occurs about the discontinuing operations.
  - Description of the discontinuing operation.
  - Business or geographical segments in which it is reported.
  - Date and nature of initial disclosure event.
  - Timing of expected completion of discontinuance.
  - Carrying amount of total assets and liabilities to be disposed of.
  - Amount of revenue and expense attributable to discontinuing operation.
  - Amount of pre-tax profit or loss and tax expense attributable to discontinuing operation.
  - Net cash flows attributable to the operating, investing financing activities of the discontinuing operation.

**Other Disclosure :**

When an enterprise disposes of assets or settles liabilities attributable to a discontinuing operation, the following other informations are also disclosed,

- Amount of gain or loss recognised on the disposal of assets or settlement of liabilities and related income-tax.
- Net selling prices from the sale of those net assets for which the enterprise has entered into binding sale agreements and the expected liming thereof and carrying amount of those assets.

**Manner of Disclosure :**

The disclosure of amount of pre-tax profit or loss and tax expense and amount of gain or loss recognised on the disposal of assets and settlement of liabilities should be disclosed on the face of statement of profits/loss accounts, other information should be disclosed in the notes to accounts.

**Updating the Disclosure :**

The disclosure required for discontinuing operation should continue in financial statements for the period upto and including the period in which the discontinuance is completed, the disclosure required should be updated.

**Recognition and Measurement :**

Standard prescribes that an enterprise should comply with the principles of recognition and measurement that are set out in other accounting standards for the purpose of deciding how and when to recognise and measure the changes in assets and liabilities and the income and expense and cash flow of discontinuing operation.

**Interim Financial Reports :**

Interim financial reports should disclose in its notes any significant activity or event since the end of the most recent annual reporting relating to discontinuing operation and any significant change in the amount, or timing of cash flows relating to assets and liabilities to be disposed /settled.

**Significant difference between AS-24, IFRS/IAS-5 and USGAAP (FASB-144) :**

- AS-24 has been tilted as "discontinuing operation" whereas the corresponding IFRS-5 is named as "Non-current assets held for sale and discontinued operation", corresponding US GAAP (FASB-144) issued in 2001 is titled as "Accounting for the impairment of Disposed of Long-lived Assets".
- IAS-35 has been superseded by IFRS-5, AS-24 is based on IAS-35. Perhaps, ICAI shall also revise the AS-24 in line with IFRS-5. Reason for issuing the IFRS-5 was to converge the US GAAP with IFRS to the extent possible.
- As per AS-24 (Indian GAAP) the disclosure for 'discontinuing operation' is to be made after the initial disclosure event; whereas as per IFRS-5 the disclosure for 'discontinuing operation' is done after the classification of non-current asset as 'held for sale'. The way the 'held for sale' is defined under US GAAP (FASB-144), the disclosure for 'discontinuing operation" will be earlier as compared to IFRS-5 and AS-24.
- As per IFRS-5 and US GAAP (FASB-144) after the non-current assets are classified as 'held for sale' these will be carried at lower of carrying amount and fair value, whereas as per AS-24 these assets are to be carried at cost less depreciation less impairment loss.
- As per IFRS-5, Assets/ Liabilities classified as 'held for sale' are to be presented separately on the face of the balance sheet, similarly income pertaining to discontinuing operation to be separately disclosed on the face of the income statement. However, AS-24 and US GAAP do not prescribe so and, disclosure is made through notes to accounts.

## PRACTICAL EXAMPLES

### Example 1

Ambuja Ltd., a textile company, has a subsidiary Branny Ltd. Ambuja Ltd. holds 80% share in Branny Ltd. During 2015-16, Ambuja sold its entire investment in Branny Ltd. Can it be called discontinuing operation ? If yes, what disclosure as per AS-24 is required ?

### Answer

No, Disclosure as per AS-24 is not required.

### Example 2

Camlin Ltd. has two divisions Computer and Cloths. During the year by demerger the computer division was separated by forming a new company Dodex Ltd. Is it a discounting operation as per AS-24 ?

### Answer

Yes, it is a discontinuing operation.

### Example 3

Is there a separate method provided by AS-24 for "Recognition of Revenue and Expenses, Assets and Liabilities ?

### Answer

No, there is no separate method for the same.

**Example 4**

The objective of AS-24 is to disclose the information about,

a) discontinued operation.
b) discontinuing operation.
c) discontinued operation is not covered.
d) business operation.

**Answer**

b) Discontinuing operation.

**Example 5**

Essar Ltd produces a single product. It has changed its geographical segments for the product as follows :

| Period | North India Monthly Units | East India Monthly Units |
| --- | --- | --- |
| January, 2015 to September, 2015 | 4,00,000 | 4,00,000 |
| October, 2015 to December, 2015 | 2,00,000 | 6,00,000 |
| January, 2016 to March, 2016 | – | 8,00,000 |

Earlier, the company was marketing the production in two geographic segments. Because of stiff competition and falling margin in the North Indian market, it had gradually closed down its operations in North India and shifted all its activities to East India.

Should this event form a part of discontinuing operations ?

**Answer**

In response to market forces, this change is merely a shifting of marketing activities from North India to East India. As per para 3, a **discontinuing operation** is a component of an enterprise :

a) that the enterprise, pursuant to a single plan, is –
   i) disposing of substantially in its entirety, such as by selling the component in a single transaction or by demerger or spin-off of ownership of the component to the enterprise's shareholders, or
   ii) disposing of piecemeal, such as by selling off the component's assets and settling its liabilities individually; or
   iii) terminating through abandonment; and
b) that represents a separate major line of business or geographical area of operations; and
c) that can be distinguished operationally and for financial reporting purposes.

From the above, it can be concluded that a discontinuing operation should result in a change in component of an enterprise. Therefore, this gradual phasing out of a geographical segment is not a discontinuing operation, since it does not meet the above definition criteria.

## 1.16 AS-25 : INTERIM FINANCIAL REPORTING (1-4-2002)

**Introduction :**

This Standard deals with the minimum content of interim financial report and prescribes the principles for recognition and measurement in complete or condensed financial statements for an interim period. This standard does not indicate anything about the frequency of such reporting.

**Meaning :**

**Interim Financial Reporting** is the reporting for periods of less than a year generally for a period of 3 months. As per clause 41 of listing agreement the companies are required to publish the financial results on a quarterly basis.

As per this standard, **Interim Financial Report** means a financial report containing either a complete set of financial statement or a set of condensed financial statement for an interim period. Interim period is a period of reporting shorter than full financial year.

A complete set of **Financial Statements** normally includes Balance Sheet, Statement of Profit and Loss Account, Cash Flow Statement and Notes to Accounts and Accounting Policies.

**Need :**

In general the basic objective of **Interim Financial Reporting** is to provide frequent and timely assessment of enterprise performance. However, interim reporting has inherent limitation, which is not the case of annual accounts as the reporting period is shortened, the effect of errors in estimations and allocation are magnified. The proper allocation of operation expenses is a significant concern. The main problems involved are :

- Proper allocation of operating expenses.
- Some operating expenses may be incurred in one interim period and yet benefit the full year operation. e.g. advertising, repair and maintenance etc.
- Seasonal fluctuation - for some enterprises revenue may be seasonal or cyclical and therefore, concentrated in certain interim period.
- Year-end events. e.g. Bonus, Incentive based on annual sales target etc.
- Determination of appropriate amount of provision e.g. pension, gratuity, litigation, contingencies etc.
- Income-Tax Expenses - one interim period may have profit and next interim period may have losses.

**Objective :**

The objective of this standard is to prescribe the minimum content of Interim Financial Report and to prescribe the principles for recognition and measurement in a complete or condensed financial statement for an interim period. As the reporting period is shortened, the effect of errors in estimations and allocation increases.

**Principles of Recognition and Measurements :**

As the objective of this Accounting Standard is to prescribe the principle for recognition and measurement of income, expenses, assets and liabilities in a complete or condensed financial statements i.e. Balance Sheet, Profit and Loss Account, Cash flow Statements and Accounting Notes and Policies, there may be two distinctive principles or views of recognition and measurement of income and expenses in interim financial reporting i.e. i) Integral View and ii) Discrete View.

**i)  Integral View :**

An approach to measuring interim period income by viewing each interim period as an integral part of the annual (Financial) period. Expenses are recognised in proportion to revenues earned through the use of special accruals and deferrals.

**ii)  Discrete View :**

An approach to measuring interim period income by viewing each interim period separately.

AS-25 resolves the debate by prescribing the discrete view in general. As per the standard – Income and expenses should be recognised/measured on year to date basis for interim reporting.

Year to date basis means financial reporting for the period, which begins on the first day of the fiscal and year ends on the given interim date.

**Estimated Annual Effecting Tax Rate :**

An expected annual tax rate which reflects estimates of annual earnings tax rate, tax credits etc.

Interim period income-tax expense is accrued using the tax rate that would be applicable to expected total annual earnings, that is, the estimated average annual effective income-tax rate applied to the pretax income of the interim period.

**Accounting Policies :**

An enterprise should apply the same accounting policies in the interim financial statements as are applied in the annual financial statements.

**Minimum Components of Interim Financial Report :**

An interim financial report should contain at least the following components :

- Condensed Balance Sheet
- Condensed Profit and Loss Account
- Condensed Cash Flow Statement
- Selected Explanatory Notes

Reporting interim financial statements in condensed manner has been prescribed on cost consideration and for timely release of the information. However, an enterprise may release complete financial statements.

**Form and Contents of Interim Financial Statements :**

An interim financial report can contain either a complete set of financial statements or a set of Condensed Financial statements.

**i)  Complete Financial Statements :**

If an enterprise opts to prepare and presents a complete set of financial statements in the interim financial reporting. It should be prepared in the same format and as per the contents and requirements of annual financial statements.

**ii) Condensed Financial Statements :**

A condensed interim financial reporting should contain the following minimum information :

- Headings and sub-totals that were included. In the most recent annual financial statements.
- Selected Explanatory Notes.
- Additional items or notes if their missing makes the interim financial reporting misleading.
- Basic and diluted earning per share for the interim period as per AS-20 (not to be annualised) (on the face of Profit and Loss Statements).

The format of condensed financial statements is given in the Annexure.

**Selection of Explanatory Notes :**

Criteria adopted for selection of explanatory notes to be included in interim financial report is updating the financial information, it is assumed that the users of interim financial report are having access to the most recent annual financial statements therefore notes to interim financial report should provide information on financial year to date basis. However, it is necessary to disclose any events or transactions, which are material for understanding the interim financial reporting.

**Minimum Disclosure of Notes :**

Following minimum disclosure of notes and explanatory statements should be made :

- A statement that the same accounting policies are followed in the Interim Financial Statements as these followed in the most recent statements or if these policies have been changed, a description of the nature and effect of the change.
- Description about the seasonal or cyclical effect on interim financial year.
- Unusual factors that affected assets, liabilities, equity, net income, and cash flow.

- Effect of change in estimates.
- Change in debt and equity through issuance, repurchase and repayments.
- Details of dividend payment.
- Segment revenue, segment result for business segment or geographical segment, whichever is the primary basis of the reporting entity.
- Material event that occurred after the end of interim period.
- Effect of changes in composition of the enterprise during interim period - change in composition include business combination, acquisition, restructuring disposal of subsidiaries etc.
- Material changes in contingent liabilities since the last Balance Sheet date.

**Materiality :**

Materiality is one of the most fundamental concepts underlying financial report. Therefore, para 21 of the standard provides that in deciding how to recognise, measure, classify or disclose an item for interim financial reporting purposes, materiality should be assessed in relation to the interim period financial data.

Information is material if its misstatement that is omission or error could influence the economic decisions of users taken on the basis of the financial information.

The overriding objective is to ensure that an interim financial report includes all information that is relevant to understanding an enterprise's financial position and performance during the interim period.

AS-25 also focuses on following points :

- Seasonal/Occasional Revenue.
- Change in Estimates.
- Change in Accounting Policy.
- Cost incurred unevenly during the financial year.
- Major planned periodic maintenance or overhaul.
- Depreciation and amortisation.
- Applicability of Interim Financial results (ASI-27).
- Significant differences among AS-25, IFRS/IAS-34 and USGAAP (APB-28).

**ANNEXURE**

**Illustrative Format of Condensed Financial Statements for an Enterprise other than a Bank**

**A) Condensed Balance Sheet**

| Particulars | Figure at the end of the Current Interim Period ₹ | Figure at the end of the Previous Accounting Year ₹ |
|---|---|---|
| **I.  Source of Funds :** | | |
| 1.  Capital | | |
| 2.  Reserves and Surplus | | |
| 3.  Minority interest (in case of consolidated financial statements) | | |
| 4.  Loan Funds : | | |
|     a)  Secured Loans | | |
|     b)  Unsecured Loans | | |

| | | |
|---|---|---|
| **Total** | | |
| **II.  Application of Funds :** | | |
| 1.  Fixed Assets : | | |
| a)  Tangible Fixed Assets | | |
| b)  Intangible Fixed Assets | | |
| 2.  Investments | | |
| 3.  Current Assets, Loans and Advances | | |
| a)  Inventories | | |
| b)  Sundry Debtors | | |
| c)  Cash and Bank Balances | | |
| d)  Loans and Advances | | |
| e)  Others | | |
| **Less :** Current Liabilities and Provisions | | |
| a)  Liabilities | | |
| b)  Provisions | | |
| Net Current Assets | | |
| 4.  Miscellaneous Expenditure to the extent not written off or adjusted. | | |
| 5.  Profit and Loss Account | | |

### (B)  Condensed Statements of Profit and Loss

| Particulars | Three months ended ₹ | Corresponding three months of the previous accounting year ₹ | Year-to-date figures for current period ₹ | Year-to-date figures for the previous year ₹ |
|---|---|---|---|---|
| 1.  Turnover | | | | |
| 2.  Other Income | | | | |
| **Total** | | | | |
| 3.  Changes in Inventories of Finished Goods and Work-in-Progress | | | | |
| 4.  Cost of Raw Material and Consumables used | | | | |
| 5.  Salaries, Wages and Other Staff Costs | | | | |
| 6.  Other Expenses | | | | |
| 7.  Interest | | | | |
| 8.  Depreciation and Amortisation | | | | |
| **Total** | | | | |
| 9.  Profit or Loss from ordinary activities before tax | | | | |
| 10.  Extraordinary items | | | | |
| 11.  Profit or Loss Before Tax | | | | |
| 12.  Tax Expenses | | | | |

| | | | |
|---|---|---|---|
| 13. Profit or Loss After Tax | | | |
| 14. Minority Interests (in case of consolidated financial statements) | | | |
| 15. Net Profit or Loss for the period | | | |
| Earnings Per Share | | | |
| 1. Basic Earnings Per Share | | | |
| 2. Diluted Earnings Per Share | | | |

### (C) Condensed Cash Flow Statement

| Particulars | Year-to-date figures for the current period ₹ | Year-to-date figures for the previous year ₹ |
|---|---|---|
| 1. Cash Flows from Operating Activities | | |
| 2. Cash Flows from Investing Activities | | |
| 3. Cash Flows from Financing Activities | | |
| 4. Net increase/decrease in cash and cash equivalents | | |
| 5. Cash and cash equivalents at the beginning of the period | | |
| 6. Cash and cash equivalents at the end of the period. | | |

### (D) Selected Explanatory Notes

This part should contain selected explanatory notes as required by paragraph 16 of this standard.

**Illustrative Format of Condensed Financial Statement for a Bank :**

### (A) Condensed Balance Sheet

| Particulars | Figure at the end of the Current Interim Period ₹ | Figure at the end of the Previous Accounting Year ₹ |
|---|---|---|
| **I. Capital and Liabilities :** | | |
|   1. Capital | | |
|   2. Reserves and Surplus | | |
|   3. Minority interest (in case of consolidated financial statements) | | |
|   4. Deposits | | |
|   5. Borrowings | | |
|   6. Other Liabilities and Provisions | | |
| **Total** | | |
| **II. Assets :** | | |
|   1. Cash and balances with Reserve Bank of India | | |
|   2. Balances with banks and money at call and short notice | | |
|   3. Investments | | |
|   4. Advances | | |
|   5. Fixed Assets | | |
|     a) Tangible Fixed Assets | | |
|     b) Intangible Fixed Assets | | |
|   6. Other Assets | | |
| **Total** | | |

**(B) Condensed Statements of Profit and Loss**

| Particulars | Three months ended ₹ | Corresponding three months of the previous accounting year ₹ | Year-to-date figures for current period ₹ | Year-to-date figures for the previous year ₹ |
|---|---|---|---|---|
| **1. Interest Earned** | | | | |
|   a) Interest/discount on advances/bill | | | | |
|   b) Interest on investments | | | | |
|   c) Interest on balances with Reserve Bank of India and other banks funds | | | | |
|   d) Others | | | | |
| **2. Other Income :** | | | | |
| **Total Income**    (+) | | | | |
|   1. Interest Expended | | | | |
|   2. Operating Expenses | | | | |
|     a) Payments to and provisions for employees | | | | |
|     b) Other Operating expenses | | | | |
|   3. Total Expenses (Excluding provisions and contingencies) | | | | |
|   4. Operating Profit (Profit before provision and contingencies) | | | | |
|   5. Provisions and Contingencies | | | | |
|   6. Profit or Loss from ordinary activities before tax | | | | |
|   7. Extraordinary Items | | | | |
|   8. Profit or Loss Before Tax | | | | |
|   9. Tax Expenses | | | | |
|   10. Profit or Loss After Tax | | | | |
|   11. Minority Interest (In case of consolidated financial statements) | | | | |
|   12. Net Profit or Loss for the period. | | | | |
| *Earnings Per Share* | | | | |
|   1. Basic Earnings Per Share | | | | |
|   2. Diluted Earnings Per Share | | | | |

### (C) Condensed Cash Flow Statement

| Particulars | Year-to-date figures for the current period ₹ | Year-to-date figures for the previous year ₹ |
|---|---|---|
| 1. Cash Flows from Operating Activities | | |
| 2. Cash Flows from Investing Activities | | |
| 3. Cash Flows from Financing Activities | | |
| 4. Net increase/decrease in cash and cash equivalents | | |
| 5. Cash and cash equivalents at the beginning of the period | | |
| 6. Cash and cash equivalents at the end of the period. | | |

## PRACTICAL EXAMPLES

### Example 1

Ajanta Ltd. has ₹ 47,500 net income for the quarter ended 31st December, 2015 including the following details :

- ₹ 30,000 extraordinary gain received on 30th July, 2015, was allocated equally to the second, third and fourth quarter of financial years 2015-16.
- ₹ 8,000 cumulative effect loss resulting from change in method of inventory valuation method was recognised on 2nd November, 2015. Out of this loss ₹ 5,000 relates to previous quarters.

You are required to calculate the profit as per AS-25 for the quarter ended 31st December, 2015 of Ajanta Ltd.

### Answer

₹ 42,500; result of the previous year will be restated.

### Example 2

Does AS-25 apply to quarterly accounts of listed companies who are required to publish them as per SEBI rules ?

### Answer

In such a case, the recognition and measurement principles as laid down in AS-25 are applied in respect of such information, unless otherwise specified in the statute or by the regulator. The disclosure requirements under AS-25 do not apply to quarterly results published under SEBI rules, since SEBI has prescribed the format of the accounts and the format does not meet the definition of an "interim financial report" as per the AS-25. However, as already mentioned, the recognition and measurement principles would be applicable (See ASI-27).

### Example 3

"AS-25 adopts more of the discrete view though the integral view is also adopted in a few cases". Do you agree with this statement.

### Answer

In case of a income tax provision, volume rebates and other anticipated price changes etc. AS-25 departs from the discrete approach. For example, income tax expenses are calculated based on the annual effective tax rate because income tax is essentially an annual phenomenon. By and large AS-25 has eliminated the possibilities of smoothing results during the interim period.

## PRACTICAL EXAMPLES

### Example 1

The following data applies to Aspro India Ltd., Ajmer's defined benefit pension plan for the year 2015-2016.

| Particulars | Amount ₹ |
|---|---|
| Fair market value of Plan Assets (beginning of year) | 4,00,000 |
| Fair market value of Plans Assets (end of year) | 5,70,000 |
| Employer Contribution | 1,40,000 |
| Benefit Paid | 1,00,000 |

Calculate the Actual Return on Plan Assets.

### Answer

**In the books of Aspro India Ltd.; Ajmer**

**Statement showing Actual Return on Plan Assets**

| | Particulars | | Amount ₹ |
|---|---|---|---|
| | Fair market value of plan assets at the end of year | | 5,70,000 |
| **Less :** | Fair market value of plan assets at the beginning of year | (–) | 4,00,000 |
| ∴ | Change in plan assets | | 1,70,000 |
| **Less :** | Adjustments for : | | 40,000 |
| | Employer Contribution | 1,40,000 | |
| **Less :** | Benefit Paid | (–) 1,00,000 | |
| ∴ | Actual Return on Plan Assets | | 1,30,000 |

### Example 2

Bokaro Tools Ltd.; Bikaner reports the following information regarding Pension Plan Assets. Calculate the Fair Value of Plan Assets.

| Particulars | Amount ₹ |
|---|---|
| Fair market value of Plan Assets (beginning of year) | 7,00,000 |
| Employer Contribution | 1,00,000 |
| Actual return on Plan Assets | 50,0000 |
| Benefits payments to retirees | 40,000 |

Answer

**In the books of Bokaro Tools Ltd., Bikaner**

**Statement showing Fair Value of Plan Assets**

| | Particulars | | Amount ₹ |
|---|---|---|---|
| | Fair market value of Plan Assets at the beginning of year | | 7,00,000 |
| **Add :** | Employer Contribution | (+) | 1,00,000 |
| | | | 8,00,000 |
| **Add :** | Actual return on Plan Assets | (+) | 50,000 |
| | | | 8,50,000 |
| **Less :** | Benefit payments to retirees | (−) | 40,000 |
| ∴ | Fair market value of Plan Assets | | 8,10,000 |

**Example 3**

**Answer the following :**

Chandrika Ltd., Chennai reviewed an actuarial valuation for the first time for its Pension Scheme, which revalued a surplus of ₹ 12,00,000. They want to spread the same over the next two years by reducing the annual contribution to ₹ 4,00,000 instead of ₹ 10,00,000. The average remaining life of the employees, if estimated to by six years, you are required to advise the Company considering the AS-5 and AS-15.

Answer

As per AS-15 (Revised 2005), on "Employee Benefits, any actuarial gains and losses should be recognised immediately in the statement of Profit and 'Loss Account as income or expense". The amount of ₹ 12,00,000. (Surplus on valuation of Pension Scheme) should be credited to the Profit and Loss Account of the current year and not be adjusted from the amount of annual contribution.

The change relating to actuarial valuation for its pension scheme should be treated as a change in accounting policy and disclosed in accordance with AS-5. The financial statements should disclose,

i)    the method for determination of these retirements benefit costs,

ii)    whether the actuarial valuation was made at the end of the period or at an earlier date, specifying such dates and

iii)    method by which the accrual for the period has been determined, if the same is not based on the report of actuary.

| Example 4 |

What are the components of pension expense for defined Benefit Pension Plan ?

| Answer |

The components of pension expenses for defined benefits pension plan are as follows :

Current service Cost, Interest Cost, Actuarial gains and losses, Past Service Cost, the effect of any curtailment re-settlements, Effect of recognition of over funding (assets) of defined benefit plan at lower of over funding amount and present value of any economic benefits available in the plan or reduction in future contribution to the plan and Expected return on any plan assets or any reimbursement rights.

| Example 5 |

Explain the treatment of cost arising from Alteration in Retirement Benefit Cost as per AS-15.

| Answer |

Alteration in the retirement benefit cost will arise from introduction of a retirement benefit scheme for existing employees or because of improving to all the existing schemes.

According to AS-15 any Alteration in Retirement Benefit Cost arising from changes in the actuarial method used or assumption adopted should be charged or credited to the statement of profit or loss as they arise in accordance with AS-5 net profit or net loss for the period, prior period items and changes in Accounting Policies.

In accordance with AS-5, a change in the actuarial method should be treated as a change in accounting policy and disclosed. The cost of additional benefits provided to retired employees due to amendments in the retirement benefit scheme should also be treated in the same way.

| Example 6 |

Dastur India Ltd., Delhi employs only three employees A, B and C, whose monthly salaries are ₹ 16,000, ₹ 12,000 and ₹ 10,000 respectively. From 1.1.2015, the firm has decided to introduce a death-cum-retirement gratuity scheme, to be funded out of its own resources. Under the scheme, each employee is entitled to half month's salaries for each completed year of service. In this connection, salary means monthly salary last drawn by concerned worker. The firm decided to evaluate gratuity obligations assuming that all employees retire at the end of each year. On 1.1.2015, number of completed years of service in respect of three employees A, B, and C were eight, six and four respectively.

You are required to compute Unfunded Past Service Cost and Retirement Benefit Cost of the year 2015.

| Answer |

As per para 28 (i) of AS-15, if the employer has chosen to make payment for retirement benefits out of its own funds, an appropriate charge to the statement of profit and loss for the year should be made through a provision for the accruing liability. The accruing liability should be calculated according to actuarial valuation. However, those enterprises which employ only a few persons may calculate the accrued liability by reference to any other rational method, e.g., a method based on the assumption that such benefits are payable to all employees at the end of the accounting year.

**In the books of Dastur India Ltd., Delhi**

**Computation of Death-cum-Retirement Gratuity Obligation up to 1.1.2015**

| Employees | Monthly Salary ₹ | Completed Years of Service | | Gratuity ₹ |
|---|---|---|---|---|
| A | 16,000 | 8 | | 64,000 |
| B | 12,000 | 6 | | 36,000 |
| C | 10,000 | 4 | (+) | 20,000 |
| | | | | 1,20,000 |

**Computation of Death-cum-Retirement Gratuity Obligation up to 31.2.2015**

| Employees | Monthly Salary ₹ | Completed Years of Service | | Gratuity ₹ |
|---|---|---|---|---|
| A | 16,000 | 9 | | 72,000 |
| B | 12,000 | 7 | | 42,000 |
| C | 10,000 | 15 | (+) | 25,000 |
| | | | | 1,39,000 |

(Gratuity = Half of monthly Salary × Completed years of service)

The death-cum-retirement benefit cost is ₹ 19,000 (₹ 1,39,000 – ₹ 1,20,000) for the year 2015. The total amount to be charged to the statement of Profit and Loss Account for the year 2015 regarding retirement benefit cost (including past service cost) is ₹ 1,39,000.

## QUESTIONS FOR SELF-STUDY

(1) What is Accounting Standards? Explain the objectives of Accounting Standards.

(2) Define the term "Accounting Standards" and explain the functions of Accounting Standard Board (ASB).

(3) What are the advantages of setting of the Accounting Standards?

(4) What are Government Grants ? State the kinds of Government Grants.

(5) Explain how AS.3 deals with the financial statement which summarises for a given period and the sources and applications of funds of an enterprise?

(6) Explain the terms: (a) Operating activities, (b) Investing activities and (c) Financial activities with reference to AS.3.

(7)   Write a detailed note on AS.3: "Cash Flow Statements".

(8)   Discuss the meaning, applicability and features of AS.3: "Cash Flow Statements".

(9)   What is 'Construction Contract as per AS-7 ? Explain the types of construction contract.

(10) Define the term 'Government Grants' as per AS-12. What is recognition of Government Grants ?

(11) What are 'Employee Benefits' as per AS-15 ? State the applicability of AS-15.

(12) Explain the treatment of costing arising from alternation in Retirement Benefit Cost as per AS-15.

(13) Difference between:

    (i)   Cash Flow from Operating and Financial Activities

    (ii)  Investment Activities and Financial Activities

    (iii) Current Investment and Long-term Investment

    (iv) Accounting Profit and Tax Profit

    (v)  Monetary Government Grants and Non-monetary Government Grants

(14) Write short notes on:

    (i)   Objectives of Accounting Standard

    (ii)  Accounting Standard Board (ASB)

    (iii) Advantages of Accounting Standard

    (iv) Applicability of AS.3

    (v)  Cash Flow from Operating Activities

    (vi) Auditor's Duties in relation to Mandatory Accounting Standards

    (vii) Tax on Income

    (viii) Types of Employee Benefits

    (ix) Objectives of AS-7 Construction Contracts

    (x)  Types of Construction Contract

    (xi) Contract Revenue

    (xii) Contract Cost

**✳✳✳**

# FINAL ACCOUNTS OF BANKING COMPANIES

**SYNOPSIS**



Etymologically, the word **'Bank'** can be traced to the French word **"Banque"** and the Italian word **"Banco"** meaning **"chest"** and **"bench"** respectively. These words sum up the two basic functions that **Commercial Banks** perform. **Chest** is a place where valuables are kept, it denotes the safekeeping function. A modern Bank's chest is the portfolio of earning assets. These are the life-blood of a Bank. The word **"Banco"** suggests a table, a counter or a place of transacting business. With reference to a Bank, these benches consist of a teller's window, a loan officer's desk, a Bank manager's cabin, desk and so on. These benches provide the customers a medium to approach the bank for conducting banking transactions. Viewed thus, the two basic functions of Commercial Banks consist of (a) providing safekeeping functions and (b) furnishing place for transacting business in money.

Commercial Banks are Joint Stock Companies dealing in money and credit. **Banking Companies in India** are governed by the Banking Regulation Act, 1949. However, provisions of the Companies Act, 1956 are also applicable to Banking Companies, provided no special provisions are made in the Banking Regulation Act, to that effect.

Ordinary rules and regulations of Book-keeping are also applicable in maintaining the books of accounts of Banking Companies. However, because of the special nature of the transactions of the Banking Company, there are some typical items which require, explanation. Further, revised formats for preparation of Balance Sheet and Profit and Loss Account have been introduced from the year 1991-92. Hence, we are going to discuss important legal provisions, as well as revised formats of Balance Sheet and Profit and Loss Account of the Banking Companies Act, 1949 as per Banking Regulations.

## 2.1 INTRODUCTION TO BANKING COMPANY

The Banking Regulation Act, 1949 defines **Banking Company** as any company which transacts the business of Banking in India. Section 5 (b) defines Banking as "accepting for the purpose of lending or investment, of deposits of money from the public, to be payable on demand or otherwise and withdrawable by cheque, draft, order or otherwise". Thus, the main functions of a banking company are, (1) to accept deposits of money from the public; and (2) to lend or invest these deposits.

Section 6 of the Act, provides that in addition to the business of banking, the **Banking Company** may also engage in any one or more forms of business, viz.

(a) the borrowing, raising, or taking up of money; the lending or advancing of money either upon or without security; the drawing, making, accepting, discounting, buying, selling, collecting and dealing in bills of exchange, promissory notes, coupons, drafts, bills of lading, railway receipts, warrants, debentures, certificates and other instruments and securities whether transferable or negotiable or not; the granting and issuing of letters of credit, traveller's cheques and circular notes; the buying, selling and dealing in million and specially the buying and selling of foreign exchange including foreign bank notes; the acquiring, holding, issuing on commission, underwriting and dealing in stock, funds, shares, debentures, stock, bonds, obligations, securities and investments of all kinds; the purchasing and selling of bonds, scrips or other forms of securities on behalf of constituents or others, the negotiating of loans and advances; the receiving of all kinds of bonds, scrips or valuables on deposit or for safe custody or otherwise; the providing of safe deposit vaults; the collecting and transmitting of money and securities;

(b) acting as agents for any Government or local authority or any other person or persons; the carrying on of agency business of any description including the clearing and forwarding of goods, giving of receipts and discharges and otherwise acting as an attorney on behalf of customers but excluding the business (of a Managing Agent or Secretary and Treasurer) of a company;

(c) contracting for public and private loans and negotiating and issuing the same;

(d) the effecting insuring, guaranteeing, underwriting, participating in managing and carrying out of any issue, public or private, of state, municipal or other loans or shares, stock, debentures, or debenture stock of any company, corporation or association and lending of money for the purpose of any such issue;

(e) carrying on the transacting of every kind of guarantee and indemnity business;

(f) managing, selling and realising any property which may come into the possession of the company in satisfaction or part satisfaction of any of its claims;

(g) acquiring and holding and generally dealing with any property or any right, title or interest in any such property which may form the security or part of the security for any loans or advances or which may be connected with any such security;

(h) undertaking and executing trusts;

(i) undertaking the administration of estates as executor, trustee or otherwise.

(j) establishing and supporting or aiding in the establishment and support of associations, institutions, funds, trusts and conveniences calculated to benefit employees or ex-employees of the company or the dependents or connections of such persons; granting pensions and allowances and making payments towards insurance subscribing to or guaranteeing moneys for charitable or benevolent objects or for any exhibition or for any public, general or useful object;

(k) the acquisition, construction, maintenance and alteration of any Buildings or Works necessary or convenient for the purposes of the company;

(l) selling, improving, managing, developing, exchanging, leasing, mortgaging, disposing, of or turning into account or otherwise dealing with all or any part of the property and rights of the company;

(m) acquiring and undertaking the whole or any part of the business of any person or company, when such business is of a nature enumerated or described in this sub-section;

(n) doing all such other things as are incidental or conducive to the promotion or advancement of the business or the company; or

(o) any other form of business which the Central Government may by notification in the Official Gazette specify as a form of business in which it is lawful for a Banking Company to engage.

## 2.2 LEGAL PROVISIONS

**Important Legal Provisions of the Banking Regulation Act 1949 are as follows :**
**a)** **Restriction on Business :**
Section 8 of the Act imposes certain restrictions on the business of a Banking Company. These **restrictions** are as follows.

i) No Banking Company can, directly or indirectly, deal in the buying or selling or bartering of goods except in connection with the realisation of security given to it or held by it.

ii) No Banking Company can engage in any trade, or buy or sell or barter goods for others except in connection with bills of exchange.

iii) No Banking Company can hold shares in any company other than its own subsidiary company, whether as pledges, mortgages or absolute owner, of an amount exceeding 30% of the paid up share capital of the other company or 30% of its own paid-up share capital and reserves, whichever is less.

**b)** **Non-Banking Assets and its Disposal :**
A Banking Company cannot acquire certain assets, but it can lend money against the security of such assets. Naturally, if the borrower fails to repay the loan, the Banking Company may take possession of such assets offered as security. Such assets are called **Non-Banking Assets** and must be shown separately in the Balance-Sheet as **"Non-Banking Assets"** in Schedule 11. Any income from such assets must be shown separately in the Profit and Loss Account of the Bank.

Section 9 of the Banking Regulation Act, 1949 provides that a Banking Company must dispose off any immovable property however acquired, except that required for its own use, within a period of seven years from the date of acquisition of such assets. However, the Reserve Bank can extend this time for its disposal upto a further period of 5 years. It is important to note here that, if the Bank acquires such assets which are allowed to be held by a bank (i.e. Government Securities), it can continue to hold them for an indefinite period. Such assets are not to be treated as Non-Banking Assets and need not be disposed off.

**c)    Capital Structure :**
Section 12 of the Banking Regulation Act, 1949 provides, that,
   i)      the subscribed capital of a Banking Company must not be less than 50% of its Authorised Capital; and
   ii)     its paid-up capital must not be less than 50% of its subscribed capital.

This section further provides that the share capital of a Banking Company should consist only  ordinary or equity shares and the voting rights of any single shareholder should not exceed 1% of the total voting rights.

**d)  Reserve Fund**
   i)      Every Banking Company incorporated in India shall create a **Reserve Fund** and [***] shall, out of the balance of profit of each year; as disclosed in the Profit and Loss Account prepared under Section 29 and before any dividend is declared, transfer to the Reserve Fund a sum equivalent to not less than **twenty percent** of such profit.
   ia)     Notwithstanding anything contained in sub-section i), the Central Government may, on the recommendation of the Reserve Bank and having regard to the adequacy of the paid-up capital and reserves of a Banking Company in relation to its deposit liabilities, declare by order in writing that the provisions of sub-section i) shall not apply to the Banking Company for such period as may be specified in the order :
   **Provided that** no such order shall be made unless, at the time it is made, the amount in the Reserve Fund under sub-section i), together with the amount in the Share Premium Account is not less than the paid-up capital of the Banking Company.
   ii)     Where a Banking Company appropriates any sum or sums from the Reserve Fund or the Share Premium Account, it shall, within twenty-one days from the date of such appropriation, report the fact to the Reserve Bank explaining the circumstances relating to such appropriation :
   **Provided that** the Reserve Bank may, in any particular case, extend the said period of twenty-one days by such period as it thinks fit or condone any delay in the making of such report.
   [**]   Certain words omitted by Act 36 of 1962, section 3 (w.e.f. 16-9-1962).
   [*]    Inserted by Act 36  of 1962, w.e.f. 1-10-1959. section 3.

**e)    Statutory Reserve :**
Section 17 of the Banking Regulation Act, 1949 makes it obligatory for a Banking Company incorporated in India to create a **Reserve Fund** and transfer to it **at least 20%** of its annual profits as disclosed by its Profit and Loss Account before declaration of dividend. Such transfer of profits to the Reserve Fund should be continued even after the aggregate amount of Reserve Fund and the Share Premium Account, if any, exceeds its paid-up capital. The Central Government may, however, grant an exemption in this regard on the recommendation of the Reserve Bank of India. If any amount from this statutory Reserve Fund is used, it must be reported to the Reserve Bank within 21 days of such use.

**f)    Cash Reserve :**
Section 42 of the Reserve Bank of India Act, 1934 requires that a scheduled bank should maintain with the Reserve Bank of India an average daily balance of at least 3% of its total time and demand liabilities in India. But the Reserve Bank of India has been given powers under Section 42 of the Reserve Bank of India Act to raise the **Cash Reserve** upto 20%.

According to Section 18 of the Banking Act, every non-scheduled bank is also required to maintain a Cash Reserve with itself or with Reserve Bank of India a sum equal to at least 3% of its total time and demand liabilities in India.

Over and above the Cash Reserve, under Section 24, every Banking Company is required to maintain in India at least 20% not exceeding 40% of its total time and demand liabilities in cash, gold or unencumbered approved securities valued at a price not exceeding the current market price. This is known as **Statutory Liquidity Reserve requirement**. However, this percentage changes from time to time on the basis of general economic conditions of the country.

**g)   Restriction on Loans and Advances :**

Section 20 of the Banking Regulation Act, 1949 as amended by the Banking Laws (Amendment) Act, 1968 provides that –

i)    no Banking Company can grant any loans or advances on the security of its own shares; and

ii)   no Banking Company can enter into any commitment for granting any loan or advance to or on behalf of –

    (a)   any of its directors, or

    (b)   any firm in which any of its directors is interested as partner, manager, employee or guarantor, or

    (c)   any company (other than a subsidiary of the Banking Company or a company registered under Section 25 of the Companies Act or a Government Company) of which any of its directors is a director, manager, employee or guarantor or in which he holds substantial interest, or

    (d)   any individual in respect of whom any of its directors is a partner or guarantor.

**h)  Bills for Collection**

Today selling is considered to be a very simple activity even though the seller and the buyer stays at different places and are unknown to each other, through a special service provided by the Bank to them viz. **Bills for Collection being Bills Receivables**. As per the purchase order the seller will supply specific type of goods to the buyer through railway or motor lorry or ship transport, but the important documents viz. railway or motor lorry receipt or bill of lading together with a bill of exchange drawn on the buyer, to their Bank. The buyer's Bank after receiving all these documents requests the buyer to honour the bill and deposit the amounts of bill in the Bank immediately. After receiving the necessary amount, the Bank hands over the concerned documents to the buyer who ultimately submits these documents to the transport authority and gets the delivery of the goods. The Bank after receiving the amount from the buyer's Bank, pays the same to the seller. For rendering this typical service of collecting the amount on behalf of the seller, the bank charges a certain commission. It is more advantageous to the buyer as well as to the seller, as the seller gets the sale amount without which goods are not delivered to the buyer and as the buyer gets the required goods when he pays the necessary amount to the Bank. Thus, Bills for Collection are certain bills received by the Bank from their customers to collect them on their due dates from the acceptors and credit the amount to their customers Current Account. These bills are recorded separately in a special book viz. "Bills for Collection Register" on collection of cash from the buyer the following journal entry is passed :

Cash A/c     Dr. (Total amount received)

    To Customer's Current A/c (The amount of bill lags commission charged)

    To Commission on Bills for Collection A/c (The amount of commission charged)

At the end of the year the bills for collection still to be collected are shown separately as Bills for Collection, after contingent liability as outside the Balance-Sheet.

**i) Acceptances, Endorsements and Other Obligations**

A Bank may accept bills on behalf of its customers and give advantage of its credit to the customers. On maturity, the Bank collects the amount of such bills from the respective customers and honours them on due dates. However, if the Bank could not collect the amount from the customer for whom it was accepted, the bank has to honour the bill on the due date by paying its own money.

The bank incurs the second liability either by accepting the bills on behalf of clients, or by endorsing the bills accepted by the clients, or by standing surety or guarantee on behalf of the clients. (The term **'other obligations'** includes letters of credit issued and guarantee given by the bank on behalf of its customers). This item is shown as a Contingent Liability outside the Balance Sheet.

**j) Rebate on Bills Discounted**

A Bank may purchase a bills receivable at a discount in which case the journal entry is passed as under :

Bills Receivable A/c            Dr.

     To Customer's Current A/c      (If on credit)

     To Bank A/c                (If for cash)

     To Discount Received A/c

Hence, as per the entry the entire amount of discount is credited to 'Discount Received Account'. However, it is possible that the maturity date of the bills discounted fails during the next financial year. Hence, the total amount of discount received should not be considered as revenue income of the current financial year. The proportionate amount of total discount relating to next year and not of the current year. Therefore, this amount relating to next year, being an 'discount received in advance' is to be carried forward as a 'other liability' and termed as 'Rebate on Bills Discounted or 'Unexpired Discount'. The following example will clarify the concept well.

A Bill of Exchange drawn and accepted on 1st January, 2016 ₹ 50,000 maturing on 31st May, 2016 is discounted @ 15%. The discounting entry will be as follows :

Bills Receivable A/c            Dr. 50,000

     To Bank A/c                     46,875

     To Discount Received A/c        3,125

Out of the total discount of ₹ 3,125, ₹ 1,875 (i.e. for 3 months for January, February and March) relates to current year, whereas for ₹ 1,250 (i.e. for 2 months for April and May) relates to next year. Hence, out of ₹ 3,125, ₹ 1,250 being discount received in advance must be transferred to Rebate on Bills Discounted Account from Discount Received Account by passing the adjusting entry as follows :

Discount Received A/c          Dr. 1,250

     To Rebate on Bills Discounted A/c      1,250

Hence, ₹ 1,250 will be deducted from interest and Discount Account in the Profit and Loss Account and shown as a 'other liability' in the Balance-Sheet.

**Accounting Treatment :**

    i)      If it is given in Trial Balance, Rebate on Bills Discounted is to be shown only on the liability side of the Balance-Sheet as 'Other Liabilities'.

    ii)     If an opening balance is given in the Trial Balance, Rebate on Bills Discounted is to be only added to 'Interest and Discount Account' in Profit and Loss Account.

   iii)     If it is given for adjustment, Rebate on Bills Discounted is to be deducted from 'Interest and Discount Account' in Profit and Loss Account and shown as 'Other Liabilities' in the Balance-Sheet on the liability side.

**EXAMPLE**

Calculate rebate on bills discounted as on 31st March, 2016 from the following information.

| Sr. No. | Date of Bill | Amount ₹ | Period | Rate of Discount |
|---|---|---|---|---|
| a) | 15.1.2016 | 25,000 | 5 Months | 8% |
| b) | 10.2.2016 | 15,000 | 4 Months | 7% |
| c) | 25.2.2016 | 20,000 | 4 Months | 7% |
| d) | 20.3.2016 | 30,000 | 3 Months | 9% |

**ANSWER**

### Statement showing Calculation of Rebate on Bills Discounted as on 31-3-2016

| Sr. No. | Date of Bill | Period | Due date (after days of grace) | Days beyond 31.3.2016 | Amount of Bill ₹ | Rate of Discount | Amount of Discount ₹ |
|---|---|---|---|---|---|---|---|
| a) | 15.1.2016 | 5 Months | 18.6.2016 | 79 | 25,000 | 8% | 432.88 |
| b) | 10.2.1010 | 4 Months | 13.6.2016 | 74 | 15,000 | 7% | 212.88 |
| c) | 25.2.2016 | 4 Months | 28.6.2016 | 89 | 20,000 | 7% | 341.37 |
| d) | 20.3.2016 | 3 Months | 23.6.2016 | 84 | 30,000 | 9% | 621.37 |
| | Total | | | | | | 1,608.50 |

**Working Notes :**

**i)** **Calculation of Days beyond 31.3.2016.**

| | April | | May | | June | | Total |
|---|---|---|---|---|---|---|---|
| a) | 30 | + | 31 | + | 18 | = | 79 |
| b) | 30 | + | 31 | + | 13 | = | 74 |
| c) | 30 | + | 31 | + | 28 | = | 89 |
| d) | 30 | + | 31 | + | 23 | = | 84 |

**ii)** **Journal Entry :**

Interest and Discount A/c        Dr.  1,608.50

    To Rebate on Bills Discount A/c        1,608.50

**k)** **Letters of Credit and Travellers' Cheques :**

Letters of Credit or Circular Letters or Circular Notes are letters addressed by a banker to correspondents certifying that a person named therein is entitled to draw on him or his credit upto a certain sum.

A person desiring to have such instrument of credit from a Bank is required to deposit full value of such instrument with the issuing Bank. Therefore, any of such instruments remaining unpaid on the date of a Balance Sheet form a liability of the Bank.

**l)** **Bills Payable :**

Bills Payable include the unpaid Bank drafts, telegraphic transfers, Bankers cheque, mail transfers and travellers cheque etc. issued by a bank on another bank or its own branch. Any such instruments remaining unpaid on the date of a Balance Sheet form liabilities of the Bank.

**m)** **Interest on Doubtful Debts :**

Interest earned on doubtful debts may be treated in any of the following ways :

    **i)** **Interest Suspense Method :** Such interest is credited to Interest Suspense Account.

    **ii)** **Cash Method :** No entry is to be passed till cash is received.

    **iii)** **Accrual Method :** Full amount is credited to Interest Account and a provision for bad and doubtful debts is made with adequate amount.

**n) Provision for Bad and Doubtful Debts**

The amount of bad debts and provision for bad debts is to be charged under the heading "Provisions and Contingencies" in the Profit and Loss Account and in the Balance Sheet. The Advances are shown after deduction of these items.

**o)  Provision for Taxation :**

The amount of Provision for Taxation has to be charged to the Profit and Loss Account under the heading "Provisions and Contingencies". In the Balance Sheet it is shown under the heading "Other Liabilities and Provisions" on the liabilities side.

**p)  Provisions and Contingencies :**

It includes all provisions made for bad and doubtful debts, provision for taxation, provisions for dimunition in the value of investments, transfer to contingencies and other similar items.

**q)  Accounting Year :**

Every Banking Company should prepare a Balance Sheet and Profit and Loss Account - as on 31st March of each year in the form set out in the Third Schedule of the Banking Regulation Act or the one as near thereto, as the circumstances admit w.e.f. 1989. But in the case of a foreign Banking, Company, the Profit and Loss Account may be prepared as on a date not earlier than two months before 31st December.

## 2.3 Non-Performing Assets (NPA)

An Asset Account becomes **non-performing when it ceases to generate income for a Bank.** Assets are classified in two categories i.e. i)  Performing Assets and ii)  Non-Performing Assets. A chart given below in Figure 2.1 shows the Classification of Assets of Banking Companies.

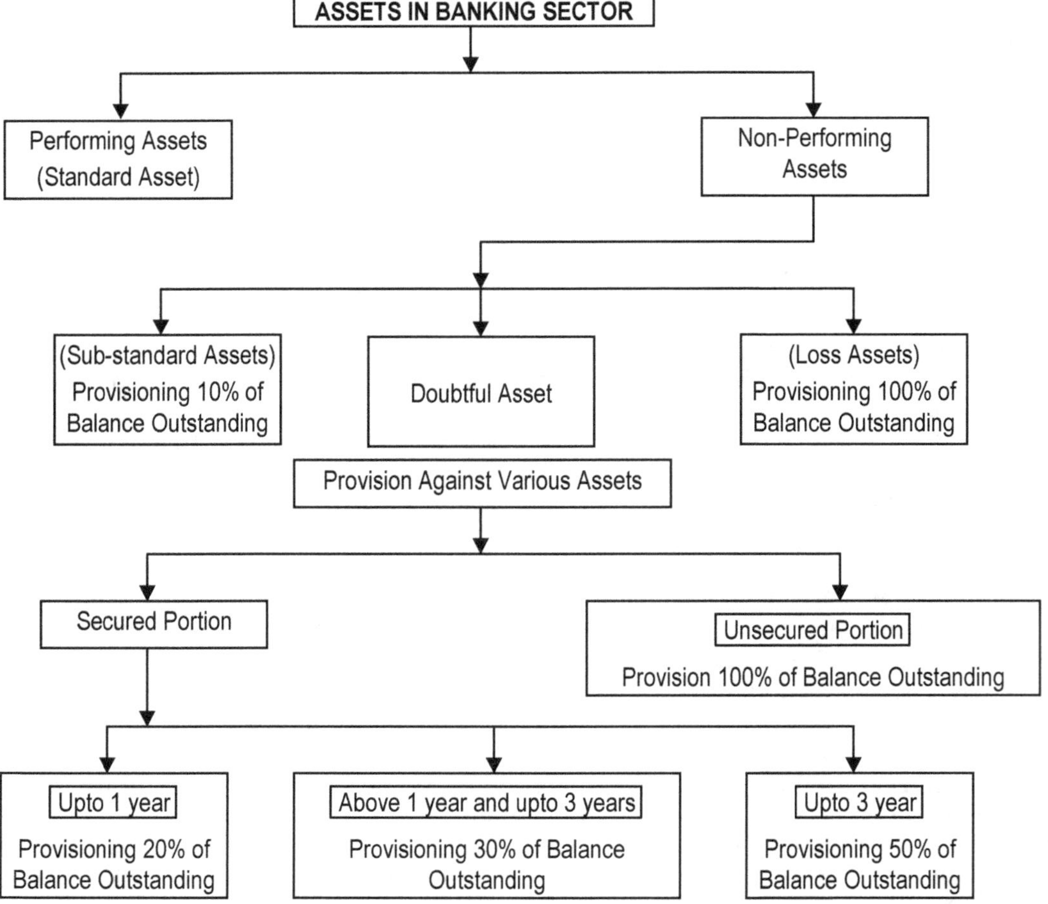


**Fig. 2.1 : Classification of Assets of Banking Companies**

**Performing Assets and Non-Performing Assets (NPA) :**

**i) Meaning :**

Assets which are not non-performing are performing assets. An asset becomes non-performing when it ceases to generate income for Bank. The term non-performing assets means a credit facility in respect of which the interest or installment remains **'past due'** for a period of two quarters i.e. six months. An amount under any of the credit facilities i.e. term loans, cash credit and overdrafts, bills purchased and discounted etc. is to be treated as **'past due'** when it has remained outstanding for thirty days beyond the due date. Moreover, if one of the account has become a non-performing asset, all the accounts of the borrower will be treated as non-performing assets. However, credit facilities backed by Government guarantee though **'past due'** should not be treated as non-performing assets. Assets of the banks are classified as performing assets and non-performing assets for the purpose of "income recognition".

**ii) Instructions from R.B.I. for 'Income Recognition' :**

Banks have been advised by the Reserve Bank of India that they should identify the non-performing assets and ensure that interest on such non-performing assets is not recognised as income and taken to the Profit and Loss Account. Banks are to recognise their income on Accrual Basis in respect of income on performing assets and on Cash Basis in respect of income on non-performing assets. Any interest accrued and credited to income account must be cancelled by a reverse entry once the credit facility comes under the category of non-performing assets.

**iii) Classification of Assets :**

Banks are required to classify the loan assets (advances) into four categories viz. :

a) Standard Assets; b) Sub-Standard Assets; c) Doubtful Assets; and d) Loss Assets.

**a) Standard Assets :**

Standard Asset is one which does not disclose, any problem and which does not carry more than normal risk attached to the business. Such asset is considered as performing asset.

**b) Subs-standard Assets :**

Sub-standard Asset is one which has been classified as a non-performing asset (NPA) for a period not exceeding two years. There is no promise of recovering the dues in full, having regard to the value of security or current networth of the borrower or guarantor, hence the possibility of loss in realising such debts.

Term loans in respect of which installments of principal are overdue for more than one year are treated as sub-standard assets. Also, the assets where the terms of loans agreement regarding payment of interest and principal have been re-negotiated or re-scheduled after commencement of production, should be treated as sub-standard assets. These assets may again be graded upto standard asset, if at least two years payments of principal and interest are made according to re-scheduled terms to the satisfaction of the banks.

**c) Doubtful Assets :**

A doubtful asset is one which has remained as a non-performing asset (NPA) for a period exceeding two years. Term Loans in respect of which installments of principal remains overdue for more than two years should be treated as doubtful. Moreover, assets rescheduling does not entitle the bank to upgrade the quality of advance automatically.

**d) Loss Assets :**

A loss asset is one where loss has been identified by the Bank or internal auditors or the RBI inspection but the amount has not been written off, wholly or partly. Such an asset is not realisable, although there may be some salvage or recovery value.

**iv) Provision Against Various Assets :**

The purpose of classification of Bank assets is to make adequate provision on the basis of quality of assets, the realisation of the security and the erosion in the value of security. It has been directed that the banks should make provision against the various assets on the following basis :

**a)**    **Standard Assets :**
No provision is required.

**b)**    **Sub-standard Assets :**
A provision of 10% of total outstanding is made.

**c)**    **Doubtful Assets :**
- To the extent the debt is not covered by realisable value of the security, 100% provision is to be made.
- In addition to above, for the secured portion of the doubtful assets, provision is required to be made between 20% and 50% depending upon the period for which the asset has remained doubtful as given below :

| Period for which the advance has been considered doubtful | Percentage of Provision |
|---|---|
| Upto one year | 20% |
| More than one year but upto three years | 30% |
| Above three years | 50% |

**d)**    **Loss Assets :**
The entire assets should be written off or if the assets are to be retained in the books for any reason, 100% provision is required to be made.

**v)**    **Calculation of "Income Recognition" :**
It has been advised by RBI that Banks are to recognise their income on **"Accrual Basis"** in respect of income on performing assets and on **"Cash Basis"** in respect of **income on non-performing assets.**

**EXAMPLE**

Following are the statements of interest on advances in respect of performing and non-performing assets of Samrudhi Bank Ltd. Find out the income to be recognised for the year ended 31-3-2015.

(₹ in Lakhs)

| Particulars | Interest Earned ₹ | Interest Received ₹ |
|---|---|---|
| Performing Assets : | | |
| i) Term Loans | 720 | 480 |
| ii) Cash Credit and Overdrafts | 2,700 | 1,590 |
| iii) Bills Purchased and Discounted | 1,050 | 725 |
| Non-performing Assets : | | |
| i) Term Loans | 450 | 60 |
| ii) Cash Credit and Overdrafts | 675 | 105 |
| iii) Bills Purchased and Discounted | 525 | 54 |

**ANSWER**

Interest on performing assets should be recognised on **accrual basis**, but **interest on non-performing assets** should be recognised on **cash basis.**

**Statement showing Calculation of Interest Income for the year ended 31-3-2016.**

(₹ in Lakhs)

| Particulars | | Amount ₹ |
|---|---|---|
| Interest on : | | |
| (i) Term Loans (₹ 720 + ₹ 60) | | 780 |
| (ii) Cash Credit and Overdrafts (₹ 2,700 + ₹ 105) | | 2,805 |
| (iii) Bills Purchased and Discounted (₹ 1,050 + ₹ 54) | (+) | 1,104 |
| ∴ **Interest Income** | | **4,689** |

**vi) Provision to be made in Profit and Loss Account on the basis of quality of Assets :**

**EXAMPLE**

With the help of the following information, compute the amount of provision to be made in the Profit and Loss Account of Samrudhi Bank Ltd. for the year 2015-2016.

(₹ in Lakhs)

| Particulars | ₹ |
|---|---|
| Assets : | |
|    Standard | 16,000 |
|    Sub-standard | 12,000 |
|    Doubtful : | |
|     •   for one year (secured) | 4,800 |
|     •   for two to three years (secured) | 3,600 |
|     •   for more than three years | 1,800 |
|       (secured by mortgage of Plant and Machinery worth ₹ 1,000 lakhs) | |
|    Non-recoverable assets | 3,000 |
| ∴   Total | **41,200** |

**ANSWER**

### Statement showing Calculation of Provisions against Advances

(₹ in Lakhs)

| Particulars | Amount ₹ | % Provisions Percentage | Provisions ₹ |
|---|---|---|---|
| Standard | 16,000 | – | – |
| Sub-standard | 12,000 | 10% | 1,200 |
| Doubtful for one year | 4,800 | 20% | 960 |
| Doubtful for two to three years | 3,600 | 30% | 1,080 |
| Doubtful for more than 3 years | 1,800 | Unsecured portion + 50% of secured portion | 1,300 |
| Loss Assets (Non-recoverable Assets) | 3,000 | 100% | 3,000 |
| ∴   Total | 41,200 | | 7,540 |

**vii) Policy-Changes in IRAC (Income Recognition and Assets Classification) norms in connection with NPAs –**

As per the guidelines received from the RBI, the following policy changes in IRAC norms are to be implemented for the year 2015-2016.

**Past Due Concept :**

To dispense with **'Past Due'** concept w.e.f. March 31, 2016.

Accordingly, Non-Performing asset shall be an advance where

i)     Interest and/or installment of principal remains overdue for a period of more than 180 days, in respect of term loan,

ii)    The account remains 'out of order' for a period of more than 180 days, in respect of an overdraft or cash credit,

iii)   The bills remain overdue for a period of more than 180 days in the case of bills purchased and discounted.

iv)   Interest and/or installment of principal remains overdue for two harvest seasons but for a period not exceeding two and half years in the case of an advance granted for agricultural purposes and

v)    any amount to be received remains overdue for a period of more than 180 days in respect of other accounts.

With implementation of the above guidelines, it will have to be ensured that interest debited and instalments fallen due upto September, 2015 are recovered for maintaining performing status of the account as of 31st March, 2015.

Since it has been decided to adopt the guidelines w.e.f. December 2015 for identifying NPAs as per above norms, suitable changes have been made in CREAM software provided to Regional Offices for updating the data as 31st December, 2015. This will enable the branches to identify the probable slippages and initiate necessary measures for recovery of critical amount due/overdues.

**Sub-standard Assets :**

An Asset should be classified as Doubtful, if it has remained in Sub-standard category for 18 months instead of 24 months, as at present, by March 31, 2016.

## Memorandum of Instructions from Narasimham Committee in connection with NPA (Non-Performing Assets) :

1. **Instructions regarding Meaning and Definition :**

1.1    According to the **Narasimham Committee**, income from non-performing assets (NPA) should not be recognised on accrual basis but should be booked as income only when it is actually received. An Asset Account becomes non-performing when it ceases to generate income for a Bank. The Committee has defined **non-performing asset** (NPA) as advances where, as on the date of the Balance-Sheet (a) in respect of term loans, interest remains past due for a period of more than 180 days, (b) in respect of overdrafts and cash credit accounts, they remain out of order for a period of more than 180 days, (c) in respect of bills purchased and discounted, the bills remain overdue and unpaid for a period of more than 180 days, and (d) in respect of other accounts, any amount to be received remains past due for a period of more than 180 days. According to the Committee, an account is considered "past due" when it remains outstanding for 30 days beyond the due date.

1.2    The Committee's recommendations have been examined and it has been decided that a **'non-performing asset'** (NPA) should be defined as a credit facility or an advance, as on the date of Balance Sheet, in respect of which interest has remained unpaid for a period of 4 quarters during the year ending 31st March, 1993, for three quarters during the year ending 31st March, 1994, and for two quarters during the year ending 31st March, 1995 and onwards. The basis for treating a credit facility as non-performing is given in Annexure-I. Banks should not charge and take to income account interest on all non-performing assets.

1.3    It has also been decided that an amount under any of the credit facilities granted by the bank is to be treated as 'past due' when it remains outstanding for 30 days beyond the due date, i.e. it remains overdue beyond 30 days. Thus, while interest may become "due" on say 31st March, 1992 it becomes 'Past due' (If not paid within 30 days) on 30th April, 1992.

1.4    It is clarified that availability of security or networth of borrower/guarantor should not be taken into account for the purpose of treating an advance as a non-performing asset or otherwise as income recognition is based on record of recovery.

1.5    The interest accrued and credited to income account in a prior accounting period with respect to NPA should be provided for in the current accounting period, if uncollected. If interest debited to an account on March 31, 1992 is not collected by March 31, 1993, the advances become NPA as on March 31, 1993. If interest debited prior to March 31, 1992 and credited to Income Account is also not collected, it should be provided for when the accounts are finalised for the year ending 31st March, 1993.

1.6    If interest income from assets in respect of a borrower becomes subject to non-accrual, fees, commission and similar income with respect to same borrower that have been accrued should cease to accrue in the current period and should be reversed or provided for with respect to past periods if uncollected.

1.7    Fees and commissions earned by banks as result of renegotiations or rescheduling of outstanding debts should be recognised on an accrual basis over the period of time covered by the renegotiated or rescheduling extension of credit.

**2.    Classification of Assets for making provisions :**

The Committee has recommended that for the purpose of making provisions for bad and doubtful debts, loans and advances of the Banks should be classified into the following broad groups, viz. (i) Standard assets, (ii) Sub-standard assets, (iii) Doubtful assets and (iv) Loss assets. Broadly speaking classification of assets into the above categories is to be done taking into account the degree of well-defined credit weaknesses and extent of dependence on collateral security for realisation of dues. The details are given in Annexure-II and should be carefully noted.

Classification given in Annexure - II is intended to provide the basis for determining provisions for loan losses. It is clarified that the above classification is not intended to replace the existing Health Code classification which would continue as a management information tool.

**3.    Provisioning for loans and advances :**

Taking into account the time lag between an account becoming doubtful of recovery, its recognition as such, the realisation of the security and the erosion over time in the value of security charged to the banks, it has been decided that the banks should make provisions against loss assets, doubtful assets and sub-standard assets, atleast to the extent of the amount indicated as follows.

**i)    Loss Assets :**    The entire assets should be written off. If the assets are permitted to remain in the books for any reason, 100% of the outstanding should be provided for.

**ii)    Doubtful Assets :**    (a)    100% of the extent to which the advance is not covered by the realisable value of the security to which the banks has a valid recourse and the realisable value is estimated on the realistic basis.

(b)    Over and above item (a) above, depending upon the period for which the asset has remained doubtful, 20% – 50% of the secured portion (i.e. estimated realisable value of the outstandings) on the following basis.

| Period for which the advance has been considered as doubtful | Percentage of Provision |
|---|---|
| Upto one year | 20 |
| One to three years | 30 |
| More than three years | 50 |

**iii)    Sub-standard Assets**    A general provision of 10% of total outstandings.

**N.B. :**

(1)    There is no objection if the bank creates bad and doubtful debts reserve, beyond the specified limits on their own or if provided in the respective State Co-operative Societies Acts.

(2)    With a view to determining whether outstanding balance in excess of realisable value of security only could be treated as loss assets and not the entire outstanding, the position is illustrated below.

If dues to the bank are, say ₹ 1 lakh, and the salvage value of the security available is ₹ 0.01 lakh, then provision should be made for ₹ 1.00 lakh and not for ₹ 0.99 lakh. If, on the other hand, dues to the bank are ₹ 1.00 lakh and realisable value of the security is ₹ 0.80 lakh and auditor, either internal or external, or the RBI inspection has not treated the security as unrealisable, the credit facility should be treated as doubtful and a 100% provision on the uncovered portion i.e. ₹ 0.20 lakh should be made and on the balance of ₹ 0.80 lakh, the provisioning requirement will be as follows.

| Status as doubtful assets | Status as NPA | Provision required on secured portion (i.e. ₹ 0.80 lakh) | Provision for unsecured portion (i.e. 0.20 lakh) | Aggregate provision required |
|---|---|---|---|---|
| Upto 1 year | Upto and including 3 years | 20% of ₹ 0.80 lakh i.e. ₹ 0.16 lakh | Being 100% i.e. ₹ 0.20 lakh | ₹ 0.36 lakh |
| 1 to 3 year | 3 to 5 year | 30% of ₹ 0.80 lakh i.e. ₹ 0.24 lakh | ₹ 0.20 lakh | ₹ 0.44 lakh |
| More than 3 years | More than 5 years | 50% of ₹ 0.80 lakh i.e. ₹ 0.40 lakh | ₹ 0.20 lakh | ₹ 0.60 lakh |

**4. Valuation of Foreign Exchange Transactions :**

Foreign currency assets and liabilities and unmatured spot and forward foreign exchange transactions should be revalued on a monthly spot and forward transactions should be revalued at the prevailing spot and forward foreign exchange rates, respectively. Long or short positions should be revalued as per regulations currently in force. Gains and losses arising from the above valuations should be reported on a net basis in the income statement and should not be aggregated with any other type of income or expenses.

**5. Project Financing :**

In case of Bank finance given for industrial projects where moratorium is given as regards payment of interest, the payment of interest becomes 'due' only after the moratorium or gestation is over. Therefore, such amounts of interest do not become "Past due" and hence NPA, with reference to the date of debit of interest. They become 'past due' if interest is not paid within 30 days after due date for payment of interest. Similarly, in the case of housing loans or similar advances granted to staff members where interest is payable after recovery of principal, interest need not be considered as "past due" from the first quarter onwards. Such loans and advances should be classified as NPA only when there is a default in payment of interest on the date of payment. e.g.

| Date of sanction MDUL or availment | Payment of Interest | NPA Status | | |
|---|---|---|---|---|
| | | As on 31-3-1993 | As on 31-3-1994 | As on 30-4-1995 |
| 1-1-1991 | 31-3-1995 (As per Moratorium / Gestation period for payment of interest) | Not past due or NPA | Not past due or NPA | Past due (if interest is not paid) |

**6. Credit facilities backed by guarantees by EOGC/DIOGC/Govt. of India/State Govt. :**

In the case of advances guaranteed by EOGC/DICGC, provision should be made only for the balance i.e. over and above the amount guaranteed by these corporation. Similarly, credit facilities backed by Government Guarantees, though 'Past due', should not be treated as non-performing assets.

**7. Consortium advances :**

In order to bring about uniformity in approach regarding a borrowing unit, classification adopted by the leader of the consortium should be adopted by the members.

**8. Depreciation on investments :**

While advising accounting system, the banks have been advised vide circular UBD. No. Plan. 13 / UB. 81 / 1992-93 dated 15th September 1992 to make a suitable provision representing the difference between the cost or market value out of current profits of the bank and show the same as "Investment and Depreciation Reserve" (vide item 2 (vii) of the Capital and Liabilities column of Form 'A' (Balance Sheet). Banks are required to show the investments at book value (with details as to face value and market value) vide item 4 of 'Property and Assets' column of Form 'A' (Balance Sheet) as provided in the Third Schedule to the Banking Regulation Act, 1949 (As Applicable to Co-operative Societies)

**9. Treatment of non-performing asset-borrowerwise or facilitywise :**

In the case of health code classification, the banks follow the principle that a borrower falls in the category of satisfactory, irregular etc. and not a particular credit facility. Similarly, while making claims to Deposit Insurance and Credit Guarantee Corporation, banks are required to make a consolidated claim in respect of all dues from a borrower and not in respect of dues under a facility. On the same analogy, it has been decided that all the facilities granted to a borrower will have to be treated as non-performing assets and not the particular facility or part thereof which has become irregular.

**10. Provisioning for other purposes :**

Banks may have retirement benefit schemes for its staff, e.g. Provident Fund, Gratuity and Pension etc. It is necessary that the liabilities on account of Provident Fund, Pension, Gratuity etc. are estimated on actuarial basis and full provision should be made every year for the purpose in the Profit and Loss Account by the primary co-operative banks.

**Identification of NPA (As per R.B.I. Master Circular No. 19/12-05.05)**

An asset becomes non-performing when it ceases to generate income for the Bank. Earlier an asset was considered as non-performing asset (NPA) based on the concept of *'Past Due'*. A 'non-performing asset' (NPA) was defined as credit in respect of which interest and/or instalment of principal has remained past due for a specific period of time. The specific period was reduced in a phased manner as under :

| | |
|---|---|
| Year ending 31st 'March | Specific period |
| 1993 | 4 quarters |
| 1994 | 3 quarters |
| 1995 | 2 quarters |

An amount is considered as past due, when it remains outstanding for 30 days beyond the due date. However, with effect from 31st March, 2001 the 'past due' concept has been dispensed with. Accordingly, as from that date, a non-performing asset (NPA) is an advance, where :

i)      Interest and/or instalment of principal remain overdue* for a period of more than 180 days in respect of a Term Loan.

ii)      The account remains 'Out of order' for a period of more than 180 days, in respect of an Overdraft/Cash Credit (OD/CC).

iii)      The bill remains overdue for a period of more than 180 days, in the case of bills purchased and discounted.

iv)      Interest and/or instalment of principal remain overdue for two harvest Seasons but for a period not exceeding two half years in the case of an advance granted for agricultural purposes as indicated in Annexure I, and in respect of agriculture loans, other than those specified in Annexure I identification of NPAs would he done on the same basis its non-agricultural advances.

v)      Any amount to be received remains overdue for a period of more than 180 clays in respect of other accounts.

*      Any amount due to the bank under any credit facility, if not paid by the due date fixed by the bank becomes overdue.

[**Note :** Equipment leasing and hire-purchasing financing activities should be treated at par with grant of loans and advances and extant guidelines on incomerecognition, asset classification and provisioning would be applicable for these activities].

With a view to moving towards international best practices and to ensure greater transparency, it has been decided to adopt the '90 days' overdue norms for identification of NPAs, from the year ending 31st March, 2004. However, gold loans and small loans up to ₹ One lakh have been exempted from the 90 days norm for recognition of loan impairement. Such loans would continue to be governed by 180 days norms for classification as NPAs even after this date. Accordingly, with effect from 31st March, 2004, a non-performing asset (except gold loans/ small loans up to ₹ one lakh) shall be a loan or an advance where:

i) Interest and/or instalment of principal remain *'overdue'* for a period of more than 90 days in respect of a Term Loan.

ii) The account remains 'Out of order'@ for a period of more than 90 days, in respect of an Overdraft/Cash Credit (OD/CC).

iii) The bill remains *'overdue'* for a period of more than 90 days in the case of bill purchased and discounted.

iv) Interest and/or instalment of principal remains overdue for two harvest seasons but for a period not exceeding two half in the case of advance granted for agricultural purposes, and in respect of agriculture loans, other than those specified in Annexure I, identification of NPAs would be done on the same basis as non-agricultural advances.

v) Any amount to be received remains 'overdue' for a period of more than 90 days in respect of other accounts.

@ "An account should be treated as *'out of order'* if the outstanding balance remains continuously in excess of the sanctioned limit/drawing power. In cases where the outstanding balance in the principal operating account is less than the sanctioned limit/drawing 9 power, but there are no credits continuously for 180 days (90 days from 3 1.03.2004) or credits are not enough to cover the interest debited during the same period, these accounts should be treated as *'out of order'''*.

**Norms applicable to Agricultural Advances :**

With effect from 30th September, 2004 the following, revised norms will be applicable to *all direct agricultural advances* (as listed in the Annexure I) :

a) A loan granted for short duration crops will be treated as NPA, if the instalment of principal or interest thereon remains overdue for two crop seasons.

b) A loan granted for long duration crops will be treated as NPA, if the instalment of principal or interest thereon remains overdue for one crop season.

i) For the purpose of these guidelines, "long duration" crops would be crops with crop season longer than one year and crops, which are not "long duration" crops would be treated as "short duration" crops.

ii) The crop season for each crop, which means the period up to harvesting of the crops raised, Would be as determined by the State Level Bankers' Committee in each state.

iii) Depending upon the duration of crops raised by an agriculturist, the above NPA norms would also be made applicable to agricultural term loans availed of by him. In respect of agricultural loans, other than those specified in the Annexure I and term loans given to non-agriculturalists, identification of NPAs would be done on the same basis as non-agricultural advances which, at present, is the 90 days delinquency norm. The relaxation granted to small loans gold loans) up to ₹ One lakh would remain Unchanged and that such loans would continue to be governed by 180 days impairment norms.

iv) Banks should ensure that while granting loans and advances, realistic repayment schedules are fixed on the basis of cash flows/fluidity with the borrowers.

## Identification of assets as NPAs should be done on an ongoing basis

The system should ensure that identification of NPAs is done on an on-going basis and doubts in asset classification due to any reason are settled through specified internal channels within one month from the date on which the account would have been classified as NPA as per prescribed norms. Banks should also make provisions for NPAs as at the end of each calendar quarter, i.e., as at the end of March/June/September/December, so that the Income and Expenditure Account for the respective quarters as well as the Profit and Loss Account and Balance Sheet for the year end reflects the provision made for NPAs.

### Guidelines for Identification of NPA at a Glance

| Type of Credit Facility | NPA Criteria |
|---|---|
| i)   Term Loan | The interest and/or installment of principal remain *'overdue'* for a period of more than 90 days. |
| ii)   Cash Credit and Overdraft | The account remains 'out of order' for a period of more than 90 days. |
| iii)   Bills Purchased and Discounted | The bill remain *'overdue'* for a period more than 90 days. |
| iv)   All Direct Agricultural Advances | **i)   Short duration crops** <br> The installment of principal or interest thereon remains *'overdue'* for two crop seasons. <br> **ii)   Long duration crops** <br> The installment of principal or interest thereon remains *'overdue'* for one crop season |
| v)   Other Loan Accounts | Any amount to be received remains *'overdue'* for a period of more than 90 days. |

**EXAMPLE**

The following two term loan accounts were sanctioned by ABC Bank, Mumbai on 1st January, 2015. The details are given below :

| Particulars | | Loan Account A & Co. | Loan Account B & Co. |
|---|---|---|---|
| i)   Amount of loan | ₹ | 6,00,000 | 10,00,000 |
| ii)   Period | Years | 5 | 5 |
| iii)   Basis of Instalment | | Quarterly | Half yearly |
| iv)   Rate of Interest | (%) | 12 | 12 |
| v)   Amount of Instalments | ₹ | 30,000 + Interest | 1,00,000 + Interest |

You are required to find out the date on which these accounts will become NPA. Assume that there is no recovery.

**ANSWER**

### Statement showing Calculation of Date of NPA

| Particulars | Loan Account A & Co. | Loan Account B & Co. |
|---|---|---|
| Date of Loan | 1.1.2015 | 1.1.2015 |
| Basis of Installment | Quarterly | Half yearly |
| Due Date for 1st Installment | 31.3.2015 | 30.06.2015 |
| Overdue Starts | 1.4.2015 | 1.7.2015 |
| Date of NPA Symptom (Exact date of NPA > 90 days) | 26.6.2015 | 28.9.2015 |

## ANNEXURE – I

### Basis for treating a credit facility as Non-Performing Asset (NPA)

| Type of Credit facility | For the year ending on .......... | | |
|---|---|---|---|
| | 31-3-1993 | 31-3-1994 | 31-3-1995 |
| **(i) Term Loan** <br> If interest remains past due for a period of | 4 quarters | 3 quarters | 2 quarters |
| **(ii) Cash credit and overdraft accounts** <br> If the outstanding balance remains continuously in excess of the sanctioned limit / drawing power or there are no credits continuously for six months as on the date of balance sheet or credits are not enough to cover the interest debited during the same period (i.e. if the account remains out of order) for a period of | 4 quarters | 3 quarters | 2 quarters |
| **(iii) Bills purchased and discounted :** <br> If the bill remains overdue and unpaid for a period of | 4 quarters | 3 quarters | 2 quarters |
| **(iv) Any other credit facility :** <br> If any amount to be received in respect of any other credit facility remains past due for a period of | 4 quarters | 3 quarters | 2 quarters |

Any other income received such as fees, commission, etc. on these accounts should be treated as income only when it is actually received by the bank.

## ANNEXURE - II

### Classification of Assets for provisioning

**i) Standard Assets :**

It is not a non-performing asset (NPA). It does not disclose any problems and which does not carry more than normal risk attached to the business.

**ii) Sub-standard Assets :**

It is an asset which has remained as non-performing asset for a period not exceeding two years. In such cases, the current net-worth of the borrower or guarantor or the current market value of the security charged is not enough to ensure recovery of the dues to the bank in full. In other words, such an asset will have well-defined credit weaknesses that jeopardise the liquidation of the debt and are characterised by the distinct possibility that the bank will sustain some loss, if deficiencies are not corrected.

In the case of term loans, where instalments are overdues for periods exceeding one year but not exceeding two years should be treated as sub-standard.

An account where the terms of the loan agreement regarding interest and principal have been renegotiated or rescheduled after commencement of production should be classified as sub-standard and should remain in such category for atleast two years of satisfactory performance under the renegotiated or rescheduled terms. In other words, the classification of an asset should not be upgraded merely as result of rescheduling unless there is satisfactory compliance of the above condition.

**iii) Doubtful Assets :**

An asset which has remained non-performing asset for a period exceeding two years will be treated as a doubtful asset.

In the case of term loans, those where instalments of principal have remained overdue for a period exceeding two years should be treated as doubtful. As in the case of sub-standard assets, rescheduling of the overdue loan does not entitle a bank to upgrade the quality of the loan or advance automatically.

A loan classified as doubtful has all the weaknesses inherent in that classified as sub-standard with the added characteristic that the weaknesses make collection or liquidation in full, on the basis of currently known facts, conditions and values, highly questionable and improbable.

**iv) Loss Assets :**

A loss asset is one where the loss has been identified by the bank or by internal or external auditors or by the Co-operation Department or by the Reserve Bank of India inspection but the amount has not been written off, wholly or partly. In other words, such an asset is considered uncollectable and its continuance as a bankable asset is not warranted although there may be some salvage or recovery value.

**Directives of the RBI in connection with Disclosure of Accounting Policies :**

With a view that the financial position of banks represents a true and fair view, the RBI has directed the banks to disclose the accounting policies regarding the key areas of operations alongwith notes of account in their financial statements for the accounting year ending 31st March, 1991 and onwards on a regular basis.

The accounting policies disclosed may contain the following aspects subject to modification by individual banks :

**i) General :**

The accompanying financial statements have been prepared on the historical cost basis and confirm to the statutory provisions and practices prevailing in the country.

**ii) Transactions involving Foreign Exchange :**

   a) Monetary assets and liabilities have been translated at the exchange rates prevailing at the close of the year. Non-monetary assets have been carried in the books at the historical cost.

   b) Income and expenditure items in respect of Indian branches have been translated at the exchange rates ruling on the date of the transaction and in respect of overseas branches at the exchange rates prevailing at the close of the year.

   c) Profit or loss on percing forward contracts has been accounted for.

**iii) Investments :**

   a) Investments in Governments and other approved securities in India are valued at the lower cost or market value.

   b) Investments in subsidiary companies and associate companies (i.e. companies in which the bank holds atleast 25% of the share capital) have been accounted for on the historical cost basis.

   c) All other investments are valued at the lower cost or market value.

**iv) Advances :**

   a) Provisions for doubtful advances have been made to the satisfaction of the auditors;

      i) In respect of identified advances, based on periodic review of advances and after taking into account the portion of advance guaranteed by the Deposit Insurance and Credit Guarantee Corporation, the Export Credit and Guarantee Corporation and similar statutory bodies;

      ii) In respect of general advances, as a percentage of total advances taking into account guidelines issued by the Government of India and determined on the basis of such revaluation made by the professional values, profit arising on revaluation has been credited to Capital Reserve.

   b) Depreciation has been provided for on the straight line or diminishing balance method.

   c) In respect of revalued assets, depreciation is provided for on the revalued figures and an amount equal to the additional depreciation consequent on revaluation is transferred annually from the Capital Reserve to the General Reserve Account or Profit and Loss Account.

**v)   Staff Benefits :**

Provisions for gratuity or pension benefits to staff has been made on an accrual or cash basis. Separate funds for gratuity or pension have been created.

**vi)   Net Profit :**
- a)   The net profit disclosed in the Profit and Loss Account is after :
  - i)   Provisions for taxes on income in accordance with statutory requirements.
  - ii)   Provisions for doubtful advances.
  - iii)   Adjustments to the value of "current" investments in Government and other approved securities in India valued at lower of cost or market value.
  - iv)   Transfers to contingency funds.
  - v)   Other usual or necessary provisions.
- b)   Contingency funds have been grouped in the Balance Sheet under the head "Other Liabilities and Provisions".

## THE BANKING REGULATION ACT, 1949

**Schedule I**
**(See Section 55)**
**Amendments**

| Year (1) | No. (2) | Short Title (3) | Amendments (4) |
|---|---|---|---|
| 1934 | 2 | The Reserve Bank of India Act, 1934 | (1)   In Section 17, to clause (15A), the following shall be added namely : "and under the Banking Companies Act, 1949".<br>(2)   (a)   Section 18 shall be renumbered as sub-section (1) of that Section and in sub-section (1), as so renumbered.<br>    (i)   in clause (3), after the words "of that section", the following words shall be added, "or, when the loan or advance, is made to a Banking Company as defined in the Banking Companies Act, 1949, against such other form of security as the Bank may consider sufficient".<br>    (ii)   for the words "under this section" wherever they occur, the words "under this sub-section" shall be substituted.<br>  (b)   after sub-section (1) as so renumbered, the following sub-section shall be inserted viz. :<br>    "(2)   Where a Banking Company to which a loan or advance has been made under the provisions of clause (3) of sub-section (1) is wound up, any sums due to the Bank in respect of such loan or advance, shall, subject only to the claims, if any, of other Banking Company in respect of any prior loan or advance made by such Banking Company against any security, be a first charge on the assets of the Banking Company.<br>    (3)   In Section 42, for sub-section (6), the following sub-section shall be substituted, viz :<br>    "(6)   The Bank shall, save as hereinafter provided, by notification in the Gazette of India, |

(a) direct the inclusion in the Second Schedule of any Bank not already so included which carries on the business of Banking in any Province of India and which

    (i) has a paid-up capital and reserves of an aggregate value of not less than five lakhs of rupees, and

    (ii) satisfies the Bank that its affairs are not being conducted in manner detrimental to the interests of its depositors; and

    (iii) is a company as defined in Clause (2) of Section 2 of the Indian Companies Act, 1913 (7 of 1913) or a Corporation or a company incorporated by or under any law in force in any place outside by the Provinces of India;

(b) direct the exclusion from that Schedule of any Scheduled Bank –

    (i) the aggregate value of whose paid-up-capital and reserves becomes at any time less than five lakhs of rupees; or

    (ii) which is, in the opinion of the Bank after making an inspection under Section 35 of the Banking Companies Act, 1949, conducting its affairs to the detriment of the interests of its depositors, or

    (iii) which goes into liquidation or otherwise ceases to carry on Banking Business;

Provided that the Bank may, on application of the Scheduled Bank concerned and subject to such conditions, if any, as it may impose, defer the making of a direction under sub-clause (i) or sub-clause (ii) of clause (b) for such period as the Bank considers reasonable to give the Scheduled Bank an opportunity of increasing the aggregate value of its paid-up capital and reserves to not less than five lakhs of rupees, or, as the case may, of removing the defects in the conduct of its affairs :

(c) alter the description in that schedule whenever any Scheduled Bank changes its name.

**Explanation :** In this sub-section the expression 'value' means the real or exchangeable value and not the nominal value which may be shown in the books of the Bank concerned; and if any dispute arises in computing the aggregate value of the paid-up capital and reserves of a Bank, a determination thereof by the Bank shall be final for the purposes of this sub-section".

**Additional Disclosures by Banks in Notes to Accounts :**

RBI/2009-10/347                                     15th March, 2010

DBOB.BP.BC.No. 79 /21.04.018/2009-10

The Chairman/Chief Executives of

All Commercial Banks

(excluding RRBs)


Dear Sir,

### Additional Disclosures by banks in Notes to Accounts

The Reserve Bank has been taking several steps from time to time to enhance the transparency in the operations of banks by stipulating comprehensive disclosures in tune with the international best practices. On a review of the existing disclosures, it has been decided to prescribe the following additional disclosures in the 'Notes to Accounts' in the banks' balance sheets, from the year ending March 2010.

    I.     Concentration of Deposits, Advances, Exposures and NPAs.

    II.    Sector-wise NPAs.

    III.   Movement of NPAs.

    IV.   Overseas assets, NPAs and revenue.

    V.    Off-balance sheet SPVs sponsored by banks.

The prescribed formats are furnished in Annex.


Yours faithfully,


(B. Mahapatra)

Chief General Manager.

---

**Annex**

**I.    Concentration of Deposits, Advances, Exposures and NPAs**

**Concentration of Deposits**

**(Amount in Rupees Crores)**

| | |
|---|---|
| Total Deposits of twenty largest depositors | |
| Percentage of Deposits of twenty largest depositors to Total Deposits of the bank | |

**Concentration of Advances***

**(Amount in Rupees Crores)**

| | |
|---|---|
| Total Advances of twenty largest borrowers | |
| Percentage of Advances to twenty largest borrowers to Total Advances of the bank | |

- Advances should be computed as per definition of Credit Exposure including derivatives furnished in our Master Circular on Exposure Norms DBOD.No.Dir.BC.15/13.03.00/ 2015-10 dated July 1, 2015.

**Concentration of Exposures****

**(Amount in Rupees Crores)**

| | |
|---|---|
| Total Exposure to twenty largest borrowers/customers | |
| Percentage of Exposures to twenty largest borrowers/customers to Total Exposure of the bank on borrowers/customers | |

**     Exposures should be computed based on credit and investment exposure as prescribed in our Master Circular on Exposure Norms DBOD.No.Dir.BC.15/13.03.2015-10 dated July 1, 2015.

**Concentration of NPAs**

**(Amount in Rupees Crores)**

| | |
|---|---|
| Total Exposure of top four NPA accounts | |

**II.   Sector-wise NPAs**

| Sl. No. | Sector | Percentage of NPAs to Total Advances in that sector |
|---|---|---|
| 1. | Agriculture and Allied Activities | |
| 2. | Industry (Micro and small, Medium and Large) | |
| 3. | Services | |
| 4. | Personal Loans | |

**III.   Movement of NPAs**

| Particulars | Amount in ₹ Crores |
|---|---|
| Gross NPAs* as on 1st April of particular year (Opening Balance) | |
| Additions (Fresh NPAs) during the year | |
| Sub-total (A) | |
| **Less :** | |
| i)     Upgradations | |
| ii)    Recoveries (excluding recoveries made from upgraded accounts) | |
| iii)   Write-offs | |
| Sub-total (B) | |
| Gross NPAs as on 31st March of the following year (closing balance (A − B) | |

*     Gross NPAs as per item 2 of Annex to DBOD Circular DBOD.BP.BC.No. 46/21.04/048/2015-10 dated September 24, 2015.

**IV.   Overseas Assets, NPAs and Revenue**

| Particulars | Amount in (Rupees Crores) |
|---|---|
| Total Assets | |
| Total NPAs | |
| Total Revenue | |

**V.   Off-Balance Sheet SPVs sponsored (which are required to be consolidated as per accounting norms).**

| Name of the SPV sponsored | |
|---|---|
| Domestic | Overseas |

## 2.4 BOOKS OF ACCOUNTS

A Banking Company follows the principle of double entry in recording its transactions in the books of account. Although the Cash Book and the General Ledger are the principal books of account of any bank, a number of subsidiary books are maintained by the bank which are as follows :

   i)    Receiving Cashier's Counter Cash Book.

   ii)   Paying Cashier's Counter Cash Book.

   iii)  Current Accounts Ledger.

   iv)  Savings Bank Accounts Ledger.

   v)   Fixed Deposit Accounts Ledger.

   vi)  Fixed Deposit Interest Ledger.

   vii)  Recurring Deposit Accounts Ledger.

  viii)  Investments Ledger.

   ix)  Loan Ledger.

   x)   Bills Discounted and Purchased Ledger.

   xi)  Consumer's Acceptances, Endorsements and Guarantee Ledger.

In addition to the above subsidiary books, there are various other books and registers in a bank for the day-to-day recording of different matters. These books and registers do not, however, form part of double entry principle. These books are as follows :

   i)    Bills for Collection Register.

   ii)   Securities Register.

   iii)  Demand Draft Register.

   iv)  Safe Deposit Vault Register.

   v)   Bills Register.

   vi)  Jewellery Register.

   vii)  Standing Order Register.

  viii)  Dishonoured Cheques Register.

   ix)  Documents Register.

   x)   Letters of Credit Register, etc.

## 2.5 PREPARATION OF FINAL ACCOUNTS

The Third Schedule under Section 29 of the Banking Regulation Act, 1949, regarding the format of Balance Sheet and Profit and Loss Account has been ammended by the Government of India by a notification on 18th January, 1991 and subsequently on 19th December, 1991. The new formats would come into force with effect from 19th March, 1992. Thus, as per the new format of accounting, vertical forms of Balance Sheet and Profit and Loss Account should be followed w.e.f. accounting year ending 31st March, 1992. The Balance Sheet is prepared in Form-A while the Profit and Loss Account is prepared in Form B of the Third Schedule in vertical form.

The prescribed vertical form of the Balance Sheet and Profit and Loss Account are given below :

### THE THIRD SCHEDULE
*(See Section 29)*
**Form 'A'**
**Form of Balance Sheet**

Balance Sheet of ................................................................................ (here enter the name of the Banking Company).

Balance Sheet as on 31st March ............... (year)                      (000's omitted)

| | Schedule No. | As on 31-3-...... (Current Year) | As on 31-3-........ (Previous Year) |
|---|---|---|---|
| **Capital and Liabilities :** | | | |
| Capital | 1 | | |
| Reserves and Surplus | 2 | | |
| Deposits | 3 | | |
| Borrowings | 4 | | |
| Other Liabilities and Provisions | 5 | | |
| **Total** | | | |
| **Assets :** | | | |
| Cash and Balances with Reserve Bank of India | 6 | | |
| Balances with Banks and Money At Call and Short Notices | 7 | | |
| Investments | 8 | | |
| Advances | 9 | | |
| Fixed Assets | 10 | | |
| Other Assets | 11 | | |
| **Total** | | | |
| Contingent Liabilities | 12 | | |
| Bills for Collection | | | |

### Schedule – I – Capital

| | As on 31-3-...... (Current Year) | As on 31-3-...... (Previous Year) |
|---|---|---|
| **I.  For Nationalised Banks :** | | |
| Capital (Fully owned by Central Government) | | |
| | | |
| **II.  For Banks Incorporated Outside India :** | | |
| Capital | | |
| i)  (The amount brought in by banks by way of start-up capital as prescribed by RBI should be shown under this head). | | |
| ii)  Amount of deposit kept with the RBI under Section 11 (2) of the Banking Regulation Act, 1949 | | |
| **Total** | | |

| | | | |
|---|---|---|---|
| **III.** | **For Other Banks :** | | |
| | Authorised Capital | | |
| | (....... shares of ₹ ....... each) | | |
| | Issued Capital | | |
| | (....... shares of ₹ ....... each) | | |
| | Subscribed Capital | | |
| | (....... shares of ₹ ....... each) | | |
| | Called-up Capital | | |
| | (....... shares of ₹ ....... each) | | |
| | **Less :**   Calls Unpaid | | |
| | **Add :**   Forfeited shares | | |

Schedule – 2 – Reserves and Surplus

| | | As on 31-3-....... (Current Year) | As on 31-3-....... (Previous Year) |
|---|---|---|---|
| **I.** | **Statutory Reserves** | | |
| | Opening Balance | | |
| **Add :** | Additions during the year | | |
| **Less :** | Deductions during the year | | |
| **II.** | **Capital Reserves** | | |
| | Opening Balance | | |
| **Add :** | Additions during the year | | |
| **Less :** | Deductions during the year | | |
| **III.** | **Share Premium** | | |
| | Opening Balance | | |
| **Add :** | Additions during the year | | |
| **Less :** | Deductions during the year | | |
| **IV.** | **Revenue and Other Reserves** | | |
| | Opening Balance | | |
| **Add :** | Additions during the year | | |
| **Less :** | Deductions during the year | | |
| **V.** | **Balance in Profit and Loss Account** | | |
| | **Total   (I, II, III, IV and V)** | | |

Schedule – 3 – Deposits

| | | | As on 31-3-....... (Current Year) | As on 31-3-....... (Previous Year) |
|---|---|---|---|---|
| **A.** | **I.** | **Demand Deposits** | | |
| | | i)   From Bank | | |
| | | ii)   From Others | | |
| | **II.** | **Savings Bank Deposits** | | |
| | **III.** | **Term Deposits** | | |
| | | i)   From Banks | | |
| | | ii)   From Others | | |
| | | **Total   (I, II and III)** | | |
| **B.** | i) | Deposits of Branches in India | | |
| | ii) | Deposits of Branches Outside India | | |
| | | **Total** | | |

### Schedule – 4 – Borrowings

| | As on 31-3-......<br>(Current Year) | As on 31-3-......<br>(Previous Year) |
|---|---|---|
| **I. Borrowings in India** | | |
|  i) Reserve Bank of India | | |
|  ii) Other Banks | | |
|  iii) Other institutions and agencies | | |
| **II. Borrowings outside India** | | |
|   **Total (I and II)** | | |
| Secured borrowings in I and II above – ₹ | | |

### Schedule – 5 – Other Liabilities and Provisions

| | As on 31-3-.........<br>(Current Year) | As on 31-3-......<br>(Previous Year) |
|---|---|---|
| I. Bills Payable | | |
| II. Inter-office adjustments (net) | | |
| III. Interest Accrued | | |
| II. Other (Including Provisions) | | |
|   **Total** | | |

### Schedule – 6 – Cash and Balance with Reserve Bank of India

| | As on 31-3-.........<br>(Current Year) | As on 31-3-.........<br>(Previous Year) |
|---|---|---|
| **I. Cash in hand** | | |
| (including foreign currency notes) | | |
| **II. Balance with Reserve Bank of India** | | |
|  i) In Current Accounts | | |
|  ii) In Other Accounts | | |
|   **Total (I and II)** | | |

### Schedule – 7 – Balances with Banks and Money at Call and Short Notice

| | As on 31-3-.........<br>(Current Year) | As on 31-3-.........<br>(Previous Year) |
|---|---|---|
| **I. In India** | | |
|  **i) Balances with Banks** | | |
|   a) in Current Accounts | | |
|   b) in Other Deposit Accounts | | |
|  **ii) Money at Call and Short Notice** | | |
|   a) With Banks | | |
|   b) With Other Institutions | | |
|   **Total (I and II)** | | |
| **II. Outside India** | | |
|  i) In Current Accounts | | |
|  ii) In Other Deposit Accounts | | |
|  iii) Money at Call and Short Notice | | |
|   **Total** | | |
|   **Grand Total (I and II)** | | |

Schedule – 8 – Investments

| | | | As on 31-3-........ (Current Year) | As on 31-3-........ (Pervious Year) |
|---|---|---|---|---|
| **I.** | **Investments in India in** | | | |
| | i) | Government Securities | | |
| | ii) | Other Approved Securities | | |
| | iii) | Shares | | |
| | iv) | Debentures and Bonds | | |
| | v) | Subsidiaries and/or Joint Ventures | | |
| | vi) | Others (to be specified) | | |
| | | **Total** | | |
| **II.** | **Investments Outside India in** | | | |
| | i) | Government Securities (including local authorities) | | |
| | ii) | Subsidiaries and/or Joint Ventures Abroad | | |
| | iii) | Other Investments (to be specified) | | |
| | | **Total** | | |
| | | **Grand Total (I and II)** | | |

Schedule – 9 – Advances

| | | | As on 31-3-........ (Current Year) | As on 31-3-........ (Previous Year) |
|---|---|---|---|---|
| **A.** | i) | Bills Purchased and Discounted | | |
| | ii) | Cash Credits, Overdrafts and Loans Repayable on Demand | | |
| | | **Total** | | |
| **B.** | i) | Secured by Tangible Assets | | |
| | ii) | Covered by Bank/Government Guarantees | | |
| | iii) | Unsecured | | |
| | | **Total** | | |
| **C.** | **I.** | **Advances in India** | | |
| | i) | Priority Sectors | | |
| | ii) | Public Sector | | |
| | iii) | Banks | | |
| | iv) | Others | | |
| | | **Total** | | |
| | **II.** | **Advances Outside India** | | |
| | i) | Due from Banks | | |
| | ii) | Due from Others | | |
| | | a) Bills Purchased and Discounted | | |
| | | b) Syndicated Loans | | |
| | | c) Others | | |
| | | **Total** | | |
| | | **Grand Total (A, B and C – I and II)** | | |

## Schedule – 10 – Fixed Assets

|  | As on 31-3-......<br>(Current Year) | As on 31-3-......<br>(Previous Year) |
|---|---|---|
| **I.**    **Premises** | | |
| At cost on 31st March of the preceding year | | |
| **Add :**   Additions during the year | | |
| **Less :**   Deductions during the year | | |
| **Less :**   Depreciation to date | | |
| **II.**    **Other Fixed Assets** (Including Furniture and Fixtures) | | |
| **Add :**   Additions during the year | | |
| **Less :**   Deductions during the year | | |
| **Less :**   Depreciation to date | | |
| **Total (I and II)** | | |

## Schedule – 11 – Other Assets

|  | As on 31-3-......<br>(Current Year) | As on 31-3-......<br>(Previous Year) |
|---|---|---|
| I.    Inter-Office Adjustments (net) | | |
| II.    Interest Accrued | | |
| III.    Tax paid in Advance or Tax deducted at source | | |
| IV.    Stationery and Stamps | | |
| V.    Non-Banking Assets acquired in satisfaction of claims | | |
| VI.    Others (a) | | |
| **Total** | | |

@    In case there is any unadjusted balance of loss the same may be shown under this item with appropriate foot-note.

## Schedule – 12 – Contingent Liabilities

|  | As on 31-3-......<br>(Current Year) | As on 31-3-......<br>(Previous Year) |
|---|---|---|
| I.    Claims against the Bank not Acknowledged as Debts | | |
| II.    Liability for partly paid Investments | | |
| III.    Liability on account of Outstanding Forward Exchange Contracts | | |
| IV.    Guarantees given on behalf of Constituents | | |
| a)    In India | | |
| b)    Outside India | | |
| V.    Acceptances, Endorsements and Other Obligations | | |
| VI.    Other items for which the Bank is Contingently liable | | |
| **Total** | | |

**Form 'B'**          (000's omitted)

**Form of Profit and Loss Account**

**for the year ended 31ˢᵗ March**

| | Schedule No. | Year ended 31-3-........ (Current Year) | Year ended 31-3-........ (Previous Year) |
|---|---|---|---|
| **I.  Income** | | | |
| Interest Earned | 13 | | |
| Other Income | 14 | | |
| **Total** | | | |
| **II.  Expenditure** | | | |
| Interest Expended | 15 | | |
| Operating Expenses | 16 | | |
| Provisions and Contingencies | | | |
| **Total** | | | |
| **III.  Profit or Loss** | | | |
| Net Profit or Loss for the year | | | |
| **Total** | | | |
| **IV.  Appropriations** | | | |
| Transfer to Statutory Reserves | | | |
| Transfer to Other Reserves | | | |
| Transfer to Government or Proposed Dividend | | | |
| Balance carried over to Balance Sheet | | | |
| **Total** | | | |

**N.B. :**

   i)     The total income includes income of foreign branches at ₹ .............

   ii)    The total expenditure includes expenditure of foreign branches at ₹ .............

   iii)   Surplus or deficit of foreign branches ₹ .............

**Schedule – 13 – Interest Earned**

| | Year ended 31-3-......... (Current Year) | Year ended 31-3-....... (Previous Year) |
|---|---|---|
| I.     Interest or Discount on Advances or Bills | | |
| II.    Income on Investments | | |
| III.   Interest on Balances with Reserve Bank of India and Other Inter-Bank Funds | | |
| IV.   Others | | |
| **Total** | | |

**Schedule 14 – Other Income**

| | Year ended 31-3-....... (Current Year) | Year ended 31-3-....... (Previous Year) |
|---|---|---|
| I.     Commission, Exchange and Brokerage | | |
| II.    Profit on Sale of Investments | | |
|        **Less :** Loss on Sale of Investments | | |
| III.   Profit on Revaluation of Investments | | |
|        **Less :** Loss on Revaluation of Investments | | |

| | | |
|---|---|---|
| IV.   Profit on Sale of Land, Buildings, and Other Assets<br>    **Less :**   Loss on Sale of Land, Buildings and Other Assets | | |
| V.   Profit on Exchange Transactions<br>    **Less :** Loss on Exchange Transactions | | |
| VI.   Income earned by way of Dividend etc. from Subsidiaries or Companies and/or Joint Ventures Abroad or in India | | |
| VII.   Miscellaneous Income | | |
| **Total** | | |

**Note :** Under items II to V loss figure may be shown in brackets.

### Schedule 15 – Interest Expended

| | Year ended<br>31-3-.........<br>(Current Year) | Year ended<br>31-3-.........<br>(Previous Year) |
|---|---|---|
| I.   Interest on Deposits | | |
| II.   Interest on Reserve Bank of India/Inter-Bank Borrowings | | |
| III.   Others | | |
| **Total** | | |

### Schedule – 16 – Operating Expenses

| | Year ended<br>31-3-.......<br>(Current Year) | Year ended<br>31-3-........<br>(Previous Year) |
|---|---|---|
| I.   Payments to and Provisions for Employees | | |
| II.   Rent, Taxes and Lighting | | |
| III.   Printing and Stationery | | |
| IV.   Advertisement and Publicity | | |
| V.   Depreciation on Bank's Property | | |
| VI.   Director's Fees, Allowances and Expenses | | |
| VII.   Auditor's Fees and Expenses (including Branch Auditor's) | | |
| VIII.   Law Charges | | |
| IX.   Postages, Telegrams, Telephones etc. | | |
| X.   Repairs and Maintenance | | |
| XI.   Insurance | | |
| XII.   Other Expenditure | | |
| **Total** | | |

## 2.6 GUIDELINES OF RBI FOR COMPILATION OF FINANCIAL STATEMENTS

### BALANCE SHEET

| Item | Schedule No. | Coverage | Notes and Instructions for compilation |
|---|---|---|---|
| Capital | 1 | **Nationalised Banks**<br>(Capital Fully owned by Central Government)<br><br>Banking Companies incorporated outside India | The Capital owned by Central Government as on the date of the Balance sheet including contribution from Government, if any, for participating in World Bank Project should be shown.<br>(i)   The amount brought in by banks by way of start-up capital as prescribed by RBI should be shown under this head.<br>(ii)   The amount of deposit kept with RBI, under sub-section 2 of Section 11 of the Banking Regulation Act, 1949 should also be shown. |

| | | | |
|---|---|---|---|
| | | **Other Banks (Indian)**<br>(Authorised Capital<br>(......... shares of ₹ ......... each)<br>Issued Capital<br>(......... shares of ₹ ......... each)<br>Subscribed Capital<br>(......... shares of ₹ ......... each)<br>Called-up Capital<br>(......... shares of ₹ ......... each)<br>**Less :** Calls unpaid<br>**Add :** Forfeited shares paid up capital | Authorised, Issued, Subscribed, Called-up Capital should be given separately. Calls-in-arrears will be deducted from Called-up Capital while the paid up value of forfeited share should be added thus arriving at the Paid-Up Capital. Where necessary items which can be combined should be shown under one head for instance 'Issued and Subscribed Capital'<br>**Notes – General**<br>The changes in the above items, if any, during the year, say, fresh contribution made by Government, fresh issue of capital, capitalisation of reserves, etc. may be explained in the notes. |
| **Reserves and Surplus** | 2 | i)   **Statutory Reserves** | Reserves created in terms of Section 17 or any other section of Banking Regulation Act must be separately disclosed. |
| | | ii)  **Capital Reserves** | The expression 'Capital Reserves' shall not include any amount regarded as free for distribution through the Profit and Loss Account. Surplus on revaluation should be treated as Capital Reserves. Surplus on translation of the financial statements of foreign branches (which includes fixed assets also) is not a revaluation reserve. |
| | | iii) **Share Premium** | Premium on issue of Share Capital may be shown separately under this head. |
| | | iv)  **Revenue and other Reserves** | The expression 'Revenue Reserve' shall mean any reserve other than capital reserve. This item will include all reserves, other than those separately classified. The expression 'Reserve' shall not include any amount written off or retained by way of providing for depreciation, renewals or diminution in value of assets or retained by way of providing for any known liability. |
| | | v)   **Balance of Profit** | Includes balance of profit after appropriations. In case of loss the balance may be shown as a deduction.<br>**Notes – General**<br>Movement in various categories of reserves should be shown as indicated in the schedule. |
| **Deposits** | 3 | A)<br>    I)    **Demand Deposits**<br>        i)    **from Banks**<br>        ii)    **from Others** | Includes all bank deposits repayable on demand. Includes all demand deposits of the non-bank sectors. Credit balances in overdrafts, cash credit accounts, deposits payable at call, overdue deposits, inoperative current accounts, matured time deposits and cash certificates, certificates of deposits, etc. are to be included under this category. |
| | | II)    **Savings Bank Deposits** | Includes all Savings Banks Deposits (including Inoperative Savings Bank Accounts). |
| | | III)   **Term Deposits**<br>       i)    **from Banks** | Includes all types of Bank Deposits repayable after a specified term. |

| | | | | |
|---|---|---|---|---|
| | | | ii) from Others | Includes all types of Deposits of Non-Bank sector repayable after a specified term. Fixed deposits, cumulative and recurring deposits, cash certificates, certificates of deposits, annuity deposits, deposits mobilised under various schemes, ordinary staff deposits, foreign currency non-resident deposits accounts etc. are to be included under this category. |
| | | B) | i) **Deposits of Branches in India** | The total of these two items will agree with the total deposits. |
| | | | ii) **Deposits of Branches outside India** | **Notes – General**<br>(a) Interest payable on deposits which is accrued but not due should be included but shown under other liabilities.<br>(b) Matured time deposits and cash certificates etc. should be treated as demand deposits.<br>(c) Deposits under special schemes should be included under term deposits if they are not payable on demand. When such deposits have matured for payment they should be shown under demand deposits.<br>(d) Deposits from banks will include deposits from the banking system in India, Co-operative Banks, Foreign banks which may or may not have a presence in India. |
| **Borrowings** | 4 | I) | **Borrowings in India**<br>i) **Reserve Bank of India** | Includes borrowings/refinance obtained from Reserve Bank of India |
| | | | ii) **Other Banks** | Includes borrowings/refinance obtained from commercial banks (including co-operative banks) |
| | | | iii) **Other Institutions and Agencies** | Includes borrowings/refinance obtained from Industrial Development Bank of India, Export-Import Bank of India, National Bank for Agriculture and Rural Development and other institutions, Agencies (including liability against participation certificates, if any) |
| | | II) | **Borrowings Outside India**<br>**Secured borrowings included above** | Includes borrowings of Indian branches abroad as well as borrowings of foreign branches.<br>This item will be shown separately. Includes secured borrowings/refinance in India and Outside India.<br>**Notes – General**<br>(i) The total of I and II will agree with the total borrowings shown in the Balance Sheet.<br>(ii) Inter-Office Transactions should not be shown as borrowings.<br>(iii) Funds raised by foreign branches by way of certificates of deposits, notes, bonds etc. should be classified depending upon documentation as 'deposits' 'borrowings' etc.<br>(iv) Refinance obtained by Banks from Reserve Bank of India and various institutions are being brought under the head 'Borrowings'. Hence, advances will be shown at the gross amount on the assets side. |
| **Other Liabilities and Provisions** | 5 | I) | **Bills Payable** | Includes drafts, telegraphic transfers, travellers' cheques, mail transfers payable, pay-slips, bankers cheques and other miscellaneous items. |
| | | II) | **Inter-office Adjustments (net)** | The Inter-Office Adjustments balance, if in credit, should be shown under this head. Only net position of inter-office accounts, inland as well as foreign, should be shown here. |
| | | III) | **Interest Accrued** | Includes interest accrued but not due on 'deposits' and 'borrowings'. |

| | | IV) **Others (including provisions)** | Includes net provision for income tax and other taxes like interest tax (less advance payment, tax deducted at source etc.) surplus in aggregate in provisions for bad debts provision account, surplus in aggregate in provisions for depreciation in securities, contingency funds which are not disclosed as reserves but are actually in the nature of reserves proposed dividend/transfer to Government. Other liabilities which are not disclosed under any of the major heads such as unclaimed dividend, provisions and funds kept for specific purposes, unexpired discount, outstanding charges like rent, conveyance etc. Certain types of deposits like staff security deposits, margin deposits etc. where the repayment is not free, should also be included under this head.<br><br>**Notes – General**<br>(i) For arriving at the net balance of inter-office adjustments all connected inter-office accounts should be aggregated and the net balance only will be shown, representing mostly items in transit and unadjusted items.<br>(ii) The interest accruing on all deposits, whether the payment is due or not, should be treated as a liability.<br>(iii) It is proposed to show only pure deposits under this head 'deposits' and hence all surplus provisions for bad and doubtful debts, contingency funds, secret reserves etc. which are not netted off against the relative assets, should be brought under the head 'Others (including provisions). |
| **Cash and Balances with the Reserve Bank of India** | 6 | I) **Cash in hand** (including foreign currency notes)<br><br>II) **Balances with Reserve Bank of India**<br>i) in Current Accounts<br>ii) in Other Accounts | Includes cash in hand including foreign currency notes and also of foreign branches in the case of banks having such branches. |
| **Balances with Banks and Money at Call and Short Notice** | 7 | I) **In India**<br>i) Balances with Banks<br>  a) in Current Accounts<br>  b) in Other Deposit Accounts<br>ii) Money at Call and Short Notice<br>  a) with Banks<br>  b) with Other Institutions<br>II) **Outside India**<br>i) Current Accounts<br>ii) Deposits Accounts<br><br><br><br><br><br><br><br>iii) Money at Call and Short Notice | Includes all balances with banks in India (including co-operative banks). Balances in Current Accounts and Deposit Accounts should be shown separately.<br>Includes deposits repayable within 15 days or less than 15 days notice lent in the inter-bank call money market.<br>Includes balances held by foreign branches and balances held by India branches of the banks outside India. Balance held with foreign branches by other branches of the bank should not be shown under this head but should be included in inter-branch accounts. The amounts held in 'Current Accounts' and 'Deposit Accounts' should be shown separately.<br>Includes deposits usually classified in foreign countries as money at call and short notice |

| **Investments** | 8 | **A)** | | **Investments in India** | Includes Central and State Government Securities and Government Treasury bills. These securities should be shown at the book value. However, the difference between the book value and market value should be given in the notes to the Balance Sheet. |
| | | i) | | **Other approved Securities** | Securities other than Government securities, which according to the Banking Regulation Act, 1949 are treated as approved securities, should be included here. |
| | | ii) | | **Shares** | Investments in shares of companies and corporations not included in item (ii) should be included here. |
| | | iii) | | **Debentures and Bonds** | Investments in debentures and bonds of companies and Corporations not included in item (ii) should be included here. |
| | | iv) | | **Investments in Subsidiaries / Joint Ventures** | Investments in subsidiaries/joint ventures (including RRBs) should be included here. |
| | | v) | | **Others** | Includes residual investments, if any, like gold, commercial paper and other instruments in the nature of shares/debentures/bonds. |
| | | **B)** | | **Investments Outside in India** | |
| | | i) | | Government Securities (including local authorities) | All foreign Government securities including securities issued by local authorities may be classified under this head. |
| | | ii) | | Subsidiaries and/or Joint Ventures Abroad | All investments made in the share capital of subsidiaries floated outside India and/or joint ventures abroad should be classified under this head. |
| | | iii) | | Others | All other investments outside India may be shown under this head. |
| **Advances** | 9 | **A)** | i) | Bills purchased and discounted | In classification under Section 'A', all outstandings in India as well as outside – less provisions made, will be classified under three heads as indicated and both secured and unsecured advances will be included under these heads. |
| | | | ii) | Cash Credits, Overdrafts and Loans repayable on demand | |
| | | | iii) | Term Loans | Including overdue instalments. |
| | | **B)** | i) | Secured by tangible assets | All advances or part of advances which are secured by tangible assets may be shown here. The item will include advances in India and outside India. |
| | | | ii) | Covered by Bank / Government Guarantee | Advances in India and outside India to the extent they are covered by guarantees of Indian and Foreign Governments and Indian and foreign banks and DICGC & ECGC are to be included. |
| | | | iii) | Unsecured | All advances not classified under (i) and (ii) will be included here. Total of 'A' should tally with total of 'B'. |
| | | **C)** | I) | **Advances in India** <br> i) Priority Sectors <br> ii) Public Sectors <br> iii) Banks <br> iv) Others | Advances should be broadly classified into 'Advances in India' and 'Advances outside India'. Advances in India will be further classified on the sectoral basis as indicated. Advances to sectors which for the time being are classified as priority sectors according to the instructions of the Reserve Bank are to be classified under the head Priority Sectors'. |

| | | | | |
|---|---|---|---|---|
| | | **II)** | **Advances Outside India** | ' Such advances should be excluded from item (ii) i.e. advances to public sector, Advances to Central and State Government and other Government undertaking including Government companies and corporations which are, according to the statutes, to be treated as public sector companies are to be included in the category 'Public Sector'. All advances to the banking sector including co-operative bank will come under the head 'Banks'. All the remaining advances will be included under the head 'Others' and typically this category will include non-priority advances to the private, joint and co-operative sectors. |
| | | i) | Due from Banks | |
| | | ii) | Due from Others | |
| | | a) | Bills purchased and discounted | |
| | | b) | Syndicated Loans | |
| | | c) | Others | |
| | | | | **Notes – General** |
| | | | | i)   The gross amount of advances including refinance and rediscounts but excluding provisions made to the satisfaction of auditors should be shown as advances. |
| | | | | ii)   Terms loans will be loans not repayable on demand. |
| | | | | iii)   Consortium advances would be shown net of share from other participating banks/institutions. |
| **Fixed Assets** | 10 | **I)** | **Premises** | Premises wholly or partly owned by banking company for the purpose of business including residential premises should be shown against 'Premises'. In the case of premises and other fixed assets, the previous balance, additions thereto and deductions therefrom during the year as also the total depreciation written off should be shown. Where sums have been written off on reduction of capital or revaluation of assets, every balance sheet after the first balance sheet subsequent to the reduction or revaluation should show the revised figures for a period of five years with the date and amount of revision made. |
| | | i) | At cost as on 31st March of the preceding year | |
| | | ii) | Additions during the year | |
| | | iii) | Deductions during the year | |
| | | iv) | Depreciation to date | |
| | | **II)** | **Other Fixed Assets** (including furniture and fixtures) | Motor Vehicles and all Other Fixed Assets other than Premises but including Furniture and Fixtures should be shown under this head. |
| | | i) | At cost 31st March of the preceding year. | |
| | | ii) | Additions during the year | |
| | | iii) | Deductions during the year | |
| | | iv) | Depreciation to date | |
| **Other Assets** | 11 | **I)** | **Inter-Office Adjustments (net)** | The Inter-Office Adjustments balance, if in debit, should be shown under this head. Only net position of inter-office accounts, inland as well as foreign should be shown here. For arriving at the net balance of inter-office adjustment accounts, all connected inter-office accounts should be aggregated and the net balance, if in debit, only should be shown representing mostly items in transit and unadjusted items. |

| | | | |
|---|---|---|---|
| | | II)    **Interest Accrued** | Interest accrued but not due on Investment and advances and interest due but not collected on investments will be the main components of this item. As banks normally debit the borrower's account with interest due on the balance sheet date, usually there may not be any amount of interest due on advances. Only such interest as can be realised in the ordinary course should be shown under this head. |
| | | III)    **Tax paid in Advance or Tax deducted at source** | The amount of tax deducted at source on securities, advance tax paid etc. to the extent that these items are not set off against relative tax provisions should be shown against this item. |
| | | IV)    **Stationery and Stamps** | Only exceptional items of expenditure on stationery like bulk purchase of security paper, loose leaf or other ledgers etc. which are shown as quasi-asset to be written off over a period of time should be shown here. The value should be on a realistic basis and cost escalation should not be taken into account, as these items are for internal use. |
| | | V)    **Non-banking Assets acquired in satisfaction of claims** | Immovable properties/tangible assets acquired in satisfaction of claims are to be shown under this head. |
| | | VI)    **Others** | This will indicate items like claims which have not been met, for instance, clearing items, debit items representing addition to asset or reduction in liabilities which have not been adjusted for technical reasons, want of particulars, etc. advances given to staff by a bank as employer and not as a banker etc. Items which are in the nature of expenses which are pending adjustments should be provided for and the provision netted against this item so that only realisable value is shown under this head. Accrued income other than interest may also be included here. |
| **Contingent Liabilities** | 12 | I)    Claims against the bank not acknowledged as debts. | – |
| | | II)    Liability for partly paid investments. | Liabilities on partly paid shares, debentures, etc. will be included in this head. |
| | | III)    Liability on account of outstanding forward exchange contracts. | Outstanding forward exchange contracts may be included here. |
| | | IV)    Guarantees given on behalf of constituents<br>(i)    in India<br>(ii)    outside India | Guarantees given for constituents in India and outside India may be shown separately. |
| | | V)    Acceptances, endorsements and other obligations. | This item will include letters of credit and bills accepted by the bank on behalf of customers. |
| | | VI)    Other items for which the Bank is contingently liable | Arrears of cumulative dividends, bills rediscounted under writing contracts estimated amounts of contracts remaining to be executed on capital account and not provided for etc. are to be included here. |
| **Bills for Collection** | | | Bills and other items in the course of collection and not adjusted will be shown against this item in the summary version only. No separate schedule is proposed. |

| | | | |
|---|---|---|---|
| **Interest earned** | 13 | **PROFIT AND LOSS ACCOUNT**<br>**I)** Interest/discount on advances / bills | Includes interest and discount on all types of loans and advances like cash credit, demand loans, overdrafts, export loans, term loans, domestic and foreign bills purchased and discounted (including those rediscounted), overdue interest and also interest subsidy, if any, relating to such advances / bills. |
| | | **II)** Income on Investments | Includes all income derived from the investment portfolio by way of interest and dividend. |
| | | **III)** Interest on balances with RBI and other Inter-Bank Funds | Includes interest on balances with Reserve Bank and other banks call loans, money market placements etc. |
| | | **IV)** Others | Includes any other interest/discount income not included in the above heads. |
| **Other Income** | 14 | **I)** Commission, Exchange and Brokerage | Includes all remuneration on services such as commission on collections, commission on exchange on remittances and transfers, commission on letters of credit, letting out of lockers and guarantees, commission on Government business, commission on other permitted agency business including consultancy and other services, brokerage etc. on securities. It does not include foreign exchange income. |
| | | **II)** Profit on sale of Investment **Less :** Loss on sale of Investment<br>**III)** Profit on revaluation of Investment **Less :** Loss on revaluation of Investments | Includes profit or Loss on sale of securities, furniture, land and buildings, motor vehicle, gold, silver etc. Only the net position should be shown. If the net position is a loss, the amount should be shown as a deduction. The net Profit or Loss on revaluation of assets may also be shown under this item. |
| | | **IV)** Profit on sale of land, buildings and other assets **Less :** Loss on sale of land, buildings and other assets | |
| | | **V)** Profit on exchange transactions **Less :** Loss on exchange transactions<br>**VI)** Income earned by way of dividends etc. from subsidiaries, companies, joint ventures abroad / in India. | Includes Profit/loss on dealing in foreign exchange, all income earned by way of foreign exchange, commission and charges on foreign exchange transactions excluding interest which will be shown under interest. Only the net position should be shown. If the net position is a loss, it is to be shown as a deduction. |
| | | **VII)** Miscellaneous Income | Includes recoveries from constituents for godown rents, income from banks properties, security charges, insurance etc. and any other miscellaneous income. In case any item under this head exceeds one percent of the total income, particulars may be given in the notes. |
| **Interest Expended** | 15 | **I)** Interest on Deposits | Includes interest paid on all types of deposits including deposits from banks and other institutions. |
| | | **II)** Interest on RBI / Inter-Bank Borrowings. | Includes discount/interest on all borrowings and refinance from RBI and other banks. |
| | | **III)** Others | Includes discount/interest on all borrowings/ refinance from financial institutions. All other payments like interest on participation certificates, penal interest paid etc. may also be included. |

| | | | | |
|---|---|---|---|---|
| **Operating Expenses** | 16 | I) | Payments to and Provisions for Employees | Includes staff salaries or wages, allowances, bonus, other staff benefit like provident fund, pension, gratuity, liveries to staff, leave concessions, staff welfare, medical allowances to staff etc. |
| | | II) | Rent, Taxes and Lighting | Includes rent paid by banks on buildings and other municipal and other taxes paid (excluding income tax and interest tax) electricity and other similar charges and levies. House rent allowances and other similar payments to staff should appear under the head 'Payments to and provisions for employees'. |
| | | III) | Printing and Stationery | Include books and forms and stationery used by the Bank and other printing charges which are not incurred by way of publicity expenditure. |
| | | IV) | Advertisement and Publicity | Includes expenditure incurred by the Bank for advertisement and publicity purpose including printing charges of publicity matter. |
| | | V) | Depreciation on Bank's Property | Includes depreciation on bank's own property, motor cars and other vehicles, furniture, electric fittings, vaults, lifts, leasehold properties, non-banking assets etc. |
| | | VI) | Director's Fees, Allowances and Expenses | Includes sitting fees and all other items of expenditure incurred on behalf of directors. The daily allowances, hotel charges, conveyance charges etc. which though in the nature of reimbursement of expenses incurred may be included under this head. Similar expenses of local Committee members may also be included under this head. |
| | | VII) | Auditor's Fees and Expenses (including Branch Auditor's Fees and Expenses) | Includes the fees paid to the statutory auditors and branch auditors for professional services rendered and all expenses for performing their duties, even though they may be in the nature of reimbursement of expenses. If external auditors have been appointed by banks themselves for internal inspections and audits and other services the expenses incurred in that context including fees may not be included under this head but shown under 'other expenditure'. |
| | | VIII) | Law Charges | All legal expenses and reimbursement of expenses incurred in connection with legal services are to be included here. |
| | | IX) | Postage, Telegrams, Telephones etc. | Includes all postal charges like stamps, telegram, telephones, teleprinter etc. |
| | | X) | Repairs and Maintenance | Includes repairs to bank's property, their maintenance charges etc. |
| | | XI) | Insurance | Includes insurance charges on bank's property, insurance premia paid to Deposit Insurance and Credit Guarantee Corporation etc. to the extent they are not recovered from the concerned parties. |
| | | XII) | Other Expenditure | All expenses other than those not included in any of the other heads like, licence fees, donations, subscriptions to papers, periodicals, entertainment expenses travel expenses etc. may be included under this head. In case any particular item under this head exceeds one percent of the total income particulars may be given in the notes. |
| **Provisions and Contingencies** | | | | Includes all provisions made for bad and doubtful debts, provisions for taxation and doubtful debts, provisions for taxation, provisions for dimunition in the value of investments, transfers to contingencies and other similar items. |

The **Final Accounts of Canara Bank as on 31st March, 2016** published in newspaper on 15th May, 2016 is shown below to understand the items and schedules incorporated therein very clearly.

## CANARA BANK
### Balance Sheet as at 31st March, 2016

| | Schedule No. | As at 31.03.2016 (₹ '000) | As at 31.03.2015 (₹ '000) |
|---|---|---|---|
| **Capital and Liabilities :** | | | |
| Capital | 1 | 410,00,000 | 410,00,000 |
| Reserves and Surplus | 2 | 6722,23,58 | 56,989,572 |
| Deposits | 3 | 11,31,132,319 | 9,31,059,186 |
| Borrowings | 4 | 25,82,40 | 114,16,42 |
| Other Liabilities and Provisions | 5 | 8860,56,70 | 7286,13,33 |
| **Total** | | **132821,85,87** | **110305,17,33** |
| **Assets :** | | | |
| Cash and Balances with Reserve Bank of India | 6 | 7913,99,57 | 4984,38,32 |
| Balances with Banks and Money At Call and Short Notice | 7 | 4909,55,90 | 3684,34,91 |
| Investments | 8 | 36974,18,30 | 38053,88,36 |
| Advances | 9 | 79425,69,98 | 60421,40,39 |
| Fixed Assets | 10 | 688,47,17 | 672,81,43 |
| Other Assets | 11 | 2909,94,95 | 2488,33,92 |
| **Total** | | **132821,85,87** | **110305,17,33** |
| Contingent Liabilities | 12 | 54900,700,90 | 57607,02,68 |
| Bills for Collection | | | |
| Notes on Accounts | 17 | 4422,58,32 | 3957,95,79 |

### Profit and Loss Account for the year ended 31st March, 2016

| | Schedule No. | For the Year ended 31.03.2016 (₹ '000) | For the year ended 31.03.2015 (₹ '000) |
|---|---|---|---|
| **I. Income :** | | | |
| Interest Earned | 13 | 8711,51,23 | 7571,96,88 |
| Other Income | 14 | 1377,51,49 | 1543,82,73 |
| **Total** | | **10089,02,72** | **9115,79,61** |
| **II. Expenditure :** | | | |
| Interest expended | 15 | 5130,00,69 | 4421,49,93 |
| Operating Expenses | 16 | 2347,13,54 | 2108,97,16 |
| Provisions and Contingencies | | 1268,66,49 | 1475,82,07 |
| **Total** | | **8745,80,72** | **8006,29,16** |
| **III. Net Profit for the year** | | 1343,22,00 | 1109,50,45 |
| **IV. Appropriations / Transfers to** | | | |
| **Statutory Reserve** | | | |
| Capital Reserve | | 340,00,00 | 280,00,000 |
| Investment Fluctuation Reserve | | 1,03,00 | 202,70,31 |
| Revenue Reserves | | (–) 1208,14,82 | 230,00,00 |
| Interim Dividend | | 1901,73,82 | 140,65,52 |
| Proposed Dividend | | – | 102,50,00 |
| Dividend Tax | | 270,60,00 | 123,00,00 |
| | | 38,00,000 | 30,64,62 |
| **Total** | | 1343,22,00 | 1109,50,45 |
| Notes on Accounts | 17 | | |
| Earnings per share | | 32.76 | 27.06 |

## 2.7 INTRODUCTION TO CORE BANKING SYSTEM

**Meaning :**

Core banking is a banking service provided by a group of networked bank branches where customers may access their bank account and perform basic transactions from any of the branch offices.

Core banking covers basic functions of bank i.e. depositing and lending money. It means core banking is often associated with retail banking and may banks treat the retail customers as their core banking customers. In core banking system, businesses are usually managed via. the corporate banking division of the institution.

The core banking services rely mainly on computer and network technology to allow a bank to centralise its record keeping and allow access from any location. It has been the development of banking software has allowed core banking solutions to be developed. In simple ways, it is doing all banking operations of branches and head office by connecting to a central computer kept at data centre.

**Basic Functions of Core Banking :**

Normal core banking will include : (i) transaction accounts, (ii) loans, (iii) mortgages and (iv) payments.

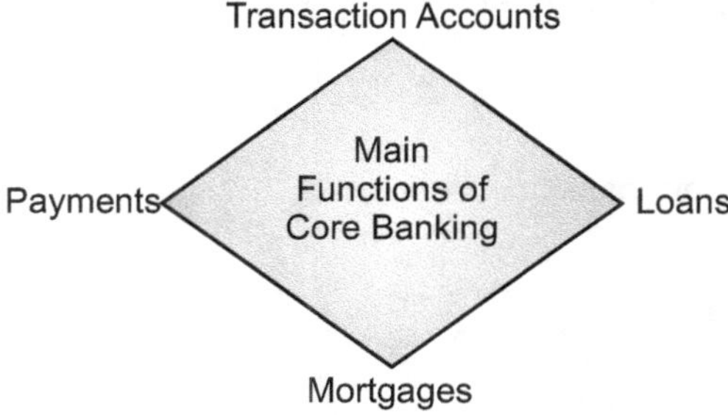


**Fig. 2.2 : Functions of Core Banking**

Now, all these banks make these functions through service available across multiple channels like ATMs, internet banking, mobile banking and branches.

A core banking system is the back-end data processing application for processing all transactions that have occurred during the day and posting update data on account balances to the mainframe. Core system typically include deposit account and CD account processing, loan and credit processing, interfaces to general ledger and reporting tools.

Now, most of Indian banks moved to core banking applications to support their operations where 'CORE' banking may stand for **"Centralised Online Real-time Exchange"**.

This basically meant that all the bank branches could access application from centralised data centres. This indicate that the deposits made were reflected immediately on the bank's servers and the customer could withdraw the deposited money from any of the bank's branches.

Core banking became possible with the advent of computer and telecommunication technology that allowed information to be shared between bank branches quickly, accurately and efficiently.

Before application of core banking services every bank used to take atleast one or two days for a transaction to reflect in the account because each branch had their local servers, and the data from server in each branch was sent in a batch to the servers in the data centre only at the end of the day.

### Definition of Core Banking

**Gartner** defines a core banking system as a back-end system that processes daily banking transactions and posts updates to accounts and other financial records. Core banking system typically include deposits, loan and credit-processing capabilities, with interfaces to general ledger systems and reporting tools. Core banking applications are often one of the largest single expenses for banks and because a legacy software issues a major issue in terms of allocating resources. Strategic spending on these systems is based on combination of service-oriented architecture and supporting technologies that create extensible architectures. The advancement is technology, especially internet and information technology has led to new ways of doing business in retail banking. These technologies have reduced manual work in banks and increasing accuracy and as well as efficiency.

### Core Banking Solutions:

The platform where communication technology and information technology are merged to suit core need of banking is known as core banking solution. Here, computer software is developed to perform core operations of banking like:

(i)     recording of transactions

(ii)    passbook maintenance

(iii)   interest calculation on loans and deposits

(iv)    customer records

(v)     balance of payments and

(vi)    withdrawals.

This software is installed at different branches of bank and then interconnected by means of computer networks based on telephones, satellite and the internet. It allows the bank customers to operate accounts from any branch if it has installed core banking solutions.

In India, many banks implement custom applications for core banking.

Others implement/customise commercial ISV packages. While it is observed that, many banks run core banking in-house, there are some which use outsourced service providers as well. There are several systems integrators like Cognizant, IMB, H.P., Capgemini, Accenture which implement these core banking packages at banks.

The elite vendors of core banking software applications for retail, private universal, wholesale and lending business functional requirements, covering core processing solutions for conventional banking and financial institutions, credit unions, MFI and co-operations banks.

### Elements of Core Banking System:

A core banking system is the software used to support a banks most common transactions.

**Elements of Core Banking include:**

(i)     Making and servicing loans.

(ii)    Opening new accounts.

(iii)   Processing cash deposits and withdrawals.

(iv)   Processing payments and cheques.

(v)    Calculating interest.

(vi)   Customer Requirement Management (CRM) and activities.

(vii)   Managing customer accounts.

(viii)   Establishing criteria for minimum balances, interest rates, number of withdrawals allowed and so on.

(ix)   Establishing interest rates.

(x)    Maintaining records for all the bank's transactions.

Core banking functions differ depending on the specific type of banks. In case of retail banking, for example, is geared towards individual customers, wholesale banking is business conducted between banks and securities trading involves the buying and selling of stocks, shares and so on.

Core banking systems are often specialised for a particular type of banking. Products that are designed to deal with multiple types of core banking functions are sometimes referred to as universal banking systems. Examples of core banking products include Infosy's, Finance, Nucleus FinnOne and Oracle's Flexcube application.

**Modern Packaged Core Banking Platforms:**

Core banking has historically meant, the critical systems that provide the basic account management features and information about customers and accounting holding. Modern packaged and core banking platforms are typically more holistic and often include these features as well as :

(i)    Customer Relationship Management (CRM) features including 360 degree customer view.

(ii)   The ability to originate new products and customers.

(iii)   Content management facilities.

(iv)   Best practice workflow processes.

(v)    Banking finance including general ledger and reporting.

(vi)   Banking channels such as teller system, side counter (sales) applications, mobile banking and online banking solutions.

(vii)   Governance and compliance capabilities such as internal control management and auditing.

(viii)   Security control and audit capabilities.

It is observed that, older core banking platforms and modern core banking platforms are quite different. Replacing these older system with modern one is often a time when bank consider strategic transformation, process revision and identifying new target operating models.

**Technical Infrastructure Required for Core Banking System:**

   (i)     Software.

   (ii)    Hardware.

   (iii)   Data centre/Disaster recovery centre.

   (iv)   Connectivity devices (BSNL/MTNL) i.e. wireless communication system.

   (v)    Connectivity service providers.

   (vi)   Security equipments.

   (vii)  Uninterrupted power supply arrangements.

   (viii) Anti-virus/Firewalls.

**Actual Functioning and Process of Core Banking System in Practice:**

In mere computerised functions each branch of bank has its own computer and branch functions are thus automated on that computer. This is called as **"Total Branch Automation"** (TBA). Backup of each branch is kept at Head Office on tapes, CD etc. Consolidation of data from different branches is done at Head Office at a decided periodically. We know that, with technology advancement particularly in 'wireless communication' and 'tele communication' it became possible to send data from one computer to another computer. Taking into advantage of this it was thought fit to connect branch computers to a centralised single computer at head office and have all transactions of all branches recorded live at one place. This is the base of core banking.

**Concept of Business Reengineering:**

As the single computer at data centre (basically at head office) get live data from branches position of the bank as a whole is available at one place at each moment. This system of operation then brought total change in traditional banking operations at branches were taken at central place. This is called **"business re-engineering"** in terms of shifting to core banking. This re-engineering process brought many advantages to bank and its customers and also changed customer service dimensions.

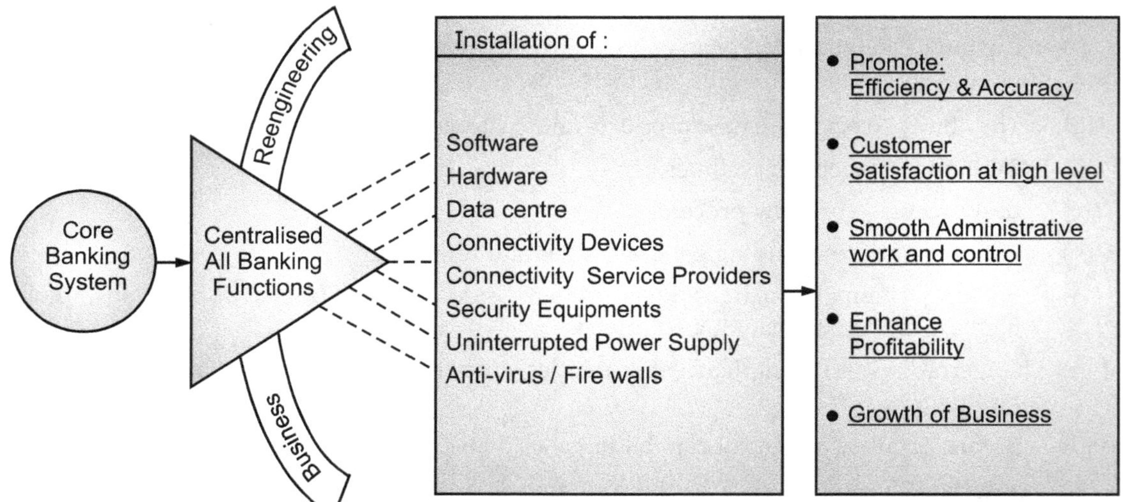


Fig. 2.3 : Core Banking Process

**Advantages of Core Banking:**

Following are the advantages of core banking.

(a)    Advantages of Centralized Accounting.

(b)    Advantages to Head Office.

(c)    Administrative Advantages.

(d)    Advantages to Customers.

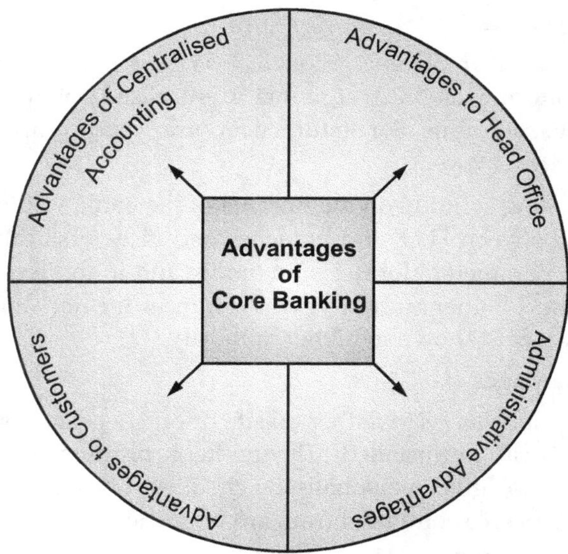


Fig. 2.4 : Advantages of Core Banking

**(a)   Advantages of Centralised Accounting :**

(i)    All the transactions of the bank directly impact the General Ledger and Profit and Loss Account. This provides a real time total picture about the financial position and situation of the bank. This helps the bank for timely effective decision making for financial management, a very critical and dynamic function in today's banking.

(ii)   Centralised accounting helps in better product analysis, monitoring and roll out. Aspects like interest rate modifications, product modification and interest application can be done centrally from one place for all the branches. Bank can quickly respond to market scenario and customer needs. This gives competitive edge to the bank.

(iii)  Any customer becomes the customer of the bank rather than of a branch. With unique ID/Account Number the accounts of customers can be viewed centrally by the bank. Such customer view gives the bank opportunity to decide directions from business development and marketing strategies.

(iv)  Present of centralised data constantly live updated at any time ensures a comprehensive report/statement generation. This facility helps in decision making as well as submission of reports to various authorities. Operational efficiency of the bank gets increased due to quick report generation for bank as a whole.

**(b)  Advantages to Head Office :**

(i)   Clearing function is centralised reducing manpower requirement at each branch for the purpose. Audit on operational aspects of the accounts can be done at a single location as entire data is available at one place.

(ii)   Better ALM, especially for short-term assets and liabilities are possible. Productwise, customerwise, customer profit based analysis and decision making is possible. Analysis of data on any aspect of banking business and control issues give scope for keeping the bank professionally healthy.

(iii)   Faster and practically real time reconciliation of accounts. Centralised marking and movement monitoring of NPA accounts. Centralised followup and co-ordination of overdue and NPA accounts. For statutory reporting and compliance no need to wait for branch compliance.

(iv)   By installing mailing solution on the intranet of the bank, written communication in the form of letters, between H.O. and branches and vice-versa can be eliminated. Mailing solution can set parameters for decision timing and if not decided in time the mail can be escalated to next higher authority. This enhances the decision making procedure and delay at any level gets known to higher authority.

**(c)  Administrative Advantages :**

(i)   Service channels such as ATM, either on site or off site, can be started. Cheques Deposit Machines (CDM) can be installed. Cheque book printing machine can be installed at central location to give personalised cheques books. Such machine is 'WAN' connectivity can receive command from any branches.

(ii)   Centralised system/I.T. administration enhances system security and user management. In Total Branch Administration (TBA) made manpower for I.T. administration is required at each branch. But in core banking it is required only at one place. This reduces in manpower need and cost. Due to single point resources available I.T. manpower is utilised properly.

(iii)   Printing of several matter such as follow-up notices, statement of accounts, etc. can be done centrally on "line printer" that reduces the printing time, printer and manpower need at each branch. Account opening and scanning of signatures can be done at central location.

(iv)   Reduced credit processing time for existing loan accounts as the credit department gets information handy. For processing of new loan accounts the information on product is available that facilitates proper decision. Corrective measures in credit portfolio can be quickly taken due to credit portfolio analysis.

(v)   In core banking system, centralised real time General Ledger and Profit and Loss Account almost eliminates accounting work. It reduces paper work, inward communication needs and work of tallying. Balance Sheet of the bank is available at any day and hour and movement.

(vi)   I.T. department becomes the focused entity and back-bone of the operations of the bank. Parameter setting, interest application and such other works being done at one place avoid chances of otherwise repetitive mistakes at different branches and then the load on I.T. department for rectification work.

(vii) Adopting proper core banking software reducing the cost of ownership, enhancing productivity, mitigating risk, expanding channels-to-market, lowering costs, improving customer service, optimising up-sell and cross-sell opportunities, driving growth and boosting profitability.

**(d) Advantages to Customers :**

(i) Customer can operate his accounts from any of the branch of the bank.

(ii) Customer service channels can be made available to the customers.

(iii) Even extension counters of branches can provide all services to the customers.

(iv) Customer gets immediate credit if the transactions is between the branches of the bank.

(v) Customer can get SMS alerts on his mobile or e-mail alerts through net for transaction taking place in his account.

(vi) Customer gets full attention and service satisfaction at the branches as the branches are freed from all back office functions, clearing functions and almost all accounting functions.

(vii) With reduced work at the branches they can focus on development of business, customer service and attendance and meaningful liaison with customer for getting new business.

**Drawbacks and Risks of Core Banking :**

(i) Total dependency on technology.

(ii) Stoppage of work has adverse effect on bank's image and reputation.

(iii) Any failure on technical ground can halt the working with uncertainty about restoring normalcy.

(iv) If not mitigated by generating profit out of benefits of core banking the recurring costs are heavy.

(v) Skilled technical person's leaving the bank poses serious problem.

(vi) Increase the capital expenditure of bank.

(vii) Bank has to face for any eventual temporary discontinuation of business activity due to technical failure beyond control.

In short, banking leaders understand that technology is critical for simplifying banking to create suitable business growth. But many are burdened with disparate host systems added piecemeal, overtime and developed on obsolute technology. These legacy systems are simply not equipped to readily respond to change. However, bankers, having growth weary of lengthy developments and ensuring business disruption, have apprehensions about transformation. A painfree approach to banking transformation with an adaptive solution at the core, will prove invaluable for banks looking to gear themselves for tomorrow. The proper core banking solution enables banks to provide a hasslefree and unified banking experience to customer that's personalised to their needs.

## SUMMARY

* Banking may be defined as "accepting for the purpose of lending or investment of deposits of money from the public, to be payable on demand or otherwise and withdrawable by cheque.

* Banking Companies in India are governed by Banking Regulation Act 1949. However, provisions of Companies Act, 1956 are also applicable to Banking Companies, ordinary rules and regulations of book-keeping are also applicable in maintaining the 'Books of Accounts' of Banking Companies.

* A revised format for preparation of Balance Sheet and Profit and Loss Account have been introduced from the year 1991-92.

  Because of special nature of transactions of Banking Company there are some typical items which requires explanation.

* Every Banking Company should prepare a Balance Sheet and Profit and Loss Account on 31$^{st}$ March of each year in the form set out in the Third Schedule of Banking Regulation Act. In the case of a foreign banking company, the Profit and Loss Account may be prepared as on a date not earlier than two months before 31$^{st}$ December.

* Assets or Accounts becomes 'non-performing' when it ceases to generate income for a bank.

* Banks are required to classify the loan assets (advances) into four categories i.e. (a) Standard Assets, (b) Sub-standard Assets, (c)  Doubtful Assets and (d) Loss Assets.

* It has been advised by RBI that Banks are to recognise their income on "Accrual Basis" in respect of income on performing assets and on "Cash Basis" in respect of income on non-performing assets.

* The new format of Balance Sheet and Profit and Loss Account has been followed w.e.f. accounting year ending 31$^{st}$ March 1992. The Balance Sheet is prepared in 'Form – A' while the Profit and Loss Account is prepared in 'Form – B' of the Third Schedule.

* 'Guidelines of RBI for completion of financial statement's are to be followed by Banking Company while preparing financial statements. These guidelines are provided for each and every item incorporated in the Balance Sheet of a Banking Company.

* Schedule No. 1 to 5 indicate the items of liabilities side of the Balance Sheet and Schedule No. 6 to 11 indicate the items of Assets side of the Balance Sheet. Schedule No. 12 indicate the items included in contingent liabilities. Schedule No. 13 to 16 indicate the items of income and expenditure of Profit and Loss Account.

## 2.8 ILLUSTRATIONS

### ILLUSTRATION 1

From the following information, prepare Profit and Loss Account of United Bank Ltd. Ulhasnagar for the year ended 31-3-2016 alongwith the necessary schedules.

| Particulars | in 000's ₹ |
|---|---|
| Interest on Term Loans | 39,00 |
| Interest on Cash Credit | 30,20 |
| Interest on Overdraft in Current Account | 13,00 |
| Discount on Bills | 15,20 |
| Interest on Fixed Deposits | 27,50 |
| Interest on Saving Bank Deposits | 8,70 |
| Commission Exchange and Brokerage | 3,00 |
| Income on Investments | 6,50 |
| Interest on balances with RBI | 1,20 |
| Interest on Inter Bank Funds | 80 |
| Profit on sale of Investments | 1,70 |
| Profit on sale of Land, Buildings and Other Assets | 40 |
| Loss on Exchange Transactions | 38 |
| Interest on RBI and Inter Bank Borrowings | 1,15 |
| Salaries, allowances and bonus to employees | 15,00 |
| Rent, Taxes and Lighting | 2,50 |
| Insurance | 40 |
| Printing and Stationery | 2,00 |
| Advertisement and Publicity | 1,10 |
| Postage, Telegrams, Telephones etc. | 65 |
| Audit Fees | 35 |
| Legal Charges | 78 |
| Director's Fees, Allowances and Expenses | 1,22 |
| Repairs and Maintenance | 48 |
| Other Income | 2,56 |
| Miscellaneous Expenditure | 1,18 |
| Profit and Loss Account (Cr.) | 6,95 |

**Additional Informations :**

i) Depreciation to be provided for the year ₹ 2,12 thousand.

ii) Rebate on bills discounted on 31-3-2015 and 31-3-2016 were ₹ 2,75 thousand and ₹ 3,15 thousand respectively.

iii) Interest on non-performing assets is as follows :

| | Earned | Collected |
|---|---|---|
| | | ₹ in 000's |
| Term Loans | 7,80 | 5,20 |
| Cash Credit | 6,90 | 4,70 |
| Overdraft | 7,50 | 3,50 |

iv) Advances of the Bank has been classified as follows :

| | (₹ in 000's) |
|---|---|
| – Substandard Assets | 7,80 |
| Secured portions of Doubtful Assets | |
| – Upto one year | 3,00 |
| – One year to three years | 2,20 |
| – More than three years | 80 |

|  |  |
|---|---|
| Unsecured portions of Doubtful Assets | 30 |
| Loss Assets | 75 |

Balance is treated as Standard Assets

Adequate provisions against the above mentioned advances is to be made

v)     Investments          32,50

Bank keeps 70% of the Investment as permanent investment. The market value of 30% investment is ₹ 8,25 thousand.

vi)    Make provision for income tax @ 55%.

vii)    The following transfers are to be made from the net profit.

      a)     20% to statutory reserve

      b)     8% to revenue reserve

viii)    Directors proposed a dividend amounting to ₹ 4,00 thousand for the year ended 31st March, 2016.

---

### SOLUTION

**In the books of United Bank Ltd., Ulhasnagar**
**Profit and Loss Account for the year ended 31-3-2016**

|  |  | Schedule No. | Year ended 31-3-2016 ₹ in '000's |
|---|---|---|---|
| **I.** | **Income** |  |  |
|  | Income Earned | 13 | 96,70 |
|  | Other Income | 14 | 7,28 |
|  | **Total** |  | **103,98** |
| **II.** | **Expenditure** |  |  |
|  | Interest Expended | 15 | 37,35 |
|  | Operating Expenses | 16 | 27,78 |
|  | Provisions and Contingencies |  | 23,61 |
|  | **Total** |  | **88,74** |
| **III.** | **Profit** |  |  |
|  | Net Profit for the year |  | 15,24 |
|  | Profit brought forward |  | 6,95 |
|  | **Total** |  | **22,19** |
| **IV.** | **Appropriations** |  |  |
|  | Transfer to Statutory Reserves |  | 3,05 |
|  | Transfer to Other Reserves |  | 1,22 |
|  | Transfer to Proposed Dividend |  | 4,00 |
|  | Balance Carried over to Balance Sheet |  | 13,92 |
|  | **Total** |  | **22,19** |

### Schedule – 13 – Interest Earned

|  |  | Year ended 31-3-2016 ₹ in 000's |
|---|---|---|
| I. | Interest or Discount on Advances/Bills | 88,20 |
| II. | Income on Investments | 6,50 |
| III. | Interest on Balance with RBI and other Inter-Bank Funds | 2,00 |
|  | **Total** | **96,70** |

## Schedule 14 – Other Income

| | | Year ended 31-3-2016 ₹ |
|---|---|---|
| I. | Commission, Exchange and Brokerage | 3,00 |
| II. | Profit on Sale of Investments | 1,70 |
| III. | Profit on Sale of Land, Buildings, and Other Assets | 40 |
| IV. | Loss on Exchange Transactions | (38) |
| V. | Other Income | 2,56 |
| | **Total** | **7,28** |

## Schedule 15 – Interest Expended

| | | Year ended 31-3-2016 ₹ |
|---|---|---|
| I. | Interest on Deposits | 36,20 |
| II. | Interest on Reserve Bank of India or Inter-Bank Borrowings | 1,15 |
| | **Total** | **37,35** |

## Schedule – 16 – Operating Expenses

| | | Year ended 31-3-2016 ₹ |
|---|---|---|
| I. | Payments and Provisions for employees | 15,00 |
| II. | Rent, Taxes and Lighting | 2,50 |
| III. | Printing and Stationery | 2,00 |
| IV. | Advertisement and Publicity | 1,10 |
| V. | Depreciation on Bank's Property | 2,12 |
| VI. | Director's Fees, Allowances and Expenses | 1,22 |
| VII. | Auditor's Fees Allowances and Expenses | 35 |
| VIII. | Law Charges | 78 |
| IX. | Postage, Telegrams, Telephones etc. | 65 |
| X. | Repairs and Maintenance | 48 |
| XI. | Insurance | 40 |
| XII. | Other Expenditure | 1,18 |
| | **Total** | **27,78** |

**Working Notes :**

**i) Calculation of Interest on Advances :**

(₹ in 000's)

| | Amount | Interest credited but not received | Net Amount |
|---|---|---|---|
| Interest on Term Loans | 39,00 | 2,60 | 36,40 |
| Interest on Cash Credit | 30,20 | 2,20 | 28,00 |
| Interest on Overdraft | 13,00 | 4,00 | 9,00 |
| **Total** | | | **73,40** |

**ii) Calculation of Discount on bills :**

| | | |
|---|---|---|
| Discount on bills | | 15,20 |
| **Add :** Rebate on bills discounted 31-3-2015 | (+) | 2,75 |
| | | 17,95 |
| **Less :** Rebate on bills discounted 31-3-2016 | (–) | 3,15 |
| **Total** | | **14,80** |

**iii) Interest/discount on advanced bills :**

| | |
|---|---|
| Interest on advances | 73,40 |
| Discount on bills | 14,80 |
| **Total** | **88,20** |

**iv) Calculation of provision against advances and investments :**

|  | Amount<br>₹ in 000's | % of provision<br>required | Amount<br>provision<br>₹ in 000's |
|---|---|---|---|
| Sub-standard asset | 7,80 | 10% | 78 |
| Secured positions of doubtful assets | | | |
|   –  Upto one year | 3,00 | 20% | 60 |
|   –  One year to 3 years | 2,20 | 30% | 66 |
|   –  More than 3 years | 80 | 50% | 40 |
|   –  Unsecured portions of doubtful assets | 30 | 100% | 30 |
|   –  Loss Assets | 75 | 100% | 75 |
| | | | **3.49** |
| Depreciation on Current Investments | | | |
| 30% of cost of Investments i.e. $\left(₹\,32,50 \times \dfrac{30}{100}\right)$ | | 9,75 | |
| **Less :** Market Value | | 8,25 | 1,50 |
| **Total provisions against advances and investments** | | | **4,99** |

**v) Calculation of Net Profit :**          ₹ in 000's

| | | | | |
|---|---|---|---|---|
| Interest Earned | | 96,70 | | |
| **Add :** Other Income | (+) | 7,28 | | 103,98 |
| **Less :** Interest Expended | | 37,35 | | |
| Operating Expenses | | 27,78 | | |
| Provision against Advances and Investments | (+) | 4,99 | (–) | 70,12 |
| ∴  Profit before Tax | | | | 33,86 |
| **Less :** Provision for Income Tax @ 55% | | | (–) | 18,62 |
| **Net Profit for the year** | | | | **15,24** |

**vi) Calculation of Provisions and Contingencies :**

| | | | |
|---|---|---|---|
| Provision against Advances and Investments | | | 4,99 |
| Provision for Income Tax | | (+) | 18,62 |
| **Total** | | | **23,61** |

---

**ILLUSTRATION 2**

The following figures are extracted from the books of Saraswati Bank Ltd. Saswad as at 31-3-2016, from which you are required to prepare Profit and Loss Account with necessary schedules.

| Particulars | ₹ |
|---|---|
| Interest on Loans | 3,10,000 |
| Interest on cash credits | 2,90,000 |
| Interest on Overdrafts | 2,00,000 |
| Interest on Balances with RBI | 40,000 |
| Income on Investments | 10,000 |
| Interest on Fixed Deposits | 2,60,000 |
| Interest on Savings Accounts | 80,000 |
| Interest on Current Accounts | 30,000 |
| Discount on Bills Discounted | 1,90,000 |
| Interest on Borrowings from other Banks | 10,000 |
| Profit on Sale of Investment | 40,000 |
| Loss on Sale of Investment | 5,000 |
| Income from Joint Ventures | 25,000 |

| | |
|---|---:|
| Profit on Revaluation of Investments | 35,000 |
| Loss on Revaluation of Investments | 10,000 |
| Dividends received from Joint Stock Companies | 25,000 |
| Salaries to Staff | 65,000 |
| Rent and Taxes | 8,000 |
| Depreciation on Bank's Assets | 21,000 |
| Sundry Income | 18,000 |
| Printing and Stationery | 17,000 |
| Repairs and Maintenance | 14,000 |
| Advertisement | 6,000 |
| Director's Fees and Allowances | 9,000 |
| Audit Fees | 6,000 |
| Law Charges | 8,000 |
| Postage and Telephone Charges | 11,000 |
| Other Expenses | 4,000 |
| Profit on 1-4-2015 | 1,20,000 |

**Adjustments :**

    i)      Write off ₹ 19,000 for Bad and Doubtful Debts.

    ii)     Provide 40% for Taxation.

    iii)    Rebate on bills discounted is to be provided for ₹ 20,000.

### SOLUTION

**In the Books of Saraswati Bank Ltd. Saswad**
**Profit and Loss Account for the year ended 31-3-2016**

| | | Schedule No. | Year ended 31-3-2016 ₹ | Year ended 31-3-2015 ₹ |
|---|---|---|---:|---:|
| **I.** | **Income** | | | |
| | Income Earned | 13 | 10,20,000 | |
| | Other Income | 14 | 1,28,000 | |
| | Total | | **11,48,000** | |
| **II.** | **Expenditure** | | | |
| | Interest Expended | 15 | 3,80,000 | |
| | Operating Expenses | 16 | 1,69,000 | |
| | Provisions and Contingencies | | 2,51,000 | |
| | Total | | **8,00,000** | |
| **III.** | **Profit** | | | |
| | Net Profit for the year | | 3,48,000 | |
| | Profit brought forward | | 1,20,000 | |
| | Total | | **4,68,000** | |

### Schedule – 13 – Interest Earned

| | | Year ended 31-3-2016 ₹ | Year ended 31-3-2015 ₹ |
|---|---|---:|---:|
| I. | Interest or Discount on Advances/Bills | 9,70,000 | |
| II. | Income on Investments | 10,000 | |
| III. | Interest on Balances with RBI and other Inter Bank Funds | 40,000 | |
| | Total | **10,20,000** | |

## Schedule 14 – Other Income

| | | | Year ended 31-3-2016 ₹ | Year ended 31-3-2015 ₹ |
|---|---|---|---|---|
| | | ₹ | | |
| (I) | Profit on Sale of Investments | 40,000 | | |
| | **Less :** Loss on Sale of Investments | (–) 5,000 | 35,000 | |
| (II) | Profit on Revaluation of Investments | 35,000 | | |
| | **Less :** Loss on Revaluation of Investments | (–) 10,000 | 25,000 | |
| (III) | Income from Joint Ventures | | 25,000 | |
| (IV) | Dividend from Joint Stock Companies | | 25,000 | |
| (V) | Sundry Income | | 18,000 | |
| | **Total** | | **1,28,000** | |

## Schedule 15 – Interest Expended

| | | Year ended 31-3-2016 ₹ | Year ended 31-3-2015 ₹ |
|---|---|---|---|
| I. | Interest on Deposits | 3,70,000 | – |
| II. | Interest on Borrowings from Banks | 10,000 | – |
| | **Total** | **3,80,000** | |

## Schedule – 16 – Operating Expenses

| | | Year ended 31-3-2016 ₹ | Year ended 31-3-2015 ₹ |
|---|---|---|---|
| I. | Payments to Employees | 65,000 | |
| II. | Rent and Taxes | 8,000 | |
| III. | Printing and Stationery | 17,000 | |
| IV. | Advertisement | 6,000 | |
| V. | Depreciation on Bank's Assets | 21,000 | |
| VI. | Director's Fees, Allowances | 9,000 | |
| VII. | Auditor's Fees | 6,000 | |
| VIII. | Law Charges | 8,000 | |
| IX. | Postage and Telegrams | 11,000 | |
| X. | Repairs and Maintenance | 14,000 | |
| XI. | Other Expenses | 4,000 | |
| | **Total** | **1,69,000** | |

---

**ILLUSTRATION 3**

Janata Bank Ltd., Jamner gives you following particulars from their books for the year ended 31st March, 2016. You are required to prepare Balance Sheet as on 31st March, 2016 in prescribed form.

| Particulars | Debit ₹ | Credit ₹ |
|---|---|---|
| Cash in hand | 1,50,000 | |
| Share Capital | | 25,00,000 |
| Investments in Equity Shares (Fully paid ₹ 3 lakhs) | | |
| Partly paid ₹ 2 lakhs) | 5,00,000 | |
| General Reserve | | 3,00,000 |

| | | |
|---|---:|---:|
| Statutory Reserve | | 6,00,000 |
| Investments in Government Securities | | |
| (Central and State Government) | 5,75,000 | |
| Interest accrued on Investments | 15,000 | |
| Balances with Reserve Bank of India | 2,00,000 | |
| Balances with Other Banks – (Current Account) | 1,50,000 | |
| Borrowings from Central Bank of India (unsecured) | | 4,00,000 |
| Bills Payable | | 2,00,000 |
| Fixed Deposits | | 25,00,000 |
| Current Account | | 40,00,000 |
| Contingency Account | | 4,00,000 |
| Loans | 50,00,000 | |
| Cash Credits | 80,00,000 | |
| Overdrafts | 7,70,000 | |
| Savings Account | | 65,00,000 |
| Unclaimed Dividends | | 25,000 |
| Bills Discounted and Purchased | 15,00,000 | |
| Branch Adjustments | | 74,000 |
| Profit and Loss Account (1-4-2015) | | 1,00,000 |
| Advances | 7,50,000 | |
| Premises (less depreciation) | 6,00,000 | |
| Furniture (less depreciation) | 2,00,000 | |
| Provision for Taxation | | 3,91,000 |
| Profit for the year 2015-2016 | | 4,20,000 |
| | **1,84,10,000** | **1,84,10,000** |

Following additional information is given :

i)      Authorised Capital is ₹ 1,00,00,000 (2,00,000 Shares of ₹ 50 each).

ii)     Issued Capital is half of the Authorised Capital. All shares are fully subscribed on which ₹ 25 per share are paid up.

iii)    Constituents Liabilities for Acceptances and Endorsements ₹ 22,00,000.

iv)    Bills for collection ₹ 15,00,000.

v)      Contingent liability for partly paid shares ₹ 2,00,000.

vi)    Provide for Doubtful loans ₹ 20,000.

vii)   Market value of Investments on 31st March, 2016.

       a)     Shares in Companies ₹ 5,25,000,      b) Government Securities ₹ 6,00,000

**SOLUTION**

**In the books of Janata Bank Ltd., Jamner**

**Balance Sheet as on 31-3-2016**

| | Schedule No. | As on 31-3-2016 ₹ | As on 31-3-2015 ₹ |
|---|:---:|---:|---:|
| **Capital and Liabilities :** | | | |
| Capital | 1 | 25,00,000 | |
| Reserves and Surplus | 2 | 14,00,000 | |
| Deposit | 3 | 1,34,00,000 | |
| Borrowings | 4 | 4,00,000 | |
| Other Liabilities and Provisions | 5 | 6,90,000 | |
| **Total** | | **1,83,90,000** | |

| | Schedule No. | As on 31-3-2016 ₹ | As on 31-3-2015 ₹ |
|---|---|---|---|
| **Assets :** | | | |
| Cash and Balances with Reserve Bank of India | 6 | 3,50,000 | |
| Balances with other Banks and Money at Call and Short Notices | 7 | 1,50,000 | |
| Investments in India | 8 | 10,75,000 | |
| Advances | 9 | 1,60,00,000 | |
| Fixed Assets | 10 | 8,00,000 | |
| Other Assets | 11 | 15,000 | |
| | | **1,83,90,000** | |
| Contingent Liabilities | 12 | 24,00,000 | |
| Bills for Collection | | 15,00,000 | |

## Schedule – 1 – Capital

| | As on 31-3-2016 ₹ | As on 31-3-2015 ₹ |
|---|---|---|
| Authorised Capital (2,00,000 Shares of ₹ 50 each) | 1,00,00,000 | |
| Issued Capital (1,00,000 Shares of ₹ 50 each) | 50,00,000 | |
| Subscribed Capital (1,00,000 Shares of ₹ 50 each) | 50,00,000 | |
| Called-up and Paid-up Capital (1,00,000 Shares of ₹ 50 each, ₹ 25 per share called and paid) | 25,00,000 | |

## Schedule – 2 – Reserves and Surplus

| | | As on 31-3-2016 ₹ | As on 31-3-2015 ₹ |
|---|---|---|---|
| Statutory Reserves | | | |
| Opening Balance | 6,00,000 | | |
| Add Additions during the year | (+) 80,000 | 6,80,000 | |
| General Reserve | | 3,00,000 | |
| Balance in Profit and Loss Account | | 4,20,000 | |
| **Total** | | **14,00,000** | |

## Schedule – 3 – Deposits

| | As on 31-3-2016 ₹ | As on 31-3-2015 ₹ |
|---|---|---|
| Current and Contingent Deposits | 44,00,000 | |
| Savings Deposits | 65,00,000 | |
| Term Deposits | 25,00,000 | |
| **Total** | **1,34,00,000** | |

## Schedule – 4 – Borrowings

| | As on 31-3-2016 ₹ | As on 31-3-2015 ₹ |
|---|---|---|
| Borrowings from other Banks and agents Central Bank of India (Unsecured) | 4,00,000 | – |
| **Total** | **4,00,000** | – |

### Schedule – 5 – Other Liabilities and Provisions

| | As on 31-3-2016 ₹ | As on 31-3-2015 ₹ |
|---|---|---|
| Bills Payable | 2,00,000 | |
| Inter-Office Adjustments (Net) | 74,000 | |
| Interest Accrued | – | |
| Unclaimed Dividend | 25,000 | |
| Provision for Taxation | 3,91,000 | |
| **Total** | **6,90,000** | |

### Schedule – 6 – Cash and Balances with Reserve Bank of India

| | As on 31-3-2016 ₹ | As on 31-3-2015 ₹ |
|---|---|---|
| Cash in hand | 1,50,000 | |
| Balances with Reserve Bank of India   (+) | 2,00,000 | |
| **Total** | **3,50,000** | |

### Schedule – 7 – Balances with Banks and Money at Call and Short Notice

| | | As on 31-3-2016 ₹ | As on 31-3-2015 ₹ |
|---|---|---|---|
| i) | Balances with other Banks in Current Accounts | 1,50,000 | |
| ii) | Money at Call and Short Notice | – | |
| | **Total** | **1,50,000** | |

### Schedule – 8 – Investments

| | | As on 31-3-2016 ₹ | As on 31-3-2015 ₹ |
|---|---|---|---|
| I. | Investments in India in | | |
| i) | Government Securities (State and Central Governments Market Value ₹ 6,00,000) | 5,75,000 | |
| ii) | Other Approved Securities | – | |
| iii) | Equity, Shares fully paid (Market Price ₹ 5,25,000 Partly paid Equity shares) | 3,00,000 | |
| iv) | Debenture and Bonds | 2,00,000 | |
| v) | Subsidiaries and/or Joint Ventures | | |
| vi) | Others | | |
| | **Total** | **10,75,000** | |

### Schedule – 9 – Advances

| | | As on 31-3-2016 ₹ | As on 31-3-2015 ₹ |
|---|---|---|---|
| A. | i) Bills Purchased and Discounted | 15,00,000 | |
| | ii) Cash Credits, Overdrafts and Loans Repayable on Demand | 1,45,00,000 | |
| | iii) Term Loans | – | |
| | **Total** | **1,60,00,000** | |
| B. | i) Secured by Tangible Assets | 1,60,00,000 | |
| | ii) Covered by Bank/Government Guarantees | – | |
| | iii) Unsecured | – | |
| | **Total** | **1,60,00,000** | |

| | | | As on 31-3-2016 | As on 31-3-2015 |
|---|---|---|---|---|
| **C.** | **I.** | **Advances in India** | | |
| | i) | Priority Sectors | – | |
| | ii) | Public Sectors | 1,00,00,000 | |
| | iii) | Banks | 30,00,000 | |
| | iv) | Others | 30,00,000 | |
| | | **Total** | **1,60,00,000** | |
| | **II.** | **Advances Outside India** | | |
| | | (* Imaginary figures are taken) | – | |

### Schedule – 10 – Fixed Assets

| | | As on 31-3-2016 ₹ | As on 31-3-2015 ₹ |
|---|---|---|---|
| **I.** | **Premises** | | |
| | At cost on 31st March of the preceding year | | |
| **Add :** | Addition during the year | | |
| **Less :** | Deductions during the year | | |
| **Less :** | Depreciation to date | 6,00,000 | |
| **II.** | **Other Fixed Assets** | | – |
| | Furniture at cost on 31$^{st}$ March of the preceding year | | |
| **Add :** | Additions during the year | | |
| **Less :** | Deductions during the year | | |
| **Less :** | Depreciation to date | 2,00,000 | |
| | **Total** | **8,00,000** | |

### Schedule – 11 – Other Assets

| | | As on 31-3-2016 ₹ | As on 31-3-2015 ₹ |
|---|---|---|---|
| I. | Inter-Office Adjustments (net) | – | |
| II. | Interest Accrued on Investments | 15,000 | |
| III. | Tax paid in Advance/Tax deducted at source | – | |
| IV. | Stationery and Stamps | – | |
| V. | Non-banking Assets Acquired in Satisfaction of Claims | – | |
| VI. | Others | – | |
| | **Total** | **15,000** | |

### Schedule – 12 – Contingent Liabilities

| | | As on 31-3-2016 ₹ | As on 31-3-2015 ₹ |
|---|---|---|---|
| I. | Claims against the Bank not acknowledged as Debts | – | |
| II. | Liability for Partly paid shares | 2,00,000 | |
| III. | Liability on account of outstanding forward exchange contracts | – | |
| IV. | Guarantees given on behalf of Constituents | – | |
| V. | Acceptances, Endorsements and Other Obligations | 22,00,000 | |
| VI. | Other items for which the Bank is Contingently liable | | |
| | **Total** | **24,00,000** | |

**ILLUSTRATION 4**

From the books of accounts of Navabharat Bank Ltd., Nashik as on 31-3-2015, the following particulars regarding loans and advances given by the Bank are available.

| Advances to | ₹ |
|---|---|
| • Priority Sector | 45,00,000 |
| • Public Sector | 15,00,000 |
| • Others | 5,00,000 |
| – Banks in India | 50,00,000 |
| – Other parties | |

| The details of the above advances | |
|---|---|
| Bills Purchased and discounted | 22,00,000 |
| (including ₹ 2,00,000 outside India) | |
| Cash Credits, Overdrafts and Loans - | |
| Payable on Demand | 50,00,000 |
| Term Loans | 45,00,000 |

Out of the above advances, 75 lakhs were secured by tangible assets while those of ₹ 30 lakhs were secured by Bank and Government Securities. The rest were unsecured. Show how these items will appear in the Balance Sheet as at 31st March, 2015.

**SOLUTION**

**In the books of Navbharat Bank Ltd., Nashik**
**Balance Sheet (Asset Side)**

| | | | As on 31-3-2015 ₹ | As on 31-3-2014 ₹ |
|---|---|---|---|---|
| **A.** | i) | Bills Purchased and Discounted | 22,00,000 | |
| | ii) | Cash Credits, Overdrafts and Loans payable on Demand | 50,00,000 | |
| | iii) | Term Loans | 45,00,000 | |
| | | **Total** | **1,17,00,000** | |
| **B.** | i) | Secured by Tangible Assets | 75,00,000 | |
| | ii) | Covered by Bank and Government Securities | 30,00,000 | |
| | iii) | Unsecured | 12,00,000 | |
| | | **Total** | **1,17,00,000** | |
| **C.** | **I.** | **Advances in India** | | |
| | i) | Priority Sector Advances | 45,00,000 | |
| | ii) | Public Sector Advances | 15,00,000 | |
| | iii) | Banks | 5,00,000 | |
| | iv) | Others | 50,00,000 | |
| | | **Total** | **1,15,00,000** | |
| | **II.** | **Advances Outside India** | | |
| | i) | Due from Banks | – | |
| | ii) | Due from Others | 2,00,000 | |
| | | a) Bills Purchased and Discounted | | |
| | | b) Syndicated Loans | – | |
| | | c) Others | – | |
| | | **Total** | **2,00,000** | |
| | | **Grand Total (C. I and C. II)** | **1,17,00,000** | |

## ILLUSTRATION 5

The following is the Trial Balance of Dhanvikas Bank Ltd., Dharangaon as on 31-3-2016.

### Trial Balance as on 31-3-2016

| Particulars | Debit ₹ | Credit ₹ |
|---|---|---|
| Subscribed Capital : 50,000 Equity Shares of ₹ 10 each fully paid | | 5,00,000 |
| Reserve Fund | | 2,50,000 |
| Loans, Cash Credits and Overdrafts | 2,85,000 | |
| Premises | 50,000 | |
| India Govt. Securities | 4,00,000 | |
| Current Deposits | | 1,00,000 |
| Fixed Deposits | | 1,25,000 |
| Savings Bank Deposits | | 1,50,000 |
| Salaries | 28,000 | |
| General Expenses | 27,400 | |
| Rent, Rates and Taxes | 2,300 | |
| Director's Fees | 1,800 | |
| Profit and Loss Account on 1-4-2015 | | 16,000 |
| Interest and Discount | | 1,28,000 |
| Stock of Stationery | 8,500 | |
| Bills Purchased and Discounted | 46,000 | |
| Interim dividend paid | 17,000 | |
| Recurring deposits | | 20,000 |
| Shares | 1,50,000 | |
| Cash in Hand and with RBI | 1,93,000 | |
| Money at Call and Short Notice | 80,000 | |
| | **12,89,000** | **12,89,000** |

The following information should be considered :

i) Provision for bad and doubtful debts is required to be made at ₹ 5,000.

ii) Interest accrued on investments was ₹ 8,000.

iii) Unexpired discount (Rebate on bills discounted) amounted to ₹ 380.

iv) Interim dividend declared was 4% actual.

v) Endorsements made on behalf of customers totalled ₹ 1,15,000.

vi) Authorised capital was 80,000 Equity Shares of ₹ 10 each.

vii) ₹ 10,000 were added to the Premises during the year. Depreciation @ 5% on the opening balance is required.

viii) Market value of Indian Govt. Securities was ₹ 3,90,000.

Prepare Profit and Loss Account for the year ending 31-3-2016 and Balance Sheet as at that date in the prescribed form.

**SOLUTION**

### In the books of Dhanvikas Bank Ltd., Dharangaon
### Balance Sheet as on 31-3-2016

| | Schedule No. | As on 31-3-2016 ₹ | As on 31-3-2015 ₹ |
|---|---|---|---|
| **Capital and Liabilities :** | | | |
| Capital | 1 | 5,00,000 | |
| Reserves and Surplus | 2 | 3,05,120 | |
| Deposit | 3 | 3,95,000 | |
| Borrowings | 4 | – | |
| Other Liabilities and Provisions | 5 | 3,380 | |
| **Total** | | **12,03,500** | |
| **Assets :** | | | |
| Cash and balances with Reserve Bank of India | 6 | 1,93,000 | |
| Balances with other Banks and Money At Call and Short Notices | 7 | 80,000 | |
| Investments | 8 | 5,40,000 | |
| Advances | 9 | 3,26,000 | |
| Fixed Assets | 10 | 48,000 | |
| Other Assets | 11 | 16,500 | |
| **Total** | | **12,03,500** | |
| Contingent Liabilities | 12 | 1,15,000 | |
| Bills for Collection | | – | |

N.B. : (Difference between Market value and Book value of Govt. Securities is ₹ 10,000 as Market value is ₹ 3,90,000).

### Schedule – 1 – Capital

| | As on 31-3-2016 ₹ | As on 31-3-2015 ₹ |
|---|---|---|
| Authorised Capital | | |
| (80,000 shares of ₹ 10 each) | 8,00,000 | |
| Issued Capital | | |
| (50,000 shares of ₹ 10 each) | 5,00,000 | |
| Subscribed, Called up and Paid-up Capital : | | |
| (50,000 shares of ₹ 10 each fully called and paid) | 5,00,000 | |
| **Less :** Calls unpaid | – | |
| **Add :** Forfeited shares | – | |
| **Total** | **5,00,000** | |

### Schedule – 2 – Reserves and Surplus

| | | As on 31-3-2016 ₹ | As on 31-3-2015 ₹ |
|---|---|---|---|
| i) | Statutory Reserve – Balance | 2,50,000 | |
| | **Add :** Additions during the year | 13,824 | |
| ii) | Capital Reserve | – | |
| iii) | Share Premium | – | |
| iv) | Other Reserves | – | |
| v) | Balance in Profit and Loss Account | 41,296 | |
| | **Total** | **3,05,120** | |

## Schedule – 3 – Deposits

| | | | As on 31-3-2016 ₹ | As on 31-3-2015 ₹ |
|---|---|---|---:|---:|
| A. | I. | Demand Deposits | | |
| | | i) From Bank | | |
| | | ii) From Others | 1,00,000 | |
| | II. | Savings Bank Deposits | 1,50,000 | |
| | III. | Term Deposits | | |
| | | i) From Banks | – | |
| | | ii) From Others | 1,45,000 | |
| | | **Total** | **3,95,000** | |

## Schedule – 4 – Borrowings

| | | As on 31-3-2016 ₹ | As on 31-3-2015 ₹ |
|---|---|---:|---:|
| I. | Borrowings in India | – | |
| II. | Borrowings outside India | | |

## Schedule – 5 – Other Liabilities and Provisions

| | | As on 31-3-2016 ₹ | As on 31-3-2015 ₹ |
|---|---|---:|---:|
| I. | Bills Payable | – | |
| II. | Inter-Office Adjustments | – | |
| III. | Interest Accrued | – | |
| IV. | Unclaimed Dividend | 3,000 | |
| V. | Unexpired Discount | 380 | |
| | | **3,380** | |

## Schedule – 6 – Cash and Balances with Reserve Bank of India

| | | As on 31-3-2015 ₹ | As on 31-3-2014 ₹ |
|---|---|---:|---:|
| I. | Cash in hand | – | |
| II. | Balances with Reserve Bank of India | 1,93,000 | |
| | | **1,93,000** | |

## Schedule – 7 – Balances with Banks and Money at Call and Short Notices

| | As on 31-3-2016 ₹ | As on 31-3-2015 ₹ |
|---|---:|---:|
| Balances with Banks | – | |
| Money at Call and Short Notices | 80,000 | |
| | **80,000** | |

## Schedule – 8 – Investments

| | As on 31-3-2016 ₹ | As on 31-3-2015 ₹ |
|---|---:|---:|
| Investments in India | | |
| • Government Securities (Cost ₹ 4,00,000) | 3,90,000 | |
| • Shares | 1,50,000 | |
| | **5,40,000** | |

## Schedule – 9 – Advances

| | | | As on 31-3-2016 ₹ | As on 31-3-2015 ₹ |
|---|---|---|---|---|
| A. | Bills Purchased and Discounted | | 46,000 | |
| | Cash credits, overdrafts and loans | | 2,80,000 | |
| | | **Total** | **3,26,000** | |
| B. | | | – | |
| C. | | | – | |
| | | **Total** | **3,26,000** | |
| | Advances outside India | | – | |

## Schedule – 10 – Fixed Assets

| | | | As on 31-3-2016 ₹ | As on 31-3-2015 ₹ |
|---|---|---|---|---|
| I. | Premises | | | |
| | At cost on 31st March, 2015 | | 40,000 | 40,000 |
| | **Add :** Addition during the year | (+) | 10,000 | – |
| | | | 50,000 | |
| | **Less :** Depreciation to date | (–) | 2,000 | – |
| | | **Total** | **48,000** | – |
| II. | Other Fixed Assets | | – | – |
| | | | **48,000** | |

## Schedule – 11 – Other Assets

| | As on 31-3-2016 ₹ | As on 31-3-2015 ₹ |
|---|---|---|
| Interest Accrued | 8,000 | |
| Stationery and Stamps | 8,500 | |
| | 16,500 | |

## Schedule – 12 – Contingent Liabilities

| | As on 31-3-2016 ₹ | As on 31-3-2015 ₹ |
|---|---|---|
| Acceptances, Endorsements and Other Obligations | 1,15,000 | |
| **Total** | **1,15,000** | |

## Profit and Loss Account for the year ended 31-3-2015

| | | Schedule No. | Year ended 31-3-2016 ₹ | Year ended 31-3-2015 ₹ |
|---|---|---|---|---|
| I. | **Income** | | | |
| | Interest Earned | 13 | 1,35,620 | |
| | Other Income | 14 | (– 10,000) | |
| | **Total** | | **1,25,620** | |
| II. | **Expenditure** | | | |
| | Interest Expended | 15 | NIL | |
| | Operating expenses | 16 | 61,500 | |
| | Provisions and Contingencies | | 5,000 | |
| | **Total** | | **66,500** | |
| III. | **Profit or Loss** | | | |
| | Net Profit/Loss (–) for the year | | 59,120 | |
| | * Profit brought forward | | 16,000 | |
| | **Total** | | **75,120** | |
| IV. | **Appropriations** | | | |
| | Transfer to Statutory Reserves | | 13,824 | |
| | Transfer to Other Reserves | | – | |
| | Interim Dividend | | 20,000 | |
| | Balance carried over to Balance Sheet | | 41,296 | |
| | **Total** | | **75,120** | |

## Schedule – 13 – Interest Earned

| | | Year ended 31-3-2016 ₹ | Year ended 31-3-2015 ₹ |
|---|---|---|---|
| I. | Interest/discount on advance/bills | 1,35,620 | – |
| II. | Income on Investments | | |
| III. | Interest on balances with Reserve Bank of India and other inter-bank funds | – | |
| IV. | Others | – | |
| | **Total** | 1,35,620 | |

## Schedule – 14 – Other Income

| | | Year ended 31-3-2016 ₹ | Year ended 31-3-2015 ₹ |
|---|---|---|---|
| I. | Commission, Exchange and Brokerage | – | |
| II. | Profit on Sale of Investments | – | |
| | **Less :** Loss on Sale of Investments | (10,000) | |
| III. | Profit on Revaluation of Investments | – | |
| | **Less :** Loss on Revaluation of Investments | – | |
| | **Total** | (10,000) | |

**N.B. :** Under items II to V loss figures may be shown in brackets.

## Schedule – 15 – Interest Expended – NIL

## Schedule – 16 – Operating Expenses

| | | Year ended 31-3-2016 ₹ | Year ended 31-3-2015 ₹ |
|---|---|---|---|
| I. | Payments to and Provisions for employees | 28,000 | – |
| II. | Rent, Taxes and Lighting | 2,300 | |
| III. | Printing and Stationery | – | |
| IV. | Advertisement and Publicity | – | |
| V. | Depreciation on Bank's Property | 2,000 | |
| VI. | Director's Fees, Allowances and Expenses | 1,800 | |
| VII. | Auditor's fees and expenses (including branch auditors) | – | |
| VIII. | Law Charges | – | |
| IX. | Postage, Telegrams, Telephones etc. | – | |
| X. | Repairs and Maintenance | – | |
| XI. | Insurance | – | |
| XII. | Other expenditure (General Expenses) | 27,400 | |
| | **Total** | 61,500 | |

## ILLUSTRATION 6

Following is the Trial Balance of Vidya Bank Ltd., Vapi as on 31-3-2016.

### Trial Balance as on 31-3-2016

| Particulars | Debit ₹ | Credit ₹ |
|---|---|---|
| Premises **Less** Depreciation | 1,85,000 | – |
| Money at Call and Short Notice | 2,15,000 | – |
| Furniture **Less** Depreciation | 30,000 | – |
| Depreciation on Bank's Assets | 11,000 | – |
| Non Banking Assets Acquired in Settlement of Claims | 20,000 | – |
| Cash in Hand | 3,00,000 | – |
| Cash at Banks | 2,50,000 | – |
| Investments | 3,50,000 | – |
| Loans, Cash Credit and Overdrafts | 12,65,000 | – |
| Interest on Deposits and Borrowings | 2,00,000 | – |
| Audit Fees | 4,500 | – |
| Salaries and Allowances to Staff | 40,500 | – |
| Director's Fees | 4,000 | – |
| Postage and Telegrams | 1,350 | – |
| Printing and Stationery | 3,700 | – |
| Other Expenditure | 2,450 | – |
| Interest and Discounts | – | 3,67,500 |

| | | |
|---|---:|---:|
| **Share Capital :** | | |
| **Authorised :** 7,500 Equity Shares of ₹ 100 each | – | – |
| Issued and Subscribed 6,000 Equity Shares of ₹ 100 each fully paid | – | 6,00,000 |
| Statutory Reserve | – | 1,20,000 |
| Deposits | – | 12,50,000 |
| Provident Funds | – | 1,35,000 |
| Borrowings from Maharaja Bank Ltd. | – | 2,55,000 |
| Unclaimed Dividend | – | 4,000 |
| Commission and Exchange | – | 37,500 |
| Profit on Sale of Non-Banking Assets | – | 1,200 |
| Profit and Loss Account as on 1-4-2015 | – | 1,12,300 |
| Total | **28,82,500** | **28,82,500** |

## Adjustments :

i)      Provide ₹ 10,000 for Bad and Doubtful Debts.

ii)      Bills for collection amounted to ₹ 1,05,000.

iii)      Acceptances, Endorsements and Other obligations amounted to ₹ 52,000.

iv)      Provide ₹ 1,500 for Rebate on Bills discounted.

v)      Provide ₹ 10,500 for taxation.

vi)      Postage stamps of ₹ 160 and Stationery of ₹ 700 was in hand on 31-3-2016.

Prepare Profit and Loss Account for the year ended 31-3-2016 and the Balance Sheet as on that date as per the Banking Regulation Act.

SOLUTION

### In the books of Vidya Bank Ltd., Vapi
### Balance Sheet as on 31-3-2016

| | Schedule No. | As on 31-3-2016 ₹ | As on 31-3-2015 ₹ |
|---|:---:|---:|---:|
| **Capital and Liabilities :** | | | |
| Capital | 1 | 6,00,000 | |
| Reserves and Surplus | 2 | 3,49,860 | |
| Deposits | 3 | 12,50,000 | |
| Borrowings | 4 | 2,55,000 | |
| Other Liabilities and Provisions | 5 | 1,51,000 | |
| **Total** | | **26,05,860** | |
| **Assets :** | | | |
| Cash and balances with Reserve Bank of India | 6 | 3,00,000 | |
| Balances with other Banks and Money at Call and Short Notices | 7 | 4,65,000 | |
| Investments | 8 | 3,50,000 | |
| Advances | 9 | 12,55,000 | |
| Fixed Assets | 10 | 2,15,000 | |
| Other Assets | 11 | 20,860 | |
| **Total** | | **26,05,860** | |
| Contingent Liabilities | 12 | 52,000 | |
| Bills for Collection | | | |

## Schedule – 1 – Capital

|  |  | As on 31-3-2016 ₹ | As on 31-3-2015 ₹ |
|---|---|---|---|
| **III.** | **For Other Banks** |  |  |
|  | Authorised Capital |  |  |
|  | (7,500 Shares of ₹ 100 each) | 7,50,000 |  |
|  | Issued Capital |  |  |
|  | (6,000 Shares of ₹ 100 each) | 6,00,000 |  |
|  | Subscribed Capital |  |  |
|  | (6,000 Shares of ₹ 100 each) | 6,00,000 |  |
|  | Called-up Capital |  |  |
|  | (6,000 Shares of ₹ 100 each) | 6,00,000 |  |
|  | **Less :** Calls unpaid |  |  |
|  | **Add :** Forfeited Shares |  |  |
|  |  | 6,00,000 |  |

## Schedule – 2 – Reserves and Surplus

|  |  | As on 31-3-2016 ₹ | As on 31-3-2015 ₹ |
|---|---|---|---|
| **I.** | **Statutory Reserves** |  |  |
|  | Opening Balance | 1,20,000 |  |
| **Add :** | Additions during the year | 23,512 |  |
| **Less :** | Deductions during the year |  |  |
| **II.** | **Capital Reserves** |  |  |
|  | Opening Balance | – |  |
| **Add :** | Additions during the year |  |  |
| **Less :** | Deductions during the year |  |  |
| **III.** | **Share Premium** |  |  |
|  | Opening Balance |  |  |
| **Add :** | Additions during the year | – |  |
| **Less :** | Deductions during the year |  |  |
| **IV.** | **Revenue and Other Reserves** |  |  |
|  | Opening Balance |  |  |
| **Add :** | Additions during the year |  |  |
| **Less :** | Deductions during the year |  |  |
| **V.** | **Balance in Profit and Loss Account** | 2,06,348 |  |
|  | **Total (I, II, III, IV and V)** | 3,49,860 |  |

## Schedule – 3 – Deposits

|  |  |  | As on 31-3-2016 ₹ | As on 31-3-2015 ₹ |
|---|---|---|---|---|
| **A.** | **I.** | **Demand Deposits** |  |  |
|  |  | i) From Banks | – |  |
|  |  | ii) From Others | – |  |
|  | **II.** | **Savings Bank Deposits** | 12,50,000 |  |
|  | **III.** | **Term Deposits** |  |  |
|  |  | i) From Banks | – |  |
|  |  | ii) From Others | – |  |
|  |  | **Total (I, II and III)** | 12,50,000 |  |
| **B.** | i) | Deposits of Branches in India |  |  |
|  | ii) | Deposits of Branches Outside India |  |  |
|  |  |  | 12,50,000 |  |

### Schedule – 4 – Borrowings

| | | As on 31-3-2016 ₹ | As on 31-3-2015 ₹ |
|---|---|---|---|
| I. | **Borrowings in India** | | |
| | i)  Reserve Bank of India | | |
| | ii)  Other Banks | 2,55,000 | – |
| | iii)  Other institutions and agencies | | |
| II. | **Borrowings outside India** | | |
| | **Total (I and II)** | 2,55,000 | – |

### Schedule – 5 – Other Liabilities and Provisions

| | | | As on 31-3-2016 ₹ | As on 31-3-2015 ₹ |
|---|---|---|---|---|
| I. | **Bills Payable** | | | |
| II. | **Others (Including Provisions)** | | | |
| | Provident Fund | 1,35,000 | | |
| | Unclaimed Dividend | 4,000 | | |
| | Provision for Taxation | 10,500 | | |
| | Unexpired Discount | (+)  1,500 | 1,51,000 | |
| | **Total** | | 1,51,000 | |

### Schedule – 6 – Cash and Balances with Reserve Bank of India

| | | As on 31-3-2016 ₹ | As on 31-3-2015 ₹ |
|---|---|---|---|
| I. | **Cash in hand** | 3,00,000 | |
| | (including foreign currency notes) | | |
| II. | **Balance with Reserve Bank of India** | | |
| | i)  In Current Accounts | – | |
| | ii)  In Other Accounts | | |
| | **Total (i and ii)** | 3,00,000 | |

### Schedule – 7 – Balances with Banks and Money at Call and Short Notice

| | | As on 31-3-2016 ₹ | As on 31-3-2015 ₹ |
|---|---|---|---|
| I. | **In India** | | |
| | i)  **Balances with Banks** | 2,50,000 | |
| |    a)  in Current Accounts | | |
| |    b)  in Other Deposit Accounts | | |
| | ii)  **Money at Call and Short Notice** | 2,15,000 | |
| |    a)  With Banks | | |
| |    b)  With Other Institutions | | |
| | **Total (i and ii)** | 4,65,000 | |
| II. | **Outside India** | | |
| | i)  In Current Accounts | – | |
| | ii)  In Other Deposit Accounts | – | |
| | iii)  Money at Call and Short Notice | – | |
| | **Total (i and ii)** | 4,65,000 | |

### Schedule – 8 – Investments

| | | As on 31-3-2016 ₹ | As on 31-3-2015 ₹ |
|---|---|---|---|
| I. | **Investments in India in** | | |
| | i)  Government Securities | | |
| | ii)  Other Approved Securities | | |
| | iii)  Shares | | |
| | iv)  Debentures and Bonds | | |
| | v)  Subsidiaries and/or Joint Ventures | | |
| | vi)  Others (to be specified) | 3,50,000 | |
| | **Total** | 3,50,000 | |
| II. | **Investments Outside India in** | | |
| | i)  Government Securities (including local authorities) | | |
| | ii)  Subsidiaries and/or Joint Ventures Abroad | | |
| | iii) Other Investments (to be specified) | | |
| | **Total** | | |
| | **Grand Total (I and II)** | 3,50,000 | |

### Schedule – 9 – Advances

| | | | | As on 31-3-2016 ₹ | As on 31-3-2015 ₹ |
|---|---|---|---|---|---|
| **A.** | i) | Bills Purchased and Discounted | | – | |
| | ii) | Cash Credits, Overdrafts and Loans Repayable on Demand | | 12,55,000 | |
| | iii) | Term Loans | | – | |
| | | | **Total** | **12,55,000** | |
| **B.** | i) | Secured by Tangible Assets | | – | |
| | ii) | Covered by Bank/Government Guarantees | | – | |
| | iii) | Unsecured | | – | |
| | | | **Total** | **12,55,000** | |

### Schedule – 10 – Fixed Assets

| | | As on 31-3-2016 ₹ | As on 31-3-2015 ₹ |
|---|---|---|---|
| **I.** | **Premises** | 1,85,000 | |
| | At cost on 31$^{st}$ March of the preceding year | | |
| **Add :** | Additions during the year | | |
| **Less :** | Deductions during the year | | |
| **Less :** | Depreciation to date | | |
| **II.** | **Other Fixed Assets** (Including Furniture and Fixtures) | | – |
| **Add :** | At Cost on 31$^{st}$ March of the preceding year | 30,000 | |
| **Add :** | Additions during the year | | |
| **Less :** | Deductions during the year | | |
| **Less :** | Depreciation to date | | |
| | **Total (I and II)** | **2,15,000** | |

### Schedule – 11 – Other Assets

| | | As on 31-3-2016 ₹ | As on 31-3-2015 ₹ |
|---|---|---|---|
| I. | Inter-Office Adjustments (net) | – | |
| II. | Interest Accrued | – | |
| III. | Tax paid in Advance or Tax deducted at source | – | |
| IV. | Stationery and Stamps | 860 | |
| V. | Non-Banking Assets Acquired in Satisfaction of Claims | 20,000 | |
| VI. | Other @ | | |
| | **Total** | **20,860** | |

@ In case there is any unadjusted balance of loss the same may be shown under this item with appropriate foot-note.

### Schedule – 12 – Contingent Liability

| | | As on 31-3-2016 | As on 31-3-2015 |
|---|---|---|---|
| I. | Claims against the Bank not Acknowledged as Debts | | |
| II. | Liability for Partly paid Investments | | |
| III. | Liability on account of outstanding forward exchange contracts | | |
| IV. | Guarantees given on behalf of Constituents | | |
| | a) In India | | |
| | b) Outside India | | |
| V. | Acceptances, Endorsements and Other Obligations | 52,000 | |
| VI. | Other items for which the Bank is Contingently liable | | |
| | **Total** | **52,000** | |

### Profit and Loss Account for the year ended 31-3-2015

| | | Schedule No. | Year ended 31-3-2016 | Year ended 31-3-2015 |
|---|---|---|---|---|
| **I.** | **Income** | | | |
| | Income Earned | 13 | 3,66,000 | |
| | Other Income | 14 | 38,700 | |
| | Total | | **4,04,700** | |
| **II.** | **Expenditure** | | | |
| | Interest Expended | 15 | 2,00,000 | |
| | Operating Expenses | 16 | 66,640 | |
| | Provisions and Contingencies | | 20,500 | |
| | Total | | **2,87,140** | |
| **III.** | **Profit/Loss** | | | |
| | Net Profit or Loss (–) for the year | | 1,17,560 | |
| | Net Profit b/f | | 1,12,300 | |
| | Total | | **2,29,860** | |
| **IV.** | **Appropriations** | | | |
| | Transfer to Statutory Reserves | | 23,512 | |
| | Transfer to Other Reserves | | | |
| | Transfer to Government or Proposed Dividend | | | |
| | Balance Carried over to Balance Sheet | | 2,06,348 | |
| | Total | | **2,29,860** | |

### Schedule – 13 – Interest Earned

| | | Year ended 31-3-2016 | Year ended 31-3-2015 |
|---|---|---|---|
| I. | Interest or Discount on Advances or Bills | 3,66,000 | – |
| II. | Income on Investments | – | |
| III. | Interest on Balances with Reserve Bank | – | |
| | Total | **3,66,000** | |

### Schedule 14 – Other Income

| | | Year ended 31-3-2016 | Year ended 31-3-2015 |
|---|---|---|---|
| I. | Commission, Exchange and Brokerage | 37,500 | |
| II. | Profit on Sale of Investments | | |
| | **Less :** Loss on Sale of Investments | | |
| III. | Profit on Revaluation of Investments | | |
| | **Less :** Loss on Revaluation of Investments | | |
| IV. | Profit on Sale of Land, Buildings, and Other Assets (Non-Banking) | 1,200 | |
| | **Less :** Loss on Sale of Land, Buildings and Other Assets | | |
| V. | Profit on Exchange Transactions | | |
| | **Less :** Loss on Exchange Transactions | | |
| VI. | Income earned by way of Dividend etc. from Subsidiaries /Companies and/or Joint Ventures abroad/in India | | |
| VII. | Miscellaneous Income | | |
| | Total | **38,700** | |

### Schedule 15 – Interest Earned

| | | Year ended 31-3-2016 | Year ended 31-3-2015 |
|---|---|---|---|
| I. | Interest on Deposits | 2,00,000 | |
| II. | Interest on Reserve Bank of India or Inter-Bank Borrowings | | |
| III. | Others | | |
| | **Total** | **2,00,000** | |

### Schedule – 16 – Operating Expenses

| | | Year ended 31-3-2016 | Year ended 31-3-2015 |
|---|---|---|---|
| I. | Payments to and Provisions for employees | 40,500 | |
| II. | Rent, Taxes and Lighting | – | |
| III. | Printing and Stationery | 3,000 | |
| IV. | Advertisement and Publicity | – | |
| V. | Depreciation on Bank's Property | 11,000 | |
| VI. | Director's Fees, Allowances and Expenses | 4,000 | |
| VII. | Auditor's Fees and Expenses (including branch auditors) | 4,500 | |
| VIII. | Law Charges | – | |
| IX. | Postages, Telegrams, Telephones etc. | 1,190 | |
| X. | Repairs and Maintenance | – | |
| XI. | Insurance | – | |
| XII. | Other Expenditure | 2,450 | |
| | **Total** | **66,640** | |

## ILLUSTRATION 7

From the following Trial Balance of Laxmi Bank Ltd. Lasalgaon on 31-3-2015 prepare Profit and Loss Account and Balance Sheet as on that date.

### Trial Balance as on 31-3-2015

| Particulars | Debit ₹ | Credit ₹ |
|---|---|---|
| Equity Share Capital of ₹ 100 each ₹ 50 paid up | – | 4,00,000 |
| Profit and Loss on Account 1-4-2015 | – | 1,60,000 |
| Current Deposit Account | – | 13,64,000 |
| Fixed Deposit Account | – | 15,60,000 |
| Savings Bank Account | – | 10,26,000 |
| Director's Fees | 18,000 | – |
| Audit Fees | 4,000 | – |
| Furniture (Cost ₹ 4,00,000) | 3,48,000 | – |
| Interest and Discount Received | – | 8,40,000 |
| Commission and Exchange | – | 4,00,000 |
| Reserve Fund | – | 1,40,000 |
| Printing and Stationery | 16,000 | – |
| Rent and Taxes | 34,000 | – |
| Salary | 2,80,000 | – |
| Buildings (Cost ₹ 12,00,000) | 9,00,000 | – |
| Law Charges | 6,000 | – |
| Cash in Hand | 64,000 | – |
| Cash with RBI | 14,00,000 | – |
| Cash with other Bank | 13,00,000 | – |
| Investment at Cost | 4,80,000 | – |
| Loans, Cash Credits and Overdrafts | 12,00,000 | – |
| Bills Discounted and Purchased | 5,60,000 | – |
| Interest Paid | 6,00,000 | – |
| Borrowing from Brahmadeo Bank | | 8,00,000 |
| Branch Adjustment Account | | 5,20,000 |
| **Total** | **72,10,000** | **72,10,000** |

**Following additional information is available**

i) The Bank has accepted on behalf of the customers bills worth ₹ 6,00,000 against the securities of ₹ 7,60,000 lodged with the bank.

ii) Rebate on bills discounted ₹ 22,000.

iii) Provide depreciation on Buildings 10% and Furnitures @ 5% on cost.

iv) Provide ₹ 6,000 for Bad and Doubtful Debts.

**SOLUTION**

**In the books of Laxmi Bank Ltd., Lasalgaon**
**Balance Sheet as on 31-3-2016**

| | Schedule No. | As on 31-3-2016 ₹ | As on 31-3-2015 ₹ |
|---|---|---|---|
| **Capital and Liabilities :** | | | |
| Capital | 1 | 4,00,000 | |
| Reserves and Surplus | 2 | 4,14,000 | |
| Deposits | 3 | 39,50,000 | |
| Borrowings | 4 | 8,00,000 | |
| Other Liabilities and Provisions | 5 | 5,42,000 | |
| **Total** | | **61,06,000** | |
| **Assets :** | | | |
| Cash and Balances with Reserve Bank of India | 6 | 14,64,000 | |
| Balances with other Banks and money at call and short notice | 7 | 13,00,000 | |
| Investments | 8 | 4,80,000 | |
| Advances | 9 | 17,54,000 | |
| Fixed Assets | 10 | 11,08,000 | |
| Other Assets | 11 | NIL | |
| **Total** | | **61,06,000** | |
| Contingent Liabilities | 12 | – | |
| Bills for Collection | – | | |

**Schedule – I – Capital**

| | As on 31-3-2016 ₹ | As on 31-3-2015 ₹ |
|---|---|---|
| Authorised Capital | | |
| (8,000 Shares of ₹ 100 each) | 8,00,000 | |
| Issued Capital | | |
| (8,000 Shares of ₹ 100 each) | 8,00,000 | |
| Subscribed Capital | | |
| (8,000 Shares of ₹ 100 each) | 8,00,000 | |
| Called-up Capital | | |
| (8,000 Shares of ₹ 100 each ₹ 50 share paid) | 4,00,000 | |
| **Less :** Calls Unpaid | | |
| **Add :** Forfeited Shares | – | |
| **Total** | **4,00,000** | |

## Schedule – 2 – Reserves and Surplus

| | | As on 31-3-2016 ₹ | As on 31-3-2015 ₹ |
|---|---|---:|---:|
| **I.** | **Statutory Reserves** | | |
| | Opening Balance | | |
| **Add :** | Additions during the year | 22,800 | |
| **Less :** | Deductions during the year | | |
| **II.** | **Capital Reserves** | | |
| | Opening Balance | – | |
| **Add :** | Additions during the year | | |
| **Less :** | Deductions during the year | | |
| **III.** | **Share Premium** | | |
| | Opening Balance | | |
| **Add :** | Additions during the year | | |
| **Less :** | Deductions during the year | | |
| **IV.** | **Revenue and Other Reserves** | | |
| | Opening Balance | 1,40,000 | |
| **Add :** | Additions during the year | | |
| **Less :** | Deductions during the year | | |
| **V.** | **Balance in Profit and Loss Account** | 2,51,200 | |
| | **Total  (I, II, III, IV and V)** | **61,06,000** | |

## Schedule – 3 – Deposits

| | | | As on 31-3-2016 ₹ | As on 31-3-2015 ₹ |
|---|---|---|---:|---:|
| **A.** | **I.** | **Demand Deposits** | | |
| | | i)  From Bank | | |
| | | ii)  From Others | 13,64,000 | |
| | **II.** | **Savings Bank Deposits** | 10,26,000 | |
| | **III.** | **Term Deposits** | | |
| | | i)  From Banks | | |
| | | ii)  From Others | 15,60,000 | |
| | | **Total  (I, II and III)** | **39,50,000** | |
| **B.** | i) | Deposits of Branches in India | – | |
| | ii) | Deposits of Branches Outside India | – | |
| | | **Total** | **39,50,000** | |

## Schedule – 4 – Borrowings

| | | As on 31-3-2016 ₹ | As on 31-3-2015 ₹ |
|---|---|---:|---:|
| **I.** | **Borrowings in India** | | |
| | (i)  Reserve Bank of India | | |
| | (ii)  Other Banks | 8,00,000 | – |
| | (iii) Other institutions and agencies | | |
| **II.** | **Borrowings outside India** | | |
| | **Total (I and II)** | **8,00,000** | **–** |
| | Secured borrowings in I and II above ₹ | | |

### Schedule – 5 – Other Liabilities and Provisions

| | | As on 31-3-2016 ₹ | As on 31-3-2015 ₹ |
|---|---|---|---|
| I. | Bills Payable | | |
| II. | Inter-office Adjustments (Net) | 5,20,000 | – |
| III. | Interest Accrued | | |
| IV. | Others (including provisions) | 22,000 | |
| | (Unexpired Discount) | | |
| | **Total** | **5,42,000** | |

### Schedule – 6 – Cash and Balances with Reserve Bank of India

| | | As on 31-3-2016 ₹ | As on 31-3-2015 ₹ |
|---|---|---|---|
| I. | **Cash in hand** | 64,000 | |
| | (including foreign currency notes) | | |
| II. | **Balance with Reserve Bank of India** | | |
| | i)    In Current Account | 14,00,000 | |
| | ii)   In Other Accounts | | |
| | **Total (I and II)** | **14,64,000** | |

### Schedule – 7 – Balances with Banks and Money at Call and Short Notice

| | | As on 31-3-2016 ₹ | As on 31-3-2015 ₹ |
|---|---|---|---|
| I. | **In India** | | |
| | i)   **Balances with Banks** | | |
| |     a)   in Current Accounts | 13,00,000 | |
| |     b)   in Other Deposit Accounts | | |
| | ii)   **Money at Call and Short Notice** | | |
| |     a)   With Banks | | |
| |     b)   With Other Institutions | | |
| | **Total (I and II)** | **13,00,000** | |
| II. | **Outside India** | | |
| | i)   In Current Accounts | | |
| | ii)   In Other Deposit Accounts | – | |
| | iii) Money at Call and Short Notice | | |
| | **Grand Total (I and II)** | **13,00,000** | |

### Schedule – 8 – Investments

| | | As on 31-3-2016 ₹ | As on 31-3-2015 ₹ |
|---|---|---|---|
| I. | **Investments in India in** | | |
| | i)    Government Securities | | |
| | ii)   Other Approved Securities | | |
| | iii)  Shares | | |
| | iv)   Debentures and Bonds | | |
| | v)    Subsidiaries and/or Joint Ventures | | |
| | vi)   Others | 4,80,000 | |
| |       (to be specified) | | |
| | **Total** | **4,80,000** | |
| II. | **Investments outside India in** | | |
| | i)    Government Securities (including local authorities) | | |
| | ii)   Subsidiaries and/or Joint Ventures Abroad | | |
| | iii)  Other Investments (to be specified) | | |
| | **Total** | | |
| | **Grand Total (I and II)** | **4,80,000** | |

Schedule – 9 – Advances

|  |  |  | As on 31-3-2016 ₹ | As on 31-3-2015 ₹ |
|---|---|---|---|---|
| **A.** | i) | Bills Purchased and Discounted | 5,60,000 | – |
|  | ii) | Cash Credits, Overdrafts and |  |  |
|  |  | Loans Repayable on Demand | 11,94,000 |  |
|  | iii) | Term Loans | – |  |
|  |  | **Total** | **17,54,000** |  |
| **B.** | i) | Secured by Tangible Assets |  |  |
|  | ii) | Covered by Bank/Government Guarantees |  |  |
|  | iii) | Unsecured |  |  |
|  |  | **Total** |  |  |
| **C.** | **I.** | **Advances in India** |  |  |
|  | i) | Priority Sectors |  |  |
|  | ii) | Public Sectors |  |  |
|  | iii) | Banks |  |  |
|  | iv) | Others |  |  |
|  |  | **Total** |  |  |
|  | **II.** | **Advances Outside India** |  |  |
|  | i) | Due from Banks |  |  |
|  | ii) | Due from Others |  |  |
|  | | a) Bills Purchased and Discounted |  |  |
|  | | b) Syndicated Loans |  |  |
|  | | c) Others |  |  |
|  |  | **Total** |  |  |
|  |  | **Grand Total (I and II)** | **17,54,000** |  |

Schedule – 10 – Fixed Assets

|  |  | As on 31-3-2016 ₹ | As on 31-3-2015 ₹ |
|---|---|---|---|
| **I.** | **Building** |  |  |
|  | At cost on 31$^{st}$ March of the preceding year | 12,00,000 |  |
| **Add :** | Additions during the year |  |  |
| **Less :** | Deductions during the year |  |  |
| **Less :** | Depreciation to date | 4,20,000 |  |
|  | **Total** | **7,80,000** |  |
| **II.** | **Other Fixed Assets** (Including Furniture |  |  |
|  | and Fixtures) | 4,00,000 |  |
| **Add :** | Addition during the year |  |  |
| **Less :** | Deductions during the year |  |  |
| **Less :** | Depreciation to date | 72,000 |  |
|  | **Total (I and II)** | **3,28,000** |  |
|  | **Total** | **11,08,000** |  |

### Profit and Loss Account for the year ended 31-3-2016

| | Schedule No. | Year ended 31-3-2016 ₹ | Year ended 31-3-2015 ₹ |
|---|---|---|---|
| **I.** **Income** | | | |
| Income Earned | 13 | 8,18,000 | |
| Other Income | 14 | 4,00,000 | |
| **Total** | | **12,18,000** | |
| **II.** **Expenditure** | | | |
| Interest Expended | 15 | 6,00,000 | |
| Operating Expenses | 16 | 4,98,000 | |
| Provisions and Contingencies | | 6,000 | |
| **Total** | | **11,04,000** | |
| **III.** **Profit/Loss** | | | |
| Net Profit or Loss for the year | | 1,14,000 | |
| Net Profit B/F | | 1,60,000 | |
| **Total** | | **2,74,000** | |
| **IV.** **Appropriations** | | | |
| Transfer to Statutory Reserves | | 22,800 | |
| Transfer to Other Reserves | | – | |
| Transfer to Government or Proposed Dividend | | – | |
| Balance Carried over to Balance Sheet | | 2,51,200 | |
| **Total** | | **2,74,000** | |

### Schedule – 13 – Interest Earned

| | | Year ended 31-3-2016 ₹ | Year ended 31-3-2015 ₹ |
|---|---|---|---|
| I. | Interest or Discount on Advances/Bills | 8,18,000 | – |
| II. | Income on Investments | | |
| III. | Interest on Balances with Reserve Bank of India and Other Inter-bank funds | | |
| IV. | Others | | |
| | **Total** | 8,18,000 | |

### Schedule 14 – Other Income

| | | Year ended 31-3-2016 ₹ | Year ended 31-3-2015 ₹ |
|---|---|---|---|
| I. | Commission, Exchange and Brokerage | 4,00,000 | |
| II. | Profit on Sale of Investments | | |
| | **Less :** Loss on Sale of Investments | | |
| III. | Profit on Revaluation of Investments | | |
| | **Less :** Loss on Revaluation of Investments | | |
| IV. | Profit on Sale of Land, Buildings, and Other Assets | | |
| | **Less :** Loss on Sale of Land, Buildings and Other Assets | | |
| V. | Profit on Exchange Transactions | | |
| | **Less :** Loss on Exchange Transactions | | |
| VI. | Income earned by way of Dividend etc. from Subsidiaries /Companies and/or Joint Ventures abroad/in India | | |
| VII. | Miscellaneous Income | | |
| | **Total** | 4,00,000 | |

**N.B. :** Under items II to V loss figures may be shown in brackets.

## Schedule 15 – Interest Earned

| | | Year ended 31-3-2016 ₹ | Year ended 31-3-2015 ₹ |
|---|---|---|---|
| I. | Interest on Deposits | 6,00,000 | |
| II. | Interest on Reserve Bank of India/Inter-Bank Borrowings | | |
| III. | Others | | |
| | **Total** | **6,00,000** | |

## Schedule – 16 – Operating Expenses

| | | Year ended 31-3-2016 ₹ | Year ended 31-3-2015 ₹ |
|---|---|---|---|
| I. | Payments to and Provisions for employees | 2,80,000 | |
| II. | Rent, Taxes and Lighting | 34,000 | |
| III. | Printing and Stationery | 16,000 | |
| IV. | Advertisement and Publicity | | |
| V. | Depreciation on Bank's Property | | |
| | a) Buildings | 1,20,000 | |
| | b) Furniture | 20,000 | |
| VI. | Director's Fees, Allowances and Expenses | 18,000 | |
| VII. | Auditor's Fees and Expenses (including branch auditors) | 4,000 | |
| VIII. | Low Charges | 6,000 | |
| IX. | Postages, Telegrams, Telephones etc. | | |
| X. | Repairs and Maintenance | | |
| XI. | Insurance | | |
| XII. | Other expenditure | | |
| | **Total** | **4,98,000** | |

---

### ILLUSTRATION 8

Following is the Trial Balance of Shri-Ganesh Co-operative Bank Ltd., Shahada as on 31-3-2016.

### Trial Balance as on 31-3-2016

| Particulars | Debit ₹ | Credit ₹ |
|---|---|---|
| Subscribed Capital | | |
|    56,250 Equity Share of ₹ 10 each fully paid | – | 5,62,500 |
| Reserve Fund | – | 2,81,250 |
| Loan, Cash Credit and Overdraft | 2,44,125 | |
| Premises | 86,250 | – |
| Indian Government Securities | 4,50,000 | – |
| Current Deposits | – | 1,12,500 |
| Fixed Deposits | – | 1,40,625 |
| Saving Bank Deposits | – | 86,250 |
| Salaries | 31,500 | – |
| General Expenses | 30,375 | – |
| Rent and Taxes | 3,375 | – |
| Director's Fees | 2,250 | – |
| Profit and Loss Account on 1-4-2015 | – | 20,250 |
| Interest and Discount Received | – | 1,40,625 |
| Stock of Stationery | 9,000 | – |
| Bills purchased and discounted | 51,750 | – |
| Interim Dividend Paid | 19,125 | – |
| Shares of Company | 56,250 | – |
| Cash-in-hand and with Reserve Bank of India | 2,13,750 | – |
| Money at Call and Short Notice | 90,000 | – |
| Interest Paid | 56,250 | – |
| **Total** | **13,44,000** | **13,44,000** |

**Adjustments :**
- i) Provide rebate on bills discounted ₹ 1,125.
- ii) Provide ₹ 3,375 for doubtful debts.
- iii) Authorised Capital was 1,20,000 Equity Shares of ₹ 10 each.
- iv) Provide ₹ 9,000 for Taxation Reserve.

You are required to prepare Profit and Loss Account for the year ended 31-3-2016 and the Balance Sheet as on that date as per Banking Companies Regulation Act with necessary Schedules.

SOLUTION

**In the books of Shri Ganesh Co-operative Bank Ltd., Shahada**
**Balance Sheet as on 31-3-2016**

| | Schedule No. | As on 31-3-2016 ₹ | As on 31-3-2015 ₹ |
|---|---|---|---|
| **Capital and Liabilities :** | | | |
| Capital | 1 | 5,62,500 | |
| Reserves and Surplus | 2 | 2,85,750 | |
| Deposit | 3 | 3,39,375 | |
| Borrowings | 4 | – | |
| Other Liabilities and Provisions | 5 | 10,125 | |
| **Total** | | **11,97,750** | |
| **Assets :** | | | |
| Cash in Hand and with Reserve Bank of India | 6 | 2,13,750 | |
| Balances with Banks and Money at Call and Short Notice | 7 | 90,000 | |
| Investments | 8 | 5,06,250 | |
| Advances | 9 | 2,92,500 | |
| Fixed Assets | 10 | 86,250 | |
| Other Assets | 11 | 9,000 | |
| **Total** | | **11,97,750** | |
| Contingent Liabilities | 12 | | |
| Bills for Collection | – | | |

**Schedule – 1 – Capital**

| | As on 31-3-2016 ₹ | As on 31-3-2015 ₹ |
|---|---|---|
| **I.**    **For Other Banks** | | |
| Authorised Capital | | |
| (1,20,000 Shares of ₹ 10 each) | 12,00,000 | |
| Issued Capital | | |
| (56,250 Shares of ₹ 10 each) | 5,62,250 | |
| Subscribed Capital | | |
| (56,250 Shares of ₹ 10 each) | 5,62,250 | |
| Called-up Capital | | |
| (56,250 Shares of ₹ 10 each) | 5,62,250 | |
| **Less :**   Calls Unpaid | – | |
| **Add :**   Forfeited Shares | – | |
| **Total** | **5,62,500** | |

Schedule – 2 – Reserves and Surplus

|  |  | As on 31-3-2016 ₹ | As on 31-3-2015 ₹ |
|---|---|---|---|
| I. | **Statutory Reserves** |  |  |
|  | Opening Balance |  |  |
| **Add :** | Additions during the year |  |  |
| **Less :** | Deductions during the year |  |  |
| II. | **Capital Reserves** |  |  |
|  | Opening Balance |  |  |
| **Add :** | Additions during the year |  |  |
| **Less :** | Deductions during the year |  |  |
| III. | **Share Premium** |  |  |
|  | Opening Balance |  |  |
| **Add :** | Additions during the year |  |  |
| **Less :** | Deductions during the year |  |  |
| IV. | **Revenue and Other Reserves** |  |  |
|  | Opening Balance | 2,81,250 |  |
| **Add :** | Additions during the year |  |  |
| **Less :** | Deductions during the year |  |  |
| V. | **Balance in Profit and Loss Account** | 4,500 |  |
|  | **Total  (I, II, III, IV and V)** | **2,85,750** |  |

Schedule – 3 – Deposits

|  |  |  | As on 31-3-2016 ₹ | As on 31-3-2015 ₹ |
|---|---|---|---|---|
| A. | I. | **Demand Deposits** |  |  |
|  |  | i)  From Banks |  |  |
|  |  | ii)  From Others | 1,12,500 |  |
|  | II. | **Savings Bank Deposits** | 86,250 |  |
|  | III. | **Term Deposits** |  |  |
|  |  | i)  From Banks |  |  |
|  |  | ii)  From Others | 1,40,625 |  |
|  |  | **Total  (I, II and III)** | **3,39,375** |  |
| B. | i) | Deposits of Branches in India | – |  |
|  | ii) | Deposits of Branches Outside India | – |  |
|  |  | **Total** | **3,39,375** |  |

Schedule – 4 – Borrowings

|  |  | As on 31-3-2016 ₹ | As on 31-3-2015 ₹ |
|---|---|---|---|
| I. | **Borrowings in India** | – | – |
| II. | **Borrowings outside India** | – | – |

Schedule – 5 – Other Liabilities and Provisions

|  |  | As on 31-3-2016 ₹ | As on 31-3-2015 ₹ |
|---|---|---|---|
| I. | Bills Payable | – |  |
| II. | Others |  |  |
| III. | Unexpired Discount | 1,125 |  |
| IV. | Provision for Taxation | 9,000 |  |
|  | **Total** | **10,125** |  |

### Schedule – 6 – Cash and Balances with Reserve Bank of India

| | | As on 31-3-2016 ₹ | As on 31-3-2015 ₹ |
|---|---|---|---|
| I. | **Cash in hand** | – | |
| | (including foreign currency notes) | | |
| II. | **Balances with Reserve Bank of India** | | |
| | i)    In Current Accounts | 2,13,750 | |
| | ii)   In Other Accounts | | |
| | **Total (I and II)** | **2,13,750** | |

### Schedule – 7 – Balances with Banks and Money at Call and Short Notice

| | | As on 31-3-2016 ₹ | As on 31-3-2015 ₹ |
|---|---|---|---|
| I. | **In India** | | |
| | **i)   Balances with Banks** | | |
| |     a)   in Current Accounts | – | |
| |     b)   in Other Deposit Accounts | – | |
| | **ii)   Money at Call and Short Notice** | | |
| |     a)   With Banks | – | |
| |     b)   With Other Institutions | 90,000 | |
| | **Total (I and II)** | **90,000** | |
| II. | **Outside India** | | |
| | i)   In Current Accounts | | |
| | ii)   In Other Deposit Accounts | | |
| | iii)   Money at Call and Short Notice | – | |
| | **Grand Total (I and II)** | **90,000** | |

### Schedule – 8 – Investments

| | | As on 31-3-2016 ₹ | As on 31-3-2015 ₹ |
|---|---|---|---|
| I. | **Investments in India in** | | |
| | i)    Government Securities | 4,50,000 | |
| | ii)   Other Approved Securities | – | |
| | iii)   Shares | 56,250 | |
| | iv)   Debentures and Bonds | – | |
| | v)   Subsidiaries and/or Joint Ventures | – | |
| | vi)   Others | | |
| |     (to be specified) | – | |
| | **Total** | **5,06,250** | |
| II. | **Investments Outside India in** | | |
| | i)   Government Securities (including local authorities) | | |
| | ii)   Subsidiaries and/or Joint Ventures Abroad | | |
| | iii)   Other Investments | | |
| |     (to be specified) | | |
| | **Total** | | |
| | **Grand Total (I and II)** | **5,06,250** | |

## Schedule – 9 – Advances

| | | | | As on 31-3-2016 ₹ | As on 31-3-2015 ₹ |
|---|---|---|---|---|---|
| A. | i) | Bills Purchased and Discounted | | 51,750 | – |
| | ii) | Cash Credits, Overdrafts and Loans Repayable on Demand | | 2,40,750 | |
| | iii) | Term Loans | | – | |
| | | | **Total** | **2,92,500** | |
| B. | i) | Secured by Tangible Assets | | | |
| | ii) | Covered by Bank/Government Guarantees | | – | |
| | iii) | Unsecured | | – | |
| | | | **Total** | | |
| C. | I. | **Advances in India** | | | |
| | i) | Priority Sectors | | – | |
| | ii) | Public Sectors | | – | |
| | iii) | Banks | | – | |
| | iv) | Others | | – | |
| | | | **Total** | | |
| | II. | **Advances Outside India** | | | |
| | i) | Due from Banks | | – | |
| | ii) | Due from Others | | | |
| | | a) Bills Purchased and Discounted | | – | |
| | | b) Syndicated Loans | | – | |
| | | c) Others | | – | |
| | | | **Total** | | |
| | | | **Grand Total (I and II)** | **2,92,500** | |

## Schedule – 10 – Fixed Assets

| | | As on 31-3-2016 ₹ | As on 31-3-2015 ₹ |
|---|---|---|---|
| I. | **Premises** | | |
| | At cost on 31$^{st}$March of the preceding year | 86,250 | |
| **Add :** | Additions during the year | | |
| **Less :** | Deductions during the year | | |
| **Less :** | Depreciation to date | | |
| II. | **Other Fixed Assets** (Including Furniture and Fixtures) | | |
| | At Cost on 31$^{st}$ March of the preceding year | | |
| **Add :** | Additions during the year | | |
| **Less :** | Deductions during the year | | |
| **Less :** | Depreciation to date | | |
| | **Total (I and II)** | 86,250 | |
| | **Total** | | |

## Schedule – 11 – Other Assets

| | | As on 31-3-2016 ₹ | As on 31-3-2015 ₹ |
|---|---|---|---|
| I. | Inter-Office Adjustments (net) | – | |
| II. | Interest Accrued | – | |
| III. | Tax paid in Advance/Tax deducted at source | – | |
| IV. | Stationery and Stamps | 9,000 | |
| V. | Non-Banking Assets Acquired in Satisfaction of Claims | – | |
| VI. | Other @ | – | |
| | **Total** | **9,000** | |

@ In case there is any unadjusted balance of loss, the same may be shown under this item with appropriate foot-note.

## Schedule – 12 – Contingent Liabilities

| | As on 31-3-2016 ₹ | As on 31-3-2015 ₹ |
|---|---|---|
| | – | – |
| | – | – |
| **Total** | | |

## Profit and Loss Account for the year ended 31-3-2016

| | | Schedule No. | Year ended 31-3-2016 ₹ | Year ended 31-3-2015 ₹ |
|---|---|---|---|---|
| **I.** | **Income** | | | |
| | Income Earned | 13 | 1,39,500 | |
| | Other Income | 14 | – | |
| | **Total** | | **1,39,500** | |
| **II.** | **Expenditure** | | | |
| | Interest Expended | 15 | 56,250 | |
| | Operating Expenses | 16 | 67,500 | |
| | Provisions and Contingencies | | 12,375 | |
| | **Total** | | **1,36,125** | |
| **III.** | **Profit/Loss** | | | |
| | Net Profit/Loss (–) for the year | | 3,375 | |
| | B/F from last year | | 20,250 | |
| | **Total** | | **23,625** | |
| **IV.** | **Appropriations** | | | |
| | Transfer to Statutory Reserves | | – | |
| | Transfer to Other Reserves | | – | |
| | Interim Dividend | | 19,125 | |
| | Balance Carried over to Balance Sheet | | 4,500 | |
| | **Total** | | **23,625** | |

### Schedule – 13 – Interest Earned

| | | Year ended 31-3-2016 ₹ | Year ended 31-3-2015 ₹ |
|---|---|---|---|
| I. | Interest/Discount on Advances/Bills | 1,39,500 | |
| II. | Income on Investments | | |
| III. | Interest on Balances with Reserve Bank of India and Other Inter-bank funds | – | |
| IV. | Others | – | |
| | **Total** | **1,39,500** | |

### Schedule 14 – Interest Expended

| | | Year ended 31-3-2016 ₹ | Year ended 31-3-2015 ₹ |
|---|---|---|---|
| I. | Interest on Deposits | 56,250 | |
| II. | Interest on Reserve Bank of India/Inter-Bank Borrowings | – | |
| III. | Others | – | |
| | **Total** | **56,250** | |

### Schedule 15 – Operating Expenses

| | | Year ended 31-3-2016 ₹ | Year ended 31-3-2015 ₹ |
|---|---|---|---|
| I. | Payments to and Provisions for employees | 31,500 | |
| II. | Rent, Taxes and Lighting | 3,375 | |
| III. | Printing and Stationery | – | |
| IV. | Advertisement and Publicity | – | |
| V. | Depreciation on Bank's Property | – | |
| VI. | Director's Fees, Allowances and Expenses | 2,250 | |
| VII. | Auditor's Fees and Expenses (including branch auditors) | | |
| VIII. | Law Charges | | |
| IX. | Postage, Telegrams, Telephones etc. | | |
| X. | Repairs and Maintenance | | |
| XI. | Insurance | | |
| XII. | Other Expenditure | 30,375 | |
| | **Total** | **67,500** | |

## QUESTIONS FOR SELF STUDY

**I.   Theory Questions :**

1) Explain the legal meaning of Bank and give the important legal provisions of Banking Regulation Act, 1949.

2) Define the term Non-Performing Assets (NPA) and explain the Memorandum of Instructions from Narasimhan Committee in connection with NPA.

3) Write short notes on :
   i) Non-Banking Assets and Disposal, ii) Statutory Report, iii) Restriction on loans and Advances, iv) Acceptance, Endorsement and other Obligations, v) Rebate on Bills Discounted, vi) Non-Performing Assets, vii) Classification of Assets, viii) Standard Assets, ix) Sub-Standard Assets, x) Doubtful Assets, xi) Loss Assets, xii)  Directives of the RBI in connection with disclosure of accounting policies, (xiii) Books of Account.

4) Give the form of Balance Sheet as per Section 29.

5) Give the form of Profit and Loss Account as per section 29.

6) Define the term 'Core Banking'. What are the elements of core banking system ?

7) Explain how core banking stands for "Centralised Online Real Time Exchange".

8) Explain functioning and process of core banking system in practice.

9) Define 'core banking and give various advantages of core banking.

10) Explain how core banking system related to business reengineering ?

11) Write short notes on :
   i)   Modern packaged core banking platforms
   ii)  Technical infrastructure required for core banking
   iii) Business reeingineering
   iv)  Advantages of core banking
   v)   Drawback and risks of core banking
   vi)  Administrative advantages of core banking
   vii) Core banking advantages to H.O.
   viii) Advantages of centralised accounting
   ix)  Process of core banking
   x)   Core banking advantages to customers.

**II. Practical Problems**

1) From the following balances extracted from the books of Gajalaxmi Bank Ltd. Nasik, prepare the Profit and Loss Account for the year ended 31-3-2016 and the Balance Sheet as on that date.

| Particulars | ₹ |
|---|---|
| Share Capital (Authorised and Issued) | |
|     40,000 shares of ₹ 25 each, ₹ 15 paid | 6,00,000 |
| Reserve Fund | 2,00,000 |
| Money at call and short notice | 3,00,000 |
| Investments at cost | 20,00,000 |
| Interest paid on Deposits and Borrowings | 1,40,000 |
| Law Charges | 4,000 |
| Postage and Telegrams | 6,000 |
| Salaries (including remuneration to Manager ₹ 22,000 and  Director's Fees ₹ 12,000) | 90,000 |
| Rent, Taxes and Insurance | 8,000 |
| General Expenses (including Stationery ₹ 4,000; Audit Fees ₹ 10,000 and Other Expenditure ₹ 6,000) | 20,000 |
| Deposits :  i)    Fixed | 10,00,000 |
|          ii)   Savings | 4,00,000 |
|          iii)  Current | 46,00,000 |
| Premises (after Depreciation upto 31-3-2015 ₹ 50,000) | 3,50,000 |
| Furniture (after Depreciation upto 31-3-2015 ₹ 10,000) | 30,000 |
| Cash in hand | 70,000 |
| Cash with RBI | 6,00,000 |
| Cash with SBI | 4,00,000 |
| Borrowings from Bank of Baroda | 7,50,000 |
| Interest and Discount | 4,46,500 |
| Profit and Loss Account (Credit Balance on 1-4-2015) | 1,00,000 |
| Dividend paid for the year 2015-2016 | 60,000 |

| | ₹ |
|---|---|
| Loans, Cash Credits and Overdrafts | 32,28,500 |
| Bills Payables | 50,000 |
| Bills discounted and purchased | 7,50,000 |
| Rebate on Bills Discounted (on 31-3-2015) | 10,000 |
| Branch Adjustments (credit) | 25,000 |
| Commission, Exchange received | 45,000 |
| Library-Books | 12,000 |
| Repairs to Bank Property | 8,000 |
| Gold Bullion | 1,50,000 |

**Adjustments :**

i) Provide depreciation @ 5% on Premises and @ 10% on Furniture (on original cost of such assets).

ii) Provide ₹ 58,000 for Taxation.

iii) Rebate on Bills Discounted as 31-3-2016 amounted to ₹ 16,500 for unexpired period.

iv) Loans advanced by Bank included a sum of ₹ 1,00,000 due from a customer against the mortgage of his machinery. As the client is unable to pay the amounts, the Bank takes over the machinery at the market value of ₹ 70,000 in full satisfaction of its claim on the date of Trial Balance.

2) The balances extracted from the books of Dhanlakshmi Bank Ltd., Dombivali on 31-3-2016 were as follows :

| Particulars | ₹ |
|---|---|
| Paid-up Capital | 1,00,00,000 |
| Local bills discounted | 90,00,000 |
| Reserve Fund | 38,50,000 |
| Cash, Credit and Overdrafts | 1,40,00,000 |
| Unclaimed Dividends | 50,000 |
| Loans | 2,30,00,000 |
| Current and Saving Deposits | 2,50,00,000 |
| Furniture | 2,00,000 |
| Fixed Deposits | 11,00,000 |
| Profit and Loss Account (Cr.) | |
| Stamps and Stationery (in hand) | 50,000 |
| Cash in Hand | 25,00,000 |
| Cash at Bank | 65,00,000 |
| Investments at Cost | 47,50,000 |

Out of total debts, debts for ₹ 28,50,000 were doubtful and rest were considered good. Out of debts considered good, ₹ 2,40,00,000 were fully secured and for debts amounting to ₹ 40,00,000 (including ₹ 11,50,000 due by a director) the Bank held personal securities of one or more persons in addition to the personal security of the debtors and for rest the bank held no securities other than the debtor's personal security. The Directors require the bank's investments to be shown in Balance Sheet at Market Value which is ₹ 52,50,000. The Authorised Capital of Bank is 1,20,00,000.

Prepare Balance Sheet as on 31-3-2016.

3) From the following particulars you are required to show the assets side of the Balance Sheet of Rajlakhsmi Bank Ltd., Raipur as on 31-3-2016 in the prescribed form.

| Particulars | ₹ |
|---|---|
| Government Securities at Cost | 1,90,00,000 |
| Shares and Debentures | 1,30,00,000 |
| Bills Discounted | 1,00,00,000 |
| Bills Purchased | 1,50,00,000 |
| Premises | 1,10,00,000 |
| Advances to Customers | 2,00,00,000 |
| Cash Credit (Debit) | 1,20,00,000 |
| Cash in Hand | 1,00,00,000 |
| Money at Call and Short Notice | 1,90,00,000 |
| Constituents Liabilities for acceptances, endorsements and other obligations as per contra | 1,51,00,000 |

4)     The following figures are extracted from the books of City Bank Ltd., Chembur as on 31-3-2016.

| Particulars | ₹ |
|---|---:|
| Interest and discount received | 3,69,57,380 |
| Interest paid on deposits | 2,03,24,520 |
| Issued and Subscribed Capital | 1,00,00,000 |
| Reserve Fund under Section 17 | 80,00,000 |
| Commission, Exchange and Brokerage | 20,00,000 |
| Rent received | 5,50,000 |
| Profit on sale of investments | 20,00,000 |
| Salaries and Allowances | 20,00,000 |
| Director's Fees and Allowances | 3,00,000 |
| Rent and Taxes paid | 10,00,000 |
| Postage and Telegrams | 5,02,860 |
| Depreciation on Bank's properties | 3,00,000 |
| Stationery | 5,00,000 |
| Preliminary Expenses | 1,50,000 |
| Audit Fees | 50,000 |

The following further information is given :

i)     A customer to whom a sum of ₹ 1,00,00,000 has been advanced has become insolvent and it is expected only 50% can be recovered from his estate. Interest due at 18% on his debt has not been provided in the Books.

ii)     There were also other debts for which a provision of ₹ 15,00,000 was found necessary by the auditors.

iii)     Rebate on bills discounted as on 1-4-2015 to ₹ 1,20,000.
       Rebate on bills discounted as on 31-3-2016 to ₹ 1,60,000.

iv)     Provide ₹ 65,00,000 for Income-Tax.

v)     The Directors desire to declare 10% dividend.
       Prepare the Profit and Loss Account for the last year ended 31-3-2016 in accordance with the Law. Make necessary assumptions.

5)     The following Trial Balance was extracted from the books of Janseva Bank Ltd., Junnar, as on 31-3-2016.

| Particulars | Debit ₹ | Credit ₹ |
|---|---:|---:|
| Share Capital | | 50,00,000 |
| Cash on hand and with Banks | 4,63,500 | |
| Investment in Govt. of India Bonds | 19,43,700 | |
| Other Investments | 15,56,300 | |
| Gold Bullion | 1,51,300 | |
| Interest accrued on Investment | 2,46,200 | |
| Savings Account Balance | | 74,200 |
| Current Account Ledger/Control Account | | 9,70,000 |
| Fixed Deposit | | 2,30,500 |
| Share Premium Account | | 9,00,000 |
| Statutory Reserve | | 14,00,000 |
| Silver Bullion | 20,000 | |
| Constituents Liability for Acceptances and Endorsements | 5,65,000 | |
| Security Deposits of Employees | | 1,50,000 |
| Buildings | 6,00,000 | |
| Furniture | 1,00,000 | |

| Particulars | | |
|---|---:|---:|
| Borrowings from Banks | | 7,72,300 |
| Money at call and Short Notice | 2,60,000 | |
| Profit and Loss Account | | 65,000 |
| Bills Discounted and Purchased | 1,25,000 | |
| Bills for Collection | | 4,35,000 |
| Acceptances and endorsements | | 5,65,000 |
| Interest | 79,500 | 7,20,000 |
| Commission and Brokerage | | 2,53,000 |
| Constituent's Liability for Bills for Collection | 4,35,000 | |
| Discount | | 4,20,000 |
| Audit Fees | 30,000 | |
| Loss on Sale of Furniture | 10,000 | |
| Director's Fees | 32,000 | |
| Salaries | 2,10,000 | |
| Postage | 2,500 | |
| Rents | | 6,000 |
| Profit on Bullion | | 12,000 |
| Managing Directors' Remuneration | 1,20,000 | |
| Miscellaneous Income | | 27,000 |
| Loss on Sale of Investments | 3,00,000 | |
| Deposit with Reserve Bank of India | 7,50,000 | |
| Advances | 40,00,000 | |
| **Total** | **1,20,00,000** | **1,20,00,000** |

You are required to prepare a Profit and Loss Account for the year ended 31st March 2016 and a Balance Sheet as at that date after considering the following.

i) Provide Rebate on Bills discounted ₹ 50,000.

ii) A Scrutiny of the Current Account Ledger reveals that there are accounts overdrawn to the extent of ₹ 2,50,000 and the total of the credit balance is ₹ 12,20,000.

iii) Claim by employees for Banks ₹ 1,80,000 is pending a word of arbitration.

iv) Directors State that Assets are over depreciated.

6) Syndicate Bank Ltd., Surat is incorporated with Authorised Capital of Rupees Three Crores divided into Equity Shares of ₹ 50 each. Prepare a Balance Sheet as at 31-3-2016 as required by the Banking Companies Act, 1949 from the following particulars made available.

| Particulars | ₹ |
|---|---:|
| Share Capital in Equity Shares of ₹ 50 each | 1,50,00,000 |
| ₹ 29 per share paid-up (Reserve liability of shareholders ₹ 25 per share) | |
| Reserve Fund | 1,10,00,000 |
| Profit and Loss Account as on 31-3-2014 (Cr.) | 28,80,000 |

| | |
|---|---:|
| U.K. Loans (Dr.) | 14,25,000 |
| Saving Bank Deposits | 22,50,000 |
| Call Deposits | 20,75,000 |
| Buildings **Less** Depreciation | 74,45,000 |
| Furniture and Fixtures **Less :** Depreciation | 17,20,000 |
| Bills for collection | 11,25,000 |
| Acceptances and endorsements on behalf of customers | 9,50,000 |
| Gold | 90,000 |
| Reserve for doubtful debts | 7,50,000 |
| Gold ornaments (received as security for Loans) | 45,000 |
| Cash certificates and Fixed Deposits | 12,50,000 |
| Loans, Cash credits, Overdrafts etc. | 1,58,50,000 |
| Current Accounts | 1,20,75,000 |
| Bills discounted and purchased | 17,50,000 |
| Silver | 6,00,000 |
| Investments in fully paid Equity Shares of Public Companies | 13,50,000 |
| Stamps and Stationery | 4,25,000 |
| Cash with Reserve Bank of India | 1,15,00,000 |
| Cash with other Banks | 13,00,000 |
| Money at Call and Short Notice | 63,30,000 |
| Cash in hand | 5,45,000 |
| Development Rebate, Reserve | 5,75,000 |
| Borrowings from Banks | 15,10,000 |
| State Government Securities (Face Value ₹ 20,00,000) | 13,30,000 |
| Unclaimed Dividends | 3,80,000 |
| Bills Payable | 90,000 |
| Branch Adjustment (Cr.) | 17,50,000 |
| Municipal Debentures (Face Value ₹ 9,00,000) | 8,75,000 |
| Share Premium | 7,50,000 |
| Amount owing to Subsidiary Company | 3,45,000 |
| Tax deducted at source on Income and Investments | 1,45,000 |

**Adjustments :**

i)    Rebate on Bills discounted and purchased for unexpired period amounted to ₹ 90,000.

ii)   Transfer ₹ 7,00,000 to Reserve Fund.

iii)  Municipal Debentures are pledged as security with a Bank for loan of ₹ 8,00,000.

iv)  Advances amounting to ₹ 1,08,00,000 are fully secured.

vi)  Liability in respect of outstanding forward Exchange Contract amounts to ₹ 12,70,000.

vi)  Liability on Bills of Exchange Re-discounted amounts to ₹ 4,00,000.

7) The following are the balances of General Ledger of Mumbai Bank Ltd., Malad as at 31-3-2015.

| Particulars | ₹ | Particulars | ₹ |
|---|---|---|---|
| Share Capital | 3,50,000 | Calls in Arrears | 250 |
| Reserve | 1,00,000 | Fixed Deposits | 6,67,500 |
| Savings Deposit | 4,16,250 | Current Deposits | 9,12,250 |
| Advances | 2,12,140 | Borrowings from Banks | 16,000 |
| Cash in hand | 3,16,540 | Cash with Reserve Bank | 1,50,000 |
| Balance with Other Banks on | | Bills Discounted | 3,15,770 |
| Current Account | 1,43,000 | Bills Payable | 5,500 |
| Fixed Deposit (Investment) | 3,00,000 | Money at Call and Short Notice | 72,600 |
| Unclaimed Dividend | 340 | Outstanding Expenses | 1,110 |
| Profit and Loss Account | 16,160 | Investments | 4,43,210 |
| Loans | 5,03,160 | Premises | 50,000 |
| Furniture | 4,400 | Silver | 1,300 |
| Non-Banking Assets | 180 | Interest and Discount (Cr.) | 46,000 |
| Commission and Exchange (Cr.) | 1,320 | Rent (Cr.) | 1,360 |
| Profit on Sale of Investments | 1,400 | Profit on Non-Banking Assets | 10 |
| Interest (Dr.) | 13,000 | Transfer Fees | 1 |
| | | Salaries and Allowances | 3,070 |
| General Manager Salary | 150 | Provident Fund Contribution | 285 |
| Director's Fees and Allowances | 1,107 | Loss on Sale of Gold | 420 |
| Municipal Tax | 56 | Income Tax paid | 5,120 |
| Postage, Telegrams and Stamps | 1,063 | Law Charges | 139 |
| Depreciation of Furniture | 36 | Auditor's Fees | 30 |
| Stationery, Printing and Advertisement | 100 | Repairs | 48 |
| | | General Expenses | 27 |

i) An analysis of Investments shows that Government Securities amount to ₹ 2,00,000 at cost (market value ₹ 2,12,000) (shares ₹ 1,43,210) (cost) (market value ₹ 1,45,000) debentures at ₹ 50,000 (cost) (market value ₹ 52,000) and gold ₹ 50,000 at cost (market value ₹ 49,000).

ii) Advances ₹ 2,12,140. Of these ₹ 1,60,000 has securities fully covering these balances ₹ 50,000 is granted on personal security of debtors concerned of which again ₹ 12,400 personal security to other persons over and above those of the debtors; ₹ 2,000 is doubtful and ₹ 140 is bad and no provision has been made for these. The loans are fully secured.

iii) Rebate on bills discounted at 31$^{st}$ March, 2016 amounted to ₹ 1,060.

iv) The Authorised Capital of the Banks is ₹ 7,00,000 divided into 7,000 Equity Shares of ₹ 100 each. All of these shares are issued and fully subscribed and are called upto the extent of ₹ 50 per share. There is an arrear of ₹ 50 per share on 10 shares.

You are required to draw up a Profit and Loss Account of the bank for the year ended 31-3-2016 under form 'B' of the Banking Companies Act and a Balance sheet as at that date under Form 'A' of the same Act.

8) Following is the trial balance of Sudhir Bank Ltd., Shahada as on 31-3-2016. You are required to prepare Profit and Loss Account for the year ended 31-3-2016 and Balance Sheet as on that date.

| Particulars | Debit ₹ | Credit ₹ |
|---|---|---|
| Share Capital | | |
| (60,000 Equity Shares of ₹ 50 each ₹ 25 paid up) | | 15,00,000 |
| Profit and Loss Account (1st April 2015) | | 1,22,250 |
| Current Deposits Accounts | | 32,16,000 |
| Fixed Deposits Accounts | | 35,14,500 |
| Savings Bank Accounts | | 16,60,500 |
| Directors' Fees | 13,950 | |
| Audit Fees | 13,200 | |
| Furniture | 1,28,850 | |
| Interest paid | 6,00,600 | |
| Interest and Discount | | 10,56,000 |
| Commission and Exchange | | 3,04,500 |
| 6% Govt. Bonds | 15,60,000 | |
| Shares in companies | 12,00,000 | |
| Branch Adjustment Account | 3,06,000 | |
| Postage and Printing | 10,350 | |
| Premises | 25,54,500 | |
| Salaries | 1,00,500 | |
| Law Charges | 7,950 | |
| Provident Fund Contribution | 16,800 | |
| Cash in hand | 3,10,500 | |
| Bills Discounted and purchased | 1,00,500 | |
| Unexpired Insurance | 4,050 | |
| Statutory Reserve Fund | | 1,27,500 |
| Loans, Cash credit and Overdrafts | 45,73,500 | |
| **Total** | **1,15,01,250** | **1,15,01,250** |

**Following additional information :**

i) Rebate on bills discounted amounted to ₹ 10,650.

ii) Provide ₹ 57,750 for Doubtful Debts.

iii) The Bank has accepted bills worth ₹ 3,75,000 on behalf of the customers against the securities of ₹ 4,65,000 lodged with the Bank.

iv) Provide depreciation on Premises ₹ 1,09,500 and on Furniture ₹ 8,850.

v) Provide for Taxation ₹ 11,250.

9) From the following figures taken from the books of Honest Bank Ltd., Hinjewadi you are require to prepare Profit and Loss Account for the year ended 31-3-2016 and Balance Sheet as on that date.

| Particulars | ₹ |
|---|---|
| Share Capital (Authorised and Issued) | |
| (20,000 Shares of ₹ 50 each ₹ 25 paid up) | 5,00,000 |
| Reserve Fund | 3,50,000 |
| Fixed Deposit Account | 9,50,000 |
| Savings Bank Deposit | 30,00,000 |
| Current Account | 80,00,000 |
| Investments (at cost) | 30,00,000 |
| Interest Accrued and paid | 2,00,000 |
| Salaries (including Salary to General Manager | |
| ₹ 24,000 and Director's Fees ₹ 9,000) | 80,000 |
| Rent | 20,000 |
| General Expenses | 10,000 |
| (Including Stationery ₹ 4,000 and Auditor's Fees ₹ 3,000) | |
| Money at Call and Short Notice | 3,00,000 |
| Profit and Loss Account (Cr.) on 1-4-2015 | 2,10,000 |
| Dividend for 2015 | 50,000 |
| Premises (after depreciation upto 31-3-2016 ₹ 10,00,000) | 12,00,000 |
| Cash in hand | 60,000 |
| Cash with Reserve Bank | 15,00,000 |
| Cash with Other Banks | 13,00,000 |
| Borrowed from Banks | 7,00,000 |
| Interest and Discounts | 7,50,000 |
| Bills discounted and purchased | 6,00,000 |
| Bills Payable | 8,00,000 |
| Loans Overdrafts and Cash Credits | 70,00,000 |
| Unclaimed Dividend | 30,000 |
| Sundry Creditors | 30,000 |
| Bills for Collection | 1,40,000 |
| Acceptances and Endorsements on behalf of customers | 2,00,000 |

Rebate on Bills discounted and purchased for unexpired term amounted to ₹ 6,000. Allow 5% depreciation on premises on original cost. A provision for doubtful debts amounting to ₹ 20,000 is required. The Bank has no business outside India. Create a provision of ₹ 1,00,000 for taxation.

10) Following balances were extracted from the books of Laxmi Bank Ltd., Lonavala as on 31-3-2016.

| Particulars | ₹ |
| --- | --- |
| Share Capital | 8,00,000 |
| Share Premium | 1,80,000 |
| Buildings | 1,30,000 |
| Deposits with RBI | 1,50,000 |
| Cash in Hand | 22,700 |
| Cash with Other Banks | 50,000 |
| Investments in Government Securities | 5,88,000 |
| Other Investments | 3,12,000 |
| Gold Bullion | 30,260 |
| Bills for Collection | 87,000 |
| Interest Accrued on Investments | 49,240 |
| Loss on Sale of Investments | 60,000 |
| Employees Security Deposits | 30,000 |
| Savings Deposits | 14,840 |
| Current Deposits | 1,94,000 |
| Fixed Deposits | 46,100 |
| Profit on Bullion | 2,400 |
| Acceptances and Endorsements | 1,13,000 |
| Miscellaneous Income | 5,400 |
| Non-Banking Assets | 4,000 |
| Statutory Reserve | 2,80,000 |
| Furniture | 10,000 |
| Postage and Telegram | 10,100 |
| Managing Director's Remuneration | 24,000 |
| Borrowing from other Banks | 1,54,460 |
| Money at Call and Short Notices | 52,000 |
| Director's Fees | 2,400 |
| Interest (Dr.) | 15,900 |
| Advances | 4,00,000 |
| Loss on Sale of Furniture | 2,000 |
| Bills Discounted and Purchased | 25,000 |
| Interest (Cr.) | 1,44,000 |
| Discount (Cr.) | 84,000 |
| Audit Fees | 10,000 |
| Salaries | 42,400 |
| Commission and Brokerage | 50,600 |
| Rent (Cr.) | 11,200 |
| Profit and Loss Account (Credit Balance) | 13,000 |

You are required to prepare Profit and Loss Account for the year ended 31-3-2016 and a Balance Sheet as on that date after considering the following :

i) Provide for Taxation ₹ 22,000.

ii) Claim by employees for Bonus ₹ 50,000 is to be provided.

iii) A scrutiny of current deposit reveals that there are three accounts overdrawn to the extent of ₹ 50,000 and total of credit balances is ₹ 2,44,000.

iv) Allow 7% depreciation on Buildings.

v) Provision for bad and doubtful debts is required amounting to ₹ 19,000.

# INSURANCE CLAIM ACCOUNTS



## 3.0 INTRODUCTION

A business may suffer abnormal losses due to different reasons such as fire, theft, burglary, flood, strike, etc. Among them, the most common which destroys or causes severe damage to the assets like Stock, Buildings, Plant, Machinery, Furniture, etc. is fire. When a fire takes place, the business naturally incurs heavy losses, and in turn, the normal business operations are disrupted. Hence, the businessmen need insurance especially in regard to cover loss of stock destroyed by fire and loss of profit during the period of disruption of normal business operations. When a business suffers a loss from an insured event, it has to notify the insurance company regarding the loss of the assets and to file a claim for compensation against those losses. Such claims are known as **Insurance Claims**. When a fire takes place, to file a claim with the insurance company for the loss of assets damaged or destroyed, a set of procedures is to be followed.

**Insurance Cover** would enable a businessman to carry on the business without much difficulty. In the absence of insurance cover, normal business operations cannot be restored. In this connection, one of the most important problems that a business has to face is the determination of the amount of the claim to be lodged.

## 3.1 TYPES OF INSURANCE CLAIM

A business takes a fire insurance policy to cover A) **Claim for Loss of Stock** and B) **Claim for Loss of Profit**. The Types of Insurance Claims are shown below in Figure 3.1.

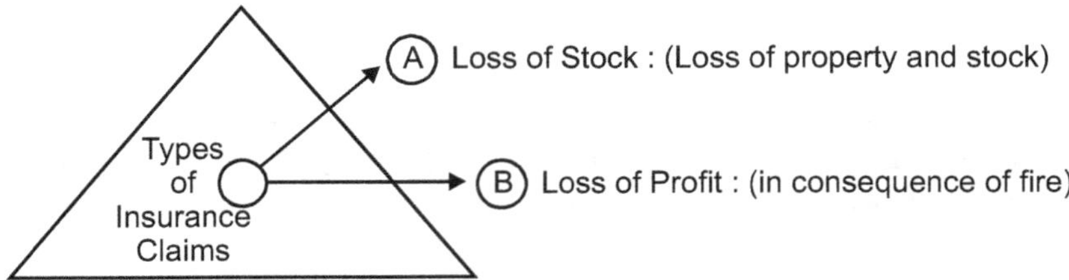


**Fig. 3.1 : Types of Insurance Claims**

## A) Claim for Loss of Stock

### Introduction

When a fixed asset is destroyed, the computation of loss is simple. The value of such assets on the date of fire can be ascertained from the books of accounts of the business because most of the businessmen usually maintain proper records of the fixed assets. Fixed assets are recorded in the books of accounts at their acquisition cost, which becomes the basis for calculation of claim for the loss of fixed assets.

When a stock is destroyed, the computation of loss is not so simple because the prices of different items of stock are seldom stable and the stock is acquired at varying rates. For most of the businesses, particularly for trading concerns, stock taking is not maintained up-to-date. Therefore, at the time of accident no readymade value of stock is available.

If the **Stock Register** is maintained properly, the value of stock lost by fire can be ascertained from it. However, the business may face a problem, even when the stock register is maintained up-to-date, if the books of accounts are also destroyed alongwith the stock.

The insured, in the event of fire accident, informs the insurer (insurance company) of the loss of property and stocks. The insurance contract is usually for a year and the insurer indemnifies the insured for the loss suffered. In response to the request of the insured, a technical expert is entrusted by the insurance company and the technical expert after investigation, sends his report by stating the amount payable by the insurance company to the insured. This report, after careful investigation must reveal the causes due to which the fire broke out and whether the claim is covered by the policy or not.

## PROCEDURE FOR CALCULATION

There are two situations in which claims can be calculated and lodged.

1) When proper records are available and the information of stock lying with the business on the date of fire is known.

2) When proper records are not available and there is difficulty in ascertaining the value of stock on the date of fire.

**1) When proper records are available :**

When proper records are available, the following would be the steps for lodging claim with the insurance company.

a) Ascertain the value of stock lying with the business concern on the date of fire.

b) Ascertain the value of stock salvaged from fire.

c) Find out the stock destroyed by fire by deducting the stock salvaged from the stock value on the date of fire i.e. a) and b) as stated above, would give the figure of stock destroyed by fire.

d) The amount of claim would be equal to the stock destroyed by fire (provided there is no under insurance and application of average clause).

**2)** **When proper records are not available, the following procedure is followed to ascertain the value of stock on the date of fire :**

**i)** **Find out the percentage of Gross Profit for the previous year or the average of Gross Profit for the previous years :**

This is done by preparing the Trading Account of the previous year which gives the figure of Gross Profit. The usual format of Trading Account is as follows.

**Dr.**            **Trading Account for the period ended ............**            **Cr.**

| Particulars | ₹ | Particulars | ₹ |
|---|---|---|---|
| To Opening Stock | | By Sales | |
| To Purchases | | **Less :** Returns Inward | |
| **Less :** Returns Outward | | By Closing Stock | |
| To Direct Expenses | | | |
| To Carriage and Freight Inward | | | |
| To Wages | | | |
| To Gross Profit C/D * | | | |
| (Balancing Figure) | | | |

**Calculation of percentage of Gross Profit to Sales :**

If Sales = Gross Profit

$\therefore$      100 =     ?

$$= \frac{100 \times \text{Gross Profit}}{\text{Sales}}$$

**ii)** **Find out the Value of the Stock on the date of Fire by constructing a separate Memorandum Trading Account :**

When it is not possible to ascertain the exact value of stock destroyed by fire from the stock register, the value of stock on the date of fire can be ascertained by constructing a Memorandum Trading Account for a period starting from the first day of the ascertaining period and ending on the date of fire. The following is a specimen of the Memorandum Trading Account.

**Memorandum Trading Account**

**Dr.**      **For the period from 1ˢᵗ day of the accounting year to the date of fire**      **Cr.**

| Particulars | ₹ | Particulars | ₹ |
|---|---|---|---|
| To Opening Stock | | By Sales | |
| To Purchases | | **Less :** Returns Inward | |
| **Less :** Returns Outward | | By Closing Stock* | |
| To Direct Expenses | | (Balancing Figure) | |
| To Carriage and Freight Inward | | | |
| To Wages | | | |
| To Gross Profit C/D | | | |
| (% on Sales) | | | |

**Debit Side :**

- **Opening Stock :**

  It is nothing but the Closing Stock of the last accounting period. Therefore, it can be ascertained from the Balance Sheet of the last accounting period.

- **Purchases :**

  These can be ascertained from the Purchase Day Book i.e. Credit Purchases and Cash Book i.e. Cash Purchases.

- **Returns Outward :**

  It can be ascertained from the Returns Outward Book.

- **Direct Expenses :**

These can be ascertained from the Cash Book.

- **Carriage and Freight Inward :**

It can be ascertained from the Cash Book.

- **Wages :**

These can be ascertained from the Wages Register and Cash Book.

- **Gross Profit :**

It is calculated on sales, based on usual gross profit percentage of the last few years.

At the time of calculation of **percentage of Gross Profit on Sales,** all the necessary adjustments must be made for i) the slow moving items; ii) goods distributed as free sample; iii) goods taken by the proprietor/partners for personal use; and iv) over-valuation or under-valuation of stock.

**Credit Side :**

- **Sales :**

These can be ascertained from the Sales Day Book i.e. Credit Sales and from the Cash Book i.e. Cash Sales.

- **Returns Inward :**

It can be ascertained from the Returns Inward Book.

The difference between the debit side total and credit side total of the Memorandum Trading Account represents the estimated **Closing Stock on the date of fire.**

The Memorandum Trading Account shows the value of stock which is supposed to exist at the time of fire. Therefore, to ascertain the actual amount of claim to be lodged, deduct the value of stock salvaged from the estimated value of closing stock on the date of fire, as ascertained from the Memorandum Trading Account.

**iii) Calculation of Actual Amount of Claim to be Lodged :**

The amount of loss to be compensated by the insurance company is always stipulated in the Insurance Policy, but under no circumstances, the claim for loss can exceed the actual loss suffered by the business. When the business is fully compensated by the insurance company for the Loss of Stock, the insurance company becomes the owner of the stock, salvaged (saved), if any. The actual amount of claim to be lodged is calculated as follows :

Statement showing Claim for Loss of Stock as on ......

| Particulars | | ₹ |
|---|---|---:|
| | Book Value of Stock | |
| | (as per Memorandum Trading Account) | ........ |
| **Less :** | Stock Salvaged | |
| | (Retained by the Business)    (–) | ........ |
| | | ........ |
| | **Loss of Stock** (Claim to be lodged)* | |

- Subject to Average Clause.

The following **example** will clarify the steps to be followed in the calculation of claims to be lodged under loss of stock policy, well.

## EXAMPLE

The godown of Burkle Ltd., Baroda caught fire on 15th June, 2016. Records saved from fire showed the following particulars.

| Particulars | ₹ | Particulars | ₹ |
|---|---|---|---|
| Stock at cost on 1st January, 2015 | 60,000 | Sales Less Returns for the year 2015 | 7,20,000 |
| Stock at cost on 31st December, 2015 | 84,000 | Purchases Less Returns from January 1 to June 15, 2016 | 1,80,000 |
| Purchases Less Returns for the year 2015 | 5,08,000 | Sales Less Returns from January 1, to June 15, 2016 | 2,46,000 |
| Wages for the year 2015 | 20,000 | Wages from January 1 to June 15, 2016 | 16,200 |

Gross Profit remained at a uniform rate. The Stocks Salvaged amounted to ₹ 8,000 and it was retained by Burkle Ltd. The godown was insured.

Calculate the amount of claim to be lodged with the insurance company.

## ANSWER

**In the Books of Burkle Ltd., Baroda**

Dr.      **Trading Account for the year ended 31st December, 2015**      Cr.

| Particulars | ₹ | Particulars | ₹ |
|---|---|---|---|
| To Opening Stock | 60,000 | By Sales Less Returns | 7,20,000 |
| To Purchases Less Returns | 5,08,000 | By Closing Stock | 84,000 |
| To Wages | 20,000 | | |
| To Gross Profit C/D* | 2,16,000 | | |
| (Balancing Figure) | | | |
| | **8,04,000** | | **8,04,000** |

**Working Notes :**

1) **Calculation of rate of Gross Profit on Sales :**

      If ₹ 7,20,000 Sales = ₹ 2,16,000 Gross Profit

∴        100 = ?

$$= \frac{100 \times Rs.\ 2,16,000}{₹\ 7,20,000}$$

= 30%

Dr.      **Memorandum Trading Account for the period 1st January, 2016 to 15th June, 2016**  Cr.

| Particulars | ₹ | Particulars | ₹ |
|---|---|---|---|
| To Opening Stock | 84,000 | By Sales Less Returns | 2,46,000 |
| To Purchases Less Returns | 1,80,000 | By Closing Stock* | 1,08,000 |
| To Wages | 16,200 | (Balancing Figure) | |
| To Gross Profit C/D | | | |
| (30% on Sales i.e. ₹ 2,46,000) | 73,800 | | |
| | **3,54,000** | | **3,54,000** |

**Statement showing Claim for Loss of Stock as on 15th June, 2016**

| Particulars | | ₹ |
|---|---|---|
| Book Value of Stock on the date of fire | | 1,08,000 |
| **Less :** Salvaged Stock | (−) | 8,000 |
| ∴  **Claim to be Lodged** | | **1,00,000** |

## AVERAGE CLAUSE

**Average Clause** applies in case of under insurance. **Average Clause** means the claim for the loss of stock is proportionately reduced having regard to under insurance of stock.

The amount of insurance premium to be paid at regular intervals depends on the value of stock insured. More the value of stock insured, more is the amount of premium to be paid. To reduce the burden of insurance premium, the Average Stock of a business may not be adequately insured with the assumption that fire may not destroy the whole stock. When a business takes an insurance policy, the value of which is less than the value of the Average Stock lying in the godown, it is known as **"Under-Insurance"**. Generally, Fire Insurance Policies contain an "Average Clause" to discourage under-insurance. At the time of calculating insurance claim, this clause is applicable if the value of stock on the date of fire was more than the policy value. In the event of a partial loss, the insurance company pays a proportional amount of claim. The net claim under average clause is calculated as follows :

$$\text{Net Claim} \ = \ \frac{\text{Value of Insurance Policy}}{\text{Value of Stock on the date of Fire}} \times \text{Loss of Stock}$$

## UNDER OR OVER-VALUATION OF STOCKS

If the stock values made available are not at cost price and are under or above cost, the Valuation of Stock must be made more accurately as per the accounting principles. Hence, it is necessary to convert these useless prices into useful cost price before calculating the exact percentage of gross profit to sales. The following example will clarify the concepts well.

## EXAMPLE

Due to a fire in the godown of Godrej Co., Gondiya on 30th September 2016, the entire stock was burnt except some stock costing ₹ 70,000. The books were, however, saved. From the information available, it was found that –

i)    The company's average gross profit was 25% on sales.

ii)    The stock on 31st March, 2016 valued at 10% above cost was ₹ 2,20,000.

iii)    The purchases and sales from 1st April, 2016 upto the date of fire were ₹ 3,00,000 and ₹ 6,80,000 respectively.

iv)    The wages for the same period amounted to ₹ 1,44,000.

v)    The company got the stock insured for ₹ 1,20,000.

vi)    The policy had an Average Clause.

You are required to prepare a statement showing the amount of stock lost by fire and the amount of claim to be lodged with the insurance company.

ANSWER

**In the Books of Godrej Co. Ltd., Gondiya**

**Dr.  Memorandum Trading Account for the period 1st April, 2016 to 30th September, 2016   Cr.**

| Particulars | ₹ | Particulars | ₹ |
|---|---|---|---|
| To Opening Stock | 2,00,000 | By Sales | 6,80,000 |
| To Purchases | 3,00,000 | By Closing Stock* | 1,34,000 |
| To Wages | 1,44,000 | (Balancing Figure) | |
| To Gross Profit C/D | 1,70,000 | | |
| (25% of ₹ 6,80,000) | | | |
| | **8,14,000** | | **8,14,000** |

**Working Notes :**

1) **Valuation of Stock on 1st April, 2016 :**

Since Stocks on 1-4-2016 are valued at 10% above cost, their cost price is calculated as under :

$$\underset{100}{\underset{\text{Price}}{\text{Cost}}} \overset{(+)}{} \underset{10}{\underset{\text{above cost}}{\text{Valuation at 10\%}}} = \underset{100}{\underset{\text{Cost}}{\text{Overvalued}}}$$

$$\text{If } 110 = ₹ 2,20,000$$

$$\therefore \qquad 100 = ?$$

$$= \frac{₹ 2,20,000 \times 100}{110}$$

$$= ₹ 2,00,000$$

**Statement showing Claim for Loss of Stock as on 30th September, 2016**

| Particulars | | ₹ |
|---|---|---|
| Book Value of Stock on the date of fire | | 1,34,000 |
| **Less :** Salvaged Stock | (−) | 70,000 |
| ∴ **Loss of Stock** | | **64,000** |

The insurance policy was taken for ₹ 1,20,000 but the value of stock on the date of fire was ₹ 1,34,000. Therefore, the average clause is applicable.

$$\textbf{Net Claim} = \frac{\text{Value of Insurance Policy}}{\text{Value of Stock on the date of Fire}} \times \text{Loss of Stock}$$

$$= \frac{₹ 1,20,000}{₹ 1,34,000} \times ₹ 64,000$$

$$= ₹ 57,313$$

∴    Amount of Claim to be Lodged = **₹ 57,313.**

## TREATMENT OF ABNORMAL ITEMS OF GOODS

The Gross Profit percentage gets disturbed due to existence of abnormal item of Purchases and Sales. **Abnormal items** means items which do not carry the normal price tag due to the reasons that they are defective or of poor quality, or slow moving items etc. such items are therefore, required to be separated from other normal items so as to reflect the correct gross profit percentage.

It is quite possible that there may be some poor-selling goods included in the stock. These goods are generally valued at below cost and, in effect, gross profit is reduced. To determine the normal rate of gross profit, the stock and sales proceeds of these goods are to be eliminated from the total sales and stock. In this case, Trading Account is prepared in columnar form to show separately normal and abnormal items. The following example will clarify the concept well.

### EXAMPLE

On 1st October, 2015, the godown of Charminar Co., Churchgate was destroyed by fire. The record of the company revealed the following :

| | ₹ |
|---|---|
| Stock on 1st April, 2014 | 9,50,000 |
| Stock on 31st March, 2015 | 8,00,000 |
| Purchases for the year ended 31st March, 2015 | 31,00,000 |
| Sales for the year ended 31st March, 2015 | 40,00,000 |
| Purchases from 1st April, 2015 to the date of fire | 7,50,000 |
| Sales from 1st April, 2015 to the date of fire | 10,00,000 |

While valuing stock on 31st March, 2016, a sum of ₹ 10,000 was written-off on the goods, cost of which was ₹ 48,000. A part of this Stock was sold in June, 2015 at a loss of ₹ 4,000 on the original cost of ₹ 24,000. The remainder of this Stock was now estimated to be worth the original cost. Subject to the above exception, gross profit remained at a uniform rate throughout. Stock salvaged was ₹ 40,000. The godown was fully insured.

Calculate the amount of the insurance claim for the loss.

### ANSWER

**In the Books of Charminar Co., Churchgate**

Dr.         **Trading Account for the year ended 31st March, 2015**

| Particulars | ₹ | Particulars | ₹ |
|---|---|---|---|
| To Opening Stock | 9,50,000 | By Sales | 40,00,000 |
| To Purchases | 31,00,000 | By Closing Stock | 7,62,000 |
| To Gross Profit* C/D | 7,60,000 | (Normal Items only) | |
| (Balancing Figure) | | (₹ 8,00,000 – ₹ 38,000) | |
| | | By Abnormal Items (Cost) | 48,000 |
| | 48,10,000 | | 48,10,000 |

**Working Notes :**

1) **Calculation of Gross Profit Rate :**

If ₹ 40,00,000 Sales = ₹ 7,60,000 Gross Profit

∴            100 = ?

$$= \frac{100 \times ₹\,7,60,000}{₹\,40,00,000}$$

= 19%

**Dr.**    **Memorandum Trading Account for the period 1st April, 2015 to 1st October, 2015**    **Cr.**

| Particulars | Normal Items ₹ | Abnormal Items ₹ | Total ₹ | Particulars | Normal Items ₹ | Abnormal Items ₹ | Total ₹ |
|---|---|---|---|---|---|---|---|
| To Opening Stock | 7,62,000 | 48,000 | 8,10,000 | By Sales | 9,80,000 | 20,000 | 10,00,000 |
| To Purchases | 7,50,000 | – | 7,50,000 | By Loss | – | 4,000 | 4,000 |
| To Gross Profit C/D | 1,86,200 | – | 1,86,200 | By Closing Stock | 7,18,200 | 24,000 | 7,42,200 |
| (19% of ₹ 9,80,000) | | | | (Balancing Figure) | | | |
| | **16,98,200** | **48,000** | **17,46,200** | | **16,98,200** | **48,000** | **17,46,200** |

**Statement showing Claim for Loss of Stock as on 1st October, 2015**

| Particulars | | ₹ |
|---|---|---|
| | Book Value of Stock on the date of fire | 7,42,200 |
| **Less :** | Salvaged Stock | (–) 40,000 |
| ∴ | **Loss of Stock** | **7,02,200** |

## B) Claim for Loss of Profit

### Introduction

When a fire occurs, it not only destroys its assets but also dislocates the normal working conditions for sometime. The business is disorganised for a certain period of time and the normal business cannot be achieved. During this period of dislocation, the sales are comparatively less than what they are supposed to be under normal working conditions.

Besides insuring against loss of stocks or assets, businesses often take out **loss of profit insurance or consequential loss of profit insurance** to cover them against loss of profits if a fire (or other perils) interrupts their business. This insurance is designed to provide for indemnification of the insured for losses ensuing from the interruption, wholly or in part, of the normal business activities consequent upon a fire or other perils. Therefore, a loss of profit insurance is an insured protection against loss of gross profit, insuring from interruption of or interference as a result of destruction of or damage to any building or any other property of the insured premise by fire.

When sales are reduced; the corresponding profits are also reduced. Therefore, reduction of sales during the dislocation period leads to loss of profit on those reduced sales during that period. Hence, an insurance policy is taken out to cover the loss of profit on the reduced sales during the period of dislocation.

While a **fire policy** covers loss of or damage to insured property, a **loss of profit policy** covers loss of gross profit sustained as a consequence of a business interruption.

The term of such policies vary widely, but they are usually framed to meet the requirements of the insured. A business interruption due to destruction of or damage to property by fire is likely to result in :

i) the reduction in turnover during the period of indemnity and

ii) the increased cost of working incurred for the purpose of avoiding or reducing the reduction in turnover.

The claim for loss of profit insurance is granted only when the insured has a valid claim in respect of the property, the loss of/or damage to which results in interruption, being admissible under a corresponding fire policy. Therefore, it is a basic condition that a business unit cannot have a loss of profit insurance policy without the presence of a fire policy covering property damage, giving rise to the loss of profit claim.

**Steps for working out the Claim and application of Average Clause :**

The following steps are to be adopted for arriving at the amount of Claim for Consequential Loss of Profit.

**i)  Calculation of Short Sales :**

The short sales i.e. the reduced sales during the period of indemnity or period of dislocation whichever is less is calculated as follows :  ₹

Sales during the corresponding period of dislocation or indemnity

during the previous year  .............

**Add :**  Expected percentage increase during the current period.  (+) ............

.............

**Deduct :**  The sales during the indemnity period or period of dislocation.  (−) ............

∴  **Short Sales**  .............

**ii)  Calculation of the Gross Profit Percentage :**

The gross profit percentage is found out by applying the following formula :

$$\text{Gross Profit \%} = \frac{\text{Net Profit of the previous year} + \text{Insured Standing charges of the previous year}}{\text{Sales during the previous year}} \times 100$$

**iii)  Claim = Percentage of Gross Profit × Short Sales**

When the actual insurance cover taken is less than Insurance cover required, then there is a case of **Under Insurance**; which attracts the application of **Average Clause**.

**Application of Average Clause :**

$$\text{Claim} = \frac{\text{Actual Insurance taken}}{\text{Insurance cover required}} \times \text{Gross Claim}$$

**Insurance Cover Required** is calculated out as follows :

**Insurance Cover Required** = Gross Profit Rate × Sales (Turnover) for the 12 months ending on the date of fire (adjusted for expected increase if, any).

## INDEMNITY UNDER POLICY

The period for which a policy is taken out is known as **Indemnity Period. Indemnity Period** is the expected period during which the business is likely to be disorganised resulting in lower sales and accordingly covered for insurance. The lesser of the two period i.e. indemnity period or dislocation period would be reckoned for calculation of the claim by the insurance company. The **Period of Indemnity** is the contemplated period of disorganisation for which loss of insurance policy is effected. The length of this period may vary with the nature of the business and required time to obtain new plant and machinery.

## SOME IMPORTANT TERMS

**i)   Indemnity Period :**

The period beginning with the occurrence of the damage and ending not later than 12 months thereafter during which the results of the business shall be affected as consequence of the damage.

**ii)   Rate of Gross Profit :**

The **Rate of Gross Profit** earned on the turnover during the financial year immediately before the date of the damage.

**iii)   Annual Turnover :**

The turnover during the twelve months immediately before the date of the damage.

**iv)   Standard Turnover :**

The turnover during that period in the twelve months immediately before the date of damage which corresponds with the indemnity period to which such adjustments shall be made as may be necessary to provide for the trend of the business and for variations in or special circumstances affecting the business either before or after the damage or which would have affected the business had the damage not occurred, so that the figures thus adjusted shall represent as nearly as which but for the damage would have been obtained during the relative period after the damage.

**v)   Gross Profit :**

For loss of profit insurance purposes Gross Profit is sum produced by the amount of the insured standing charges to the net profit.

If there is net loss, Gross Profit is the amount of insured standing charges less such a proportion of any net trading loss as the amount of the insured standard charges bears to all the standing charges (insured + uninsured) of the business.

**vi)   Net Profit :**

The net trading profit (exclusive of all capital receipts and accretions and all outlay properly chargeable to Capital) resulting from the business of the insured at the premises after due provision has been made for all standing and other charges including depreciation but before the deduction of any taxation chargeable on profits.

**vii)   Insured Standing Charges :**

The insured standing charges are those charges specified in the policy which the insured desires to recover in the case of an accident. It may include the following :

Rent, Rates and Taxes (not related with the profit of the business); Interest on debentures and loans; Salaries of permanent staff; Wages of skilled workers; Directors' fees; Auditors' fees; Advertising; Traveling; and Unspecified standing charges (not exceeding 5% of the amount of specified standing charges), etc.

**viii)   Turnover :**

The money paid or payable to the insured for goods sold and delivered and for services rendered in course of the business at the premises.

**xi) Memo 1 :**

If during the Indemnity Period, goods shall be sold or services shall be rendered elsewhere than at the premises for the benefit of the business either by the insured or by others on his behalf the money paid or payable in respect of such sales or services shall be brought into account arriving at the turnover during the Indemnity Period.

**x) Memo 2 :**

If any standing charges of the business be not insured by this policy, then in computing the amount recoverable hereunder as increase in cost of working that proportion only of the additional expenditure shall be brought into account which the sum of the net profit and the insured standard charges bears to the sum of the net profit and all standing charges.

## PROCEDURE FOR ASCERTAINING CLAIMS

Usually, the following steps are followed to arrive at the amount of a Claim under Loss of Profit Insurance.

 i) Calculate rate of Gross Profit (adjust to provide for the trend of the business, if any).

 ii) Calculate Short Sales. (It is the difference between the Standard Sales (adjusted) and Actual Sales of dislocated period).

 iii) Calculate Gross Profit on Short Sales.

 iv) Calculate the amount of admissible additional expenses as follows :

  The least of the following shall be taken as admissible additional expenses.

  a) Actual expenses incurred

  b) Gross Profit on additional sales

  c) $\text{Additional Expenses} \times \dfrac{\text{Gross Profit on Annual Turnover}}{\text{Gross Profit on Annual Turnover} + \text{Uninsured Standing Charges}}$

  OR

  $\text{Additional Expenses} \times \dfrac{\text{Net Profit} + \text{Insured Standing Charges}}{\text{Net Profit} + \text{All Standing Charges}}$

 v) Deduct from the sum of iii) and iv) any savings in insured standing charges during the period of indemnity.

 vi) Apply Average Clause :

  $\text{Net Claim} = \text{Claim} \times \dfrac{\text{Policy Value}}{\text{Gross Profit on Annual Turnover}}$

The following example will simplify the procedure for ascertaining claims under Loss of Profit Insurance.

## EXAMPLE

A businessman took out a Loss of Profit insurance policy for ₹ 40,000 with an indemnity period of 6 months. The financial year of the business ended on 30th June. Gross Profit for the last financial year was ₹ 50,000 and turnover for that period was ₹ 2,00,000. Turnover for the

12 months immediately preceding the fire was ₹ 2,20,000. A fire occured on 31st March 2016. Turnover for 6 months immediately following the fire, compared with the turnover of corresponding months in the previous year was :

| Year | | April | May | June | July | August | September |
|---|---|---|---|---|---|---|---|
| 2014 | ₹ | 16,000 | 17,000 | 18,000 | 16,000 | 17,000 | 19,000 |
| 2015 | ₹ | – | 6,000 | 9,000 | 14,000 | 16,000 | 18,000 |

₹ 1,000 were spent on putting the fire out. During the indemnity period, increase in the cost of working directly attributable to sales amounted to ₹ 8,050. All standing charges of the business were insured and paid.

From the above particulars, you are required to assess the loss and the amount payable by the insurance company as claim under the Loss of Profit Insurance Policy.

**ANSWER**

**i)** **Gross Profit Ratio :**

$$= \frac{\text{Gross Profit}}{\text{Sales}} \times 100$$

$$= \frac{₹\,50,000}{₹\,2,00,000} \times 100$$

$$= 25\%$$

**ii)** **Short Sales :**

| | Particulars | | ₹ |
|---|---|---|---|
| (a) | Sales from 1.4.2014 to 30.9.2014 | | 1,03,000 |
| **Add :** | 10% increase | (+) | 10,300 |
| | ∴ **Standard Sales** | | **1,13,300** |

| | Particulars | | ₹ |
|---|---|---|---|
| (b) | Standard Sales | | 1,13,300 |
| **Less :** | Actual Sales from April to September, 2015 | (–) | 63,000 |
| | ∴ **Short Sales** | | **50,300** |

**iii)** **Loss of Gross Profit :**

$$= \text{Short Sales} \times \text{Gross Profit}$$

$$= ₹\,50,300 \times 25\%$$

$$= ₹\,12.575$$

**iv)** **Admissible Increased Working Cost :**

Lower of the following :

a) Gross Profit on Additional Sales

$$= 25\% \text{ of } ₹\,63,000$$

$$= ₹\,15,750.$$

b)   Additional Expenses $\times \dfrac{\text{Gross Profit on Annual Turnover (Adjusted)}}{\text{Gross Profit on Annual Turnover (Adjusted)} + \text{Uninsured Standing Charges}}$

$$= ₹\,8,050 \times \frac{₹\,55,000}{₹\,55,000 + \text{Nil}}$$

$$= ₹\,8,050$$

**v)**                            **Statement of Claim**

| Particulars | | ₹ |
|---|---|---|
| Loss of Gross Profit | | 12,575 |
| **Add :**   Admissible insured Working Cost | (+) | 8,050 |
| ∴ **Gross Claim** | | **20,625** |

**vi) Application of Average Clause :**

$$\textbf{Net Claim} \;=\; \text{Gross Claim} \times \frac{\text{Policy Value}}{\text{Gross Profit on Annual Sales}}$$

$$= ₹\,20,625 \times \frac{₹\,40,000}{₹\,55,000}$$

$$= ₹\,15,000$$

**vii) Total Claim :**                         ₹

Amount of Claim under Policy             15,000

**Add :** Expenses for putting off fire         (+) <u>1,000</u>

∴     Claim for Loss of Profit Policy        <u>**16,000**</u>

(Insurance company is liable to pay all expenses for putting off fire. Hence, these expenses are added in total claim).

**Working Notes :**

**i) Calculation of Upward Trend in Turnover :**

Turnover for the 12 months immediately preceding fire was ₹ 2,20,000 and Sales of the previous accounting period were ₹ 2,00,000. Hence, increase in Sales amounted to ₹ 20,000.

Therefore, % of increase

$$= \frac{₹\,20,000}{₹\,2,00,000} \times 100$$

$$= \quad 10\%$$

**Journal Entries in the Books of the Insured**

**1) When expenses are paid for repairs, fire brigade charges, etc. :**

| | |
|---|---|
| Repairs to Plant A/c | Dr. [Actual Amount] |
| Repairs to Factory A/c | Dr. [Actual Amount] |
| Fire Brigade Charges A/c | Dr. [Actual Amount] |
|      To Bank A/c | |

**2)  When Stock is damaged or destroyed :**

Stock Destroyed A/c                          Dr. [Actual Loss]

Stock Damaged A/c                           Dr. [Actual Loss]

    To Trading A/c

**3)  When claims are admitted by the Insurance Company for Stock, Assets, Expenses, etc. :**

Insurance Company A/c                        Dr. [Total amount of claim admitted]

    To Stock Destroyed A/c

    To Stock Damaged A/c

    To Fire Brigade Charges A/c

    To Repairs to Plant A/c

    To Repairs to Factory A/c

    To Assets A/c

**4)  When Actual Cash is received from Insurance Company :**

Bank A/c                                     Dr.

    To Insurance Company A/c

**5)  If the actual loss or expenses are more than the amount admitted by the Insurance Company, the difference (unadmitted amount) is transferred to Profit and Loss Account :**

Profit and Loss A/c                          Dr. [Total unadmitted amount]

    To Stock Destroyed A/c

    To Stock Damaged A/c                      (Unadmitted amount)

    To Repairs to Plant A/c

    To Assets A/c

**6)  When the amount of admitted is more than the written-down value of the assets :**

Assets A/c                                   Dr.

    To General Reserve A/c

**7)  When the amount admitted is more than the original cost, the difference between original cost and the amount admitted is transferred to Capital Reserve and the difference between written-down value and original cost is transferred to General Reserve.**

## C)  CLAIM FOR LOSS OF FIXED ASSETS

**Introduction :**

A business may suffer abnormal losses due to different causes such as fire, theft, burglary, strike etc. Among them the most common which destroys or causes several damage to the assets like stock, building, plant, machinery, furniture and fixtures etc. is fire. When a fire takes place, the business naturally incurs heavy losses. To cover the risk of losses from such events, a business may take on insurance policy with an insurance company.

When a fixed asset is destroyed, the computation of loss is simple. The value of such assets on the date of fire can be ascertained from the books of accounts of the business because most of them usually maintain proper records of fixed assets. Normally, fixed assets are recorded in the books of accounts at their acquisition cost, which becomes the basis for calculation for the loss of fixed assets.

**Important Terms:**

**(i) Consumption of Fixed Capital (CFC) :** Consumption of Fixed Capital (CFC) is the term used in business accounts, tax assessments, income claims and national accounts for depreciation of fixed assets. CFC is used in preference to "depreciation" to emphasise that fixed capital is used up in the process of generating new output and because unlike depreciation is not valued at historical cost but a current market value. CFC may also include other expenses incurred using or utilising or installing fixed assets beyond actual depreciation charges.

Consumption fixed capital is declined during the course of the accounting period, the current value of the stock of fixed assets owned and used by a producer as a result of physical deterioration, normal obsolescence or normal accidental damage.

**(ii) Tangible Fixed Assets :** These include things such as land, buildings, equipments, leasehold on equipments, vehicles, signs and furniture and fixtures.

**(iii) Intangible Assets :** These can include goodwill, patents, registered or trademarks names and even telephone numbers, intellectual property and websites if you ever plan on selling your business.

**(iv) "Partial Losses":** Fires that damage but do not completely destroy a building create special insurance claim issues. These claims are often called **"Partial Losses"** because the building has only been partially destroyed. Things to watch our for with partial losses include :

- Hidden damage (water, smoke, ash, mold, air quality, dusts).
- Inadequate or improper cleaning and repairing methods.
- Delays : Particular after disasters, partial losses can be low priority for overworked insurance adjusters.
- Disputes over "matching" and line of sight: Repairs should return your property to a "uniform and consistent appearance" even if that means replacing undamaged items such as roof tiles or carpeting.

[In any property loss situation, there are basic steps to follow to make the insurance, recovery process go more smoothly. Document everything that was damaged or destroyed, file a timely claim, learn and asset your rights to full and fair payment and get help if and when you need it.

**(v) Value as New :** The base of insurance value of the asset, based on acquisition/ production costs. This value can be indexed annually to give current insurance value. It can also incorporate the indexed value of transactions that affect the asset value.

**(vi) Market Value :** The current market value of the asset. Assets automatically calculated current value from net book value of the asset, incorporating indexing factors and the indexed value of any transactions that affect the asset value.

**(vii) Manual Value :** You can manually enter an insurance value for an asset, usually in agreement with the insurance company. With this calculation method you can also manually enter updates to the asset insurance values.

**Procedure for ascertaining claims :**

The financial report standard codifies much of existing accounting practice.

Its objective is to ensure that tangible fixed assets are accounted for on a consistent basis and where a policy of revaluation is adopted, that revaluations are kept up-to-date.

Whether acquired or self constructed, a tangible fixed asset should initially be measured at its cost. Only 'costs' that are directly attributable to bringing the asset into working condition for its intended use should be included. Such costs should be capitalised only for the period in which the activities that are necessary to get the asset ready for use are in progress.

The capitalisation of finance costs, including interest is optional. However, if an entity adopts such a policy then it should be applied consistently. All finance costs that are directly attributable to the construction of a tangible fixed asset should be capitalised as part of the cost of that asset, subject to the proviso that the total amount of finance costs capitalised during a period should not exceed the amount of finance costs incurred during the period.

If the amount recognised when a tangible fixed asset is acquired or constructed exceeds its recoverable amount, it should be written down to recoverable amount. Subsequent expenditure undertaken to ensure that the asset maintains its previously assessed standard of performance. For example, routine repairs and maintenance expenditure, should be recognized in the profit and loss account as it is incurred.

**Valuation :**

An 'entity' has the option of revaluating its tangible fixed assets. However, where such a policy is adopted it should be applied consistently to all tangible fixed assets of the same class.

Where a tangible fixed asset is revalued its carrying amount should be its current value at the balance sheet.

Where a tangible fixed asset are revalued the following valuation bases for unimpaired assets should be used :

- **Non-specified properties :** Existing use value, with additional of notional directly attributable acquisition costs where material.

- **Specialised properties :** Depreciated replacement cost.

- **Properties surplus to an entity's requirement :** Open market value after deducting expected directly attributable selling costs, where material.

- **Tangible fixed assets other than properties :** Market value or depreciated replacement cost where market value is not available.

In general, it seems that assets should be written off at a loss and the cost of replacement assets written up as again. Reimbursed expenses would be wash. Business interruption/loss of income would be a gain.

**Accounting treatment : Insurance claim : Loss of fixed assets (Different Issues)**

**(i) If insurance claim for replacement value received is excess of book value**

Plant and Machinery lost in fire          – Insured for replacement value. Insurance

claim received in for replacement value is excess of written down value.

We have to break down this incident as two separate events (a) Lost of asset and (b) Insurance claim and receipt of cash, these two events should be recorded separately also.

The entry for the claim recovered from the fire insurance depend on the exact assets that were destroyed in the fire and what extent the insurance company were covered.

For example : A storeroom and its contents valued ₹ 1,20,000 were destroyed by fire, the insurance company pays ₹ 1,20,000.

In this case the entry would be :

| | | |
|---|---|---|
| Insurance Co. A/c | Dr. ₹ 1,20,000 | |
|  To Storeroom (Assets) A/c | | ₹ 1,20,000 |

Later:

| | | |
|---|---|---|
| Bank A/c | Dr. 1,20,000 | |
|  To Insurance Co. A/c | | ₹ 1,20,000 |

If insurance company agreed amount of claim was ₹ 1,00,000 instead of ₹ 1,20,000.

The journal entry will be :

| | | |
|---|---|---|
| Insurance Co. A/c | Dr. ₹ 1,00,000 | |
| Loss A/c | Dr. ₹ 20,000 | |
|  To Storeroom (Assets) A/c | | ₹ 1,20,000 |

If insurance company agreed amount of claim was ₹ 1,40,000 instead of ₹ 1,20,000 (Excess Book Value)

The journal will be :

| | | |
|---|---|---|
| Insurance Co. A/c | Dr. ₹ 1,40,000 | |
|  To Storeroom (Assets) A/c | | ₹ 1,20,000 |
|  To Profit A/c | | ₹ 20,000 |

Later :

| | | |
|---|---|---|
| Bank A/c | Dr. ₹ 1,40,000 | |
|  To Insurance Co. A/c | | ₹ 1,40,000 |

**(ii) Pending Insurance Claim :**

If asset loss on any date of the financial year and the claim could not be settled at the end of the financial year then the effect of particular asset should be included as normal asset or under the head of "fixed asset under insurance claim" and the final adjustments entry should be passed in the year in which the claim settled.

**(iii) Entry for difference in loss by fire and partial insurance claim received :**

If a company bear losses of assets by fire ₹ 5,00,000 but company received ₹ 3,00,000 only for assets. The relative entries in Profit and Loss Account and Balance Sheet of the company in the year when loss is incurred and supposing the insurance claim is received in the next financial year.

If during the first financial year partially, we expect to receive the insurance claim for ₹ 1,80,000 we can record a receivable amount in first financial year as under :

| | |
|---|---|
| Insurance Receivable A/c | Dr. 1,80,000 |
| Loss of Assets A/c | Dr. 3,20,000 |
|    To Assets | 5,00,000 |

Next Year :

| | |
|---|---|
| Bank A/c | Dr. 1,80,000 |
|    To Insurance Receivable A/c | 1,80,000 |

If we are not sure in that first year is if we were going to received any insurance then we would record the full loss in that year. And the next year we would record it as an income.

| | |
|---|---|
| Loss of Assets A/c | Dr. 2,00,000 |
|    To Assets A/c | 2,00,000 |

Next year :

| | |
|---|---|
| Bank A/c | Dr. 1,80,000 |
|    To Insurance Claim Received (Income) | 1,80,000 |

The accounting entries to be passed in the books of the insured in respect of fire claim for the loss of fixed assets will be as follows :

1. For the claim amount admitted by Insurance Company

   Insurance Company A/c          Dr.

      To Concerned Asset A/c

   (With the amount of claim admitted)

2. For the claim amount received from insurance company

   Bank or Cash A/c          Dr.

      To Insurance Company A/c

   (With the amount of claim received)

3. For transfer of Profit on any fixed assets :

   Concerned Asset A/c          Dr.

      To Profit and Loss A/c

   (With the amount of profit on any fixed assets)

4. For transfer of loss on any fixed assets :

   Profit and Loss A/c or Capital Reserve A/c Dr.

      To Concerned Assets A/c

   (With the amount of loss, if any).

**Illustration :** The Nashik Factory Ltd. fully insured their factory which was damaged by fire on 31st March, 2016. The Management asks you to file insurance claim for the damaged from the following particular available from the Balance Sheet as on 30th November, 2015.

Stock ₹ 3,64,956  Machinery ₹ 1,85,820

Building ₹ 1,38,420  Furniture ₹ 8,400

Transaction from 1st December, 2015 to 31st March 2016 were

Purchases ₹ 5,88,276   Sales 3,38,829

Wages ₹ 1,49,538

Salvage received were :

Building ₹ 6,000
Machinery ₹ 9,000
Furniture ₹ 1,500

The average profit percentage is 23% of sales.

Draw up a statement of claim.

**Solution :**

### Memorandum Trading Account
### for the period from 1.12.2015 to 31.03.2016

| Particulars | ₹ | Particulars | ₹ |
|---|---|---|---|
| To Opening Stock (30.11.2014) | 3,64,956 | By Sales | 3,38,829 |
| To Purchases | 5,88,276 | By Closing Stock | 8,41,872 |
| To Wages | 1,49,538 | (Balancing Figure) | |
| To Gross Profit | 77,931 | | |
| (23% of 3,38,829) | | | |
| | 11,80,701 | | 11,80,701 |

### Statement of Fire Claim

| | ₹ | ₹ |
|---|---|---|
| **In respect of stock :** (Value on the date of fire) | 8,41,872 | |
| **Less :** Stock of salvage | Nil | 8,41,872 |
| **In respect of Building :** (Value of the date of fire) | 1,38,420 | |
| **Less :** Value of Building salvaged | 6,000 | 1,32,420 |
| **In respect of Machinery** (Value on the date of fire) | 1,85,820 | |
| **Less :** Value of Machinery Salvaged | 9,000 | 1,76,820 |
| **In respect of Furniture :** (Value on the date of fire) | 8,400 | |
| **Less :** Value of furniture salvaged | 1,500 | 6,900 |
| **Total Amount of Fire Claim** | | 11,58,012 |

### SUMMARY

A businessman needs insurance especially in regard to the following :

a) To cover loss of stock destroyed by fire.

b) To cover loss of profit during the period of disruption of normal business operations.

**(A) Loss of Stock Policy :**

There are two situations in which claims can be lodged.

a)    When proper records are available and the information of stock lying with the business on the date of fire is known.

b)    When proper records are not available and there is difficulty in ascertaining the value of stock on the date of fire.

### a)    When records are available :

When proper records are available, the following would be the steps for lodging claim with the insurance company.

i)    Ascertain the value of stock lying with the business concern on the date of fire.

ii)    Ascertain the value of stock salvaged from fire.

iii)    Find out the stock destroyed by fire by deducting the stock salvaged from the stock value on the date of fire i.e. i) and ii) as stated above, would give the figure of stock destroyed by fire.

iv)    The amount of claim would be equal to the stock destroyed by fire. (provided there is no under insurance and application of average clause).

### b)    When proper records are not available, the following procedure is followed to ascertain the value of stock on the date of fire :

**i)    Find out the percentage of Gross Profit for the previous year or the average of Gross Profit for the previous years.**

This is done by preparing the Trading Account of the previous year which gives the figure of Gross Profit.

**ii)    The second stage consists of the following steps :**

*    Prepare Memorandum Trading Account for the period from the opening date of the year (Closing date of previous year) to the date of fire.

*    The figure of Gross Profit is ascertained by applying the Gross Profit percentage of the previous year as ascertained above to the sales for the current period.

*    Having obtained the figure of Gross Profit, the Trading Account is balanced and the balancing figure would represent the figure of Stock lying with the business concern on the date of fire.

**iii)    The amount of claim now is equal to the value of stock lying on the date of fire minus the stock salvaged if any, (provided there is no under insurance and application of average clause).**

### Existence of Abnormal items of Purchases and Sales :

Abnormal items means items which do not carry the normal price tag due to the reasons that they are defective or of poor quality, or slow moving items etc. Such items are therefore  required to be separated from other normal items so as to reflect the correct gross profit percentage.

### Average Clause :

Average Clause applies in case of under insurance. Average clause means that the claim for the loss of stock is proportionately reduced having regard to the under insurance of stock. This is done by applying the following formula :

$$\text{Claim} = \frac{\text{Value of Insurance Policy}}{\text{Value of the stock on the date of fire}} \times \text{Loss of Stock}$$

### (B)    Loss of Profit Policy :

When a fire occurs, it not only destroys its assets but also dislocates the normal working conditions for sometime. When sales are reduced; the corresponding profits are also reduced. Hence, an insurance policy is taken out to cover the loss of profit on the reduced sales during the period of dislocation.

**Indemnity period :**

The period for which the policy is taken out is known as indemnity period. Indemnity period is the expected period during which the business is likely to be disorganised resulting in lower sales and accordingly covered for insurance. The lesser of the two periods i.e. indemnity period or dislocation period would be reckoned for calculation of the claim by the insurance company.

**Steps for working out the claim and application of average clause :**

The following steps are to be adopted for arriving at the amount of claim for consequential loss of profit insurance policy.

    i)    **Calculation of Short Sales.**

    ii)    **Calculation of the Gross Profit percentage.**

The Gross Profit percentage is found out by applying the following formula :

$$\text{Gross Profit \%} = \frac{\text{Net Profit of the previous year} + \begin{array}{c}\text{Insured Standing charges}\\ \text{of the previous year}\end{array}}{\text{Sales during the previous year}} \times 100$$

    iii)   **Claim = The percentage of Gross Profit × Short Sales in i) above**

When the actual insurance cover taken is less than the Insurance cover required, then there is a case of under insurance; which attracts the application of average clause.

**Application of Average Clause :**

$$\text{Claim} = \frac{\text{Actual Insurance taken}}{\text{Insurance cover required}} \times \text{Gross Claim}$$

Insurance cover required is worked out as follows :

Insurance cover required = Gross Profit Rate × Sales (turnover) for the 12 months ending on the date of fire (adjusted for expected increase, if any).

## 3.2 ILLUSTRATIONS

### (A) * LOSS OF STOCK POLICY *

**ILLUSTRATION 1**

A fire broke out in the premises of Maharaja Co. Malegaon on 1st July 2016 and Stock of the value of ₹ 1,57,500 was salvaged and the books and records were saved.

| The following information was obtained : | ₹ |
|---|---|
| Stock on 31st March 2015 | 4,20,000 |
| Stock on 31st March 2016 | 4,20,000 |
| Sales from 1st April to 30th June 2016 | 5,10,000 |
| Purchases from 1st April to 30th June 2016 | 3,15,000 |
| Sales for the year ended 31st March 2016 | 15,00,000 |
| Purchases for the year ended 31st March 2016 | 9,00,000 |

Calculate the amount of claim to be submitted to the Insurance Company in respect of the Loss of Stock.

SOLUTION

**In the books of Maharaja Co., Malegaon**

Dr.  **Trading Account for the year ended 31-3-2015**  Cr.

| Particulars | ₹ | Particulars | ₹ |
|---|---|---|---|
| To Opening Stock (1-4-2014) | 4,20,000 | By Sales | 15,00,000 |
| To Purchases | 9,00,000 | By Closing Stock (31-3-2015) | 4,20,000 |
| To Gross Profit C/D * | 6,00,000 | | |
| (Balancing figure) | | | |
| | 19,20,000 | | 19,20,000 |

**Calculation of Rate of Gross Profit on Sales :**

$$= \frac{\text{Gross Profit}}{\text{Sales}} \times 100$$

$$= \frac{₹\,6,00,000}{₹\,15,00,000} \times 100$$

$$= 40\%$$

Dr. **Memorandum Trading Account for the period 1-4-2015 to 1-7-2015 i.e. to the date of fire** Cr.

| Particulars | ₹ | Particulars | ₹ |
|---|---|---|---|
| To Opening Stock (1-4-2015) | 4,20,000 | By Sales | 5,10,000 |
| To Purchases | 3,15,000 | By Stock * | 4,29,000 |
| To Gross Profit C/D | 2,04,000 | (Balancing figure i.e. Value of | |
| (40% on Sales i.e. ₹ 5,10,000) | | Stock on the date of fire) | |
| | 9,39,000 | | 9,39,000 |

**1) Ascertainment of value of stock destroyed by fire :**

| | | ₹ |
|---|---|---|
| | Value of Stock on the date of fire | 4,29,000 |
| **Less :** | Value of Stock Salvaged | (–) 1,57,500 |
| | ∴ Value of stock destroyed by fire | **2,71,500** |

Hence, insurance claim will be equal to ₹ 2,71,500 in the absence of any average clause.

∴ Amount of Claim = ₹ 2,71,500.

ILLUSTRATION 2

A fire occurred in the business premises of Mumbai Traders, Mumbai on 15-10-2015. From the following particulars, ascertain the loss of stock and prepare a claim for insurance.

| | ₹ |
|---|---|
| Stock on 1-1-2014 | 34,000 |
| Purchases from 1-1-2014 to 31-12-2014 | 1,22,000 |
| Sales from 1-1-2014 to 31-12-2014 | 1,80,000 |
| Stock on 31-12-2014 | 30,000 |
| Purchases from 1-1-2015 to 14-10-2015 | 1,47,000 |
| Sales from 1-1-2015 to 14-10-2015 | 1,50,000 |

The stock salvaged was worth ₹ 18,000. The amount of policy was ₹ 63,000. There was an average clause in the policy.

**SOLUTION**

**In the books of Mumbai Traders, Mumbai**

**Dr.**         **Trading Account for the year ended 31-12-2014**         **Cr.**

| Particulars | ₹ | Particulars | ₹ |
|---|---|---|---|
| To Opening Stock (1-1-2014) | 34,000 | By Sales | 1,80,000 |
| To Purchases | 1,22,000 | By Closing Stock (31-12-2014) | 30,000 |
| To Gross Profit C/D * | 54,000 | | |
| (Balancing Figure) | | | |
| | **2,10,000** | | **2,10,000** |

*** Calculation of Rate of Gross Profit on Sales :**

$$= \frac{\text{Gross Profit}}{\text{Sales}} \times 100$$

$$= \frac{₹\,54,000}{₹\,1,80,000} \times 100$$

$$= 30\%$$

**Dr.**     **Memorandum Trading Account for the period 1-1-2015 to 15-10-2015**     **Cr.**

| Particulars | ₹ | Particulars | ₹ |
|---|---|---|---|
| To Opening Stock (1-1-2014) | 30,000 | By Sales | 1,50,000 |
| To Purchases | 1,47,000 | By Stock* | 72,000 |
| To Gross Profit C/D * | 45,000 | (Balancing Figure i.e. Value of | |
| (30% on Sales i.e. ₹ 1,50,000) | | Stock on the date of fire) | |
| | **2,22,000** | | **2,22,000** |

1. **Ascertainment of value of stock destroyed by fire :**

|  |  | ₹ |
|---|---|---|
| | Value of Stock on the date of fire | 72,000 |
| **Less :** | Stock Salvaged | (–) 18,000 |
| | ∴ Value of Stock destroyed by fire | **54,000** |

2. **Application of the Average Clause :**

$$\text{Claim} = \frac{\text{Value of Insurance Policy}}{\text{Value of Stock on the date of fire}} \times \text{Loss of Stock}$$

$$= \frac{₹\,63,000}{₹\,72,000} \times ₹\,54,000$$

$$= ₹\,47,250$$

(*** N.B. :** Insurance cover required should be equal to the value of stock on the date of fire).

∴ Amount of Claim = ₹ 47,250.

**ILLUSTRATION 3**

There was a fire in the business premises of Baroda Traders, Baroda on 15-10-2015. From the following particulars, ascertain the loss of stock and prepare a claim for insurance.

|  | ₹ |
|---|---|
| Stock on 1-1-2014 | 15,300 |
| Purchases from 1-1-2014 to 31-12-2014 | 61,000 |
| Sales from 1-1-2014 to 31-12-2014 | 90,000 |
| Stock on 31-12-2014 | 13,500 |
| Purchases from 1-1-2015 to 14-10-2015 | 73,500 |
| Sales from 1-1-2015 to 14-10-2015 | 75,000 |

The stocks were always valued at 90% of the cost. The stock saved was worth ₹ 9,000. The amount of the policy was ₹ 31,500. There was an average clause in the policy.

**SOLUTION**

**Valuation of Stock :**

Since stocks are valued at 90% of cost, their cost price is calculated as under :

$$\begin{matrix} \text{Cost} \\ \text{Price} \end{matrix} \ (-) \ \begin{matrix} \text{Valuation at 10\%} \\ \text{below Cost} \end{matrix} = \begin{matrix} \text{Under Valued} \\ \text{Cost} \end{matrix}$$

$$100 \quad\quad 10 \quad\quad = \quad 90$$

**i) Stock on 1-1-2014 :**

$$\text{If } 90 = ₹\ 15,300$$
$$\therefore \ 100 = ?$$
$$= \frac{100 \times ₹\ 15,300}{90}$$
$$= ₹\ 17,000$$

**ii) Stock on 31-12-2014 :**

$$\text{If } 90 = 13,500$$
$$\therefore \ 100 = ?$$
$$= \frac{100 \times 13,500}{90}$$
$$= ₹\ 15,000$$

**In the books of Baroda Traders, Baroda**

**Dr.**       **Trading Account for the year ended 31-12-2014**       **Cr.**

| Particulars | ₹ | Particulars | ₹ |
|---|---|---|---|
| To Opening Stock | 17,000 | By Sales | 90,000 |
| To Purchases | 61,000 | By Closing Stock | 15,000 |
| To Gross Profit C/D * | 27,000 | | |
| (Balancing Figure) | | | |
| | **1,05,000** | | **1,05,000** |

**Calculation of Rate of Gross Profit on Sales :**

$$= \frac{\text{Gross Profit}}{\text{Sales}} \times 100$$

$$= \frac{₹\ 27,000}{₹\ 90,000} \times 100$$

$$= 30\%$$

**Dr.**       **Memorandum Trading Account for the period**       **Cr.**

**1-1-2015 to 15-10-2015 i.e. to the date of fire**

| Particulars | ₹ | Particulars | ₹ |
|---|---|---|---|
| To Opening Stock | 15,000 | By Sales | 75,000 |
| To Purchases | 73,500 | By Stock* | 36,000 |
| To Gross Profit C/D | 22,500 | (Balancing figure i.e. value of | |
| (30% on Sales i.e. ₹ 75,000) | | stock on the date of fire) | |
| | **1,11,000** | | **1,11,000** |

**1. Ascertainment of value of stock destroyed by fire :**

|  | ₹ |
|---|---|
| Value of Stock on the date of fire | 36,000 |
| **Less :** Stock Salvaged | (−) 9,000 |
| Value of Stock destroyed by fire | **27,000** |

2. **Application of the Average Clause :**

$$\text{Claim} = \frac{\text{Value of Insurance Policy}}{\text{Value of Stock on the date of fire}} \times \text{Loss of Stock}$$

$$= \frac{₹\,31,500}{₹\,36,000} \times ₹\,27,000$$

$$= ₹\,23,625$$

(Insurance cover required should be equal to the value of stock on the date of fire).

∴    Amount of Claim = ₹ 23,625.

---

**ILLUSTRATION 4**

There was a fire in the godown of Atlas Trading Co., Ahmedabad on 31st December, 2015 but the accounting records and subsidiary books were saved. The following accounting information was made available.

|  | ₹ |
|---|---|
| Stock on 1st July, 2014 | 44,000 |
| Purchases for the year ended 30th June, 2015 | 51,800 |
| Returns Outward for the year 2014-15 | 800 |
| Carriage Inward for the year 2014-15 | 9,000 |
| Sales for the year ended 30th June, 2015 | 90,700 |
| Returns Inward for the year 2014-15 | 700 |
| Stock on 30th June, 2015 | 30,800 |
| Purchases from 1st July, 2015 to 31st December, 2015 | 32,400 |
| Returns to suppliers from 1st July, 2015 to 31st December, 2015 | 400 |
| Carriage Inward for the period 1st July, 2015 to 31st December, 2015 | 4,000 |
| Sales from 1st July, 2015 to 31st December, 2015 | 50,800 |
| Returns from Customers from 1st July, 2015 to 31st December, 2015 | 800 |

There was a practice in the firm to value stock at 10% above cost. Stock worth ₹ 4,000 was saved. The amount of the policy was ₹ 21,000 incorporating an average clause in the policy.

Calculate the insurance claim to be lodged with the insurance company for loss of stock by fire.

---

**SOLUTION**

Since stocks are valued at 10% above cost, their cost price is calculated as under :

| Cost Price | (+) | Valuation at 10% above cost | = | Overvalued Cost |
|---|---|---|---|---|
| 100 | | 10 | | 110 |

i)  **Stock on 1st July, 2014 :**

    If 110  =  ₹ 44,000

    ∴ 100  =  ?

$$= \frac{100 \times ₹\,44,000}{110}$$

    =  ₹ 40,000

ii)  **Stock on 30th June, 2015 :**

    If 110  =  ₹ 30,800

    ∴ 100  =  ?

$$= \frac{₹\,30,800 \times 100}{110}$$

    =  ₹ 28,000

**In the books of Atlas Trading Co., Ahmedabad**

Dr.      **Trading Account for the year ended 30th June, 2015**      Cr.

| Particulars | ₹ | ₹ | Particulars | ₹ | ₹ |
|---|---|---|---|---|---|
| To Opening Stock | | 40,000 | By Sales | 90,700 | 90,000 |
| To Purchases | 51,800 | 51,000 | **Less :** Returns Inward  (–) | 700 | |
| **Less :** Returns Outwards(–) | 800 | | By Closing Stock | | 28,000 |
| To Carriage Inward | | 9,000 | | | |
| To Gross Profit C/D* | | 18,000 | | | |
| (Balancing Figure) | | | | | |
| | | 1,18,000 | | | 1,18,000 |

**Calculation of Rate of Gross Profit on Sales :**

$$= \frac{\text{Gross Profit}}{\text{Sales}} \times 100$$

$$= \frac{₹\ 18,000}{₹\ 90,000} \times 100$$

$$= ₹\ 20\%$$

Dr.      **Memorandum Trading Account for the period 1-7-2015 to 31-12-2015**      Cr.

| Particulars | ₹ | ₹ | Particulars | ₹ | ₹ |
|---|---|---|---|---|---|
| To Opening Stock | | 28,000 | By Sales | 50,800 | 50,000 |
| To Purchases | 32,400 | 32,000 | **Less :** Returns Inward  (–) | 800 | |
| **Less :** Returns Outwards(–) | 400 | | By Stock* | | 24,000 |
| To Carriage Inward | | 4,000 | (Balancing Figure i.e. | | |
| To Gross Profit C/D* | | 10,000 | Value of Stock on the date | | |
| (20% on Sales | | | of fire) | | |
| i.e. ₹ 50,000) | | | | | |
| | | 74,000 | | | 74,000 |

**1)   Ascertainment of value of Stock destroyed by fire :**

| | ₹ |
|---|---|
| Value of Stock on the date of fire | 24,000 |
| **Less :**   Stock saved | (–) 4,000 |
| ∴   Value of Stock destroyed by fire | 20,000 |

**2)   Application of Average Clause :**

$$\text{Claim} = \frac{\text{Value of Insurance Policy}}{\text{Value of Stock on the date of fire}} \times \text{Loss of Stock}$$

$$= \frac{₹\ 21,000}{₹\ 24,000} \times ₹\ 20,000$$

$$= ₹\ 17,500.$$

∴     Amount of Claim = ₹ 17,500.

---

**ILLUSTRATION 5**

Comet Stationers, Chalisgaon closed their books every year on 31st March. On 30th April, 2015 their premises and stock were destroyed by fire. From books of account and other records, the following information is obtained. Every year the stock on hand is valued at 10% less than the cost.

| Particulars | 2013-14 ₹ | 2014-15 ₹ | 2015-16 ₹ | 1-4-2016 to 30-4-2016 |
|---|---|---|---|---|
| Opening Stock | 2,70,900 | 3,24,000 | 3,60,000 | 3,69,000 |
| Purchases **Less** Returns | 7,49,000 | 8,00,000 | 8,10,000 | 60,000 |
| Sales **Less** Returns | 12,00,000 | 13,20,000 | 14,00,000 | 1,20,000 |
| Wages | 2,10,000 | 2,30,000 | 2,50,000 | 20,000 |
| Closing Stock | 3,24,000 | 3,60,000 | 3,69,000 | – |

They have taken fire insurance policy of ₹ 3,50,000 and there is an average clause in the policy. The salvaged goods amounted to ₹ 10,000.

Find out the amount of claim to be submitted to the Insurance Company.

### SOLUTION

**Valuation of Stock :**

Since stocks are valued at 10% less than the cost, their cost price is calculated as under :

$$\dfrac{\text{Cost Price}}{100} \;(-)\; \dfrac{\text{Valuation at 10\% less than the cost}}{10} \;=\; \dfrac{\text{Under Valued Cost}}{90}$$

**1) Opening Stock 2013-14 :**

$$\text{If } 90 = 2,70,900$$
$$\therefore 100 = ?$$
$$= \dfrac{₹\, 2,70,900 \times 100}{90}$$
$$= ₹\, 3,01,000$$

**2) Opening Stock 2013-14 :**

$$\text{If } 90 = ₹\, 3,24,000$$
$$\therefore 100 = ?$$
$$= \dfrac{100 \times ₹\, 3,24,000}{90}$$
$$= ₹\, 3,60,000$$

**3) Opening Stock 2014-15 :**

$$\text{If } 90 = ₹\, 3,60,000$$
$$\therefore 100 = ?$$
$$= \dfrac{₹\, 100 \times ₹\, 3,60,000}{90}$$
$$= ₹\, 4,00,000$$

**4) Opening Stock 2015-16 :**

$$\text{If } 90 = ₹\, 3,69,000$$
$$\therefore 100 = ?$$
$$= \dfrac{100 \times ₹\, 3,69,000}{90}$$
$$= ₹,\, 4,10,000$$

### In the books of Comet Stationers, Chalisgaon

**Dr.**      Trading Account for the year 2013-14, 2014-15 and 2015-16      **Cr.**

| Particulars | 2013-14 ₹ | 2014-15 ₹ | 2015-16 ₹ | Particulars | 2013-14 ₹ | 2014-15 ₹ | 2015-16 ₹ |
|---|---|---|---|---|---|---|---|
| To Opening Stock | 3,01,000 | 3,60,000 | 4,00,000 | By Sales | 12,00,000 | 13,20,000 | 14,00,000 |
| | | | | **Less :** Returns | | | |
| To Purchase | 7,49,000 | 8,00,000 | 8,10,000 | By Closing Stock | 3,60,000 | 4,00,000 | 4,10,000 |
| **Less :** Returns | | | | | | | |
| To Wages | 2,10,000 | 2,30,000 | 2,50,000 | | | | |
| To Gross Profit C/D* | 3,00,000 | 3,30,000 | 3,50,000 | | | | |
| (Balancing figure) | | | | | | | |
| | **15,60,000** | **17,20,000** | **18,10,000** | | **15,60,000** | **17,20,000** | **18,10,000** |

**Calculation of Rate of Gross Profit on Sales :**

|  | 2013-14 | 2014-15 | 2015-16 |
|---|---|---|---|
| $= \dfrac{\text{Gross Profit}}{\text{Sales}} \times 100$ | $= \dfrac{₹\,3,00,000}{₹\,12,00,000} \times 100$ | $= \dfrac{₹\,3,30,000}{₹\,13,20,000} \times 100$ | $= \dfrac{₹\,3,50,000}{₹\,14,00,000} \times 100$ |
| | $= 25\%$ | $= 25\%$ | $= 25\%$ |

Hence, average percentage of Gross Profit to Sales will be,

$$= \frac{25 + 25 + 25}{3} = \frac{75}{3} = 25\%$$

**Dr.**     Memorandum Trading Account (for the period from 1-4-2016 to 30-4-2016 i.e. to date of fire)     **Cr.**

| Particulars | ₹ | Particulars | ₹ |
|---|---|---|---|
| To Opening Stock (at cost) | 4,10,000 | By Sales **Less :** Returns | 1,20,000 |
| To Purchases **Less :** Returns | 60,000 | By Stock * | 4,00,000 |
| To Wages | 20,000 | (Balancing Figure i.e. value of stock | |
| To Gross Profit C/D | 30,000 | on the date of fire) | |
| (25% on Sales i.e. 1,20,000) | | | |
| | **5,20,000** | | **5,20,000** |

**1) Ascertainment of value of stock destroyed by fire :**

|  | ₹ |
|---|---|
| Value of Stock on the date of Fire | 4,00,000 |
| **Less :** Stock Salvaged | (–) 10,000 |
| ∴ Stock destroyed by fire | **3,90,000** |

**2) Application of the Average Clause :**

$$\text{Claim} = \frac{\text{Value of Insurance Policy}}{\text{Value of Stock on the date of fire}} \times \text{Loss of Stock}$$

$$= \frac{₹\,3,50,000}{₹\,4,00,000} \times ₹\,3,90,000$$

$$= ₹\,3,41,250$$

∴ Amount of Claim = ₹ 3,41,250.

## ILLUSTRATION 6

Find out the amount of claim to be lodged with the Insurance Company from the following information relating to Ahura Bros., Amaravati.

| Particulars | 2013 ₹ | 2014 ₹ | 2015 ₹ | 1-1-2016 upto the date of fire ₹ |
|---|---|---|---|---|
| Opening Stock | 15,000 | – | – | – |
| Purchases **Less :** Returns | 50,000 | 75,000 | 90,000 | 60,000 |
| Sales **Less :** Returns | 60,000 | 80,000 | 1,30,000 | 84,000 |
| Wages | 3,000 | 5,000 | 6,000 | 4,000 |
| Closing Stock | 20,000 | 40,000 | 50,000 | – |

During the year 2015, the closing stock included goods purchased but not recorded ₹ 5,000. The salvaged stock was valued at ₹ 9,000. The amount of policy was ₹ 34,000. There was an average clause in the policy. The firm closes its books on 31st December every year.

## SOLUTION

**In the books of Ahura Bros., Amaravati**

Dr.          **Trading Account for the year 2013, 2014, 2015**          Cr.

| Particulars | 2013 ₹ | 2014 ₹ | 2015 ₹ | Particulars | 2013 ₹ | 2014 ₹ | 2015 ₹ |
|---|---|---|---|---|---|---|---|
| To Opening Stock | 15,000 | 20,000 | 40,000 | By Sales | 60,000 | 80,000 | 1,30,000 |
| | | | | **Less** Returns | | | |
| To Purchases | 50,000 | 75,000 | 95,000 * | By Closing Stock | 20,000 | 40,000 | 50,000 |
| **Less** Returns | | | | | | | |
| **Add :** Unrecorded Purchases | | | | | | | |
| To Wages | 3,000 | 5,000 | 6,000 | | | | |
| To Gross Profit C/D* | 12,000 | 20,000 | 39,000 | | | | |
| (Balancing Figure) | | | | | | | |
| | 80,000 | 1,20,000 | 1,80,000 | | 80,000 | 1,20,000 | 1,80,000 |

**Calculation of of Gross Profit on Sales :**

| | 2013 | 2014 | 2015 |
|---|---|---|---|
| $= \dfrac{\text{Gross Profit}}{\text{Sales}} \times 100$ | $= \dfrac{₹\,12,000}{₹\,60,000} \times ₹\,100$ | $= \dfrac{₹\,20,000}{₹\,80,000} \times 100$ | $= \dfrac{₹\,39,000}{₹\,1,30,000} \times 100$ |
| | 20% | 25% | 30% |

Hence, average percentage of Gross Profit to Sales will be,

$$= \frac{20 + 25 + 30}{3} = \frac{75}{3} = 25\%$$

Dr.     **Memorandum Trading Account for the period from 1-1-2016 to the date of fire**     Cr.

| Particulars | ₹ | Particulars | ₹ |
|---|---|---|---|
| To Opening Stock (1-1-2016) | 50,000 | By Sales **Less** Returns | 84,000 |
| To Purchases **Less** Returns | 60,000 | By Stock * | 51,000 |
| To Wages | 4,000 | (Balancing figure i.e. value of stock | |
| To Gross Profit C/D | 21,000 | on the date of fire) | |
| (25% on Sales) | | | |
| | 1,35,000 | | 1,35,000 |

**1. Ascertainment of value of stock destroyed by fire :**

|  |  | ₹ |
|---|---|---|
| | Stock as on the date of fire | 51,000 |
| **Less :** Value of Salvaged Stock | | (–) 9,000 |
| ∴ Stock destroyed by fire | | **42,000** |

**2. Application of the Average Clause :**

$$\text{Claim} = \frac{\text{Value of Insurance Policy}}{\text{Value of Stock on the Stock date of fire}} \times \text{Loss of Stock}$$

$$= \frac{₹\,34,000}{₹\,51,000} \times ₹\,42,000$$

$$= ₹\,28,000$$

∴ Amount of Claim = ₹ 28,000.

### ILLUSTRATION 7

On 15th September 2015, the premises of Landmark Ltd., Lasalgaon were destroyed by fire and stock of ₹ 1,500 was salvaged and reclaimed by the insured. The business books and records were saved from which the following information is obtained.

|  | ₹ |
|---|---|
| Stock as on 1st January, 2014 | 12,500 |
| Stock on 31st December, 2014 | 17,500 |
| Purchases for the year ended 31st December 2014 | 1,18,500 |
| Sales for the year ended 31st December 2014 | 1,50,000 |
| Purchases from 1st January 2015 to 15th September 2015 | 37,500 |
| Sales from 1st January to 15th September 2015 | 51,250 |

In valuing the stock as on 31st December 2014, ₹ 1,000 had been written off certain stock having cost of ₹ 2,250. Half of these goods were sold in July 2015 for ₹ 1,250. The balance is estimated to be worth the original cost. Subject to the above exception, Gross Profit had remained at the uniform rate. On 14th September, 2015, goods worth ₹ 1,000 had been received by the godown keeper but had not been entered in the Purchases Account.

Show the amount of claim.

### SOLUTION

**In the books of Landmark Ltd., Lasalgaon**

**Dr.**     **Trading Account for the year ended 31-12-2014**     **Cr.**

| Particulars | ₹ | Particulars | | ₹ |
|---|---|---|---|---|
| To Opening Stock (1-1-2014) | 12,500 | By Sales | | 1,50,000 |
| To Purchases | 1,18,500 | By Closing Stock | | |
| To Gross Profit C/D * | 37,500 | (31-12-2014) | 17,500 | |
| | | **Add :** Amount written off | | |
| | | certain item of Stock   (+) | 1,000 | 18,500 |
| | **1,68,500** | | | **1,68,500** |

**Calculation of Gross Profit on Sales :**

$$= \frac{\text{Gross Profit}}{\text{Sales}} \times 100$$

$$= \frac{₹\,37,500}{₹\,1,50,000} \times 100$$

$$= 25\%$$

**Dr.**      **Memorandum Trading Account**      **Cr.**

**for the period from 1-1-2015 to 15-9-2015 i.e. to the date of fire**

| Particulars | ₹ | ₹ | Particulars | ₹ | ₹ |
|---|---|---|---|---|---|
| To Opening Stock (1-1-2014) | 18,500 | | By Sales | 51,250 | |
| **Less :** Total cost of Abnormal | | | **Less :** Sale proceeds of half | | |
| item | (–) 2,250 | 16,250 | of Abnormal item | (–) 1,250 | 50,000 |
| To Purchases | 37,500 | | | | |
| **Add :** Unrecorded Purchases | (+) 1,000 | 38,500 | By Stock * | | 17,250 |
| To Gross Profit C/D | | 12,500 | (Balancing figure i.e. value of | | |
| (25% on Sales i.e. ₹ 50,000) | | | stock on the date of fire) | | |
| | | 67,250 | | | 67,250 |

**1) Value of Stock destroyed by fire :**

| | | ₹ |
|---|---|---|
| | Normal Stock | 17,250 |
| **Add :** | Abnormal Stock (50% of ₹ 2,250) | (+) 1,125 |
| | | 18,375 |
| **Less:** | Stock Salvaged | (–) 1,500 |
| | Value of stock destroyed by fire | 16,875 |

Insurance Claim will be equal to ₹ 16,875 in the absence of any average clause.

∴    Amount of Claim = ₹ 16,875.

### ILLUSTRATION 8

On 15th September 2015, the premises of Rexona Ltd., Raipur were destroyed by fire and a stock of ₹ 12,000 was salvaged and retained by the insured. The business books and records were saved from which the following information is obtained.

| Particulars | ₹ |
|---|---|
| Stock as on 1-1-2014 | 1,00,000 |
| Stock on 31-12-2014 | 1,40,000 |
| Purchases for the year ended 31-12-2014 | 9,48,000 |
| Sales for the year ended 31-12-2014 | 12,00,000 |
| Purchases from 1-1-2015 to 15-9-2015 | 3,00,000 |
| Sales from 1-1-2015 to 15-9-2015 | 4,10,000 |

In valuing the stock as on 31-12-2014, ₹ 8,000 had been written off certain stock having cost of ₹ 18,000.

Half of these goods were sold in July 2015 for ₹ 10,000. The balance is estimated to be worth the original cost. Subject to the above exception, gross profit had remained at the uniform rate.

On 14th September, 2015, goods worth ₹ 8,000 had been received by the godown keeper but had not been entered in the Purchase Account.

Show the statement of claim for loss of stock.

### SOLUTION

**In the books of Rexona Ltd., Raipur**

**Dr.**      **Trading Account for the year ended 31-12-2014**      **Cr.**

| Particulars | ₹ | Particulars | | ₹ |
|---|---|---|---|---|
| To Opening Stock (1-1-2014) | 1,00,000 | By Sales | | 12,00,000 |
| To Purchases | 9,48,000 | By Stock (31-12-2014) | 1,40,000 | |
| To Gross Profit C/D | 3,00,000 | | | |
| (Balancing figure) | | **Add :** Amount written off | | |
| | | previously | (+) 8,000 | 1,48,000 |
| | 13,48,000 | | | 13,48,000 |

**Calculation of Rate of Gross Profit on Sales :**

$$= \frac{\text{Gross Profit}}{\text{Sales}} \times 100$$

$$= \frac{₹\,3,00,000}{₹\,12,00,000} \times 100$$

$$= 25\%$$

**Dr.**            **Memorandum Trading Account**            **Cr.**

**for the period from 1-1-2015 to 15-9-2015 i.e. to the date of fire**

| Particulars | | ₹ | ₹ | Particulars | | ₹ | ₹ |
|---|---|---|---|---|---|---|---|
| To Stock (1-1-2015) | | 1,48,000 | | By Sales | | 4,10,000 | |
| **Less :** Abnormal item at | | | | **Less :** Sale proceeds of | | | |
| original cost | (–) | 18,000 | 1,30,000 | Abnormal item (50%) | (–) | 10,000 | 4,,00,000 |
| To Purchases | | 3,00,000 | | By Stock * | | | 1,38,000 |
| **Add :** Unrecorded Purchases | | | | (Balancing figure i.e. value | | | |
| at cost | (+) | 8,000 | 3,08,000 | of stock on the date of fire) | | | |
| To Gross Profit C/D | | | 1,00,000 | | | | |
| (25% on Sales i.e. ₹ 4,00,000) | | | | | | | |
| | | | 5,38,000 | | | | 5,38,000 |

**1) Ascertainment of Value of Stock destroyed by fire :**

|  |  |  | ₹ |
|---|---|---|---|
| | Normal Stock | | 1,38,000 |
| **Add :** | Abnormal items at original cost | | |
| | (1/2 of ₹ 18,000) | | (+) 9,000 |
| | | | 1,47,000 |
| **Less :** | Value of Stock salvaged | | (–) 12,000 |
| | ∴ Value of stock destroyed by fire | | **1,35,000** |

Insurance Claim will be equal to ₹ 1,35,000 in the absence of any average clause.

∴     Amount of Claim = ₹ 1,35,000.

---

### ILLUSTRATION 9

On 16th May 2016, the premises of Panchavati Ltd., Nasik were destroyed by fire but sufficient records were saved from which the following information was ascertained :

| | ₹ |
|---|---|
| Stock on 1-1-2015 | 76,800 |
| Purchases during the year 2015 | 3,20,000 |
| Sales during the year 2015 | 4,05,200 |
| Stock on 31-12-2015 | 63,600 |
| Purchase from 1-1-2016 to 16-5-2016 | 1,08,000 |
| Sales from 1-1-2016 to 16-5-2016 | 1,22,800 |

An item of Stock purchased in 2014 at cost of ₹ 20,000 was valued at ₹ 12,000 on 31-12-2014. Half of this Stock was sold in 2015 for ₹ 5,200, the remaining was valued at ₹ 4,800 on 31-12-2015. One-fourth of the Original Stock was sold on 15-3-2016 for ₹ 2,800 and the remaining stock was considered to be worth 60% of the original cost. The salvaged stock was worth ₹ 24,000. The amount of Policy was ₹ 60,000 and there was an average clause in the policy.

Find the amount of claim.

**SOLUTION**

**In the books of Panchavati Ltd., Nasik**

Dr.     **Trading Account for the year ended 31-12-2015**     Cr.

| Particulars | ₹ | ₹ | Particulars | ₹ | ₹ |
|---|---|---|---|---|---|
| To Stock (1-1-2015) | 76,800 | | By Sales | 4,05,200 | |
| **Less :** Value of Abnormal item (–) 12,000 | | 64,800 | **Less :** Sale of half of | | |
| To Purchases | | 3,20,000 | Abnormal item | (–) 5,200 | 4,00,000 |
| To Gross Profit C/D * | | 74,000 | By Stock (31-12-2015) | 63,600 | |
| (Balancing figure) | | | **Less :** Value of remaining | | |
| | | | Abnormal item | (–) 4,800 | 58,800 |
| | | **4,58,800** | | | **4,58,800** |

**Calculation of Rate Gross Profit on Sales :**

$$= \frac{\text{Gross Profit}}{\text{Sales}} \times 100$$

$$= \frac{₹\,74,000}{₹\,4,00,000} \times 100$$

$$= 18.5\%$$

Dr.     **Memorandum Trading Account**     Cr.

**for the period from 1-1-2016 to 16-5-2016 i.e. to the date of fire**

| Particulars | ₹ | ₹ | Particulars | | ₹ |
|---|---|---|---|---|---|
| To Stock (1-1-2014) | | 58,800 | By Sales | 1,22,800 | |
| To Purchases | | 1,08,000 | **Less :** Sale of Abnormal item | | |
| To Gross Profit C/D | | 22,200 | (remaining half) (–) 2,800 | | 1,20,000 |
| (18.5% on Sales i.e. ₹ 1,20,000) | | | By Stock * | | 69,000 |
| | | | (Balancing figure i.e. value of | | |
| | | | stock on the date of fire) | | |
| | | **1,89,000** | | | **1,89,000** |

**1) Ascertainment of Value of Stock destroyed by fire :**

| | ₹ |
|---|---|
| Normal Stock | 69,000 |
| (As per Memorandum Trading Account) | |
| **Add :** Abnormal Items | |
| (60% of ₹ 5,000) | (+) 3,000 |
| ∴ Value of Stock on the date of Fire | 72,000 |
| **Less :** Stock salvaged | (–) 24,000 |
| Value of Stock destroyed by Fire | **48,000** |

**2) Application of Average Clause :**

$$\text{Claim} = \frac{\text{Value of Insurance Policy}}{\text{Value of Stock as on the date of fire}} \times \text{Loss of Stock}$$

$$= \frac{₹\,60,000}{₹\,72,000} \times ₹\,48,000 = ₹\,40,000$$

∴    Amount of Claim = ₹ 40,000.

**Note on Abnormal Item :**

| | | ₹ |
|---|---|---|
| i) | Total cost of Abnormal item | 20,000 |
| ii) | Half of this stock was sold in 2015 | 5,200 |
| iii) | Half of the remaining half (i.e. 1/4th) was sold in March 2014 at ₹ 5,000 | 2,800 |
| iv) | Remaining 1/4th was considered to be valued for claim at 60% of the original cost | 3,000 |

**ILLUSTRATION 10**

The premises of Rambharose Traders, Rajkot were destroyed by fire on 30-6-2016. The following figures were however, collected from available sources. Prepare a Statement of claim in respect of the loss of stock for submission to the insurance company explaining basis of your claim. The firm closes its books on 31$^{st}$ December each year.

| Particulars | 2013 ₹ | 2014 ₹ | 2015 ₹ | 2016 (30-6-2016) |
|---|---|---|---|---|
| Opening Stock | 20,000 | 22,000 | 11,800 | 34,020 |
| Purchases | 1,78,000 | 1,50,000 | 1,77,000 | 36,000 |
| Sales | 2,22,500 | 2,02,500 | 1,93,500 | 28,000 |
| Purchase Return | 18,000 | 5,000 | 7,000 | 1,000 |
| Sales Return | 22,000 | 4,000 | 6,000 | 2,000 |
| Freight Inward | 5,000 | 3,000 | 5,000 | 1,000 |
| Closing Stock | 22,000 | 11,800 | 34,020 | – |

In 2013, while valuing closing stock, a slow moving item costing ₹ 5,000 was valued at ₹ 4000. This was sold for ₹ 4,500 in 2014. In 2014, an item costing ₹ 6,000 was wrongly valued at ₹ 7,000. This was sold for ₹ 5,500 in 2015. In 2015 slow moving item, costing ₹ 12,000 was valued at ₹ 10,000, 50% of which was sold before 30$^{th}$ June 2016 for ₹ 6,000. The value of salvage was ₹ 8,000.

**In the books of Rambharose Traders, Rajkot**

**Dr.**   **Trading Account for the year ended 31-12-2013**   **Cr.**

| Particulars | | ₹ | Particulars | | | ₹ |
|---|---|---|---|---|---|---|
| To Stock (1-1-2013) | | 20,000 | By Sales | | 2,22,000 | |
| To Purchases | 1,78,000 | | **Less :** Returns Inward | (–) | 22,000 | 2,00,000 |
| **Less :** Returns Outward (–) | 18,000 | 1,60,000 | By Stock (31-12-2013) | | 22,000 | |
| To Freight Inward | | 5,000 | **Add :** Adjustment for | | | |
| To Gross Profit C/D * | | 38,000 | under valuation | (+) | 1,000 | 23,000 |
| (Balancing figure) | | | | | | |
| | | **2,23,000** | | | | **2,23,000** |

**Calculation of Rate of Gross Profit on Sales :**

$$= \frac{\text{Gross Profit}}{\text{Sales}} \times 100$$

$$= \frac{₹\,38,000}{₹\,2,00,000} \times 100$$

$$= 19\%$$

**Dr.**   **Trading Account for the year ended 31-12-2014**   **Cr.**

| Particulars | | ₹ | Particulars | | | ₹ |
|---|---|---|---|---|---|---|
| To Stock (1-1-2014) | 23,000 | | By Sales | | 2,02,500 | |
| **Less :** Full Cost of Abnormal | | 18,000 | **Less :** Sale proceeds of | | | |
| item | 5,000 | | Abnormal item | (–) | 4,500 | |
| To Purchases | 1,50,000 | | | | | |
| **Less :** Returns Outward (–) | 5,000 | 1,45,000 | | | 1,98,000 | |
| To Freight Inward | | 3,000 | **Less :** Returns Inward | (–) | 4,000 | 1,94,000 |
| To Gross Profit C/D * | | 38,800 | By Stock (31-12-2014) | | 11,800 | |
| (Balancing figure) | | | **Less :** Adjustment for over- | | | |
| | | | valuation of an item of | | 1,000 | 10,800 |
| | | | stock | (–) | | |
| | | **2,04,800** | | | | **2,04,800** |

**Calculation of Rate of Gross Profit on Sales :**

$$= \frac{\text{Gross Profit}}{\text{Sales}} \times 100$$

$$= \frac{₹\ 38,800}{₹\ 1,94,000} \times 100$$

$$= 20\%$$

**Dr.**  **Trading Account  for the year ended 31-12-2015**  **Cr.**

| Particulars | ₹ | ₹ | Particulars | ₹ | ₹ |
|---|---|---|---|---|---|
| To Stock  (1-1-2015) | 10,800 | | By Sales | 1,93,500 | |
| **Less :** Elimination of the full cost | | | **Less :** Sale proceeds of | | |
| of Abnormal item    (–) | 6,000 | 4,800 | Abnormal item    (–) | 5,500 | |
| To Purchases | 1,77,000 | | | 1,88,000 | |
| **Less :** Returns Outward  (–) | 7,000 | 1,70,000 | **Less :** Returns Inward  (–) | 6,000 | 1,82,000 |
| To Freight Inward | | 5,000 | By Stock (31-12-2015) | 34,020 | |
| To Gross Profit C/D * | | 38,220 | **Add :** Adjustment for under- | | |
| (Balancing figure) | | | valuation of an item of stock (+) | 2,000 | 36,020 |
| | | **2,18,020** | | | **2,18,020** |

**Calculation of Rate of Gross Profit on Sales :**

$$= \frac{\text{Gross Profit}}{\text{Sales}} \times 100$$

$$= \frac{₹\ 38,220}{₹\ 1,82,000} \times 100$$

$$= 21\%$$

Hence, average percentage of rate of Gross Profit to Sales will be,

$$= \frac{19 + 20 + 21}{3}$$

$$= \frac{60}{3}$$

$$= 20\%$$

Memorandum Trading Account

**Dr.**  **for the period from 1-1-2016 to 30-6-2016 i.e. to the date of fire**  **Cr.**

| Particulars | ₹ | ₹ | Particulars | ₹ | ₹ |
|---|---|---|---|---|---|
| To Stock  (1-1-2016) | 36,020 | | By Sales | 28,000 | |
| **Less :** Original Cost of Abnormal | | | **Less :** Sale proceeds of | | |
| item    (–) | 12,000 | 24,020 | Abnormal item  (1/2)  (–) | 6,000 | |
| To Purchases | 36,000 | | | 22,000 | |
| **Less :** Returns Outward  (–) | 1,000 | 35,000 | **Less :** Returns Inward  (–) | 2,000 | 20,000 |
| To Freight Inward | | 1,000 | By Stock * | | 44,020 |
| To Gross Profit C/D | | 4,000 | (Balancing figure i.e. value of | | |
| (20% on Sales i.e. ₹ 20,000) | | | stock on the date of fire) | | |
| | | **64,020** | | | **64,020** |

**1) Ascertainment of Value of Stock destroyed by fire :**

| | | ₹ |
|---|---|---:|
| | Normal Items | 44,020 |
| **Add :** | Abnormal items | (+) 6,000 |
| | ∴ Value of Stock on the date of fire | 50,020 |
| **Less :** | Value of Stock Salvaged | (−) 8,000 |
| ∴ | Value of Stock destroyed by fire | **42,020** |

Insurance Claim will be equal to ₹ 42,020 in the absence of any average clause.

∴      Amount of Claim = ₹ 42,020.

## * (B) LOSS OF PROFIT POLICY *

### ILLUSTRATION 1

From the following information, calculate the amount of Claim under Loss of Profit Policy.

i)      Date of Fire 1-4-2015

ii)     Period of Indemnity : 4 months

iii)    Policy amount ₹ 3,00,000

iv)    Sales from 1-1-2015 to 31-12-2015 – ₹ 18,00,000

v)     Sales from 1-4-2015 to 31-3-2016 – ₹ 20,00,000

vi)    Net Profit for the year 2015 – ₹ 2,00,000 and Standing charges : ₹ 2,00,000 (out of which ₹ 40,000 were uninsured)

vii)   Sales during the dislocation period ₹ 2,00,000 and during the corresponding period in the last year : ₹ 6,00,000

### SOLUTION

**1. Calculation of Short Sales :**

| | | ₹ |
|---|---|---:|
| | Sales from 1-4-2015 to 31-7-2015 | 6,00,000 |
| **Less :** | Sales from 1-4-2016 to 31-7-2016 | (−) 2,00,000 |
| | ∴ **Short Sales** | **4,00,000** |

**2. Calculation of Gross Profit Rate :**

$$= \frac{\text{Net Profit + Insured Standing Charges}}{\text{Sales of the previous year}} \times 100$$

$$= \frac{₹\,2,00,000 + ₹\,1,60,000}{₹\,18,00,000} \times 100$$

$$= 20\%$$

**3. Loss of Profit on Sales :**

$$= \text{Gross Profit Rate} \times \text{Short Sales}$$

$$= 20\% \times ₹\,4,00,000$$

$$= ₹\,80,000$$

**4. Application of Average Clause :**

Insurance cover required   = 20% on Sales for 12 months ending on the date of fire

                                = 20% of ₹ 20,00,000

                                = ₹ 4,00,000

$$\therefore \quad \text{Claim} = \frac{\text{Amount of Policy taken}}{\text{Insurance cover required}} \times \text{Gross claim i.e. Loss of Profit}$$

$$= \frac{₹\,3,00,000}{₹\,4,00,000} \times ₹\,80,000$$

$$= ₹\,60,000$$

When the Insurance policy taken is short of the actual insurance cover required, then the loss of profit is proportionately reduced having regard to the ratio of amount of policy to insurance cover required. This is because of the under insurance being effected by the businessman.

$\therefore$ Amount of Claim = ₹ 60,000.

### ILLUSTRATION 2

From the following details, find out the claim under a Loss of Profit Policy.

| | |
|---|---:|
| Indemnity period – 6 months | |
| Policy Amount : | ₹ 4,50,000 |
| Date of fire : | 1-4-2015 |
| Dislocation upto | 1-8-2015 |
| Sales for 2015 accounting year | ₹ 18,00,000 |
| Net Profit for 2015 accounting year | ₹ 1,65,000 |
| Standing charges for 2015 accounting year (all insured) | ₹ 2,85,000 |
| Sale from 1-4-2014 upto 31-3-2015 | ₹ 24,00,000 |
| Sales from 1-4-2015 upto 1-8-2015 | ₹ 2,25,000 |
| Sales from 1-4-2014 upto 1-8-2014 | ₹ 7,50,000 |

There is a clear 10% upward trend in the business.

### SOLUTION

**1. Calculation of Short Sales :**

| | ₹ |
|---|---:|
| Sales in the period (1-4-2014 to 1-8-2014) | 7,50,000 |
| **Add :** 10% for upward trend | (+) 75,000 |
| | 8,25,000 |
| **Less :** Sales in the period (1-4-2015 to 1-8-2015) | (–) 2,25,000 |
| $\therefore$ **Short Sales** | **6,00,000** |

**2. Calculation of Gross Profit Rate :**

$$= \frac{\text{Net Profit + Insured Standing Charges}}{\text{Sales of the previous accounting year}} \times 100$$

$$= \frac{₹\,1,65,000 + ₹\,2,85,000}{₹\,18,00,000} \times 100$$

$$= 25\%$$

**3. Loss of Profit on Sales :**

$$= \text{Gross Profit Rate} \times \text{Short Sales}$$

$$= 25\% \times ₹\,6,00,000$$

$$= ₹\,\mathbf{1,50,000}$$

**4. Application of Average Clause :**

Insurance required is 25% on the Sales for the year ending on the date of fire i.e. 25% on (₹ 24,00,000 + 10%) = 25% on ₹ 26,40,000 = ₹ 6,60,000

$$\text{Claim} = \frac{\text{Amount of Policy taken}}{\text{Insurance cover required}} \times \text{Gross claim i.e. Loss of Profit}$$

$$= \frac{₹\,4,50,000}{₹\,6,60,000} \times ₹\,1,50,000$$

$$= ₹\,1,02,273$$

$\therefore$ Amount of Claim = ₹ 1,02,273.

### ILLUSTRATION 3

Sukhadiya Traders, Surat holds a loss of profit policy. From the following information, calculate the amount of claim under a loss of profit policy.

a)      The accounts are prepared annually on 31st December.

b)      The net profit plus insured standing charges for the year ended 31st December 2014 amounted to ₹ 5,00,000.

c)      A fire occurred on 30th April 2015, the period of indemnity was 6 months.

d)      The sales for the year ended 30th April 2015 were ₹ 14,00,000 and for the year ended 31st December 2014 were ₹ 12,50,000.

e)      The sales during the period of dislocation were ₹ 2,00,000 and for the corresponding period in the preceding year were ₹ 4,50,000.

f)      The expenses incurred to mitigate loss was ₹ 20,000.

g)      The saving in insured standing charges due to fire amounted to ₹ 5,000.

h)      The amount of policy was ₹ 4,00,000.

### SOLUTION

**1) Calculation of Short Sales :**

| | ₹ |
|---|---|
| Sales (from 1-5-2014 to 31-10-2014) | 4,50,000 |
| **Less :** Sales (from 1-5-2015 to 31-10-2015) | (–) 2,00,000 |
| **Short Sales** | **2,50,000** |

**2) Calculation of Gross Profit Rate :**

$$= \frac{\text{Net Profit} + \text{Insured Standing Charges}}{\text{Sales of the last accounting year}} \times 100$$

$$= \frac{₹\,5,00,000}{₹\,12,50,000} \times 100$$

$$= 40\%$$

**3) Loss of Profit on Sales :**

$$= \text{Gross Profit Rate} \times \text{Short Sales}$$

$$= 40\% \times ₹\,2,50,000$$

$$= ₹\,1,00,000$$

| | ₹ |
|---|---|
| Loss of Profit | 1,00,000 |
| **Add :** Increase in Expenses | (+) 20,000 |
| | 1,20,000 |
| **Less :** Savings in Standing charges | (–) 5,000 |
| **Gross Claim** | **1,15,000** |

**4) Application of Average Clause :**

Insurance cover required      = Gross Profit at 40% on the Sales for the 12 months ending on the date of fire (₹ 14,00,000)

                                     = 40% of ₹ 14,00,000

                                     = ₹ 5,60,000

But the sum insured is ₹ 4,00,000

Hence, the average clause applies (sum insured being less than the Gross Profit amount)

$$\text{Claim} = \frac{\text{Amount of Policy taken}}{\text{Insurance cover required}} \times \text{Gross claim i.e. Loss of Profit}$$

$$= \frac{₹\ 4,00,000}{₹\ 5,60,000} \times ₹\ 1,15,000$$

$$= ₹\ 82,143$$

∴     Amount of Claim = ₹ 82,143.

## ILLUSTRATION 4

On 31st December 2014, a fire damaged the premises of Soni Bros. Sagar. and the business of the company was disorganised until March 2015. The company was insured under a loss of profit policy for ₹ 2,60,000 with a six months period of indemnity. The company's accounts for the year ended 31st October 2014 showed a turnover of ₹ 7,00,000 with a net profit of ₹ 80,000. The amount of standing charges covered by the insurance and debited in that year was ₹ 2,00,000. The turnover for the twelve months ended 31st December 2015 was ₹ 7,80,000. The turnover during the period the business was dislocated amounted to ₹ 80,000 while during the corresponding period in the preceding year it was ₹ 1,70,000.

You are required to calculate the claim to be submitted.

## SOLUTION

**1) Calculation of Short Sales :**

|  |  | ₹ |
|---|---|---:|
| Sales during the corresponding period (from 31-12-2013 to 31-3-2014) | | 1,70,000 |
| **Less :** Sales during the period of dislocation | | (–) 80,000 |
| **Short Sales** | | **90,000** |

**2) Calculation of Gross Profit Rate :**

$$= \frac{\text{Net Profit} + \text{Standing Charges}}{\text{Sales of the previous accounting year}} \times 100$$

$$= \frac{₹\ 80,000 + ₹\ 2,00,000}{₹\ 7,00,000} \times 100$$

$$= 40\%$$

**3) Loss of Profit on Sales** = Gross Profit Rate × Short Sales

$$= 40\% \times ₹\ 90,000$$

$$= ₹\ 36,000$$

**4) Application of Average Clause :**

Gross Profit percentage on the Sales for the year ending on the date of fire

Insurance cover required = 40% of ₹ 7,80,000 = ₹ 3,12,000

However, Insurance Policy taken = ₹ 2,60,000

$$\text{Claim} = \frac{\text{Amount of Policy}}{\text{Insurance cover required}} \times \text{Gross claim i.e. Loss of Profit}$$

$$= \frac{₹\ 2,60,000}{₹\ 3,12,000} \times ₹\ 36,000$$

$$= ₹\ 30,000$$

∴     Amount of Claim = ₹ 30,000.

### ILLUSTRATION 5

From the following information find out the claim under 'Loss of Profit Policy'.

| | ₹ |
|---|---|
| Sales in 2012 | 15,00,000 |
| Sales in 2013 | 18,00,000 |
| Sales in 2014 | 21,60,000 |
| Sales in 2015 | 25,92,000 |
| Net Profit in 2015 | 1,50,000 |
| Insured Standing Charges in 2015 | 1,09,200 |
| Date of fire : 1$^{st}$ January 2016 | |
| Period of dislocation : 3 months | |
| Sales from 1-1-2015 to 31-3-2015      – | 6,48,000 |
| Sales from 1-1-2016 to 31-3-2016      – | 1,77,600 |
| Indemnity period 9 months | |
| Policy Amount      – | 7,50,000 |

### SOLUTION

Sales in 2015 have increased by ₹ 4,32,000 over the previous year which is 20%.

$$= \left( \frac{₹\,4,32,000}{₹\,21,60,000} \times 100 \right)$$

Sales in 2014 have increased by ₹ 3,60,000 over the pervious year which is 20%.

$$= \left( \frac{₹\,3,60,000}{₹\,18,00,000} \times 100 \right)$$

Sales in 2013 have increased by ₹ 3,00,000 over the previous years which is 20%

$$= \left( \frac{₹\,3,00,000}{₹\,15,00,000} \times 100 \right)$$

Therefore, there has been a consistent rise in the sales during the previous years by 20%

**1) Calculation of Short Sales :**

| | | ₹ |
|---|---|---|
| | Sales (1-1-2015 to 31-3-2015) | 6,48,000 |
| **Add :** | Increase by 20% | (+) 1,29,600 |
| | | 7,77,600 |
| **Less :** | Sales (1-1-2016 to 31-3-2016) | (–) 1,77,600 |
| | **Short Sales** | **6,00,000** |

**2) Calculation of Gross Profit Rate :**

$$= \frac{\text{Net Profit + Insured Standing Charges}}{\text{Sales for the previous year}} \times 100$$

$$= \frac{₹\,1,50,000 + ₹\,1,09,200}{₹\,25,92,000} \times 100$$

$$= 10\%$$

**3) Loss of Profit on Sales :**

$$= \text{Gross Profit Rate} \times \text{Short Sales}$$
$$= 10\% \times ₹\,6,00,000$$
$$= ₹\,60,000$$

**4)** There is no application of average clause, since the amount of policy is more than the annual profit of ₹ 3,09,600 which is calculated :

10% × (₹ 25,92,000 + 20%)

$$= 10\% \text{ of } ₹\,31,10,400$$
$$= ₹\,\mathbf{3,11,040}$$

∴    Amount of Claim = ₹ 60,000.

### ILLUSTRATION 6

Akash Traders, Ahmednagar are insured under a loss of profit policy for ₹ 1,26,000. Their books of accounts are closed on 31st December each year. The fire occurred in the premises of the business on 1-7-2015. The records saved disclosed the following information :

|  | ₹ |
|---|---|
| Turnover during the year ended 30-6-2015 | 14,40,000 |
| Turnover during the year ended 31-12-2014 | 12,00,000 |
| Turnover from 1-7-2015 to 30-9-2015 | 60,000 |
| Turnover in the corresponding period of 2014 | 3,60,000 |
| Standing charges for the year ending 31-12-2014 | 72,000 |
| Net Profit during the year ending 31-12-2014 | 48,000 |

It has been ascertained that the business has consistently shown an increase of 25% in turnover in the months preceding the fire over corresponding period of the previous year.

Calculate the amount of claim.

### SOLUTION

**1)  Calculation of Short Sales :**                                     ₹

(during the indemnity period)

|  |  |  |
|---|---|---|
| | Expected Turnover | 3,60,000 |
| **Add :** | 25% increase anticipated | (+) 90,000 |
| | | 4,50,000 |
| **Less :** | Actual turnover during the indemnity period | (−) 60,000 |
| | **Short Sales** | **3,90,000** |

**2)  Calculation of Gross Profit Rate :**

$$= \frac{\text{Net Profit during the previous accounting year} + \text{Insured Standing charges in the previous accounting year}}{\text{Sales in the last accounting year}} \times 100$$

$$= \frac{₹\,48,000 + ₹\,72,000}{₹\,12,00,000} \times 100$$

$$=\quad 10\%$$

**3)  Loss of Profit on Sales :**

$$=\quad \text{Gross Profit Rate} \times \text{Short Sales}$$

$$=\quad 10\% \times ₹\,3,90,000$$

$$=\quad ₹\,39,000$$

**4)  Application of the Average Clause :**

Insurance Covered required = 10% of ₹ 14,40,000 being sales for 12 months ending on the date of fire + 25% increase

$$= 10\%\,(₹\,14,40,000 + ₹\,3,60,000)$$

$$= 10\% \times (₹\,18,00,000)$$

$$= ₹\,1,80,000$$

$$= \frac{\text{Amount of Insurance Policy taken}}{\text{Insurance cover required}} \times \text{Gross claim i.e. Loss of Profit}$$

$$= \frac{₹\,1,26,000}{₹\,1,80,000} \times ₹\,39,000$$

$$= ₹\,27,300$$

∴    Amount of Claim = ₹ 27,300.

## QUESTIONS FOR SELF-STUDY

**I.  Theory Questions :**
1) Why insurance is necessary ?
2) Explain the necessity of loss of stock policy.
3) How to calculate claims under loss of stock policy ?
4) What is the need of loss of profit policy ?
5) Explain the steps involved in the calculation of claims under loss of profit policy.
6) Write short notes on :

   (a) Treatment of abnormal items in loss of stock, (b) Short Sales, (c) Average Clause, (d) Loss of profit policy, (e) Gross Profit Ratio, (f) Indemnity Ratio, (g) Standard Turnover, (h) Loss of stock policy.

**II.  Practical Problems :**
1) From the following particulars find out claim under the loss of profit policy.
   i) Date of fire – 1-4-2015
   ii) Value of insurance policy – ₹ 35,200
   iii) Indemnity period – 4 months
   iv) Dislocation period upto 30-9-2015
   v) Sales for 2014 accounting year – ₹ 1,20,000, Net Profit for the year 2014 – ₹ 13,000 and insured standing charges – ₹ 17,000

   | | |
   |---|---:|
   | vi) Sales from 1-4-2014 to 31-3-2015 | ₹ 1,60,000 |
   | vii) Sales from 1-4-2015 to 30-9-2015 | ₹ 20,000 |
   | viii) Sales from 1-4-2015 to 1-8-2015 | ₹ 15,000 |
   | ix) Sales from 1-4-2014 to 30-9-2014 | ₹ 35,000 |
   | x) Sales from 1-4-2014 to 1-8-2014 | ₹ 50,000 |

   There is clear upward trend of 10% in business.

2) Fire occurred in the premises of Somani Bros. Sunasgaon on 1-5-2015. They have a loss of profit policy for ₹ 1,20,000. Sales from 1-5-2014 to 30-4-2015 were ₹ 10,00,000. Sales from 1-5-2014 to 31-8-2014 were ₹ 3,00,000. During the indemnity period which lasted for four months, sales amounted to ₹ 40,000 only. The Trading and Profit and Loss Account of Somani Bros. for the year ended 31-12-2014 is given below.

| Particulars | ₹ | Particulars | ₹ |
|---|---:|---|---:|
| To Opening Stock | 1,00,000 | By Sales | 9,50,000 |
| To Purchases | 6,00,000 | By Closing Stock | 50,000 |
| To Work Expenses | 67,000 | | |
| To Variable Selling Expenses | 90,500 | | |
| To Fixed Expenses | 72,500 | | |
| To Net Profit C/D | 70,000 | | |
| | **10,00,000** | | **10,00,000** |

   Comparing the sales of the first four months of 2015 with those of 2014 it was found that sales were 20% higher in 2015. Ascertain the loss of profit to be claimed with the insurance company.

3) From the following particulars ascertain the claim to be lodged in respect of consequential loss policy.
   i) Fire occurred on 1-4-2015 and affected sales for 3 months
   ii) Sales for 3 months ending 30-6-2015 and 30-6-2016 were ₹ 3,00,000 and ₹ 1,00,000 respectively.
   iii) The policy was for ₹ 9,50,000.
   iv) Sales for 12 months ended 31-3-2016 were ₹ 3,80,000.
   v) Accounts are prepared on 31$^{st}$ December. The net profit for 2015 amounted to ₹ 5,00,000 after debiting standing charges of ₹ 2,20,000 (all insured), Sales for 2015 were ₹ 36,00,000.
   vi) A sum of ₹ 7,000 was spent as additional expenses to mitigate the effect of loss.

4) From the following particulars find out the amount of claim for loss of profit under the consequential loss policy.

   | | ₹ |
   |---|---:|
   | Date of fire : 30-6-2015 | |
   | Period of indemnity – 6 months | |
   | Sum insured | 40,000 |
   | Net profit for the accounting year ending on 31-3-2015 | 12,500 |
   | Sales for the year ended 30-6-2015 | 2,00,000 |
   | Standing charges for the accounting year ending on 31-3-2015 | 28,500 |

| | |
|---|---:|
| Turnover for the year ending 31-3-2015 | 1,98,000 |
| Turnover for the indemnity period from 1-7-2015 to 31-12-2015 | 56,000 |
| Turnover for the period from 1-7-2014 to 31-12-2014 | 1,10,000 |

The turnover of the year 2013-2014 had shown a tendency of increase of 10% over the turnover of the preceding year.

5) A fire occurred on 15-4-2016 and destroyed the business of Super and Co., Solapur. The books of accounts and the stock amounting to ₹ 1,80,000 was salvaged and the following information was made available from the books.

| | Turnover ₹ | Trading Profits ₹ |
|---|---:|---:|
| for the year ended 31-12-2011 | 86,00,000 | 21,50,000 |
| for the year ended 31-12-2012 | 71,00,000 | 21,30,000 |
| for the year ended 31-12-2013 | 60,00,000 | 20,00,000 |
| for the year ended 31-12-2014 | 55,00,000 | 18,70,000 |
| for the year ended 31-12-2015 | 48,00,000 | 16,00,000 |

On 31-12-2015, the stock on hand was valued at ₹ 9,70,000. The purchases, sales and productive wages from 1-1-2016 to 14-4-2016 were ascertained at ₹ 7,50,000, ₹ 15,90,000 and ₹ 3,00,000 respectively.

Prepare a statement of claim.

6) There was a fire on 15-9-2015 in the premises of Goodluck Ltd., Gorakhpur. From the following figures, calculate the amount of claim to be lodged with the insurance company for the loss of stock.

| | ₹ |
|---|---:|
| Stock on 1-1-2014 (at cost) | 20,000 |
| Stock on 1-1-2015 (at cost) | 30,000 |
| Purchases 2014 | 40,000 |
| Purchases from 1-1-2015 to 15-9-2015 | 88,000 |
| Sales 2014 | 60,000 |
| Sales from 1-1-2015 to 15-9-2015 | 1,05,000 |

During the current year cost of purchases have increased by 10% above last year's level. Selling price has gone up by 5%. Salvage stocks amounted to ₹ 6,000.

7) Fire occurred in the premises of Unfortunate Ltd., Ulhasnagar on 10-4-2015. From the following particulars ascertain the claim for loss of stock.

| | ₹ |
|---|---:|
| Stock on 1-1-2015 | 72,000 |
| Stock on 31-12-2015 | 45,000 |
| Purchases during 2015 | 2,90,000 |
| Sales during 2015 | 4,00,000 |
| Purchases from 1-1-2016 to 9-4-2016 | 2,92,000 |
| Sales from 1-1-2016 to 9-4-2016 | 3,78,000 |
| Salvage Stock | 14,000 |

The Company follows the practice of valuing stocks at cost less than 10%

8) On 15-6-2016, the premises of Unlucky Ltd. Udampur were destroyed by fire but sufficient records were saved from which the following particulars were ascertained.

| | ₹ |
|---|---:|
| Stock on 1-1-2015 (cost price) | 73,500 |
| Stock on 31-12-2015 (cost price) | 79,600 |
| Net purchases for the year 2015 | 3,98,000 |
| Net Sales for the year 2015 | 4,87,000 |
| Purchases less returns, 1-1-2016 to 15-6-2016 | 1,62,000 |
| Sales less returns, 1-1-2016 to 15-6-2016 | 2,31,200 |

In valuing stock on 31-12-2016 ₹ 2,300 had been written off certain stock which was of poor selling line having cost ₹ 6,900. A portion of these goods were sold in February, 2016 at a loss of ₹ 250 on the original cost of ₹ 3,450. The remainder of this stock was now estimated to be worth the original cost. Subject to the above exception, gross profit had remained at a uniform rate throughout. The stock salvaged was ₹ 3,050.

Show the amount of claim.

# Chapter 4

# FINAL ACCOUNTS OF CO-OPERATIVE SOCIETIES

**SYNOPSIS**



## 4.0 INTRODUCTION

There are different kinds of Co-operative Societies, viz. Consumer Co-operative Societies, Credit and Thrift Societies, Housing Societies and the like. The primary law governing the formation and functioning of any Co-operative Society in the Central Co-operative Societies Act of 1912. Certain states having also passed their own laws for governing the formation and functioning of the Co-operatives situated in their states. e.g. the Co-operative Act in force in Maharashtra state is the Maharashtra Co-operative Societies Act 1960, supported by situated rules. The exact nature and scope of accounting would, therefore depend on the nature of its business.

A society which as proclaimed as its objective the promotion of economic interests of its members in accordance with Co-operative principles or a Society formed with object of facilitating the functioning of such a society may be registered under the appropriate Act. On the proper registration, a society will become a 'body corporate' under the name in which it has been registered with perpetual succession and common seal and also with power to hold property, enter into contracts and so on. The Act, (in case of Maharashtra State, the M.S. Co-operative Societies Act, 1960) also provides for compulsory audit by the Registrar of Co-operative Societies or any person duly authorised by him. Property and funds of Registered Co-operative Societies are very important for both accounting and auditing purposes.

## 4.1  MEANING : CO-OPERATIVE SOCIETY

The dictionary meaning of the word co-operation is 'working together for a common purpose'. Co-operative Societies are organisations formed to take the benefits of co-operation. These Co-operative Societies are democratic, self - governing bodies. They are democratic as they are managed by the managing committee which is formed by applying the principle of one man one vote and not on the basis of shareholding. They are governed by the members themselves. However, due to this they lack in professional management. They are not formed with an intention to earn profit. Co-operative Societies are formed to provide goods or services to its members at the lowest possible prices.

Each Co-operative Society has to be registered under the Co-operative Societies Act of the concerned state. In Maharashtra, Co-operative Societies are formed and registered under the Maharashtra Co-operative Societies Act, 1960. Each Co-operative Society must have its own rules and regulations which are known as bye - laws. While registering the Society these bye - laws need to be approved by the concerned authority.

**Section 2 (9) :** 'Consumer Society' means a Society, the object of which is :
(a)   the procurement, procedures or processing and distribution of goods to or the performance of other services for its members as also other customers and
(b)   the distribution among its members and customers, in the proportion, prescribed by rules or by bye-laws of the Society of the profits accruing from such procurement, production or processing and distribution.

**Section 2 (25) :** 'Resource Society' means a Society the object of which is obtaining for its members of credit, goods or services required by them.

Agricultural Credit, Thrift and Urban Credit Societies are types of Credit Resources Societies. These societies are formed voluntarily by consumers, farmers and other weaker sections of the society. In the real sense of the term a co-operative movement can really be called as a people's movement and is promoted by the Government so as to serve the economic interests of the weaker sections of the society. 'Service', rather than 'profit', is the aim of the co-operative societies. Such societies serve primarily the interests of the members and the public in general.

## 4.2  CO-OPERATIVE LEGISLATION

The first enactment in India relating to Co-operative societies was the Co-operative Credit Societies Act, 1904. With the passing of this Act, the Co-operative credit societies were established particularly to offer credit facilities to the farmers in order to free them from the clutches of moneylenders. There has been a central legislation : The Co-operative Societies Act, 1912 which contains the fundamental law in regard to the formation and working of the Co-operative Societies. It is applicable in many states with or without amendments. Although some of the states have enacted their separate Co-operative Societies Acts, the basic principles and the framework is identical to the parent Central Act. In the State of Maharashtra, Co-operatives are governed by 'The Maharashtra Co-operative Societies Act, 1960' and the 'Maharashtra Co-operative Societies Rules, 1961' formulated under it.

## 4.3  CONSUMERS' CO-OPERATIVE SOCIETIES

**A Consumers' Co-operative Society is established with the following objects :**
(i)    the procurement, production or processing and distribution of goods to its members and also other customers.
(ii)   the distribution among its members, and customers in the proportion prescribed by rules or by the bye-laws of the society, of the profits accruing from such procurement, production or processing and distribution.

### 4.3.1 Books of Accounts for Consumer's Co-operative Societies

Following books of accounts are generally maintained by the Consumers' Co-operative Society.

(i) Cash Book, (ii) Cash Sales Subsidiary Book, (iii) Credit Sales Register (if credit sales are allowed by law), (iv) Purchase Book, (v) Stock Register, (vi) Bin-Cards for itemwise upto-date quantity records, (vii) Register of excess and shortages, (viii) General Ledger, (ix) Debtors Ledger, Creditors Ledger, (x) Journal Proper, (xi) Register of tenders, (xii) List of approved suppliers, (xiii) Register of market rates.

## 4.4 CO-OPERATIVE CREDIT SOCIETIES

The primary objects in the formation of Co-operative credit societies are: inculcation of the habit of thrift among members, promotion of savings and mutual help which will lead to the improvement of the economic conditions of the members. The Credit Co-operative Societies are basically of two types: Agricultural Credit Societies and Non-Agricultural or Urban Credit Societies. (known as Primary Co-operative Societies).

### 4.4.1 Books of Accounts for Credit Co-operative Society

According to Section 79 of the Maharashtra Co-operative Societies Act, 1960, the Registrar may direct the Co-operative Society to maintain proper accounts in relation to :

(i)     All sums of money received and expended by the society and the matters in respect of which receipts and expenditure take place.

(ii)    All sales and purchases of goods by the society and of the stock in hand and its valuation.

(iii)   The Assets and liabilities belonging to the society.

The Registrar is empowered to call the society to furnish such statements and returns and to produce such returns as he may require from time to time.

According to Rule 65 of the Maharashtra Co-operative Societies Rules, the following books of accounts and registers are to be maintained by the society.

(i) Cash Book, (ii) General Ledger and Personal Ledger, (ii) Stock Register, (iv) Property Register, (v) Register of Audit Objections and their rectifications, (vi) Such other accounts and books as from time to time be specified by the Government.

## 4.5 CO-OPERATIVE ACCOUNT KEEPING

Co-operative Societies need to maintain the books of accounts for the purpose of knowing the financial position of the Society. Normally, Co-operative Societies are governed by the people who may not be having any knowledge of the book keeping and accountancy. In view of the above, it becomes necessary to evolve and indigenous form of account-keeping, so as to suit the convenience and understanding of common man. These Societies do not follow the double entry book keeping system. Instead, they use a simplified system. Co-operative Societies do not maintain separate journals for recording journal entries. All the transactions are routed through the day book or cash book.

Under the Maharashtra Co-operative Societies Rules, 1961, Rule 61 provides that the managing committee of every Society shall prepare annual statements of accounts within 42 days of the close of the accounting year showing :

(i)     Receipts and disbursements during the previous Co-operative year.

(ii)    The Profit and Loss Account for the year, and

(iii)   The Balance Sheet as at the close of the year.

### 4.5.1  Preparation of Receipts and Payments Statement

**Day Book or Cash Book :** All the transactions, whether involving cash or not, are routed through cash book. The transactions involving receipt in cash are recorded on the receipt side and transactions involving payment of cash are recorded on the payment side of cash book. The transaction which do not involve cash are given double effect through cash book only. Suppose there are purchases on credit from say Mr. A, which do not involve payment in cash. For recording this transaction on the receipt side of cash book A's Account will be written as his account needs to be credited and on payment side purchases will be written as purchase account needs to be debited. When these entries are posted the desired effect will be achieved. Also since in the cash book a receipt as well as payment entry is recorded it will not affect the cash balance.

After such day book is written and posted in the ledger, the totaling of accounts is done. Since the Receipt and Payments Account is to be prepared from this, the accounts are not balanced but instead the total of receipts and payments of each account is kept separate. The receipts and payments account will show the total receipts from each account and total payment to each account.

Suppose, during the year some of the fixed assets are sold and some fixed assets are purchased also, in normal accounting a net balance of this account would be drawn. But in this case the total of receipts (sale proceeds of sale of assets) and payments (purchase of assets) would be shown separately. The Receipts and Payments Account will start with opening balance of cash and bank, followed by various receipts on the receipts side. On payment side after the various payments the account will close with the closing balances of cash and bank. The account thus will be tallied.

### 4.5.2  Final Accounts of Co-operative Societies

Rule No. 61 of the Maharashtra Co-operative Societies Rules 1961, provides that, the society has to prepare the following final statements within 45 days of the close of the accounting year which is 30th June.

(i)      Receipts and Payments Account during the previous Co-operative year.

(ii)      The Profit and Loss Account for the year and

(iii)      The Balance Sheet as at the close of the year.

Rule No. 62 of the Maharashtra Co-operative Societies Rules, 1961 provides that the Society has to prepare the Profit and Loss Account and the Balance Sheet in the prescribed form i.e. Form 'N'. However, the Registrar of Co-operative Societies may allow a certain Society to prepare its financial statements in some other form as he deems fit. The Final Accounts are to be prepared in the prescribed form and are to be laid down before the members of the society in their Annual General Meeting which is to be held within three months from the end of the accounting year.

### 4.5.2.1  Format (As per Maharashtra Co-operative Societies Act, 1960)

(A) Profit and Loss Account and
(B) Balance-Sheet.

According to Sec. 65 of the Maharashtra Co-operative Societies Act, 1960 read with Rule 62 (1) of the Maharashtra Co-operative Societies Rules 1961, the Balance Sheet and the Profit and Loss Account of the Society shall be prepared in form N which is as follows :

### (A) Form 'N'

**Dr.**            **Profit and Loss A/c for the year ended ......**            **Cr.**

| Previous year ₹ | Expenditures | Current year ₹ | Previous year ₹ | Income | Current year ₹ |
|---|---|---|---|---|---|
| | 1. Interest<br>  (a) Paid<br>  (b) Payable<br>2. Bank Charges<br>3. Salaries and Allowances of Staff<br>4. Contribution to Staff Provident Fund<br>5. Salary and Allowances of Managing Director<br>6. Attendance Fees and Travelling Expenses of Directors and Committee members<br>7. Travelling Expenses of staff<br>8. Rent, Rates and Taxes<br>9. Postage, Telegrams and Telephone Charges<br>10. Printing and Stationery<br>11. Audit Fees<br>12. General Expenses (Contingencies)<br>13. Bad Debts written off or provision made for bad debts<br>14. Depreciation on Fixed Assets<br>15. Land Income and Expenditure<br>16. Other items<br>17. Net profit carried to Balance Sheet | | | 1. Interest Received<br>  (a) On Loans and Advances<br>  (b) On Investments<br>2. Dividend received on Shares<br>3. Commission<br>4. Miscellaneous Income<br>  (a) Share Transfer Fees<br>  (b) Rent<br>  (c) Rebate in interest<br>  (d) Sale of forms<br>  (e) Other Items<br>5. Land Income and Expenditure | |

In case of marketing societies, consumer societies and other societies which undertake trading activities, the Profit and Loss Account, has to be divided into two parts showing separately, The Trading Account and the Profit and Loss Account. The gross profit shown by the Trading Account is to be transferred to the Profit and Loss Account.

In case of Producer's Societies, Processing Societies, Forest Labourers Societies and other Societies undertaking production activities, the manufacturing account has also to be prepared. The manufacturing and trading Accounts are to be prepared in the usual form which is adopted by Sole Proprietorship and Partnership Firms.

## (B) Form 'N'
### Balance Sheet as on ......

| Previous year ₹ | Liabilities | Current year ₹ | Previous year ₹ | Assets | Current year ₹ |
|---|---|---|---|---|---|
| | **I. Share Capital :** | | | **I. Cash / Bank Balances :** | |
| | • Authorised -- shares of ₹.-- each. | | | • Cash on Hand | |
| |  Subscribed -- shares of Rs -- each | | | • Cash in Banks : | |
| |  Less : Calls in Arrears | | |  (i) Current Account | |
| | | | |  (ii) Savings Account | |
| | | | |  (iii) Call Deposits on Banks | |
| | **II. Reserve Fund and Other Funds :** | | | **II. Investments** | |
| | • Statutory Reserve Fund | | | • Govt. Securities | |
| | • Buildings Fund | | | • Other trustee Securities | |
| | • Special Development Fund | | | • Non - trustee Securities | |
| | • Bad and Doubtful Debts Reserve | | | • Shares of other Co-op. Societies | |
| | • Investment Depreciation Fund | | | • Shares, Debentures or Bonds of companies registered under Co. Act. | |
| | • Dividend Equalisation Fund | | | • Fixed Deposits | |
| | • Bonus Equalisation Fund | | | | |
| | • Reserve for overdue interest | | | | |
| | • Other Funds | | | | |
| | **III. Staff Provident Fund :** | | | **III. Investments of Staff Provident Fund :** | |
| | | | | • Investment of Staff Provident Funds | |
| | | | | • Advances against Staff Provident Fund | |
| | **IV. Secured Loans :** | | | **IV. Loans and Advances :** | |
| | • Debentures | | | • Loans | |
| | • Loans, Overdrafts and cash credit from banks | | | • Overdrafts | |
| | • Loans from Government | | | • Cash Credit | |
| | • Other Secured Loans | | | • Loans due by Managing Committee Members ₹ _______ | |
| | | | | • Loans due by Secretary and Other Employees ₹ ____ | |
| | **V. Unsecured Loans :** | | | **V. Sundry Debtors :** | |
| | • Loans, Cash Credit and Overdraft from | | | • Credit Sales | |
| | • Central Banks | | | • Advances | |
| | • From Government | | | • Others | |
| | • From Others | | | | |
| | • Bills Payable | | | | |
| | **VI. Deposits :** | | | **VI. Current Assets :** | |
| | • Fixed Deposits | | | • Stores and spare parts | |
| | • Recurring Deposits | | | • Loose Tools | |
| | • Thrift or Saving Deposits | | | • Stock in Trade | |
| | • Current Deposits | | | • Work in Progress | |
| | • Deposits at call | | | | |
| | • Other Deposits | | | | |
| | • Credit balances in Cash Credit and Overdraft Account | | | | |

| | | | | |
|---|---|---|---|---|
| **VII. Current Liabilities and Provisions :** | | | **VII. Fixed Assets :** | |
| • Sundry Creditors | | | Land and Buildings | |
| • Outstanding Creditors : | | | Leaseholds | |
|     (i)     for purchases | | | Railway Siding | |
|     (ii)    for expenses | | | Plant and Machinery | |
| including salary of staff, rent, taxes etc. | | | Loose Tools and other equipment's | |
| • Advance recoveries, Unexpired | | | Dead Stock | |
| subscription, premium, commission etc. | | | Furniture and Fittings | |
| | | | Live Stock | |
| | | | Vehicles etc. | |
| **VIII. Unpaid Dividends :** | | | **VIII. Miscellaneous Expenditure and Losses :** | |
| | | | Goodwill | |
| | | | Preliminary Expenses | |
| | | | Expenses connected with the issue of shares and debentures including underwriting charges, brokerage etc. | |
| | | | Deferred Revenue Expenditure | |
| **IX Interest Accrued due but not paid :** | | | **IX. Other Items :** | |
| | | | Prepaid expenses | |
| | | | Interest accrued but not due | |
| | | | Other items (to be specified) | |
| **X. Other Liabilities** (to be specified) | | | **X. Profit and Loss Account :** | |
| | | | Accumulated loss not written off | |
| **XI. Profit and Loss Account :** | | | **XI. Current Losses :** | |
| • Profit for the last year | | | | |
| Less : Appropriations | | | | |
| Add : Profit for the current year | | | | |
| **Contingent Liability** | | | | |
| **Total** | | | **Total** | |

## 4.5.2.2  Notes on Items in Balance Sheet

**(Important hints as per Maharashtra State Co-operative Societies Act, 1960)**

**(A) Asset Side :**

- **Cash and Bank Balance :** Fixed deposits and call deposits with Central Banks and other approved bankers should be shown under the heading "Investments" and not under the heading "cash and bank balances".

- **Current Assets :** Mode of valuation and stock shall be stated and the amount in respect of raw-materials, partly finished and finished goods and stores required for consumption should be stated separately. Mode of valuation of work-in-progress shall be stated.

- **Fixed Assets :** Under each head the original cost and the additions thereto and deductions therefrom made during the year and the total depreciation written off or provided up to the end of the year should be stated.

- **Investments :** The nature of each investment and the mode of valuation (cost or market value) should be mentioned. If, the book value of any security is less than the market value, a remark to that effect should be made against each item.

- **Investment of Staff Provident Fund :** Quoted and un-quoted securities should be shown separately.
- **Loans and Advances :** In case of Central Banks and other federal societies, Loans due by societies and individual members should be shown separately.

**(B) Liabilities Side :**

- **Share Capital :** Share Capital contributed by Govt. and by Co-operative societies and different classes of individual members should be shown separately. Terms of redemption or conversion of any redeemable preference shares should be mentioned.

**Reserve Fund and Other Funds :**

(a)  Statutory Reserve Fund and other reserves and funds should be shown separately.

(b)  Additions and deductions since last Balance Sheet are to be shown under each of the specified head.

(c)  Funds in the nature of reserves and funds created out of any profits for specific purposes should be shown separately.

(d)  Maintain a reserve fund and a bad debt fund in respect of the profits, if any, desirable from its transactions.

(e)  Subject to the rules, any portion of the reserve fund not used is the business  of the society shall be invested or deposited as prescribed.

- **Staff Provident Fund :** Staff Provident Funds and any other insurance or Bonus Funds maintained for the benefit of the employees should be shown separately.
- **Secured Loans :** The nature of security should be specified in each case. Where Loans have been guaranteed by Government or state Co-operative or Central Banks, a mention thereof should also be made together with the maximum amount of such guarantee. Loans from Government, State Co-operative Bank or Central Bank or State Bank of India and other Banks should be shown separately.
- **Deposits :** Deposits from societies and individuals should be shown separately.
- **Contingent Liabilities** which have not been provided should also be mentioned in the Balance Sheet by way of a foot note.

## 4.6 ALLOCATION OF PROFIT AS PER CO-OPERATIVE SOCIETY ACT

When the Profit and Loss Account and Balance Sheet are prepared, they are required to be approved by the members in the Annual General Meeting. The appropriation of profit as recommended by the managing committee also need to be approved in the Annual General Meeting. Since the Annual General Meeting is held only after finalising the accounts, the effects of these appropriations are given in the accounts for the next year. This is evident in item No. XI of the liability side. It shows the profit for the last year less appropriations then added with the current profit. The various appropriations are as follows.

(a) **Dividend :** Co-operative Societies are not formed for earning profit. Their main aim is to make the goods and services available to the members at cheaper rates. These Societies therefore are not allowed to pay dividend at a rate exceeding 12%. This rate can be increased maximum upto 15% with the prior approval of the State Government. The Co-operative Societies are not allowed to pay dividend otherwise than out of profit.

**(b) Reserve Fund :** When the Society earns profit at least 25% of the net profits of each year need to be transferred to the Reserve Fund. Since this fund is required to be maintained statutorily, it is also termed as Statutory Fund. Such Reserve Fund may be used in the business of the Society or may be invested as per the directions of the State Government.

**(c) Dividend Equalisation Fund :** The profits earned by the Society will fluctuate from year to year. To avoid the fluctuations in the dividend due to the fluctuations in the profit, Dividend Equalisation Fund may be created. In the years when there is excess profit an amount may be transferred to this fund and can be utilized for maintaining the dividend for the years when the profit is low.

**(d) Building Fund :** For the purpose of construction or purchase of building for the business of the Society this fund may be created.

**(e) Co-operative Education Fund:** Recognising the need of Co-operative education, the committee of Co-operative Law (1956) recommended that each Co-operative Society should contribute to a Co-operative Education Fund. In view of the above the State Government has notified that every Co-operative Society shall contribute.

    (i)    ₹ 10 in respect of those which have suffered loss during the previous Co-operative year.

    (ii)   1/10% of the working capital in respect of those Co-operative Societies which have earned profit during the previous co-operative year, subject to maximum of ₹ 500. In the case of Primary Consumers Societies, the rate is 2 paise per ₹ 100 of the working capital subject to maximum of ₹ 1,000.

## 4.6.1 Ascertainment of Net Profit (Provisions as per Co-operative Societies Act

In accordance with Rule 49A, net profit can be arrived at, by deducting the following items from the Gross Profit :

    (i)    All interest accrued and accruing on accounts of overdue loans, excepting interest on overdue amounts of loans against fixed deposits, gold etc.

    (ii)   Interest payable on loans and deposits.

    (iii)  Establishment charges.

    (iv)  Audit fees or supervision fees.

    (v)   Working expenses inclusive of expenses such as on repairs, rent and taxes.

    (vi)  Depreciation.

    (vii)  Bonus payable to employees in accordance with the provisions of the Payment of Bonus Act, 1965.

    (viii) Provision for payment of Income Tax.

    (ix)  Amount to be paid towards the contribution to the Education Fund at the State Federal Society as notified by the State Government.

    (x)   Amount to be paid towards contribution to the Co-operative cadre employment Fund.

    (xi)  Provision for bad and doubtful debts.

    (xii)  Provision for Redemption of Share Capital Fund for the shares purchased by the Government.

    (xiii) Provision for Investment Fluctuation Fund.

    (xiv) Provision for retirement benefit to the employees of the Society.

    (xv)  Provisions for any other claims which are admissible under the provisions of any other law.

    (xvi) Provisions for bad debts and revenue losses which are not adjusted against any fund created out of profits by the society.

In addition to the above items deductible from gross profits, the following items shall be deducted from the gross profits of the society.

(i) Contribution, if any, to be made towards any sinking fund or guarantee fund constituted as per the provisions of this Act, the Rules or bye-laws of the Society in order to ensure fulfilment of guarantee given by the Government in regard to the loans raised by the Society.

(ii) Provision for depreciation in the value of any security, bonds or shares held by the society as part of its investment.

The net profit so arrived at as explained above together with the amount of profits brought forward from the last co-operative year, shall be available for appropriation. It can be used for the creation of the following :

(i)       Reserve Fund

(ii)      Development Fund

(iii)     Building Fund

(iv)     Charitable Fund

(v)      Dividend Equalisation Fund

(vi)     Any other Fund created under bye-laws of the society.

(vii)    Payment of Dividend to members on their shares on the basis of paid-up capital.

(viii)   Payment of Bonus to members and non-members on the basis of support received from them for the business of the society.

(x)      For any other purpose specified in the Rules and bye-laws.

**Any other purposes :** The other purposes for which a society may appropriate its profits shall be education and enlightenment of the members of the society as also any co-operative or charitable purpose including relief to the poor, education, medical relief and advancement of any other general public utility provided that the expenditure on such items does not exceed 10% of the net profits. Further, no part of the profits is to be appropriated without the approval of the members at the Annual General Meeting and unless it is in accordance with the Act, Rules and bye-laws.

## 4.7 IMPORTANT PROVISIONS OF LAW AS REGARD TO CERTAIN ITEMS OF BALANCE-SHEET

**(a) Reserve Fund**

Section 65 (2) provides that a society may appropriate its net profit to the reserve fund or any other fund for payment of dividend to members on their shares. It further provides that no part of the profit shall be appropriated except with the approval of the General Body. According to section 66, every society has to carry at least one fourth of the net profits of each year to the reserve fund. The reserve fund so created can be used by the society for :

(i) the business of the society, or

(ii) invested as provided under section 70, or

(iii) be used in part for some public purpose, with the prior approval of the State Government, or

(iv) for some such purpose of the state or local interest.

The Reserve Fund cannot be utilised for payment of dividend or bonus. The Reserve Fund not used in the business of the society shall be invested or deposited as prescribed. (subject to the rules).

**(b) Education Fund**

According to Section 68, every society is required to contribute annually towards the education fund of the State Federal Society. Such a contribution is to be made at prescribed rates. Presently, a Primary Consumers Society has to contribute 2 paise per ₹ 100 of the working capital subject to a maximum of ₹ 1,000. For credit Co-operative Societies these rates are : ₹ 100 in case of those societies who have suffered loss in the last year. And for the Credit Co-operative Societies which have earned profits, the contribution is 10 percent of their working capital subject to a maximum of ₹ 500.

**(c) Bonus Equalisation Fund**

A Co-operative Society may create a Bonus Equalisation Fund out of its net profits for payment of bonus to persons other than its paid employees, who are not its members.

**(d) Guarantee Fund**

A Co-operative Society may raise debenture capital or loan which is guaranteed by the State Government. Therefore, a society may require to contribute a portion of its profits towards 'guarantee fund'.

**(e) Dividend**

According to section 67 of the Act, no society can pay dividend to its members at a rate exceeding 12% on the paid-up share capital, except with the prior sanction of the State Government. No dividend shall be paid by a society with shares and unlimited liability without the previous sanction of the Registrar.

No dividend or rebate shall be paid by any Co-operative Society unless such dividend or rebate is recommended by the Managing Committee and approved in the general meeting.

**(f) Dividend Equalisation Fund**

This fund is created in order to enable the Society to pay dividend at a certain rate every year. A co-operative society may credit a sum not exceeding 2% of the paid-up share capital in any year, until the total fund amounts to 9% of the paid-up share capital. The law provides that dividend is to be paid only from net profit of that year or from the Dividend Equalisation Fund. Therefore, when the profits are not adequate in a particular year, this fund can be utilised for payment of dividend at a certain rate.

**(g) Investment of Funds**

Section 70 provides that a Co-operative Society can invest or deposit its funds in one or more of the following

(a) a Central Bank or the State Co-operative Bank.

(b) in any of the securities specified under section 20 of the Indian Trust Act.

(c) in the shares or securities of any other registered society with limited liability.

(d) in any other Co-operative Bank or banking company approved for this purpose by the Registrar. or

(e) any other mode permitted by the rules or special order of the State Government.

**(h) Share Capital Redemption Fund**

There may be some shares purchased by the Government which are to be redeemed after a certain period. For this purpose, share capital redemption fund may be created out of the net profits of the society.

**(i) Writing off Bad Debts**

Rule 49 provides that all loans including interest and recovery charges which are found irrecoverable and are certified as Bad Debts by the auditor can be written off against the Reserve for Bad Debts and the balance bad debts will be debited to Profit and Loss Account or may be written off against the Reserve Fund. Any debt considered bad shall, if so approved by the Registrar, be written off by general meeting in the following order against :

(a) the Bad Debt Fund, or any other fund created out of profits, for writing off bad debts but not earmarked for any other specific purpose;

(b) the Reserve Fund created as per law.

## 4.8 ILLUSTRATIONS

# Final Accounts of Credit-Co-operative Societies

### Illustration 1

From the following information relating to Urban Credit Co-operative Society Ltd., Pune you are required to prepare Profit and Loss Account for the year ended 31st March, 2016 and Balance-Sheet as on that date :

**Balance sheet as on 1st April, 2015**

| Liabilities | ₹ | Assets | ₹ |
|---|---|---|---|
| Share Capital | 25,000 | Cash in hand | 250 |
| Reserve Fund | 2,500 | Bank Current Account | 1,600 |
| Dividend Equalisation fund | 1,000 | Shares in PDCC Bank | 150 |
| Members Deposit | 13,500 | Members Loan | 57,000 |
| Loan from Dena Bank | 21,500 | Furniture | 5,000 |
| Outstanding Salary | 500 | Fixed Deposits | 10,000 |
| Profit and Loss Account | 10,000 | | |
| Opening Bal. (1-4-2014)        2,000 | | | |
| Add Profits (2014-15)    (+)  8,000 | | | |
| | **74,000** | | **74,000** |

| Dr. | Receipts and Payments Account for the year ended 31st March, 2016 | | Cr. |
|---|---|---|---|
| **Receipts** | ₹ | **Payments** | ₹ |
| Balance on 1-4-2015 : | | Bank Current Account | 12,600 |
| • Cash in hand | 250 | Bank Loans | 14,000 |
| • Bank Current Account | 15,500 | Share Capital | 700 |
| Loan from PDCC Bank | 25,000 | Furniture | 1,000 |
| Share Capital | 2,500 | Typewriter | 4,000 |
| Deposits from Members | 4,000 | Member Deposit | 500 |
| Members short Term Loans | 4,500 | Salaries | 2,000 |
| Entrance Fees | 100 | Printing and Stationery | 500 |
| Commission | 350 | Rent and Taxes | 1,000 |
| Interest on Loan | 13,500 | Travelling Expenses | 1,100 |
| Interest on Fixed Deposits | 1,000 | Allowances | 1,500 |
| Dividend | 50 | Interest on Bank Loan | 1,250 |
| | | Member Short Term Loans | 18,500 |
| | | Audit Fees | 250 |
| | | Cash in hand | 7,850 |
| | **66,750** | | **66,750** |

**Adjustments :**

1. Salary payable, on 31st March, 2016 amounted to ₹ 600.
2. Provide depreciation @ 10% p.a. on Furniture and Typewriter.
3. Outstanding interest on loan to members amounted to ₹ 2,100.
4. Directors recommended dividend @ 10% on Share Capital as on 1st April, 2015.

**Solution**

**In the books of Urban Credit Co-operative Society Ltd, Pune**

Dr.      **Profit and Loss A/c for the year ended 31st March 2016**      Cr.

| Expenditure | ₹ | Income | ₹ |
|---|---|---|---|
| 1. Interest | 1,250 | 1. Interest received | 16,600 |
|    (a) Paid on Deposit | |    (a) On Loans and | |
|    (b) Paid on Bank Loan  (+) 1,250 | |       Advances   13,500 | |
| | |    (b) On Investment | |
| | |       (Fixed Deposit)  (+) 1,000 | |
| | |          14,500 | |
| | | Add : Outstanding interest | |
| | | on Loan to Members  (+) 2,100 | |
| 2. Bank charges | | 2. Dividend received on shares | 50 |
| 3. Salaries and Allowances of Staff | | 3. Commision | 350 |
|    Salaries      2,000 | 2,100 | 4. Miscellaneous income | |
|    Less : Outstanding | |    (a) Share Transfer Fees | |
|    (2014-15)     (–) 500 | |    (b) Rent | |
|       1,500 | |    (c) Rebate in Interest | |
|    Add : Outstanding  (+) 600 | |    (d) Sale of forms | |
|    • Allowances | 1,500 |    (e) Other Items | |
| | |       (i) Entrance fees | 100 |
| 4. Contribution to Staff | | 5. Land Income and Expenditure | |
|    Provident Fund | | | |
| 5. Salaries & Allowances | | | |
|    of Managing Director | | | |
| 6. Attendance Fees and Travelling Expenses of Directors and Committee members | | | |
| 7. Travelling Expenses of staff | 1,100 | | |
| 8. Rent, Rates and Taxes | 1,000 | | |
| 9. Postage, Telegram and Telephone charges | | | |
| 10. Printing and Stationery | 500 | | |
| 11. Audit Fees | 250 | | |
| 12. General Expenses | | | |
| 13. Bad debts written off or provision for bad and doubtful debts. | | | |
| 14. Depreciation on fixed Assets | | | |
|    • Furniture @10% p.a. | 600 | | |
|    • Typewriter @10% p.a. | 400 | | |
| 15. Land Income and Expenditure | | | |
| 16. Other items | | | |
| Net Profit carried to Balance-sheet | 8,400 | | |
| | **17,100** | | **17,100** |

## Balance Sheet as on 31st March, 2016

| Liabilities | ₹ | ₹ | Assets | ₹ | ₹ |
|---|---|---|---|---|---|
| **1. Share Capital** | | | **1. Cash and Bank** | | |
| **(A) Authorised Capital** | | – | • Cash in hand | | |
| **(B) Issued & Subscribed** | | 26,800 | | | 7,850 |
| (25,000 + 2,500 – 700) | | | | | |
| **2. Reserve Fund and Other** | | | **2. Investments** | | |
| • Reserve Fund | | | • Shares in P.D.C.C. Bank | | 150 |
| Add : 25% Profits of 2012-13 | 2,500 | 4,500 | • Fixed Deposits | | 10,000 |
| transferred to Reserve fund | | | **3. Investments of Staff** | | |
| | (+) 2,000 | | **Provident Fund** | | |
| • Dividend Equalisation | | 1,000 | **4. Loans and Advances** | | |
| Fund | | | Members Loan | | 71,000 |
| | | | (57,000 – 4,500 + 18,500) | | |
| **3. Staff Providend Fund** | | | **5. Sundry Debtors** | | |
| **4. Secured Loans** | | | **6. Current Assets** | | |
| Bank Loans | | 32,500 | | | |
| (21,500 + 25,000 – 14,000) | | | | | |
| **5. Unsecured Loans** | | | **7. Fixed Assets** | | |
| Bank Overdraft | | | • Furniture | 5,000 | 5,400 |
| (15,500 – 12,600 – 1,600) | | 1,300 | Add : Additions | (+) 1,000 | |
| **6. Deposits** | | | | 6,000 | |
| Members Deposit | | 17,000 | Less : Depre. @10% p.a. | (–) 600 | |
| (13,500 + 4,000 – 500) | | | • Typewriter | 4,000 | 3,600 |
| | | | Less Depre. @10% p.a. | (–) 400 | |
| **7. Current Liabilities and** | | | **8. Miscellaneous Expenses** | | |
| **Provisions** | | 600 | | | |
| • Salary Payable | | | | | |
| **8. Unpaid Dividends** | | 2,500 | **9. Other Items** | | |
| ⎛Provision – Paid⎞ | | | Outstanding Interest | | |
| ⎝ 2,500 – Nil ⎠ | | | | | 2,100 |
| **9. Interest Accrued due but** | | | **10. Profit and Loss Account** | | |
| **10. Other Liabilities** | | | **11. Current Losses** | | |
| **11. Profit and Loss A/c** | | 13,900 | | | |
| Profit and Loss Account | | | | | |
| balance as on 1-4-2014 | 2,000 | | | | |
| Add : Profits for the year | (+) 8,000 | | | | |
| | 10,000 | | | | |
| Less : Proposed Dividend | (–) 2,500 | | | | |
| | 7,500 | | | | |
| Less : 25% profit of 2014-15 | (–) 2,000 | | | | |
| | 5,500 | | | | |
| Add : Profits for 2015-16 | (+) 8,400 | | | | |
| **Contingent Liability** | | | | | |
| | | 1,00,100 | | | 1,00,100 |

| Illustration 2 |

From the following Trial Balance of Pimpri People's Co-operative Credit Society Ltd., Pimpri as on 31st March, 2016 and other adjustments, prepare Profit and Loss Account for the year ended 31st March, 2016 and a Balance-Sheet as on that date.

**Trial Balance as on 31st March, 2016**

| Particulars | Debit ₹ | Credit ₹ |
|---|---|---|
| Cash in hand | 170 | |
| Cast at Bank | 1,300 | |
| Fixed Deposit | 15,000 | |
| Furniture | 1,200 | |
| Interest on Deposits | 8,000 | |
| Outstanding interest on Loans | 800 | |
| Salary | 3,000 | |
| Establishment Charges | 200 | |
| Printing and Stationery | 150 | |
| Travelling Expenses of Staff | 200 | |
| Insurance charges | 150 | |
| Contribution to Staff Provident Fund | 200 | |
| Loan due from members | 3,00,000 | |
| Share Capital | | 70,000 |
| Reserve Fund | | 10,000 |
| Members Deposit | | 2,10,875 |
| Unpaid Dividend | | 1,010 |
| Dividend Equalisation Reserve | | 1,000 |
| Staff Provided Fund | | 2,000 |
| Profit & Loss Appropriation Account (Balance as on 1-4-2016) | | 1,000 |
| Profits for the year 2014-2015 | | 16,000 |
| Interest | | 17,000 |
| Commission | | 1,000 |
| Share Transfer Fees | | 200 |
| Co-operative Development fund | | 200 |
| Education fund | | 85 |
| | 3,30,370 | 3,30,370 |

**Other Adjustments :**
1. Interest due to members deposit was ₹ 500.
2. Interest accrued due but not received was ₹ 200.
3. Additions to furniture during year amounted to ₹ 100. Provide depreciation @10% p.a. on closing balance.
4. Salary outstanding and prepaid amounted to ₹ 30 and ₹ 50 respectively.
5. Audit fees due but not paid for the year amounted to ₹ 300.
6. Authorised share capital of the society was 10,000 shares of ₹ 10 each.
7. Directors proposed the following appropriations for the year 2014-2015.
   (a) Dividend to shareholders @5% on share capital.
   (b) 25% to Reserve Fund.
   (c) Additions to Dividend Equalisation Reserve ₹ 500.
   (d) Additions to Building Fund ₹ 1,000.

Solution

**In the books of Pimpri People's Co-operative Credit Society Ltd., Pimpri**

Dr.      **Profit and Loss Account for the year ended 31st March 2016**      Cr.

| Expenditure | ₹ | Income | ₹ |
|---|---|---|---|
| 1. Interest | 8,500 | 1. Interest received | 17,200 |
|   (a) Paid on Deposit    8,000 | |   (a) On Loans and | |
|      Add : Interest due | |      Advances    17,000 | |
|      to Members | |   (b) On Investment    17,000 | |
|      Deposit      (+)    500 | |      Add : Interest accrued | |
| 2. Bank Charges | |      due but not received (+)    200 | |
| | | | |
| 3. Salaries and Allowances | | 2. Dividend received on shares | |
|      of Staff      3,000 | 2,980 | 3. Commision | 1,000 |
|      Add : Outstanding | | 4. Miscellaneous income | |
|      Salary      (+)    30 | |   (a) Share Transfer fees | 200 |
|          3,030 | |   (b) Rent | |
|      Less : Prepaid Salary (−)   50 | |   (c) Rebate in Interest | |
| 4. Contribution to staff | |   (d) Sale of forms | |
|      Provident Fund | 200 |   (e) Other Items | |
| 5. Salaries and Allowances | | 5. Land Income and Expenditure | |
|      of Managing Director | | | |
| 6. Attendance Fees and | | | |
|      Travelling Expenses of | | | |
|      Directors and Committee | | | |
|      members | | | |
| 7. Travelling Expenses of staff | 200 | | |
| 8. Rent, Rates and Taxes | | | |
| 9. Postage, Telegram and | | | |
|      Telephone charges | | | |
| 10. Printing and Stationery | 150 | | |
| 11. Audit Fees | | | |
|    • Outstanding Audit fees | 300 | | |
| 12. General Expenses | | | |
| 13. Bad debts written off or provision for bad and doubtful debts. | | | |
| 14. Depreciation on Fixed Assets | | | |
|    • Furniture @10% p.a. | 120 | | |
| 15. Land Income and | | | |
|      Expenditure Account | | | |
| 16. Other items | | | |
|    • Establishment charges | 200 | | |
|    • Insurance charges | 150 | | |
| Net Profit carried to Balance-Sheet | 5,600 | | |
| | **18,400** | | **18,400** |

### Balance Sheet as on 31st March, 2016

| Liabilities | ₹ | ₹ | Assets | ₹ | ₹ |
|---|---|---|---|---|---|
| **1. Share Capital** | | | **1. Cash and Bank Balance** | | |
| **(A) Authorised Capital** | | 1,00,000 | Cash in hand | | |
| 10,000 shares of ₹ 10 each | 1,00,000 | | Cash at Bank | | 170 |
| **(B) Issued & Subscribed Capital** | | 70,000 | **2. Investments** | | 1,300 |
| | | | Fixed Deposits | | |
| 7,000 shares of ₹ 10 each fully called-up and paid-up | 70,000 | | **3. Investments of Staff Provident Fund** | | 15,000 |
| **2. Reserve Fund and Other Funds** | | | **4. Loans and Advances** | | |
| • Reserve Fund | 10,000 | 14,000 | Loan due from Members | | 3,00,000 |
| Add : 25% Profits of 2014-15 transferred to Reserve fund | (+) 4,000 | | **5. Sundry Debtors** | | |
| • Dividend Equalisation Reserve | 1,000 | 1,500 | **6. Current Assets** | | |
| Add : Additions | (+) 500 | | **7. Fixed Assets** | | |
| | | | Furniture | 1,100 | 1,080 |
| • Co-operative Development Fund | | 200 | Add : Additions | (+) 100 | |
| • Education Fund | | 85 | | 1,200 | |
| • Additions to Building fund | | 1,000 | Less : Depre. @10% p.a. | (−) 120 | |
| **3. Staff Provident Fund** | | 2,000 | **8. Miscellaneous Expenses & Losses** | | |
| **4. Secured Loans** | | | **9. Other Items** | | |
| **5. Unsecured Loans** | | | Interest accrued due but not received | | 200 |
| **6. Deposits** | | | Prepaid Salary | | |
| Members Deposit | | 2,10,875 | **10. Profit and Loss Account** | | 800 |
| **7. Current Liabilities and Provisions** | | | **11. Current Losses** | | 50 |
| • Outstanding Salary | | 30 | | | |
| • Outstanding Audit Fees | | 300 | | | |
| **8. Unpaid Dividends** | | 1,010 | | | |
| Proposed Dividend @5% on | | 3,500 | | | |
| **9. Interest Accrued due but not paid** | | | | | |
| **10. Other Liabilities** | | 500 | | | |
| **11. Profit and Loss Account** | | 13,600 | | | |
| Profit & Loss Appropriation A/c balance as on 1-4-2014 | 1,000 | | | | |
| Add : Profits for the year 2014-15 | (+ 16,000 | | | | |
| | 17,000 | | | | |
| Less : Proposed Dividend @5% on Share Capital i.e. ₹ 70,000 | (−) 3,500 | | | | |
| | 13,500 | | | | |
| Less : 25% profits of 2014-15 transferred to Reserve fund | (−) 4,000 | | | | |
| | 9,500 | | | | |
| Less : Additions to Dividend Equalisation Reserve | (−) 500 | | | | |
| | 9,000 | | | | |
| Less Additions to Building fund | (−) 1,000 | | | | |
| | 8,000 | | | | |
| Add Profits for 2015-16 | (+) 5,600 | | | | |
| **Contingent Liability** | | | | | |
| | | 3,18,600 | | | 3,18,600 |

### Illustration 3

From the following Trial Balance of Pune People's Co-operative Credit Society Ltd., Pune as on 31st March, 2016 and other information, prepare Profit and Loss Account for the year ended 31st March, 2016 and a Balance-Sheet as on that date.

**Trial Balance as on 31st March, 2016**

| Particulars | Debit ₹ | Credit ₹ |
|---|---|---|
| Share Capital called-up and paid-up | | 7,50,000 |
| Cash in hand | 3,600 | |
| Cast at Bank | 14,000 | |
| Fixed Deposit with Maharashtra State Co-operative Bank | 1,55,000 | |
| Reserve Fund | | 50,000 |
| Members Deposit | | 22,47,750 |
| Office Furniture | 7,000 | |
| Interest on Deposits | 80,000 | |
| Interest due on Loans | 8,000 | |
| Salary and Allowances | 30,000 | |
| Office Expenses | 5,000 | |
| Printing and Stationery | 400 | |
| Travelling and Conveyance | 600 | |
| Insurance Premium | 1,000 | |
| Contribution to Provident Fund | 2,000 | |
| Loan due from Members | 30,00,000 | |
| Dividend paid | 35,000 | |
| Dividend Equalisation Reserve | | 18,000 |
| Staff Providend Fund | | 20,000 |
| Profit & Loss Appropriation Account (balance as on 1st April, 2014) | | 11,000 |
| Profits for the year 2014-2015 | | 60,000 |
| Interest received | | 1,78,000 |
| Commission | | 4,000 |
| Sundry Income | | 300 |
| Co-operative Development Fund | | 2,550 |
| | 33,41,600 | 33,41,600 |

**Other Adjustments :**

1. Authorised Share Capital of the society was ₹ 10,00,000 divided into 1,00,000 shares of ₹ 10 each.
2. Interest due to members deposit amounted to ₹ 5,000.
3. Interest accrued due but not received was ₹ 2,000.
4. Salary due but not paid was ₹ 300.
5. Charge depreciation @10% p.a. of office furniture.
6. Audit fees due unpaid for the year amounted to ₹ 3,000.
7. Directors made the following appropriations for the year 2014-2015.
   (i) Dividend @5% on paid-up share capital.
   (ii) Additions to Co-operative Development fund by ₹ 3,000.
8. Directors proposed 5% dividend for the year 2015-16.

Solution

**In the books of Pune People's Co-operative Credit Society Ltd., Pune**

Dr.        **Profit and Loss Account for the year ended 31st March 2016**        Cr.

| Expenditure | ₹ | Income | ₹ |
|---|---|---|---|
| 1. Interest | 93,000 | 1. Interest received | 1,80,000 |
|    (a) Paid on Deposit    80,000 | |    (a) On Loans and | |
|    (b) Interest due | |        Advances    1,78,000 | |
|       on loans    8,000 | |    (b) On Investment | |
|    Add : Interest due | |        1,78,000 | |
|    on members Deposit (+) 5,000 | |    Add : Interest accrued | |
| 2. Bank Charges | |    due but not received (+) 2,000 | |
| 3. Salaries and Allowances of | | 2. Dividend received on Shares | |
|    Staff    30,000 | 30,300 | 3. Commision | 4,000 |
|    Add : Salary due but | | 4. Miscellaneous Income | |
|    not paid    (+) 300 | |    (a) Share Transfer Fees | |
| 4. Contribution to Staff | |    (b) Rent | |
|    Provident Fund | 2,000 |    (c) Rebate in Interest | |
| 5. Salaries & Allowances | |    (d) Sale of forms | |
|    of Managing Director | |    (e) Other Items | |
| 6. Attendance Fees and | |    (i) Sundry Income | 300 |
|    Travelling Expenses of | | 5. Land Income and Expenditure | |
|    Directors and Committee | | | |
|    members | | | |
| 7. Travelling Expenses of staff | 600 | | |
| 8. Rent, Rates and Taxes | | | |
| 9. Postage, Telegram and | | | |
|         Telephone charges | | | |
| 10. Printing and Stationery | 400 | | |
| 11. Unpaid Audit Fees | 3,000 | | |
| 12. General Expenses | | | |
| 13. Bad debts written off or | | | |
|    provision for bad and | | | |
|    doubtful debts. | | | |
| 14. Depreciation on Fixed Assets | | | |
|    • Office Furniture @10% | 700 | | |
|       p.a. | | | |
| 15. Land Income and | | | |
|    Expenditure | | | |
| 16. Other items | | | |
|    • Office Expenses | 5,000 | | |
|    • Insurance Premium | 1,000 | | |
| Net Profit carried to Balance-Sheet | 48,300 | | |
| | **1,84,300** | | **1,84,300** |

### Balance Sheet as on 31st March, 2016

| Liabilities | ₹ | ₹ | Assets | ₹ | ₹ |
|---|---|---|---|---|---|
| **1. Share Capital** | | 10,00,000 | **1. Cash and Bank** | | |
| **(A) Authorised Capital** | | | • Cash in hand | | |
| 1,00,000 shares of ₹ 10 | | | • Cash at Bank | | 3,600 |
| **(B) Issued & Subscribed** | 10,00,000 | | **2. Investments** | | 14,000 |
| 75,000 shares of ₹ 10 each fully | | 7,50,000 | Fixed Deposit with Maharashtra | | |
| called-up and paid-up | | | State Co-operative Bank | | |
| | 7,50,000 | | | | 1,55,000 |
| **2. Reserve Fund and Other** | | | **3. Investments of Staff** | | |
| •   Reserve Fund | 50,000 | 65,000 | **4. Loans and Advances** | | |
| Add : 25% Profits of 2014-15 | (+) 15,000 | | • Loan due from Members | | |
| transferred to Reserve fund | | | **5.   Sundry Debtors** | | 30,00,000 |
| •   Dividend Equalisation Reserve | | 18,000 | **6.   Curent Assets** | | |
| •   Co-operative Development | | 5,550 | **7.   Fixed Assets** | | |
| Fund | 2,550 | | Office Furntiure | 7,000 | 6,300 |
| Add : Additions | (+) 3,000 | | Less Depre. @10% p.a. | (–) 700 | |
| | | | **8.   Miscellaneous Expenses** | | |
| **3. Staff Providend Fund** | | 20,000 | **    & Losses** | | |
| **4. Secured Loans** | | | **9.   Other Items** | | |
| **5. Unsecured Loans** | | | Interest accrued due but | | 2,000 |
| **6.   Deposits** | | | not received | | |
| Members Deposit | | 22,47,750 | **10.   Profit and Loss A/c** | | |
| **7. Current Liabilities &** | | | | | |
| •   Salary due but not paid | | | **11.   Current Losses** | | |
| •   Unpaid Audit fees | | 300 | | | |
| | | 3,000 | | | |
| **8. Unpaid Dividends** | | 2,500 | | | |
| (Provision   Paid | | | | | |
| 37,500 – 35,000 ) | | | | | |
| **9. Interest accrued due but not paid** | | | | | |
| **10.   Other Liabilities** | | 5,000 | | | |
| **11.   Profit and Loss Account** | 11,000 | 63,800 | | | |
| Profit & Loss Appropriation A/c | | | | | |
| balance as on 1-4-2014 | (+) 60,000 | | | | |
| Add : Profits for the year 2014-15 | 71,000 | | | | |
| Less : Proposed Dividend @5% on | (–) 37,500 | | | | |
| paid up share capital for 2014-15 | 33,500 | | | | |
| i.e. ₹ 7,50,000 | | | | | |
| Less : Additions to | (–) 3,000 | | | | |
| Co-operative Development | 30,500 | | | | |
| Less : 25% profits of 2014-15 | (–) 15,000 | | | | |
| | 15,500 | | | | |
| Add : Profits for 2015-16 | 48,300 | | | | |
| **Contingent Liability** | | | | | |
| | | **31,80,900** | | | **31,80,900** |

### Calculation and Notes :

1. Appropriations of the profit cannot be made without the approval of Annual General Meeting and as such dividend proposed @5% for the year 2015-16 is not shown in final accounts prepared on 31st March, 2016.
2. As per the statutory provisions every society has to appropriate 25% to Reserve fund (i.e. 25% of ₹ 60,000 – profits of the year 2014-15).

### Illustration 4

From the following Trial Balance of Urban Vikas Co-operative Credit Society Ltd., Pune prepare Profit and Loss Account for the year ended 31-03-2016 and a Balance Sheet as on that date.

Trial Balance as on 31-03-2016

| Particulars | Debit ₹ | Credit ₹ |
|---|---|---|
| Salaries and Honorarium | 79,600 | |
| Interest on deposits and loans | 3,32,000 | |
| Postage | 1,000 | |
| Printing and Stationary | 7,200 | |
| Office Expenses | 7,500 | |
| Office Rent | 6,300 | |
| Travelling Expenses | 7,600 | |
| Meeting Expenses | 1,600 | |
| Audit Fees | 1,000 | |
| Telephone Charges | 4,000 | |
| Advertisments | 1,400 | |
| Commission | 120 | |
| Donation | 200 | |
| Legal Charges | 3,000 | |
| Insurance | 1,600 | |
| Motor Tax | 2,200 | |
| Sundry Expenses | 1,400 | |
| Share Capital | | 10,00,000 |
| Interest Received | | 5,80,900 |
| Commission Received | | 900 |
| Dividend Received | | 8,700 |
| Reserve Fund | | 71,000 |
| Dividend Equalisation Reserve | | 6,000 |
| Deposits : | | |
| (i) Fixed | | 9,16,000 |
| (ii) Savings | | 1,30,,000 |
| Loans and Overdrafts | | 16,00,000 |
| Development Fund | | 29,000 |
| Cash in hand | 16,000 | |
| Cash at Bank | 2,91,000 | |
| Dividend paid | 40,000 | |
| P.D.C.C. Bank Shares | 2,00,000 | |
| Loans | 32,60,000 | |
| Motor Car | 1,15,000 | |
| Stock | 30,000 | |
| Profits for the year 2014-15 | | 67,220 |
| | 44,09,720 | 44,09,720 |

**Additional Information :**

1. Provide depreciation on Motor Car ₹ 16,000
2. Outstanding Expenses were - Electricity Charges ₹ 300, Office Rent ₹ 500.
3. Prepaid Insurance amounted to ₹ 200
4. Outstanding interest on loan to members ₹ 5,000.

5. Dividend at 5% was declared on Share Capital of ₹ 9,00,000 as on 31-3- 2015.
6. Transfer 25 % of the profits of 2014-15 to Reserve Fund.

Solution

**In the books of Urban Vikas Co-operative Credit Society Ltd, Pune.**

Dr.              **Profit and Loss A/c for the year ended 31st March 2016**              Cr.

| Expenditure | | ₹ | Income | | ₹ |
|---|---|---|---|---|---|
| 1. | **Interest** | 3,32,000 | 1 | **Interest received** | |
| | (a) Paid on deposits & | | | (a) On Loans and  Advances | |
| | Loans          3,32,000 | | | (b) On Investment     5,80,900 | |
| | (b) Payable            – | | | Add Outstanding | 5,85,900 |
| 2. | **Bank Charges** | | | Interest on Loans  to | |
| | | | | Members          (+)  5,000 | |
| 3. | **Salaries & Allowances of** | | 2. | **Dividend Received on Shares** | 8,700 |
| | **Staff** | 79,600 | 3. | **Commission** | 900 |
| | Salaries  and Honorarium | | 4. | **Miscellaneous Income** | |
| 4. | **Contribution to Staff** | | | (a) Share Transfer fees | |
| | **Providend Fund** | | | (b) Rent | |
| 5. | **Salaries and Allowances of** | | | (c) Rebate in Interest | |
| | **Managing Director** | | | (d) Sales of forms | |
| 6. | **Attendance Fees and** | | | (e) Other items | |
| | **Travelling Expenses of** | | 5. | **Land Income and** | |
| | **Directors** | | | **Expenditure** | |
| 7. | **Travelling Expenses of staff** | | | | |
| | • Travelling Expenses | 7,600 | | | |
| 8. | **Rent, Rates and Taxes** | | | | |
| | • Office Rent         6,300 | 6,800 | | | |
| | Add Outstanding | | | | |
| | Office rent      (+)   500 | | | | |
| | • Motor Tax | 2,200 | | | |
| 9. | **Postage Telegram &** | | | | |
| | **Telephone Charges –** | | | | |
| | Postage | 1,000 | | | |
| | Telephone Charges | 4,000 | | | |
| 10. | **Printing and Stationery** | 7,200 | | | |
| 11. | **Audit Fees** | 1,000 | | | |
| 12. | **General Expenses** | | | | |
| | Sundry Expenses | 1,400 | | | |
| 13. | **Bad Debts or Provision for** | | | | |
| | **bad debts** | | | | |
| 14. | **Depre. on Fixed Assests** | | | | |
| | • Motor Car | 16,000 | | | |
| 15. | **Land Income and** | | | | |
| | **Expenditure** | | | | |
| 16. | **Other Items** | | | | |
| | • Office Expenses | 7,500 | | | |
| | • Meeting Expenses | 1,600 | | | |
| | • Advertisements | 1,400 | | | |
| | • Commission | 120 | | | |

| | ₹ | | | ₹ |
|---|---|---|---|---|
| • Donations | | 200 | | |
| • Legal Charges | | 3,000 | | |
| • Insurance | 1,600 | | | |
| Less Prepaid | (–) 200 | 1,400 | | |
| • Outstanding Electricity Charges | | 300 | | |
| **Net Profit carried to Balance Sheet** | | 1,21,180 | | |
| | | **5,95,500** | | **5,95,500** |

## Balance Sheet as on 31st March, 2016

| | Liabilities | ₹ | ₹ | | Assets | ₹ | ₹ |
|---|---|---|---|---|---|---|---|
| 1. | **Share Capital** | | | 1. | **Cash and Bank Balances** | | |
| | (a) Authorised Capital | | 10,00,000 | | • Cash in Hand | | 16,000 |
| | (b) Issued & Subscribed Capital | | | | • Cash at Bank | | 2,91,000 |
| 2. | **Reserve Fund and Other Funds** | | | 2. | **Investments** | | |
| | | | | | P.D.C.C. Bank Shares | | 2,00,000 |
| | • Reserve Fund | 71,000 | 87805 | 3. | **Investments of Staff Providend Fund** | | |
| | Add 25% transfer to R.F. | (+) 16,805 | | 4. | **Loans And Advances** | | |
| | • Dividend Equalisation Reserve | | 6,000 | | Loans | | 32,60,000 |
| | Development Fund | | 29,000 | 5. | **Sundry Debtors** | | |
| 3. | **Staff Providend Fund** | | | 6. | **Current Assets** | | |
| 4. | **Secured Loans** | | | | • Stock | | 30,000 |
| 5. | **Unsecured Loans** | | | 7. | **Fixed Assets** | | 99,000 |
| | • Loans and Overdrafts | | 16,00,000 | | • Motor Car | 1,15,000 | |
| 6. | **Deposits** | | | | Less Depreciation | (–) 16,000 | |
| | • Fixed Deposits | | 9,16,000 | 8. | **Miscellaneous Expenses & Losses** | | |
| | • Saving Deposits | | 1,30,000 | 9. | **Other Items** | | |
| 7. | **Current Liabilities and Provisions** | | | | • Prepaid Insurance | | 200 |
| | • Outstanding Electricity Charges | | 300 | | • Outstanding Interest on Loan to Members | | 5,000 |
| | • Outstanding Office Rent | | 500 | 10. | **Profit and Loss Account** | | |
| 8. | **Unpaid Dividends** | | 5,000 | 11. | **Current Losses** | | |
| | $\begin{pmatrix} \text{Provision} - \text{Paid} \\ 45,000 \quad - \quad 40,000 \end{pmatrix}$ | | | | | | |
| 9. | **Interest Accrued due but not paid** | | | | | | |
| 10. | **Other Liabilities** | | | | | | |
| 11. | **Profit and Loss Account** | | 1,26,595 | | | | |
| | Profit for the year 2014-15 | 67,220 | | | | | |
| | Less Dividend (5% of ₹ 9,00,000) | – 45,000 | | | | | |
| | | 22,220 | | | | | |
| | Less 25% Profits transferred to Reserve Fund (25% of ₹ 67,220) | – 16,805 | | | | | |
| | | 5,415 | | | | | |
| | Add Profits for 2015-16 | (+) 1,21,180 | | | | | |
| | **Contingent Liability** | | | | | | |
| | | | **39,01,200** | | | | **39,01,200** |

## Illustration 5

The Trial Balance of Self-Help Co-operative Credit Society Ltd., Sholapur as on 31.3.2016 is as follows.

### Trial Balance as on 31-3-2016

| Particulars | | Debit ₹ | Credit ₹ |
|---|---|---|---|
| Cash in Hand | | 2,700 | |
| Cash with S.D.C.C. Bank | | 10,000 | |
| Balance with Dena Bank | | 9,900 | |
| Investments | | 1,55,000 | |
| Loan due from Members | | 30,00,000 | |
| Office Furniture | | 10,000 | |
| Share Capital | | | 7,50,000 |
| Reserve Fund | | | 35,000 |
| Dividend Equalisation Reserve | | | 20,000 |
| Staff Provident Fund | | | 20,000 |
| Deposits from Members | | | 22,48,000 |
| Dividend | | 31,000 | |
| Profit and Loss A/c | | | |
|   (i) Balance on 1-4-2014 | 23,000 | | 83,000 |
|   (ii) Profits for the year 2014-15 | (+) 60,000 | | |
| Interest on Investment and Loan | | | 1,75,000 |
| Renewal Fees | | | 4,000 |
| Sundry Income | | | 2,300 |
| Salaries and allowances of staff | | 29,700 | |
| Establishment charges for a executive office | | 5,000 | |
| Printing and Stationery | | 400 | |
| Travelling Expenses | | 600 | |
| Insurance Premium | | 1,000 | |
| Contribution to Provident Fund | | 2,000 | |
| Interest paid on Deposits | | 80,000 | |
| | | 33,37,300 | 33,37,300 |

**Adjustments :**

1. Interest payable on members deposits amounted to ₹ 5,000
2. Interest receivable on members loan ₹ 8,000 and on investments ₹ 2,000
3. Outstanding expenses were as follows : Salaries - ₹ 300; Audit Fees - ₹ 3,000.
4. Dividend at 5% was declared on Share Capital of ₹ 7,00,000 as on 31-3-2015 out of profits of 2014-15.
5. Transfer 25% profit of 2014-15 to Reserve Fund.

   Prepare Profit and Loss A/c for the year ended 31-03-2016 and a Balance Sheet as on that date.

**Solution**

**In the books of Self Help Co-operative Credit Society Ltd, Sholapur**

Dr.      **Profit and Loss Account for the year ended 31st March 2016**      Cr.

| Expenditure | ₹ | Income | ₹ |
|---|---|---|---|
| 1. **Interest** | 85,000 | 1. **Interest received** | 1,85,000 |
|   (a) Paid on Deposits    80,000 | |   (a) On Loans & Advances ⎫ | |
|   (b) Payable        (+) 5,000 | |   (b) On Investment     ⎭ | |
| 2. **Bank Charges** | |                    1,75,000 | |
| 3. **Salaries & Allowances to staff** | |   Add : Interest | |
|   Salaries & Allowances | 30,000 |   receivable on | |
|   to staff          29,700 | |   (a) Members Loan   (+) 8,000 | |
|   Add : Outstanding | |   (b) Investments     (+ 2,000 | |
|   salaries        (+) 300 | | 2. **Dividend received on Shares** | |
| 4. **Contribution to Staff** | | 3. **Commission** | |
|   **Providend Fund** | 2,000 | 4. **Miscellaneous Income** | |
| 5. **Salaries and allowances of** | |   (a) Share Transfer Fees | |
|   **Managing Director** | |   (b) Rent | |
| 6. **Attendance Fees & Travelling** | |   (c) Rebate in Interest | |
|   **expenses of directors** | |   (d) Sale of forms | |
| 7. **Travelling expenses of staff** | |   (e) Other Items | |
|   Travelling Expenses | 600 |     • Renewal Fees | 4,000 |
| 8. **Rent, Rates and Taxes** | |     • Sundry Income | 2,300 |
| 9. **Postage, Telegram and** | | 5. **Land Income and Expenditure** | |
|   **Telephone charges** | | | |
| 10. **Printing and Stationery** | | | |
|   Printing and Stationery | 400 | | |
| 11. **Audit Fees** | | | |
|   • Outstanding Audit Fees | 3,000 | | |
| 12. **General Expenses** | | | |
| 13. **Bad debts or provision for Bad** | | | |
|   **debts** | | | |
| 14. **Depreciation on Fixed assets** | | | |
| 15. **Land Income and Expenditure** | | | |
| 16. **Other Items** | | | |
|   • Establishment charges for a | | | |
|     executive office | 5,000 | | |
|   • Insurance Premium | 1,000 | | |
|   **Net Profit carried to Balance** | 64,300 | | |
|   **Sheet** | | | |
| | **1,91,300** | | **1,91,300** |

## Balance Sheet as on 31st March 2016

| Liabilities | ₹ | ₹ | Assets | ₹ | ₹ |
|---|---|---|---|---|---|
| **1. Share Capital** | | | **1. Cash & Bank Balances** | | |
| (a) Authorised Capital | | | • Cash in Hand | | 2,700 |
| (b) Issued and Subscribed Capital | | 7,50,000 | • Cash at with S.D.C.C. Bank | | 10,000 |
| **2. Reserve Fund & Other Funds** | | | • Balance with Dena Bank | | 9,900 |
| • Reserve Fund | 35,000 | 50,000 | **2. Investments** | | |
| Add 25% transferred to R.F. | (+) 15,000 | | • Investments | | 1,55,000 |
| • Dividend Equalisation Reserve | | 20,000 | **3. Investments of Staff Providend Fund** | | |
| **3. Staff Providend Fund** | | | **4. Loans & Advances** | | |
| Staff Provident Fund | | 20,000 | Loan due from Members | | 30,00,000 |
| **4. Secured Loans** | | | **5. Sundry Debtors** | | |
| **5. Unsecured Loans** | | | **6. Current Assets** | | |
| **6. Deposits** | | | **7. Fixed Assets** | | |
| Deposits from Members | | 22,48,000 | • Office Furniture | | 10,000 |
| **7. Current Liabilities & Provisions** | | | **8. Miscellaneous Expenses & Losses** | | |
| • Outstanding Salaries | | 300 | **9. Other Items** | | |
| • Outstanding Audit fees | | 3,000 | • Interest receivable on | | |
| **8. Unpaid Dividends** | | | (a) Members Loan | 8,000 | |
| $\left(\begin{array}{ll}\text{Provision} & - & \text{Paid} \\ 35,000 & - & 31,000\end{array}\right)$ | | 4,000 | (b) Investment | (+) 2,000 | 10,000 |
| | | | **10. Profit and Loss Account** | | |
| **9. Interest accrued due but not paid** | | | **11. Current Losses** | | |
| • Interest payable on members deposit | | 5,000 | | | |
| **10. Other Liabilities** | | | | | |
| **11. Profit and Loss Account** | | 97,300 | | | |
| Profit and Loss A/c | | | | | |
| Balance on 1.4.2014 | 23,000 | | | | |
| Profits for the year 2014-15 | (+) 60,000 | | | | |
| | 83,000 | | | | |
| Less : Dividends | (–) 35,000 | | | | |
| (5% of ₹ 7,00,000) | 48,000 | | | | |
| 25% Profit transferred to Reserve Fund | (–) 15,000 | | | | |
| (25% of ₹ 60,000) | 33,000 | | | | |
| Add : Profits for 2015-16 | (+) 64,300 | | | | |
| **Contingent Liability** | | | | | |
| | | 31,97,600 | | | 31,97,600 |

| Illustration 6 |

From the following Trial Balance of Shivaji Co-operative Credit Society Ltd., Kolhapur as on 31-03-2016 prepare Profit and Loss Account for the year ended 31-03-2016 and Balance Sheet as on that date after considering the adjustments given thereafter.

### Trial Balance as on 31-03-2016

| Particulars | Debit ₹ | Credit ₹ |
|---|---|---|
| Share Capital | | |
| (i) Authorised | | 10,00,000 |
| (ii) Paid up | | 6,00,000 |
| Cash Credit (K.D.C.C. Bank) | | 1,35,000 |
| Interest on Loan | | 1,20,000 |
| Sale of Loan forms | | 200 |
| Dividend on Shares | | 4,000 |
| Interest on Fixed Deposits | | 7,000 |
| Dividend Equalisation Fund | | 10,000 |
| Reserve Fund | | 80,000 |
| Common Good Fund | | 5,000 |
| Building Fund | | 10,000 |
| Balance of Profit (2014-15) | | 23,200 |
| Loan to members | | |
| (i) Medium term | 8,20,000 | |
| (ii) Emergency | 10,000 | |
| Investment of Reserve Fund in Fixed Deposits | 80,000 | |
| Investment in Shares of K.D.C.C. Bank | 40,000 | |
| Interest on Cash Credit | 16,000 | |
| Honorarium to Secretary | 4,000 | |
| Printing and Stationery | 1,500 | |
| Annual General Meeting Expenses | 1,800 | |
| Postage and Telegrams | 100 | |
| Audit Fees | 800 | |
| Travelling Expenses | 400 | |
| General Expenses | 500 | |
| Furniture | 3,000 | |
| Advertisement | 500 | |
| Insurance | 600 | |
| Cash at Bank | 15,000 | |
| Cash in Hand | 200 | |
| | **9,94,400** | **9,94,400** |

**Adjustments :**
1. Provide depreciation at 10% p.a. on Furniture.
2. Interest accrued on Investment amounted to ₹ 1,000.
3. Honorarium payable to Secretary ₹ 400.
4. Stock of Stationery on 31-03-2016 was ₹ 500.
5. Provide for bad and doubtful debts ₹ 500.

**Solution**

**In the books of Shivaji Co-operative Credit Society Ltd, Kolhapur**

Dr.     **Profit and Loss A/c for the year ended 31st March 2016**     Cr.

| Expenditure | ₹ | Income | ₹ |
|---|---|---|---|
| 1. **Interest** | | 1. **Interest received** | |
|   (a) Paid on cash credit | 16,000 |   (a) On Loans & Advances | 1,28,000 |
|   (b) Payable | |                1,20,000 | |
| 2. **Bank Charges** | |   (b) On Investment | |
| 3. **Salaries & Allowances of staff** | |      (Fixed Deposits)     7,000 | |
| | |   Add : Interest accrued | |
| | |   on Investment     (+) 1,000 | |
|   Honorarium to Secretary | | 2. **Dividend received on Shares** | 4,000 |
|                4,000 | | 3. **Commission** | |
|   Add : Hon. payable | | 4. **Miscellaneous Income** | |
|   to secretary       (+) 400 | 4,400 |   (a)   Share Transfer Fees | |
| 4. **Contribution to Staff Providend Fund** | |   (b)   Rent | |
| 5. **Salaries & Allowances of Managing Director** | |   (c)   Debate in Interest | |
| | |   (d)   Sales of Loan Forms | 200 |
| 6. **Attendance Fees and Travelling Expenses of Directors** | |   (e)   Other items | |
| 7. **Travelling Expenses of Staff** | | 5. **Land Income and Expenditure** | |
|   • Travelling Expenses | 400 | | |
| 8. **Rent, Rates & Taxes** | | | |
| 9. **Postage, Telegram and Telephone Charges** | | | |
|   • Postage and Telegrams | 100 | | |
| 10. **Printing & Stationery** | | | |
|   Printing & Stationery     1,500 | | | |
|   Less Stock of Stationery (-) 500 | 1,000 | | |
| 11. **Audit Fees** | | | |
|   • Audit Fees | 800 | | |
| 12. **General Expenses** | | | |
|   • General Expenses | 500 | | |
| 13. **Bad debts or Provision for bad debts** | | | |
|   Provision for Bad and doubtful debts | 500 | | |
| 14. **Depreciation on Fixed Assets** | | | |
|   • Furniture at 10 % p.a. | 300 | | |
| 15. **Land Income and Expenditure** | | | |
| 16. **Other items** | | | |
|   • Annual General Meeting Expenses | 1,800 | | |
|   • Advertisement | 500 | | |
|   • Insurance | 600 | | |
| **Net Profit carried to Balance Sheet** | 1,05,300 | | |
| | **1,32,200** | | **1,32,200** |

## Balance Sheet as on 31st March, 2016

| Liabilities | ₹ | ₹ | Assets | ₹ | ₹ |
|---|---|---|---|---|---|
| **1. Share Capital** | | | **1. Cash & Bank Balances** | | |
|   (a) Authorised Capital | | 10,00,000 |   • Cash in Hand | | 15,000 |
|   (b) Issued and Subscribed | | 6,00,000 |   • Cash at Bank | | 200 |
|     Capital (Paid up) | | | **2. Investments** | | |
| **2 Reserve Fund & Other** | | |   • Investment of Reserve | | |
| **Funds** | | |     Fund in Fixed Deposits | | 80,000 |
|   • Dividend Equalisation Fund | | 10,000 |   • Investment in Share of | | |
|   • Reserve Fund | 80,000 | 85,800 |     K.D.C.C. Bank | | 40,000 |
|     Add 25% transferred to R.F. | (+) 5,800 | | **3. Investments of Staff** | | |
|   • Common Good Fund | | 5,000 | **Provident Fund** | | |
|   • Building Fund | | 10,000 | **4. Loans & Advances** | | |
|   • Provision for Bad & | | |   • Loan to Members | | |
|     doubtful debts | | 500 |   (i) Medium Term | | 8,20,000 |
| **3. Staff Providend Fund** | | |   (ii) Emergency | | 10,000 |
| **4. Secured Loans** | | | **5. Sundry Debtors** | | |
| **5. Unsecured Loans** | | | **6. Current Assets** | | 500 |
|   Cash Credit (K.D.C.C. Bank) | | 1,35,000 |   Stock of Stationery | | |
| | | | **7. Fixed Assets** | | |
| **6. Deposits** | | |   • Furniture | 3,000 | |
| **7. Current Liabilities &** | | |     Less Depre. @10 % p.a. | (–) 300 | 2,700 |
| **Provisions** | | | **8. Miscellaneous Expenses** | | |
|   • Honorarium payable to | | 400 | **& Losses** | | |
|     secretary | | | **9. Other Items** | | |
| **8. Unpaid Dividends** | | |   • Interest accrued on | | 1,000 |
| **9. Interest accrued due but** | | |     Investment | | |
| **not paid** | | | **10. Profit & Loss A/c** | | |
| **10. Other Liabilities** | | | **11. Current Losses** | | |
| **11. Profit & Loss A/c** | | | | | |
|   Balance of Profit 2014-15 | 23,200 | 1,22,700 | | | |
|   Less 25% profit transferred | | | | | |
|   to Reserve Fund | (–) 5,800 | | | | |
| | 17,400 | | | | |
|   Add Profits for 2015-16 | (+) 1,05,300 | | | | |
| | | **9,69,400** | | | **9,69,400** |

# Final Accounts of Consumer's Co-operative Societies

**ILLUSTRATION 1**

From the following Trial Balance as on 31-03-2016 and the adjustments given in respect of Jay - Vijay Consumer's Co-operative Society Ltd., Jalna. Prepare Trading Account and Profit and Loss Account for the year ended 31-03-2016 and a Balance Sheet as on that date.

**Trial Balance as on 31-03-2016**

| Particulars | Debit ₹ | Credit ₹ |
|---|---|---|
| Stock of Fertilizers and Machinery | 10,000 | |
| Share Capital : | | |
| 7,500 shares of ₹ 10 each fully paid - up. | | 75,000 |
| Deposits from Members | | 90,000 |
| Printing Charges | 2,500 | |
| Investments : | | |
| (i)  in Shares – J.D.C.C. Bank | 60,000 | |
| (ii) in Shares of Co-operative Purchase and Sales Society | 36,000 | |
| Stationery purchased | 500 | |
| Loan from Bank (unsecured) | | 92,000 |
| Loan to members | 1,35,000 | |
| Interest earned on Loan | | 45,000 |
| Purchases of Fertilizers and Machinery | 3,70,000 | |
| Sales of Fertilizers and Machinery | | 4,50,000 |
| Office Equipments | 25,000 | |
| Office Rent | 5,000 | |
| Salaries | 25,000 | |
| Travelling Expenses | 5,000 | |
| Profits for the year 2014-15 | | 1,00,000 |
| Carriage Inward | 3,500 | |
| Freight | 1,500 | |
| Interest Paid | 8,000 | |
| Reserve Fund | | 86,000 |
| Cash in Hand | 51,000 | |
| Cash at Bank | 1,00,000 | |
| Sundry Debtors | 1,00,000 | |
| | 9,38,000 | 93,8,000 |

**Adjustments :**

1. Closing stock of Fertilizers and Machinery as on 31-03-2016 was ₹ 70,000 at cost.
2. Office Rent payable was ₹ 1,000
3. Office Equipments are to be depreciated at 5% p.a.
4. Create a reserve for bad and doubtful debts for ₹ 4,500.
5. Audit fees are to be paid to ₹ 2,000.
6. Directors declared a dividend to members at 8% on its paid-up capital on 1st April, 2015.

**Solution**

**In the books of Jay-Vijay Consumer's Co-operative Society Ltd, Jalna**

Dr.      **Trading Account for the year ended 31st March, 2016**      Cr.

| Expenditure | ₹ | Income | ₹ |
|---|---|---|---|
| To Opening stock of Fertilizers and Machinery | 10,000 | By Sales of Fertilizers and Machinery    4,50,000 | 4,50,000 |
| | | Less : Returns Inward   (–)   NIL | |
| To Purchases of Fertilizers and Machinery    3,70,000 | 3,70,000 | By Closing stock of Fertilizers and Machinery | 70,000 |
| Less : Returns Outwards(–)   NIL | | | |
| To Carriage Inward | 3,500 | | |
| To Freight | 1,500 | | |
| To Gross Profit transferred to Profit and Loss A/c | 1,35,000 | | |
| | **5,20,000** | | **5,20,000** |

Dr.      **Profit and Loss Account for the year ended 31st March 2016**      Cr.

| Expenditure | ₹ | Income | ₹ |
|---|---|---|---|
| 1.   **Interest** | 8,000 | 1.   **Interest received** | 45,000 |
|    (a)   Paid    8,000 | |    (a)   On Loans and | |
|    (b)   Payable    – | |      Advances    45,000 | |
| 2.   **Bank Charges** | |    (b)   On Investments (–)   NIL | |
| 3.   **Salaries & Allowances of staff** | | 2.   **Dividend Received on shares** | |
|    Salaries | 25,000 | 3.   **Commission** | |
| 4.   **Contribution to Staff Providend Fund** | | 4.   **Miscellaneous Income** | |
| | |    (a)   Share Transfer Fees | |
| 5.   **Salaries and allowances of Managing Director** | |    (b)   Rent | |
| 6.   **Attendance Fees and Travelling Expenses of Directors and Committee Members** | |    (c)   Rebate in Interest | |
| | |    (d)   Sale of Forms | |
| | |    (e)   Other Items | |
| | | 5.   **Land Income and Expenditure** | |
| 7.   **Travelling Expenses of Staff** | |    Gross Profit B/D | 1,35,000 |
|    • Travelling Expenses | 5,000 | | |
| 8.   **Rent Rates and Taxes** | | | |
|    • Office Rent    5,000 | 6,000 | | |
|    Add Office Rent payable    (+) 1,000 | | | |
| 9.   **Postage, Telegram and Telephone Charges** | | | |
| 10. **Printing and Stationery** | | | |
|    • Printing Charges | 2,500 | | |
|    • Stationery purchased | 500 | | |
| 11. **Audit Fees** | | | |
|    • Outstanding Audit Fees | 2,000 | | |

| | | | | |
|---|---|---|---|---|
| 12. **General Expenses** | | | | |
| 13. **Bad Debts or Provision for bad debts** | | | | |
|    Reserve for bad and doubtful debts | 4,500 | | | |
| 14. **Depreciation on Fixed Assets** | | | | |
|    • Office Equip. @ 5% p.a. | 1,250 | | | |
| 15. **Land Income and Expenditure** | | | | |
| 16. **Other items** | | | | |
|    **Net Profit carried to Balance Sheet** | 1,25,250 | | | |
| | **1,80,000** | | | **1,80,000** |

## Balance Sheet as on 31st March 2016

| Liabilities | ₹ | ₹ | Assets | ₹ | ₹ |
|---|---|---|---|---|---|
| 1. **Share Capital** | | | 1. **Cash & Bank Balances** | | |
|   (a)  Authorised Capital | | – |   • Cash in Hand | | 51,000 |
|   (b)  Issued & Subscribed Capital | | 75,000 |   • Cash at Bank | | 1,00,000 |
|     7,500 Shares of ₹ 10 each fully called up | | | 2. **Investments** | | |
|     and paid up | (+) 75,000 | |   • In shares of J.D.C.C. Bank | | 60,000 |
| 2. **Reserve Fund & Other Funds** | | |   • In Shares of Co-op. Purchase and Sales Society | | 36,000 |
|   • Reserve Fund | 86,000 | 1,11,000 | 3. **Investments of Staff Providend Fund** | | |
|     Add : 25% transferred | (+) 25,000 | | 4. **Loans & Advances** | | |
|   • Reserve for Bad and Doubtful Debts | | 4,500 |   Loans to members | | 1,35,000 |
| 3. **Staff Providend Fund** | | | 5. **Sundry Debtors** | | |
| 4. **Secured Loans** | | |   Sundry Debtors | | 1,00,000 |
| 5. **Unsecured Loans** | | | 6. **Curent Assets** | | |
|   • Loans from Banks (unsecured) | | 92,000 |   Closing Stock of Fertilizers and Machinery | | 70,000 |
| 6. **Deposits** | | | 7. **Fixed Assets** | | |
|   • Deposits from Members | | 90,000 |   Office Equipments | 25,000 | 23,750 |
| | | |   Less : Depre. @ 5% p.a. | (–) 1,250 | |
| 7. **Current Liabilities & Provisions** | | | 8. **Miscellaneous Expenses & Losses** | | |
|   • Office Rent payable | | 1,000 | 9. **Other Items** | | |
|   • Outstanding Audit Fees | | 2,000 | 10. **Profit and Loss Account** | | |
| 8. **Unpaid Dividends** | | | 11. **Current Losses** | | |
|   $\left(\begin{array}{cc}\text{Provision} & - & \text{Paid} \\ 6,000 & - & \text{Nil}\end{array}\right)$ | | 6,000 | | | |
| 9. **Interest accrued due but not paid** | | | | | |
| 10. **Other Liabilities** | | | | | |
| 11. **Profit and Loss Account** | | 1,94,250 | | | |
|   Profit for the year 2014-15 | 1,00,000 | | | | |
|   Less : Dividend (8% of ₹ 75,000) | (–) 6,000 | | | | |
| | 94,000 | | | | |
|   Less : 25% Profits transferred to Reserve Fund (25% of ₹ 1,00,000) | (–) 25,000 | | | | |
|   Add : Profits for 2015-16 | 69,000 | | | | |
| | (+) 1,25,250 | | | | |
| **Contingent Liability** | | | | | |
| | | **5,75,750** | | | **5,75,750** |

Illustration 2

From the following Trial Balance for the year ended 31st March, 2016 and the adjustments in respect of Bhusawal Consumer's Co–operative Society Ltd., Bhusawal prepare Trading Account and Profit and Loss Account for the year ended 31.03.2016 and a Balance-Sheet as on that date.

**Trial Balance as on 31-03-2016**

| Particulars | Debit ₹ | Credit ₹ |
|---|---|---|
| Share Capital | | 8,00,000 |
| Reserve Fund | | 2,00,000 |
| Purchases | 12,00,000 | |
| Stock on 1st March, 2015 | 2,00,000 | |
| Carriage Inward | 4,000 | |
| Salaries and Allowances of staff | 1,40,000 | |
| Building Fund | | 1,40,000 |
| Capital Redemption Fund | | 25,000 |
| Contribution to Staff Providend Fund | 10,000 | |
| Staff Provident Fund | | 34,000 |
| Sales | | 16,00,000 |
| Custom and Duty | 4,000 | |
| Octroi | 2,000 | |
| Bad debts | 8,000 | |
| Provision for bad debts | | 8,000 |
| Postage | 6,000 | |
| Machinery at cost | 28,000 | |
| Travelling Expenses | 10,000 | |
| Bonus to employee | 10,000 | |
| Printing and Stationery | 3,500 | |
| Insurance | 11,000 | |
| Buildings at cost | 6,00,000 | |
| Furniture at cost | 1,00,000 | |
| Depreciation Fund | | 90,000 |
| Sundry Debtors | 2,00,000 | |
| Sundry Creditors | | 37,000 |
| Investments in Shares of Credit Co–operative Society | 1,20,000 | |
| Investments of Staff Provident Fund | 34,000 | |
| Fixed Deposits with B.D.C.C. Bank | 1,60,000 | |
| Miscellaneous Expenses | 10,000 | |
| Repairs to Building | 20,000 | |
| Interest on Fixed Deposit | | 16,000 |
| Dividend received on shares | | 12,000 |
| Share Transfer Fees | | 5,000 |
| Profit and Loss A/c (2014-15) | | 20,000 |
| Cash in Hand | 6,500 | |
| Cash at Bank | 1,00,000 | |
| | **29,87,000** | **29,87,000** |

**Adjustments :**

1. Closing Stock as on 31.03.2016 was ₹ 3,20,000.
2. Salaries unpaid on 31.03.2016 was ₹ 8,000.
3. Prepaid insurance amounted to ₹ 1,500.
4. Provide for bad and doubtful debts at 5% on Sundry Debtors.
5. Depreciation as per depreciation fund method for the year to be provided as under :
   (i) Buildings – ₹ 30,000
   (ii) Furniture – ₹ 10,000
   (iii) Machinery – ₹ 2,800
6. Transfer ₹ 1,000 to Education Fund and ₹ 3,000 to Capital Redemption Fund from the profits of 2014-15.
7. Audit Fees due but not paid amounted to ₹ 5,000
8. Directors declared a dividend to members at 1% on paid up capital on 1st April, 2015.

**Solution**

**In the books of Bhusawal Consumer's Co-operative Society Ltd., Bhusawal**

Dr.      **Trading Account for the year ended 31st March 2016**      Cr.

| Expenditure | ₹ | | Income | | ₹ |
|---|---|---|---|---|---|
| To Opening stock on 01.04.2015 | | 2,00,000 | By Sales | 16,00,000 | 16,00,000 |
| To Purchases 12,00,000 | | 12,00,000 | | | |
| Less : Returns Outward (–) Nil | | | Less : Returns Inward (–) Nil | | |
| To Carriage Inward | | 4,000 | By Closing Stock on 31.03.2016 | | 3,20,000 |
| To Custom and Duty | | 4,000 | | | |
| To Octroi | | 2,000 | | | |
| To Gross Profit transferred to Profit and Loss A/c | | 5,10,000 | | | |
| | | 19,20,000 | | | 19,20,000 |

Dr.      **Profit and Loss Account for the year ended 31st March 2016**      Cr.

| Expenditure | ₹ | | Income | | ₹ |
|---|---|---|---|---|---|
| 1. **Interest** | | | 1. **Interest received** | | 16,000 |
| (a) Paid on deposits | | | (a) On Loans and Advances | | |
| (b) Payable | | | (b) On Investment | | |
| 2. **Bank Charges** | | | • Interest on Fixed Deposits (+) 16,000 | | |
| 3. **Salaries and Allowances of staff :** | | | 2. **Dividend Received on Shares** | | |
| • Salaries and Allowances of staff 1,40,000 | 1,48,000 | | • Dividend received on shares | | 12,000 |
| Add : Salaries unpaid (+) 8,000 | | | 3. **Commission** | | |
| Bonus to Employees | 10,000 | | 4. **Miscellaneous Income** | | |
| 4. **Contribution to Staff Provident Fund** | 10,000 | | (a) Share Transfer Fees | | 5,000 |
| 5. **Salaries and Allowances of Managing Director** | | | (b) Rent | | |
| | | | (c) Rebate in Interest | | |
| 6. **Attendance fees & Travelling expenses of Directors** | | | (d) Sale of Forms | | |
| | | | (e) Other Items | | |

| | | ₹ | | | ₹ |
|---|---|---|---|---|---|
| 7. | **Travelling Expenses of Staff** | | 5. | **Land Income and Expenditure** | |
| | • Travelling Expenses | 10,000 | | | |
| 8. | **Rent Rates and Taxes** | | | | |
| 9. | **Postage, Telegram and Telephone charges** | | | | |
| | • Postage | 6,000 | | | |
| 10. | **Printing and Stationery** | | | | |
| | • Printing and Stationery | 3,500 | | | |
| 11. | **Audit Fees** | | | | |
| | Audit fees due but not paid | 5,000 | | | |
| 12. | **General Expenses** | | | | |
| | Miscellaneous Expenses | 10,000 | | | |
| 13. | **Bad debts or provision for bad debts** | | | | |
| | Bad debts or | 8,000 | | | |
| | Provision for bad debts | 2,000 | | | |
| | New Reserve    10,000 | | | | |
| | (@ 5% of ₹ 2,00,000) | | | | |
| | Less : Old Reserve    (–) 8,000 | | | Gross Profit B/D | 5,10,000 |
| 14. | **Depreciation on Fixed Assets** | | | | |
| | (i)    Building | 30,000 | | | |
| | (ii)    Furniture | 10,000 | | | |
| | (iii)    Machinery | 2,800 | | | |
| 15. | **Land Income and Expenditure** | | | | |
| 16. | **Other Items** | | | | |
| | • Insurance    11,000 | 9,500 | | | |
| | Less : Prepaid Insurance    (–) 1,500 | | | | |
| | Repairs to building | 20,000 | | | |
| | **Net Profit carried to Balance Sheet** | 2,58,200 | | | |
| | | **5,43,000** | | | **5,43,000** |

## Balance Sheet as on 31st March 2016

| | Liabilities | ₹ | ₹ | | Assets | ₹ | ₹ |
|---|---|---|---|---|---|---|---|
| 1. | **Share Capital** | | | 1. | **Cash and Bank Balances** | | |
| | (a)   Authorised Capital | | | | • Cash in Hand | | 6,500 |
| | (b)   Issued   &   Subscribed Capital | | 8,00,000 | | • Cash at Bank | | 1,00,000 |
| 2. | **Reserve Fund & Other   Funds** | | | 2. | **Investments** | | |
| | • Reserve Fund | 2,00,000 | | | In shares of credit | | |
| | Add : 25% transferred | (+) 5,000 | 2,05,000 | | Co–operative Society | | 1,20,000 |
| | | | | | Fixed Deposits with    B.D.C.C. Bank | | 1,60,000 |

| | | | | | | |
|---|---|---:|---|---|---:|---:|
| | • Building Fund | | 1,40,000 | **3.** | **Investments of Staff** | |
| | • Capital Redemption Fund | 25,000 | 28,000 | | **Provident Fund** | |
| | Add : Transferred | (+) 3,000 | | | Investments of Staff   Provident | 34,000 |
| | • Transfer to Edu. Fund | | 1,000 | | Fund | |
| | • Depreciation Fund | 90,000 | 1,32,800 | **4.** | **Loans & Advances** | |
| | Add : Depreciation | | | **5.** | **Sundry Debtors** | |
| | (i) Building | 30,000 | | | Sundry Debtors | 2,00,000 |
| | (ii) Furniture | 10,000 | | **6.** | **Current Assets** | |
| | (iii)  Machinery | (+) 2,800 | | | Closing Stock | 3,20,000 |
| | • Provision for bad and doubtful | | | **7.** | **Fixed Assets** | |
| | debts @ 5% on Sundry Debtors | | 10,000 | | Machinery at cost | 28,000 |
| | | | | | Building at cost | 6,00,000 |
| **3.** | **Staff Provident Fund** | | | | Furniture at cost | 1,00,000 |
| | • Staff Provident Fund | | 34,000 | **8.** | **Miscellaneous Expenses** | |
| **4.** | **Secured Loans** | | | | **& Losses** | |
| **5.** | **Unsecured Loans** | | | **9.** | **Other  Items** | |
| **6.** | **Deposits** | | | | • Prepaid Insurance | |
| **7.** | **Current Liabilities &** | | | **10.** | **Profit and Loss Account** | 1,500 |
| | **Provisions** | | | **11.** | **Current Losses** | |
| | •   Sundry Creditors | | 37,000 | | | |
| | •   Salaries Unpaid | | 8,000 | | | |
| | •   Audit Fees due but not | | 5,000 | | | |
| | paid | | | | | |
| **8.** | **Unpaid Dividends** | | | | | |
| | $\left(\begin{array}{cc}\text{Provision} - & \text{Paid} \\ 8,000 \; - & \text{Nil}\end{array}\right)$ | | 8,000 | | | |
| **9.** | **Interest accrued  due but    not** | | | | | |
| | **paid** | | | | | |
| **10.** | **Other Liabilities** | | | | | |
| **11.** | **Profit and Loss Account** | | 2,61,200 | | | |
| | Profit & Loss A/c (2014-15) | 20,000 | | | | |
| | Less : Transferred to Education | | | | | |
| | Fund | (−) 1,000 | | | | |
| | Less : Transferred to | 19,000 | | | | |
| | Capital Redemption Fund | (−) 3,000 | | | | |
| | Less : Dividend | 16,000 | | | | |
| | (1% of ₹ 8,00,000) | (−) 8,000 | | | | |
| | Less : 25% transferred to | 8,000 | | | | |
| | Reserve fund | | | | | |
| | (25% of ₹ 20,000) | (−) 5,000 | | | | |
| | | 3,000 | | | | |
| | Add : Profits for 2015-16 | (+) 2,58,200 | | | | |
| | **Contingent Liability** | | | | | |
| | | | 16,70,000 | | | 16,70,000 |

### Illustration 3

The following is a statement of Receipts and Payments of Modern Education Society's Consumers Co–operative Store Ltd., Pune for the first year ended 31ˢᵗ March, 2016.

**Statement of Receipts and Payments as on 31ˢᵗ March, 2016**

| Receipts | ₹ | Payments | ₹ |
|---|---|---|---|
| Share Capital | 15,000 | Purchases | |
| Admission Fees | ,300 | (i)  Consumers Goods | 24,000 |
| Sales   (i)   Consumers Goods | 42,720 | (ii)  Books | 6,000 |
|       (ii)  Books | 5,000 | | |
| Loans recovered from Members | 18,000 | Printing and Stationery | 300 |
| P.D.C.C. Bank Current A/c. | 9,000 | Loan to members | 39,000 |
| Interest received on Members Loan | 2,000 | Other Expenses | 1,000 |
| | | Furniture | 5,000 |
| Renewal Fees | 2,500 | Postage | 50 |
| Sale of Empties | ,100 | P.D.C.C. Bank Current A/c | 15,000 |
| Loan from P.D.C.C. Bank | 5,000 | Carriage and Freight | ,500 |
| | | Shares in P.D.C.C. Bank | 2,000 |
| | | Shares in Consumers Federation | 1,000 |
| | | Rent | 1,000 |
| | | Electricity Charges | 70 |
| | | Salary | 500 |
| | | Managing Committee meeting expenses | 600 |
| | | Taxes | 1,500 |
| | | Travelling Expenses | 100 |
| | | Cash in hand closing | 2,000 |
| | **99,620** | | **99,620** |

**Adjustments :**

1. Provide depreciation @ 10% p.a. on Furniture
2. Prepaid rent amounted to ₹ 200.
3. Salary due but not paid ₹ 300.
4. Closing stock as  on 31.03.2016 was (i) Consumers Goods ₹ 6,000  (ii) Books ₹ 2,000

### Solution

**In the books of Modern Education Society's Consumers Co-operative Stores Ltd., Pune**

**Dr.**            **Trading Account for the year ended 31st March 2016**            **Cr.**

| Expenditure | | ₹ | Income | | ₹ |
|---|---|---|---|---|---|
| To Opening stock | | – | By Sales | | 47,720 |
| To Purchases | | 30,000 | (i)  Consumers Goods | 42,720 | |
| (i)  Consumers Goods | 24,000 | | (ii)  Books | (+) 5,000 | |
| (ii)  Books | (+) 6,000 | | | 47,720 | |
| | 30,000 | | | | |
| Less : Returns Outward | (–) Nil | | Less : Returns Inward | (–) Nil | |
| To Carriage and Freight | | 500 | By Closing Stock | | 8,000 |
| | | | (i)  Consumer's Goods | 6,000 | |
| | | | (ii)  Books | (+) 2,000 | |
| To Gross Profit transferred to Profit and Loss A/c | | 25,320 | By Sale of Empties | | 100 |
| | | **55,820** | | | **55,820** |

**Dr.**      **Profit and Loss Account for the year ended 31st March 2016**      **Cr.**

| Expenditure | ₹ | Income | ₹ |
|---|---|---|---|
| 1. **Interest** | | 1. **Interest Received** | 2,000 |
|    (a) Paid | |    (a) On Loans and | |
|    (b) Payable | |         Advances     2,000 | |
| 2. **Bank Charges** | |    (b) On Investment (+)   Nil | |
| 3. **Salaries & Allowances of staff** | | 2. **Dividend Received on shares** | |
|     Salary         500 | 800 | 3. **Commission** | |
|     Add : Salaries due but | | 4. **Miscellaneous Income** | |
|     not paid      (+) 300 | |    (a) Share Transfer Fees | |
| 4. **Contribution to Staff Provident Fund** | |    (b) Rent | |
| 5. **Salaries and Allowances of Managing Director** | |    (c) Rebate in Interest | |
| 6. **Attendance Fees & Travelling expenses of Directors** | |    (d) Sale of forms | |
| | |    (e) Other items | |
| 7. **Travelling Expenses of Staff** | |    (i) Admission Fees | 300 |
|    • Travelling Expenses | 100 |    (ii) Renewal Fees | 2,500 |
| 8. **Rent, Rates and Taxes** | | 5. **Land Income and Expenditure** | |
|    • Rent         1,000 | 800 | | |
|     Less : Prepaid Rent (−) 200 | | | |
|    • Taxes | 1,500 | | |
| 9. **Postage, Telegram and Telephone charges** | | | |
|     Postage | 50 | | |
| 10. **Printing and Stationery** | | | |
|    • Printing and Stationery | 300 | Gross Profit B/D | 25,320 |
| 11. **Audit Fees** | | | |
| 12. **General Expenses** | | | |
|    • Other expenses | 1,000 | | |
| 13. **Bad debts or provision for bad debts** | | | |
| 14. **Depreciation on Fixed Assets** | 500 | | |
|     Furniture @10% p.a. | | | |
| 15. **Land Income and Expenditure** | | | |
| 16. **Other Items** | | | |
|    • Electricity Charges | 70 | | |
|    • Managing Committee Meeting Expenses | 600 | | |
| **Net Profit carried to Balance Sheet** | 24,400 | | |
| | **30,120** | | **30,120** |

### Balance Sheet as on 31st March 2016

| Liabilities | ₹ | ₹ | Assets | ₹ | ₹ |
|---|---|---|---|---|---|
| **1. Share Capital** | | | **1. Cash & Bank Balances** | | |
| (a) Authorised Capital | | | • P.D.C.C. Bank | | |
| (b) Issued and Subscribed | | | Current A/c | | |
| Capital | | 15,000 | (15,000 – 9,000) | | 6,000 |
| **2. Reserve Fund & Other Funds** | | | • Cash in Hand | | 2,000 |
| | | | **2. Investments** | | |
| **3. Staff Provident Fund** | | | • Shares in P.D.D.C. Bank | | 2,000 |
| **4. Secured Loans** | | | • Shares in Consumers | | 1,000 |
| **5. Unsecured Loans** | | | Federation | | |
| • Loan from P.D.C.C. Bank | | 5,000 | **3. Investments of Staff** | | |
| **6. Deposits** | | | **Provident Fund** | | |
| **7. Current Liabilities &** | | | **4. Loans & Advances** | | |
| **Provisions** | | | Loan to members | | 21,000 |
| • Salaries due but not paid | | 300 | $\left(\begin{array}{cc}\text{Given} & \text{Recovered} \\ 39,000 & 18,000\end{array}\right)$ | | |
| **8. Unpaid Dividends** | | | | | |
| **9. Interest accrued due but not** | | | **5. Sundry Debtors** | | |
| **paid** | | | **6. Current Assets** | | |
| **10. Other Liabilities** | | | • Closing Stock – | | |
| **11. Profit and Loss Account** | | | (i) Consumers Goods | | 6,000 |
| • Profits for 2015-16 | | 24,400 | (ii) Books | | 2,000 |
| **Contingent Liability** | | | **7. Fixed Assets** | | |
| | | | • Furniture | 5,000 | 4,500 |
| | | | Less : Depre. @ 10% p.a. | (–) 500 | |
| | | | **8. Miscellaneous Expenses and** | | |
| | | | **Losses** | | |
| | | | **9. Other Items** | | |
| | | | • Prepaid Rent | | 200 |
| | | | **10. Profit and Loss Account** | | |
| | | | **11. Current Losses** | | |
| | | **44'700** | | | **44'700** |

---

## Illustration 4

From the following Trial Balance of Pune District Consumers Co–operative Society Ltd., Pune as on 31st March 2016 prepare Trading Account and Profit and Loss Account for the year ended 31.03.2016 and a Balance Sheet as on that date after considering the adjustment given thereafter.

### Trial Balance as on 31-03-2016

| Particulars | Debit ₹ | Credit ₹ |
|---|---|---|
| Share Capital | | 1,68,000 |
| Reserve Fund | | 30,000 |
| Sundry Creditors | | 20,000 |
| Profit and Loss A/c as on 1st April, 2014 | | 8,000 |
| Profit for the year 2014-15 | | 80,000 |
| Opening Stock | 1,96,000 | |
| Furniture and Equipments | 62,000 | |
| Container Deposit | 16,000 | |
| Sundry Debtors | 30,000 | |
| Salaries | 1,50,000 | |

| | | |
|---|---:|---:|
| Commission | 4,40,000 | |
| Rent and Taxes | 23,000 | |
| Postage | 4,000 | |
| Travelling Expenses | 9,000 | |
| Printing and Stationery | 7,000 | |
| Dividend paid for 2014-15 | 7,900 | |
| Admission Fees | | ,'000 |
| Purchases | 31,72,000 | |
| Excise Duty | 80,000 | |
| Investments | 1,20,000 | |
| Sales | | 38,13,000 |
| Purchases Returns | | 2,000 |
| Cash in hand | 2,100 | |
| Bank balance | 2,00,000 | |
| Sales Returns | 3,000 | |
| Development Fund | | 4,000 |
| | **41,26,000** | **41,26,000** |

**Adjustments :**

1. Closing Stock on 31st March, 2016 is valued at ₹ 2,20,000

2. Outstanding rent amounts to ₹ 2,000 and commission payable ₹ 10,000.

3. ₹ 4,000 salary was paid as advance on 31.03.2016.

4. The society declared 5% dividend on its paid up capital as on 31.03.2016 for the year 2015-16. The society transferred 25% of its profit for the year ended 31.03.2016 to Reserve Fund and also transferred ₹ 4,000 to Development Fund approved in the Annual General Meeting held on 31st July, 2015.

5. Provide for outstanding Audit Fees ₹ 8,000.

6. Accrued interest on investment amounted to ₹ 10,000.

7. The directors recommended 10% dividend for the current year.

8. Provide depreciation at 10% on Furniture and Equipments.

Solution

**In the books of Pune District Consumers Co-operative Society Ltd' Pune.**

Dr.        **Trading Account for the year ended 31st March 2016**        Cr.

| Expenditure | | ₹ | Income | | ₹ |
|---|---:|---:|---|---:|---:|
| To Opening Stock | | 1,96,000 | By Sales | 38,13,000 | 38,10,000 |
| To Purchases | 31,72,000 | 31,70,000 | | | |
| Less: Purchases Returns | (–) 2,000 | | Less: Sales Returns | (–) 3,000 | |
| To Excess Duty | | 80,000 | By Closing Stock | | 2,20,000 |
| To Gross Profit transferred to | | | | | |
| Profit and Loss A/c | | 5,84,000 | | | |
| | | **40,30,000** | | | **40,30,000** |

**Dr.**      **Profit and Loss Account for the year ended 31st March 2016**      **Cr.**

| Expenditure | ₹ | Income | ₹ |
|---|---|---|---|
| **1. Interest** | | **1. Interest received** | |
|   (a) Paid on deposits | |   (a) On Loans and | 10,000 |
|   (b) Payable | |        Advances | |
| **2. Bank Charges** | |   (b) On Investment    Nil | |
| **3. Salaries & Allowances of** | |   Add : Accrued interest on | |
|    **staff** | 1,46,000 |        Investments   (+) <u>10,000</u> | |
|   Salaries         1,50,000 | | **2. Dividend Received on Shares** | |
|   Less : Advance Salary (–) <u>4,000</u> | | **3. Commission** | |
| **4. Contribution to Staff Provident** | | **4. Miscellaneous Income** | |
|    **Fund** | |   (a) Share Transfer Fees | |
| **5. Salaries and allowances of** | |   (b) Rent | |
|    **Managing Directors** | |   (c) Rebate in Interest | |
| **6. Attendance Fees & Travelling** | |   (d) Sale of forms | |
|    **expenses of Directors** | |   (e) Other Items | |
| **7. Travelling Expenses of Staff** | |       (i) Admission Fees | 1,000 |
|   • Travelling Expenses | 9,000 | **5. Land Income and** | |
| **8. Rent, Rates & Taxes** | 25,000 |    **Expenditure** | |
|   • Rent and Taxes      23,000 | | | |
|   Add : Outstanding Rent (+) <u>2,000</u> | | | |
| **9. Postage, Telegram and** | | | |
|    **Telephone charges** | | | |
|   • Postage | 4,000 | | |
| **10. Printing and Stationery** | | Gross Profit B/D | 5,84,000 |
|   • Printing and Stationery | 7,000 | | |
| **11. Audit Fees** | | | |
|   • Outstanding Audit Fees | 8,000 | | |
| **12. General Expenses** | | | |
| **13. Bad debts or provision for Bad** | | | |
|    **debts** | | | |
| **14. Depreciation on Fixed Assets** | | | |
|   • Furniture and Equipments | | | |
|     @10 % p.a. | 6,200 | | |
| **15. Land Income and** | | | |
|    **Expenditure** | | | |
| **16. Other Items** | | | |
|   • Commission      44,000 | 54,000 | | |
|    Add : Commission | | | |
|        payable    (+) <u>10,000</u> | | | |
| **Net profit carried to** | 3,35,800 | | |
| **Balance Sheet** | | | |
| | **5,95,000** | | **5,95,000** |

### Balance Sheet as on 31st March 2016

| Liabilities | ₹ | ₹ | Assets | ₹ | ₹ |
|---|---|---|---|---|---|
| **1. Share Capital** | | | **1. Cash and Bank Balances** | | |
| (a) Authorised Capital | | | • Cash in Hand | | 2,100 |
| (b) Issued and Subscribed | | | • Bank Balance | | 2,00,000 |
| Capital | | 1,68,000 | | | |
| **2. Reserve Fund and Other** | | | **2. Investments** | | |
| **Funds** | | | • Investments | | 1,20,000 |
| • Reserve Fund | 30,000 | 50,000 | **3. Investments of Staff** | | |
| Add : 25% transferred | (+) 20,000 | | **Provident Fund** | | |
| • Development Fund | 4,000 | 8,000 | **4. Loans and Advances** | | |
| Add : Transferred | (+) 4,000 | | • Container Deposit | | 16,000 |
| **3. Staff Provident Fund** | | | **5. Sundry Debtors** | | |
| **4. Secured Loans** | | | • Sundry Debtors | | 30,000 |
| **5. Unsecured Loans** | | | **6. Current Assets** | | |
| **6. Deposits** | | | • Closing Stock | | 2,20,000 |
| **7. Current Liabilities and** | | | **7. Fixed Assets** | | |
| **Provisions** | | | • Furniture & Equipments | 62,000 | 55,800 |
| • Sundry Creditors | | 20,000 | Less : Depre. @10% p.a | (−) 6,200 | |
| • Outstanding Rent | | 2,000 | **8. Miscellaneous Expenses and** | | |
| • Commission Payable | | 10,000 | **Losses** | | |
| • Outstanding Audit Fees | | 8,000 | | | |
| **8. Unpaid Dividends** | | 500 | **9. Other Items** | | |
| $\begin{pmatrix} \text{Provision} & \text{Paid} \\ 8,400 & - & 7,900 \end{pmatrix}$ | | | • Advance Salary | | 4,000 |
| | | | • Accrued interest on | | |
| | | | investments | | 10,000 |
| **9. Interest accrued due but not** | | | **10. Profit and Loss Account** | | |
| **paid** | | | **11. Current Losses** | | |
| **10. Other Liabilities** | | | | | |
| **11. Profit and Loss Account** | | 3,91,400 | | | |
| Profit and Loss A/c as on | | | | | |
| 01-04-2014 | 8,000 | | | | |
| Add : Profits for the year 2014-15 | | | | | |
| | (+) 80,000 | | | | |
| | 88,000 | | | | |
| Less : Dividend | | | | | |
| (5% of ₹ 1,68,000) | (−) 8,400 | | | | |
| | 79,600 | | | | |
| Less : 25% profit transferred | | | | | |
| to Reserve Fund | | | | | |
| (25% of ₹ 80,000) | (−) 20,000 | | | | |
| | 59,600 | | | | |
| Less : Transferred to | | | | | |
| Development Fund | (−) 4,000 | | | | |
| | 55,600 | | | | |
| Add : Profits for the year | (+) 3,35,800 | | | | |
| 2015-2016 | | | | | |
| **Contingent Liability** | | | | | |
| | | **6,57,900** | | | **6,57,900** |

**N.B. :** The recommendations made by the directors to declare a divided at 10% for the current year will have to be sanctioned by the general body in the Annual General Meeting hence no effect of this adjustment will be shown in the above mentioned final accounts prepared on 31st March, 2016.

**Illustration 5**

From the following Trial Balance of Bharati Consumers Co–operative Society Ltd., Pune as on 31st March, 2016, prepare Trading Account and Profit and Loss Account for the year ended 31.03.2016 and a Balance Sheet as on that date.

Trial Balance as on 31-03-2016

| Particulars | Debit ₹ | Credit ₹ |
|---|---|---|
| Share Capital | | 1,60,000 |
| Calls in Arrears | 10,000 | |
| Reserve Fund | | 15,000 |
| Common Good Fund | | 5,000 |
| Opening Stock of Consumers Goods | 1,10,000 | |
| Furniture | 48,000 | |
| Education Fund | | 8,000 |
| Sundry Creditors | | 20,000 |
| Sundry Debtors | 30,000 | |
| Taxes payable | | 4,000 |
| Salaries | 71,000 | |
| Commission | 17,400 | |
| Rent and Rates | 20,000 | |
| Postage | 12,100 | |
| Land | 9,000 | |
| Interest on Investment | | 10,000 |
| Equipments | 20,000 | |
| Purchases | 16,40,000 | |
| Investment | 1,00,000 | |
| Sales | | 19,60,500 |
| Cash in Hand | 25,000 | |
| Cash at Bank | 1,70,000 | |
| Profits for the year 2014-15 | | 1,00,000 |
| | 22,82,500 | 22,82,500 |

**Adjustments :**

1. Rent payable on 31.03.2016 was ₹ 1,000.
2. Charge depreciation @ 5% p.a. on Furniture.
3. Closing stock of Consumers Goods is valued at cost ₹ 1,40,000.
4. Interest accrued on investment ₹ 2,000.
5. Outstanding salary on 31.03.2016 was ₹ 2,000 and ₹ 3,000 paid in advance.
6. Authorised Capital was 20,000 shares of ₹ 10 each.

**Solution**

### In the books of Bharati Consumers Co-operative Society Ltd, Pune.

**Dr.**      **Trading Account for the year ended 31st March 2016**      **Cr.**

| Expenditure | ₹ | Income | ₹ |
|---|---|---|---|
| To Opening stock of Consumers Goods | 1,10,000 | By Sales | 19,60,500 |
| To Purchases    16,40,000 | 16,40,000 | Less : Returns Inward    (–) Nil | |
| Less : Returns Outward (–) ___ Nil | | By Closing Stock of Consumers Goods | 1,40,000 |
| To Gross Profit not transferred to Profit and Loss A/c. | 3,50,500 | | |
| | 21,00,500 | | 21,00,500 |

**Dr.**      **Profit and Loss Account for the year ended 31st March 2016**      **Cr.**

| Expenditure | ₹ | Income | ₹ |
|---|---|---|---|
| 1. **Interest** | | 1. **Interest received** | 12,000 |
|   (a) Paid | |   (a) On Loans and Advances | |
|   (b) Payable | |   (b) On Investments (+) 10,000 | |
| 2. **Bank Charges** | |      10,000 | |
| 3. **Salaries and Allowances of Staff** | 70,000 |   Add : Interest accrued | |
|   Salaries    71,000 | |     on Investment (+) 2,000 | |
|   Add : Outstanding Sal. (+) 2,000 | | 2. **Dividend Received on Shares** | |
|      73,000 | | 3. **Commission** | |
|   Less : Advance Salary (–) 3,000 | | 4. **Miscellaneous Income** | |
| 4. **Contribution to Staff Provident Fund** | |   (a) Share Transfers | |
| 5. **Salaries and Allowances of Managing Director** | |   (b) Rent | |
| | |   (c) Rebate in Interest | |
| 6. **Attendance Fees and Travelling Expenses of Directors** | |   (d) Sale of forms | |
| | |   (e) Other items | |
| 7. **Travelling Expenses of Staff** | | 5. **Land Income and Expenditure** | |
| 8. **Rent, Rates and Taxes** | 21,000 | By Gross Profit B/D | 3,50,000 |
|   • Rent and Rates    20,000 | | | |
|   Add : Rent Payable    (+) 1,000 | | | |
| 9. **Postage, Telegram and Telephone Charges** | | | |
|   Postage | | | |
| 10 **Printing and Stationery** | 12,100 | | |
| 11. **Audit Fees** | | | |
| 12. **General Expenses** | | | |
| 13. **Bad debts or Provision for Bad debts** | | | |
| 14. **Depreciation on Fixed Assets** | | | |
|   • Fixed Assets @ 5% p.a. | 2,400 | | |
| 15. **Land Income and Expenditure** | | | |
| 16. **Other items** | | | |
|   • Commission | 17,400 | | |
|   **Net Profit Carried to Balance Sheet** | 2,39,600 | | |
| | 3,62,500 | | 3,62,500 |

## Balance Sheet as on 31st March 2016

| | Liabilities | ₹ | ₹ | | Assets | ₹ | ₹ |
|---|---|---|---|---|---|---|---|
| 1. | **Share Capital** | | | 1. | **Cash & Bank Balances** | | |
| | (a) Authorised Capital | | 2,00,000 | | • Cash in Hand | | 25,000 |
| | 20,000 shares of | | | | • Cash at Bank | | 1,70,000 |
| | ₹ 10 each | 2,00,000 | | 2. | **Investments** | | |
| | (b) Issued & Subscribed | | | | • Investments | | |
| | Capital | | | 3. | **Investments of Staff** | | 1,00,000 |
| | 16,000 shares of | | | | **Provident Fund** | | |
| | ₹ 10 each fully | | | 4. | **Loans and Advances** | | |
| | called up | 1,60,000 | 1,50,000 | 5. | **Sundry Debtors** | | |
| | Less : Calls in arrears | (–) 10,000 | | | • Sundry Debtors | | 30,000 |
| 2. | **Reserve Fund and Other** | | | 6. | **Current Assets** | | |
| | **Funds** | | | | • Closing Stock of | | |
| | • Reserve Fund | 15,000 | 40,000 | | Consumers Goods | | 1,40,000 |
| | Add : 25% transferred | (+) 25,000 | | 7. | **Fixed Assets** | | |
| | • Common Good Fund | | 5,000 | | • Furniture | 48,000 | 45,600 |
| | • Education Fund | | 8,000 | | Less : Depr. @ 5% p.a. | (–) 2,400 | |
| 3. | **Staff Provident Fund** | | | | • Land | | 9,000 |
| 4. | **Secured Loans** | | | | • Equipments | | 20,000 |
| 5. | **Unsecured Loans** | | | 8. | **Miscellaneous Expenses** | | |
| 6. | **Deposits** | | | | **and Losses** | | |
| 7. | **Current Liabilities And** | | | 9. | **Other Items** | | |
| | **Provisions** | | | | • Interest accrued on | | |
| | • Sundry Creditors | | 20,000 | | Investment | | 2,000 |
| | • Taxes Payable | | 4,000 | | • Advance Salary | | 3,000 |
| | • Rent Payable | | 1,000 | 10. | **Profit and Loss Account** | | |
| | • Outstanding Salary | | 2,000 | 11. | **Current Losses** | | |
| 8. | **Unpaid Dividends** | | | | | | |
| 9. | **Interest accrued due but** | | | | | | |
| | **not paid** | | | | | | |
| 10. | **Other Liabilities** | | | | | | |
| 11. | **Profit and Loss Account** | | | | | | |
| | Profit for the year 2014-15 | 1,00,000 | 3,14,600 | | | | |
| | Less 25% Profit transferred | (–) 25,000 | | | | | |
| | to Reserve Fund | 75,000 | | | | | |
| | (25% of ₹ 1,00,000) | | | | | | |
| | Add : Profits for the year | (+) 2,39,600 | | | | | |
| | 2015-16 | | | | | | |
| | **Contingent Liability** | | | | | | |
| | | | **5,44,600** | | | | **5,44,600** |

Illustration 6

From the following Trial Balance as on 31st March, 2016 and the information given thereafter of Jalgaon Consumer's Co–operative Society Ltd., Jalgaon, prepare Trading Account and Profit and Loss Account for the year ended 31.03.2016 and a Balance Sheet as on that date.

**Trial Balance as on 31-03-2016**

| Particulars | Debit ₹ | Credit ₹ |
|---|---|---|
| Share Capital as on 1st April, 2015 | | 10,000 |
| Reserve Fund | | 1,500 |
| Co–operative Development Fund | | 500 |
| Stock of Consumer's Goods as on 1st April, 2015 | 11,250 | |
| Office Furniture | 5,300 | |
| Price Fluctuation fund | | 800 |
| Sundry Creditors for purchases | | 2,000 |
| Sundry Debtors for sales | 3,000 | |
| Salaries | 7,500 | |
| Commission | 2,700 | |
| Commission Payable | | 500 |
| Rent and Taxes | 2,600 | |
| Postage | 1,250 | |
| Travelling and conveyance | 200 | |
| Printing and Stationary | 400 | |
| Calls in arrears as on 1st April, 2015 | 600 | |
| Dividend for 2014-15 | 470 | |
| Audit Fees | 400 | |
| Interest on Investment | | 1,100 |
| Profits for the year 2014-15 | | 5,000 |
| Equipments | 1,800 | |
| Admission Fees | | 50 |
| Purchases | 1,58,500 | |
| Carriage and Cartage | 4,000 | |
| Investments | 10,000 | |
| Sales | | 2,05,000 |
| Cash in Hand | 1,480 | |
| Cash at Bank | 15,000 | |
| | **2,26,450** | **2,26,450** |

**Additional Information :**

1. Closing Stock of Consumer's Goods as on 31.03.2016 is valued at cost price ₹ 12,500 and at market price ₹ 14,000.

2. Outstanding expenses on 31.03.2016 were as follows :
   (i)　Rent ₹ 100
   (ii)　Salary ₹ 200
3. Salary  prepaid amounted to ₹ 300
4. Interest accrued on investments was ₹ 200.
5. Charge 5% depreciation on office furniture.
6. The society declared 10% dividend on its paid–up capital as on 31.03.2016. The society also transferred 25% of their profits for the year ended 31.03.2016 to Reserve Fund and transferred ₹ 310 to Co-operative Development Fund as approved in the Annual General Meeting held on 31st July, 2016.

**Solution**

**In the books of Jalgaon Consumer's Co-operative Society Ltd., Jalgaon**

Dr.　　　　　　　　**Trading Account for the year ended 31st March 2016**　　　　　　　Cr.

| Expenditure | ₹ | Income | | ₹ |
|---|---|---|---|---|
| To Stock of Consumer's Goods as on 1st April, 2015 | 11,250 | By Sales | 2,05,000 | 2,05,000 |
| To Purchases　　　　1,58,500 | 1,58,500 | | | |
| Less : Returns Outward (–)　Nil | | Less : Returns Inward　(–)　Nil | | |
| To Carriage and Freight | 4,000 | By Closing Stock of Consumer's Goods | | 12,500 |
| To Gross Profit transferred to Profit and Loss A/c | 43,750 | | | |
| | 2,17,500 | | | 2,17,500 |

Dr.　　　　　　**Profit and Loss Account for the year ended 31st March 2016**　　　　　　Cr.

| Expenditure | ₹ | Income | ₹ |
|---|---|---|---|
| **1.　Interest** | | **1.　Interest received :** | 1,300 |
| 　(a)　Paid | | 　　(a)　On Loans and  Advances | |
| 　(b)　Payable | | 　　(b)　On Investment　(+)　1,100 | |
| **2.　Bank Charges** | | | |
| **3.　Salaries & Allowances of Staff** | 7,400 | 　　Add : Interest accrued on | |
| 　• Salaries　　　　7,500 | | 　　　　Investments　　(+)　200 | |
| 　Add : Outstanding | | **2.　Dividend Received  on Shares** | |
| 　　Salary　　　(+)　200 | | | |
| 　　　　　　　7,700 | | **3.　Commission** | |
| 　Less : Salary prepaid　(–)　300 | | **4.　Miscellaneous Income :** | |
| | | 　　(a)　Share Transfer Fees | |
| | | 　　(b)　Rent | |
| **4.　Contribution to Staff Provident Fund** | | 　　(c)　Rebate in Interest | |
| | | 　　(d)　Sale of Forms | |
| **5.　Salaries and allowances of Managing Director** | | 　　(e)　Other items | |
| | | 　　　　(i)　Admission Fees | 50 |

| | | | | | |
|---|---|---|---|---|---|
| 6. | **Attendance Fees and Travelling Expenses of directors** | | 5. | **Land Income and Expenditure** | |
| 7. | **Travelling Expenses of Directors** | | | | |
| | • Travelling and Conveyance | 200 | | | |
| 8. | **Rent Rates and Taxes** | | | | |
| | • Rent and Taxes    2,600 | | | | |
| | Add: Outstanding Rent (+) 100 | 2,700 | | | |
| 9. | **Postage, Telegram and Telephone charges** | | | | |
| | • Postage | 1,250 | | | |
| 10. | **Printing and Stationery** | 400 | | Gross Profit B/D | 43,750 |
| 11. | **Audit Fees** | | | | |
| | • Audit fees | 400 | | | |
| 12. | **General Expenses** | | | | |
| 13. | **Bad debts or provision for Bad debts** | | | | |
| 14. | **Depreciation on Fixed Assets** | | | | |
| | • Office Furniture @5% p.a. | 265 | | | |
| 15. | **Land Income and Expenditure** | | | | |
| 16. | **Other items** | | | | |
| | • Commission | 2,700 | | | |
| | **Net profit carried to Balance Sheet** | 29,785 | | | |
| | | **45,100** | | | **45,100** |

Balance Sheet as on 31st March 2016

| | **Liabilities** | ₹ | ₹ | | **Assets** | ₹ | ₹ |
|---|---|---|---|---|---|---|---|
| 1. | **Share Capital** | | | 1. | **Cash and Bank Balances** | | |
| | (a)   Authorised Capital | | | | • Cash in Hand | | 1,480 |
| | (b)   Issued & Subscribed | | | | • Cash at Bank | | 15,000 |
| |      Capital | 10,000 | | 2. | **Investments** | | |
| | Less : Calls in arrears | (–) 600 | 9,400 | | • Investments | | 10,000 |
| 2. | **Reserve Fund and Other Funds** | | | 3. | **Investments of Staff Provident Fund** | | |
| | • Reserve Fund | 1,500 | 2,750 | 4. | **Loans and Advances** | | |
| | Add : 25% transferred | (+) 1250 | | 5. | **Sundry Debtors** | | |
| | • Co–operative | | | | • Sundry Drs, for sales | | 3,000 |
| |    Development Fund | 500 | 810 | 6. | **Current Assets** | | |
| | Add : Transferred | (+) 310 | | | • Closing Stock of Consumer's | | |
| | • Price Fluctuation Fund | | 800 | | Goods | | 12,500 |

| | | | | | | |
|---|---|---|---:|---|---:|---:|
| 3. | **Staff Provident Fund** | | | 7. | **Fixed Assets** | |
| 4. | **Secured Loans** | | | | • Office Furniture    5,300 | 5,035 |
| 5. | **Unsecured Loans** | | | | Less : Depre. @ 5% p.a.    (–) 265 | |
| 6. | **Deposits** | | | | Equipments | 1,800 |
| 7. | **Current Liabilities and Provisions** | | | 8. | **Miscellaneous Expenses and Losses** | |
| | • Sundry Creditors for purchases | | 2,000 | 9. | **Other Items** | |
| | • Commission Payable | | 500 | | • Salary prepaid | 300 |
| | • Outstanding Rent | | 100 | | • Interest accrued on Investments | 200 |
| | • Outstanding Salary | | 200 | 10. | **Profit and Loss Account** | |
| 8. | **Unpaid Dividends** | | 470 | 11. | **Current Losses** | |

$$\left( \begin{array}{cc} \text{Provision} & - & \text{Paid} \\ 940 & - & 470 \end{array} \right)$$

| | | | |
|---|---|---:|---:|
| 9. | **Interest accrued due but not paid** | | |
| 10. | **Other Liabilities** | | |
| 11. | **Profit and Loss Account** | | |
| | Profit for the year 2014-15 | 5,000 | |
| | Less : Dividend (10% on ₹ 9,400) | (–) 940 | |
| | | 4,060 | |
| | Less : 25% profits transferred to Reserve Fund (25% of ₹ 5,000) | (–) 1,250 | |
| | | 2,810 | |
| | Less : Transferred to Co–operative Develop. Fund | (–) 310 | |
| | | 2,500 | |
| | Add : Profits for the year 2015-16 | (+) 29,785 | 32,285 |
| | **Contingent Liability** | | |
| | | | **49,315** |

Asset side total: **49,315**

## QUESTIONS FOR SELF STUDY

**I. Theory Questions :**

1. What is Co-operative Society ? Explain the difference between Credit Co-operative Society and Consumers Co-operative Society.
2. What are the books of accounts to be maintained by Co-operative Societies ?
3. Explain the procedure of Co-operative account keeping.
4. How the profits are allocated as per Co-operative Society Act ?
5. Write Short Notes on :
    (i) Final Accounts of Credit Co-operative Societies
    (ii) Final Accounts of Consumers Co-operative Societies
    (iii) Statutory Reserve Fund
    (iv) Dividend Equalisation Fund
    (v) Education Fund
    (vi) Buildings Fund
    (vii) Dividend
    (viii) Writing of Bad Debts
    (ix) Day Book of Co-operative Society.

**II. Practical Problems**

1. From the following Trial Balance of Modern Education Society's Credit Co-operative Society Ltd., Pune prepare Profit and Loss A/c for the year ended 31$^{st}$ March 2016 and a Balance Sheet as on that date.

| Debit balances | ₹ | Credit Balances | ₹ |
|---|---|---|---|
| Loans due from members | 3,60,000 | Share Capital | 90,000 |
| Contribution to Staff Provident Fund | 240 | Reserve Fund | 6,000 |
| Insurance | 120 | Members Deposits | 2,69,730 |
| Travelling Expenses | 72 | Unpaid Dividend | 252 |
| Printing | 48 | Dividend Equalisation Fund | 2,160 |
| Administration Expenses | 600 | Staff Provident Fund | 2,400 |
| Salary and Allowances | 3,600 | Profit and Loss A/c 2014-15 | 3,720 |
| Interest due on Loans | 960 | Interest | 21,360 |
| Interest on Deposits | 9,600 | Renewal Fees | 480 |
| Furniture | 840 | Miscellaneous Income | 36 |
| Fixed Deposits | 18,600 | Co-operative Development Fund | 246 |
| Cash with Bank | 1,680 | Education Fund | 60 |
| Cash in Hand | 84 | | |
| | **3,96,444** | | **3,96,444** |

**Adjustments :**

     (i) Interest due on members deposits ₹ 500.
     (ii) Interest accrued due but not received ₹ 240.
     (iii) Salary outstanding as on 31-03-2016 ₹ 60.
     (iv) Audit fees unpaid ₹ 360.
     (v) Authorised Capital 10,000 Shares of ₹ 10 each.
     (vi) Directors propose to pay a dividend at 2% on Share Capital as on 31-03-2016.

2. Following is the Trial Balance of Bahinabai Mahila Nagari Sahakari Pat Sanstha Ltd., Warje for the year ended 31st March 2016, prepare Profit and Loss Account for the year ended 31st March 2016 and a Balance Sheet as on that date.

### Trial Balance as on 31st March 2016

| Particulars | Debit ₹ | Credit ₹ |
|---|---|---|
| Interest Received | | 2,04,480 |
| Discount Received | | 1,202 |
| Sundry Expenses | 5,166 | |
| Office Rent | 7,200 | |
| Telephone Charges | 935 | |
| Identity Cards | 1,000 | |
| Depreciation | 2,164 | |
| Lighting | 593 | |
| Insurance | 879 | |
| Share Capital | | 2,49,150 |
| Reserve Fund | | 6,000 |
| Building Fund | | 53,295 |
| Cash in hand | 5,385 | |
| Cash in P.D.C.C. Bank | 10,000 | |
| Cash in Bank of Maharashtra | 1,31,433 | |
| Shares in P.D.C.C. Bank | 100 | |
| Salaries of Staff | 18,085 | |
| Meeting Expenses | 4,331 | |
| Advertisement | 18,954 | |
| Pigmi Commission | 63,544 | |
| Saving Deposits | | 94,054 |
| Pigmi Deposits | | 13,67,070 |
| Recurring Deposits | | 12,944 |
| Damduppat Deposits | | 3,45,938 |
| Time Deposits | | 1,07,678 |
| Compulsory Deposits | | 5,430 |
| Loans on Personal Credits | 1,49,504 | |
| Loans against security of Vehicles | 1,51,695 | |
| Loans against various securities | 13,77,939 | |
| Loans against security of Gold | 2,74,797 | |
| Loans against Deposit | 1,57,553 | |
| Locker Rent | 100 | |
| Subscription to newspapers | 408 | |
| Printing and Stationery | 28,413 | |
| Postage and Telegram | 100 | |
| Interest | 38,985 | |
| Repairs | 3,502 | |
| Dead Stock | 19,476 | |
| Office Deposit | 15,000 | |
| Profits for 2014-15 | | 40,000 |
| | 24,87,241 | 24,87,241 |

**Adjustment :**

1. Salary and Audit Fees payable ₹ 4,895 and ₹ 500 respectively.
2. Interest accrued on loans ₹ 56,327 and due but not received ₹ 6,415.
3. Provide for bad and doubtful debts ₹ 86,000.
4. Stock of Stationery amounted to ₹ 8,413.

3. From the following Trial Balance of Pravara Engineering College Employee's Co-operative Credit Society Ltd., Pravaranagar, you are required to prepare Profit and Loss Account for the year ended 31st March 2016 and a Balance Sheet as on that date.

**Trial Balance as on 31st March 2016**

| Particulars | Debit ₹ | Credit ₹ |
|---|---:|---:|
| Share Capital | | 4,00,000 |
| General Reserve | | 18,000 |
| Dividend Equilisation Fund | | 1,500 |
| Silver Jubilee Fund | | 2,500 |
| Welfare Fund | | 5,000 |
| Deposits | | 1,00,000 |
| Cash Credit and Overdraft | | 12,45,000 |
| Interest payable on Fixed Deposits | | 23,000 |
| Dividend payable | | 52,000 |
| Profits for 2014-15 | | 1,100 |
| Loans | 18,00,000 | |
| Furniture | 95,000 | |
| Cash at Bank | 30,000 | |
| Interest on Bank Deposits | | 3,600 |
| Dividend received | | 7,400 |
| Interest received on Loans | | 3,48,000 |
| Commission | | 1,000 |
| Other receipts | | 1,400 |
| Interest paid on Loans | 2,56,000 | |
| Interest paid on Deposits | 2,300 | |
| Salaries | 16,000 | |
| Printing and Stationery | 4,800 | |
| Meeting Expenses | 600 | |
| Foundation Day Expenses | 400 | |
| Audit Fees | 1,600 | |
| Other Expenditure | 2,800 | |
| | **22,09,500** | **22,09,500** |

**Other Information :**

(i) Charge depreciation on Furniture ₹ 2,000.

(ii) Outstanding Audit Fees ₹ 500 and Outstanding Premium ₹ 2,000

(iii) Transfer ₹ 500 to Education Fund and ₹ 500 to Employees Provident Fund.

4. Jamner Cotton Ginening and Pressing Co-operative Society Ltd's Trial Balance as on 31-03-2016 is given as follows :

**Trial balance as on 31-03-2016**

| Particulars | Debit ₹ | Credit ₹ |
|---|---|---|
| Share Capital : 70,000 Equity Shares of ₹ 10. each | | 7,00,000 |
| Calls in Arrears | 10,000 | |
| Advances for Share Capital | | 5,000 |
| Loans from Bank | | 35,000 |
| Reserve Fund | | 40,000 |
| Dividend Equalisation Fund | | 5,000 |
| Co-operative Development Fund | | 5,000 |
| Sales - Cotton Bales and Cotton Seeds | | 30,00,000 |
| Opening Stock - Cotton Bales and Seeds | 70,000 | |
| Purchases of Cotton | 27,50,000 | |
| Cartage and Weighing Charges | 4,000 | |
| Ginning Expenses | 40,500 | |
| Pressing Expenses | 36,000 | |
| Selling Expenses | 26,800 | |
| Insurance Premium | 11,300 | |
| Manufacturing Wages | 16,800 | |
| Interest on Loan | 45,600 | |
| Salaries and Allowances and Provident Fund Contributions | 25,400 | |
| Directors Sitting Fees and Allowances | 3,000 | |
| Ground Rent | 2,000 | |
| Printing and Stationery | 7,200 | |
| Dividend paid | 30,000 | |
| Profits for the year 2014-15 | | 1,05,000 |
| Sundry Debtors | 90,000 | |
| Audit Fees | 7,000 | |
| Sundry Expenses | 15,600 | |
| Factory Building | 1,50,000 | |
| Ginening and Pressing Machinery | 3,20,000 | |
| Furniture and Fixtures | 35,000 | |
| Electric Motors and Electric Instruments | 25,000 | |
| Stores and Spare Parts | 1,15,000 | |
| Cash and Bank Balances | 1,33,800 | |
| Provident Fund | | 20,000 |
| Investment of Provident Fund | 20,000 | |
| Creditors for Purchases | | 75,000 |
| | 39,90,000 | 39,90,000 |

**Adjustments :**

(i) Closing stock of Cotton Bales and Cotton Seeds valued at ₹ 1,10,000.

(ii) Provide for reserve for doubtful debts at 5% on debtors.

(iii) Provide 5% depreciation on Machinery and 2% depreciation on Building.

(iv) 5% dividend was declared against profit of 2014-15 and 25% of the profit of 2014-15 was to be transferred to Reserve Fund as approved in the Annual General Meeting held in December 2015.

Prepare Trading Account and Profit and Loss Account for the year ended 31st March 2016 and a Balance Sheet as on that date.

5. Following is the Trial Balance of Sadhana Consumers Co-operative Society Sangli as on 31st March 2016.

**Trial Balance as on 31st March, 2016**

| Particulars | Debit ₹ | Credit ₹ |
|---|---|---|
| Share Capital | | 80,000 |
| Deposits from members | | 50,000 |
| Sales | | 12,50,000 |
| Purchase returns | | 5,000 |
| Credit Suppliers | | 10,000 |
| Interest on investment | | 12,000 |
| Rebate received | | 3,000 |
| Common Good Fund | | 4,000 |
| Price Fluctuation Fund | | 8,000 |
| Reserve Fund | | 20,000 |
| Cash in hand | 400 | |
| Cash at Bank | 86,000 | |
| Furniture | 6,000 | |
| Purchases | 10,05,000 | |
| Credit Customers | 30,000 | |
| Carriage Inward | 5,000 | |
| Sales Return | 2,000 | |
| Rent | 10,000 | |
| Audit Fees | 2,000 | |
| Sale Tax | 3,000 | |
| Staff Salary | 50,000 | |
| Printing and Stationary | 10,000 | |
| Investment | 2,00,000 | |
| Stock in Trade | 30,000 | |
| Interest paid | 2,600 | |
| | 14,42,000 | 14,42,000 |

**Adjustments :**

(i)   Value of closing stock on 31-03-2016 was ₹ 60,000.

(ii)  Provide depreciation on Furniture @ 10% p.a.

(iii) Interest accrued on deposits ₹ 1,500 and on investment ₹ 6,000.

(iv) Outstanding expenses were - Salary ₹ 3,000 and Sales Tax ₹ 1,000.

Prepare Trading Account and Profit and Loss Account for the year ended 31st March 2016 and a Balance Sheet as on that date.

6.    Following is the Trial Balance of Nagari Consumer's Co-operative Society Ltd. Amalner as on 31st March 2016 :

### Trial Balance as on 31-03-2016

| Particulars | Debit ₹ | Credit ₹ |
|---|---|---|
| Share Capital | | 15,000 |
| Deposits from members | | 30,000 |
| Dead Stock | 7,000 | |
| Printing and Stationery | 1,000 | |
| Investment in A.D.C.C. Bank | 25,000 | |
| Investment in shares of Jamner Consumer Society | 12,000 | |
| Loan from Bank (unsecured) | | 31,000 |
| Loan to Members | 45,000 | |
| Interest earned on Members Loan | | 15,000 |
| Purchases of Fertilizers and Machinery | 1,20,000 | |
| Sale of Fertilizers and Machinery | | 1,50,000 |
| Office Rent | 9,000 | |
| Office Salaries | 8,000 | |
| Travelling Expenses | 1,500 | |
| Carriage Inward | 1,300 | |
| Freight | 1,900 | |
| Bank Current A/c | 45,600 | |
| Bank Interest | 8,300 | |
| Reserve Fund | | 59,000 |
| Cash in hand | 4,400 | |
| Bank Saving A/c | 10,000 | |
| | **3,00,000** | **3,00,000** |

**Adjustment :**

(i)   Closing stock of Fertilizers and Machinery as on 31st March 2016 was ₹ 20,000.

(ii)   Outstanding office rent amounted to ₹ 3,000.

(iii) Provide depreciation @ 5% on Dead stock.

(iv) Create provision for bad and doubtful debts ₹ 1,500.

(v)   Provide for Audit Fees ₹ 600.

You are required to prepare Trading Account and Profit and Loss Account for the year ending on 31st March 2016 and Balance Sheet as on that date.

7. Mumbai Co-operative Society rendering loans and rationing facilities to its members. The Trial Balance of the Society as on 31st March, 2016 is as follows :

### Trial Balance as on 31st March, 2016

| Particulars | Debit ₹ | Credit ₹ |
|---|---|---|
| Members Share Capital | | 5,640 |
| Members Deposits | | 12,000 |
| Dead Stock | 2,800 | |
| Stationery and Printing | 300 | |
| Bank Loans (Simple) | | 12,400 |
| Members Loans | 33,300 | |
| Bank Share Purchased | 2,000 | |
| Sahakari Sangh Shares Purchased | 800 | |
| Interest on Members Loans | | 21,300 |
| Purchase of Rationing Grains | 48,000 | |
| Sales of Rationing Grains | | 51,000 |
| Office Rent | 3,600 | |
| Salary | 4,220 | |
| Travelling Expenses | 500 | |
| Freight | 520 | |
| Coolie Charges | 360 | |
| Bank Current A/c | 13,400 | |
| Bank Interest | 10,500 | |
| Reserve and Other Funds | | 18,000 |
| Cash Balance | 40 | |
| | 1,20,340 | 1,20,340 |

**Adjustments :**

(i) Closing stock of Rationing Grains on 31st March, 2016 ₹ 1,400.

(ii) Outstanding Office Rent is ₹ 400.

(iii) Provide for Audit Fees due to ₹ 240.

(iv) Provide depreciation on Dead Stock @ 5% p.a.

(v) Transfer ₹ 880 to Reserve Fund.

You are required to prepare Trading Account, Profit and Loss Account for the year ending 31st March 2016 and Balance Sheet as on that date.

*Chapter* **5**

# COMPUTERISED ACCOUNTING PRACTICES

**SYNOPSIS**

5.1  VAT

5.2  Service Tax

5.3  Central Value Added Tax

5.4  Income Tax - Tax Deducted at Source (TDS)

Including Entries with the help of Accounting Software

•  Questions for Self-Study

## 5.1 VAT

Value Added Tax (VAT) is a multipoint sales tax with set off for tax paid on purchase. It is basically a tax on the value addition on the product. The burden of tax is ultimately borne by the customer of goods. In many aspects, it is equivalent to last point of sales tax. It can also be called as a multipoint sales tax levied as a proportion of value added. It is a general tax that applies, in principle, to all commercial activities involving the production and distribution of goods and provision of services. It is not a charge on companies. It is charged as a percentage of price.

**Working of VAT (Value Added Tax)**

A trader registered for VAT effectively pays VAT only at one stage when he sells his goods. This tax is the only amount, which has effect on his selling price which includes VAT. The VAT that he has paid as a part of his purchase price is charged on him by his suppliers. This is not a cost to him because he gets it back by deducting it from tax on his sales (output tax). Therefore, VAT should have a minimum impact on his selling prices.

For example,

(i)  **Manufacturer :** The manufacturing company XYZ Pvt. Ltd. has purchased raw material worth ₹ 1,00,000 after paying state tax of ₹ 4,000 @ 4%. The labour contents are ₹ 80,000 and the margin towards administrative and selling expenses and profit are ₹ 20,000, hence total sale price ₹ 2,00,000. Suppose the tax rate is 12.5% he will charge ₹ 25,000 as tax from the wholesaler. Since he has already paid ₹ 4,000 on the raw materials hence his net tax liability ₹ 21,000 after getting a credit of ₹ 4,000 tax paid by him on raw material. This is VAT for manufacturer.

(ii)  **Wholesaler :** The wholesaler "Swastik Shoe Seller" has purchased goods worth ₹ 2,00,000 after paying tax of ₹ 25,000 as mentioned above. Let us assume his margin for profit and expenses is ₹ 14,000 then he will sell the goods for ₹ 2,14,000 to the retailer and also charge tax of ₹ 26,750 from the retailer.

Since he has already paid the tax of ₹ 25,000 on his purchases hence his net tax liability will be ₹ 26,750 (−) 25,000 = ₹ 1,750. We can verify it as 12.5% of ₹ 14,000. Since the value added by the wholesaler is ₹ 14,000.

**(iii) Retailer :** The retailer 'M/s Aher Shoe Mart' has purchased goods for ₹ 2,14,000 after paying tax of ₹ 26,750. Suppose his margin for profit and expenses is ₹ 20,000 thus he will sell the goods to the customer at ₹ 2,34,000 and will charge tax of ₹ 29,250. His net tax liability will be ₹ 29,250 (−) ₹ 26,750 = ₹ 2,500. We can verify it as 12.5% of ₹ 20,000 since the value added by the retailer is ₹ 20,000.

### VAT Returns :

VAT returns are filed every month or every quarter depending on the amount of VAT you pay. The normal rule is that if you pay less than ₹ 15,000 for every month, a VAT return is to be filed every quarter. It is all at the discretion of the VAT officer. A monthly or quarterly intervals on your VAT return, you should subtract your input tax (attributable to taxable supplies only) from your output tax and pay the difference to the VAT commissioner.

If your input tax is greater than your output tax, you can carry over the difference as a credit to your next VAT return. In certain circumstances, the commissioner may pay you any excess if he is satisfied that such an excess is a regular feature of your business.

### Issuing Tax Bills and Invoices :

According to VAT law, you cannot sell any goods without a sales document. This document can be small cash memo or cash sale or a bill for cash transaction issued at or before the time when the cash is received.

The price mentioned on these sale documents should include VAT and the words "Price includes VAT" must be printed on them. These documents are suitable for retailer such as grocers and medical stores. You must give the original to the customer and keep a duplicate. At the end of each business day, you can total the cash sales and enter it in your sales ledger. For selling on credit, you are required to provide the purchaser with a tax invoice at the time of supply in respect of that supply. When you received a deposit as advance payment for a booking, a tax invoice should be issued at the time such deposit is received. All tax invoices should be serially numbered and issued in serial number order.

### VAT Details :

 **(i)** **Input VAT :** Amount paid by a buyer as a percentage of the gross purchase price for goods or services used in production.

 **(ii)** **Output Vat :** Amount received by a seller as a percentage of the gross sale price of goods or services.

 **(iii)** **Zero Rated :** Transactions in which the seller collects no output tax and the corresponding input tax is fully refundable. Exports are zero rated.

 **(iv)** **Exempt :** Transactions in which the seller collects no output tax but the corresponding input tax is non-refundable and absorbed by the seller. Financial services are commonly exempt.

### VAT Rates and Goods Exempted from VAT :

For different commodities VAT rates are calculated as 1%, 4%, 12.5% and a specific category is exempted from VAT.

**Goods Exempted from VAT :**

(i) Agricultural implements manually operated or animal drives notified by the state government.

(ii) Aquatic food, cattle food, poultry food, animal food supplements.

(iii) Books including almanacs, panchangs, time tables for passenger transport services.

(iv) Cereals and pulses (during period from 01.04.2005 to 31.03.2006) in whole grain.

(v) Chalk stick, charcoal and badaml, charcoal, charkha implements used in production of handspun yarn.

(vi) Firewood, fishnet fabrics, contraceptives of all types.

## VAT (Value Added Tax)

## Enabling in Tally ERP9

To enable VAT in Tally ERP9.

Go to gateway of Tally > F11: Features > F3 : Statutory and Taxation.

**1. In the Statutory and Taxation Features**

- Set Enable Value Added (VAT) to Yes.

- Enable Set/Alter VAT Details.

| Company : ABC Company | | | | |
|---|---|---|---|---|
| **Statutory and Taxation** | | | | |
| **Enable Excise** ? | No. | **Enable Tax Deduction at Source (TDS)** ? | | No. |
| **Set/Alter Excise Details** ? | No. | **Set/Alter TDS Details** | ? | No. |
| **(Note: Enable Maintain** | | **Enable Tax Collected at Source (TCS)** | ? | No. |
| **Godowns for Multiple Excise Units)** | | **Set/Alter TCS Details** | | |
| **Follow Excise rules for invoicing?** | No. | | | |
| **Enable Value Added Tax (VAT)** ? | Yes | **Enable Fringe Benefit Tax (FBT)** | ? | No. |
| **Set/Alter Service Tax Details** | Yes | **Set/Alter FBT Details** | ? | No. |
| **Enable Service Tax** | No. | **Enable MCA Reports** | ? | No. |
| **Set/Alter Service Tax Details** ? | No. | | | |
| | **Tax Information** | | | |
| | **VAT TIN Composition :** | | | |
| | **VAT TIN (Regular) :** | | | |
| | **Local Sales Tax Number :** | | | |
| | **Inter State Sales-Tax Number :** | | | |
| | **PAN/Income Tax No. :** | | | |
| **F1 : Accounts, F2 : Inventory, F3 : Statutory, F6 : Add-Ons** | | | | |

**2.** **Press 'Enter' to view the Company VAT Details Screen**

**Note :** The procedure for providing the appropriate details in respective of **Company VAT Details** screen is given with respect to Maharashtra State. You can select the required state from the list of the states displayed to import the state-specific statutory masters.

**3.** In the **Company VAT Details** screen, specify the VAT details and return form specific additional information.

- Under VAT details section.
- Select the state as 'Maharashtra'.
- Select the "Type of Dealer" as applicable based on the type of registration made by the dealer's with the VAT Department. In this section, the procedure pertaining to regular dealer is being explained. Hence, select the **"Type of Dealer"** as **Regular.**

<table>
<tr><td colspan="3" align="center">VAT Details</td></tr>
<tr><td>State</td><td>:</td><td>Maharashtra</td></tr>
<tr><td>Type of Dealer</td><td>?</td><td>Regular</td></tr>
<tr><td>Regular VAT Applicable from</td><td>:</td><td>01.04.2013</td></tr>
<tr><td colspan="3" align="center">Additional Information</td></tr>
<tr><td>LVO/VSO Code</td><td>:</td><td>LVO 011</td></tr>
<tr><td>Authorised person</td><td>:</td><td>Madhav Kulkarni</td></tr>
<tr><td>Status/Designation</td><td>:</td><td>Accounts Officer</td></tr>
<tr><td>Place</td><td>:</td><td>Nashik</td></tr>
</table>

Enter the date from which the Vat provisions are applicable for the dealer in the **'Regular VAT Applicable from' field.**

- **Under Addition Information Section :**
  - **LVO/VSO Code :** Enter the local VAT office/Local sub-VAT office code in this field.
  - **Authorised person :** Enter the name of person authorized to sign the return form.
  - **Status/Designation :** Enter the status/designation of the authorized person in this field.
  - **Place :** Enter the name of place where the return is being filed.

Press **"Enter"** to save the details and return to the **'Company Operations Alterations'** screen.

The details entered in the additional information field will be captured in the **'Report Generation'** screen of **'return forms'** and **'annexures'**.

In the **'Report Generation'** screen of Return Forms and Annexures, the details in the field - Authorised Person, Status/Designation and Place can be changed as per requirement. On existing the screen, the temporarily modified details will not be saved. Every time the report is generated, the information entered in **'Company VAT Details'** screen of **F3: Statutory and Taxation Features** will be displayed.

**4.** A brief description on the fields pertaining to **'Tax Information'** that appears in this screen is given below :

- **VAT TIN (Composition) :** This field will be skipped on selecting the **'Type of Dealer'** as **Regular.** The **VAT TIN** can be entered in this field only when the **Type of Dealer** is selected as **'Composite'.**
- **VAT TIN (Regular) :** Enter the Tax Identification Number (TIN) in this field, the TIN is 11 digit number.

- **Local Sales Tax Number :** This field will be skipped on selecting the **Type of Dealer as Regular**. This number will be provided only for dealer who does not posses a VAT/TIN.

- **Inter-State Sales Tax Number :** Enter the Inter-state Sales Tax Number.

- **PAN/Income Tax Number :** Enter the Permanent Account Number in this field. The PAN is a 10 digit alphanumeric number.

**Note :** The detailed explanation on the procedure of enabling VAT, recording transactions and making the adjustment entries as per state specified statutory requirements can be obtained in the **Statutory Reference Manual**. The same can be downloaded by clicking on the download button in website **www.tallysolutions.com**.

**Purchase Ledger :**

To create a purchase ledger :

Go to Gateway of Tally 7 Accounts Info > Ledgers > Create

- Enter the **'Name'** of the Purchase Ledger.

- In the **'Under'** field, select **"Purchase Accounts"** from the 'list of Groups'.

- Set the field **'Inventory Values are affected'** to **Yes**.

- Select the 'Type of Ledger as 'Not Applicable'.

- Set the field **"Used in VAT Returns"** to **Yes**.

| Ledger     Creation | | National |
|---|---|---|
| **Name :** Purchases @ 5.5%<br>(alias) | | Total Opening Balance |
| **Under** | **Purchase Account** | |
| **Inventory values are affected** | ?     Yes | |
| **Use for Assessable Value Calculation** | ?     No | |
| **Statutory Information** | ?     Yes | |
| **Used in VAT Returns** | ?     No | |
| **Or For assessable value calculation** | ? | |
| Opening Balance (on 1st April, 2015) | | |

- Select the required VAT/Tax class from the list displayed.

**Note :** The VAT/Tax classification pertaining to purchases will be displayed for selection based on the **'State'** and **'Type of Dealer'** pre-defined in the **F3 : 'Statutory and Taxation Features'**. The VAT/Tax classification displayed for purchases in this example pertains to **Maharashtra State**.

- Accept the purchase ledger.

To create an input VAT ledger.

Go to Gateway of Tally > Accounts Info > Ledgers > Create

- Enter the **Name** of the input VAT ledger.
- In the **'Under'** field, select **"Duties and Taxes"** from the **"List of Groups"**.
- Select **VAT** in the **Type of Duty/Tax field**.
- In **'VAT Sub Type'** select **"Input VAT"** from the **'List of VAT Sub Types'** screen.
- Select the input VAT classification in the **'VAT/Tax Class'** field.
- The **'Percentage of Calculation'** and the **"Method of Calculation'** will be diaplayed based on the **VAT/Tax** class selected.

| Ledger          Creation | | National |
|---|---|---|
| Name : Input VAT @ 5.5% <br> (alias) | | Total Opening Balance |
| **Under** | **Duties and Taxes** <br> **(Current Liabilities)** | |
| **Type of Duty/Tax** | : VAT | |
| **VAT Sub Type** | : Input VAT | |
| **VAT/Tax Class** | : Input VAT @ 5.5% | |
| **Inventory values are affected**    ? | : No | |
| **Percentage of calculation (e.g. 5)**    ? | : 5.50% | |
| **Method of Calculation** | : On VAT rate | |
| **Rounding method** | : Not applicable | |
| | | Accept ? <br> Yes or No |
| Opening Balance (on 1st April, 2015) | | |

- **Accept the Input VAT ledger**

**Note :** The VAT/Tax classifications pertaining to input tax will be displayed for selection based on the **State** and **'Type of Dealer'** pre defined in the **F3 : Statutory and Taxation Features'**. The VAT/Tax classification displayed for input tax in this example pertains to Maharashtra State.

**Sales Ledger :**

To create a Sales Ledger

Go to Gateway of Tally > Accounts Info ? Ledgers > Create

- Enter the **'Name'** of the Sales Ledger.
- In the **Under** field, select the **Sales Accounts** from the **'List of Groups'**.
- Set the field **Inventory values are affected to Yes**.
- Select the **'Type of Ledger'** as **'Not Applicable'**.
- Set the field **'Used in VAT Returns to Yes**.

| Ledger Creation | National |
|---|---|
| **Name :** Sales (@ 5.5%) <br> (alias) | Total Opening Balance |

| | | |
|---|---|---|
| **Under** | | Purchase Account |
| **Inventory values are affected** | ? | Yes |
| **Type of Ledger** | ? | Not Applicable |
| | **Statutory Information** | |
| **Used in VAT Returns** | ? | Yes |
| **Use for Assessable Value Calculation** | ? | No |

Opening Balance (on 1st April, 2015)

- **Select the required VAT/Tax Class from the list displayed**.
- Accept the Sales ledger.

  **Note :** The VAT/Tax classification pertaining to sales will be displayed for selection based on the state and the **'Type of Dealer'** pre-determined in **F3 : Statutory and Taxation Features**. The VAT/Tax classification displayed for sales in this example pertains to Maharashtra State.

**Output VAT Ledger :**

To create on output VAT ledger

Go to Gateway of Tally > Accounts Info > Ledgers > Create

- Enter the **Name** of the **Output VAT Ledger**.
- In the **Under** field, select **"Duties and Taxes"** from the **'List of Groups'**.
- Select VAT in the **Type of Duty/Tax Field**.
- In **'VAT Sub "Type'** select **Output VAT** from the **List of VAT Sub Types Screen**.
- Select the output VAT classification in the **VAT/Tax Class** field.
- The **Percentage of Calculation** and the **Method of Calculation** will be displayed on the VAT/Tax class selected.

| Ledger Creation | National |
|---|---|
| **Name :** Output VAT (@ 5.5%) <br> (alias) | Total Opening Balance |

| | | |
|---|---|---|
| **Under** | | Duties and Taxes <br> Current Liabilities |
| Type of Duty/Tax | : | VAT |
| VAT Sub Type | : | Output VAT |
| **VAT/Tax Class** | : | Output VAT @ 5.5% |
| **Inventory values are affected** | ? : | No |
| **Percentage of calculation (e.g. 5)** | ? : | 5.50% |
| **Method of Calculation** | : | On VAT rate |
| **Rounding method** | : | Not applicable |
| | | Accept ? <br> Yes or No |

Opening Balance (on 1st April, 2015)

- **Accept the Output VAT ledger**

**Note :** The VAT/Tax classification pertaining to output tax will be displayed for selection based on the **State** and **'Type of Dealer's** pre-defined. **F3 : Statutory and Taxation Features.** The VAT/Tax classification displayed for output tax in this example pertains to Maharashtra State.

**Current Asset Ledger :**

In excise and VAT enabled company, if the excise ledger is grouped under "Current Assets" the field - **Type of Duty/Tax** will be displayed. On setting **'CENVAT'** as the **Type of Duty/Tax** the ledger values entered in purchase entry gets apportioned to purchase cost. VAT will be calculated on the apportioned assessable value.

In **Current Asset** ledger master, if the **Type of Duty/Tax** is set to **'Not Applicable'** in Excise and VAT enable company, the field - Use for **'Assessable Value Calculation'** will be displayed. On enabling it, the field **"Apportion for"** and **Method of Apportion** gets enabled. Select **VAT** in Apportion for field and set the **'Method of Apportion'** to either **'Based on Quality/'Based on Value'.** This will be apportion the excise duty to purchase cost for calculation of VAT on apportioned assessable amount of purchases based on quantity/value as selected in ledger master.

In the ledger creation screen of Excise and VAT enable company,

- Enter the **'Name'** as Excise duty.

- Select **Current Assets** as the group name in the **Under** field.

- Set the option **"Use for Assessable Value Calculation"** to **Yes.**

- On enabling this option, the additional field - **Apportion for and Method of Apportion** will be displayed.

- In the **'Apportion for'** field select **VAT** and set the **Method of Apportion** to **Based on Quantity**. The value entered for this ledger while recording entries will be apportioned to the assessable value as per the method, selected for apportionment.

| Ledger Creation | | National Traders |
|---|---|---|
| **Name :**       Excise Duty | | Total Opening Balance |
| (alias) | | |
| **Under :**      **Current Assets** | | |
| **Type of Duty/Tax**    :   Not Applicable | | |
| **Inventory values are affected**   ?   :   No | | |
| **Use for Assessable Value Calculation**   :   Yes | | |
| **Apportion for**    ?   :   VAT | | |
| **Method of Apportion**    :   Based on Value | | |
| | | Method of Apportion<br>Based on Quantity<br>Based on Value |
| Opening Balance (on 1st April, 2015) | | |

- **Accept the ledger creation screen**

**Additional Expenses Ledger :**

To create a ledger for packing materials.

Go to Gateway of Tally > Accounts Info > Ledger > Create.

- Enter the **'Name'** as **Package Material**.

- Select **Direct/Indirect Expenses** as the group name in the **Under** field.

- The option **'Inventory values are affected'** is set to **'No'** by default.

- Set the **Type of Ledger** field to **'Not Applicable'**.

- Set the option **'Use Assessment Value Calculation'** to **Yes**. On enabling this option, the addition field **'Apportion for'** and **'Method of Apportion'** will be displayed. The value entered for this ledger while recording entries will be apportioned to the assessable value as per the method selected for apportionment.

- In the **'Apportion for'** field select **VAT** and set **'Method of Apportion'** to **Based on Quantity**.

| Ledger Creation | | National |
|---|---|---|
| Name :            Package Material<br>(alias) | | Total Opening Balance |
| **Under :** | **Current Assets** | |
| **Inventory values are affected**        ?   :   No | | |
| **Type of Ledger**        ?   :   Not Applicable | | |
| **Statutory Information** | | |
| **Used in VAT Returns**        ?   :   No | | |
| **Use for Assessable Value Calculation** ?   :   Yes | | |
| **Apportion for**        ?   :   VAT | | |
| **Method of Apportion**        :   Based on Value | | |
| | | Accept ?<br>Yes or No |
| Opening Balance (on 1st April, 2015) | | |

- **Press Y or Enter to accept and save.**

**Creation of VAT Commodity :**

To create a VAT commodity,

Go to Gateway of Tally > Inventory Info > VAT Commodity > Create

- Enter the **Name** of the VAT commodity.

- Select **VAT** in the **User for** field.

- On selecting VAT in **'Use for'** field the cursor will skip 'HSN Code' and promote to enter the information under VAT section.

- Under **VAT** Section, enter **"Commodity Code" Schedule Number** and **Schedule Serial Number** as applicable.

| **Ledger Commodity Creation** | | **National Traders** |
|---|---|---|
| **Name :**     Computer Peripherals | | Total Opening Balance |
| (alias) | | |
| **Used for** | :   VAT | |
| **HSN Code** | : | |
| **VAT** | | |
| **Commodity Code** | :   2015 | |
| **Schedule Number** | :   5 | |
| **Schedule Serial Number** | :   12 | |
| Notes | | |

- Enter the notes if required and accept the **VAT Commodity Creation Screen**.

**Creation of Stock Item :**

Go to Gateway of Tally > Inventory Info > Stock Items > Create

- Enter the **Name** of the stock item.
- Select the group name in the **Under** field.
- Select the unit of measurement of the stock in item in the units field.
- In the **Commodity** field, select the required **VAT Commodity**.
- The VAT commodity code will also be displayed if entered while creating VAT commodity along with the commodity name in the **List of VAT Commodity**.
- Enter the **Rate of VAT** for the stock item.
- Enter the Opening Balance (Quantity and rate of the stock item) if any.

| **Stock Item Creation** | | **National Traders** | |
|---|---|---|---|
| **Name :**     Computer | | | |
| (alias) | | | |
| **Under**    :   Primary | | **Tax Information** | |
| **Units**    :   Numbers | | **Tariff Classification**    :   Not Applicable | |
| | | **Rate of Duty (e.g. 5)**    :   0 | |
| | | **VAT Details** | |
| | | **Commodity**    :   Computer Peripherals | |
| | | **Rate of VAT (%)**    :   5-50 | |
| **Quantity** | **Rate Per** | | **Value** |
| | | | Accept ?<br>Yes or No |

- Press Y or Enter to accept and save.

**VAT Adjustment Class for Journal**

To create a VAT Adjustment Class.

Go to Gateway of Tally > Account Info > Voucher Type > Alter > Journal

- In the **Voucher Type Alternation** screen, enter the **Name of Class**. For e.g. **VAT Adjustment Class.**

| Voucher Type Alteration | ABC Company | | Ctrl + M |
|---|---|---|---|
| **Name** : Journal<br>(alias) | | | |
| **General** | **Printing** | | **Name of Class** |
| **Type of Voucher** : Journal<br>**Abbr** : Jrnl | **Print after Saving Voucher ? :** No | | **VAT Adjustment Class** |
| **Method of Voucher Numbering ? :** | Automatic | | |
| **Use Advance Configuration ? :** | No | | |
| **Make 'Optional' as default ? :** | No | | |
| **Use Common Narration ? :** | Yes | | |
| **Narration for each entry ? :** | No | | |

- **Set Use Class for VAT Adjustments to Yes.**

| Voucher Type Class | ABC Company | Ctrl + M | X |
|---|---|---|---|
| **Name : Journal**<br>(alias) | Class : VAT Adjustment Class<br><br>Use class for VAT Adjustment ? Yes<br><br>Ledger amount to use | | |
| | **Ledger Name** | | |

- Press **Enter** to go back to **Voucher Type Alteration** screen.
- **Accept the journal Voucher Type Alteration Screen.**

**Tax Invoice Voucher Type**

G to Gateway of Tally > Accounts Info > Voucher Types > Create

- Enter the **Name** of the **Voucher Type**. For e.g. **'Tax Invoice'.**
- Select the **Type of Voucher**. For e.g. **Sales** from the **"List of Voucher Type"**.
- In the Abbr. field, you may abbreviate the voucher type as per your requirement or retain the same.
- Select the **Method of Voucher** Numbering as **Automatic**.
- Set **Print after saving Voucher** to **Yes** or **No as applicable**.
- Enter the **Default Print Title** as **Tax Invoice**.
- Enter the **Default** Jurisdiction as **Maharashtra**.
- Set the field is **Tax Invoice** to **Yes**.

| **Voucher Type Creation** | **ABC Company** | **Ctrl + M** |
|---|---|---|
| Name   :   Tax Invoice <br> (alias) | | |

| **General** | **1 ... 2 more** | **Name of Class** |
|---|---|---|
| **Type of Voucher**  :   Sales <br> Abbr             :   Sale | | |
| **Method of Voucher Numbering**  ? :  Automatic <br> **Use Advance Configuration**      ? :  No <br> **Use Effective Dates for Vouchers** ? :  No <br> **Make 'Optional' as default**       ? :  No <br> **Use Common Narration**          ? :  Yes <br> **Narration for each entry**       ? :  No | **Use of POS Invoicing ? :** No <br> **Default Print Title :** Tax Invoice <br> **Default Jurisdiction :** Maharashtra <br> Is a Tax Invoice ? Yes <br> Declaration : | |
| | | Accept ? <br> Yes or No |

- Press Y or Enter to accept the **Tax Invoice.**

**Note :** In the Sales Voucher type, only when the option **'Is Tax Invoice'** is set **Yes**, the invoice can be printed as Tax Invoice'.

## 5.2 SERVICE TAX

Service tax is a tax imposed by Government of India on services provided in India. The service provider collects the tax and pays the same to the government. It is charged on all services covered in the negative list (Section 66 of Finance Act, 1994) of services and services covered under Mega Exemption Notification (Notification No. 25/2012 ST dated 20:06:2012). The current rate is 14% on gross value of the service.

Budget 2012 revamped the taxation provisions for services by introducing a new system of taxation of services in India. In the new system all services, except those specified in the negative list, are subject to taxation. Earlier the levy of service tax was based on positive list specified 119 taxable services.

As per clause (34) of Section 65 B of the Finance Act, 1994, the term "Negative List" means the services which are listed in Section 66 D.

Rule 4A prescribes that taxable services shall be provided and input credit shall be distributed only on the basis of a bill, invoice or challan. Such bill, invoice or challan will also include documents used by service providers of banking services (such as pay-in-slip, debit credit advice etc.) and consignment note issued by goods transport agencies. Rule 4B provides for issuance of a consignment note to customer by the service provider in respect of goods transport booking services.

According to Rule 5 of Service Tax Rules, 1994, records include computerised data and means the record as maintained by assessee in accordance with the various laws in force from time to time. Records maintained as such shall be acceptable to Central Excise Officer. Every assessee is required to furnish to the Central Excise Officer at the time of filing his return for the first time a list of all accounts maintained by the assessee in relation to service tax including memoranda received from his branch offices. This information may be sent along with a covering letter while filing the service tax return for the first time.

Service tax is a tax levied by the Government on service providers on certain service transactions, but it is actually borne by the customers. It is charged to the individual service providers on cash basis and to companies on accrual basis.

**Enabling Service Tax in Tally ERP9 :**

To enable Service Tax

- Go to Gateway of Tally > F11 : Features > Statutory and Taxation.

- Set Enable Service Tax to Yes .

- Set Set/Alter Service Tax Details to Yes to enter the Company Service Tax Details.

**Company : www.satyamevjayate.com.**

**Statutory and Taxation**

| | | | |
|---|---|---|---|
| Enable Dealer-Excise | ? : No | Enable Tax Deduction at Source (TDS) | ? : No |
| Set/Alter Dealer-Excise Details | ? : No | Set/Alter TDS Details | ? : No |
| Follow Invoice rules for invoicing | ? : No | Enable Tax Collected at Source (TDS) | ? : No |
| Enable Value Added Tax (VAT) | ? : No | Set/Alter TCS Details | ? : No |
| Set/Alter VAT Details | ? : No | Enable Fringe Benefit Tax (FBT) | ? : No |
| Enable Service Tax | ? : Yes | Set/Alter FBT Details | ? : No |
| Set/Alter Service Tax Details | ? : Yes | | |

**Tax Information**

- **Enter the details as per the following figure**

| Company Service Tax Details | | Division | |
|---|---|---|---|
| Service Tax Registration No. : | ABC123456BLS | Code | : 123 NMC |
| Date of Registration | : 1st Jan. 2011 | Name | : KULKARNI |
| Assessee Code | : 123XYZA | Range | : |
| Premises Code No | : ALP | Code | : 12345 |
| Type of Organisation | : Registered Private Ltd. Co. | Name | : Maharashtra |
| Is large tax payer ? | : No | Commissionerate | : |
| Large tax payer unit | : | Code | : 222222 |
| | | Name | : Madhav Kulkarni |

| Focal Bank Details | | |
|---|---|---|
| Focal Bank Code | : | CBIN4444 |
| Focal Bank Name | : | Central Bank of India |
| Focal Bank Address | : | Main Road, Nashik. |

It is one time configuration for service tax features to be enable in Tally ERP9 follow the steps given below to configure service tax for a new company Satyamevjayate Pvt. Ltd.

To enable service tax for companies which are already created in Tally ERP9. Follow the instruction provided under the head **Enable Service Tax**. Satyamev Jayate (P) Ltd. is a company engaged in providing multiple services to their clients. The services provided by Satyamev Jayate (P) Ltd., fall within the ambit of tax net and are taxable @ 14%.

### Step 1 : Create Company

Go to Gateway of Tally > Alt + F3 : Company Info > Create Company

- In the Company Creation Screen,

Specific **Satyamev Jayate (P) Ltd.,** as the company **Name and Address** details **Select India** in the **Statutory Compliance** for field specify the State, Pin Code and **Account with or without** inventory details.

The Completed Company Creation Screen displays as shown.

| Company Creation | | Ctrl + M |
|---|---|---|
| Directory | : C:/Tally.ERP9\Data | |
| Name | : Satyamev Jayate (P) Ltd. | |
| | **Mailing and Contact Details** | **Company Details** |
| Mailing Name | Satyamev Jayate (P) Ltd. | Currency Symbol : ₹ |
| Address | # 56/1 | Maintain : Accounts with Inventory |
| | M.G. Road | Financial Year from : 1-4-2015 |
| | Bangalore | Books beginning from : 1-4-2015 |
| | | **Security Control** |
| Statutory compliance for | : India | TallyVault Password (if any) : |
| State | : Maharashtra | Repeat Password  : |
| PIN Code | : 560085 | (WARNING : Forgetting your TallyVault password with render your data unusable!!) |
| Telephone No. | : 22589651 | Use Security Control |
| Mobile No. | : 9985745142 | (Enable Security to avail Tally.Net Features) |
| E-mail | : sales@satyamevjayate | |
| | **Auto Backup Details** | |
| Enable Auto Back | : Yes | |
| | **Base Currency Information** | |
| Base Currency Symbol | : ₹ | Show Amounts in Millions ? No |
| Formal Name | : INR | Put a SPACE between Amount and Symbol ? Yes |
| Number of Decimal Places | : 2 | Decimal Places for Printing Amounts in words |
| Is Symbol SUFFIXED to Amounts ? No | | |
| Symbol for Decimal Portion | : Paise | |
| | | Accept ? Yes or No |

Press **Enter** to Save.

**Fig. 5.1 : Company Creation Screen**

### Step 2 : Enable Service Tax

**Enable Service Tax Feature in F11 : Features**

**Go to Gateway of Tally > F11 : Features > Statutory and Taxation**

**Set Enable Service Tax** to Yes .

**Enable Set/Alter Service Tax Details** to Yes .

| Company Satyamev Jayate (P) Ltd. | | | |
|---|---|---|---|
| **Statutory and Taxation** | | | |
| Enable Excise | ? No | Enable Tax Deducted at Source (TDS) | ? No |
| Set/Alter Excise Details | ? No | Set/Alter TDS Details | ? No |
| (Note : Enable Maintain Multiple Godowns' | | Enable Tax Collected at Source (TCS) | ? No |
| for Multiple Excise Units) | | Set/Alter TCS Details | ? No |
| Follow Excise Added Tax (VAT) | ? No | Enable Fringe Benefit Tax (FBT) | ? No |
| Set/Alter VAT Details | ? No | Set/Alter FBT Details | ? No |
| Enable Service Tax | ? Yes | | |
| Set/Alter Service Tax Details | ? Yes | | |

**Tax Information**

Local Sales Tax Number

Inter-state Sales Tax Number

PAN/Income-Tax No.

F1 : Accounts    F2 : Inventory    F3 : Statutory

**Fig. 5.2 : F11 : Statutory and Taxation Features**

**The Company Service Tax Details Sub Form appears as shown.**

| Company Service Tax Details | | |
|---|---|---|
| Service Tax Registration No. | | Assessee Code |
| Date of Registration | | Premises Code No |
| Type of Organisation | | Is Large Tax Payer ? No |
| Enable Service Tax Round Off | Yes | Large Tax Payer Unit |
| **Range** | **Division** | **Commissionerate** |
| Code | Code | Code |
| Name | Name | Name |

(Note : All the above details will be used in Challan, Forms and Returns)

**Fig. 5.3 : Company Service Tax Details Screen**

**In Company Service Tax Details screen are the following details.**

1. **Service Tax Registration Number :** In this field, enter the Service Tax Registration Number of the company allotted by the department (before the Circular No. 35/3/2001. dated 27.08.2001).

2. **Date of Registration :** Specify the Date of Service Tax Registration of the Company e.g. 15.8.2015.

3. **Type of Organisation :** In this field, select the appropriate organisation type from the list of organisation. e.g. Registered Private Ltd. Company.

4. **Enable Service Tax Refund Off :** By default, this option will be set to ⎡Yes⎤.

   If this option is ⎡Yes⎤, service tax will get rounded off to nearest rupee and such round off will happen for each tax head. Set this option to : No if rounding off is not necessary. In this case, Satyamev Jayate (P) Ltd. does not want to round off the service tax amount, hence this option is set to No.

   If the option Enable Service Tax Round off is enable (set to yes) and for a service bill, the tax is calculated as shown below, then each tax head gets rounded off.

   Service Tax of 1012.85 to 1013

   Education Cess of 20.53 to 21.

   Secondary Education Cess of 10.12 to 10.

   If the option Enable Service Tax Round off is disable (set to No) and for a service bill the tax is calculated as shown below then each tax head will not be rounded off.

   Service Tax of 1012.85.

   Education Cess of 20.53.

   Secondary Education Cess of 10.12.

   While creating the company, if you had enabled the option Enable Service Tax Round off and recorded few transactions in the books of accounts. Later because of accounting requirements if you change the settings to Enable Service Tax Round off (set to No).

   On altering the existing Service Tax transactions, the application will automatically change the present round off values into values with decimals.

5. **Assessee Code :** In this field, enter the Service Tax Assessee Code of the company e.g. ABCDE188PNT001.

6. **Premises Code No :** In this field, enter company's premises code allowed by department. e.g. MSG500014.

   Premises code is the identification number provided to the premises of the Service Tax payers. Premises code is issues to an assessee under S. No. 5 of the Certificate for Registration (ST 2).

7. **Is the Large Tax Payer :** This will be set to ⎡Yes/No.⎤ based on the amount of tax paid by the asessee. Set this option to No.

   Large tax payers are those assesses who pay large amount of tax. They are the eligible tax payer for the purposes of being saved by the LTO. For e.g. ₹ 5 crores.

8. **Large Tax Payer Unit :** Enter the name of the unit where the large tax payers pay service tax.

   Tally ERP9 skips large tax payer unit when the option is large tax payer is set to no.

9. Under Range, Enter Code and Name under which your company falls.

10. Under Division, enter the Division Code and name of the Commissionerate of Service Tax.

11. Under commissionerate, enter code and name of the company's registered office is located.

   The completed Company Service Tax Details screen appears as shown.

<table>
<tr><td colspan="3" align="center">**Company Service Tax Details**</td></tr>
<tr><td>Service Tax Registration No.</td><td>: ASDCE1588PST001</td><td>Assessee Code   : ASDCE1588PST001</td></tr>
<tr><td>Date of Registration</td><td>: 15-Mar-2002</td><td>Premises Code No  : SC0500012</td></tr>
<tr><td>Type of Organisation</td><td>: Registered Private Ltd. Company</td><td>Is Large Tax Payer  : ? No</td></tr>
<tr><td>Enable Service Tax Round Off</td><td>: No</td><td></td></tr>
<tr><td>**Range**</td><td>**Division**</td><td>**Commissionerate**</td></tr>
<tr><td>Code : 06</td><td>Code : 02</td><td>Code : 09</td></tr>
<tr><td>Name : Bommanahalli</td><td>Name : Division II</td><td>Name : Maharashtra</td></tr>
</table>

(Note : All the above details will be used in Challan, Forms and Returns)

**Fig. 5.4 : Completed Company Service Tax Details Screen**

12. Accept the 'Company Service Tax Details' screen.

13. In the **PAN/Income Tax Number field**, enter the **Permanent Account Number (PAN)** of the company.

   The completed Statutory and Taxation Screen is displayed as shown.

<table>
<tr><td colspan="4" align="center">**Company Satyamev Jayate (P) Ltd.**</td></tr>
<tr><td colspan="4" align="center">**Statutory and Taxation**</td></tr>
<tr><td>Enable Excise</td><td>? No</td><td>Enable Tax Deducted at Source (TDS)</td><td>? No</td></tr>
<tr><td>Set/Alter Excise Details</td><td>? No</td><td>Set/Alter TDS Details</td><td>? No</td></tr>
<tr><td>(Note : Enable Maintain Multiple Godowns'</td><td></td><td>Enable Tax Collected at Source (TCS)</td><td>? No</td></tr>
<tr><td>for Multiple Excise Units)</td><td></td><td>Set/Alter TCS Details</td><td>? No</td></tr>
<tr><td>Follow Excise rules for Invoicing</td><td>? No</td><td>Enable Fringe Benefit Tax (FBT)</td><td>? No</td></tr>
<tr><td>Enable Value Added Tax (VAT)</td><td>? No</td><td>Set/Alter FBT Details</td><td>? No</td></tr>
<tr><td>Set/Alter VAT Details</td><td>? No</td><td></td><td></td></tr>
<tr><td>Enable Service Tax</td><td>? Yes</td><td></td><td></td></tr>
<tr><td>Set/Alter Service Tax Details</td><td>? Yes</td><td></td><td></td></tr>
<tr><td colspan="4" align="center">**Tax Information**</td></tr>
<tr><td colspan="4" align="center">Local Sales Tax Number</td></tr>
<tr><td colspan="4" align="center">Inter-state Sales Tax Number</td></tr>
<tr><td colspan="4" align="center">PAN/Income-Tax No.</td></tr>
<tr><td colspan="4" align="center">F1 : Accounts     F2 : Inventory     F3 : Statutory</td></tr>
</table>

14. Press **'Enter'** to save.

**Fig. 5.5 : Completed Statutory and Taxation Features Screen**

To create a Customer Ledger :

Go to Gateway of Tally > Accounts Info > Ledger > Create

- In the **Name** field enter the Name of the Company to which the services are provided. e.g. ABC Co.
- In **Under** field select **"Sundry Debtors"** from the **'List of Groups'**.
- Set maintain **balances bill-by-bill** to **Yes**.
- Enter details in the **Default Credit Period** if applicable.
- Set **Is Service Tax Applicable to Yes** to view the **Exemption Details** screen to display.

| | | |
|---|---|---|
| | | |
| **Under** | **Sundry Debtors** | **Mailing Details** |
| | **(Current Assets)** | **Name :** Shriram Computers |
| **Maintain balances bill-by-bill** | ? : Yes | **Address :** 11, Gole Colony, Nashik. |
| **Default Credit Period** | : | |
| **Inventory Values are affected** | ? : No | |
| **Statutory Information** | | |
| **Is Service Tax applicable** | ? : Yes | |

1. In the **Exemption Details** screen.
2. In **type of Classification** select **Not Applicable**. The option **"Exempt"** will be selected when the tax is not payable.

| **Exemption details** | **ABC Company** | **Ctrl + M** |
|---|---|---|
| Exemption Details<br>**Type of Classification :** Not Applicable | | |
| Classification | | |
| √   Not Applicable | | |
| Exempt | | |

3. Enter the Mailing Details and Tax Information (Mentioned as above).

- Accept the screen to save.

Similarly, you can create Supplier Ledger.

**To Create Service Tax Ledger :**

Go to **Gateway of Tally > Accounts Info > Ledger > Create**

1. In the **Name** field enter the **Name of the Ledger**.
2. Select the Group **Duties and Taxes** in the **Under** field.

3.    In **Type of Duty** field select **'Service Tax'** from the list of **Types of Duty/Tax**.

4.    In **Category Name** files select **'Accounting Services (619)** from the **List of Services Categories**.

| Ledger Creation | | ABC Company | Ctrl + M (X) **List of Service Categories** |
|---|---|---|---|
| **Name** : Tax (@ 6%) <br> (alias) | | | ↓ <br> ↓ <br> ↓ |
| **Under**      : **Duties and Taxes** <br>        **(Current Liabilities)** <br> **Type of Duty**    : Service Tax <br> **Category Name**    : Accounting Services (619) <br> **Inventory Values are affected** : ? No | | **Name** <br> **Address** | ↓ <br> ↓ <br> ↓ <br> ↓ |
| **Opening Balance (1ˢᵗ April 2015)** | | | |

-   **Set Inventory Values are affected to number,** which can be set to yes if applicable.
-   Accept the screen to save.

**To create Sales Ledgers for Services :**

Go to Gateway of Tally > Accounts Info > Ledgers > Create

1.    In the **Name** field enter the name of the Ledger. e.g. **Sales Accounting Services**.

2.    Select the **Group Sales Accounts** from the **List of Group** in the **Under** field.

3.    Set **Inventory Values are affected** to : No.

4.    Set **'Service Tax Applicable'** to **Yes** to view **Category Name Screen**.

5.    In the **'Category Name'** field select **Accounting Services** (619) from the **List of Service Categories**.

| Category Name | ABC Company | Ctrl + M [X] |
|---|---|---|
| | [Category Name] <br><br> [Accounting Services (619)] <br><br> [List of Service Categories] <br> ↓ <br> ↓ <br> ↓ <br> ↓ | |

- **Set Used in Sales Tax to No.**

- **Accept the Screen to Save.**

   Similarly, you can create Ledgers for various services

**Creating Ledger for Indirect Expenses :**

   An **'Expenses'** Ledger has to be created to **claim the expenses.**

   **Go to Gateway of Tally > Accounts Info > Ledgers > Create.**

   1.  In the **Name** field enter the expenses ledger name. e.g. **General Expenses.**

   2.  Select the Group of **Indirect Expenses** from the **'List of Groups'** in the **Under** field.

   3.  Set **Inventory Values are affected** to **'No'.**

   4.  Set **'Service Tax Applicable'** to **Yes** to view **Category Name Screen.**

   5.  In the **'Category Name'** screen select **Accounting Services (619)** from the **List of Service Categories.**

| Category Name | ABC Company | Ctrl + M [X] |
|---|---|---|
| | Category Name <br> Accounting Services (619) | |
| Under : **Indirect Expenses** | | |

- **Accept the screen to save.**

## 5.3   CENTRAL VALUE ADDED TAX

Cenvat (Central Value Added Tax) has its origin in the system of VAT (Value Added Tax), which is common in West European countries. Concept of VAT was developed to avoid cascading effect of taxes. VAT was found to be a very good and transparent tax collection system, which reduces tax evasion, ensure better tax compliance and increase tax revenue.

MODVAT (Modified Value Added Tax) was introduced in India in 1986 (MODVAT was renamed Cenvat w.e.f. 1-4-2000). The system was termed as MODVAT, as it was restricted upto manufacturing stage and credit of only excise duty paid on manufacturing products (and corresponding (VD paid on imported goods) was available.

'Cenvat' is called as basic excise duty. Every manufacturer is liable to pay excise duty in various kinds namely Basic Excise Duty, Special Excise Duty, Additional Excise Duty etc. so to reduce the tax burden of the end user, the Government of India introduced the MODVAT scheme which is now called CENVAT scheme.

**Business Exhibition (Demonstration) :** Business exhibition means an exhibition : (a) to market, or (b) to promote, (c) to advertise or (d) to showcase, any product or service, intended for the growth in business of the producer or provider of such product or service, as the case may be, (Section 65 (19a) of the Finance Act, 1994).

'Taxable Service' means any service provided or to be provided to an exhibitor, by the organisor of the business, in relation to business exhibition, (Section 65 (105) (ZZ) of the Finance Act, 1994).

**Hands on Experience :** Hands on mean someone who has hands on experience of something has done or used it rather than just read or learned about it. Knowledge or skill that someone gets from doing something rather than just reading about it or seeing it being done.

**Meaning of Hands on Experience :**

Hands on experience means, knowledge or skill that someone gets from doing something rather than just reading or observing about it or seeing it being done. They will participate in workshops and get hands on experience leading classes. He always said, he learned more about newspapers from hands-on experience than he did in the classroom. Someone with a hands-on experience may be doing things becomes closely involved in meaning and organising things and in making decisions. Someone who has hands-on experience of something has done or used it rather than just read or learned about it. Many employers consider hand-on experience to be as useful as academic qualifications.

**'Hands-on' involving active participation :**

Someone with a hands-on way of doing (things closely involved in managing and organising things and in making decisions.

'Hands-on investor' is an investor who has a large stake in a corporation and takes on active role in its management.

**New CENVAT Scheme :**

MODVAT credit scheme was introduced in 1986 vide rules 57A to 57U. Such rules can be amended easily by Central Government, the scheme remains flexible and hence can be modified quickly as per changing requirements. CENVAT was introduced in place of MODVAT w.e.f. 01.07.2001. These were replaced by CENVAT Credit Rules 2002. These are now replaced by Central Credit Rules, 2004 w.e.f. 10.09.2004.

**Merging of CENVAT and Service Tax Rules :** Cenvat Credit Rules 2004 have been issued by superseding Cenvat Credit Rules, 2004 w.e.f. 10.09.2004.

**Procedure and Records for Cenvat :**

The main procedures are :

Maintaining records of input and capital goods.

Maintaining records of credit received and utilised.

Submit returns of details of Cenvat Credit availed, Principal Inputs and utilisation of Principal Input in form ER-1 to ER-6.

**Returns :** A manufacturer has to submit returns to Range Superintendent of Central Excise in the prescribed form ER-1 to ER-6 in respect of Cenvat Availed, Principal Inputs, Utilisation of Principal Inputs etc.

Quarterly return of first stage/second stage dealer within 15 days from the close of quarter.

Half yearly return within one month from close of half year by provider of output service.

Half yearly return within one month from close of half year by Input Service Distributor.

**Central (Excise) for Manufacturer in Tally ERP9 :**

**A. Enabling Excise in Tally ERP9 :**

**B. Excise transactions to generate G.A.R. 7**

**1. Excise Purchases (Purchase of Raw Materials)**

    **Step 1 : Create Masters.**

    (i)    **Party Ledger.**

    (ii)    CENVAT Type Duty Ledgers.

        (a)  Basic Excise Duty (CENVAT).

        (b)  Education Cess (CENVAT).

        (c)  Secondary Education Cess (CENVAT).

   (iii)    Purchases Ledger.

    **Step 2 :** 'Create' Excise Purchase Voucher Type.

    **Step 3 :** 'Create' Tariff Classification.

    **Step 4 :** 'Create' Stock Item.

    **Step 5 :** Record a Excise Purchase Voucher.

**2. Availing CENVAT Credit on Purchases**

    **Step 1 :** 'Create' Voucher Class in Debit Note Voucher.

    **Step 2 :** Record a Debit Note Voucher.

**3. Manufacturer of Finished Goods**

    **Step 1 :** 'Create' Manufacturing Journal Voucher Type.

    **Step 2 :** Create Stock Item.

    **Step 3 :** Record a Manufacturing Journal.

**4. Excise Sales**

    **Step 1 :** Create Masters

    (i)    Customer Ledger

    (ii)    Sales Ledger

    (iii)  VAT Duty Ledger

    **Step 2 :** Create Excise Voucher Type.

    **Step 3 :** Record a Excise Sales Voucher.

    •    Printing Excise Sales Invoice.

**5. Adjustment of CENVAT credit availed against the Duty Payable**

    **Step 1 :** Create Voucher Class in Journal Voucher.

    **Step 2 :** Record a Journal Voucher.

6.   **Payment of Excise Duty**

7.   **Generating G.A.R. 7.**

**Enabling Dealer Excise in Tally 9 :**

Excise Duty is a tax on goods produced or manufactured in India and intended for home consumption i.e. sale in India. Excise Duty is chargeable at the time of production or manufacturing, but for convenience it is charged at the time of removal. It is an indirect tax on the manufacturers or producer which is passed on the ultimate consumer.

Tally's "Dealer Excise" module facilities complete excise accounting for dealers engaged in trading of excisable goods and designing to issue **'cenvatable'** invoices. It minimises the possibilities of erroneous data entity and ensures transparency and better level of compliance with statutues.

**Step 1 :**

- Go to Gateway of Tally → Press F11 : Company Features → Statutory and Taxation.
- Set Enable Dealer - Excise to Yes.
- Set. Set/Alter Dealer Excise Details to Yes.
- Press Y or Enter to view 'Company Excise Details'.

**In Company Excise Details :**

- Specify the ECC/PAN Based Regulation/Code Number allotted to premises.
- **Range :** Enter the Code, Name and Address of the Range which has jurisdiction over the premises.
- **Commissionerate :** Enter the name of the Commissionerate of the Central Excise Department under which the address of your registered premises is located.
- **Division :** Enter the Code, Name and Address of the Division and Name under which your company falls.

Ensure that the completed company excise details screen displays as shown.

**Company Excise Details :**

| ECC/PAN Based/Code No. NHSIM123456 | | Commissionerate : NASHIK ((MAHARASHTRA) | |
|---|---|---|---|
| **Range :** | | **Division** | |
| **Code :** | XXX | **Code :** | XXX |
| **Name :** | MADHAV | **Name :** | MADHAV |
| **Address :** | COLLEGE ROAD | **Address :** | COLLEGE ROAD |
| | NASHIK (MAHARASHTRA) | | NASHIK |

1.   Set **Enable Value Added Tax** (VAT) to **Yes.**

2.   Set. Set/Alter VAT details to Yes. Press **'Enter'** to view the **VAT details.**

3.   In **VAT details** screen, specify the state, **Type of Dealer Regular** and **Enter** 1.4.2014 in **regular VAT applicable form.**

4.   Under **Tax Information Centre :**

- **VAT TIN (Regular) :** 110001122334.
- **Inter-State Sales Tax Number :** 123456.
- **PAN/Income Tax No. :** NASH 6182H.

The complete company operation alteration screen displays as shown.

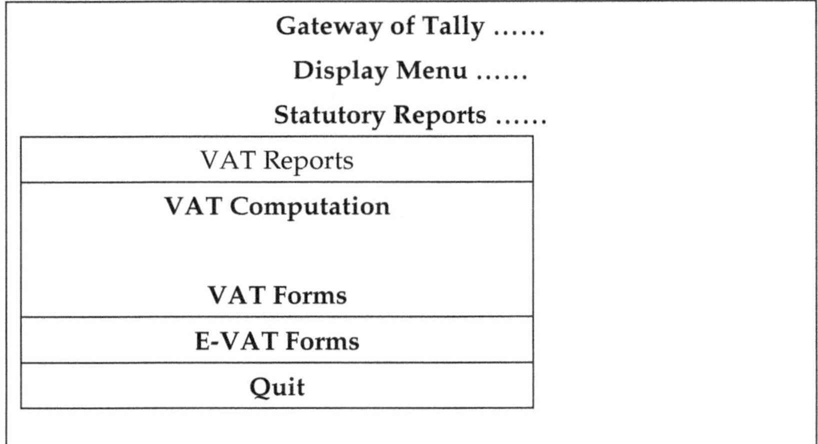


- Press Y or Enter to accept the screen.

### 'E' Filing Form 201 and Annexures

To view the E-VAT means for generating the excel files from Tally ERP9 for filing e-returns.

- Go to Gateway of Tally > Display > Statutory Reports > VAT Reports.

**Gateway of Tally ......**

**Display Menu ......**

**Statutory Reports ......**

| |
|---|
| VAT Reports |
| **VAT Computation** |
| **VAT Forms** |
| **E-VAT Forms** |
| **Quit** |

Press 'Enter' Key on E-VAT Forms to view the e-VAT forms menu.

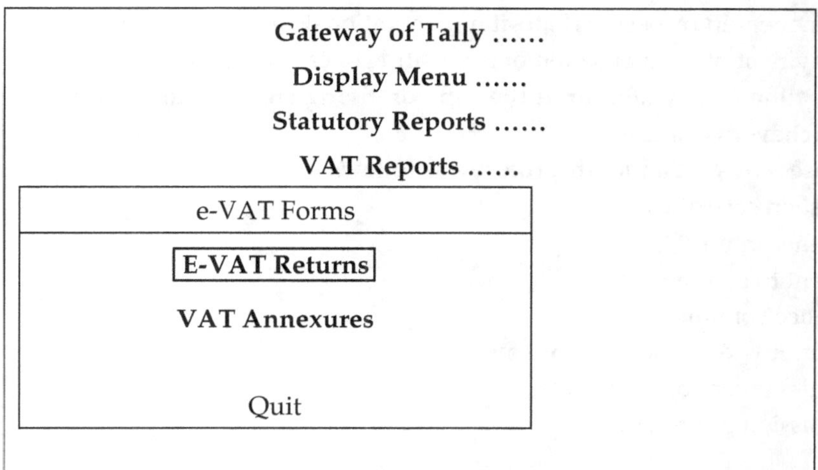


The E-VAT Forms menu consists of :

- E-VAT Returns.
- VAT Annexures.

## 5.4 INCOME TAX : TAX DEDUCTED AT SOURCE (TDS)

In order to check tax evasion by the recipient of income, government requires that  person making such payment must deduct the tax at prescribed rates and pay only the net amount to the person who has earned the income. The amount so deducted is called *Tax Deducted at Source* or *TDS*. The tax deducted is required to be deposited by the payer in the Government Treasury within the stipulated time. The recipient of such net income is issued a certificate in Form 16 or 16 A or 16 AA as the case may be, within one month from the end of the month during which the payment is made. The payee will get credit for the tax so paid. From his total tax liability for the concerned year, the TDS will be deducted and he will be required to pay only the balance. If the TDS is more than the tax liability, he can claim refund from the Government in the prescribed form. TDS enables quick and effective collection of tax.

**Incomes on which TDS Scheme is Applicable**

TDS scheme is applicable on the following incomes :

1. Salary to resident/non-resident.
2. Other incomes such as interest, deemed interest, deemed dividends, rent, commission/ brokerage, lottery, winnings, winnings of races, technical/ professional fees, royalty, compulsory acquisition compensation, payment to contractors, royalty etc.

**Time of TDS**

Tax is deducted at source either at the time of payment or at the time of giving credit to the recipient.

1. **At the time of payment :** In the following cases, tax is deducted at the time of payment.
   - Salary
   - Deemed dividend
   - Winnings from lottery/crossword puzzle, horse races

> ➢ Payment in respect of deposit under National Saving Scheme
>
> ➢ Payment of compensation or acquisition of capital asset

**2. At the time of payment or at the time of giving credit to the recipient in the books of the payer, whichever is earlier.**

The cases covered under this rule are as follows :

➢ Interest on securities

➢ Any other interest

➢ Payment to contractors

➢ Insurance commission

➢ Payment to non-resident sportsmen

➢ Commission on lottery tickets

➢ Commission or brokerage

➢ Rent

➢ Fees for professional/ technical services royalty

➢ Payment to non-resident/foreign companies

**Limit of Income up to which TDS Scheme is Not Applicable**

Tax is deducted at source for the incomes mentioned above only if the amount of income earned by the assessee is more than the prescribed limit. The limit of income up to which tax is not deducted at source is stated below :

1. Salary - If taxable salary exceeds ₹ 15,833/₹ 20,000/₹ 13,333 especially for woman, senior citizens and others respectively.

| | | | |
|---|---|---:|---:|
| 2. | Bank/Co-operative Bank/ Post office interest | ₹ | 10,000 |
| 3. | Any other interest | ₹ | 5,000 |
| 4. | Interest on compensation awarded by motor accidents claims tribunal ₹ | | 50,000 |
| 5. | Winnings from lottery/crossword puzzles | ₹ | 10,000 |
| 6. | Winnings from Horse Races | ₹ | 5,000 |
| 7. | Payment to contractor (single contract) | ₹ | 30,000 |
| 8. | Payment to contractor (aggregate consideration for a financial year) | ₹ | 75,000 |
| 9. | Insurance commission | ₹ | 20,000 |
| 10. | Deposit under NSS Scheme | ₹ | 2500 |
| 11. | Lottery commission | ₹ | 1000 |
| 12. | Commission/brokerage | ₹ | 5000 |
| 13. | Rent | ₹ | 180,000 |
| 14. | Professional fees | ₹ | 30,000 |
| 15. | Technical fees | ₹ | 30,000 |
| 16. | Royalty | ₹ | 30,000 |
| 17. | Compulsory acquisition payment | ₹ | 100,000 |
| 18. | Commission of sale of lottery tickets | ₹ | 1000 |

**Time for Deposit of TDS**

The tax deducted at source should be deposited within 7 days from the end of the month in which tax is deducted/collected. Exceptions to the rate are as given as follows.

(a)  The amount should be deposited on the same day in cases where the tax is deducted by an office of Government and when tax is to be deposited without production of income tax Challan.

(b)  Tax deducted in the month of March should be deposited by 30th April after the end of the financial year (other than office of Government).

(c)  In some cases the Assessing officer may permit quarterly deposit of TDS. In such cases, the amount collected as TDS should be deposited within 7 days from the end of each quarter. In case of the fourth quarter, the amount should be deposited by 30th April after the end of the financial year.

## Quarterly Statements

The person deducting tax at source should submit quarterly statements of TDS in Form No. 24Q, 27Q, 26Q, 27EQ as applicable. These statements are to be submitted within 15 days from the end of each quarter. The fourth quarter return should be submitted on or before May 15th of the immediately preceding financial year.

## Mode of Submission of Quarterly Statements

TDS return can be submitted either electronically or in paper format. The collector/deductor in office of the Government, principal officer of a company, person required to get his account audited under Section 44AB and when the number of deductees is 20 or more, the submission of quarterly return must be made electronically.

## Rate of TDS

TDS is deducted at the prescribed rates, stated below :
1.  Salary at the rates prescribed in the Finance Act.
2.  Interest on securities - @ 10%.
3.  Other interest - @ 10%
4.  Winnings from lottery, cross-word puzzles or card game and other games - @ 30%
5.  Winnings from Horse races - @ 30%.
6.  Payments contractors, @ 1% it undivided HUF contractors and @ 2% to other persons.
7.  Insurance commission - @ 10%
8.  Payments out of deposits under NSS - 20%
9.  Repurchase of units - @ 20%
10.  Commission on sale of lottery tickets - @ 10%
11.  Commission on brokerage payable - @ 10%
12.  Rent - of machinery plant etc. - @ 20%
    land and building - @ 20%
13.  Fees for professional services or technical services - @ 10%.
14.  Payment of compensation on acquisition of land / building - @10%.

## Applicability of Surcharge and Education Cess while computing TDS

**Surcharge** on TDS in applicable only when the recipient is a foreign company and the amount subject to TDS is **more than ₹ 1 crore.**

**Education Cess** of 2% of TDS and secondary  and higher education cess at the rate of 1% of TDS is applicable only when the recipient is a non-resident or a foreign  company or in the case of payment of salary to any person.

**PAN :** If PAN  is not intimated, tax will be deducted at either the normal rate given or at the rate of 20%, whichever is higher.

## QUESTIONS FOR SELF-STUDY

1. What is VAT? How it works? Give the details of VAT.

2. How a company's Statutory and Taxation and Tax Information is display in computer ? Give the practical details.

3. How VAT details and statutory and taxation features will be displayed in computer ?

4. Apply an computer software and create a purchase ledger for VAT Returns.

5. Give the example of VAT/Tax Classification Displayed for purchases pertains to Maharashtra State.

6. Create an input VAT Ledger and give the practical examples.

7. Create a 'Sales Ledger' and give the practical examples.

8. Create an Output VAT Ledger and give the practical examples.

9. Create a Current Asset Ledger and set the method of apportion to based on quality.

10. Create Additional Expenses Ledger for Packing Material and give the practical examples.

11. Explain the computerized process for creation of VAT Commodity.

12. Create a VAT adjustment class and enter the details.

13. Create a Tax Invoice Voucher Type and enter the details.

14. What is Service Tax ? How company's Statutory and Taxation and Tax Information is displayed in computer ? Give the practical examples.

15. Create a "Service Tax Ledger" and give the practical examples.

16. Create a Sales Ledger for Services and give the practical examples.

17. Create ledger for indirect expenses and give the practical examples.

18. What is CENVAT ? Define demonstration and Hands-on Experience.

19. Explain with the help of computer new cenvat scheme.

20. Create excise purchase and create purchase ledger and the practical details.

21. Set enable Dealer-excise and set enable VAT on computer screen.

22. Create VAT forms on computer screen with the help of practical details.

23. Create VAT return on computer screen with the help of software.

Chapter 6

# BRANCH ACCOUNTS



## 6.0 INTRODUCTION

A **Branch** is a subordinate division of a central office. The concept of branch *presupposes* the existence of a head office. As per the provision of Section 2(9) of the Companies Act, 1956, Branch Office in relation to a Company means,

i) any establishment described as a branch by the company; or

ii) any establishment carrying on either the same or substantially the same activity as that carried on by the head office of the company; or

iii) any establishment engaged in any production, processing or manufacture.

but does not include any establishment specified in any order made by the Central Government under Section 8 of the Companies Act, 1956.

**Meaning :**

A **Branch** is a section of an enterprise, geographically separated from the rest of the business, controlled by a **head office,** and generally carrying on the same activities as of the enterprise. As a business grows, it may open up branches in different towns and cities in order to market its products or services over a large territory and thus increase its profits.

## 6.1 DEFINITION AND NEED FOR BRANCH ACCOUNTING

**Definitions :**

According to **Pickles,**

"**Branch** is a section of a business segregated physically from the main section".

"Head office is the main section or central office or parent shop which control the subsidiary establishment, to earn huge amount of profits".

From an accounting point of view, a **Branch** is a clearly identifiable profit centre of a business house. In order to exercise greater control over the branches, it is necessary to ascertain profit or loss made by such branches separately. Apart from this, specialised accounting techniques have to be adopted for controlling various branch activities and for their smooth running, both at the branch level and at the head office level. The systems of accounting vary between different enterprises in accordance with their type of activities, methods of operation, the preferences of their managements and the nature of the business.

It is necessary that the head office and the branch obtain information from either side at regular intervals about the proper functioning of the branch. This requires the head office and the branch to keep proper books of accounts.

**Need for Branch Accounting :**

The accurate accounting record of every individual branch is required to be maintained by the head office to know exact trading results of the branch at the end of the accounting period.

The **need for systematic and scientific branch accounting** arises as,

i)      to incorporate the profit or loss made by the branch and its assets and liabilities in the firm's final accounts,

ii)      to ascertain the requirements of stock and cash for each branch,

iii)      to ascertain whether the branch is yielding a satisfactory rate of return on capital invested in it,

iv)      to ascertain whether the branch should be expanded or closed,

v)      to ascertain the quantity of stock held by each branch at the end of that accounting period,

vi)      to ascertain the amount of commission payable to the manager, if that is based on profits.

vii)      to ascertain the profitability of each branch separately for a particular accounting period,

viii)      to ascertain the financial position of each branch separately at the end of the accounting period,

ix)      to assess the progress and performances of each branch,

x)      to fulfill the audit requirements under Section 228 of the Companies Act, 1956 and

xi)      to transfer the different Branch Expenditure Accounts to Profit and Loss Account of the head office.

## 6.2 TYPES OF BRANCH ACCOUNTING

For accounting conveniences generally the branches are divided into the following types as shown in Figure 7.1.

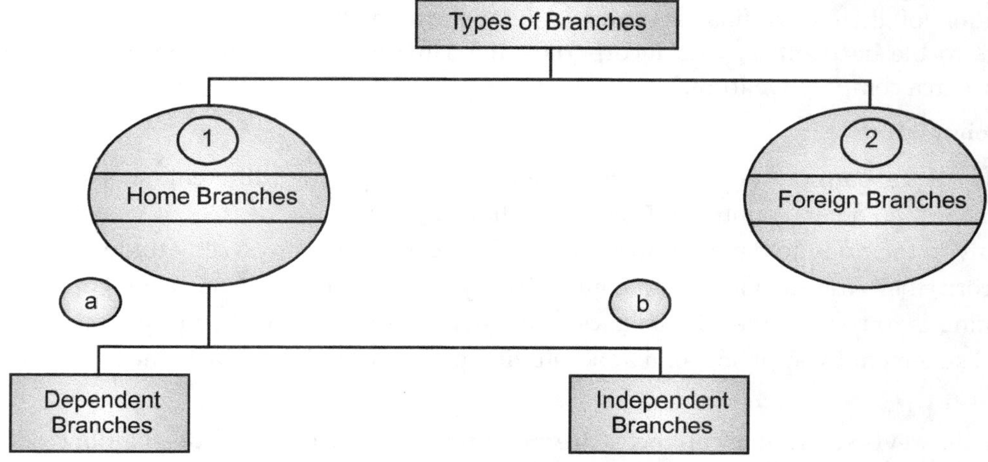


**Fig. 6.1 : Types of Branches**

**1)   Home Branches :**

It is the expansion of a business enterprise by opening different shops and offices i.e. branches, in different parts of the city and in different cities of the country. **Home Branches** are also termed as inland branches, as the business opens their new branches at various market places in the same country, to cater the demand in the local, state and even in national market, in the most economical and profitable manner. These branches are classified according to the degree of power and autonomy enjoyed by them as follows :

**a)   Dependent Branches :**

These branches are totally **dependent** on head office hence they are also termed as Agency Branches. They work in actual practice like agents of head office. The important features of these branches are listed as follows :

i)      they are not allowed to make their own purchases from open market and pay for their expenses,

ii)     they are supposed to sell only those goods which are supplied by the head office, at cost or above cost, for cash or on credit basis as the case may be,

iii)    fixed expenses of the branch are paid directly by the head office through branch,

iv)    variable expenses of the branch are paid by themselves out of petty cash received from head office on monthly basis for this purpose.

v)     the proceeds of cash sales and collection from debtors must be remitted promptly by the branch to head office.

vi)    these branches do not maintain any account as such but submits the periodical accounting data regularly to the head office, as the complete accounting record of the dependent branch is maintained at the head office, separately.

**b)  Independent Branches :**

These branches are totally **independent** and autonomous as they are allowed to make their own purchases from open market and pay for their expenses. These branches keep their books of accounts independently. A trial balance is prepared by the branch, which ultimately leads to preparation of their own final accounts. All independent branches are to submit their final accounts to the head office, who incorporates the same in the overall statement of a business enterprise in a comparative form.

**2)  Foreign Branches :**

It is the expansion of a business enterprise by opening different shops and offices i.e. branches in other countries. These branches enjoy highest degree of powers and total autonomy in their day to day working. **Foreign Branches** almost invariably trade independently and record their transactions in foreign currency. The important feature of Foreign Branch Accounting is to convert the trial balance in the home currency and then to prepare the overall financial statement by applying similar accounting principles followed by home branch at central head office.

(As the revised syllabus of the concerned subject restricts the understanding of **Branch Accounting Methods for Dependent Branches** only the detail discussions are made for the same accordingly).

## 6.3 ACCOUNTING METHODS FOR DEPENDENT BRANCHES

As per the accounting principles, the dependent branches submits only the required accounting information regularly to the head office. Ultimately, the systematic accounting record is maintained at a head office separately. The suitable accounting method for these branches depends upon the number of factors e.g. actual number of branches opened, the frequency of transactions transacted by them, the degree of control required to be exercised etc. The accounting methods commonly used for dependent branches are shown below in Fig. 6.2.

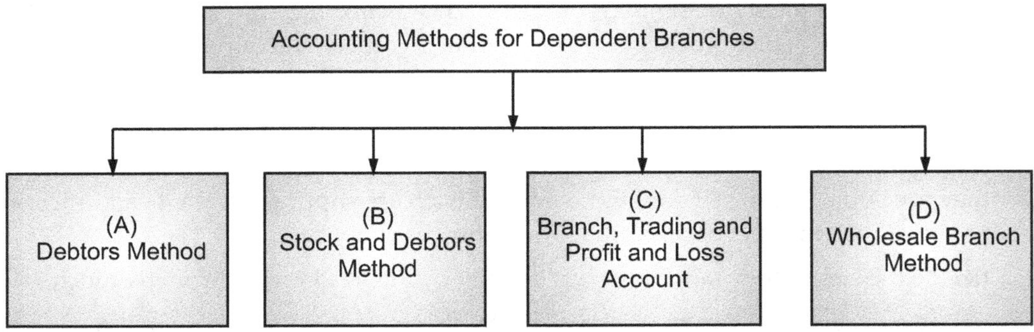


**Fig. 6.2 : Accounting Methods for Dependent Branches**

**1) Debtors Method**

**Debtors Method** also known as Synthetic Method is usually adopted when the branch is of the small size. Under this method, the head office maintains separate a Branch Account for each branch. Such Branch Account is of nominal nature. This system of accounting is suitable for the small-size branches. Under this, a Branch Account is opened for each branch in the head office ledger. All transactions relating to that branch are recorded in this account. The Branch Account is prepared in such a way that it discloses the profit or loss of the branch.

Head Office may send goods to branch either at **"cost price"** or **"selling price"** (also called invoice price). The accounting procedure in these two cases is slightly different. Therefore, we will discuss them separately.

**i)**     **Accounting Treatment when Head Office supplies goods to Branch at Cost Price :**

At the beginning of the year the Branch Account is debited with the opening balances of Assets such as Stock (at Cost), Debtors, Petty Cash, Furniture, Prepaid Expenses, Accrued Income, etc., lying with the branch. Similarly, it is credited with the opening balances of Liabilities of the branch such as Creditors, Outstanding Salaries, Rent, etc.

The Branch Account is then debited with the amount of goods sent to the Branch (at Cost) and other amounts remitted to meet various expenses such as Salaries, Rent, Rates and Taxes, etc. Likewise, the Branch Account is credited with the return of goods (at Cost) by the Branch, and Receipts from Debtors and Cash Sales. At the year end, Branch Account is debited with the closing values of liabilities and credited with the closing values of Assets. The difference between the two sides represents profit or loss for the branch for a particular period.

**The proforma journal entries passed in the books of Head Office under Debtors Method are as follows :**

Proforma Journal Entries

i)     Opening Balances of Assets at the Branch

      Branch A/c                 Dr.

           To (Individual) Branch Assets A/c

ii)    Opening Balances of Liabilities at the Branch :

      (Individual) Branch Liabilities A/c       Dr.

           To Branch A/c

iii)   Goods sent to Branch :

      Branch A/c                 Dr.     [At Cost]

           To Goods Sent to Branch A/c

iv)    Return of goods by Branch to the Head Office :

      Goods Sent to Branch A/c           Dr.

           To Branch A/c

v)     Remittance of cash or cheque to Branch for expenses

      (e.g. Salary, Rent, Petty Expenses, etc.)

      Branch A/c                 Dr.     [Actual]

           To Cash/Bank A/c

vi)    Cash or cheque received from Branch

      (e.g. Cash Sales and Collection from Debtors) :

      Cash or Bank A/c            Dr.     [Actual including direct from debtors]

           To Branch A/c

vii) 'Closing Balances of Assets' at the Branch :

 (Individual) Branch Assets A/c   Dr.

  To Branch A/c

viii) 'Closing Balances of Liabilities' at the Branch :

 Branch A/c   Dr.

  To Liabilities (Individual) A/c

ix) Closing balance in Goods sent to Branch Account adjusted :

 Goods Sent to Branch A/c   Dr.

  To Purchases A/c   [Trader]

  To Trading A/c   [Manufacturer]

x) Credit Sales :

 [No Entry]

xi) Normal Loss :

 [No Entry]

xii) Goods returned by customers :

 [No Entry]

xiii) Abnormal Loss

 • Abnormal Loss A/c   Dr. [Total]

   To Branch A/c

 • General Profit and Loss A/c   Dr. [Loss]

  Insurance Claim A/c   Dr. [Claim]

   To Abnormal Loss A/c   [Total]

xiv) Pilferage :

One of the common feature of retail trade is 'shoplifting' and this has come to be regarded as a normal business loss, hence no entry is required for it.

xv) Branch Expenses paid by the Branch :

 [No Entry]

xvi) Bad Debts, Discount Allowed to Debtors :

 [No Entry]

xvii) For transferring profit or loss of the Branch:

 • **If Profit :**

 Branch A/c   Dr.

  To General Profit and Loss A/c

 • **If Loss :**

 General Profit and Loss A/c   Dr.

  To Branch A/c

A general format of Branch Account is given below :

**In the Books of Head Office**
**Branch Account for the period ended ......**

Dr.                                                                   Cr.

| Particulars | ₹ | Particulars | ₹ |
|---|---|---|---|
| To Balance B/D | | By Balance B/D | |
| •   Stock | xxx | •   Creditors | xxx |
| •   Debtors | xxx | •   Outstanding Expenses | xxx |
| •   Petty Cash | xxx | By Bank | |
| •   Fixed Assets | xxx | •   By Branch | xxx |
| •   Prepaid Expenses | xxx | •   By Branch Debtors directly | |
| To Goods sent to Branch or | |      to Head Office | xxx |
| Goods sent by Head Office or | | (Remittances to Head Office) | |
| Goods sent by Other Branches | xxx | By Goods sent to Branch or | |
| To Bank | xxx | Returned by Branch or | xxx |
| (Remittances by Head Office) | | Returned by Branch Debtors directly to | |
| To Balance C/D | | Head Office or | |
| •   Creditors | xxx | Sent to Other Branches | xxx |
| •   Outstanding Expenses | xxx | By Balance C/D | |
| To Net Profit transferred to General | | •   Stock | xxx |
| Profit and Loss A/c | xxx | •   Debtors | xxx |
| | | •   Petty Cash | xxx |
| | | •   Fixed Assets | xxx |
| | | •   Prepaid Expenses | xxx |
| | | By Net Loss transferred to General | |
| | | Profit and Loss A/c | xxx |
| | **xxx** | | **xxx** |

**Points to Remember**

i)    **The following transactions do not appear in the Branch Account :**
     a) **Petty Expenses met by Branch out of Cash,** since either cash balance at the end is decreased or the liability at the end is increased.
     b) **Purchase of Goods or Fixed Assets by Branch,** since book value of goods or fixed assets at the end is increased and either the amount of remittances is reduced or the creditors at the end are increased.
     c) **Sale of Goods or Fixed Assets by Branch** since book value of Goods or Fixed Assets at the end is decreased and either the amount of remittances is increased or the debtors at the end are increased.
     d) **Bad Debts, Discount Allowed, Sales Returns by Customers to Branch, Cash Received by Branch from Branch Debtors, etc.,** since the debtors at the end appear at the adjusted figure.
     e) **Depreciation and Profit/Loss on Sale of Fixed Assets** since Fixed Assets at the end appear at the adjusted figure.
     f) **Abnormal Losses** since stock at the end appears at the adjusted figure.

ii)    **When the Branch is not authorised to keep any sum of collection, expenses met by Branch out of Petty Cash maintained may be dealt with as follows :**
     a) In case the Petty Cash is maintained on Imprest System, the expenses met by the Branch are to be shown in the same manner as the Branch Expenses met by the

Head Office. In such a case, Petty Cash Balance at the end appears at the same amount at which it appears in the beginning.

b) In case the Petty Cash is not maintained on Imprest System, the expenses met by the Branch are automatically charged to the Branch Account since the Petty Cash at the end appears at the adjusted figure.

**iii) When goods are returned either by Branch Debtors to the Head Office or are sent by one branch to another branch, the entry is made in the same manner as in the case of goods returned by the Branch to the Head Office.**

iv) In case any Insurance Claim is admitted and paid to the Branch, either the Bank Balance at the end will increase or the remittances to Head Office will increase. In case, the Insurance Claim is admitted but not paid, the Insurance Company will appear as a debtor at the end.

v) To ascertain any missing figure relating to Stock and/or Debtors, Memorandum Branch Stock Account and Memorandum Branch Debtors Account may be prepared.

**vi) Accounting Treatment of different items :**

| | Item | Treatment in Branch Account | Treatment in Memorandum Account |
|---|---|---|---|
| a) | Goods returned by Branch Customers directly to Head Office | Treat like goods returned by Branch to Head Office and thus, show the Cost/Invoice price (as the case may be) of these goods on credit side of Branch Account. | Treat like goods returned by Branch to Head Office and thus, show the Cost/Invoice price (as the case may be) of these goods on credit side of Branch Stock Account. |
| b) | Cash remitted by Branch Customers directly to Head Office | Treat like cash remitted by Branch to Head Office and thus, show on the credit side of Branch Account. | Treat like cash collected from Debtors and thus, show on the credit side of Branch Debtors Account. |
| c) | Goods sent to another branch. | Treat like goods returned to Head Office and thus, show on the credit side of Branch Account. | Treat like goods returned to Head Office and thus, show on the credit side of Branch Stock Account. |
| d) | Goods received from another branch | Treat like goods received from Head Office and thus, show on the debit side of Branch Account. | Treat like goods received from Head Office and thus, show on the debit side of Branch Stock Account. |
| e) | Normal Loss | Normal Loss does not appear in the Branch Account since the Closing Stock appears at the adjusted figure. | Cost/Invoice price (as the case may be) of Normal Loss appears on the credit side of Branch Stock Account in order to reduce the figure of Closing Stock. |
| f) | Abnormal Loss | Abnormal Loss does not appear in the Branch Account since the Closing Stock appears at the adjusted figure. | Cost/Invoice price (as the case may be) of Abnormal Loss appears on the credit side of Branch Stock Account in order to reduce the figure of Closing Stock. |

| g) | Insurance Claim : | | |
|---|---|---|---|
| | • Admitted and received | Show on the credit side of Branch Account by way of increased Closing either Cash/Bank Balance or remittance to Head Office. | No Treatment |
| | • Admitted but not yet received | Show Insurance Company as a Debtor at the end on the credit side of Branch Account. | No Treatment |
| h) | Agreed Allowance or Trade Discount | Agreed Allowance or Trade Discount does not appear in the Branch Account since the Closing Debtors appear at the adjusted figure. | Cost/Invoice Price (as the case may be) of Agreed Allowance or Trade Discount appears on the credit side of Branch Stock Account. |

**Calculation of Commission to Branch Manager :**

Commission may be allowed as a percentage of Net Profit before charging such commission or after charging such commission.

• **Commission as a % of Net Profit before charging such Commission :**

$$= \quad \text{Net Profit before Commission} \times \frac{\text{Rate of Commission}}{100}$$

• **Commission as a % of Net Profit after charging such Commission :**

$$= \quad \text{Net Profit before Commission} \times \frac{\text{Rate of Commission}}{100 + \text{Rate of Commission}}$$

**Accounting Treatment of Branch Manager's Commission :**

Outstanding Branch Manager's Commission appears on the debit side of Branch Account.

---

**EXAMPLE**

From the following details relating to the Mumbai Branch for the year ending on 31st March, 2016, prepare Mumbai Branch Account in the books of Ashoka Ltd., Ahmedabad.

| Particulars | ₹ | Particulars | ₹ |
|---|---|---|---|
| Opening Stock | 25,000 | Cash Received from Debtors | 65,000 |
| Opening Debtors | 10,000 | Cash paid by Debtors directly to : | |
| Opening Furniture | 6,000 | Head Office | 5,000 |
| Opening Petty Cash | 1,000 | Closing Stock | 15,000 |
| Prepaid Insurance in the beginning | 300 | Goods returned by Branch | 2,000 |
| Salaries Outstanding in the beginning | 4,000 | Goods returned by Debtors | 1,000 |
| Goods sent to Branch | 2,00,000 | Cash sent to Branch for Expenses | |
| Cash Sales during the year | 2,70,000 | •    Rent (₹ 800 per month) | 9,600 |
| Total Sales | 3,50,000 | •    Salary (₹ 4,000 per month) | 48,000 |
| Petty Cash Expenses | 2,200 | •    Petty Cash | 2,000 |
| Discount Allowed to Debtors | 500 | •    Insurance (upto June, 2016) | 1,200 |

Goods costing ₹ 2,500 were damaged in transit and a sum of ₹ 2,000 was recovered from the Insurance Company in full settlement of the claim. Depreciate Furniture @ 10% p.a. The Branch Manager is entitled to a commission of 5% of profit of Branch after charging such commission.

**ANSWER**

### In the books of Ashoka Ltd., Ahmedabad

**Dr.**      Memorandum Branch Debtors Account      **Cr.**

| Particulars | ₹ | Particulars | ₹ |
|---|---|---|---|
| To Balance B/D | 10,000 | By Cash | 5,000 |
| To Credit Sales | 80,000 | (Collection by Head Office) | |
| | | By Branch Cash | 65,000 |
| | | (Collection by Branch) | |
| | | By Returns Inwards | 1,000 |
| | | By Discount Allowed | 500 |
| | | By Balance C/D* | 18,500 |
| | | (Balancing Figure) | |
| | **90,000** | | **90,000** |

**Dr.**      Memorandum Branch Petty Cash Account      **Cr.**

| Particulars | ₹ | Particulars | ₹ |
|---|---|---|---|
| To Balance B/D | 1,000 | By Petty Expenses | 2,200 |
| To Branch Cash | 2,000 | By Balance C/D* | 800 |
| | | (Balancing Figure) | |
| | **3,000** | | **3,000** |

**Dr.**      Memorandum Branch Cash Account      **Cr.**

| Particulars | ₹ | Particulars | ₹ |
|---|---|---|---|
| To Cash Sales | 2,70,000 | By Salaries for the previous  year | 4,000 |
| To Collection from Debtors | 65,000 | By Rent | 9,600 |
| To Remittance from Head Office | 60,800 | By Salaries for Current Year | 44,000 |
| To Claim from Insurance Company | 2,000 | By Petty Cash | 2,000 |
| | | By Insurance | 1,200 |
| | | By Remittance to Head Office* | 3,37,000 |
| | | (Balancing Figure) | |
| | **3,97,800** | | **3,97,800** |

**Dr.**      Mumbai Branch Account for the year ended 31st March, 2016      **Cr.**

| Particulars | ₹ | Particulars | ₹ |
|---|---|---|---|
| To Balance B/D | | By Outstanding Salary | 4,000 |
| • Stock | 25,000 | By Bank | |
| • Debtors | 10,000 | • By Branch | |
| • Petty Cash | 1,000 | • By Branch Debtors directly to | 3,37,000 |
| • Furniture | 6,000 | Head Office | |
| • Prepaid Insurance | 300 | (Remittances) | |
| To Goods sent to Branch | 2,00,000 | By Goods sent to Branch | 5,000 |
| To Bank | 60,800 | (Returns by Branch) | 2,000 |
| (Remittances by Head Office) | | By Balance C/D | |
| To Outstanding Salary | 4,000 | • Stock | 15,000 |
| To Branch Manager's Commission | | • Debtors | 18,500 |
| [₹ 80,900 × 5/105] | 3,852 | • Petty Cash | 800 |
| To Net Profit transferred to General | | • Furniture | 5,400 |
| Profit and Loss | 77,048 | • Prepaid Insurance | 300 |
| | **3,88,000** | | **3,88,000** |

## 2) Accounting Treatment when Head Office supplies goods to Branch at Invoice Price :

**Invoice Price and Loading :**

Sometimes, the consignor does not want to reveal the cost of goods to the consignee and therefore, invoices goods at a price which is higher than the Cost Price (CP). Such price is known as **'Invoice Price'** (IP) and the difference between the Invoice Price (IP) and the Cost Price (CP) is called **'Loading'**.

**Removal of Loading :**

When goods are sent at invoice price, to ascertain correct profit or loss on consignment, the items recorded at invoice price should be brought down to Cost Price level. For this purpose, the loading included in various items (like Opening Stock, Goods Sent to Branch, Goods Returned by Branch, Closing Stock) should be eliminated by passing the following adjusting entries.

**a)** **To remove loading from the account of Net Goods sent to Branch i.e. Goods sent to Branch *Less* : Returns by Branch (or Branch Customers) to Head Office :**

Goods sent to Branch A/c          Dr.

       To Branch A/c

**b)** **To remove loading from the amount of Closing Stock at Branch :**

Branch A/c          Dr.

       To Branch Stock Reserve A/c

The Closing Stock at the end of current accounting period becomes the Opening Stock of the next accounting period. The aforesaid entry will be reversed in the beginning of the next accounting period as follows :

Branch Stock Reserve A/c          Dr.

       To Branch A/c

After passing the aforesaid adjusting entries, the relevant items will appear in the Branch Account as follows :

**Dr.**        **An Extract of Branch Account**        **Cr.**

| Particulars | ₹ | Particulars | ₹ |
|---|---|---|---|
| To Opening Stock (At Invoice Price) | xxx | By Stock Reserve (Loading on Opening Stock) | xxx |
| To Goods sent to Branch (At Invoice Price) | xxx | By Goods Sent to Branch (Returns at Invoice Price) | xxx |
| To Stock Reserve (Loading on Closing Stock) | xxx | By Goods sent to Branch (Loading on Net Goods sent to Branch) | xxx |
| To Goods Sent to Branch (Loading on goods return) | | By Closing Stock (At Invoice Price) | xxx |
| | **xxx** | | **xxx** |

| Points to Remember |
| --- |

i)    Unless otherwise stated, Goods sent to Branch and Branch Stock are deemed to be at invoice price.

ii)    Stock at Branch (at Cost to Branch) or Stock at Branch at its Cost means Stock at Invoice Price.

### EXAMPLE

**Calculate the invoice price and loading separately for the following branch transactions.**

   i)    Goods sent to Branch (at Cost) ₹ 1,20,000. Goods are invoiced to the Branch to give a Gross Margin of **20% on sale price**.

   ii)   Goods sent to Branch (at Cost to Branch) ₹ 1,50,000. Goods are invoiced to the Branch at **25% above the cost**.

   iii)  Goods received from Head Office ₹ 1,00,000. Goods in transit from Head Office ₹ 50,000. Goods are invoiced to the Branch at **cost plus 25%**.

### ANSWER

| Sr. No. | Invoice Price = Cost Price + Profit | Profit (Loading) = Total Invoice Price $\times \dfrac{\text{Profit}}{\text{Invoice Price}}$ |
|---|---|---|
| i) | IP $=$ CP + P <br> 100 $=$ 80 + 20 <br> $=$ ₹ 1,20,000 $\times \dfrac{100}{80} =$ ₹ 1,50,000 | $=$ ₹ 1,50,000 $\times \dfrac{20}{100} =$ ₹ 30,000 |
| ii) | IP $=$ CP + P <br> 125 $=$ 100 + 25 <br> ₹ 1,50,000 (at Cost to Branch means Invoice Price) | $=$ ₹ 1,50,000 $\times \dfrac{25}{125} =$ ₹ 30,000 |
| iii) | IP $=$ CP + P <br> 125 $=$ 100 + 25 <br> ₹ 1,00,000 + ₹ 50,000 = ₹ 1,50,000 | $=$ ₹ 150,000 $\times \dfrac{25}{125} =$ ₹ 30,000 |

### EXAMPLE

Apollo Ltd., Ajmer has a Head Office and many retail branches to which goods are supplied from the Head Office at 20% profit on sales price. Accounts are kept at Head Office where all expenses (except Petty Expenses) are paid. Such Petty Expenses are paid by the Branches which are allowed to maintain Petty Cash Balance of ₹ 300 on Imprest System. From the following balances, as shown by the books, prepare Tatanagar Branch Account for the year ended 31-3-2016.

| Particulars | ₹ | Particulars | ₹ |
|---|---|---|---|
| **Balance as on 1st April 2015 :** | | Cash Purchases by the Branch | 10,500 |
| • Petty Cash in Hand at Branch | 300 | (With permission) | |
| • Stock at Branch at its Invoice Price | 20,000 | Credit Purchases by the Branch | 9,800 |
| • Sundry Debtors at Branches | 5,000 | (With permission) | |
| • Sundry Creditors at Branches | 1,200 | **Payments made by the Head Office :** | |
| • Furniture and Fixtures at Branch | 8,000 | Rent for one year (paid on 1.7.2015) | 1,800 |
| Rent Prepaid (upto 30th June, 2016) | 300 | Salaries | 2,000 |
| **Transactions for the year :** | | Insurance paid for the year ending on | |
| Goods sent to Branch | 1,04,000 | 30th June, 2015 | 360 |
| Cash Sales at Branch | | **Payments made by the Branch :** | |
| 64% of Total Sales | | Petty Expenses | 180 |
| Credit Sales at Branch | 45,000 | **Balance as on 31st March, 2016 :** | |
| Allowances to Debtors | 500 | •   Stock at Cost Price | 30,000 |
| Bad Debts to be written off | 200 | •   Creditors at the end | 3,000 |
| | | •   Debtors at the end | 9,300 |

Write off 10% depreciation on Furniture. The Branch Manager is entitled to a commission at 5% of Profit of Branch after charging such commission.

ANSWER

**Working Notes :**

1) **Calculation of Closing Stock at invoice price :**

$$IP = CP + P$$
$$100 = 80 + 20$$

If 80 CP $=$ 100 IP

$\therefore$ ₹ 30,000 CP $=$ ?

$$= \frac{\text{Rs. } 30,000 \times 100}{80}$$

$$= ₹ 37,500$$

**In the Books of Apollo Ltd.; Ajmer**

**Dr.**      **Memorandum Branch Debtors Account**      **Cr.**

| Particulars | ₹ | Particulars | ₹ |
|---|---|---|---|
| To Balance B/D | 5,000 | By Allowances | 500 |
| To Sales Credit | 45,000 | By Bad Debts | 200 |
| | | By Cash Received from Debtors* | 40,000 |
| | | (Balancing Figure) | |
| | | By Balance C/D | 9,300 |
| | **50,000** | | **50,000** |

**Dr.**      **Memorandum Branch Creditors Account**      **Cr.**

| Particulars | ₹ | Particulars | ₹ |
|---|---|---|---|
| To Cash paid to Creditors* | 8,000 | By Balance B/D | 1,200 |
| (Balancing Figure) | | By Purchases Credit | 9,800 |
| To Balance C/D | 3,000 | | |
| | **11,000** | | **11,000** |

**Dr.**      **Memorandum Branch Cash Account**      **Cr.**

| Particulars | ₹ | Particulars | ₹ |
|---|---|---|---|
| To Cash Sales | 80,000 | By Cash Purchases | 10,500 |
| To Cash Collection from Debtors | 40,000 | By Payments Creditors | 8,000 |
| | | By Petty Cash | 180 |
| | | By Cash remitted to Head Office* | 1,01,320 |
| | | (Balancing Figure) | |
| | **1,20,000** | | **1,20,000** |

**Dr.**      **Memorandum Branch Petty Cash Account**      **Cr.**

| Particulars | ₹ | Particulars | ₹ |
|---|---|---|---|
| To Balance B/D | 300 | By Petty Expenses | 180 |
| To Cash | 180 | By Balance C/D* | 300 |
| | | (Balancing Figure) | |
| | **480** | | **480** |

**Dr.**    **Tatanagar Branch Account for the year ended 31-3-2016**    **Cr.**

| Particulars | ₹ | Particulars | ₹ |
|---|---|---|---|
| To Balance B/D | | By Balance B/D | 1,200 |
|  • Petty Cash | 300 | (Creditors) | |
|  • Stock | 20,000 | By Remittances | 1,01,320 |
|  • Debtors | 5,000 | By Stock Reserve | 4,000 |
|  • Furniture | 8,000 | (Loading For Opening Stock) | |
|  • Rent Prepaid | 300 | By Goods sent to Branch | 20,800 |
| To Goods sent to Branch | 1,04,000 | Loading for goods sent to Branch | |
| To Bank : | | By Balance C/D | |
|  • Rent 1,800 | |  • Stock | 37,500 |
|  • Salaries 2,000 | |  • Debtors | 9,300 |
|  • Insurance (+) 360 | 4,160 |  • Petty Cash | 300 |
| To Stock Reserve | 7,500 |  • Furniture | 7,200 |
| (Loading for Closing Stock) | |  • Rent Prepaid | 450 |
| To Balance C/D | 3,000 |  • Insurance | 90 |
| (Creditors) | | | |
| To Branch Manager's Commission | 1,424 | | |
|  [₹ 29,900 × 5/105] | | | |
| To Net Profit transferred to | | | |
| General Profit and Loss | 28,476 | | |
| | **1,82,160** | | **1,82,160** |

## 2) Stock and Debtors Method

  **Stock and Debtors Method** also known as Analytical Method is generally used,
  i) When goods are sent to branch at an invoice price,
  ii) When size of the branch is sufficiently large,
  iii) Where turnover at the branch is substantially high and
  iv) Where there is a need to maintain the branch accounts on elaborative method.

  Under this method a few central accounts are maintained separately to exercise stricter control over the numerous transactions transacted by the branch. Generally, the central accounts prepared and their basic purposes are listed as under :

| Accounts | Purpose |
|---|---|
| 1. Branch Stock Account | To ascertain any shortage or surplus in stock. |
| 2. Branch Debtors Account | To ascertain opening balance of Debtors or Credit Sales or Collection from Debtors or Closing balance of Debtors. |
| 3. Branch Petty Cash Account | To ascertain actual Petty Expenses paid |
| 4. Branch Expenses Account | To ascertain total expenses incurred at Branch. |
| 5. Goods sent to Branch Account | To ascertain net cost of goods sent to the Branch. |
| 6. Branch Fixed Assets Account | To know the position of Fixed Assets at Branch. |
| 7. Branch Cash Account | To know the position of Cash at Branch. |
| 8. Branch Adjustment Account | To know Gross Profit or Gross Loss at Branch. |
| 9. Branch Profit and Loss Account | To know Net Profit or Net Loss at Branch. |

## 1) Branch Stock Account :

Branch Stock Account is a practical means of controlling Stock at Branch. This account records the transactions in regard to the stock in the branch, at **invoice price.** The debit side of this account records the inflow of stock into the branch and credit side records its outflow from the branch.

The Branch Stock Account is opened with the opening value of stock at branch and in transit (at invoice price) and debited with the invoice value of goods sent to branch and goods returned by the customers.

This account is credited with the total Sales (cash and credit) and Goods returned to the Head Office (at invoice price). Ultimately, this account is credited with the Closing Stock of the branch at invoice price. Sometimes, it is also credited with goods in transit at the end of the year (at invoice price).

The format of Branch Stock Account is given below :

**In the books of Head Office**

Dr.                               **(1) Branch Stock Account**                            Cr.

| Particulars | ₹ | Particulars | ₹ |
|---|---|---|---|
| To Balance B/D. | xxx | By Branch Cash | xxx |
| To Goods sent to Branch | xxx | (Cash Sales) | |
| (Goods supplied to Branch) | | By Branch Debtors | xxx |
| To Branch Debtors | xxx | (Credit Sales) | |
| (Returns by Customers to Branch) | | By Goods Sent to Branch | xxx |
| To Goods sent to Branch | xxx | (Returns to Head Office) | |
| (Transfer of goods from other Branch) | | By Goods Sent to Branch | xxx |
| To Branch Adjustment | xxx | (Transfer of Goods to other Branch) | |
| (Surplus Stock) | | By Branch Adjustment | xxx |
| | | (Load on Abnormal Loss due to fire) | |
| | | By Branch Profit and Loss | xxx |
| | | (Cost of Abnormal Loss due to fire) | |
| | | By Branch Adjustment | xxx |
| | | (Normal Loss) | |
| | | By Balance C/D | |
| | |   •   In Hand | xxx |
| | |   •   In Transit | xxx |
| | **xxx** | | **xxx** |

**Dr.**            **(2) Branch Debtors Account**            **Cr.**

| Particulars | ₹ | Particulars | ₹ |
|---|---|---|---|
| To Balance B/D | xxx | By Branch Cash | xxx |
| To Branch Stock | xxx | (Cash Collection from Debtors) | |
| (Credit Sales) | | By Bills Receivable | xxx |
| To Bills Receivable | xxx | (Bills Receivable received) | |
| (Bills Receivable Dishonoured) | | By Branch Stock | xxx |
| | | (Returns by customers) | |
| | | By Goods sent to Branch | xxx |
| | | (Goods returned to Head Office) | |
| | | By Branch Expenses | |
| | | i) Discount Allowed | xxx |
| | | ii) Allowance given to Debtors | xxx |
| | | iii) Bad Debts written off | xxx |
| | | By Balance C/D | xxx |
| | xxx | | xxx |

**Dr.**            **(3) Branch Petty Cash Acount**            **Cr.**

| Particulars | ₹ | Particulars | ₹ |
|---|---|---|---|
| To Balance B/D | xxx | By Branch Expenses | xxx |
| To Cash | xxx | (Actual Petty Expenses) | |
| (Remittances for Petty Cash) | | By Balance C/D | xxx |
| | xxx | | xxx |

**Dr.**            **(4) Branch Expenses Account**            **Cr.**

| Particulars | ₹ | Particulars | ₹ |
|---|---|---|---|
| To Branch Cash : | xxx | By Branch Profit and Loss | xxx |
| i)    Salaries | | (Total Branch Expenses transferred | |
| ii)   Rent | | to Branch Profit and Loss Account) | |
| iii)  Taxes | | | |
| To Branch Debtors : | xxx | | |
| i)    Discount Allowed | | | |
| ii)   Allowance given to Debtors | | | |
| iii)  Bad Debts written off | | | |
| To Branch Petty Cash | xxx | | |
| i)    Actual Petty Expenses | | | |
| To Branch Fixed Assets | xxx | | |
| i)    Depreciation | | | |
| | xxx | | xxx |

**Dr.**            **(5) Goods Sent to Branch Account**            **Cr.**

| Particulars | ₹ | Particulars | ₹ |
|---|---|---|---|
| To Branch Stock | xxx | By Branch Stock | xxx |
| (Returns to Head Office) | | (Goods supplied to Branch) | |
| To Branch Adjustment | xxx | | |
| (Load on Net Goods sent) | | | |
| To Purchases/Trading | xxx | | |
| | xxx | | xxx |

**Branch Fixed Assets Account :**

The head office may maintain separate Asset Account for each fixed asset. This account is debited with the opening value of Asset and Purchase of an Asset, if any. This account is credited with the depreciation provided on the Asset. The balance of the account represents the closing value of Fixed Asset. The format of Branch Fixed Asset Account is given below :

**Dr.**            **(6) Branch Fixed Assets Account**            **Cr.**

| Particulars | ₹ | Particulars | ₹ |
|---|---|---|---|
| To Balance B/D | xxx | By Branch Expenses | xxx |
| To Cash | xxx | (Depreciation on Fixed Assets) | |
| (Purchases of Fixed Asset) | | By Balance C/D | xxx |
| | xxx | | xxx |

**Dr.**            **(7) Branch Cash Account**            **Cr.**

| Particulars | ₹ | Particulars | ₹ |
|---|---|---|---|
| To Balance B/D | xxx | By Branch Expenses | xxx |
| To Branch Debtors | xxx | i)    Salary | |
| (Cash Collection from Debtors) | | ii)   Rent | |
| To Branch Stock | xxx | iii)  Taxes | |
| (Cash Sales) | | By Branch Fixed Assets | xxx |
| To Bank | xxx | (Purchases of Fixed Assets) | |
| (Transfer from other Branch) | | By Bank | xxx |
| | | (Remittance of Cash to | |
| | | Head Office) | |
| | | By Branch Petty Cash | |
| | | (Remittance for Petty Cash) | |
| | | By Bank | xxx |
| | | (Transfer to other Branch) | |
| | | By Balance C/D | xxx |
| | xxx | | xxx |

**Dr.**            **(8) Branch Adjustment Account**            **Cr.**

| Particulars | ₹ | Particulars | ₹ |
|---|---|---|---|
| To Branch Stock | xxx | By Stock Reserve | xxx |
| (Load on Abnormal Loss due to fire) | | (Load on Opening Stock) | |
| To Branch Stock | xxx | By Goods sent to Branch | xxx |
| (Normal Loss) | | (Load on Net Goods sent) | |
| To Stock Reserve | xxx | By Branch Stock | xxx |
| (Load on Closing Stock) | | (Surplus Stock) | |
| To Branch Profit and Loss | xxx | | |
| (Gross Profit C/D) | | | |
| | xxx | | xxx |

**Dr.**            **(9) Branch Profit and Loss Account**            **Cr.**

| Particulars | ₹ | Particulars | ₹ |
|---|---|---|---|
| To Branch Stock | xxx | By Branch Adjustment | xxx |
| (Cost of Abnormal Loss) | | (Gross Profit B/D) | |
| To Branch Expenses | xxx | By Branch Cash | xxx |
| * To Net Profit transferred to | | (Insurance Claim Received)/ | |
| General Profit and Loss | xxx | By Insurance Company. | |
| | | (Insurance Claim admitted but not | |
| | | received) | |
| | | * By Net Loss transferred to General | |
| | | Profit and Loss | xxx |
| | xxx | | xxx |

**The proforma journal entries passed in the books of Head Office under Stock and Debtors Method are as follows :**

### Proforma Journal Entries

i)   Goods sent to Branch :
Branch Stock A/c       Dr.   [Invoice Price]
    To Goods Sent to Branch A/c

ii)   Goods returned by Branch to Head Office :
Goods Sent to Branch A/c       Dr.   [Invoice Price]
    To Branch Stock A/c

iii)   Goods received from other Branches :
Branch Stock A/c       Dr.   [Invoice Price]
    To Goods sent to Branch A/c

iv)   Goods transferred to other Branches on advice of Head Office :
Goods Sent to Branch A/c       Dr.   [Invoice Price]
    To Branch Stock A/c

v)   Cash Sales :
Bank A/c       Dr.   [Actual Sales Proceeds]
    To Branch Stock A/c

vi)   Credit Sales :
Branch Debtors A/c       Dr.
    To Branch Stock A/c

vii)   Bills accepted by Branch Debtors :
Bills Receivable A/c       Dr.
    To Branch Debtors A/c

viii)   Cash collection from Debtors :
Bank A/c       Dr.
    To Branch Debtors A/c

ix)   Bad Debts, Discount Allowed, Allowance Given etc. :
Branch Expenses A/c       Dr.
    To Branch Debtors A/c

x)   Depreciation on Branch Fixed Assets :
Branch Expenses A/c       Dr.
    To Branch Fixed Assets A/c

xi)   Branch Expenses incurred in cash :
Branch Expenses A/c       Dr.
    To Branch Cash A/c

xii)   Transfer of Branch Expenses to Branch Profit and Loss Account :
Branch Profit and Loss A/c       Dr.
    To Branch Expenses A/c

xiii)   Shortage in Stock or Pilferage or Theft :
-   Shortage in Stock/Pilferage/Theft A/c       Dr.   [Invoice Price]
    To Branch Stock A/c
-   Branch Adjustment A/c       Dr.   [Loading]
   Branch Profit and Loss A/c       Dr.   [Cost]
    To Shortage in Stock/Pilferage/Theft A/c

xiv) Loss by Fire/Loss in Transit :

-  Accidental Loss A/c    Dr. [Invoice Price]
     To Branch Stock A/c

-  Branch Adjustment A/c   Dr. [Loading]
   Bank A/c (Insurance Claim Received) Dr.
   Insurance Company A/c   Dr.
   (Claim yet to receive)
   General Profit and Loss A/c  Dr. [Loss]
     To Accidental Loss A/c

xv) Loading on Opening Stock including Stock in Transit at the beginning :

Stock Reserve A/c     Dr. [Loading]
   To Branch Adjustment A/c

xvi) Loading on Net Goods sent :

Goods Sent to Branch A/c   Dr. [Loading]
   To Branch Adjustment A/c

xvii) Loading on Closing Stock including Stock-in-transit at the end :

Branch Adjustment A/c    Dr. [Loading]
   To Stock Reserve A/c

[In the Balance Sheet of Head Office, the Stock Reserve is shown as a deduction from Branch Stock at the end].

xviii) Transfer of Gross Profit :

Branch Adjustment A/c    Dr.
   To Branch Profit and Loss Account

xix) Transfer of Net Profit at the Branch :

Branch Profit and Loss A/c   Dr.
   To General Profit and Loss A/c
(Reverse Entry for Net Loss)

xx) Closing balance in Goods sent to Branch Account adjusted :

Goods Sent to Branch A/c   Dr.
  To Purchases A/c    [Trader]
  To Trading A/c     [Manufacturer]

**Accounting Treatment for some Typical Items**

**i) Normal Loss :**

No treatment is required even if it is given specifically in the examination problem. However, for calculating Branch Closing Stock (when it is not given) Normal Loss is credited to Branch Stock Account at invoice price. Normal Loss Account is closed by debiting to Branch Adjustment Account.

**ii) Pilferage/Theft :**

In retail trade, pilferage or shoplifting is very common and this has come to be regarded as a normal business loss. The loading of such goods is charged to Branch Adjustment and cost is charged to Branch Profit and Loss Account.

**iii) Shortage in Stock :**

Shortage in Stock may be due to spoilage, leakage, sales in small quantity, etc. Loading on shortage in stock should be charged to Branch Adjustment Account and cost of such goods should be charged to Branch Profit and Loss Account.

**iv) Surplus in Stock :**

Loading on surplus in stock is credited to Branch Adjustment Account and cost of such goods is credited to Branch Profit and Loss Account.

**v) Loss by Fire/Loss-in-Transit :**

Loading on goods lost by fire or in-transit should be charged to Branch Adjustment Account and the cost of such goods should be charged to **General Profit and Loss Account.**

**i) Inter-Branch Transfer of Goods :**

Sometimes, goods may be transferred by one branch to another branch. At the time of making entry for transferring branch, it should be treated as a transfer to head office (though the goods are actually transferred to a particular branch). Similarly, for receiving branch it will be treated as received from head office.

- For the transferring branch, the entry will be :

Goods Sent to Branch A/c                 Dr.    [Invoice Price]

     To Branch Stock A/c

- For the receiving branch, the entry will be :

Branch Stock A/c                     Dr.    [Invoice Price]

     To Goods Sent to Branch A/c

---

**EXAMPLE**

Ambika Ltd., Chennai, has a Branch at Pune to which goods are sent @ 20% above cost. The Branch makes both cash and credit sales. Branch Expenses are met partly from Head Office and partly by the Branch. The statement of expenses incurred by the branch every month is sent to Head Office for recording. Following further details are given for the year ended 31st December 2015.

| | ₹ |
|---|---|
| Goods sent to Branch at Cost | 2,00,000 |
| Goods received by Branch till 31.12.2015 at invoice price | 2,20,000 |
| Credit Sales for the year at invoice price | 1,65,000 |
| Cash Sales for the year at invoice price | 59,000 |
| Cash remitted to Head Office | 2,22,500 |
| Expenses paid by Head Office | 12,000 |
| Bad Debts written off | 750 |

| Balances as on : | 1.1.2015 | 31.12.2015 |
|---|---|---|
| • Stock | 25,000 | 28,000 |
| | (Cost Price) | (Invoice Price) |
| • Debtors | 32,750 | 26,000 |
| • Cash in Hand | 5,000 | 2,500 |

Show necessary ledger in the books of Ambika Ltd., Chennai and determine the profit and loss of the Branch for the year ended 31st December, 2015 (A) Under Debtors Method, and (B) Under Stock and Debtors Method.

ANSWER

**Working Notes :**

1) **Calculation of Opening Stock at Invoice Price :**

    Cost Price     +     Profit     =     Invoice Price

    100         20% above cost       120

    ₹ 25,000 = ?

    If 100 CP = 120 IP

∴      ₹ 25,000 = ?

$$= \frac{Rs.\ 25,000 \times 120}{100}$$

$$= ₹\ 30,000$$

2) **Calculation of Goods sent to Branch at Invoice Price :**

    Cost Price     +     Profit     =     Invoice Price

    100         20% above cost       120

    ₹ 2,00,000                         ?

    If 100 CP = 120 IP

∴      ₹ 2,00,000 = ?

$$= \frac{Rs.\ 2,00,000 \times 120}{100}$$

$$= ₹\ 2,40,000$$

**(A) Under Debtors Method :**

**In the books of Ambika Ltd., Chennai, (Head Office)**

Dr.        **Memorandum Branch Stock Account**        Cr.

| Particulars | ₹ | Particulars | ₹ |
|---|---|---|---|
| To Balance B/D | 30,000 | By Branch Debtors | 1,65,000 |
| To Goods Sent to Branch | 2,40,000 | (Credit Sales) | |
| To Branch Adjustment* | 2,000 | By Branch Cash | 59,000 |
| (Surplus in Stock i.e. Balancing | | (Cash Sales) | |
| Figure) | | By Balance C/D | |
| | | • Goods-in-transit | 20,000 |
| | | [₹ 2,40,000 – ₹ 2,20,000] | |
| | | • Stock at Branch | 28,000 |
| | **2,72,000** | | **2,72,000** |

**Dr.**     **Memorandum Branch Debtors Account**     **Cr.**

| Particulars | ₹ | Particulars | ₹ |
|---|---|---|---|
| To Balance B/D | 32,750 | By Bad Debt written off | 750 |
| To Branch Stock | 1,65,000 | By Branch Cash* | 1,71,000 |
| (Credit Sales) | | (Cash Collection from Debtors i.e. | |
| | | Balancing Figure) | |
| | | By Balance C/D | 26,000 |
| | **1,97,750** | | **1,97,750** |

**Dr.**     **Memorandum Branch Cash Account**     **Cr.**

| Particulars | ₹ | Particulars | ₹ |
|---|---|---|---|
| To Balance B/D | 5,000 | By Bank | 2,22,500 |
| To Branch Stock | 59,000 | (Remittance to Head Office) | |
| (Cash Sales) | | By Expenses | 12,000 |
| To Branch Debtors | 1,71,000 | (Paid by Head Office) | |
| (Collection from Debtors) | | By Expenses* | 10,000 |
| To Bank | 12,000 | Expenses Paid by Branch | |
| (Remittance from Head Office) | | i.e. Balancing Figure) | |
| | | By Balance C/D | 2,500 |
| | **2,47,000** | | **2,47,000** |

**Dr.**     **Pune Branch Account for the year ended 31-12-2015**     **Cr.**

| Particulars | ₹ | Particulars | ₹ |
|---|---|---|---|
| To Balance B/D | | By Stock Reserve | 5,000 |
| • Stock | 30,000 | [₹ 30,000 × 20/120] | |
| • Debtors | 32,750 | By Goods Sent to Branch | 40,000 |
| • Cash | 5,000 | [₹ 2,40,000 × 20/120] | |
| To Goods Sent to Branch | 2,40,000 | By Bank | 2,22,500 |
| To Bank | 12,000 | i) Cash Sales    59,000 | |
| (Expenses paid by Head Office) | | ii) Collection from | |
| To Stock Reserve | 8,000 | Debtors    (+) 1,63,500 | |
| (Loading on Closing Stock) | | ⎡ Total Cash − Cash ⎤ | |
| (₹ 48,000 × 20/120) | | ⎢ Remittances   Sales ⎥ | |
| To Net Profit transferred to General | | ⎣ ₹ 2,22,500   ₹ 59,000 ⎦ | |
| Profit and Loss | 16,250 | (Remittances received from | |
| | | Branch) | |
| | | By Balance C/D | |
| | | • Stock (including Transit) | 48,000 |
| | | • Debtors | 26,000 |
| | | • Cash | 2,500 |
| | **3,44,000** | | **3,44,000** |

## B) Under Stock and Debtors Method

**Dr.**        **Branch Stock Account**        **Cr.**

| Particulars | ₹ | Particulars | ₹ |
|---|---|---|---|
| To Balance B/D | 30,000 | By Branch Debtors | 1,65,000 |
| To Goods Sent to Branch | 2,40,000 | By Branch Bank | 59,000 |
| To Branch Adjustment | 2,000 | By Balance C/D | |
| (Surplus in Stock i.e. Balancing | | • Goods in Transit | 20,000 |
| Figure) | | (₹ 2,40,000 – ₹ 2,20,000) | |
| | | • Stock at Branch | 28,000 |
| | **2,72,000** | | **2,72,000** |

**Dr.**        **Branch Debtors Account**        **Cr.**

| Particulars | ₹ | Particulars | ₹ |
|---|---|---|---|
| To Balance B/D | 32,750 | By Bad Debts | 750 |
| To Branch Stock | 1,65,000 | By Branch Cash | 1,71,000 |
| | | (Collection from Debtors | |
| | | i.e. Balancing Figure) | |
| | | By Balance C/D | 26,000 |
| | **1,97,750** | | **1,97,750** |

**Dr.**        **Goods Sent to Branch Account**        **Cr.**

| Particulars | ₹ | Particulars | ₹ |
|---|---|---|---|
| To Branch Adjustment | 40,000 | By Branch to Stock | 2,40,000 |
| (Load on Goods sent to Branch) | | (Goods sent to Branch) | |
| To Purchase* | 2,00,000 | | |
| (Balancing Figure) | | | |
| | **2,40,000** | | **2,40,000** |

**Dr.**        **Branch Cash Account**        **Cr.**

| Particulars | ₹ | Particulars | ₹ |
|---|---|---|---|
| To Balance B/D | 5,000 | By Bank Remittance to Head Office | 2,22,500 |
| To Branch Stock | 59,000 | By Branch Adjustment | 12,000 |
| (Cash Sales) | | (Expenses paid by Head Office) | |
| To Bank | 12,000 | By Branch Adjustment* | 10,000 |
| (As per contra) | | (Expenses paid by Branch | |
| To Branch Debtors | 1,71,000 | i.e. Balancing Figure) | |
| (Collection from Debtors) | | By Balance C/D | 2,500 |
| | **2,47,000** | | **2,47,000** |

**Dr.**   **Branch Adjustment Account**   **Cr.**

| Particulars | ₹ | Particulars | ₹ |
|---|---|---|---|
| To Stock Reserve (Load on Closing Stock i.e. ₹ 48,000 × 20/120) | 8,000 | By Stock Reserve (Load on Opening Stock i.e., ₹ 30,000 × 20/130) | 5,000 |
| | | By Goods Sent to Branch (Load on Goods sent to Branch) | 40,000 |
| | | By Branch Stock | 2,000 |
| To Gross Profit C/D | 39,000 | (Surplus in Stock) | |
| | **47,000** | | **47,000** |

**Dr.**   **Branch Profit and Loss Account**   **Cr.**

| Particulars | | ₹ | Particulars | ₹ |
|---|---|---|---|---|
| To Branch Expenses | | 22,000 | By Gross Profit B/D | 39,000 |
| i) By Ho | 12,000 | | | |
| ii) By Br. | 10,000 | | | |
| To Branch Debtors | | 750 | | |
| (Bad Debts) | | | | |
| To Net Profit transfer to General Profit and Loss | | 16,250 | | |
| | | **39,000** | | **39,000** |

---

### 3) Branch Trading and Profit and Loss Account Method

The Head Office may also prepare a **Memorandum Branch Trading and Profit and Loss Account** to find out the profit or loss of a branch, apart from preparing the Branch Account. Here, the Trading and Profit and Loss Account is prepared in the usual manner, after converting all figures to cost price. The reason for preparing the Memorandum Trading and Profit and Loss Account is to consider detail information of all transactions which are ignored under **Debtors System.**

Following are some of the important points which are to be considered while preparing Branch Trading and Profit and Loss Account.

 i) All items of stock in Trading and Profit and Loss Account are to be converted into cost price, if these are given at an invoice price.

 ii) Branch Account will be a simple Personal Account in nature. It will show only the mutual transactions between Head Office and the Branch. The balance of Branch Account is nothing but net assets of the Branch at the end of the accounting year.

 iii) Branch Trading and Profit and Loss Account is merely a Memorandum Account and therefore, the entries made therein do not have any double-entry effect. The only object of this account is to disclose profit made or loss incurred by the branch for a particular period.

### EXAMPLE

Adwani Ltd. having its Head Office at Mumbai has a branch at Kolkata. You are given the following particulars relating to the Kolkata Branch for the year ending 31.12.2015.

| Particulars | ₹ | Particulars | ₹ |
|---|---|---|---|
| Stock at Branch on 1.1.2015 | 15,700 | Petty Cash at Branch 1.1.2015 | 110 |
| Goods sent to the Branch during 2015 | 45,600 | Goods Returned by Branch | 3,900 |
| Total Sales at Branch | 73,300 | **Cash Sent to Branch for Expenses :** | |
| (including ₹ 19,700 for Cash Sales) | | i) Salary | 12,800 |
| Cash Received from Debtors | 52,200 | ii) Petty Cash | 2,600 |
| Branch Debtors on 1.1.2015 | 16,900 | iii) Rent | 3,000 |
| | | Stock at Branch on 31.12.2015 | 18,800 |
| | | Petty Cash at Branch on 31.12.2015 | 90 |

Prepare Kolkata Branch Account for the year ended 31-12-2015 and Memorandum Branch Trading and Profit and Loss Account for the year ended 31-12-2015 in the Head Office books.

ANSWER

### In the Books of Adwani Ltd., Mumbai, Head Office

**Dr.**      **Kolkata Branch Account for the year ended 31-12.2015**

| Particulars | ₹ | Particulars | ₹ |
|---|---|---|---|
| To Balance B/D | | By Bank | |
| • Stock | 15,700 | i) Cash Sales | 19,700 |
| • Debtors | 16,900 | ii) Collection from Debtors | 52,200 |
| • Petty Cash | 110 | By Goods Sent to Branch | 3,900 |
| (Opening Balances) | | (goods returned by Branch) | |
| To Goods Sent to Branch | 45,600 | By Balance C/D | |
| (Goods sent to Branch) | | • Stock | 18,800 |
| To Bank | | • Debtors | 18,300 |
| • Salary | 12,800 | • Petty Cash | 90 |
| • Petty Cash | 2,600 | (Closing Balances) | |
| • Rent | 3,000 | | |
| (Remittances for Expenses) | | | |
| To Net Profit transferred to General Profit and Loss | 16,280 | | |
| | **1,12,990** | | **1,12,990** |

**Dr.**      **Memorandum Branch Trading and Profit and Loss Account**      **Cr.**

**for the year ended 31st December, 2015**

| Particulars | | ₹ | Particulars | ₹ |
|---|---|---|---|---|
| To Opening Stock | | 15,700 | By Sales : | |
| To Goods Sent to Branch | 45,600 | | • Cash | 19,700 |
| **Less :** Returned to HO | (–) 3,900 | 41,700 | • Credit | 53,600 |
| To Gross Profit C/D | | 34,700 | By Closing Stock | 18,800 |
| | | **92,100** | | **92,100** |
| To Salaries | | 12,800 | By Gross Profit B/D | 34,700 |
| To Rent | | 3,000 | | |
| To Petty Expenses | | 2,620 | | |
| To General Profit and Loss | | 16,280 | | |
| (Net Profit C/D) | | | | |
| | | **34,700** | | **34,700** |

**Dr.**        **Branch Debtors Account**        **Cr.**

| Particulars | ₹ | Particulars | ₹ |
|---|---|---|---|
| To Balance B/D | 16,900 | By Collection from Debtors | 52,200 |
| To Sales Credit | 53,600 | By Balance C/D | 18,300 |
| | **70,500** | | **70,500** |

**Dr.**        **Branch Petty Cash Account**        **Cr.**

| Particulars | ₹ | Particulars | ₹ |
|---|---|---|---|
| To Balance B/D | 110 | By Petty Expenses | 2,620 |
| To Bank | 2,600 | (Balancing Figure) | |
| (Remittances) | | By Balance C/D | 90 |
| | **2,710** | | **2,710** |

**D) Wholesale Branch Method :**

Usually, the manufacturers open their own retail branches for selling the goods in addition to selling of goods through wholesalers. Under such circumstances, the head office sends the goods to branch at wholesale price and branches sell the goods to their customers at retail price. The difference between the wholesale price and the retail price is considered as the profit on retailing. If all goods received by the branch are sold, the profit becomes earned profits. But if part of the goods remain unsold at branch at the end of the accounting year, adjustments are necessary to record the unsold goods at the reduced cost price.

## 6.4 GOODS SUPPLY AT COST AND INVOICE PRICE METHOD

In branch accounting, head office sends the goods to branch on invoice price instead of cost price because with this company can hide its profit margin from branch employees. In the invoice price, there are two prices included one is cost price and second is profit %. So, it is necessary to use invoice price method for maintaining branch accounting.

It is also necessary to adjust the stock of company when it supplies to branch at invoice price. Actually H.O. are not selling the product to their branch. Branch is small part of company (H.O.). So for deducting the profit from stock, H.O. will pass the reverse entry of stock reserve which is relating to adjustment of opening stock, closing stock and goods sent to branch. For example, H.O. have ₹ 1,000 opening stock in branch. In this ₹ 1,000, ₹ 200 is profit of company, so it is necessary to deduct ₹ 200 from ₹ 1,000 from opening stock. Same procedure will apply on closing stock also.

Following accounting entries are essential :

(i) For adjustment in the value of opening stock

     Stock Reserve Account        Dr. (Invoice Cost – Cost value)

         To Branch A/c

(ii) For adjustment in the value of goods sent to branch less return

  Goods sent to Branch Account    Dr. (Invoice Cost  – Cost Value)

   To Branch A/c

(iii) For adjustment in the value of Closing Stock

  Branch Account      Dr. (Invoice Value – Cost Values)

   To Stock Reserve A/c

**Opening of Branch Account :**

Branch Account (Invoice Price Method)

| Debit Side | | Credit Side | |
|---|---|---|---|
| To Balance B/D | ...... | By Balance B/D | ...... |
| (Opening Stock of Assets) | | (Opening Stock of Liabilities) | |
| Cash in Hand | ...... | Bank Account | ...... |
| Stock in Trade (Invoice price) | ...... | Cash Sales | ...... |
| Sundry Debtors | ...... | Cash Received from Debtors | ...... |
| Furniture | ...... | By Balance C/D | ...... |
| Prepaid Insurance | ...... | (Closing Stock of Assets) | |
| To Goods sent to Branch (Less) | ...... | Cash in Hand | ...... |
| Returns (Invoice price) | ...... | Stock in Trade (Invoice Prices) | ...... |
| To Bank Account | ...... | Sundry Debtors | ...... |
| (Expenses paid by H.O.) | ...... | Furniture | ...... |
| To Stock Reserve on Closing Stock | ...... | Prepaid Insurance | ...... |
| To Balance C/D | ...... | By Stock Reserve on Opening Stock | ...... |
| (Closing Stock of Liabilities) | | By Goods sent to Branch (Adjustments) | ...... |
| To General Profit and Loss A/c (Profit) | ...... | By General Profit and Loss A/c (Loss) | ...... |
| | ...... | | ...... |

**Accounting Entries in the Books of H.O. :**

1. **For opening balance of assets at the branch**

  Branch Account      Dr.

   To Branch Assets A/c (Individual Accounts)

2. **For opening balances of liabilities at the branch**

  Branch Liabilities A/c (Individual Accounts) Dr.

   To Branch Account

3.  **For goods sent to Branch A/c (At Proforma invoice price)**
    Branch Account                                    Dr.
        To Goods sent to Branch A/c

4.  **For Return of goods from Branch (At Proforma invoice price)**
    Goods sent to Branch A/c                          Dr.
        To Branch Account

5.  **For reversal of loading on (net) goods sent to Branch (With an amount of loading)**
    Goods sent to Branch A/c                          Dr.
        To Branch Account

6.  **For remittance for cash or cheques to the Branch**
    Branch A/c                                        Dr.
        To Cash/Bank A/c

7.  **For cash or cheque received from Branch**
    Cash/Bank Account                                 Dr.
        To Branch Account

8.  **For Closing Balances of Assets at Branch**
    Branch Assets A/c (Individual Accounts)           Dr.
        To Branch A/c

9.  **For Closing Balances of Liabilities at Branch**
    Branch Account                                    Dr.
        To Branch Liabilities (Individual Accounts)

10. **For Closing Goods sent to Branch Account**
    Goods sent to Branch A/c                          Dr.
        To Purchases A/c

11. **For Closing Branch Account into Profit and Loss Account**
    **In case of profit :**
        Branch A/c                                    Dr.
            To Profit and Loss A/c

    **In case of loss :**
        Profit and Loss A/c                           Dr.
            To Branch A/c

12. **For Abnormal Loss (should always be accounted for at cost)**

    Abnormal Loss A/c (At Cost)                       Dr.

        To Branch A/c

    Insurance Claim A/c (claim admitted)              Dr.

        To Profit and Loss A/c

    (Balance if not admitted by the Insurance Company).

        To Abnormal Loss A/c (Cost of Abnormal Loss)

**Note :** No accounting entry is required for normal losses.

### ILLUSTRATION

Vishal Garments of Mumbai has a branch at Nashik. Goods are supplied to the branch at cost. The expenses of the branch are paid from Mumbai and the branch keeps a sales journal and debtors' ledger only. From the following information supplied by the branch, prepare a Branch Account in the books of Head Office. Goods are sent to branch at proforma invoice price which is cost plus 20% (All figures in ₹).

| Particulars | ₹ |
|---|---|
| Opening Stock (at proforma invoice) | 28,800 |
| Closing Stock (at proforma invoice) | 21,600 |
| Closing Debtors | 9,160 |
| Opening Debtors | ? |
| Goods received from H.O. (at proforma invoice) | 40,320 |
| Bad Debts | 140 |
| Credit Sales | 41,000 |
| Expenses paid by H.O. | 10,400 |
| Cash Sales | 17,500 |
| Cash received from Debtors | 37,900 |
| Pilferage of goods by the employees (Normal loss) | 2,000 |

### SOLUTION

**In the books of Head Office (Mumbai)**

**Nashik Branch Account (Debtors System)**

| Particulars | ₹ | Particulars | ₹ |
|---|---|---|---|
| To Opening Stock | 24,000 | By Cash Received from Branch | 17,500 |
| To Opening Debtors | 6,200 | By Cash Received from Debtors | 37,900 |
| To Cash sent to Branch | 10,400 | By Goods sent to Branch | 6,720 |
| To Goods sent to Branch A/c | 40,320 | (Loading) | |
| To General Profit and Loss A/c | 8,360 | By Closing Stock | 18,000 |
| | | By Closing Debtors | 9,160 |
| | **89,280** | | **89,280** |

**Working Notes :**

**Debtors A/c**

| Particulars | ₹ | Particulars | ₹ |
|---|---|---|---|
| To Opening Balance | 6,200 | By Cash Received from Debtors | 37,900 |
| (Balancing Figure) | | By Bad Debts | 140 |
| To Sales | 41,000 | By Closing Balance of (Debtors) | 9,160 |
| | **47,200** | | **47,200** |

- **Loading in Opening Stock :**

  28,800 × 100/1,200 = 24,000 (Proforma invoice × % of cost by % proforma invoice)

- **Loading in Closing Stock**

  21,600 × 100/120 = 18,000 (Proforma invoice × % of cost by % proforma invoice)

- **Loading in Goods sent to Branch A/c (Net)**

  | | |
  |---|---:|
  | Goods sent to Branch (at proforma invoice) | ₹ 40,320 |
  | **Less :** Goods Returns | — |
  | Net goods sent | 40,320 |

  ₹ 40,320 × 20/120 = 6,720.

## SUMMARY

A well established or large sized business may have its Head Office in one city and its branches located in different cities. It is the Head Office that records all business transactions of its branches. The Head Office may follow the **'Debtors System'** of maintaining accounts, in which case a 'Branch Account' records all major business transactions and shows the final profit or loss made by the Branch.

It may adopt the **'Stock and Debtors System** in which the various accounts are prepared such as 'Branch Stock Account', 'Branch Expenses Account', Branch Adjustment Account', etc. The final profit of the Branch is disclosed either by 'Branch Adjustment Account' or by 'Branch Profit and Loss Account', as the case may be.

The Head Office may send goods to its Branch at cost price or invoice price. In case of goods sent at invoice price, the hidden profit (loading) included in the invoice price is to be found and cancelled by passing the opposite debit or credit entry for it.

The head office may also prepare a Branch Trading and Profit and Loss Account to find out the true profit or loss of a branch, apart from preparing a Branch Account. Under this method, Branch Trading and Profit and Loss Account is prepared in the usual manner after converting all items of stock from invoice price to cost price.

## 6.5 ILLUSTRATIONS

### (A) : Debtors Method – Goods sent to Branch at Cost Price

### ILLUSTRATION 1

To a branch at Mumbai goods are supplied by Henley Co., Pune Head Office at cost, to be sold for cash only. The expenses of branch are paid by Head Office. From the following particulars, prepare Mumbai Branch Account for the year ended 31-3-2016 in the books of the Head Office.

|  | ₹ |
|---|---|

Opening balances as on 1-4-2015 :

| | | ₹ |
|---|---|---|
| i) | Stock at Branch | 60,000 |
| ii) | Petty Cash | 500 |
| iii) | Furniture at Branch | |
| | (Original cost ₹ 8,000) | 6,400 |
| | Goods supplied to Branch | 4,00,000 |
| | Goods supplied by Branch - Returned | 10,000 |
| | Stock at Branch as on 31-3-2016 | 40,000 |
| | Cash sent to Branch for expenses : | |
| i) | Rent | 28,800 |
| ii) | Other Expenses | 37,400 |
| iii) | Salaries | 4,000 |
| iv) | Advertisement | 7,000 |
| v) | Petty Cash | 1,500 |
| | Cash sent to Head Office | 4,78,000 |

Furniture is to be depreciated @ 10% p.a. on Straight Line Method. Actual petty expenses paid by branch amounted to ₹ 1,000.

SOLUTION

**Working Notes :**

A) Missing items :

    i) Closing balance of Branch Petty Cash Account

    ii) Closing balance of Furniture Account

B) Closing Balance of Furniture Account can be calculated as follows :

| Particulars | | Amount |
|---|---|---|
| | | ₹ |
| Furniture as on 1-4-2015 | | 6,400 |
| (Original Cost ₹ 8,000) | | |
| **Less :** Depreciation @ 10% p.a. on S.L.M. i.e., ₹ 8,000 | (–) | 800 |
| ∴ Closing balance of Furniture Account as on 31-3-2016 | | 5,600 |

**In the books of Henley Co. Pune, Head Office**

Dr.     **Mumbai Branch Account for the year ended 31-3-2016**     Cr.

| Particulars | | ₹ | Particulars | | ₹ |
|---|---|---|---|---|---|
| To Opening Balances : | | 66,900 | By Bank | | 4,78,000 |
| i) Stock | 60,000 | | i) Cash Sales (+) 4,78,000 | | |
| ii) Petty Cash | 500 | | | | |
| iii) Furniture (+) | 6,400 | | | | |
| (Original Cost ₹ 8,000) | | | | | |
| To Goods sent to Branch | | 4,00,000 | By Goods sent to Br. Less Returned | | 10,000 |
| To Bank : | | 78,700 | By Closing Balances | | 46,600 |
| i) Rent | 28,800 | | i) Stock | 40,000 | |
| ii) Other Expenses | 37,400 | | ii) Petty Cash | 1,000 | |
| iii) Salaries | 4,000 | | iii) Furniture (+) | 5,600 | |
| iv) Advertisement | 7,000 | | By General Profit and Loss * | | 11,000 |
| v) Petty Cash (+) | 1,500 | | (Net Loss C/D) | | |
| | | **5,45,600** | | | **5,45,600** |

Dr.     **Branch Petty Cash Account**     Cr.

| Particulars | ₹ | Particulars | ₹ |
|---|---|---|---|
| To Balance B/D | 500 | By Actual Petty expenses | 1,000 |
| To Cash sent to Branch | 1,500 | By Balance C/D * | 1,000 |
| | | (Balancing Figure) | |
| | **2,000** | | **2,000** |

---

## (A) Debtors Method – Goods sent to Branch at Invoice Price

**ILLUSTRATION 2**

Jain Brothers, Jalgaon has a branch at Dhulia. All goods required for sale at Dhulia are supplied from Jalgaon at cost plus 25% and all cash received at the branch is banked daily in the Head Office Account opened in a Bank at Dhulia. From the following particulars prepare Dhulia Branch Account in the books of Jain Brothers, Jalgaon, Head Office for the year ended 31-3-2016.

|  |  | ₹ |
|---|---|---|
| Balances as on 1-4-2015 | | |
| i) | Stock | 79,000 |
| ii) | Debtors | 1,13,000 |
| iii) | Petty Cash | 900 |
| | Returns from customers | 4,000 |
| | Returned goods to Head Office | 10,000 |
| | Bad Debts written-off | 1,000 |
| | Bad Debts provision | 2,100 |
| | Selling for cash | 14,000 |
| | Rent payable on 31-03-2016 | 1,000 |

| | |
|---|---:|
| Allowances given | 4,500 |
| Branch expenses paid by Head Office | |
|   i)    Rent | 14,000 |
|   ii)   Salary | 15,000 |
|   iii)  Sundries | 7,000 |
| Petty cash expenses at Branch | 2,400 |
| Total Sales | 3,49,000 |
| Petty cash remittances | 2,800 |
| Balances as on 31-3-2016 | |
|   i)    Stock | 84,000 |
|   ii)   Debtors | 1,95,100 |
| Goods invoiced to Branch | 2,50,000 |

## SOLUTION

**Working Notes :**

**A) Missing items**

  i)    Collection from Debtors

  ii)   Closing balance of Branch Petty Cash Account

  iii)  Credit Sales

$$\text{Total Sales} - \text{Cash Sales} = \text{Credit Sales}$$
$$₹\,3,49,000 - ₹\,14,000 = ₹\,3,35,000$$

**B) Calculation of Loading i.e. cost plus 25%**

$$SP = CP + P$$
$$125 = 100 + 25$$
$$\therefore \quad \frac{P}{SP} = \frac{25}{125} = \frac{1}{5}$$

**C)** Bad Debts Provisions are to be debited to Branch Account.

**D)** Rent Payable i.e. outstanding rent for current year are to be debited to Branch Account.

### In the books of Jain Brothers, Jalgaon Head Office

**Dr.**          **Branch Debtors Account**          **Cr.**

| Particulars | ₹ | Particulars | ₹ |
|---|---:|---|---:|
| To Balance B/D | 1,13,000 | By Returns from customers | 4,000 |
| To Credit Sales | 3,35,000 | By Bad Debts written off | 1,000 |
| | | By Allowances given | 4,500 |
| | | By Cash collection from Debtors * | 2,43,400 |
| | | (Balancing Figure) | |
| | | By Balance C/D | 1,95,100 |
| | **4,48,000** | | **4,48,000** |

**Dr.**     **Branch Petty Cash Account**     **Cr.**

| Particulars | ₹ | Particulars | ₹ |
|---|---|---|---|
| To Balance B/D | 900 | By Petty Cash expenses | 2,400 |
| To Petty Cash remittance | 2,800 | | |
| | | By Balance C/D * | 1,300 |
| | | (Balancing Figure) | |
| | **3,700** | | **3,700** |

**Dr.**     **Dhulia Branch Account for the year ended 31-3-2016**     **Cr.**

| Particulars | | ₹ | Particulars | | ₹ |
|---|---|---|---|---|---|
| To Opening Balances : | | 1,92,900 | By Stock Reserve | | 15,800 |
| i)    Stock | 79,000 | | By Bank | | 2,57,400 |
| ii)   Debtors | 1,13,000 | | i)   Cash Sales | 14,000 | |
| iii)   Petty cash    (+) | 900 | | ii) Collection from Debtors (+) 2,43,400 | | |
| To Goods sent to Branch | | 2,50,000 | By Goods sent to Br. Less Returned | | 10,000 |
| To Bad Debts provision | | 2,100 | | | |
| To Rent payable on 31-3-2015 | | 1,000 | | | |
| To Bank Account | | 38,800 | By Closing Balances : | | 2,80,400 |
| i)    Rent | 14,000 | | i)    Stock | 84,000 | |
| ii)   Salary | 15,000 | | ii)   Debtors | 1,95,100 | |
| iii)   Sundries | 7,000 | | iii)   Petty Cash    (+) | 1,300 | |
| iv)   Petty Cash    (+) | 2,800 | | By Goods sent to Branch | | 50,000 |
| To Goods sent to Branch | | 2,000 | (Loading) | | |
| (Loading) – Returned | | | | | |
| To Stock Reserve | | 16,800 | | | |
| To General Profit and Loss* | | 1,10,000 | | | |
| (Net Profit C/D) | | | | | |
| | | **6,13,600** | | | **6,13,600** |

## ILLUSTRATION 3

Bharat Traders, Baroda has a branch at Surat to which goods are supplied by Head Office at 25% on cost price. Branch remits all cash received by the Head Office and all expenses, except petty cash expenses of the branch are paid by the Head Office by cheques. Prepare Surat Branch Account in the books of Bharat Traders, Baroda taking into consideration the following information for the year 2015-2016.

| Particulars | Balances as on 1-4-2015 ₹ | Balances as on 31-3-2016 ₹ |
|---|---|---|
| Stock-in-Trade | 1,00,000 | 57,600 |
| Debtors | 10,000 | 54,000 |
| Cash in Hand | 100 | – |

| | ₹ |
|---|---|
| Goods sent to Branch | 2,00,000 |
| Total Sales | 3,00,000 |
| Cash received from Debtors | 1,90,000 |
| Goods returned by Debtors | 2,000 |
| Discount allowed to customers | 4,000 |
| Allowances to customers | 2,000 |
| Bad debts written off | 4,000 |
| Bills receivable from Debtors | 4,000 |
| Cheques sent to Branch for expenses : | |
| i)   Salaries | 9,530 |
| ii)  Rent | 2,400 |
| iii) Advertisement | 1,200 |
| Petty Expenses by Branch | 950 |
| Petty Cash remittances to Branch | 1,000 |

The branch manager is entitled to a commission of 10% on branch profits before charging such commission.

$\boxed{\text{SOLUTION}}$

**Working Notes :**

**A)   Missing items :**

i)   Credit Sales

ii)  Closing balance of Branch Petty Cash Account

iii) Cash Sales

$$\text{Total Sales} - \text{Credit Sales} = \text{Cash Sales}$$
$$₹\,3,00,000 - ₹\,2,50,000 = ₹\,50,000$$

**B)   Calculation of Loading i.e. 25% on Cost Price**

$$SP = CP + P$$
$$125 = 100 + 25$$
$$\therefore \quad \frac{P}{SP} = \frac{25}{125} = \frac{1}{5}$$

**C)   Bills Receivable from debtors are to be credited to Branch Account**

**D)   Calculation of Manager's Commission :**

i)   Calculation of rough profit :

$$\text{Total Income} - \text{Total Expenses} = \text{Rough Profit}$$
$$₹\,4,15,750 - ₹\,3,35,750 = ₹\,80,000$$

ii)   Calculation of Manager's Commission @ 10% on branch profits before charging such commission i.e. 10% of ₹ 80,000 = ₹ 8,000

Therefore,

| | | | |
|---|---|---|---|
| i) | Total Rough Profits | = | ₹ 80,000 |
| ii) | Manager's Commission | = | ₹ 8,000 |
| iii) | Actual Net Profits | = | ₹ 72,000 |

**In the books of Bharat Traders, Baroda, Head Office**

**Dr.**      **Surat Branch Account for the year ended 31-3-2016**      **Cr.**

| Particulars | | ₹ | Particulars | | ₹ |
|---|---|---|---|---|---|
| To Opening Balances : | | 1,10,100 | By Stock Reserve | | 20,000 |
| i) Stock-in-Trade | 1,00,000 | | By Bank : | | 2,40,000 |
| ii) Debtors | 10,000 | | i) Cash Sales | 50,000 | |
| iii) Cash in hand (+) | 100 | | ii) Collection from | | |
| | | | Debtors (+) | 1,90,000 | |
| To Goods sent to Branch | | 2,00,000 | | | |
| To Bank | | 14,130 | By Closing Balances | | 1,11,750 |
| i) Salaries | 9,530 | | i) Stock-in-Trade | 57,600 | |
| ii) Rent | 2,400 | | ii) Debtors | 54,000 | |
| iii) Advertisement | 1,200 | | iii) Cash in hand (+) | 150 | |
| iv) Petty Cash (+) | 1,000 | | | | |
| To Stock Reserve | | 11,520 | By Bills Receivable from | | |
| To Manager's Commission | | 8,000 | Debtors | | 4,000 |
| To General Profit and Loss * | | 72,000 | By Goods sent to Branch | | 40,000 |
| (Net Profit C/D) | | | (Loading) | | |
| | | 4,15,750 | | | 4,15,750 |

**Dr.**      **Branch Debtors Account**      **Cr.**

| Particulars | ₹ | Particulars | ₹ |
|---|---|---|---|
| To Balance B/D | 10,000 | By Cash received from Debtors | 1,90,000 |
| To Credit Sales * | 2,50,000 | By Goods returned by Debtors | 2,000 |
| (Balancing figure) | | By Discount Allowed to customers | 4,000 |
| | | By Allowances to customers | 2,000 |
| | | By Bad Debts written off | 4,000 |
| | | By Bills Receivable from Debtors | 4,000 |
| | | By Balance C/D | 54,000 |
| | 2,60,000 | | 2,60,000 |

**Dr.**        **Branch Petty Cash Account**        **Cr.**

| Particulars | ₹ | Particulars | ₹ |
|---|---|---|---|
| To Balance B/D | 100 | By Petty Expenses | 950 |
| To Petty Cash remittances | 1,000 | | |
| | | By Balance C/D * | 150 |
| | | (Balancing Figure) | |
| | **1,100** | | **1,100** |

### ILLUSTRATION 4

Cibaca Ltd., Kolkata invoiced goods to its branch at Nagpur at 20% on inflated price. Prepare Nagpur Branch Account in the books of the Head Office from the following information for the year ended 2015-2016.

| | ₹ |
|---|---|
| Debtors on 1-4-2015 | 26,200 |
| Debtors on 31-3-2016 | 33,100 |
| Stock on 1-4-2015 | 15,000 |
| Stock on 31-3-2016 | 13,900 |
| Goods received from Head Office | 50,800 |
| Cash Sales | 33,500 |
| Allowances to customers | 320 |
| Yearly Turnover | 93,500 |
| Goods returned to Head Office | 700 |
| Goods returned by customers | 580 |
| Discount Allowed | 2,400 |
| Bad Debts | 600 |
| Rent and Taxes | 1,800 |
| Wages and Salaries | 1,540 |
| Carriage and Cartage | 1,300 |

The branch manager is entitled to a commission of 10% on branch profits after charging such commission.

### SOLUTION

**Working Notes :**

**A) Missing items :**

    i)    Collection from Debtors

    ii)    Credit Sales

$$\text{Total Sales} - \text{Cash Sales} = \text{Credit Sales}$$

i.e. (Yearly turnover)

$$₹\,93,500 - ₹\,33,500 = ₹\,60,000$$

**B) Calculation of Loading i.e. 20% on inflated price**

$$SP = CP + P$$

(Inflated price)

$$100 = 80 + 20$$

$$\therefore \quad \frac{P}{SP} = \frac{20}{100} = \frac{1}{5}$$

**C) Calculation of Manager's Commission :**

i) Calculation of Rough Profit –

$$\text{Total Income} - \text{Total Expenses} = \text{Rough Profit}$$
$$₹\,1,43,560 \quad - \quad ₹\,99,560 = ₹\,44,000$$

ii) Calculation of Manager's Commission @ 10% on branch profits after charging such commission i.e. (100 + 10 = 110)

$$\text{If } ₹\,110 \text{ Profits} = ₹\,10 \text{ Commission}$$
$$\therefore \quad ₹\,44,000 \text{ Profits} = ?$$
$$= \frac{₹\,44,000 \times ₹\,10}{₹\,110}$$
$$= ₹\,4,000$$

Therefore,

| | | |
|---|---|---|
| i) | Total Rough Profits | = ₹ 44,000 |
| ii) | Manager's Commission | = ₹ 4,000 |
| iii) | Actual Net Profit | = ₹ 40,000 |

**In the books of Cibaca Ltd., Kolkata Head Office**

**Dr.**      **Branch Debtors Account**      **Cr.**

| Particulars | ₹ | Particulars | ₹ |
|---|---|---|---|
| To Balance B/D | 26,200 | By Allowances to customers | 320 |
| To Credit Sales * | 60,000 | By Goods returned by customers | 580 |
| (Balancing figure) | | By Discount Allowed | 2,400 |
| | | By Bad Debts | 600 |
| | | By Collection from Debtors * | |
| | |     (Balancing Figure) | 49,200 |
| | | By Balance C/D | 33,100 |
| | **86,200** | | **86,200** |

**Dr.**      **Nagpur Branch Account for the year ended 31-03-2016**      **Cr.**

| Particulars | | ₹ | Particulars | | ₹ |
|---|---|---|---|---|---|
| To Opening Balances : | | 41,200 | By Stock Reserve | | 3,000 |
| i) Debtors | 26,200 | | By Bank : | | 82,700 |
| ii) Stock | (+) 15,000 | | i) Cash Sales | 33,500 | |
| | | | ii) Collection from Debtors (+) | 49,200 | |
| To Goods sent to Branch | | 50,800 | By Goods sent to Br. less | | |
| | | | Returned | | 700 |
| To Bank : | | 4,640 | By Closing Balances : | | 47,000 |
| i) Rent and Rates | 1,800 | | i) Debtors | 33,100 | |
| ii) Wages and Salaries | 1,540 | | ii) Stock | (+) 13,900 | |
| iii) Carriage and Cartage (+) | 1,300 | | | | |
| To Goods sent to Branch | | 140 | By Goods sent to Branch | | 10,160 |
| Less Returned (Loading) | | | (Loading) | | |
| To Stock Reserve | | 2,780 | | | |
| To Manager's Commission | | 4,000 | | | |
| To General Profit and Loss * | | 40,000 | | | |
| (Net Profit C/D) | | | | | |
| | | **1,43,560** | | | **1,43,560** |

## ILLUSTRATION 5

Rexona Ltd. Raipur has a branch at Agra. Goods are invoiced to the Agra branch at cost plus 50%. Branch remits all cash received to the Head Office and all expenses are met by the Head Office. Following particulars are available.

| | ₹ |
|---|---:|
| Stock on 1-4-2015 (Invoice Price) | 18,600 |
| Debtors on 1-4-2015 | 13,600 |
| Petty cash on 31-3-2016 | 160 |
| Goods invoiced to Branch (invoice price) | 1,06,200 |
| Sales at Branch : | |
| i)     Cash sales | 50,020 |
| ii)    Credit Sales | 62,000 |
| Goods returned by debtors | 2,400 |
| Cash collected from debtors | 60,800 |
| Goods transferred from Delhi to Agra branch (invoice price) | 3,000 |
| Goods returned by branch to Head Office (invoice price) | 3,000 |
| Discount allowed to customers | 300 |
| Irrecoverable debts | 100 |
| Expenses at Branch : | |
| i)   Rent | 6,000 |
| ii)  Salary | 4,000 |
| iii) Office expenses | 800 |
| iv) Petty cash | 400 |
| Actual petty expenses by Branch Manager | 340 |

You are required to prepare Agra Branch Account in the books of Rexona Ltd., Raipur.

Also prepare :

i)   Branch Debtors Account

ii)  Branch Petty Cash Account and

iii) Branch Stock Account for the year ended 31-3-2016.

## SOLUTION

**Working Notes :**

**(A)  Missing items :**

    i)   Closing balance of Branch Debtors Account

    ii)  Opening balance of Branch Petty Cash Account

    iii) Closing balance of Branch Stock Account.

**B)  Calculation of Loading i.e. cost plus 50%.**

$$SP = CP + P$$
$$150 = 100 + 50$$
$$\therefore \quad \frac{P}{SP} = \frac{50}{150} = \frac{1}{3}$$

**C)** Goods transferred from Delhi Branch to Agra Branch are to be debited to Agra Branch Account.

## In the books of Rexona Ltd., Raipur (Head Office)

**Dr.**    **Branch Debtors Account**    **Dr.**

| Particulars | ₹ | Particulars | ₹ |
|---|---|---|---|
| To Balance B/D | 13,600 | By Goods returned by Debtors | 2,400 |
| To Credit Sales | 62,000 | By Cash collected from Debtors | 60,800 |
| | | By Discount allowed to customers | 300 |
| | | By Irrecoverable Debts | 100 |
| | | By Balance C/D * | 12,000 |
| | | (Balancing Figure) | |
| | **75,600** | | **75,600** |

**Dr.**    **Branch Petty Cash Account**    **Cr.**

| Particulars | ₹ | Particulars | ₹ |
|---|---|---|---|
| To Balance B/D * | 100 | By Actual Petty Expenses | 340 |
| (Balancing Figure) | | | |
| To Petty Cash Remittances | 400 | By Balance C/D | 160 |
| | **500** | | **500** |

**Dr.**    **Branch Stock Account**    **Cr.**

| Particulars | ₹ | Particulars | ₹ |
|---|---|---|---|
| To Balance b/d | 18,600 | By Cash Sales | 50,020 |
| To Goods invoiced to Branch | 1,06,200 | By Credit Sales | 62,000 |
| To Goods returned by Debtors | 2,400 | By Goods returned by branch to head office | 3,000 |
| To Goods transferred from Delhi to Agra Branch | 3,000 | By Balance c/d * (Balancing Figure) | 15,180 |
| | **1,30,200** | | **1,30,200** |

**Dr.**    **Agra Branch Account for the year ended 31-3-2016**    **Cr.**

| Particulars | | ₹ | Particulars | | ₹ |
|---|---|---|---|---|---|
| To Opening Balances : | | 32,300 | By Stock Reserve | | 6,200 |
| i) Stock | 18,600 | | By Bank : | | 1,10,820 |
| ii) Debtors | 13,600 | | i) Cash Sales | 50,020 | |
| iii) Petty Cash (+) | 100 | | ii) Collection from Debtors (+) | 60,800 | |
| To Goods sent to Branch | | 1,06,200 | By Goods sent to Branch less Returned | | 3,000 |
| To Goods transferred from Delhi to Agra Branch | | 3,000 | | | |
| To Bank : | | 11,200 | By Closing Balances : | | 27,340 |
| i) Rent | 6,000 | | i) Stock | 15,180 | |
| ii) Salary | 4,000 | | ii) Debtors | 12,000 | |
| iii) Office Expenses | 800 | | iii) Petty Cash (+) | 160 | |
| iv) Petty Cash (+) | 400 | | | | |
| To Goods sent to Branch Less Returned (Loading) | | 1,000 | By Goods sent to Branch (Loading) | | 35,400 |
| To Stock Reserve | | 5,060 | By Goods transferred from Delhi to Agra Branch (Loading) | | 1,000 |
| To General Profit and Loss (Net Profit C/D) | | 25,000 | | | |
| | | **1,83,760** | | | **1,83,760** |

## ILLUSTRATION 6

Godrej Corporation, Dadar has a branch at Chinchwad. The Head Office invoices goods to its branch at cost plus $1/3$. The branch transfers all cash received to head office daily. All branch expenses are paid from the head office. From the following information prepare :

1. Chinchwad Branch Account
2. Branch Debtors Account
3. Branch Petty Cash Account
4. Goods sent to Branch Account
5. Stock Reserve Account,

in the books of Godrej Corporation, Dadar, Head Office.

| | ₹ |
|---|---:|
| Branch stock at invoice price on 1-4-2015 | 80,000 |
| Branch Debtors on 1-4-2015 | 20,000 |
| Branch Petty cash on 1-4-2015 | 2,000 |
| Cash Sales | 30,000 |
| Discount allowed to credit customers | 4,000 |
| Book debts becoming bad and written off | 3,000 |
| Returns Inward | 1,500 |
| Cash received from Branch Debtors | 1,20,000 |
| Goods sent to branch at invoice price | 2,00,000 |
| Goods returned to head office | 16,000 |
| Credit Sales | 1,50,000 |
| Branch Stock at invoice price on 31-3-2016 | 1,00,000 |
| Cheques received from Head Office for expenses : | |
| i)    Salaries | 12,000 |
| ii)   Advertisement | 5,000 |
| iii)  Petty cash | 3,000 |
| iv)  Annual taxes upto 1-7-2016 | 6,000 |
| Actual expenses incurred by Branch | 4,000 |

## SOLUTION

**Working Notes :**

**A) Missing items :**

    i)    Closing balance of Branch Debtors Account

    ii)   Closing balance of Branch Petty Cash Account

**B) Calculation of Loading i.e. cost plus $1/3$**

$$SP = CP + P$$

$$133\,{}^1/_3 = 100 + 33\,{}^1/_3 \text{ (i.e. } {}^1/_3 \text{ of CP)}$$

$$\therefore \quad \frac{P}{SP} = \frac{33\,{}^1/_3}{133\,{}^1/_3} = \frac{1}{4} \text{ or } 25\%$$

**C)** Taxes paid in advance i.e. prepaid taxes for 3 months are to be credited to Branch Account.

### In the books of Godrej Corporation, Dadar (Head Office)

**Dr.**      **Branch Debtors Account**      **Cr.**

| Particulars | ₹ | Particulars | ₹ |
|---|---|---|---|
| To Balance B/D | 20,000 | By Discount Allowed | 4,000 |
| To Credit Sales | 1,50,000 | By Bad Debts written off | 3,000 |
| | | By Returns Inward | 1,500 |
| | | By Cash received from Debtors | 1,20,000 |
| | | By Balance C/D * | 41,500 |
| | | (Balancing Figure) | |
| | **1,70,000** | | **1,70,000** |

**Dr.**      **Branch Petty Cash Account**      **Cr.**

| Particulars | ₹ | Particulars | ₹ |
|---|---|---|---|
| To Balance B/D | 2,000 | By Actual Petty Expenses | 4,000 |
| To Cheque for Petty Cash | 3,000 | By Balance C/D * | 1,000 |
| | | (Balancing Figure) | |
| | **5,000** | | **5,000** |

**Dr.**      **Goods sent to Branch Account**      **Cr.**

| Particulars | ₹ | Particulars | ₹ |
|---|---|---|---|
| To Chinchwad Branch | 16,000 | By Chinchwad Branch | 2,00,000 |
| (Goods returned) | | (Goods sent) | |
| To Chinchwad Branch | 50,000 | By Chinchwad Branch | 4,000 |
| (Loading in goods sent) | | (Loading in goods returned) | |
| To Trading * | 1,38,000 | | |
| (Balancing Figure) | | | |
| | **2,04,000** | | **2,04,000** |

**Dr.**      **Stock Reserve Account**      **Cr.**

| Particulars | ₹ | Particulars | ₹ |
|---|---|---|---|
| To Chinchwad Branch | 20,000 | By Balance B/D | 20,000 |
| To Balance C/D * | 25,000 | By Chinchwad Branch | 25,000 |
| (Balancing Figure) | | | |
| | **45,000** | | **45,000** |

**Dr.**      **Chinchwad Branch Account for the year ended 31-03-2016**      **Cr.**

| Particulars | | ₹ | Particulars | | ₹ |
|---|---|---|---|---|---|
| To Opening Balances : | | 1,02,000 | By Stock Reserve | | 20,000 |
| i)   Stock | 80,000 | | By Bank : | | 1,50,000 |
| ii)  Debtors | 20,000 | | i)   Cash Sales | 30,000 | |
| iii) Petty Cash   (+) | 2,000 | | ii)  Cash received from | | |
| | | |      Debtors    (+) | 1,20,000 | |
| To Goods sent to Branch | | 2,00,000 | By Goods sent to Branch | | 16,000 |
| | | | Less Return | | |
| To Bank : | | 26,000 | By Closing Balances : | | 1,42,500 |
| i)   Salaries | 12,000 | | i)   Stock | 1,00,000 | |
| ii)  Advertisement | 5,000 | | ii)  Debtors | 41,500 | |
| iii) Petty Cash | 3,000 | | iii) Petty Cash   (+) | 1,000 | |
| iv) Taxes   (+) | 6,000 | | | | |
| To Goods sent to Branch | | 4,000 | By Prepaid Taxes | | 1,500 |
| Less Return Loading | | | | | |
| To Stock Reserve | | 25,000 | By Goods sent to  Branch | | 50,000 |
| To General Profit and Loss | | 23,000 | (Loading) | | |
| (Net Profit C/D) | | | | | |
| | | **3,80,000** | | | **3,80,000** |

### ILLUSTRATION 7

Siddhartha Traders, Nasik has a branch at Aurangabad, to which goods are invoiced at cost plus 33 $\frac{1}{3}$ %. The branch remits all cash received to Head Office daily. All branch expenses are paid from the Head Office.

| | ₹ |
|---|---|
| Branch Stock (1-4-2015) at Invoice Price | 2,40,000 |
| Branch Debtors  (1-4-2015) | 60,000 |
| Petty Cash (1-4-2015) | 8,000 |
| Furniture purchased for the Branch on 1-10-2015 | 40,000 |
| Cash Sales | 1,32,000 |
| Discount to Debtors | 18,000 |
| Bad Debts Written off | 12,000 |
| Returns from Debtors | 6,000 |
| Collection from Debtors | 4,80,000 |
| Goods from Head Office (Invoice Price) | 8,40,000 |
| Goods return to Head Office (Invoice Price) | 72,000 |
| Credit Sales | 6,00,000 |
| Closing Stock (31-3-2016) (Invoice Price) | 2,64,000 |
| Cheques received from H.O. for expenses : | |
|     Petty Cash | 12,000 |
|     Salaries | 8,000 |
|     Rent and Rates | 16,000 |
|     Advertisement | 20,000 |
|     Actual Petty Expenses incurred by the Branch | 14,000 |

Provide depreciation on Branch Fixed Assets @ 5% p.a. as per Written Down Value method.

Prepare Branch Account, Branch Debtors Account and Branch Petty Cash Account as it would appear in the books of Head Office. Also pass the necessary journal entries for cancellation of loading.

| SOLUTION |

**Working Notes :**

**A) Missing items :**

    i)     Closing balance of Branch Debtors Account

    ii)     Closing balance of Branch Petty Cash Account

**B) Calculation of Loading i.e. cost plus 33 $\frac{1}{3}$ %**

$$SP = CP + P$$
$$133\tfrac{1}{3} = 100 + 33\tfrac{1}{3}$$
$$\therefore \quad \frac{P}{SP} = \frac{33\tfrac{1}{3}}{133\tfrac{1}{3}} = \frac{1}{4}$$

**C)** Calculation of depreciation on branch fixed assets i.e. Furniture @ 5% p.a. for 6 months as per Written Down Value method : 5% of ₹ 40,000 for 6 months = ₹ 1,000.

**In the books of Siddartha Traders, Nasik (Head Office)**

**Dr.**          **Aurangabad Branch Account for the year ended 31-3-2016**          **Cr.**

| Particulars | | ₹ | Particulars | | ₹ |
|---|---|---|---|---|---|
| To Opening Balances : | | 3,08,000 | By Stock Reserve | | 60,000 |
| i) Stock | 2,40,000 | | By Bank : | | 6,12,000 |
| ii) Debtors | 60,000 | | i) Cash Sales | 1,32,000 | |
| iii) Petty Cash (+) | 8,000 | | ii) Cash from Debtors | 4,80,000 | |
| | | | By Goods sent to Br. Less Returned | | 72,000 |
| To Bank : | | 96,000 | By Closing Balances : | | 4,53,000 |
| i) Furniture | 40,000 | | i) Stock | 2,64,000 | |
| ii) Petty Cash | 12,000 | | ii) Debtors | 1,44,000 | |
| iii) Salaries | 8,000 | | iii) Petty Cash | 6,000 | |
| iv) Rent and Rates | 16,000 | | iv) Furniture (+) | 39,000 | |
| v) Advertisement (+) | 20,000 | | | | |
| To Goods sent to Branch | | 8,40,000 | By Goods sent to Branch (Loading) | | 2,10,000 |
| To Stock Reserve | | 66,000 | | | |
| To Goods sent to Branch Less Returned (Loading) | | 18,000 | | | |
| To General Profit and Loss * (Net Profit C/D) | | 79,000 | | | |
| | | 14,07,000 | | | 14,07,000 |

**Dr.**          **Branch Debtors Account**          **Cr.**

| Particulars | ₹ | Particulars | ₹ |
|---|---|---|---|
| To Balance B/D | 60,000 | By Discount to Debtors | 18,000 |
| To Credit Sales | 6,00,000 | By Bad Debts | 12,000 |
| | | By Returns from Debtors | 6,000 |
| | | By Collection from Debtors | 4,80,000 |
| | | By Balance C/D * (Balancing Figure) | 1,44,000 |
| | **6,60,000** | | **6,60,000** |

**Dr.**          **Branch Petty Cash Account**          **Cr.**

| Particulars | ₹ | Particulars | ₹ |
|---|---|---|---|
| To Balance B/D | 8,000 | By Actual Petty expenses | 14,000 |
| To Cheque sent to Branch for Petty Cash | 12,000 | | |
| | | By Balance C/D * (Balancing Figure) | 6,000 |
| | **20,000** | | **20,000** |

### Journal Entries for Cancellation of Loading

| Date | Particulars | L.F. | Debit ₹ | Credit ₹ |
|---|---|---|---|---|
| 31-3-2016 | | | | |
| i) | Aurangabad Branch A/c      Dr. | – | 18,000 | |
| |     To Goods sent to Branch A/c | – | | 18,000 |
| | *(Being the journal entry for cancellation of loading in goods returned by branch)* | | | |
| ii) | Aurangabad Branch A/c      Dr. | – | 66,000 | |
| |     To Stock Reserve A/c | – | | 66,000 |
| | *(Being the journal entry for cancellation of loading in closing branch stock)* | | | |
| iii) | Goods sent to Branch A/c      Dr. | – | 2,10,000 | |
| |     To Aurangabad Branch A/c | – | | 2,10,000 |
| | *(Being the journal entry for cancellation of loading in goods supplied to branch)* | | | |
| iv) | Stock Reserve A/c      Dr. | – | 60,000 | |
| |     To Aurangabad Branch A/c | – | | 60,000 |
| | *(Being the journal entry for cancellation of loading in Opening Branch Stock)* | | | |

## (B) Stock and Debtors Method

### ILLUSTRATION 8

Hindustan Traders, Baramati has a branch at Shahapur. Goods are invoiced to branch at cost plus 50%. Branch remits all cash received to head office and all expenses are met by head office. From the following particulars prepare necessary ledger accounts on Stock and Debtors system to show the profits earned at the branch.

|  | ₹ |
|---|---|
| Stock on 1-4-2015, invoice price | 9,300 |
| Debtors on 1-4-2015 | 6,800 |
| Cash in hand on 1-4-2015 | 100 |
| Goods invoiced to branch, cost price | 34,000 |
| Sales at branch : | |
|     i)    Cash | 25,010 |
|     ii)   Credit | 31,000 |
| Petty cash remittance to branch | 400 |
| Cash received on ledger accounts | 30,400 |
| Goods returned by credit customers | 1,200 |
| Goods returned by branch to head office, invoice price | 1,500 |
| Actual petty expenses by branch | 370 |
| Allowances to Debtors | 400 |
| Goods transferred from Shrirampur branch to Shahapur branch | 2,100 |
| Bad debts written off | 600 |
| Shortage of goods | 450 |
| Discount allowed to customers | 200 |
| Rent and Taxes | 3,000 |
| Salaries and Wages | 2,000 |
| Advertisement | 400 |
| Interest charged on the overdues of credit customers | 1,000 |

### SOLUTION

**Working Notes :**

**A) Calculation of Loading i.e. cost plus 50%.**

$$SP = CP + P$$
$$150 = 100 + 50$$
$$\therefore \quad \frac{P}{SP} = \frac{50}{150} = \frac{1}{3}$$

**B) Calculation of invoice price of goods invoiced to branch**

$$IP = CP + P$$
$$₹\,51,000 = ₹\,34,000 + ₹\,17,000 \text{ (i.e. 50\% of CP)}$$

**C)** The entire amount of shortage of goods will be transferred to Branch Adjustment Account.

**D)** Total branch expenses will be transferred to Branch Adjustment Account.

**In the books of Hindustan Trades, Baramati (Head Office)**

**Ledger accounts of Shahapur Branch for the year 2015-2016**

Dr.     **Branch Stock Account**     Cr.

| Particulars | ₹ | Particulars | ₹ |
|---|---|---|---|
| To  Balance B/D | 9,300 | By  Cash | 25,010 |
| To  Goods sent to Branch | 51,000 | (Cash Sales) | |
| (Goods sent to branch) | | By Branch  Debtors | 31,000 |
| To  Branch Debtors | 1,200 | (Credit Sales) | |
| (Return by customers) | | By Goods sent to Branch | 1,500 |
| To  Shrirampur Branch | 2,100 | (Return by branch) | |
| (Goods from Shrirampur) | | By Branch Adjustment | 450 |
| | | (Shortage of goods) | |
| | | By Balance C/D * | 5,640 |
| | | (Balancing Figure) | |
| | **63,600** | | **63,600** |

Dr.     **Branch Petty Cash Account**     Cr.

| Particulars | ₹ | Particulars | ₹ |
|---|---|---|---|
| To Balance B/D | 100 | By Branch Expenses | 370 |
| To Cash | 400 | (Actual Petty Cash Expenses) | |
| (Petty Cash remittances) | | By Balance C/D * | 130 |
| | | (Balancing Figure) | |
| | **500** | | **500** |

Dr.     **Branch Debtors Account**     Cr.

| Particulars | ₹ | Particulars | ₹ |
|---|---|---|---|
| To Balance B/D | 6,800 | By Cash | 30,400 |
| To Branch Stock | 31,000 | (Cash received on ledger accounts) | |
| (Credit Sales) | | By Branch Stock | 1,200 |
| To Branch Adjustment | 1,000 | (Returns by customers) | |
| (Interest charged) | | By Branch Expenses : | 1,200 |
| | | i)  Allowances to debtors  400 | |
| | | ii)  Bad debts written off  600 | |
| | | iii) Discount allowed to | |
| | |   customers  (+) <u>200</u> | |
| | | By Balance C/D * | 6,000 |
| | | (Balancing Figure) | |
| | **38,800** | | **38,800** |

**Dr.**        **Branch Expenses Account**        **Cr.**

| Particulars | | ₹ | Particulars | ₹ |
|---|---|---|---|---|
| To Branch Petty Cash : | | 370 | By Branch Adjustment * | 6,970 |
| i)   Actual Petty Expenses  (+) | 370 | | (Total Branch Expenses transferred) | |
| To Branch Debtors : | | 1,200 | | |
| i)   Allowances to Debtors | 400 | | | |
| ii)  Bad debts written off | 600 | | | |
| iii) Discount allowed to | | | | |
|      customers       (+) | 200 | | | |
| To Cash | | 5,400 | | |
| i)   Rent and Taxes | 3,000 | | | |
| ii)  Salaries & Wages | 2,000 | | | |
| iii) Advertisement | | | | |
| (Expenses for Branch)    (+) | 400 | | | |
| | | **6,970** | | **6,970** |

**Dr.**        **Branch Adjustment Account**        **Cr.**

| Particulars | ₹ | Particulars | ₹ |
|---|---|---|---|
| To Branch Stock | 450 | By Branch Debtors | 1,000 |
| (Shortage of goods) | | (Interest charged) | |
| To Branch Expenses | 6,970 | By Stock Reserve | 3,100 |
| (Total branch expenses) | | (Loading in Opening Stock) | |
| To Goods sent to Branch | 500 | By Goods sent to Branch | 17,000 |
| (Loading in goods returned by branch) | | (Loading in goods sent to branch) | |
| To Stock Reserve | 1,880 | By Shrirampur Branch | 700 |
| (Loading in Closing stock) | | (Loading in goods from | |
| To General Profit and Loss | 12,000 | Shrirampur) | |
| (Net Profit C/D) | | | |
| | **21,800** | | **21,800** |

### ILLUSTRATION 9

Sammy Ltd., Patna has a branch at Bilaspur to which goods are supplied at cost plus 20% profit. Prepare Branch Stock Account, Branch Debtors Account, Branch Petty Cash Account, Branch Expenses Account, and Branch Adjustment Account in the books of Sammy Ltd., Patna-Head Office. Also pass the necessary journal entries to record the undermentioned information relating to Bilaspur Branch for the year 2015-2016.

|  | | ₹ |
|---|---|---|
| Opening balances as on 1-4-2015 : | | |
| i) | Stock of Goods | 42,000 |
| ii) | Debtors | 75,600 |
| iii) | Petty cash | 1,200 |
| Good invoiced to branch | | 2,52,000 |
| Goods returned by branch | | 6,000 |

| | |
|---|---:|
| Cash Turnover | 1,05,000 |
| Sales to credit customers | 1,70,400 |
| Surplus in stock | 23,400 |
| Cash received from debtors | 1,71,000 |
| Allowances to customers | 1,200 |
| Discount allowed to branch debtors | 9,000 |
| Bad debts written off | 3,000 |
| Returns from customers | 3,000 |
| Advertisement | 6,000 |
| Salaries | 20,000 |
| Rent (Including prepaid for 2016-2017 ₹ 800) | 8,000 |
| Cash sent to branch for petty expenses | 2,400 |
| Commission paid | 6,000 |
| Closing balances as on 31-3-2016 | |
|     i)    Debtors | 58,800 |
|     ii)    Petty cash | 600 |

## SOLUTION

**Working Notes :**

**A)** **Calculation of Loading i.e. cost plus 20%.**

$$SP = CP + P$$
$$120 = 100 + 20$$
$$\therefore \quad \frac{P}{SP} = \frac{20}{120} = \frac{1}{6}$$

**B)** Prepaid Rent for 2016-2017 is to be credited to Branch Expenses Account.

**C)** The entire amount of Surplus in Stock will be transferred to Branch Adjustment Account.

**D)** Total Branch Expenses will be transferred to Branch Adjustment Account.

**In the books of Sammy Ltd., Patna (Head Office)**

**Ledger Accounts of Bilaspur Branch for the year 2015-2016**

**Dr.**                            **Branch Stock Account**                            **Cr.**

| Particulars | ₹ | Particulars | ₹ |
|---|---:|---|---:|
| To Balance B/D | 42,000 | By Goods sent to Branch | 6,000 |
| To Goods sent to Branch | 2,52,000 | (Return by Branch) | |
| (Goods invoiced to Branch) | | By Cash | 1,05,000 |
| To Branch Adjustment | 23,400 | (Cash turnover) | |
| (Surplus in Stock) | | By Branch Debtors | 1,70,400 |
| To Branch Debtors | 3,000 | (Credit Sales) | |
| (Returns from customers) | | By Balance C/D * | 39,000 |
| | | (Balancing Figure) | |
| | **3,20,400** | | **3,20,400** |

**Dr.**     **Branch Debtors Account**     **Cr.**

| Particulars | ₹ | Particulars | ₹ |
|---|---|---|---|
| To Balance B/D | 75,600 | By Cash | 1,71,000 |
| To Branch Stock | 1,70,400 | (Cash received from debtors) | |
| (Credit Sales) | | By Branch Expenses : | 13,200 |
| | | i)    Allowances to customers    1,200 | |
| | | ii)    Discount Allowed to Branch    9,000 Debtors | |
| | | iii)    Bad debts written off    (+)    3,000 | |
| | | By Branch Stock | 3,000 |
| | | (Returns from customers) | |
| | | By Balance C/D | 58,800 |
| | **2,46,000** | | **2,46,000** |

**Dr.**     **Branch Petty Cash Account**     **Cr.**

| Particulars | ₹ | Particulars | ₹ |
|---|---|---|---|
| To Balance B/D | 1,200 | By Branch Expenses * | 3,000 |
| To Cash | 2,400 | (Balancing Figure) | |
| (Cash sent to branch for petty expenses) | | By Balance C/D | 600 |
| | **3,600** | | **3,600** |

**Dr.**     **Branch Expenses Account**     **Cr.**

| Particulars | | ₹ | Particulars | ₹ |
|---|---|---|---|---|
| To Branch Debtors : | | 13,200 | By Prepaid Rent | 800 |
| i)   Allowances to Customers | 1,200 | | (Prepaid Rent for 2015-2016 adjusted) | |
| ii)   Discount Allowed to Branch Debtors | 9,000 | | By Branch Adjustment * | 55,400 |
| iii)   Bad debts written off   (+) | 3,000 | | (Total Branch expenses transferred) | |
| To Cash : | | 40,000 | | |
| i)   Advertisement | 6,000 | | | |
| ii)   Salaries | 20,000 | | | |
| iii)   Rent | 8,000 | | | |
| iv)   Commission   (+) | 6,000 | | | |
|     (Expenses for branch) | | | | |
| To Branch Petty Cash : | | 3,000 | | |
| i)   Actual Petty Expenses   (+) | 3,000 | | | |
| | | **56,200** | | **56,200** |

Dr.      **Branch Adjustment Account**      Cr.

| Particulars | ₹ | Particulars | ₹ |
|---|---|---|---|
| To Branch Expenses (Total Branch Expenses) | 55,400 | By Branch Stock (Surplus in Stock) | 23,400 |
| To Goods sent to Branch (Loading in goods returned by branch) | 1,000 | By Stock Reserve (Loading in Opening Stock) | 7,000 |
| To Stock Reserve (Loading in Closing stock) | 6,500 | By Goods sent to Branch (Loading in goods sent to branch) | 42,000 |
| To General Profit and Loss A/c * (Net Profit C/D) | 9,500 | | |
| | 72,400 | | 72,400 |

### Journal Entries in the books of Sammy Ltd., Patna (Head Office)

| Date 2015-2016 | Particulars | L.F. | Debit ₹ | Credit ₹ |
|---|---|---|---|---|
| 1. | Branch Stock A/c    Dr. | – | 2,52,000 | |
| |    To Goods sent to Branch A/c | – | | 2,52,000 |
| | (Being goods invoiced to Branch) | | | |
| 2. | Goods sent to Branch A/c    Dr. | – | 6,000 | |
| |    To Branch Stock A/c | – | | 6,000 |
| | (Being goods returned by Branch) | | | |
| 3. | Cash A/c    Dr. | – | 1,05,000 | |
| |    To Branch Stock A/c | – | | 1,05,000 |
| | (Being cash turnover made) | | | |
| 4. | Branch Debtors A/c    Dr. | – | 1,70,400 | |
| |    To Branch Stock A/c | – | | 1,70,400 |
| | (Being goods sold to credit customers) | | | |
| 5. | Branch Stock A/c    Dr. | – | 23,400 | |
| |    To Branch Adjustment A/c | – | | 23,400 |
| | (Being surplus in stock recorded) | | | |
| 6. | Cash A/c    Dr. | – | 1,71,000 | |
| |    To Branch Debtors A/c | – | | 1,71,000 |
| | (Being cash received from Debtors) | | | |
| 7. | Branch Expenses A/c    Dr. | – | 13,200 | |
| |    To Branch Debtors A/c | – | | 13,200 |
| | (Being allowances to debtors, discount allowed to debtors and the bad debts written-off transferred to Branch Expenses A/c). | | | |
| 8. | Branch Stock A/c    Dr. | – | 3,000 | |
| |    To Branch Debtors A/c | – | | 3,000 |
| | (Being returns from customer's recorded) | | | |

| Date<br>2015-<br>2016 | Particulars | L.F. | Debit<br>₹ | Credit<br>₹ |
|---|---|---|---|---|
| 9. | Branch Expenses A/c      Dr. | – | 40,000 | |
| | To Cash A/c | – | | 40,000 |
| | (Being Advertisement, Salaries, Rent and Commission paid for branch) | | | |
| 10. | Prepaid Rent A/c      Dr. | – | 800 | |
| | To Branch Expenses A/c | – | | 800 |
| | (Being Prepaid rent for 2015-2016 adjusted) | | | |
| 11. | Branch Petty Cash A/c      Dr. | – | 2,400 | |
| | To Cash A/c | – | | 2,400 |
| | (Being cash sent to branch for petty expenses) | | | |
| 12. | Branch Expenses A/c      Dr. | – | 3,000 | |
| | To Branch Petty Cash A/c | – | | 3,000 |
| | (Being actual petty expenses transferred from Branch Petty Cash A/c) | | | |
| 13. | Branch Adjustment A/c      Dr. | – | 55,400 | |
| | To Branch Expenses A/c | – | | 55,400 |
| | (Being Total Branch expenses transferred to Branch Adjustment A/c) | | | |
| 14. | Stock Reserve A/c      Dr. | – | 7,000 | |
| | To Branch Adjustment A/c | – | | 7,000 |
| | (Being the journal entry for cancellation of loading in opening stock) | | | |
| 15. | Goods sent to Branch A/c      Dr. | – | 42,000 | |
| | To Branch Adjustment A/c | – | | 42,000 |
| | (Being the journal entry for cancellation of loading in goods sent to branch) | | | |
| 16. | Branch Adjustment A/c      Dr. | – | 1,000 | |
| | To Goods sent to Branch A/c | – | | 1,000 |
| | (Being the journal entry for cancellation of loading in goods returned by branch) | | | |
| 17. | Branch Adjustment A/c      Dr. | – | 6,500 | |
| | To Stock Reserve A/c | – | | 6,500 |
| | (Being the journal entry for cancellation of loading in closing stock) | | | |
| 18. | Branch Adjustment A/c      Dr. | – | 9,500 | |
| | To General Profit and Loss A/c | – | | 9,500 |
| | (Being net profit transferred to General Profit and Loss Account) | | | |

## ILLUSTRATION 10

Tobacco Co., Talegaon has a branch at Malegaon to which goods are invoiced at $33\tfrac{1}{3}\%$ profit on loaded price. Branch remits all cash received to head office and expenses are met by head office. From the following particulars prepare Branch Stock Account, Branch Debtors Account, Branch Expenses Account, Branch Adjustment Account and Branch Profit and Loss Account in the ledger of Tobacco Co., Talegaon, Head Office for 2015-2016.

|  |  | ₹ |
|---|---|---|
| Opening balances as on 1-4-2015 : |  |  |
| i) | Stock | 2,67,000 |
| ii) | Debtors | 14,000 |
| iii) | Furniture | 10,000 |
| Selling for cash | | 7,29,400 |
| Cash collection from credit customers | | 28,000 |
| Goods returned by branch to head office | | 11,700 |
| Goods returned by customers to branch | | 5,700 |
| Discount allowed | | 1,200 |
| Goods transferred by Malegaon Branch to Manmad Branch | | 45,000 |
| Goods supplied to Branch | | 7,83,000 |
| Bad debts written off | | 1,500 |
| Publicity charges | | 15,600 |
| Miscellaneous expenses | | 5,000 |
| Salaries and Wages | | 30,000 |
| Closing balances as on 31-3-2016 : |  |  |
| i) | Debtors | 9,600 |
| ii) | Furniture | 9,000 |

Goods at the invoice price of ₹ 6,600 were destroyed in transit from Talegaon Head Office to Malegaon Branch. A claim was made with the Insurance Company for loss of stock and ₹ 5,800 were accepted in settlement of the claim.

## SOLUTION

**Working Notes :**

**A)** **Calculation of Loading i.e. $33\tfrac{1}{3}$ % on loaded price**

$$SP = CP + P$$
$$\text{(i.e. loaded price) } 100 = 66\tfrac{2}{3} + 33\tfrac{1}{3}$$
$$\therefore \quad \frac{P}{SP} = \frac{33\tfrac{1}{3}}{100} = \frac{1}{3}$$

**B)** Goods transferred by Malegaon Branch to Manmad Branch will be credited to Branch Stock Account.

**C)** Goods destroyed in transit credited to Branch Stock Account will be adjusted as follows :

(i) Loading (i.e. $\tfrac{1}{3}$) will be transferred to Branch Adjustment Account.

(ii) Cost price (i.e. $\tfrac{2}{3}$) will be transferred to Branch Profit and Loss Account.

**D)** Total Branch Expenses will be transferred to Branch Profit and Loss Account.

## In the books of Tobacco Co., Talegaon (Head Office)

### Ledger accounts of Malegaon Branch for the year 2015-2016

**Dr.**            **Branch Stock Account**            **Cr.**

| Particulars | ₹ | Particulars | ₹ |
|---|---|---|---|
| To Balance B/D | 2,67,000 | By Cash | 7,29,400 |
| To Branch Debtors | 5,700 | (Cash Sales) | |
| (Returned by customers) | | By Goods sent to Branch | 11,700 |
| To Goods sent to Branch | 7,83,000 | (Goods returned by Branch) | |
| (Goods supplied to branch) | | By Goods sent to Branch | 45,000 |
| | | (Transfer to Manmad Branch) | |
| | | By Goods destroyed in Transit | 6,600 |
| | | i)  Branch Adjustment ($^1/_3$)  2,200 | |
| | | ii) Branch Profit and Loss ($^2/_3$)  (+) 4,400 | |
| | | By Branch Debtors | 32,000 |
| | | (Credit Sales) | |
| | | By Balance C/D * | 2,31,000 |
| | | (Balancing Figure) | |
| | **10,55,700** | | **10,55,700** |

**Dr.**            **Branch Debtors Account**            **Cr.**

| Particulars | ₹ | Particulars | ₹ |
|---|---|---|---|
| To Balance B/D | 14,000 | By Cash | 28,000 |
| To Branch Stock * | 32,000 | (Collection from Debtors) | |
| (Balancing figure i.e. Credit | | By Branch Stock | 5,700 |
| Sales) | | (Returned by customers) | |
| | | By Branch Expenses | 2,700 |
| | | i)    Discount Allowed  1,200 | |
| | | ii)   Bad Debts written off  (+) 1,500 | |
| | | By Balance C/D | 9,600 |
| | **46,000** | | **46,000** |

**Dr.**            **Branch Expenses Account**            **Cr.**

| Particulars | ₹ | Particulars | ₹ |
|---|---|---|---|
| To Branch Debtors : | 2,700 | By Branch Profit and Loss | 53,300 |
| i)    Discount Allowed  1,200 | | (Total Branch Expenses transferred) | |
| ii)   Bad Debts written off  (+) 1,500 | | | |
| To Cash : | 50,600 | | |
| i)    Publicity charges  15,600 | | | |
| ii)   Miscellaneous expenses  5,000 | | | |
| iii)  Salaries and Wages  (+) 30,000 | | | |
|    (Expenses for Branch) | | | |
| | **53,300** | | **53,300** |

**Dr.**          **Branch Adjustment Account**          **Cr.**

| Particulars | ₹ | Particulars | ₹ |
|---|---|---|---|
| To Branch Stock (Goods destroyed in transit) | 2,200 | By Stock Reserve (Loading in Opening Stock) | 89,000 |
| To Goods sent to Branch (Loading in goods returned by Branch) | 3,900 | By Goods sent to Branch (Loading in goods supplied to Branch) | 2,61,000 |
| To Goods sent to Branch (Loading in goods transferred to Manmad Branch) | 15,000 | | |
| To Stock Reserve (Loading in Closing stock) | 77,000 | | |
| To Gross Profit C/D * | 2,51,900 | | |
| | **3,50,000** | | **3,50,000** |

**Dr.**          **Branch Profit and Loss Account**          **Cr.**

| Particulars | ₹ | Particulars | ₹ |
|---|---|---|---|
| To Branch Stock (Goods destroyed in transit) | 4,400 | By Cash (Recovery of claim from Insurance Company) | 5,800 |
| To Branch Expenses (Total Branch Expenses) | 53,300 | By Gross Profit B/D | 2,51,900 |
| To Depreciation on Furniture $\left(\begin{array}{ccc}\text{Opening} & \text{Closing} & \text{Dep.}\\ \text{Rs. 10,000} - \text{Rs. 9,000} = \text{Rs. 1,000}\end{array}\right)$ | 1,000 | | |
| To General Profit and Loss * (Net Profit C/D) | 1,99,000 | | |
| | **2,57,700** | | **2,57,700** |

## ILLUSTRATION 11

Texmo Ltd., Bengaluru has a branch at Porbandar to which goods are invoiced so as to have 10% bearing on market price. The Porbandar Branch has sent the following figures for the year 2015-2016.

| | ₹ |
|---|---|
| Stock on 1-4-2015 | 15,000 |
| Stock on 31-3-2016 | 13,900 |
| Debtors on 1-4-2015 | 26,200 |
| Debtors on 31-3-2016 | 33,100 |
| Goods received from head office | 80,800 |
| Goods returned to head office | 700 |
| Cash Sales | 31,400 |
| Credit Sales | 60,000 |
| Allowances to Customers | 580 |
| Returns from Customers | 200 |
| Discount Allowed to Customers | 2,400 |

| | |
|---|---:|
| Bad debts | 600 |
| Rent | 1,800 |
| Salaries | 6,000 |
| General charges | 1,300 |
| Rent due but not paid for 2015-2016 | 100 |
| Miscellaneous Income | 660 |

All items of stock are at invoice price. All expenses are paid by head office and all cash received is daily banked into the head office account.

You are required to prepare,

i)    Branch Stock Account
ii)   Goods sent to Branch Account
iii)  Stock Reserve Account
iv)   Branch Debtors Account
v)    Branch Expenses Account
vi)   Branch Adjustment Account
vii)  Branch Profit and Loss Account

### SOLUTION

**Working Notes :**

**A)   Calculation of Loading i.e. 10% on Market Price**

$$\text{SP (i.e. market price 100)} = \text{CP} + \text{P}$$
$$100 = 90 + 10$$
$$\therefore \quad \frac{P}{SP} = \frac{10}{100} + \frac{1}{10}$$

**B)**   Rent due but not paid for 2015-2016 is to be debited to Branch Expenses Account.

**C)**   The difference in Branch Stock Account i.e. surplus in stock will be adjusted as follows :

i)    Loading (i.e. $^1/_{10}$) will be transferred to Branch Adjustment Account.

ii)   Cost Price (i.e. $^9/_{10}$) will be transferred to Branch Profit and Loss Account.

**D)**   Total Branch Expenses will be transferred to Branch Profit and Loss Account.

**E)**   Miscellaneous Income is to be credited to Branch Profit and Loss Account.

**In the books of Texmo Ltd., Bengaluru (H.O.)**

**Ledger Accounts of Porbandar Branch for the year 2015-2016**

Dr.                                **Branch Stock Account**                                Cr.

| Particulars | ₹ | Particulars | ₹ |
|---|---:|---|---:|
| To Balance B/D | 15,000 | By  Goods sent to Branch | 700 |
| To  Goods sent to Branch | 80,800 | By  Bank | 31,400 |
| (Goods from H.O.) | | (Cash Sales) | |
| To Branch  Debtors | 200 | By  Branch Debtors | 60,000 |
| (Returns from customers) | | (Credit Sales) | |
| To  Surplus in Stock * | 10,000 | | |
| i)   Branch Adjustment ($^1/_{10}$) 1,000 | | | |
| ii)  Branch Profit and Loss A/c | | | |
| (+) ($^9/_{10}$) 9,000 | | | |
| (Balancing Figure) | | By  Balance C/D | 13,900 |
| | 1,06,000 | | 1,06,000 |

**Dr.**        **Branch Debtors Account**        **Cr.**

| Particulars | ₹ | Particulars | ₹ |
|---|---|---|---|
| To Balance B/D | 26,200 | By Branch Expenses : | 3,580 |
| To Branch Stock | 60,000 | i) Allowances to Customers 580 | |
| (Credit Sales) | | ii) Discount Allowed to cust. 2,400 | |
| | | iii) Bad Debts (+) 600 | |
| | | By Branch Stock | 200 |
| | | (Returns from customers) | |
| | | By Cash * | 49,320 |
| | | (Balancing Figure i.e. collection | |
| | | from debtors) | |
| | | By Balance C/D | 33,100 |
| | **86,200** | | **86,200** |

**Dr.**        **Goods Sent to Branch Account**        **Cr.**

| Particulars | ₹ | Particulars | ₹ |
|---|---|---|---|
| To Branch Stock | 700 | By Branch Stock | 80,800 |
| (Goods returned to H.O.) | | (Goods from H.O.) | |
| To Branch Adjustment | 8,080 | By Branch Adjustment | 70 |
| (Loading in goods from H.O.) | | (Loading in goods returned to H.O.) | |
| To Trading A/c * | 72,090 | | |
| (Balancing Figure) | | | |
| | **80,870** | | **80,870** |

**Dr.**        **Branch Expenses Account**        **Cr.**

| Particulars | ₹ | Particulars | ₹ |
|---|---|---|---|
| To Branch Debtors : | 3,580 | By Branch Profit and Loss * | 12,780 |
| i) Allowances to Customers 580 | | (Total branch expenses | |
| ii) Disc. Allowed to Customers 2,400 | | transferred) | |
| iii) Bad Debts (+) 600 | | | |
| To Bank : | 9,100 | | |
| i) Rent 1,800 | | | |
| ii) Salaries 6,000 | | | |
| iii) General charges (+) 1,300 | | | |
| (Expenses for Branch) | | | |
| To Rent due but not paid for 2015-2016 | 100 | | |
| (Outstanding rent for 2015-16 adjusted) | | | |
| | **12,780** | | **12,780** |

**Dr.**        **Branch Adjustment Account**        **Cr.**

| Particulars | ₹ | Particulars | ₹ |
|---|---|---|---|
| To Goods sent to Branch | 70 | By Branch Stock | 1,000 |
| (Loading in goods returned to H.O.) | | (Surplus in Stock) | |
| To Stock Reserve | 1,390 | By Stock Reserve | 1,500 |
| (Loading in Closing Stock) | | (Loading in Opening Stock) | |
| | | By Goods sent to Branch | 8,080 |
| | | (Loading in goods from H.O.) | |
| To Gross Profit C/D * | 9,120 | | |
| | **10,580** | | **10,580** |

**Dr.**      **Branch Profit and Loss Account**      **Cr.**

| Particulars | ₹ | Particulars | ₹ |
|---|---|---|---|
| To Branch Expenses | 12,780 | By Branch Stock | 9,000 |
| (Total Branch Expenses) | | (Surplus in Stock) | |
| | | By Gross Profit B/D | 9,120 |
| To General Profit and Loss A/c * | 6,000 | By Miscellaneous Income | 660 |
| (Net Profit C/D) | | | |
| | **18,780** | | **18,780** |

**Dr.**      **Stock Reserve Account**      **Cr.**

| Particulars | ₹ | Particulars | ₹ |
|---|---|---|---|
| To Branch Adjustment | 1,500 | By Balance B/D | 1,500 |
| (Loading in Opening Stock) | | | |
| To Balance C/D * | 1,390 | By Branch Adjustment | 1,390 |
| (Balancing Figure) | | (Loading in Closing Stock) | |
| | **2,890** | | **2,890** |

## (C) Branch Trading and Profit and Loss Account Method

### ILLUSTRATION 12

Sarda Bros., Chennai, has a branch at Shahapur. Branch sells the goods for cash and credit. Goods are supplied from Chennai at cost price and all expenses are paid by Head Office only. From the following particulars prepare Shahapur Branch Trading and Profit and Loss Account and a Shahapur Branch Account in the books of the Head Office.

|  | ₹ |
|---|---|
| Opening balances as on 1-4-2015 | |
|     i)   Stock at cost price | 9,000 |
|     ii)  Debtors | 23,000 |
|     iii) Petty cash | 300 |
| Goods from Head Office | 57,000 |
| Goods returned by customers | 500 |
| Total turnover during the year | 80,000 |
| Goods returned to Head Office | 700 |
| Cash Sales | 24,000 |
| Discount allowed to customers | 2,300 |
| Allowances to Debtors | 300 |
| Bad Debts | 400 |
| Rent and Rates | 1,800 |
| Salaries | 3,000 |
| Wages | 2,200 |
| Petty expenses paid by Branch | 1,500 |
| Loss of goods at Branch Office | 1,200 |
| Closing balances as on 31-3-2016 | |
|     (i)   Stock at cost price | 12,000 |
|     (ii)  Debtors | 24,000 |
|     (iii) Petty cash | 200 |

SOLUTION

**In the books of Sarda Bros., Chennai, (Head Office)**

**Dr.**      Shahapur Branch Trading Account for the year ended 31-3-2016      **Cr.**

| Particulars | | ₹ | Particulars | | | ₹ |
|---|---|---|---|---|---|---|
| To Opening Stock | | 9,000 | By Sales | | | 79,500 |
| To Purchases | 57,000 | 56,300 | (i) Credit | | 56,000 | |
| Less : Returns Outward(–) | 700 | | (ii) Cash | (+) | 24,000 | |
| | | | | | 80,000 | |
| | | | Less : Returns Inward | (–) | 500 | |
| To Wages | | 2,200 | By Closing Stock | | | 12,000 |
| To Gross Profit C/D * | | 25,200 | By Loss of goods | | | 1,200 |
| | | **92,700** | | | | **92,700** |

**Dr.**      Shahapur Branch Profit and Loss Account for the year ended 31-3-2016      **Cr.**

| Particulars | ₹ | Particulars | ₹ |
|---|---|---|---|
| To Discount Allowed | 2,300 | By Gross Profit B/D | 25,200 |
| To Allowances to Debtors | 300 | | |
| To Bad Debts | 400 | | |
| To Rent and Rates | 1,800 | | |
| To Salaries | 3,000 | | |
| To Petty Expenses | 1,500 | | |
| To Loss of goods | 1,200 | | |
| To General Profit and Loss | | | |
| (Net Profit C/D *) | 14,700 | | |
| | **25,200** | | **25,200** |

**Working Notes :**

**A)**   **Missing items :**
   i)     Cash sent to Branch for Petty expenses.
   ii)    Collection from Debtors.
   iii)   Credit Sales :    Total Sales – Cash Sales = Credit Sales
                    ₹ 80,000   –   ₹ 24,000 =   ₹ 56,000

**Dr.**      Shahapur Branch Account for the year ended 31-03-2016      **Cr.**

| Particulars | | ₹ | Particulars | | ₹ |
|---|---|---|---|---|---|
| To Opening Balances : | | 32,300 | By Bank : | | 75,500 |
| i)   Stock | 9,000 | | i)   Cash Sales | 24,000 | |
| ii)   Debtors | 23,000 | | ii) Collection from Debtors (+) | 51,500 | |
| 3.   Petty cash   (+) | 300 | | | | |
| To Goods sent to Branch | | 57,000 | By Goods sent to Branch Less Returned | | 700 |
| To Bank : | | 8,400 | | | |
| i)   Rent and Rates | 1,800 | | By Closing Balances : | | 36,200 |
| ii)   Salaries | 3,000 | | i)    Stock | 12,000 | |
| iii) Wages | 2,200 | | ii)   Debtors | 24,000 | |
| iv) Petty Cash   (+) | 1,400 | | iii) Petty Cash   (+) | 200 | |
| To Net Profit transferred | | 14,700 | | | |
| to General Profit and Loss | | | | | |
| | | **1,12,400** | | | **1,12,400** |

**Dr.**       **Branch Petty Cash Account**       **Cr.**

| Particulars | ₹ | Particulars | ₹ |
|---|---|---|---|
| To Balance B/D | 300 | By Petty expenses by Branch | 1,500 |
| To Goods sent to Branch for Petty expenses * (Balancing Figure) | 1,400 | By Balance C/D | 200 |
| | **1,700** | | **1,700** |

**Dr.**       **Branch Debtors Account**       **Cr.**

| Particulars | ₹ | Particulars | ₹ |
|---|---|---|---|
| To Balance B/D | 23,000 | By Goods returned by customers | 500 |
| To Credit Sales | 56,000 | By Discount allowed to customers | 2,300 |
| | | By Allowances to Debtors | 300 |
| | | By Bad Debts | 400 |
| | | By Collection from Debtors * (Balancing Figure) | 51,500 |
| | | By Balance C/D | 24,000 |
| | **79,000** | | **79,000** |

### ILLUSTRATION 13

Gemini Bros, Sangli has a branch at Satara. All goods required for sale at Satara are supplied from Sangli at cost plus $1/4$. All cash received at the branch is remitted to Head Office immediately. From the following particulars prepare :

i)   Satara Branch Account.

ii)   Satara Branch Trading and Profit and Loss Account for the year ended 31-3-2016 in the books of Gemini Bros., Sangli Head Office.

| Particulars | Balances as on 1-4-2015 ₹ | Balances as on 31-03-2016 ₹ |
|---|---|---|
| Stock | 20,000 | 15,000 |
| Debtors | 15,000 | 39,500 |
| Furniture | 10,000 | 8,000 |
| Petty Cash | 200 | ? |

| | ₹ |
|---|---|
| Goods returned by Debtors | 800 |
| Goods invoiced to Branch | 50,000 |
| Goods returned by Branch | 2,000 |
| Bad Debts written off | 500 |
| Reserve for bad and doubtful debts | 3,000 |
| Cash Sales during the year | 3,000 |
| Goods destroyed in transit not insured | 1,000 |
| Allowances given | 900 |
| Branch expenses paid by head office : | |
|     i)   Wages | 1,000 |
|     ii)   Printing | 800 |
|     iii)   Rent | 3,000 |

|  |  |  |  |
|---|---|---|---|
| iv) | Salary |  | 3,000 |
| v) | Carriage |  | 600 |
| vi) | Sundry expenses |  | 1,000 |
| vii) | Trade expenses |  | 500 |
| Petty cash expenses at branch |  |  | 500 |
| Total cash remittances by branch |  |  | 43,300 |
| Remittances to branch for petty expenses |  |  | 600 |

**SOLUTION**

**Working Notes :**

**A) Missing items :**

i) Credit Sales

ii) Closing balance of Branch Petty Cash A/c

iii) Cash collection from Debtors

Total cash remittances by branch – Cash Sales = Collection from Debtors

$$₹\,43,200 \quad - ₹\,3,000 \quad = ₹\,40,300$$

**B) Calculation of Loading i.e. cost plus $^1/_4$**

$$SP = CP + P$$
$$125 = 100 + 25 \text{ (i.e. } ^1/_4 \text{ of CP)}$$
$$\therefore \quad \frac{P}{SP} = \frac{25}{125} = \frac{1}{5}$$

**C)** Reserve for bad and doubtful debts are to be debited to Branch A/c.

**In the books of Gemini Bros. Sangli (Head Office)**

Dr.      **Branch Debtors Account**      Cr.

| Particulars | ₹ | Particulars | ₹ |
|---|---|---|---|
| To Balance B/D | 15,000 | By Goods Returned by Debtors | 800 |
| To Credit Sales * | 67,000 | By Bad Debts written off | 500 |
| (Balancing figure) |  | By Allowances given | 900 |
|  |  | By Collection from Debtors | 40,300 |
|  |  | By Balance C/D | 39,500 |
|  | **82,000** |  | **82,000** |

Dr.      **Branch Petty Cash Account**      Cr.

| Particulars | ₹ | Particulars | ₹ |
|---|---|---|---|
| To Balance B/D | 200 | By Petty Cash Expenses | 500 |
| To Remittances for Petty | 600 | By Balance C/D * | 300 |
| Expenses |  | (Balancing figure) |  |
|  | **800** |  | **800** |

**Dr.**  **Satara Branch Account for the year ended 31-3-2016**  **Cr.**

| Particulars | | ₹ | Particulars | | ₹ |
|---|---|---|---|---|---|
| To Opening Balances : | | 45,200 | By Stock Reserve | | 4,000 |
| i)   Stock | 20,000 | | By Bank : | | 43,300 |
| ii)  Debtors | 15,000 | | i)  Cash Sales | 3,000 | |
| iii) Furniture | 10,000 | | ii) Collection from | | |
| iv) Petty Cash   (+) | 200 | |     Debtors   (+) | 40,300 | |
| To Goods sent to Branch | | 50,000 | By Goods sent to Branch Less Returned | | 2,000 |
| To Bank : | | 10,500 | By Closing Balances : | | 62,800 |
| i)   Wages | 1,000 | | i)   Stock | 15,000 | |
| ii)  Printing | 800 | | ii)  Debtors | 39,500 | |
| iii) Rent | 3,000 | | iii) Furniture | 8,000 | |
| iv) Salary | 3,000 | | iv) Petty Cash  (+) | 300 | |
| v)   Carriage | 600 | | | | |
| vi) Sundry Expenses | 1,000 | | | | |
| vii) Trade Expenses | 500 | | | | |
| viii)Petty Expenses  (+) | 600 | | | | |
| To Reserve for bad and doubtful debts | | 3,000 | By Goods sent to Branch (Loading) | | 10,000 |
| To Goods sent to Branch Less Returned (Loading) | | 400 | | | |
| To Stock Reserve | | 3,000 | | | |
| To Net Profit transferred to General Profit and Loss | | 10,000 | | | |
| | | **1,22,100** | | | **1,22,100** |

  In **Branch Trading Account** all items of stock i.e. Opening stock, Goods sent to Branch (i.e. purchases), Goods returned by Branch (i.e. returns outward), Closing Stock, Goods destroyed in Transit etc. **must be recorded at cost price**, which are to be calculated as follows :

    Invoice price – Loading = Cost Price.

| Particulars | | Invoice Price ₹ | Loading ₹ | Cost Price ₹ |
|---|---|---|---|---|
| Opening Stock as on 1-4-2015 | – | 20,000 | 4,000 | 16,000 |
| Goods invoiced to Branch | – | 50,000 | 10,000 | 40,000 |
| Goods returned by Branch | – | 2,000 | 400 | 1,600 |
| Closing stock as on 31-3-2016 | – | 15,000 | 3,000 | 12,000 |
| Good destroyed in Transit | – | 1,000 | 200 | 800 |

**Dr.**      **Satara Branch Trading Account for the year ended 31-3-2016**      **Cr.**

| Particulars | ₹ | Particulars | ₹ |
|---|---|---|---|
| To Opening Stock | 16,000 | By Sales | 69,200 |
| To Purchases    40,000 | 38,400 | i)   Credit    67,000 | |
| **Less :** Returns | | ii)   Cash    (+)    3,000 | |
|     Outward    (–)   1,600 | |     70,000 | |
| To Wages | 1,000 | **Less :** Returns Inward   (–)    800 | |
| To Carriage | 600 | By Closing Stock | 12,000 |
| To Trade Expenses | 500 | By   Goods destroyed in Transit | 800 |
| To Gross Profit C/D * | 25,500 | | |
| | **82,000** | | **82,000** |

**Dr.**      **Satara Branch Profit and Loss Account for the year ended 31-3-2016**      **Cr.**

| Particulars | ₹ | Particulars | ₹ |
|---|---|---|---|
| To Bad Debts | 500 | By Gross Profit B/D | 25,500 |
| To Reserve for bad and doubtful debts | 3,000 | | |
| To Goods destroyed in transit | 800 | | |
| To Allowances | 900 | | |
| To Printing | 800 | | |
| To Rent | 3,000 | | |
| To Salary | 3,000 | | |
| To Sundry Expenses | 1,000 | | |
| To Petty Cash Expenses | 500 | | |
| To Depreciation on Furniture : | 2,000 | | |
|      Opening    10,000 | | | |
| **Less :** Closing   (–)    8,000 | | | |
| To General Profit and Loss* (Net Profit C/D) | 10,000 | | |
| | **25,500** | | **25,500** |

## ILLUSTRATION 14

Anant Trade Centre of Delhi has a branch at Agra to which goods are supplied at fixed selling price which is 25% on cost. All expenses of the branch are met by the Head Office and all cash received by the branch is remitted to the Head Office only.

From the following transactions relating to Agra Branch for the year 2015-2016, prepare Branch Account, Branch Trading and Profit and Loss Account for the year ended 31st March 2016 in the books of Head Office.

|  | ₹ |
|---|---|
| Stock as on 1.4.2015 (Invoice Price) | 30,000 |
| Branch Debtors as on 1.4.2015 | 16,000 |
| Petty Cash as on 1.4.2015 | 400 |
| Furniture as on 1.4.2015 | 10,000 |
| Goods sent by Head Office (Invoice Price) | 2,50,000 |

Cheques sent for Branch expenses :

| | ₹ | ₹ |
|---|---|---|
| • Petty Cash | 1,200 | |
| • Salaries and Wages | 10,000 | |
| • Rent | (+) 6,000 | 17,200 |

| | ₹ |
|---|---|
| Goods returned to Head Office at Invoice Price | 2,000 |
| Cash Sales | 26,000 |
| Cash collected from Debtors | 1,60,000 |
| Credit Sales | 1,74,000 |
| Bad Debts written off | 2,000 |
| Discount Allowed | 1,600 |
| Credit Sales returned | 2,400 |
| Goods sent by Head Office at Invoice price but not received by the branch upto 31.3.2016 | 10,000 |
| Shortage in goods at Invoice price | 400 |
| Branch Debtors 31.3.2016 | 24,000 |
| Petty cash 31.3.2016 | 800 |
| Stock as on 31.3.2016 (Invoice Price) | 70,000 |

Provide depreciation on Furniture @ 10% p.a.

## SOLUTION

**Working Notes :**

A) Calculation of Loading i.e. 25% on cost

$$SP = CP + P$$
$$125 \quad 100 \quad 25$$

$$\therefore \quad \frac{P}{SP} = \frac{25}{125} = \frac{1}{5}$$

B) Goods sent by HO at invoice price but not received by the Branch upto 31.3.2016 i.e. Goods in Transit which is to be credited to the Branch Account.

**In the Books of Anant Trade Centre, Delhi (Head Office)**

Dr.        **Agra Branch Account for the year ended 31.3.2016**        Cr.

| Particulars | | ₹ | Particulars | | ₹ |
|---|---|---|---|---|---|
| To Opening Balances : | | 56,400 | By Stock Reserve | | 6,000 |
| i) Stock | 30,000 | | By Bank : | | 1,86,000 |
| ii) Debtors | 16,000 | | i) Cash sales | 26,000 | |
| iii) Petty Cash | 400 | | ii) Collection from | | |
| iv) Furniture | (+) 10,000 | | Debtors | (+) 1,60,000 | |
| To Goods sent to Branch | | 2,50,000 | By Goods sent to Branch Less | | |
| To Bank | | 17,200 | Returned | | 2,000 |
| i) Petty Cash | 1,200 | | By Closing Balances : | | 1,03,800 |
| ii) Salaries and Wages | 10,000 | | i) Stock | 70,000 | |
| iii) Rent | (+) 6,000 | | ii) Debtors | 24,000 | |
| To Goods sent to Branch Less | | | iii) Petty Cash | 800 | |
| Returned (Loading) | | 400 | iv) Furniture | (+) 9,000 | |
| To Stock Reserve | | 14,000 | | 10,000 | |
| To Goods in Transit (Loading) | | 2,000 | (–) Dep. 10% p.a. | 1,000 | |
| To Net Profit transferred to General | | 17,800 | By Goods in Transit | | 10,000 |
| Profit and Loss | | | By Goods sent to Branch | | |
| | | | (Loading) | | 50,000 |
| | | **3,57,800** | | | **3,57,800** |

In **Branch Trading Account** all items of Stock i.e. Opening stock, Goods sent to Branch (i.e. Purchases), Goods returned by Branch (i.e. Returns outward), Closing stock, Goods in Transit, Shortage in Goods etc. **must be recorded at cost price**, which are to be calculated as follows :

| Particulars | Invoice Price ₹ | Loading ₹ | Cost Price ₹ |
|---|---|---|---|
| Stock as on 1.4.2015 | 30,000 | 6,000 | 24,000 |
| Goods sent by HO | 2,50,000 | 50,000 | 2,00,000 |
| Goods returned to HO | 2,000 | 400 | 1,600 |
| Goods in Transit | 10,000 | 2,000 | 8,000 |
| Shortage in Goods | 400 | 80 | 320 |
| Stock as on 31.3.2016 | 70,000 | 14,000 | 56,000 |

**In the Books of Anant Trade Centre, Delhi (Head Office)**

Dr.        **Agra Branch Trading Account for the year ended 31.3.2016**        Cr.

| Particulars | | ₹ | Particulars | | ₹ |
|---|---|---|---|---|---|
| To Opening Stock | | 24,000 | By Sales | | 1,97,600 |
| To Purchases | 2,00,000 | 1,98,400 | i) Credit | 1,74,000 | |
| Less Returns Outward | (–) 1,600 | | ii) Cash | (+) 26,000 | |
| | | | | 2,00,000 | |
| | | | Less Returns Inward : (–) | 2,400 | |
| | | | By Closing Stock | | 56,000 |
| | | | By Goods in Transit | | 8,000 |
| To Gross Profit C/D * | | 39,520 | By Shortage in Goods | | 320 |
| | | **2,61,920** | | | **2,61,920** |

**Dr.**        **Branch Profit and Loss Account for the year ended 31.3.2016**        **Cr.**

| Particulars | ₹ | Particulars | ₹ |
|---|---|---|---|
| To Petty Expenses | 800 | By Gross Profit B/D | 39,520 |
| To Salaries and Wages | 10,000 | | |
| To Rent | 6,000 | | |
| To Bad Debts | 2,000 | | |
| To Discount Allowed | 1,600 | | |
| To Shortage in Goods | 320 | | |
| To Depreciation on | | | |
|    Furniture @10% p.a. | 1,000 | | |
| To General Profit and Loss* | 17,800 | | |
| (Net Profit C/D) | | | |
| | **39,520** | | **39,520** |

## QUESTIONS FOR SELF STUDY

**I.  Theory Questions :**
1) What is Branch ? Explain the need for Branch Accounting.
2) Define the term 'Branch'. State the types of branches from accounting point of view.
3) State the methods of maintaining the accounts of dependent branches.
4) Explain in detail the Debtors Method of maintaining accounts of dependent branches.
5) Prepare the format of Branch Account in the books of head office.
6) What is Invoice Price ? Pass the necessary journal entries for removal of loading in the items of stock.
7) What is 'Stock and Debtors Method' ? State the necessary accounts to be prepared under Stock and Debtors system with their basic purpose.
8) What is 'Final Accounts Method' ? Prepare the format of Memorandum Branch Trading and Profit and Loss Account.
9) Differentiate between :
   a) Home Branches and Foreign Branches
   b) Dependent Branches and Independent Branches
   c) Debtors System and Stock and Debtors System
10) Write short notes on :
a) Branch, b) Need for Branch Accounting, c) Dependent Branches, d) Debtors System, e) Stock and Debtors System, f) Invoice Price Method, g) Branch Final Accounts Method.

**II. Practical Problems :**
1) Maharashtra Traders has its Head Office at Pune and Branch at New Delhi. The Head Office at Pune makes purchases and sends the goods to its branch for sale.

    The Branch offices effect sales, keep their own sales ledgers, receive cash against sales, debtors and pay in the whole of their cash receipts every day to the Head Office. The Branch expenses are paid from cash remitted by the Head Office for that purpose. The transactions of the New Delhi Branch for the year ended 31st March 2016 are furnished as below :

| | ₹ |
|---|---|
| Credit Sales | 39,000 |
| Returns Inwards | 360 |
| Allowances to customers | 60 |
| Cash received on Ledger Accounts | 36,000 |

| | |
|---|---:|
| Cash Sales | 18,750 |
| Stock as on 1st April 2015 | 7,200 |
| Stock as on 31st March 2016 | 8,700 |
| Debtors as on 1st April 2015 | 18,000 |
| Debtors as on 31st March 2016 | 20,430 |
| Bad debts | 150 |
| Goods purchased by Head Office and supplied to Branch | 30,900 |
| Rent and Insurance | 1,050 |
| Wages and Miscellaneous expenses | 5,340 |

You are required to show

i)      New Delhi Branch Account as they may appear in the Head Office Books.

ii)      Profit and Loss Account showing the working results of the branch.

iii)      The net profit of the whole concern assuming that the H.O. expenses were ₹ 15,000.

2)    To a Branch at Nagpur goods are supplied by Amit Traders, Pune Head Office at cost, to be sold for cash only. The expenses of branch are paid by Head Office. From the following particulars prepare the Nagpur Branch Account for the year ended 31-12-2015 in the books of the Head Office.

| | ₹ |
|---|---:|
| Opening balances as on 1-1-2015 : | |
|      Stock at Branch | 1,20,000 |
|      Petty cash | 1,000 |
|      Furniture at Branch | |
|      (Original cost ₹ 16,000) | 12,800 |
| Goods supplied to Branch | 8,00,000 |
| Goods supplied to Branch Less Returned | 20,000 |
| Stock at Branch as on 31-12-2015 | 80,000 |
| Cash sent to Branch for expenses : | |
| •     Rent | 57,600 |
| •     Other expenses | 74,800 |
| •     Salaries | 8,000 |
| •     Advertisement | 14,000 |
| •     Petty Cash | 3,000 |
| Cash sent to Head Office | 9,56,000 |

Furniture is to be depreciated @ 10% p.a. on Straight Line Method. Actual petty expenses paid by the branch amounted to ₹ 2,000.

3)    Rosy Ltd., Kolkata invoiced goods to its Branch at Nagar at 20% on inflated price. Prepare Nagar Branch Account in the books of head office from the following information for the year 2015.

| | ₹ |
|---|---:|
| Debtors on 1-1-2015 | 52,400 |
| Debtors on 31-12-2015 | 66,200 |
| Stock as on 1-1-2015 | 30,000 |
| Stock as on 31-12-2015 | 27,800 |
| Goods received from Head Office | 1,01,600 |
| Cash sales | 67,000 |
| Allowances to customers | 640 |

| | |
|---|---:|
| Yearly turnover | 1,87,000 |
| Goods returned to Head Office | 1,400 |
| Goods returned by customers | 1,160 |
| Discount allowed | 4,800 |
| Bad debts | 1,200 |
| Rent and Taxes | 3,600 |
| Wages and Salaries | 3,080 |
| Carriage and Cartage | 2,600 |

The Branch Manager is entitled to commission of 10% on branch profits after charging such commission.

4) The following are the details of Vijay Traders, Pune having its Branch at Nasik.

| | ₹ | | ₹ |
|---|---:|---|---:|
| Goods sent to Branch at cost | 50,000 | Credit Sales | 51,000 |
| Goods returned from Branch at cost | 3,000 | Closing Stock with Branch | 17,000 |
| Expenses paid by H.O. | 10,000 | Branch Debtors (Closing Balance) | 7,700 |
| Remittances received from Branch | 45,000 | Discount allowed to customers | 1,800 |
| Received from Debtors by Branch | 42,500 | by Branch | |
| Cash Sales | 2,500 | | |

You are required to open Nasik Branch Account in the books of the Head Office.

5) Maharaja Trades has a retail branch, which is supplied with goods from Head Office and which keeps its own sales ledger and remits all the cash received daily to Head Office, the Branch expenses being paid by the Head Office by weekly cheques.

From the following particulars, draw up the Branch Account for the six months ended 31.12.2015.

| | ₹ |
|---|---:|
| Credit Sales | 2,485 |
| Cash Sales | 1,460 |
| Return Inward | 30 |
| Cash received on Ledger Accounts | 2,387 |
| Debtors as on 1.1.2015 | 1,345 |
| Stock as on 1.1.2015 | 840 |
| Stock as on 31.12.2015 | 1,280 |
| Goods received from Head Office | 2,276 |
| Bad Debts at Branch | 65 |
| Wages and Sundry Expenses | 415 |
| Rent, Rates and Taxes | 402 |

6) Sudarshan Ltd., Pune has a branch at Ulhasnagar to which goods are supplied at cost plus 20% profit. Prepare Branch Stock Account, Branch Debtors Account, Branch Petty Cash Account, Branch Expenses Account, and Branch Adjustment Account in the books of Sudarshan Ltd., Pune-Head Office. Also pass the necessary journal entries to record the undermentioned information relating to Ulhasnagar Branch for the year 2015.

|  | Opening balances as on 1-1-2015 : | ₹ |
|---|---|---|
| i) | Stock of goods | 1,68,000 |
| ii) | Debtors | 3,02,400 |
| iii) | Petty cash | 4,800 |
|  | Goods invoiced to branch | 10,08,000 |
|  | Goods returned by branch | 24,000 |
|  | Cash Turnover | 4,20,000 |
|  | Sales to credit Turnover | 6,81,600 |
|  | Surplus in stock | 93,600 |
|  | Cash received from Debtors | 6,84,000 |
|  | Allowances to Customers | 4,800 |
|  | Discount Allowed to branch Debtors | 36,000 |
|  | Bad Debts written off | 12,000 |
|  | Returns from customers | 12,000 |
|  | Advertisement | 24,000 |
|  | Salaries | 80,000 |
|  | Rent (Including prepaid for 2016 ₹ 800) | 32,000 |
|  | Cash sent to branch for petty expenses | 9,600 |
|  | Commission paid | 12,000 |
|  | Closing balances as on 31-12-2015 : |  |
| • | Debtors | 2,35,200 |
| • | Petty cash | 2,400 |

7) Maximo Ltd. Bengaluru has a branch at Porbandar to which goods are invoiced so as to have 10% bearing on market price. The Branch has sent the following figures for year 2015.

|  | ₹ |
|---|---|
| Stock as on 1-1-2015 | 45,000 |
| Stock as on 31-12-2015 | 41,700 |
| Debtors as on 1-1-2015 | 78,600 |
| Debtors as on 31-12-2015 | 99,300 |
| Goods received from head office | 2,42,400 |
| Goods returned to head office | 2,100 |
| Cash Sales | 94,200 |
| Credit Sales | 1,80,000 |
| Allowances to Customers | 1,740 |
| Returns from Customers | 600 |
| Discount Allowed to Customers | 7,200 |
| Bad Debts | 1,800 |
| Rent | 5,400 |
| Salaries | 18,000 |

| | |
|---|---:|
| General charges | 3,900 |
| Rent due but not paid for 2015 | 300 |
| Miscellaneous Income | 1,980 |

Items of stock are at invoice price. All expenses are paid by head office and all cash received is daily banked into the head office account.

You are required to prepare

i) Branch Stock Account, ii) Goods sent to Branch Account, iii) Stock Reserve Account, iv) Branch Debtors Account, v) Branch Expenses Account, vi) Branch Adjustment Account, vii) Branch Profit and Loss Account,

8. Amar Traders, Anand opened a branch at Chennai on $1^{st}$ January 2015. Goods were invoiced at selling price which was cost plus 25%. From the following particulars, prepare necessary accounts under "Stock and Debtors System".

| | | ₹ |
|---|---:|---:|
| Goods sent to Branch | | 6,00,000 |
| Sales –   Cash | | 2,00,000 |
|           Credit | | 2,80,000 |
| Goods returned by Customers | | 6,000 |
| Cash received from Customers | | 1,60,000 |
| Discount allowed | | 2,000 |
| Cheques sent to branch for : | | |
|    i)      Rent and Rates | 3,200 | |
|    ii)     Sundry Expenses | 2,000 | |
|    iii)    Salaries | (+) <u>14,000</u> | 19,200 |
| Defective goods written off (at selling price) | | 2,000 |
| Goods returned by branch | | 24,000 |

9. From the following details, prepare necessary accounts of Patna Branch under Stock and Debtors System in the books of Ajanta Ltd., Bilaspur, Head Office.
On $1^{st}$ January 2015, the following balances appeared in the Head office ledger :

| | ₹ |
|---|---:|
| Branch Debtors Account | 15,000 |
| Branch Stock Account (at selling price) | 6,000 |
| Branch Adjustment Account (Credit) | 1,500 |

The following were the transactions of the branch during the year ended $31^{st}$ December 2015.

Cash Sales ₹ 8,000, Credit Sales ₹ 1,70,000, Goods from Head Office at selling price ₹ 2,00,000. Cash received from branch debtors ₹ 1,60,000, Discount allowed to branch debtors ₹ 4,000, Branch expenses paid by Head Office ₹ 27,500. The Stock at the branch on $31^{st}$ December 2015 was ₹ 24,000 at selling price. Prepare necessary ledger accounts in the books of Head Office (including Branch Profit and Loss Account) according to Stock and Debtor System. Goods are invoiced to Branch at Cost plus 33 $^1/_3$%.

Chapter **7**

# SINGLE ENTRY SYSTEM

**SYNOPSIS**

7.0 Introduction
7.1 Meaning and Classification of Single Entry System
7.2 Ascertainment of Profit or Loss of Sole Trader
7.3 Statement of Affairs Method
7.4 Conversion of Single Entry into Double Entry
7.5 Illustrations
• Capital Comparison Method
• Conversion Method
• Questions for Self-Study

## 7.0 INTRODUCTION

In India, there are many small-scale businesses which do not keep complete records for all their financial transactions because the proprietors of these business are untrained in accounting and hence consider it better to keep an additional productive employee rather than a book-keeper. They assume that without an elaborate accounting system, they can exercise control over assets, expenses, revenues and liabilities. They record a few transactions completely just like the double entry system but a majority of the transactions are recorded only partially. Therefore, it is also known as **"Accounts from Incomplete Records"**. **Incomplete Accounting Records** are those accounting records which, at present, are not complete according to double entry principles. Many authors describe it as the **'Single Entry System'** but according to a majority of accountants, it is appropriate to describe it as **'Incomplete Records'** because incomplete records contain : i) both the aspects of some of the transactions; ii) only one aspect of some of the transactions; iii) no aspect of some of the transaction.

**Reasons for Incomplete Records :**

Accounting records may be incomplete due to anyone or more of the following reasons :
i)     the businessman may be untrained in accounting;
ii)    the businessman may be ignorant of the separate legal entity assumption;
iii)   the businessman may be ignorant of the double entry accounting principles;
iv)    the businessman may not intentionally maintain proper accounts to evade taxation;
v)     destruction of the books of accounts due to fire, flood, etc. and
vi)    the businessman may assume that without double entry system he can exercise control over assets, liabilities, expenses and incomes.

The number of small-scale businesses which do not keep complete records for their business transactions is significant in India. Therefore, it is necessary to learn **'Single Entry System'** by the students of accounting and management

## 7.1 MEANING AND CLASSIFICATION OF SINGLE ENTRY SYSTEM

Many small businesses have neither the time nor the experience necessary to maintain a full set of accounting records using the double entry system; and cannot afford the expense of outside staff to keep such records. However, every business is interested to know its profit from time to time. Any set of procedures for ascertaining profits that does not provide for the analysis of each transaction in terms of double entry system of book-keeping is generally referred to as **'Single Entry System'**. In fact, **Single Entry System** is a mixture of : double entry; single entry; and no entry. Under this system, certain transactions are recorded just like the double entry system, for example, cash collected from debtors – it is recorded in the Debtors Account as well as in the Cash Account. Again, certain transactions are recorded partially e.g. cash sales, cash purchases, etc. Similarly, certain transactions are not recorded at all. e.g. bad debt, depreciation, etc.

**Definition :**

**Single Entry System** may be defined as, "a system in which accounting records are not made strictly according to the double entry principles of book-keeping".

Since all the transactions are not recorded strictly on the double entry principle, it is not possible to prepare a trial balance and check the arithmetical accuracy of the books of accounts. Strictly speaking, **Single Entry constitutes incomplete records rather than single entry accounting**. Therefore, the expression *Single Entry* does not mean that there is recording of only one entry for each transaction.

**Classification of Single Entry System :**

The Classification of Single Entry System is shown below in Figure 8.1.

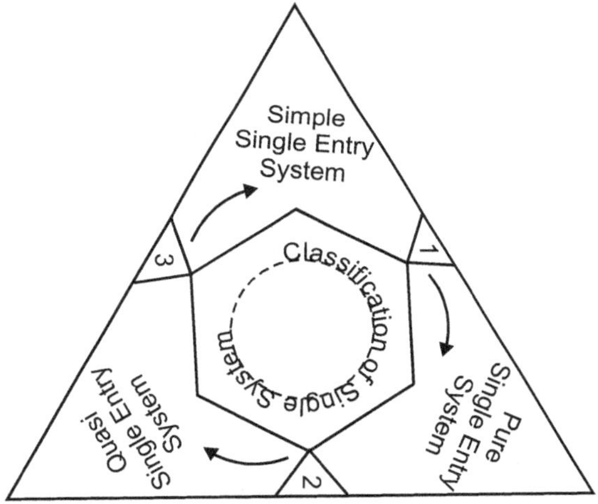


**Fig. 7.1 : Classification of Single Entry System**

The expression **'single entry'** covers a wide range of accounting records, starting from the brief notes of transactions kept by a hawker to the elaborate records kept by a large traditional enterprise. The degree of incompleteness of records differs from one business to another, according to its nature and complexity. Generally, the Single Entry System can be classified into the following three categories :

1) **Pure Single Entry System :**

   Under this system, only Personal Accounts are kept. No records are kept for Real or Nominal Accounts.

2) **Quasi Single Entry System :**

   Under this system, Personal Accounts, Cash Book; and some other Subsidiary Books are kept separately.

3) **Simple Single Entry System :**

   Under this system, Personal Accounts, and Cash Book are kept separately.

**Characteristics of Single Entry System :**

The important **characteristics of Single Entry System** are as follows :

i)     In this system, generally Personal Accounts are kept but Real and Nominal Accounts are ignored. This is because, a Single Entry takes account only of the personal transactions and leaves the impersonal transactions of the business unit entirely unrecorded.

ii)     In the absence of record of the two-fold aspect of every transaction, it is not possible to prepare a Trial Balance and check the arithmetical accuracy of the books of accounts. Similarly, no Balance Sheet can be prepared in the absence of balances in the ledger.

iii)     This system is highly changeable and flexible and is not governed by any definite rules of operation.

iv)     Under this system, the profit or loss can be found out but its comparison will not be available.

v)     This system is a mixture of : Double Entry, Single Entry, and No Entry.

vi)     This system is suitable for small businesses where the proprietor or partners can directly control the affairs of the business.

vi)     Single Entry System can be classified into : i) Pure, ii) Quasi and Simple Single Entry System.

**Limitations of Single Entry System :**

Single Entry System ignores the concept of duality and, therefore, transactions are not recorded in their two-fold aspects. As a result, the final accounts of the business concern cannot be prepared in the usual way. The other **limitations** are as under :

i)     Arithmetical accuracy of the accounts cannot be checked because no agreed Trial balance can be prepared.

ii)     True Profits or Losses cannot be ascertained because Trading and Profit and Loss Account cannot be prepared.

iii)     True financial position cannot be ascertained because Balance Sheet cannot be prepared.

iv)     It is difficult to conduct the audit of such records.

v)     It is difficult to operate internal control system.

vi)     It is difficult to operate internal check system.

vii)     It is difficult to exercise control over assets.

viii)     It is difficult to detect fraud.

ix)     Such records are not recognised by the Courts, Sales Tax and Income-Tax authorities.

x)     This system engenders a spirit of laxity and invites frauds and misappropriations.

xi)     No limited company can keep account under this system, because of legal restrictions.

xii)     Owing to incompleteness of records, proper appraisal of the financial position of the business is not possible.

**Distinction between Double Entry System and Single Entry System :**

| Sr. No. | Basis of Distinction | Double Entry System | Incomplete Records System/ Single Entry System |
|---|---|---|---|
| i) | Assumptions and Principles | It is based on certain assumptions and principles and values. Both the aspects of all transactions are recorded. | It is not based on certain assumptions and principles and rules. Both the aspects of all transactions are not recorded. |
| ii) | Both aspects of all transactions | Both the aspects of all transactions are recorded. | Both the aspects of all transactions are not recorded. |
| iii) | Preparation of Cash Book and General ledger, etc. | In this system, Cash Book, General ledger, Debtors' Ledger and Creditors' Ledger are maintained. | In this system, only Debtors' Ledger and Creditors' Ledger are kept. Cash Book is also kept but personal transactions get mixed with business transactions. |
| iv) | Nature of Accounts maintained | All types of accounts – Personal, Real and Nominal are maintained. | Usually, Cash Account and Personal Accounts are maintained. |
| v) | Trial Balance | Arithmetical accuracy of the records can be checked by preparing a Trial Balance. | Arithmetical accuracy of the records cannot be checked since Trial Balance cannot be prepared. |
| vi) | Determination of True Profit or Loss | True Profits or Losses can be determined by preparing Trading, and Profit and Loss Account. | Only estimated profits or losses can be determined since Trading and Profit and Loss Account cannot be prepared. |
| vii) | Financial Position | True financial position can be known by preparing a Balance Sheet. | Only estimated financial position can be known on the basis of Statement of Affairs. |
| viii) | Adjustments | All types of adjustments are made while preparing Final Accounts. | No special attention is given to adjustments. |
| ix) | Interpretation of Financial data | For interpretation of financial data, we can compute different types of ratios, if the accounts are maintained under this system. | Vital ratios cannot be computed (such as Gross Profit Ratio, Net Profit Ratio, etc.) if the accounts are maintained under this system. |
| x) | Utility | It is used by all types of traders. | It is used only by small traders. |
| xi) | Recognition by Government | Records maintained according to this system are recognised by the Government. | Records maintained according to this system are not recognised by the Government. |

## 7.2 ASCERTAINMENT OF PROFIT OR LOSS OF SOLE TRADER

To ascertain the results of operations and the financial position of the business, the information available from the incomplete records can be used in the following methods as shown in Figure 8.2.

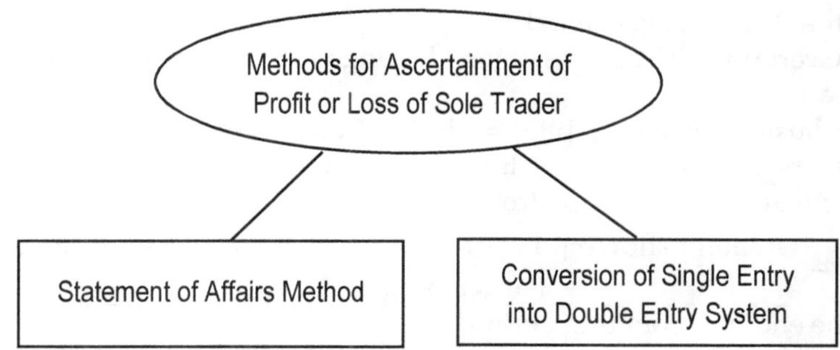


**Fig. 7.2 : Methods for Ascertainment of Profit or Loss of Sole Trader**

## 7.3 STATEMENT OF AFFAIRS METHOD

Under Statement of Affairs Method, which is also termed as Capital Comparison Method, two Statement of Affairs are prepared. One, at the beginning of the period for finding out the *Opening Capital* and the other at the end of the period for finding out the *Closing Capital.* A comparison is made between the Opening and Closing Capital. If the Closing Capital is more than the Opening Capital, it shows an increase in capital, which means a **profit**. Conversely, if the Closing Capital is less than the Opening Capital, it shows a decrease in capital, which means a **loss** for the period. In other words :

**Closing Balance Sheet :** $\dfrac{\text{Opening Balance Sheet : Assets = Liabilities + Capital}}{\text{Change in period : } \Delta \text{ Assets} = \Delta \text{ Liabilities} + \Delta \text{ Capital}}$

The change ($\Delta$) in assets may be due to change in liabilities or capital or both. The increase in assets due to increase in capital represents profit.

**Practical Steps involved in the Ascertainment of the Profit or Loss according to the Statement of Affairs Methods :**

Step 1 :     **Ascertain Opening Capital** by preparing a Statement of Affairs at the beginning of the accounting period. The usual format of Statement of Affairs is as follows :

**Statement of Affairs of ... as at ......**

| Liabilities | ₹ | Assets | ₹ |
|---|---|---|---|
| Sundry Creditors | xxx | Cash in Hand | xxx |
| Bills Payable | xxx | Cash at Bank | xxx |
| Outstanding Expenses | xxx | Sundry Debtors | xxx |
| Bank Overdraft | xxx | Bills Receivable | xxx |
| Capital | xxx | Stock in Trade | xxx |
| (Balancing Figure) | | Prepaid Expenses | xxx |
| | | Fixed Assets | xxx |
| | **xxx** | | **xxx** |

Step 2 :     **Ascertain Closing Capital** by preparing a Statement of Affairs at the end of the accounting period.

Step 3 :     **Add,** the amount of **Drawings** (whether in cash or in kind) and Interest on Drawings to the Closing Capital.

**Step 4 :**   **Deduct** the amount of **Additional Capital** introduced and Interest on Capital from the Closing Capital.

**Step 5 :**   **Ascertain Profit or Loss** by deducting Opening Capital from the Adjusted Closing Capital.

**Note :**   Adjusted Closing Capital = Closing Capital (+) Drawings (–) Additional Capital + Interest on Drawings (–) Interest on Capital.

The format of Statement showing Profit or Loss is as follows :

### Statement showing Profit or Loss for the period ending ......

| Particulars | ₹ |
|---|---|
| A)  Capital at the end of accounting period | xxx |
| B)  **Add :** Drawings (whether in cash or in kind) during the accounting period and Interest on Drawings                       (+) | xxx |
| C)  **Less :** Additional Capital introduced (whether cash or in kind) during the accounting period and Interest on Capital          (–) | xxx |
| D)  Adjusted Capital at the end of accounting period (A + B – C) | xxx |
| E)  Less : Capital at the beginning of accounting period | xxx |
| F)  Profit (if Adjusted Capital is more than the Opening Capital) or Loss (if Adjusted Capital is less than the Opening Capital) | xxx |

**Step 6 :**   **Make Adjustment** for items not yet adjusted while calculating Closing Capital.

## Important Hints :

**1)  Ascertain Opening Capital :**

**Opening Capital** can be calculated by preparing a Statement of Affairs at the beginning of the year. The Statement of Affairs is just similar to a Balance Sheet. All the Assets are shown on the right-hand side and all the Liabilities are shown on the left-hand side of the Statement of Affairs. If the total of the right-hand side is greater than the total of the left-hand side, it represents 'Opening Capital'. The Assets and Liabilities are ascertained as follows :

    i)    Amount of cash is ascertained by physical count;

    ii)   Bank Balance is ascertained from the Pass Book;

    iii)  The closing stock is ascertained by physical stock taking;

    iv)  The balances of debtors and creditors can be ascertained from the list, the trader maintains;

    v)   Regarding other assets, the trader prepares a list and values them; and

    vi)  Other relevant information is supplied by the trader from his memory and personal record.

**2)  Ascertain Closing Capital :**

It can be calculated by preparing the Closing Statement of Affairs in the same manner we prepare the Opening Statement of Affairs in Step 1. However, in the Closing Statement of Affairs, we will consider Assets and Liabilities at the end of the period (before adjustment).

**3)  Ascertain the Drawings during the period :**

Ascertainment of Drawings for a given period is the most difficult task. Drawings increase the personal capital but decrease the business capital. Since the entries are recorded from the point of the proprietor, personal affairs of the proprietor gets mixed up with the business affairs. To take an account of Drawings, all withdrawals from the business must be traced. For calculating Drawings, the following points are to be considered : (i) How much is drawn from the business at regular intervals for household or private purposes ? and (ii) How much has been utilised for household or private purposes from the sale proceeds or other receipts before depositing it into the Bank ?

**4) Ascertain the amount of additional capital introduced during the period :**

A trader may introduce new capital (in the form of Cash or Assets) during the period. The trader is to make a list of the amount of capital introduced during the period.

**5) Ascertainment of Profit or Loss :**

Preparing the two Statement of Affairs and ascertaining capital at the beginning and at the end, the two capital balances are compared and the difference is noted. If the Closing Capital is more than the Opening Capital, it cannot be stated that the difference is profit or vice-versa, because the difference may be due to the following reasons :

- i) There may be additions to capital i.e. fresh capital might have been brought.
- ii) There may be goods taken by the proprietor for his own use.
- iii) There may be drawings during the year.
- iv) Some goods or assets might have been brought into business during the year by the proprietor.

Therefore, adjustment will have to be made in respect of the above items before the capital is ascertained.

**Balance Sheet (Redrafted) :**

After ascertaining profit by following the above procedures, a Balance Sheet (Redrafted) is prepared at the end of the period after incorporating adjustment for depreciation, provision for bad debts, etc. The Balance Sheet (Redrafted) will appear as follows :

Balance Sheet as on .........

| Liabilities | | | ₹ | Assets | | | ₹ |
|---|---|---|---|---|---|---|---|
| Opening Capital | | xxx | | Plant and Machinery | | xxx | |
| **Add :** New Capital introduced (+) | | xxx | | **Less :** Depreciation | (–) | xxx | xxx |
| **Add :** Interest on capital | (+) | xxx | | Furniture | | xxx | |
| **Add :** Profit for the year | (+) | xxx | | **Less :** Depreciation | (–) | xxx | xxx |
| | | xxx | | Debtors | | xxx | |
| **Less :** Drawings | (–) | xxx | xxx | **Less :** Provision for Bad Debts | | xxx | xxx |
| **Less :** Interest on Drawings | (–) | xxx | | Stock | | | xxx |
| Creditors | | | xxx | Cash at Bank | | | xxx |
| Bills Payable | | | | Cash in Hand | | | xxx |
| Bank Overdraft | | | | | | | |
| | | | xxx | | | | xxx |

**Difference Between Statement of Affairs and Balance Sheet :**

A **Statement of Affairs** is a statement of the assets, liabilities and capital prepared from incomplete records, whereas a **Balance Sheet** is a statement of assets, liabilities and capital extracted from ledger balances maintained under the double entry system.

Under the Double Entry System, the basic purpose of the Balance Sheet is to show the financial position of the business on the last day of the accounting period. Under Single Entry, the same purpose is served by the Statement of Affairs. Also, it is used as the basis for calculating the trading results for the period.

Hence, Statement of Affairs which looks like a Balance Sheet, differs from the Balance Sheet in the following respects.

| Sr. No. | Basis of Distinction | Statement of Affairs | Balance Sheet |
|---|---|---|---|
| i) | Basis of preparation | It is prepared on the basis of some ledger accounts and estimates. | It is prepared on the basis of ledger accounts. |
| ii) | Balance of Capital Account | Balance of Capital Account is arrived at as a balancing figure. | Balance of Capital Account is taken from the ledger. |
| iii) | Omission of Assets/ Liabilities | Omission of an Asset or Liability cannot be easily traced. | Omission of an Asset or Liability can be easily traced because of non-agreement of both the sides of the Balance Sheet. |
| iv) | Estimated Vs. True Financial Position | It shows only the estimated financial position. | It shows the true financial position. |
| v) | Ratio Analysis | Vital ratios cannot be computed by the business with the help of this statement. | Different types of ratios can be computed with the help of Balance Sheet. |

**Impact of Profit or Loss on Capital :**

Under the Single Entry System, profit or loss cannot be ascertained by the regular method of preparing Trading and Profit and Loss Account. But the result of business can be estimated by computing the capitals of the proprietor at the beginning and at the close of the period. And only excess of closing capital over the opening capital is considered as a profit, provided no other transactions are there affecting the capital.

To determine the profit, it is necessary to find out the difference between the costs of the enterprise and its earning. This is an involved process with many hidden difficulties, since different ideas exist as to what are the true costs and what are the true earnings.

The owner of the business appropriates the net profit. The word "appropriate" means to take the possession of. Since the whole purpose of the business is to make profit, the owner takes possession of the profits which are added to his account, the Capital Account. We see that at the end of the trading period the owner's capital increases by the amount of net profit made during the period.

The chief advantage of the net profit percentage is that it enables us to compare one year with another, or one trading period with the previous trading period, if we take out Final Accounts more frequently.

The net profit for a period is credited to Capital Account, and if his drawings are less than that of profit, the Capital is increased by the difference. On the other hand, the net loss for a period is debited to Capital Account. His drawings amount is also debited to Capital Account.

| EXAMPLE |

Ashutosh Barve, Chennai, keeps his books by the Single Entry Method. His position on 31st December, 2014 and on 31st December, 2015, are as follows :

| Particulars | 31-12-2014 | 31-12-2015 |
|---|---|---|
| Cash in Hand | 3,000 | 2,000 |
| Cash at Bank | 25,000 | 28,000 |
| Debtors | 18,000 | 25,000 |
| Stock | 29,000 | 31,000 |
| Furniture | 5,000 | 6,000 |
| Machinery | 5,000 | 5,000 |
| Creditors for Goods | 18,000 | 25,000 |
| Expenses Outstanding | 1,500 | – |
| Prepaid Insurance | – | 400 |

On 1st July, 2015, Ashutosh introduced ₹ 5,000 as further capital in the business and withdrew on the same date ₹ 2,000 for personal use. Depreciation is to be calculated on Machinery @ 10% p.a. A provision for Doubtful Debts is to be created on Sundry Debtors @ 5%. Goods taken for personal use amounted to ₹ 1,500. Also provide Interest on Capital @ 10% p.a.

Prepare the necessary statements showing the profit or loss made by him during the year ending 31st December, 2015.

ANSWER

### In the books of Ashutosh Barve, Chennai

**Step 1 → Calculation of Opening Capital :**

#### Statement of Affairs as on 1st January, 2015

| Liabilities | ₹ | Assets | ₹ |
|---|---|---|---|
| Creditors for Goods | 18,000 | Cash in Hand | 3,000 |
| Expenses Outstanding | 1,500 | Cash at Bank | 25,000 |
| **A's Capital*** | 65,500 | Debtors | 18,000 |
| (Balancing Figure) | | Stock | 29,000 |
| | | Furniture | 5,000 |
| | | Machinery | 5,000 |
| | **85,000** | | **85,000** |

**Step 2 → Calculation of Closing Capital :**

#### Statement of Affairs as on 31st December, 2015

| Liabilities | ₹ | Assets | ₹ |
|---|---|---|---|
| Creditors for Goods | 25,000 | Cash in Hand | 2,000 |
| A's Capital* | 72,400 | Cash at Bank | 28,000 |
| (Balancing Figure) | | Debtors | 25,000 |
| | | Stock | 31,000 |
| | | Furniture | 6,000 |
| | | Machinery | 5,000 |
| | | Prepaid Insurance | 400 |
| | **97,400** | | **97,400** |

**Step 3 → Calculation of Profit or Loss :**

#### Statement showing Profit or Loss for the year ended 31st December, 2015

| | Particulars | | | ₹ |
|---|---|---|---|---|
| A. | Ashutosh's Capital at the end of the year | | | 72,400 |
| B. | **Add :** Drawings –      • Cash | | 2,000 | |
| |      • Goods | | (+) 1,500 | 3,500 |
| | | | (+) | 75,900 |
| C. | **Less :** Capital introduced on 1st July by Ashutosh | | (–) | 5,000 |
| D. | Adjusted Closing Capital of Ashutosh | | | 70,900 |
| E. | **Less :** Capital in the beginning of the year of Ashutosh | | (–) | 65,500 |
| F. | Gross Profit subject to Adjustment | | | 5,400 |
| G. | **Less :**  • Depreciation on Machinery (10% on ₹ 5,000) | | 500 | |
| |   • Provision for Doubtful Debts (5% on ₹ 25,000) | | 1,250 | |
| |   • Interest on Capital (10% on ₹ 65,500 for 12 months) – | 6,550 | | |
| |     (10% on ₹ 5,000 for 6 months) – | 250 | (+) 6,800 | 8,550 |
| H. | Net Loss | | | (–) 3,150 |

## 7.4 CONVERSION OF SINGLE ENTRY INTO DOUBLE ENTRY

Under the Single Entry System, adequate accounting information is not available and the profit disclosed by that system is not gladly accepted by the revenue authority. For better management of the business, avoiding harassment by the revenue authorities, and facing challenges of the competitors effectively, sometimes a trader may adopt the Double Entry System by giving up the Single Entry System.

In the Single Entry Systems, there are varying degrees of incompleteness, and the procedure to be adopted for conversion must depend upon the nature of the records and data available. It is not possible to give a formula which can be applied in every situation. However, as a general rule, the following steps are followed :

**Step 1 :** Prepare Cash and Bank summary i.e. **Cash Book** to ascertain the missing information (such as Opening and Closing Balance, Cash Sales or Cash Purchases, Drawings made during the period, etc.).

**Step 2 :** Prepare **Total Debtors Account** to ascertain the missing information (such as Opening or Closing Balance, Credit Sales, Collection from Debtors, Bills Receivable drawn during the period, etc.).

**Step 3 :** Prepare **Bills Receivable Account** to ascertain the missing information (such as Opening or Closing Balance, Bills Receivable drawn and collected, Bills Receivable endorsed, etc.).

**Step 4 :** Prepare **Total Creditors Account** to ascertain the missing information (such as Opening or Closing Balance, Credit Purchases, Payment made to Creditors, Bills Payable accepted during the period etc.).

**Step 5 :** Prepare **Bills Payable Account** to ascertain the missing information (such as Opening or Closing Balance, Bills Payable accepted, Bills Payable discharged, etc.).

**Step 6 :** Prepare **Stock Account** to ascertain the missing information (such as Opening Stock or Closing Stock, Total Purchases, Cost of goods sold, Shortage, etc.).

**Step 7 :** Prepare **Revenue Expense Account** to ascertain the missing information (such as Opening or Closing Balance of Outstanding or Prepaid Expenses, Expenses Paid, Current Year's Expenses, etc.).

**Step 8 :** Prepare **Revenue Income Account** to ascertain the missing information (such as Opening or Closing Balance of Accrued or Unaccrued Income Received, Current Year's Income, etc.).

**Step 9 :** Prepare **Fixed Asset Account** to ascertain the missing information (such as Opening or Closing Balance, Purchases or Sales, Depreciation provided, profit or loss on sale, etc.).

**Step 10 :** Ascertain **Opening Capital** by preparing **Statement of Affairs** at the beginning of the accounting period.

**Step 11 :** Prepare **Trial Balance** to check the arithmetical accuracy.

**Step 12 :** Prepare **Trading and Profit and Loss Account** and the **Balance Sheet**.

**Accounts from Incomplete Records :**

| Missing Information | Hints for Tracing |
|---|---|
| 1.  Cash | I.  Cash and Bank Account Summary |
|  | II.  Total Sales (–) Net Credit Sales |
| 2.  Net Credit Sales | I.  Prepare Total Debtors Account |
|  | II.  Total Sales (–) Cash Sales (–) Sales Returns |
|  | III. Closing Debtors × [(12/Credit period allowed (in months)] |
| 3.  Net Sales | I.  Cash Sales (+) Credit Sales (–) Sales Returns |
|  | II.  Cost of goods sold + Gross Profit |
|  | III. Gross Profit × 100/Rate of Gross Profit on Sale |
| 4.  Cost of Goods Sold | I.  Opening Stock (+) Purchases (+) Direct Expenses (e.g. Carriage/Cartage/Freight Inward) (–) Closing Stock |
|  | II.  Net Sales (–) Gross Profit |
|  | III. Stock Account |
| 5.  Gross Profit | I.  Net Sales × Rate of Gross Profit/100 |
|  | II.  Net Sales (–) Cost of Goods Sold |
| 6.  Cash Purchases | I.  Prepare Cash and Bank Accounting Summary |
|  | II.  Total Purchases (–) Net Credit Purchases |
| 7.  Net Credit Purchases | I.  Prepare Total Creditors Account |
|  | II.  Total Purchases (–) Cash Purchases (–) Purchase Returns |
|  | III. Closing Creditors × [(12/Credit period received in months)] |
| 8.  Net Purchases | I.  Cash Purchase (+) Credit Purchase (–) Purchases Returns |
|  | II.  Cost of Goods sold (+) Closing Stock (–) Opening Stock |
|  | III. Stock Account |
| 9.  Collection from Debtors | I.  Total Debtors Account |
|  | II.  Cash and Bank Account Summary |
| 10. Payments to Creditors | I.  Total Creditors Account |
|  | II.  Cash and Bank Account Summary |
| 11. Bills Receivable drawn | I.  Bills Receivable Account. |
|  | II.  Total Debtors Account |
| 12. Bills Payable accepted | I.  Bills Payable Account |
|  | II.  Total Creditors Account |

| | |
|---|---|
| 13. Bills Receivable collected | I.   Bills Receivable Account<br>II.  Cash and Bank Account Summary |
| 14. Bills Payable discharged | I.   Bills Payable Account<br>II.  Cash and Bank Account Summary |
| 15. Bills Receivable dishonoured | I.   Bills Receivable Account<br>II.  Total Debtors Account |
| 16. Bills Receivable endorsed dishonoured | I.   Total Debtors Account<br>II.  Total Creditors Account |
| 17. Drawings/Operating Expenses paid/Loan Repayment/ Additional Capital introduced/Loans raised/Income received. | I.   Cash and Bank Account Summary |
| 18. Cash and Bank Balance/ Cash stolen by Cashier | I.   Cash and Bank Account Summary |
| 19. Opening Capital | I.   Opening Balance Sheet |
| 20. Current Year's Sales | I.   Previous Year's Sales (±) Change due to change in Sales Price and/or Sales Volume |
| 21. Current Year's Revenue Expenses | I.   Prepare Revenue Expenses Account<br>II.  Expenses paid (+) Outstanding at the end (+) Prepaid in the Beginning (−) Outstanding in the beginning (−) Prepaid at the end. |
| 22. Current Year's Revenue Income | I.   Prepare Revenue Income Account.<br>II.  Income Received (+) Accrued at the end (+) Unaccrued in the beginning (−) Accrued in the beginning (−) Unaccrued at the end. |
| 23. Opening and Closing Balance of any other item | I.   Prepare the Account of Respective Item |

Following Proforma of Total Debtors Account, Bills Receivable Account, Total Creditors Account, Bills Payable Account are useful in this method.

**Dr.**          **Total Debtors Account**          **Cr.**

| Particulars | ₹ | Particulars | ₹ |
|---|---|---|---|
| To Balance B/D | xxx | By Cash Received | xxx |
| To Bills Received dishonoured | xxx | By Bills Receivable during the year | xxx |
| To Credit Sales | xxx | By Sales Returns | xxx |
| | | By Bad Debts | xxx |
| | | By Discount Allowed | xxx |
| | | By Allowances Given | xxx |
| | | By Balance C/D | xxx |
| | **xxx** | | **xxx** |

**Dr.**      **Bills Receivable Account**      **Cr.**

| Particulars | ₹ | Particulars | ₹ |
|---|---|---|---|
| To Balance B/D | xxx | By Creditors | xxx |
| To Sundry Debtors | xxx | (Bills Receivable Endorsed) | |
| | | By Cash Received | xxx |
| | | By Balance C/D | xxx |
| | xxx | | xxx |

**Dr.**      **Total Creditors Account**      **Cr.**

| Particulars | ₹ | Particulars | ₹ |
|---|---|---|---|
| To Cash paid | xxx | By Balance B/D | xxx |
| To Bills Payable during the year | xxx | By Bills Payable dishonoured | xxx |
| To Bills Receivable (B/R endorsed) | xxx | By Credit Purchases | xxx |
| To Purchases Returns | xxx | | |
| To Discount Received | xxx | | |
| To Balance C/D | xxx | | |
| | xxx | | xxx |

**Dr.**      **Bills Payable Account**      **Cr.**

| Particulars | ₹ | Particulars | ₹ |
|---|---|---|---|
| To Cash paid | xxx | By Balance B/D | xxx |
| To Balance C/D | xxx | By Sundry Creditors | xxx |
| | xxx | | xxx |

**Note :**

**Inter-relationship between Sundry Debtors Account and Bills Receivable Account, Sundry Creditors Account and Bills Payable Account.**

If Bills Received during the year is not given, then first this should be found and transferred to Total Debtors Account, without which Total Debtors Account cannot be completed. Total Debtors Account will disclose Credit Sales which in turn will help to prepare Trading Account.

Similarly, if Bills accepted during the year is not given, it would be found by taking the difference of Bills Payable Account and transferring this difference to Total Creditors Account. Total Creditors Account will disclose credit purchases which in turn would help to prepare the Trading Account.

**The following steps may be taken to convert Single Entry into Double Entry System.**
i)     Preparation of Opening Statement of Affairs.
ii)     Preparation of Cash Book.
iii)     Preparation of Total Debtors and Total Creditors Account.
iv)     Finding out Total Purchases and Sales.
v)     Preparation of Trading and Profit and Loss Account and Balance Sheet.

Following are certain examples which will give you the perfect understanding about the accounting procedure to be followed under Single Entry System.

### EXAMPLE

Chimandas Dongre, Edalabad, maintained his account on Single Entry System. His balances for the year ended 31st March, 2015 and 31st March, 2016, were as follows.

| Particulars | 31st March, 2015 | 31st March, 2016 |
|---|---|---|
| Bills Receivable | 2,000 | 1,200 |
| Stock | 3,950 | 4,400 |
| Creditors | 4,700 | 4,175 |
| Cash | 1,954 | 981 |
| Bills Payable | 1,736 | 2,525 |
| Debtors | 4,680 | 4,178 |
| Furniture | 1,000 | 1,000 |

From his Cash Book for the year 2015-2016 following information is available :

| Particulars | ₹ |
|---|---|
| Wages | 450 |
| Bills Payable | 1,500 |
| Bills Receivable | 2,150 |
| Miscellaneous Expenses | 350 |
| Salary | 400 |
| Investment Purchased | 500 |
| Sales | 600 |
| Purchases | 300 |
| Received from Debtors | 1,225 |
| Paid to Creditors | 712 |
| Miscellaneous Income | 15 |
| Drawings | 750 |

On enquiry you are told that in 2015-2016.

i) Discount allowed ₹ 200   ii) Discount Received ₹ 178

iii) Bills Payable issued ₹ 2,290   iv) Bills Receivable Received ₹ 1,500

v) Bad Debts written off ₹ 280   vi) Bills Receivable dishonoured ₹ 150

You are required to prepare Trading Account, Profit and Loss Account for the year ended 31.3.2016 and the Balance Sheet as on that date.

### ANSWER

**Missing Items :**

i) Credit Purchases – Sundry Creditors Account,  ii) Credit Sales – Sundry Debtors Account, iii) Opening Capital – Opening Statement of Affairs.

Hence, for finding out these missing items, it is advisable to prepare the following memorandum accounts.

### In the books of Chimandas Dongre, Edalabad

**Dr.**      **Memorandum Creditors Account**      **Cr.**

| Particulars | ₹ | Particulars | ₹ |
|---|---|---|---|
| To Cash | 712 | By Balance B/D | 4,700 |
| To Discount Received | 178 | By Purchases* | 2,655 |
| To Bills Payable issued | 2,290 | (Balancing Figure) | |
| To Balance C/D | 4,175 | | |
| | **7,355** | | **7,355** |

**Dr.**      **Memorandum Debtors Account**      **Cr.**

| Particulars | ₹ | Particulars | ₹ |
|---|---|---|---|
| To Balance B/D | 4,680 | By Cash Received | 1,225 |
| To Bills Receivable dishonoured | 150 | By Discount Allowed | 200 |
| To Sales Credit* | 2553 | By Bills Receivable received | 1,500 |
| (Balancing Figure) | | By Bad Debts written off | 280 |
| | | By Balance C/D | 4,178 |
| | **7,383** | | **7,383** |

### Statement of Affairs as on 1-4-2015

| Liabilities | ₹ | Assets | ₹ |
|---|---|---|---|
| Creditors | 4,700 | Cash | 1,954 |
| Bills Payable | 1,736 | Bills Receivable | 2,000 |
| Capital* | 7,148 | Debtors | 4,680 |
| (Balancing Figure) | | Stock | 3,950 |
| | | Furniture | 1,000 |
| | **13,584** | | **13,584** |

**Dr.**      **Trading Account and Profit and Loss Account for the year ended 31.3.2016**      **Cr.**

| Particulars | | ₹ | Particulars | | ₹ |
|---|---|---|---|---|---|
| To Opening Stock | | 3,950 | By Sales : | | |
| To Purchases : | | | • Cash Sales | 600 | |
| • Cash | 300 | | • Credit | (+) 2,533 | 3,153 |
| • Credit | (+) 2,655 | 2,955 | By Closing Stock | | 4,400 |
| To Wages | | 450 | | | |
| To Gross Profit C/D | | 198 | | | |
| | | **7,553** | | | **7,553** |
| To Salary | | 400 | By Gross Profit B/D | | 198 |
| To Discount Allowed | | 200 | By Miscellaneous Income | | 15 |
| To Bad Debts | | 280 | By Discount Received | | 178 |
| To Miscellaneous Expenses | | 350 | By Net Loss C/D | | 839 |
| | | **1,230** | | | **1,230** |

**Balance Sheet as on 31-3-2016**

| Liabilities | | ₹ | Assets | ₹ |
|---|---|---|---|---|
| Capital : | 7,148 | | Cash in Hand | 981 |
| **Less :** Net Loss | (–) 839 | | Debtors | 4,178 |
| **Less :** Drawings | (–) 750 | 5,559 | Investments | 500 |
| | | | Bills Receivable | 1,200 |
| Creditors | | 4,175 | Stock | 4,400 |
| Bills Payable | | 2,525 | Furniture | 1,000 |
| | | **12,259** | | **12,259** |

| EXAMPLE |
|---|

Balance Sheet as on 31.3.2015, is available with Bimal Chandra, Dombivali. He has supplied the following information from which you are required to prepare a Trading and Profit and Loss Account for the year ended 31st March, 2016, and a Balance Sheet as on that date.

**Balance Sheet as on 31-3-2015**

| Liabilities | ₹ | Assets | ₹ |
|---|---|---|---|
| Capital | 50,000 | Cash | 2,500 |
| Creditors | 10,000 | Bank | 5,000 |
| Bills Payable | 20,000 | Bills Receivable | 10,000 |
| | | Debtors | 12,500 |
| | | Stock | 10,000 |
| | | Furniture | 5,000 |
| | | Plant | 35,000 |
| | **80,000** | | **80,000** |

| Dr. | | | Cash Book for the year ended 31.3.2016 | | Cr. |
|---|---|---|---|---|---|
| **Receipts** | | ₹ | **Payment** | | ₹ |
| Opening Balance : | | | Drawings | | 6,000 |
| • Cash | 2,500 | | Wages | | 10,000 |
| • Bank | (+) 5,000 | 7,500 | Payment to Creditors | | 17,500 |
| Cash Sales | | 17,500 | Bills Payable Paid | | 30,000 |
| Collection from Debtors | | 40,000 | Sundry Expenses | | 15,000 |
| Bills Receivable Honoured | | 37,500 | Rent, Rates and Taxes | | 10,000 |
| | | | Closing Balance : | | |
| | | | • Cash | 1,500 | 14,000 |
| | | | • Bank | 12,500 | |
| | | **1,02,500** | | | **1,02,500** |

**Additional Information :**

| Particulars | ₹ |
|---|---|
| Debtors (31.3.2016) | 20,000 |
| Creditors (31.3.2016) | 12,500 |
| Bills Receivable (31.3.2016) | 15,000 |
| Bills Payable (31.3.2016) | 25,000 |
| Stock (31.3.2016) | 15,000 |
| Bills Receivable dishonoured during the year | 2,500 |
| Bills Payable dishonoured | 1,000 |
| Bills Receivable endorsed | 7,500 |
| Bills Receivable as endorsed dishonoured | 1,000 |
| Discount Allowed | 500 |
| Discount Received | 1,000 |

**ANSWER**

**Missing Items :**

i) Credit Sales – Sundry Debtors Account, ii) Bills Receivable received during the year – Bills Receivable Account, iii) Credit Purchases – Sundry Creditors Account, iv) Bills Payable issued during the year – Bills Payable Account.

Hence, for finding out these missing items, it is advisable to prepare the following memorandum accounts.

**In the books of Bimal Chandra, Dombivli**

Dr.       **Memorandum Bills Receivable Account**       Cr.

| Particulars | ₹ | Particulars | ₹ |
|---|---|---|---|
| To Balance B/D | 10,000 | By Cash | 37,500 |
| To Sundry Debtors* | 52,500 | By Debtors (Dishonoured) | 2,500 |
| (Balancing Figure) | | By Creditors (Endorsed) | 7,500 |
| | | By Balance C/D | 15,000 |
| | **62,500** | | **62,500** |

Dr.       **Memorandum Debtors Account**       Cr.

| Particulars | ₹ | Particulars | ₹ |
|---|---|---|---|
| To Balance B/D | 12,500 | By Cash | 40,000 |
| To Bills Receivable (Dishonoured) | 2,500 | By Discount Allowed | 500 |
| To Sundry Creditors | 1,000 | By Bills Receivable | 52,500 |
| (Endorsed dishonoured) | | By Balance C/D | 20,000 |
| To Sales Credit * | 97,000 | | |
| (Balancing Figure) | | | |
| | **1,13,000** | | **1,13,000** |

Dr.       **Memorandum Bills Payable Account**       Cr.

| Particulars | ₹ | Particulars | ₹ |
|---|---|---|---|
| To Cash | 30,000 | By Balance B/D | 20,000 |
| To Creditors (Dishonoured) | 1,000 | By Sundry Creditors* | 36,000 |
| To Balance C/D | 25,000 | (Balancing Figure) | |
| | **56,000** | | **56,000** |

**Dr.**        **Memorandum Creditors Account**        **Cr.**

| Particulars | ₹ | Particulars | ₹ |
|---|---|---|---|
| To Cash | 17,500 | By Balance B/D | 10,000 |
| To Bills Receivable (Endorsed) | 7,500 | By Bills Payable (Dishonoured) | 1,000 |
| To Discount Received | 1,000 | By Debtors | 1,000 |
| To Bills Payable | 36,000 | (Endorsed dishonoured) | |
| To Balance C/D | 12,500 | By Purchases Credit* | 62,500 |
| | | (Balancing Figure) | |
| | **74,500** | | **74,500** |

**Dr.**    **Trading Account and Profit and Loss Account for the year ended 31.3.2016**    **Cr.**

| Particulars | ₹ | Particulars | ₹ |
|---|---|---|---|
| To Opening Stock | 10,000 | By Sales : | |
| To Purchases : | 62,500 | • Cash Sales 17,500 | |
| To Wages | 10,000 | • Credit (+) 97,000 | 1,14,500 |
| To Gross Profit C/D | 47,000 | By Closing Stock | 15,000 |
| | **1,29,500** | | **1,29,500** |
| To Sundry Expenses | 15,000 | By Gross Profit B/D | 47,000 |
| To Rent, Rates and Taxes | 10,000 | By Discount Received | 1,000 |
| To Discount Allowed | 500 | | |
| To Net Profit transferred to | | | |
| Capital A/c | 22,500 | | |
| | **48,000** | | **48,000** |

**Balance Sheet as on 31st March, 2016**

| Liabilities | | ₹ | Assets | ₹ |
|---|---|---|---|---|
| Creditors | | 12,500 | Cash | 1,500 |
| Bills Payable | | 25,000 | Bank | 12,500 |
| B's Capital : | 50,000 | | Bills Receivable | 15,000 |
| **Add :** Net Profit | (+) 22,500 | | Debtors | 20,000 |
| | 72,500 | | Stock | 15,000 |
| **Less :** Drawings | (−) 6,000 | 66,500 | Furniture | 5,000 |
| | | | Plant | 35,000 |
| | | **1,04,000** | | **1,04,000** |

## SUMMARY

- The Single Entry System of maintaining accounts is defective as it does not adhere to the basic principles of Accountancy i.e. the dual aspect.
- Since only the Cash Book and Personal Accounts are maintained, it becomes difficult to find the profit and loss position.
- Ascertainment of profit or loss is therefore done with the help of the 'Statement of Affairs'.
- The Capital in the beginning and at the end of the financial year is traced out to find profit or loss.
- In the Conversion Method, Final Accounts are to be prepared by first tracing out the missing items like Bills Receivable received during the year from the Bills Receivable Account, Credit Sales from Total Debtors Account, Bills payable accepted during the year from Bills Payable Account and Credit Purchases from Total Creditors Account. These missing items, in turn, will help to complete the Final Accounts.

## 7.5 ILLUSTRATIONS

### CAPITAL COMPARISON METHOD

### ILLUSTRATION 1

Amit Bajaj, Chopda a retailer had not kept proper books of accounts but he gives the information about his assets and liabilities as follows :

| Assets and Liabilities | As on 1st April, 2015 ₹ | As on 31st March, 2016 ₹ |
|---|---|---|
| Cash in hand | 1,200 | 1,500 |
| Creditors | 16,200 | 7,500 |
| Stock | 2,400 | 2,700 |
| Bills Payable | 8,800 | 8,300 |
| Cash at Bank | 10,000 | 10,000 |
| Ms. A's Loan (Cr.) | 10,000 | 10,000 |
| Loose Tools | 3,600 | 3,600 |
| Book Debts | 13,500 | 18,000 |
| Bills Receivable | 4,300 | 5,000 |
| Machinery | 25,000 | 25,000 |

On 31st March, 2016, Amit received ₹ 5,000 as interest on his private investment which he deposited immediately into the Business Bank Account at Dena Bank as introduction of additional capital. During the year he had withdrawn from his business, cash of ₹ 1,750 and goods of ₹ 650 for his personal use. Interest on opening capital is to be provided @ 4% p.a. and charged on drawings @ 5%. No depreciation or reserve is necessary except that Machinery should be written down by 8%. Bad debts amounted to ₹ 520.

Prepare a Statement showing Profit or Loss for the year ended 31st March, 2016 and a Balance-Sheet (Redrafted) as on that date.

### SOLUTION

**In the books of Amit Bajaj, Chopda**
**Statement of Affairs**

| Liabilities | As on 1-4-2015 ₹ | As on 31-3-2016 ₹ | Assets | As on 1-4-2015 ₹ | As on 31-3-2016 ₹ |
|---|---|---|---|---|---|
| Creditors | 16,200 | 7,500 | Cash in Hand | 1,200 | 1,500 |
| Bills Payable | 8,800 | 8,300 | Stock | 2,400 | 2,700 |
| Ms. A's Loan (Cr.) | 10,000 | 10,000 | Cash at Bank | 10,000 | 10,000 |
| | | | Loose Tools | 3,600 | 3,600 |
| A's Capital* | 25,000 | 40,000 | Book Debts | 13,500 | 18,000 |
| (Balancing Figure) | | | Bills Receivable | 4,300 | 5,000 |
| | | | Machinery | 25,000 | 25,000 |
| | 60,000 | 65,800 | | 60,000 | 65,800 |

## Statement showing Profit or Loss as on 31st March, 2016

| Particulars | | | ₹ |
|---|---|---|---|
| Capital as on 31st March, 2016 | | | 40,000 |
| **Add :** i)   Drawings (Cash ₹ 1,750 + Goods ₹ 650) | 2,400 | | |
| ii)   Interest on Drawings @5% | (+) 120 | (+) 2,520 | |
| | | | 42,520 |
| **Less :** i)   Capital as on 1st April, 2015 | 25,000 | | |
| ii)   Introduction of Additional Capital | 5,000 | | |
| iii)   Interest on Capital @4% p.a. | (–) 1,000 | (–) 31,000 | |
| ∴ **Gross Profit** | | | **11,520** |
| **Add :** Business Incomes | | (+) | NIL |
| **Less :** i)   Depreciation on Machinery @ 8% p.a. | 2,000 | | |
| ii)   Bad Debts | (+) 520 | (–) 2,520 | |
| ∴ **Net Profit** | | | **9,000** |

## Balance Sheet (Redrafted) as on 31st March, 2016

| Liabilities | | ₹ | Assets | | ₹ |
|---|---|---|---|---|---|
| A's Capital | 25,000 | 37,480 | Cash in Hand | | 1,500 |
| **Add :** Introduction of | | | Stock in Trade | | 2,700 |
| Additional Capital | 5,000 | | Cash at Bank | | 10,000 |
| **Add :** Interest on Capital | | | Loose-Tools | | 3,600 |
| @ 4% p.a. | 1,000 | | Book Debts | 18,000 | 17,480 |
| **Add :** Net Profit | (+) 9,000 | | **Less :** Bad Debts | (–) 520 | |
| | 40,000 | | Bills Receivable | | 5,000 |
| **Less :** Drawings | | | Machinery | 25,000 | 23,000 |
| • Cash | 1,750 | | **Less :** Dep. @8% p.a. | (–) 2,000 | |
| • Goods (+) 650 | 2,400 | | | | |
| **Less :** Interest on | | | | | |
| Drawings @5% | (–) 120 | | | | |
| Creditors | | 7,500 | | | |
| Bills Payable | | 8,300 | | | |
| Ms. A's Loan | | 10,000 | | | |
| | | **63,280** | | | **63,280** |

---

**ILLUSTRATION 2**

Balaji Chandan, Deolali, keeps his books on Single Entry System. The following information is disclosed :

| Particulars | As on 1-4-2015 ₹ | As on 31-3-2016 ₹ |
|---|---|---|
| Cash in Hand | 2,300 | 9,000 |
| Stock in Trade | 16,000 | 28,000 |
| Debtors | 20,000 | 15,500 |
| Bank Overdraft | 6,400 | 8,000 |
| Motor Vehicles | 35,000 | 35,000 |
| Furniture and Fixtures | 10,000 | 15,000 |
| Bills Receivable | 13,000 | 10,000 |
| Creditors | 22,000 | 8,000 |
| Salary Payable | 600 | 1,000 |
| Bills Payable | 7,300 | 5,500 |

Balaji had withdrawn ₹ 2,600 for payment of rent of residential quarters. Additions to furniture were made on 30th September, 2015. Make a reserve of 6% in respect of Bills Receivables. Depreciation @ 4% p.a. on Furniture and Fixtures and @ 6% p.a. on Motor Vehicles should be provided as per written down value method. As regards debtors it is ascertained that ₹ 500 are irrecoverable and a further reserve of 6% should be made for bad and doubtful debts. Discount allowed to credit customers amounted to ₹ 100.

You are requested to prepare a Statement showing Profit or Loss for the year ended 31$^{st}$ March, 2014 and a Balance-Sheet (Redrafted) as on that date.

## SOLUTION

**In the books of Balaji Chandan, Deolali**
**Statement of Affairs**

| Liabilities | As on 1-4-2015 ₹ | As on 31-3-2016 ₹ | Assets | As on 1-4-2015 ₹ | As on 31-3-2016 ₹ |
|---|---|---|---|---|---|
| Bank Overdraft | 6,400 | 8,000 | Cash in hand | 2,300 | 9,000 |
| Creditors | 22,000 | 8,000 | Stock-in-Trade | 16,000 | 28,000 |
| Salary Payable | 600 | 1,000 | Debtors | 20,000 | 15,500 |
| Bills Payable | 7,300 | 5,500 | Motor Vehicles | 35,000 | 35,000 |
| B's Capital | 60,000 | 90,000 | Furniture & Fixtures | 10,000 | 15,000 |
| (Balancing Figure) | | | Bills Receivable | 13,000 | 10,000 |
| | 96,300 | 1,12,500 | | 96,300 | 1,12,500 |

**Statement showing Profit or Loss as on 31st March, 2016**

| Particulars | | ₹ |
|---|---|---|
| | Capital as on 31$^{st}$ March, 2016 | 90,000 |
| **Add :** | Drawings for payment of rent of residential quarters  (+) | 2,600 |
| | | 92,600 |
| **Less :** | Capital as on 1$^{st}$ April, 2015  (−) | 60,000 |
| ∴ | **Gross Profit** | 32,600 |
| **Add :** | Business Incomes  (+) | NIL |
| **Less :** | i)   Depreciation on Furniture and Fixtures @4% p.a.  500 | 4,700 |
| | ii)  Depreciation on Motor Vehicles @6% p.a.  2,100 | |
| | iii) Reserve for Bills Receivable @6%  600 | |
| | iv) Bad Debts  500 | |
| | v)  Reserve for Bad and Doubtful Debts @6%  900 | |
| | vi) Discount Allowed to credit customers  (+) 100 | |
| ∴ | **Net Profit** | **27,900** |

**Balance Sheet (Redrafted) as on 31st March, 2016**

| Liabilities | | | ₹ | Assets | | | ₹ |
|---|---|---|---|---|---|---|---|
| B's Capital | | 60,000 | 85,300 | Cash in Hand | | | 9,000 |
| **Add :** | Net Profit | (+) 27,900 | | Stock-in-Trade | | | 28,000 |
| | | 87,900 | | Debtors | | 15,500 | 14,000 |
| **Less :** | Drawings | (−) 2,600 | | **Less :** Bad Debts | | (−) 500 | |
| Bank Overdraft | | | 8,000 | | | 15,000 | |
| Creditors | | | 8,000 | **Less :** R.D.D. @ 6% | | (−) 900 | |
| Salary Payable | | | 1,000 | | | 14,100 | |
| Bills Payable | | | 5,500 | **Less :** Discount Allowed | (−) | 100 | |
| | | | | Motor Vehicles | | 35,000 | 32,900 |
| | | | | **Less :** Depre. @6% p.a. | (−) | 2,100 | |
| | | | | Furniture and Fixtures | | 10,000 | 14,500 |
| | | | | **Add :** Additions on 30.09.08 | (+) | 5,000 | |
| | | | | | | 15,000 | |
| | | | | **Less :** Depre. @4% p.a | (−) | 500 | |
| | | | | Bills Receivable | | 10,000 | 9,400 |
| | | | | **Less :** Reserve @6% | (−) | 600 | |
| | | | 1,07,800 | | | | 1,07,800 |

## ILLUSTRATION 3

Chunilal Deo, Edalabad, does not maintain his books of accounts on Double Entry System. However, he gives you the following information regarding his assets and liabilities for the year 2015-2016.

| Assets and Liabilities | As on 1-4-2015 ₹ | As on 31-3-2016 ₹ |
|---|---|---|
| Bank | 5,000 (Dr.) | 9,000 (Cr.) |
| Cash in Hand | 1,200 | 1,900 |
| Creditors | 27,000 | 20,000 |
| Stock in Trade | 25,000 | 19,100 |
| Bills Payable | 1,900 | 500 |
| Furniture | 2,000 | 1,800 |
| Loose Tools | 1,700 | 1,700 |
| Debtors | 19,000 | 16,000 |

Out of total debtors, a credit customer Maganlal became bankrupt and the balance due from him amounting to ₹ 600 could not be recovered at all. Loose Tools were revalued at ₹ 1,260 on 31st March, 2016. During the year he had withdrawn ₹ 5,000 from his business of which ₹ 4,000 were invested in purchasing 4% Govt. Bonds on 1st January, 2016, as business investment.

Find out his profit or loss for the year ended 31st March, 2016, and also prepare a Balance Sheet, (Readjusted) as on that date.

## SOLUTION

**In the Books of Chunilal Deo, Edalabad**
**Statement of Affairs**

| Liabilities | As on 1-4-2015 ₹ | As on 31-3-2016 ₹ | Assets | As on 1-4-2015 ₹ | As on 31-3-2016 ₹ |
|---|---|---|---|---|---|
| Bank (Cr.) | – | 9,000 | Bank (Dr.) | 5,000 | – |
| Creditors | 27,000 | 20,000 | Cash in hand | 1,200 | 1,900 |
| Bills Payable | 1,900 | 500 | Stock-in-Trade | 25,000 | 19,100 |
| C's Capital A/c * | 25,000 | 15,000 | Furniture | 2,000 | 1,800 |
| (Balancing Figure) | | | Loose-Tools | 1,700 | 1,700 |
| | | | Debtors | 19,000 | 16,000 |
| | | | Investment in 4% Govt. Bonds | – | 4,000 |
| | **53,900** | **44,500** | | **53,900** | **44,500** |

**Statement showing Profit or Loss as on 31st March, 2016**

| Particulars | | ₹ |
|---|---|---|
| Capital as on 31st March, 2016 | | 15,000 |
| **Add :** Drawings | | (+) 1,000 |
| | | 16,000 |
| **Less :** Capital as on 1st April, 2015 | | (–) 25,000 |
| ∴ **Gross Loss** | | 9,000 |
| **Add :** i) Bad Debts | 600 | |
|     ii) Depreciation on Loose Tools | (+) 440 | (+) 1,040 |
| | | 10,040 |
| **Less :** i) Outstanding Interest on Investment in 4% Govt. Bonds | | |
|      for 3 months | | (–) 40 |
| ∴ **Net Loss** | | 10,000 |

### Balance Sheet (Readjusted) as on 31st March, 2016

| Liabilities | | ₹ | Assets | | ₹ |
|---|---|---|---|---|---|
| C's Capital | 25,000 | 14,000 | Cash in Hand | | 1,900 |
| **Less :** Net Loss | (–) 10,000 | | Stock-in-Trade | | 19,100 |
| | 15,000 | | Furniture | | 1,800 |
| | | | Loose Tools | 1,700 | 1,260 |
| **Less :** Drawings | (–) 1,000 | | **Less :** Depr. | (–) 440 | |
| Bank (Cr.) | | 9,000 | Debtors | 16,000 | 15,400 |
| Creditors | | 20,000 | **Less :** Bad Debts | (–) 600 | |
| Bills Payable | | 500 | Investment in 4% | | 4,040 |
| | | | Govt. Bonds | 4,000 | |
| | | | **Add :** Outstanding Interest | (+) 40 | |
| | | | (4% of ₹ 4,000 for 3 months) | | |
| | | **43,500** | | | **43,500** |

## CONVERSION METHOD

### ILLUSTRATION 1

Dinesh Edke, Firozpur, keeps his books on single entry system. The following information is supplied by him for the year ended 31st March, 2016.

The particulars of assets and liabilities are disclosed as below :

| Assets and Liabilities | As on 1-4-2015 ₹ | As on 31-3-2016 ₹ |
|---|---|---|
| Spare Parts | 300 | 300 |
| Creditors | 9,400 | 8,350 |
| Bills Receivable | 4,000 | 2,400 |
| Bills Payable | 3,471 | 5,051 |
| Fixtures | 1,700 | 1,700 |
| Stock-in-Trade | 7,900 | 8,800 |
| Cash in Hand | 1,408 | 1,063 |
| Petty Cash | 500 | 500 |
| Cash at Bank | 2,000 | 400 |
| Book Debts | 9,361 | 8,355 |
| Salary Payable | 150 | 250 |

Summary of Cash Book gives the following details :

**Dr.**   Cash Book for the year ended 31st March, 2016   **Cr.**

| Receipts | ₹ | Payments | ₹ |
|---|---|---|---|
| To Balance B/D | | By Cartage | 200 |
| • Cash in hand | 1,408 | By Bills payable | 3,000 |
| • Petty cash | 500 | By Trading Expenses | 450 |
| • Cash at Bank | 2,000 | By Salary | 800 |
| To Bills Receivable | 4,300 | By Investments | 1,000 |
| To Sales | 1,200 | By Purchases | 600 |
| To Sundry Debtors | 2,450 | By General Expenses | 250 |
| To Interest on Investments | 30 | By Sundry Creditors | 1,425 |
| | | By Wages | 700 |
| | | By Medical Expenses of Mr. Dinesh | 1,500 |
| | | By Balance C/D | |
| | | • Cash in Hand | 1,063 |
| | | • Petty Cash | 500 |
| | | • Cash at Bank | 400 |
| | **11,888** | | **11,888** |

| Other additional information discloses the following facts : | ₹ |
|---|---|
| • Bad Debts | 560 |
| • Acceptances Received from Debtors ........ | 3,000 |
| • Discount Allowed to customers ........ | 400 |
| • Acceptances given to creditors ........ | 4,580 |
| • Discount Allowed by suppliers ........ | 355 |
| • Bills Receivable dishonoured ........ | 300 |

In addition to the above goods costing ₹ 94 were stolen away from the godown, no entry has been recorded for the same.

You are required to prepare Trading Account, Profit and Loss Account for the year ended 31st March, 2016, and Balance-Sheet as on that date.

### SOLUTION

**Working Notes :**

**A) Missing Items :**
   i)    Opening balance of Capital Account – Opening Statement of Affairs
   ii)   Credit Sales – Sundry Debtors Account
   iii)  Credit Purchases – Sundry Creditors Account

**In the books of Dinesh Edke, Firozpur**
**Statement of Affairs as on 1st April, 2015**

| Liabilities | ₹ | Assets | ₹ |
|---|---|---|---|
| Creditors | 9,400 | Spare Parts | 300 |
| Bills Payable | 3,471 | Bills Receivable | 4,000 |
| Salary Payable | 150 | Fixtures | 1,700 |
| | | Stock-in-Trade | 7,900 |
| Capital * | 14,148 | Cash in Hand | 1,408 |
| (Balancing Figure) | | Petty Cash | 500 |
| | | Cash at Bank | 2,000 |
| | | Book Debts | 9,361 |
| | **27,169** | | **27,169** |

| Dr. | Sundry Debtors Account | | Cr. |
|---|---|---|---|
| **Particulars** | ₹ | **Particulars** | ₹ |
| To Balance B/D | 9,361 | By Cash | 2,450 |
| To Bills Receivable | 300 | By Bad Debts | 560 |
| To Credit Sales * | 5,104 | By Bills Receivable | 3,000 |
| (Balancing Figure) | | By Discount Allowed | 400 |
| | | By Balance C/D | 8,355 |
| | **14,765** | | **14,765** |

| Dr. | Sundry Creditors Account | | Cr. |
|---|---|---|---|
| **Particulars** | ₹ | **Particulars** | ₹ |
| To Cash | 1,425 | By Balance B/D | 9,400 |
| To Bills Payable | 4,580 | By Credit Purchases* | 5,310 |
| To Discount Received | 355 | (Balancing Figure) | |
| To Balance C/D | 8,350 | | |
| | **14,710** | | **14,710** |

| Dr. | Trading Account for the year ended 31st March, 2016 | | | | Cr. |
|---|---|---|---|---|---|
| **Particulars** | | ₹ | **Particulars** | | ₹ |
| To Opening Stock | | 7,900 | By Sales | | 6,304 |
| To Purchases | | 5,910 | • Cash | 1,200 | |
| • Cash | 600 | | • Credit | (+) 5,104 | |
| • Credit | (+) 5,310 | | By Closing Stock | | 8,800 |
| To Cartage | | 200 | | | |
| To Trading Expenses | | 450 | By Loss by Theft | | 94 |
| To Wages | | 700 | | | |
| To Gross Profit C/D* | | 38 | | | |
| | | **15,198** | | | **15,198** |

| Dr. | Profit and Loss Account for the year ended 31st March, 2016 | | | Cr. |

| Particulars | | ₹ | Particulars | ₹ |
|---|---|---|---|---|
| To Salary | 800 | 900 | By Gross Profit B/D | 38 |
| **Add :** Outstanding | | | | |
| (2015-2016) | (+) 250 | | By Interest on Investments | 30 |
| | 1,050 | | By Discount Received | 355 |
| **Less :** Outstanding | | | | |
| (2014-2015) | (–) 150 | | | |
| To General Expenses | | 250 | | |
| To Bad Debts | | 560 | | |
| To Discount Allowed | | 400 | | |
| To Loss by Theft | | 94 | By Net Loss C/D* | 1,781 |
| | | **2,204** | | **2,204** |

Balance Sheet as on 31st March, 2016

| Liabilities | | ₹ | Assets | ₹ |
|---|---|---|---|---|
| E's Capital | 14,148 | 10,867 | Spare Parts | 300 |
| Less : Net Loss | (–) 1,781 | | Bills Receivable | 2,400 |
| Less : Drawings | (–) 1,500 | | Fixtures | 1,700 |
| • (Mr. E's Medical Expenses) | | | Stock-in-Trade | 8,800 |
| Creditors | | 8,350 | Cash in hand | 1,063 |
| Bills Payable | | 5,051 | Petty cash | 500 |
| Salary Payable | | 250 | Cash at Bank | 400 |
| | | | Book Debts | 8,355 |
| | | | Investments | 1,000 |
| | | **24,518** | | **24,518** |

---

**ILLUSTRATION 2**

Edward Fattelal, Gulbarga, started his business on 1st April, 2015, with a cash capital of ₹ 1,00,000 and Buildings of ₹ 80,000. He immediately purchased Furniture of ₹ 25,000 and Tools and Implements of ₹ 15,000. He does not know how to maintain the books of accounts on double entry system. He gives you the following information from which you are required to prepare his Trading Account, Profit and Loss Account for the year ended 31st March, 2016, and a Balance-Sheet as on that date.

                ₹

i) Turnover for the year 2015-2016 :

- Cash      27,500
- Credit      55,500

ii) Purchases made during the year 2015-2016

- Credit      30,500
- Cash      10,000

iii) Return of Goods :

- Returns to Suppliers      1,500
- Returns from Customers      3,000

iv) Discounts and Allowances :

- Discount allowed by Suppliers      800
- Allowances given to Debtors      450
- Discount allowed to Customers      650

v) Bills of exchange and acceptances :
- Acceptances issued to Creditors     2,500
- Bills received from Debtors     3,500

vi) Closing balances of assets and liabilities as on 31$^{st}$ March, 2016.     ₹
- Sundry Debtors     13,500
- Sundry Creditors     10,000

vii) Expenses and Incomes during the year 2015-2016

| | ₹ |
|---|---|
| Insurance for 13 months | 1,300 |
| Rent for 11 months | 550 |
| Carriage and Cartage | 1,250 |
| Advertisement and Publicity | 1,800 |
| Commission paid on Sales | 850 |
| Commission received | 1,500 |
| Salaries of Administrative staff | 12,800 |
| Personal Travelling expenses of Edward | 1,400 |
| Wages of Manufacturing and Factory Staff | 6,400 |
| Legal Fees paid to Lawyer | 900 |
| Purchase of Motor Vehicles on 31.3.2016 | 50,450 |

viii) Adjustments :
- a) Closing Stock as on 31$^{st}$ March, 2016, was :
  - Cost Price     16,000
  - Market Price     18,000
- b) Provide depreciation @5% p.a. on Buildings, @4% p.a. on Furniture and @20% p.a. on Tools and Implements.

### SOLUTION

**Working Notes**

**A) Missing Items :**
- i) Closing balance of Cash Account – Cash Book
- ii) Collection from Debtors - Sundry Debtors Account
- iii) Payment to Creditors - Sundry Creditors Account

**In the books of Edward Fattelal, Gulbarga**

Dr.     **Cash Book for the year ended 31$^{st}$ March, 2016**     Cr.

| Receipts | ₹ | Payments | ₹ |
|---|---|---|---|
| To F's Capital | 1,00,000 | By Furniture | 25,000 |
| To Cash Sales | 27,500 | By Tools and Implements | 15,000 |
| To Commission | 1,500 | By Cash Purchases | 10,000 |
| To Collection from Debtors | 34,400 | By Insurance | 1,300 |
| | | By Rent | 550 |
| | | By Carriage and Cartage | 1,250 |
| | | By Advertisement and Publicity | 1,800 |
| | | By Commission on Sales | 850 |
| | | By Salaries | 12,800 |
| | | By Wages | 6,400 |
| | | By Legal Fees | 900 |
| | | By Edward's Drawings | 1,400 |
| | | (Personal Travelling Exp. of Edward) | |
| | | By Payment to Creditors | 15,700 |
| | | By Motor Vehicles | 50,450 |
| | | By Balance C/D* | 20,000 |
| | | (Balancing Figure) | |
| | **1,63,400** | | **1,63,400** |

**Dr.**        **Sundry Debtors Account**        **Cr.**

| Particulars | ₹ | Particulars | ₹ |
|---|---|---|---|
| To Balance B/D | NIL | By Returns Inward | 3,000 |
| To Credit Sales | 55,500 | By Discount Allowed | 650 |
| | | By Allowances Given | 450 |
| | | By Bills Receivables | 3,500 |
| | | By Collection from Debtors* | 34,400 |
| | | (Balancing Figure) | |
| | | By Balance C/D | 13,500 |
| | 55,500 | | 55,500 |

**Dr.**        **Sundry Creditors Account**        **Cr.**

| Particulars | ₹ | Particulars | ₹ |
|---|---|---|---|
| To Returns Outward | 1,500 | By Balance B/D | NIL |
| To Discount Received | 800 | By Credit Purchases | 30,500 |
| To Bills Payables | 2,500 | | |
| To Payment to Creditors* | 15,700 | | |
| (Balancing Figure) | | | |
| To Balance C/D | 10,000 | | |
| | 30,500 | | 30,500 |

**Dr.**        **Trading Account for the year ended 31st March, 2016**        **Cr.**

| Particulars | ₹ | Particulars | ₹ |
|---|---|---|---|
| To Opening Stock | 39,000 | By Sales : | 80,000 |
| To Purchases : | | i)  Cash      27,500 | |
| i)  Cash      10,000 | | ii)  Credit      (+) 55,500 | |
| ii)  Credit      (+) 30,500 | |      83,000 | |
|      40,500 | | **Less :** Returns Inward   (−) 3,000 | |
| **Less :** Returns Outward   (−) 1,500 | | By Closing Stock | 16,000 |
| To Carriage and Cartage | 1,250 | | |
| To Wages | 6,400 | | |
| To Gross Profit C/D* | 49,350 | | |
| | 96,000 | | 96,000 |

**Cr.**        **Profit and Loss Account for the year ended 31st March, 2016**        **Cr.**

| Particulars | ₹ | Particulars | ₹ |
|---|---|---|---|
| To Discount Allowed | 650 | By Gross Profit B/D | 49,350 |
| To Allowances Given | 450 | By Discount Received | 800 |
| To Insurance      1,300 | 1,200 | By Commission | 1,500 |
| Less : Prepaid      (−) 100 | | | |
| To Rent      550 | 600 | | |
| Add : Outstandings      (+) 50 | | | |
| To Advertisement and Publicity | 1,800 | | |
| To Commission on Sales | 850 | | |
| To Salaries | 12,800 | | |
| To Legal Fees | 900 | | |
| To Depreciation : | 8,000 | | |
| i)  Buildings @ 5% p.a.      4,000 | | | |
| ii)  Furniture @ 4% p.a.      1,000 | | | |
| iii) Tools and Implements | | | |
|      @ 20% p.a.      (+) 3,000 | | | |
| To Net Profit C/D.* | 24,400 | | |
| | 51,650 | | 51,650 |

**Balance Sheet as on 31st March, 2016**

| Liabilities | | ₹ | Assets | | ₹ |
|---|---|---|---|---|---|
| F's Capital | 1,80,000 | | Buildings | 80,000 | 76,000 |
| Cash | 1,00,000 | 2,03,000 | **Less :** Depre. @ 5% p. a. (–) 4,000 | | |
| Buildings (+) 80,000 | | | Furniture | 25,000 | 24,000 |
| **Add :** Net Profit (+) 24,400 | | | **Less :** Depre. @ 4% p.a. (–) 1,000 | | |
| | 2,04,400 | | Tools and Implements | 15,000 | 12,000 |
| **Less :** Drawings (–) 1,400 | | | **Less :** Depre. @ 20% p.a. (–) 3,000 | | |
| (Personal Travelling Exp.) | | | Bills Receivable | | 3,500 |
| Bills Payable | | 2,500 | Sundry Debtors | | 13,500 |
| Sundry Creditors | | 10,000 | Prepaid Insurance | | 100 |
| Outstanding Rent | | 50 | Closing Stock | | 16,000 |
| | | | Motor Vehicles | | 50,450 |
| | | | (Purchased on 31.3.2016) | | |
| | | | Cash | | 20,000 |
| | | **2,15,550** | | | **2,15,550** |

### ILLUSTRATION 3

You are given with :

a)      The Balance Sheet of Fattechand Gore, Himmatpur as on 1.4.2015.
b)      The summary of cash transactions for the year 2015–2016.
c)      The remaining transactions and
(d)      Adjustments.

**a)      Balance Sheet as on 1.4.2015**

| Liabilities | ₹ | Assets | ₹ |
|---|---|---|---|
| Capital | 1,20,600 | Land and Buildings | 80,000 |
| Creditors | 69,800 | Machinery | 50,000 |
| Bills Payable | 29,000 | Patents | 20,000 |
| Loans | 30,600 | Fixtures | 15,000 |
| General Reserve | 20,000 | Stock | 44,600 |
| Outstanding Wages | 2,680 | Debtors | 49,400 |
| Bank Overdraft | 4,000 | Bills Receivable | 14,600 |
| | | Cash in hand | 3,080 |
| | **2,76,680** | | **2,76,680** |

**b)      Cash - Book for the year ended 31.3.2016**

| Particulars | ₹ | Particulars | ₹ |
|---|---|---|---|
| To Balance B/D | 3,080 | By Bank Overdraft | 4,000 |
| To Debtors | 45,980 | By Wages | 15,280 |
| To Bills Receivables | 11,400 | By Loans Paid | 10,600 |
| To Capital | 15,000 | By Creditors | 41,000 |
| To Sales (Cash) | 35,820 | By Bills Payable | 21,800 |
| To Commission | 5,000 | By Salaries | 23,400 |
| To Rent | 22,000 | By Sundry Expenses | 1,460 |
| | | By Interest on Loans | 2,000 |
| | | By Drawings | 8,940 |
| | | By 6% Investments | |
| | |      (Purchased on 1.10.2015) | 8,000 |
| | | By Balance C/D. –    • Cash | 1,580 |
| | |           • Bank | 220 |
| | **1,38,280** | | **1,38,280** |

**c)** **The remaining transactions :**

|  | ₹ |
|---|---:|
| Credit Sales | 76,000 |
| Credit Purchases | 70,000 |
| Bills receivable Received | 21,400 |
| Stock on 31.3.2016 | 59,000 |
| Discount to Customers | 1,020 |
| Discount from Suppliers | 740 |
| Bills Payable issued | 19,400 |
| Bills Receivable dishonoured | 3,000 |

**d)** **Adjustments**
i) Provide 5% for Doubtful Debts on Debtors and Bills Receivable.
ii) Depreciate Machinery by 5% and Land and Buildings by $2\frac{1}{2}\%$, Patents and Fixtures by 10%.
iii) Outstanding Wages are ₹ 1,820 and Salary outstanding amounted to ₹ 1,080.
iv) Transfer ₹ 10,000 to General Reserve.

Prepare Trading and Profit and Loss Account for the year ended 31.3.2016, and Balance as on that date.

> **SOLUTION**

**Working Notes :**

**A) Missing Items :**
i) Closing balance of Sundry Debtors Account – Sundry Debtors Account
ii) Closing balance of Bills Receivable Account – Bills Receivable Account
iii) Closing balance of Sundry Creditors Account – Sundry Creditors Account
iv) Closing balance of Bills Payable Account – Bills Payable Account

**In the Books of Fattechand Gore, Himmatpur**

**Dr.**    **Sundry Debtors Account**    **Cr.**

| Particulars | ₹ | Particulars | ₹ |
|---|---:|---|---:|
| To Balance B/D | 49,400 | By Cash | 45,980 |
| To Credit Sales | 76,000 | By Bills Receivable | |
| To Bills Receivable | 3,000 | (Bills Receivable received) | 21,400 |
| (Bills Receivable dishonoured) | | By Discount to Customers | 1,020 |
| | | By Balance C/D* | 60,000 |
| | | (Balancing Figure) | |
| | **1,28,400** | | **1,28,400** |

**Dr.**    **Bills Receivable Account**    **Cr.**

| Particulars | ₹ | Particulars | ₹ |
|---|---:|---|---:|
| To Balance B/D | 14,600 | By Cash | 11,400 |
| To Sundry Debtors | 21,400 | By Sundry Debtors | 3,000 |
| (Bills Receivable Received) | | (Bills Receivable dishonoured) | |
| | | By Balance C/D * | 21,600 |
| | | (Balancing Figure) | |
| | **36,000** | | **36,000** |

**Dr.**    **Sundry Creditors Account**    **Cr.**

| Particulars | ₹ | Particulars | ₹ |
|---|---:|---|---:|
| To Cash | 41,000 | By Balance B/D | 69,800 |
| To Discount from Suppliers | 740 | By Credit Purchases | 70,000 |
| To Bills Payable | 19,400 | | |
| (Bills Payable issued) | | | |
| To Balance C/D * | | | |
| (Balancing Figure) | 78,660 | | |
| | **1,39,800** | | **1,39,800** |

**Dr.**     **Bills Payable Account**     **Cr.**

| Particulars | ₹ | Particulars | ₹ |
|---|---|---|---|
| To Cash | 21,800 | By Balance B/D | 29,000 |
| To Balance C/D* | 26,600 | By Sundry Creditors | 19,400 |
| (Balancing Figure) | | (Bills Payable Issued) | |
| | **48,400** | | **48,400** |

**Dr.**     **Trading Account for the year ended 31st March, 2016**     **Cr.**

| Particulars | | | ₹ | Particulars | | | ₹ |
|---|---|---|---|---|---|---|---|
| To Opening Stock | | | 44,600 | By Sales : | | | 1,11,820 |
| To Purchases : | | | 70,000 | •   Cash | | 35,820 | |
| •   Cash | | – | | •   Credit | (+) | 76,000 | |
| •   Credit | (+) | 70,000 | | By Closing Stock | | | 59,000 |
| To Wages | | 15,280 | 14,420 | | | | |
| **Less** : Outstandings | | | | | | | |
| (2014-2015) | (–) | 2,680 | | | | | |
| | | 12,600 | | | | | |
| **Add** : Outstandings | | | | | | | |
| (2015-2016) | (+) | 1,820 | | | | | |
| To Gross Profit C/D * | | | 41,800 | | | | |
| | | | **1,70,820** | | | | **1,70,820** |

**Dr.**     **Profit and Loss Account for the year ended 31st March, 2016**     **Cr.**

| Particulars | | ₹ | Particulars | ₹ |
|---|---|---|---|---|
| To Salaries | 23,400 | 24,480 | By Gross Profit B/D | 41,800 |
| **Add** : Outstandings | | | By Commission | 5,000 |
| (2015-2016) | (+) 1,080 | | By Rent | 22,000 |
| To Sundry Expenses | | 1,460 | By Outstanding Interest on | |
| To Interest on Loan | | 2,000 |     6% Investments | 240 |
| To Discount to Customers | | 1,020 | To Discount from Suppliers | 740 |
| To R.D.D. @5% on Sundry Debtors | | 3,000 | | |
| To Prov. @5% on Bills Receivable | | 1,080 | | |
| To Depreciation : | | 8,000 | | |
| •   Machinery @5% p.a. | 2,500 | | | |
| •   Land and Buildings | | | | |
|    @ $2\frac{1}{2}$% p.a. | 2,000 | | | |
| •   Patents @ 10% p.a. | 2,000 | | | |
| •   Fixtures @ 10% p.a. | (+) 1,500 | | | |
| To Transfer to General Reserve | | 10,000 | | |
| To Net Profit C/D* | | 18,740 | | |
| | | **69,780** | | **69,780** |

### Balance Sheet as on 31.3.2016

| Liabilities | | ₹ | Assets | | ₹ |
|---|---|---|---|---|---|
| G's Capital | 1,20,600 | 1,45,400 | Land and Buildings | 80,000 | 78,000 |
| **Add :** Additions | (+) 15,000 | | **Less :** Dep. @ $2^1/_2$% p.a. | (−) 2,000 | |
| **Add :** Net Profit | (+) 18,740 | | Machinery | 50,000 | 47,500 |
| | 1,54,340 | | **Less :** Dep. @ 5% p.a. | (−) 2,500 | |
| **Less :** Drawings | (−) 8,940 | | Patents | 20,000 | 18,000 |
| | | | **Less :** Dep. @10% p.a. | (−) 2,000 | |
| Loans | 30,600 | 20,000 | Fixtures | 15,000 | 13,500 |
| **Less :** Loans paid | (−) 10,600 | | **Less :** Dep. @ 10% p.a. | (−) 1,500 | |
| General Reserve | 20,000 | 30,000 | 6% Investments | | |
| **Add :** Transfer | (+) 10,000 | | (Purchased on 1.10.2015) | | 8,000 |
| Sundry Creditors | | 78,660 | Outstanding Interest on 6% Invst. | | 240 |
| Bills Payable | | 26,600 | Cash | | 1,580 |
| Outstanding Wages | | 1,820 | Bank | | 220 |
| Salary Outstanding | | 1,080 | Closing Stock | | 59,000 |
| | | | Sundry Debtors | 60,000 | 57,000 |
| | | | **Less :** R.D.D. @5% | (−) 3,000 | |
| | | | Bills Receivable | 21,600 | |
| | | | **Less :** Provision @ 5% | (−) 1,080 | 20,520 |
| | | **3,03,560** | | | **3,03,560** |

## ILLUSTRATION 4

Gendalal Hazare, Ichalkaranji, keeps his books on single entry system. His Balance Sheet as on 1st April, 2015, is as follows :

| Liabilities | ₹ | Assets | ₹ |
|---|---|---|---|
| G's Capital | 14,850 | Cash | 2,250 |
| Creditors | 3,000 | Bills Receivable | 3,000 |
| Bills Payable | 6,000 | Debtors | 3,750 |
| Wages Payable | 150 | Stock-in-Trade | 3,000 |
| | | Machinery | 10,000 |
| | | Loose Tools | 2,000 |
| | **24,000** | | **24,000** |

The summary of Cash-Book discloses the following :

| Dr. | | Cash Book for the year ended 31st March, 2016 | | Cr. |
|---|---|---|---|---|
| **Receipts** | ₹ | **Payments** | | ₹ |
| To Balance B/D | 2,250 | By Creditors | | 5,250 |
| To Sales | 5,000 | By Wages | | 3,150 |
| To Debtors | 12,000 | By House Rent | | 1,650 |
| To Bills Receivable | 11,250 | By Bills payable | | 9,000 |
| To Sundry Income | 250 | By Freight | | 1,200 |
| | | By Office Rent | | 2,500 |
| | | By Octroi Duty | | 2,800 |
| | | By Factory Rent | | 1,000 |
| | | By Balance C/D | | 4,200 |
| | **30,750** | | | **30,750** |

Additional information includes balances of assets and liabilities as on 31$^{st}$ March, 2016 which are as follows :

|  |  | ₹ |
|---|---|---|
| • | Sundry Debtors | 6,000 |
| • | Bills Receivable | 6,750 |
| • | Sundry Creditors | 3,750 |
| • | Bills Payable | 7,500 |
| • | Stock | 4,500 |

The remaining transactions are :

|  |  | ₹ |
|---|---|---|
| • | Discount Allowed to Debtors | 375 |
| • | Bills Receivable endorsed | 2,250 |
| • | Discount Received from Creditors | 975 |
| • | Bills Receivable dishonoured | 750 |
| • | Bills Payable dishonoured | 300 |
| • | Bills Receivable endorsed–dishonoured | 300 |
| • | Loose Tools were revalued at | 1,650 |

- Goods amounted to ₹ 350 were used by Gendalal for his domestic purposes. No. entry is made in the books.

You are required to prepare Trading Account and Profit and Loss Account for the year ended 31$^{st}$ March, 2016 and a Balance-Sheet as on that date. Also pass necessary journal entries for the important bills of exchange transactions.

SOLUTION

**Working Notes :**

**A) Missing Items :**
- i)    Credit Sales – Sundry Debtors Account
- ii)   Bills Receivables received during the year – Bills Receivable Account
- iii)   Credit Purchases – Sundry Creditors Account
- iv)   Bills Payables issued during the year – Bills Payable Account

**Note :** Inter-relationship between Sundry Debtors Account and Bills Receivable Account, Sundry Creditors Account and Bills Payable Account.

**B) Accounting entries for the important bills of exchange transactions :**

| Date | Particulars | | L.F. | Debit ₹ | Credit ₹ |
|---|---|---|---|---|---|
| i) | **Bills Receivable endorsed ₹ 2,250 :** | | | | |
| | Sundry Creditors | Dr. | – | 2,250 | |
| |    To Bills Receivable A/c | | – | | 2,250 |
| | (Being Bills Receivable endorsed to creditors) | | | | |
| ii) | **Bills Receivable dishonoured ₹ 750 :** | | | | |
| | Sundry Debtors A/c | Dr. | – | 750 | |
| |    To Bills Receivable A/c | | – | | 750 |
| | (Being Bills receivable dishonoured) | | | | |
| iii) | **Bills Receivable endorsed - dishonoured ₹ 300 :** | | | | |
| | Sundry Debtors A/c | Dr. | – | 300 | |
| |    To Sundry Creditors A/c | | – | | 300 |
| | (Being Bills Receivable endorsed to Creditors dishonoured) | | | | |
| iv) | **Bills Payable dishonoured ₹ 300 :** | | | | |
| | Bills Payable A/c | Dr. | – | 300 | |
| |    To Sundry Creditors A/c | | – | | 300 |
| | (Being Bills Payable dishonoured) | | | | |

### In the books of Gendalal Hazare, Ichalkaranji

**Dr.**     **Sundry Debtors Account**     **Cr.**

| Particulars | ₹ | Particulars | ₹ |
|---|---|---|---|
| To Balance B/D | 3,750 | By Cash | 12,000 |
| To Bills Receivable (Dishonoured) | 750 | By Discount Allowed | 375 |
| To Sundry Creditors | 300 | By Bills Receivables | 18,000 |
| To Credit Sales* | 31,575 | By Balance C/D | 6,000 |
| (Balancing Figure) | | | |
| | **36,375** | | **36,375** |

**Dr.**     **Bills Receivable Account**     **Cr.**

| Particulars | ₹ | Particulars | ₹ |
|---|---|---|---|
| To Balance B/D | 3,000 | By Cash | 11,250 |
| To Sundry Debtors* | 18,000 | By Sundry Creditors (Endorsed) | 2,250 |
| (Balancing Figure) | | By Sundry Debtors (Dishonoured) | 750 |
| | | By Balance C/D | 6,750 |
| | **21,000** | | **21,000** |

**Dr.**     **Sundry Creditors Account**     **Cr.**

| Particulars | ₹ | Particulars | ₹ |
|---|---|---|---|
| To Cash | 5,250 | By Balance B/D | 3,000 |
| To Bills Receivable (Endorsed) | 2,250 | By Bills Payable | 300 |
| To Discount Received | 975 | By Sundry Debtors | 300 |
| To Bills Payable issued | 10,800 | By Credit Purchases* | 19,425 |
| To Balance C/D | 3,750 | (Balancing figure) | |
| | **23,025** | | **23,025** |

**Dr.**     **Bills Payable Account**     **Cr.**

| Particulars | ₹ | Particulars | ₹ |
|---|---|---|---|
| To Cash | 9,000 | By Balance B/D | 6,000 |
| To Sundry Creditors | 300 | By Sundry Creditors* | 10,800 |
| To Balance C/D | 7,500 | (Balancing Figure) | |
| | **16,800** | | **16,800** |

**Dr.**     **Trading Account for the year ended 31st March, 2016**     **Cr.**

| Particulars | | ₹ | Particulars | | ₹ |
|---|---|---|---|---|---|
| To Opening Stock | | 3,000 | By Sales : | | 36,575 |
| To Purchases : | | 19,425 | •   Cash | 5,000 | |
| •   Cash | NIL | | •   Credit | (+) 31,575 | |
| •   Credit | (+) 19,425 | | By Closing Stock | | 4,500 |
| To Wages | 3,150 | 3,000 | By G's Drawings (Goods) | | 350 |
| Less : Outstandings | | | | | |
| (2007-2014) | (–) 150 | | | | |
| To Freight | | 1,200 | | | |
| To Octroi Duty | | 2,800 | | | |
| To Factory Rent | | 1,000 | | | |
| To Gross Profit C/D * | | 11,000 | | | |
| | | **41,425** | | | **41,425** |

### Profit and Loss Account for the year ended 31st March, 2016

| Particulars | ₹ | Particulars | ₹ |
|---|---|---|---|
| To Office Rent | 2,500 | By Gross Profit B/D | 11,000 |
| To Discount Allowed | 375 | | |
| To Depre. on Loose Tools | 350 | By Sundry Income | 250 |
| To Net Profit C/D* | 9,000 | By Discount Received | 975 |
| | **12,225** | | **12,225** |

**Balance Sheet as on 31st March, 2016**

| Liabilities | | | ₹ | Assets | | | ₹ |
|---|---|---|---|---|---|---|---|
| G's Capital | | 14,850 | 21,850 | Machinery | | | 10,000 |
| Add : Net Profit | (+) | 9,000 | | Loose Tools | | 2,000 | 1,650 |
| | | 23,850 | | Less : Depreciation | (–) | 350 | |
| Less :Drawings : | (–) | 2,000 | | Cash | | | 4,200 |
| i) House Rent | - | 1,650 | | Sundry Debtors | | | 6,000 |
| ii) Goods | - (+) | 350 | | Bills Receivable | | | 6,750 |
| | | | | Stock | | | 4,500 |
| Sundry Creditors | | | 3,750 | | | | |
| Bills Payable | | | 7,500 | | | | |
| | | | **33,100** | | | | **33,100** |

ILLUSTRATION 5

Himmatlal Ingale, Jalna, keeps his books on single entry system. The summary of assets and liabilities is as follows :

| Assets and Liabilities | As on 1-4-2015 ₹ | As on 31-3-2016 ₹ |
|---|---|---|
| Cash at Bank | – | 1,700 |
| Bank Overdraft | 6,000 | – |
| Bills Receivable | 20,000 | 21,000 |
| Creditors | 15,000 | 12,500 |
| Stock-in-Trade | 4,500 | 6,000 |
| Bills Payable | 16,500 | 14,500 |
| Debtors | 24,000 | 27,000 |
| Plant and Machinery | 30,000 | 30,000 |
| Furniture and Fixtures | 6,000 | 8,000 |

The summary of cash transactions is as follows :

**Dr.**      **Cash Book for the year ended 31.03.2016**      **Cr.**

| Receipts | ₹ | Payments | ₹ |
|---|---|---|---|
| To Debtors | 68,000 | By Balance B/D | 6,000 |
| To Commission | 1,400 | (Bank Overdraft) | |
| To Sales | 23,000 | By Creditors | 40,000 |
| To Bills Receivable | 7,800 | By Purchases | 16,000 |
| | | By Bank Interest | 500 |
| | | By Wages | 6,000 |
| | | By Salary | 2,000 |
| | | By Insurance | 2,500 |
| | | By Miscellaneous Expenses | 2,000 |
| | | By Carriage Outward | 500 |
| | | By Rent | 1,000 |
| | | By H's Drawings | 4,000 |
| | | By Carriage Inward | 4,000 |
| | | By Furniture and Fixtures | 2,000 |
| | | By Bills Payable | 12,000 |
| | | By Balance C/D | 1,700 |
| | **1,00,200** | | **1,00,200** |

The other adjustments are as follows :
i)　Goods distributed as free samples for advertisement purposes amounted to ₹ 1,500.
ii)　Of Sundry Debtors ₹ 400 were to be written off as Provision for R.D.D.
iii)　Interest on Capital is to be allowed @ 5% p.a.
iv)　Provide depreciation on Plant and Machinery @ 5% and on Furniture and Fixtures @ 10% on opening balance.
v)　Discount allowed to debtors amounted to ₹ 300 whereas discount received from creditors was ₹ 300.

Prepare Trading Account and Profit and Loss Account for the year ended 31.3.2016 and Balance-Sheet as on that date.

|SOLUTION|

**Working Notes :**

**A)　Missing Items :**
i)　Opening balance of H's Capital Account – Opening Statement of Affairs
ii)　Credit Sales – Sundry Debtors Account
iii)　Bills receivables received during the year – Bills Receivable Account
iv)　Credit Purchases – Sundry Creditors Account
v)　Bills payables issued during the year – Bills Payable Account

**Note :** Inter-relationship between Sundry Debtors Account and Bills Receivable Account, Sundry Creditors Account and Bills Payable Account.

**In the books of Himmatlal Ingale, Jalna**
**Statement of Affairs as on 1.4.2015**

| Liabilities | ₹ | Assets | ₹ |
|---|---|---|---|
| Bank Overdraft | 6,000 | Bills Receivable | 20,000 |
| Sundry Creditors | 15,000 | Stock-in-Trade | 4,500 |
| Bills payable | 16,500 | Sundry Debtors | 24,000 |
| H's Capital | 47,000 | Plant and Machinery | 30,000 |
| (Balancing Figure) | | Furniture and Fixtures | 6,000 |
| | **84,500** | | **84,500** |

| Dr. | | Sundry Debtors Account | | Cr. |
|---|---|---|---|---|
| Particulars | ₹ | Particulars | | ₹ |
| To Balance B/D | 24,000 | By Cash | | 68,000 |
| To Credit Sales* | 80,100 | By Discount allowed | | 300 |
| (Balancing Figure) | | By Bills Receivables | | 8,800 |
| | | By Balance C/D | | 27,000 |
| | **1,04,100** | | | **1,04,100** |

| Dr. | | Bills Receivable Account | | Cr. |
|---|---|---|---|---|
| Particulars | ₹ | Particulars | | ₹ |
| To Balance B/D | 20,000 | By Cash | | 7,800 |
| To Sundry Debtors* | 8,800 | | | |
| (Balancing Figure) | | By Balance C/D | | 21,000 |
| | **28,800** | | | **28,800** |

| Dr. | | Sundry Creditors Account | | Cr. |
|---|---|---|---|---|
| Particulars | ₹ | Particulars | | ₹ |
| To Cash | 40,000 | By Balance B/D | | 15,000 |
| To Discount Received | 300 | By Credit Purchases * | | 47,800 |
| To Bills Payable | 10,000 | (Balancing Figure) | | |
| To Balance C/D | 12,500 | | | |
| | **62,800** | | | **62,800** |

**Dr.**            **Bills Payable Account**            **Cr.**

| Particulars | ₹ | Particulars | ₹ |
|---|---|---|---|
| To Cash | 12,000 | By Balance B/D | 16,500 |
|  |  | By Sundry Creditors* | 10,000 |
| To Balance C/D | 14,500 | (Balancing figure) |  |
|  | **26,500** |  | **26,500** |

**Dr.**      **Trading Account for the year ended 31st March, 2016**      **Cr.**

| Particulars |  | ₹ | Particulars |  | ₹ |
|---|---|---|---|---|---|
| To Opening Stock |  | 4,500 | By Sales |  | 1,03,100 |
| To Purchases : |  | 63,800 | •   Cash | 23,000 |  |
| •   Cash | 16,000 |  | •   Credit | (+) 80,100 |  |
| •   Credit | (+) 47,800 |  | By Closing Stock |  | 6,000 |
| To Wages |  | 6,000 | By Goods distributed as Free Samples |  | 1,500 |
| To Carriage Inward |  | 4,000 |  |  |  |
| To Gross Profit C/D * |  | 32,300 |  |  |  |
|  |  | **1,10,600** |  |  | **1,10,600** |

**Dr.**    **Profit and Loss Account for the year ended 31st March, 2016**    **Cr.**

| Particulars |  | ₹ | Particulars | ₹ |
|---|---|---|---|---|
| To Bank Interest |  | 500 | By Gross Profit B/D | 32,300 |
| To Salary |  | 2,000 | By Commission | 1,400 |
| To Insurance |  | 2,500 | By Discount Received | 300 |
| To Miscellaneous Expenses |  | 2,000 |  |  |
| To Carriage Outward |  | 500 |  |  |
| To Rent |  | 1,000 |  |  |
| To Goods distributed as Free Samples |  | 1,500 |  |  |
| To Bad Debts |  | 400 |  |  |
| To Interest on H's Capital @ 5% p.a. |  | 2,350 |  |  |
| To Depreciation : |  |  |  |  |
| i)   Plant and Machinery |  |  |  |  |
|     @ 5% p.a | 1,500 |  |  |  |
| ii) Furniture and Fixtures |  | 2,100 |  |  |
|     @ 10% p.a. | (+) 600 |  |  |  |
| To Discount Allowed |  | 300 |  |  |
| To Net Profit C/D* |  | 18,850 |  |  |
|  |  | **34,000** |  | **34,000** |

**Balance Sheet as on 31st March, 2016**

| Liabilities |  | ₹ | Assets |  | ₹ |
|---|---|---|---|---|---|
| H's Capital | 47,000 | 64,200 | Cash at Bank |  | 1,700 |
| **Add :** Interest on capital |  |  | Bills Receivable |  | 21,000 |
|     @ 5% p.a. | 2,350 |  | Closing Stock |  | 6,000 |
| **Add :** Net Profit | (+) 18,850 |  | Debtors | 27,000 | 26,600 |
|  | 68,200 |  | **Less :** Bad Debts R.D.D. pro. (–) | 400 |  |
| **Less :** Drawings | (–) 4,000 |  | Plant and Machinery | 30,000 | 28,500 |
| Creditors |  | 12,500 | **Less :** Depre. @ 5% p.a. (–) | 1,500 |  |
| Bills Payable |  | 14,500 | Furniture and Fixtures | 6,000 | 7,400 |
|  |  |  | **Add :** Purchases | (+) 2,000 |  |
|  |  |  |  | 8,000 |  |
|  |  |  | **Less :** Depre. @ 10% p.a. (–) | 600 |  |
|  |  | **91,200** |  |  | **91,200** |

### ILLUSTRATION 6

Ishwarlal Joshi, Kalyan, keeps his books of accounts under an unscientific method of Single Entry System. He does not know how to find out profit or loss. From the following information relating to the year 2015-2016, prepare his Trading Account and Profit and Loss Account for the year ended 31st March, 2016 and a Balance Sheet as on that date :

**A) Particulars of Assets and Liabilities :**

| Assets and Liabilities | As on 1-4-2015 ₹ | As on 31-3-2016 ₹ |
|---|---|---|
| Investments in 20% Government Bonds | 30,000 | 30,000 |
| Prepaid Insurance | – | 500 |
| Acceptances receivables | 30,000 | 27,000 |
| Wages payable | – | 1,530 |
| Acceptances payables | 12,300 | 4,200 |
| Sundry Debtors | 75,000 | 87,000 |
| Sundry Creditors | 59,100 | 53,700 |
| Stock-in-Trade | 42,300 | 34,200 |
| Outstanding Printing | – | 410 |
| Machinery | 90,000 | 90,000 |
| Loan from Mohanlal @ 10% | 45,000 | 45,000 |
| Outstanding Interest on Mohanlal's Loan | – | 4,500 |
| Cash in Hand | 15,900 | 11,400 |

**B) Summary of Cash Transactions :**

| Dr. | | Cash Book for the year ended 31.3.2016 | | Cr. |
|---|---|---|---|---|
| **Receipts** | **₹** | **Payments** | | **₹** |
| To Opening Cash in hand | 15,900 | By Sundry Creditors | | 59,100 |
| To I's Capital introduced on 1.4.2015 | 33,200 | By Bills Payable | | 45,900 |
| To Sundry Debtors | 31,900 | By Wages | | 22,470 |
| To Sales | 43,500 | By Cartage | | 1,330 |
| To Interest on Investments | | By Salaries | | 10,000 |
|     on Govt. Bonds | 5,100 | By Printing | | 1,590 |
| To Bills Receivables | 39,900 | By Postage | | 1,490 |
| | | By Accountancy Charges | | 2,120 |
| | | By Insurance | | 1,500 |
| | | By Insurance premium on | | |
| | |     Ms. I's Life Insurance Policy | | 2,600 |
| | | By Sales Promotion Expenses | | 10,000 |
| | | By Balance C/D | | 11,400 |
| | **1,69,500** | | | **1,69,500** |

**(C) Other Unrecorded transactions :**

    i)     Depreciate Machinery @ 5% p.a. on Written Down Value Method.

    ii)     Revenue Stamps of ₹ 90 were in hand on 31.03.2014.

    iii)     Interest on Capital is to be provided @ 10% p.a.

### SOLUTION

**Working Notes :**

**A) Missing Items :**

    i)     Opening balance of I's Capital Account – Opening Statement of Affairs.

    ii)     Credit Sales – Sundry Debtors Account.

    iii)     Acceptances received during the year – Bills Receivable Account.

    iv)     Credit Purchases – Sundry Creditors Account.

    v)     Acceptances issued during the year – Bills Payable Account.

(**Note** : Inter-relationship between Sundry Debtors Account and Bills Receivable Account, Sundry Creditors Account and Bills Payable Account

### In the books of Ishwarlal Joshi, Kalyan
### Statement of Affairs as on 1.4.2015

| Liabilities | ₹ | Assets | ₹ |
|---|---|---|---|
| Bills Payable | 12,300 | Investments in 20% Govt. Bonds | 30,000 |
| Sundry Creditors | 59,100 | Bills Receivable | 30,000 |
| M's Loan @ 10% | 45,000 | Sundry Debtors | 75,000 |
| | | Sock-in-Trade | 42,300 |
| I's Capital * | 1,66,800 | Machinery | 90,000 |
| (Balancing Figure) | | Cash in Hand | 15,900 |
| | **2,83,200** | | **2,83,200** |

**Dr.**    **Sundry Debtors Account**    **Cr.**

| Particulars | ₹ | Particulars | ₹ |
|---|---|---|---|
| To Balance B/D | 75,000 | By Cash | 31,900 |
| To Credit Sales* | 80,800 | By Bills Receivables | 36,900 |
| (Balancing Figure) | | By Balance C/D | 87,000 |
| | **1,55,800** | | **1,55,800** |

**Dr.**    **Bills Receivable Account**    **Cr.**

| Particulars | ₹ | Particulars | ₹ |
|---|---|---|---|
| To Balance B/D | 30,000 | By Cash | 39,900 |
| To Sundry Debtors* | 36,900 | | |
| (Balancing Figure) | | By Balance C/D | 27,000 |
| | **66,900** | | **66,900** |

**Dr.**    **Sundry Creditors Account**    **Cr.**

| Particulars | ₹ | Particulars | ₹ |
|---|---|---|---|
| To Cash | 59,100 | By Balance B/D | 59,100 |
| To Bills Payable | 37,800 | By Credit Purchases* | 91,500 |
| To Balance C/D | 53,700 | (Balancing Figure) | |
| | **1,50,600** | | **1,50,600** |

**Dr.**    **Bills Payable Account**    **Cr.**

| Particulars | ₹ | Particulars | ₹ |
|---|---|---|---|
| To Cash | 45,900 | By Balance B/D | 12,300 |
| | | By Sundry Creditors* | 37,800 |
| To Balance C/D | 4,200 | (Balancing Figure) | |
| | **50,100** | | **50,100** |

**Dr.**    **Trading Account for the year ended 31st March, 2016**    **Cr.**

| Particulars | | ₹ | Particulars | | ₹ |
|---|---|---|---|---|---|
| To Opening Stock | | 42,300 | By Sales : | | 1,24,300 |
| To Purchases : | | 91,500 | • Cash | 43,500 | |
| • Cash | NIL | | • Credit | (+) 80,800 | |
| • Credit | (+) 91,500 | | By Closing Stock | | 34,200 |
| To Wages | 22,470 | 24,000 | | | |
| **Add** : Outstanding | (+) 1,530 | | | | |
| To Cartage | | 1,330 | By Gross Loss C/D* | | 630 |
| | | **1,59,130** | | | **1,59,130** |

**Dr.**　　　　　　**Profit and Loss Account for the year ended 31st March, 2016**　　　　　　**Cr.**

| Particulars | | ₹ | Particulars | | ₹ |
|---|---|---|---|---|---|
| To Gross Loss B/D | | 630 | By Interest on Investments in 20% | | |
| To Insurance | 1,500 | 1,000 | Govt. Bonds | 5,100 | 6,000 |
| **Less :** Prepaid | (–) 500 | | **Add :** Outstanding Interest | | |
| To Printing | 1,590 | 2,000 | @ 20% p.a. | (+) 900 | |
| **Add :** Outstanding | (+) 410 | | | | |
| To Outstanding Interest on | | | | | |
| M's Loan @ 10% p.a. | | 4,500 | | | |
| To Salaries | | 10,000 | | | |
| To Postage | 1,490 | 1,400 | | | |
| **Less :** Stock of | | | | | |
| Revenue stamps | (–) 90 | | | | |
| To Accountancy Charges | | 2,120 | | | |
| To Sales Promotion Expenses | | 10,000 | | | |
| To Dep. on Machinery @5% p.a. | | 4,500 | | | |
| To Interest on I's Capital | | | | | |
| @10% p.a. | | 20,000 | | | |
| | | | By Net Loss C/D* | | 50,150 |
| | | **56,150** | | | **56,150** |

**Balance Sheet as on 31st March, 2016**

| Liabilities | | ₹ | Assets | | ₹ |
|---|---|---|---|---|---|
| I's Capital | 1,66,800 | 1,67,250 | Investments in 20% Govt. Bonds | | 30,000 |
| **Add :** Introduction of new | | | Prepaid Insurance | | 500 |
| Capital on 1.4.2015 (+) 33,200 | | | Bills Receivables | | 27,000 |
| | 2,00,000 | | Sundry Debtors | | 87,000 |
| **Add :** Interest on Capital | | | Closing Stock | | 34,200 |
| @ 10% p.a. on | | | Machinery | 90,000 | 85,500 |
| ₹ 2,00,000 | (+) 20,000 | | Less : Depre. @ 5% p.a. (–) 4,500 | | |
| | 2,20,000 | | Cash in Hand | | 11,400 |
| **Less :** Net Loss | (–) 50,150 | | Stock of Revenue Stamps | | 90 |
| **Less :** Drawings | (–) 2,600 | | Outstanding Interest on | | |
| (Insurance Premium on Ms. I's | | | Investments in Govt. Bonds | | |
| Life Insurance Policy) | | | @ 20% p.a. | | 900 |
| Wages Payable | | 1,530 | | | |
| Bills Payable | | 4,200 | | | |
| Sundry Creditors | | 53,700 | | | |
| Outstanding Printing | | 410 | | | |
| M's Loan @ 10% p.a. | 45,000 | 49,500 | | | |
| **Add :** Outstanding interest | | | | | |
| on I's Loan | (+) 4,500 | | | | |
| | | **2,76,590** | | | **2,76,590** |

## ILLUSTRATION 7

Jayesh Kulkarni, Lasalgaon, did not keep a complete set of double entry records but was able to provide you with the following information relating to the year 2015-2016.

**(A) Particulars of Assets and Liabilities :**

| Assets and Liabilities | As on 1-4-2015 ₹ | As on 31-3-2016 ₹ |
|---|---|---|
| M/s J's Loan (Cr.) | – | 20,000 |
| Book Debts | 33,000 | 38,600 |
| Salaries Payable | 1,000 | – |
| Bills Receivable | 3,000 | 4,400 |
| Wages Outstanding | – | 4,000 |
| Motor Vehicles | 8,000 | 8,000 |
| Creditors | 20,000 | 25,000 |
| Buildings | 50,000 | 70,000 |
| Bills Payable | 4,000 | 9,000 |
| Stock | 30,000 | 28,000 |
| Cash | 1,000 | 6,800 |

**(B) Summary of Cash Transactions :**

| Dr. | | Cash Book for the year ended 31st March, 2016 | | Cr. |
|---|---|---|---|---|
| **Receipts** | **₹** | **Payments** | | **₹** |
| To Balance B/D | 1,000 | By Payments to Creditors | | 74,000 |
| To Sales | 12,000 | (including bills payable honoured) | | |
| To Receipts from Debtors | 1,54,200 | By Wages | | 20,000 |
| (including bills receivable honoured) | | By Excise Duty | | 2,000 |
| To Loan from M/s Jogilal | | By Salaries | | 20,000 |
| (@ 10% p.a. on 1st Jan. 2016) | 20,000 | By Advertisement | | 5,000 |
| To General Income | | By Office Expenses | | 16,000 |
| | 600 | By College Fees of Ms. Jayesh | | 14,000 |
| | | By Fixed Deposits @ 12% p.a. | | 10,000 |
| | | (On 31st March, 2016) | | |
| | | By Additions to Buildings | | 20,000 |
| | | (on 1.10.2015) | | |
| | | By Balance C/D | | 6,800 |
| | 1,87,800 | | | 1,87,800 |

**(C) Additional information :**

(i)    Discount Allowed were ₹ 1,800 and Discount Received were ₹ 1,000.

(ii)   Reserve for Bad and Doubtful Debts should be maintained at ₹ 1,600 on Sundry Debtors.

(iii) Depreciation @ 5% p.a. on Motor Vehicles and @ 10% p.a. on Buildings should be provided.

(iv) Office Expenses included Insurance at ₹ 1,200 p.a. paid upto 1.7.2016.

(v)   Insured goods amounting to ₹ 1,000 were destroyed by fire and Insurance Company admitted the claims for ₹ 450.

(vi) Returns from Debtors and to Creditors amounted to ₹ 5,000 and ₹ 3,000 respectively.

You are required to prepare Trading Account, Profit and Loss Account for the year ended 31.3.2014 and Balance Sheet as on that date.

| SOLUTION |
|---|

**Working Notes :**

**A)   Missing Items :**
  i)   Opening balance of C's Capital Account – Opening Statement of Affairs
  ii)  Credit Sales – Sundry Debtors Account (including Bills Receivable Account)
  iii) Credit Purchases – Sundry Creditors Account (including Bills Payable Account)

**B)   Preparation of Joint Accounts :**
  i)   When Cash Collection from Debtors and Cash Received in respect of Bills Receivables honoured are not given separately a Sundry Debtors Account (including Bills Receivable A/c) will be prepared to find out Credit sales made during the year.
  ii)  When cash payment to Creditors and cash paid in respect of Bills Payable honoured are not given separately a Sundry Creditors Account (including Bills Payable Account) will be prepared to find out Credit Purchases made during the year.

**In the books of Jayesh Kulkarni, Lasalgaon**
**Statement of Affairs as on 1.4.2015**

| Liabilities | ₹ | Assets | ₹ |
|---|---|---|---|
| Salaries Payable | 1,000 | Book Debts | 33,000 |
| Creditors | 20,000 | Bills Receivable | 3,000 |
| Bills Payable | 4,000 | Motor Vehicles | 8,000 |
|  |  | Buildings | 50,000 |
| J's Capital Account* | 1,00,000 | Stock | 30,000 |
| (Balancing Figure) |  | Cash | 1,000 |
|  | **1,25,000** |  | **1,25,000** |

**Dr.        Sundry Debtors Account  (including Bills Receivable Account)        Cr.**

| Particulars | ₹ | Particulars | ₹ |
|---|---|---|---|
| To Balance B/D : |  | By Cash |  |
| (i)   Sundry Debtors | 33,000 | (including Bills Receivable honoured) | 1,54,200 |
| (ii)  Bills Receivable | 3,000 | By Discount Allowed | 1,800 |
| To Credit Sales* | 1,68,000 | By Returns from Debtors | 5,000 |
| (Balancing Figure) |  | By Balance C/D : |  |
|  |  | (i)   Sundry Debtors | 38,600 |
|  |  | (ii)  Bills Receivable | 4,400 |
|  | **2,04,000** |  | **2,04,000** |

**Dr.        Sundry Creditors Account (including Bills Payable Account)        Cr.**

| Particulars | ₹ | Particulars | ₹ |
|---|---|---|---|
| To Cash | 74,000 | By Balance B/D : |  |
| (including Bills Payable honoured) |  | i)   Sundry Creditors | 20,000 |
| To Discount Received | 1,000 | ii)  Bills Payable | 4,000 |
| To Returns to Creditors | 3,000 | By Credit Purchases* | 88,000 |
| To Balance C/D : |  | (Balancing Figure) |  |
| i)   Sundry Creditors | 25,000 |  |  |
| ii)  Bills Payable | 9,000 |  |  |
|  | **1,12,000** |  | **1,12,000** |

**Dr.        Trading Account for the year ended 31st March, 2016        Cr.**

| Particulars |  | ₹ | Particulars |  |  | ₹ |
|---|---|---|---|---|---|---|
| To Opening Stock |  | 30,000 | By Sales |  |  | 1,75,000 |
| To Purchases |  | 85,000 | i)   Cash |  | 12,000 |  |
| i)   Cash | NIL |  | ii)  Credit | (+) | 1,68,000 |  |
| ii)  Credit | (+) 88,000 |  |  |  | 1,80,000 |  |
|  | 88,000 |  | **Less :** Returns Inward | (–) | 5,000 |  |
| **Less :** Returns Outward | (–) 3,000 |  | By Closing Stock |  |  | 28,000 |
| To Wages | 20,000 | 24,000 | By Goods destroyed by fire |  |  | 1,000 |
| **Add :** Outstanding | (+) 4,000 |  |  |  |  |  |
| To Excise Duty |  | 2,000 |  |  |  |  |
| To Gross Profit C/D * |  | 63,000 |  |  |  |  |
|  |  | **2,04,000** |  |  |  | **2,04,000** |

**Dr.**      **Profit and Loss Account for the year ended 31st March, 2016**      **Cr.**

| Particulars | ₹ | Particulars | ₹ |
|---|---|---|---|
| To Salaries 20,000 | 19,000 | By Gross Profit B/D | 63,000 |
| **Less :** Payable (2012-13) (−) 1,000 | | | |
| To Advertisement | 5,000 | By General Income | 600 |
| To Office Expenses 16,000 | 15,700 | By Discount Received | 1,000 |
| **Less :** Prepaid Insurance (−) 300 | | | |
| To Discount Allowed | 1,800 | | |
| To R.D.D. on Sundry Debtors | 1,600 | | |
| To Depreciation : | 6,400 | | |
| i) Motor vehicles @ 15% p.a. 400 | | | |
| ii) Buildings @ 10% p.a. (+) 6,000 | | | |
| To Loss by Fire | 550 | | |
| To Outstanding Interest on | | | |
|     Ms. J's Loan @ 10% p.a. | | | |
|     for 3 months | 500 | | |
| To Net Profit C/D* | 14,050 | | |
| | **64,600** | | **64,600** |

**Balance Sheet as on 31st March, 2016**

| Liabilities | ₹ | Assets | ₹ |
|---|---|---|---|
| J's Capital 1,00,000 | 1,00,050 | Book Debts 38,600 | 37,000 |
| **Add :** Net Profit (+) 14,050 | | Less : R.D.D. (−) 1,600 | |
| 1,14,050 | | Bills Receivable | 4,400 |
| **Less :** Drawings | | Motor Vehicles 8,000 | 7,600 |
| (College fees of Ms. J) (−) 14,000 | | **Less :** Depre. @ 5% p.a. (−) 400 | |
| | | Buildings 50,000 | |
| Ms. J's Loan 20,000 | 20,500 | **Add :** Additions (1.10.2015) 20,000 | |
| **Add :** Outstanding Interest | | 70,000 | 64,000 |
|     @ 10% p.a. (+) 500 | | **Less :** Depre. @ 10% p.a. (−) 6,000 | |
| Outstanding Wages | 4,000 | Cash | 6,800 |
| Creditors | 25,000 | Fixed Deposits @ 12% p.a. | 10,000 |
| Bills payable | 9,000 | (31.03.2016) | |
| | | Prepaid Insurance | 300 |
| | | Outstanding claims with | |
| | | Insurance company | 450 |
| | | Closing Stock | 28,000 |
| | **1,58,550** | | **1,58,550** |

## QUESTIONS FOR SELF STUDY

**I.   Theory Questions :**

1) How is Single Entry System different from Double Entry System ?
2) What are the disadvantages of Single Entry System ?
3) Explain how profit or loss can be ascertained by comparison method in the Single Entry System.

**II. Practical Problems :**

1) Amit started a Retail store in groceries at Mumbai from 1st April 2015. He kept his books on Single Entry System. He commenced his business with ₹ 12,000 of his own and ₹ 3,000 borrowed from his wife, who is to be paid interest at the rate of 8% p.a. on her loan.

   On 31st March, 2016, an inventory of his Assets shows a total value of ₹ 25,000 whereas his Trade liabilities on that day amounted to ₹ 8,000 in addition to his wife's loan on which neither interest is paid nor any repayment is made.

   On a scrutiny of his books, the following additional information is available.

   a) On 1st November, 2015, he remitted to his son who is abroad ₹ 3,000 by Bank draft. For this purpose he had to transfer ₹ 1,200 from his business Bank Account to his personal Bank Account

   b) A friend of his borrowed from him ₹ 1,000 in August, 2015, which he paid from business cash balance. This amount was returned by the said friend in March, 2016, with interest of ₹ 50 which was deposited in the firm's Bank Account.

   c) Municipal Rates and Taxes paid by the firm include ₹ 50 paid for his residential house.

   d) Dividends of ₹ 300 for Tata Chemical Shares owned by him were paid by mistake in the firm's Bank Account.

   e) His personal drawings during the year were ₹ 3,000.

   Find out his profit or loss for the year ending on 31st March, 2016 giving detailed workings.

2) Sumit started his business with ₹ 50,000 on 1st January, 2015. He immediately purchased Furniture worth ₹ 2,000, Machinery worth ₹ 32,000 and Land worth ₹ 20,000 by taking ₹ 10,000 as a Loan from the Bank of Maharashtra which was not paid in 2015. On 1st July, 2014 he further introduced ₹ 7,000 in the business as fresh capital and on 1st October, 2015, he received a dividend of ₹ 1,500 on his private investment which he put in the bank account of his business. On 31st, December 2015, his position was as follows :

| Particulars | ₹ |
|---|---|
| Cash in hand | 1,400 |
| Cash at Bank | 7,400 |
| Debtors | 10,730 |
| Stock | 5,470 |
| Bills Receivables | 2,700 |
| Creditors | 2,900 |

   Sumit withdrew ₹ 400 per month for his personal expenses and spent ₹ 4,300 for his daughter's marriage from his business.

   Depreciate Furniture at 10%, Machinery at $7\frac{1}{2}$% and Land at $2\frac{1}{2}$%. On 31st December, 2015 Outstanding Rent was ₹ 320 and Outstanding salaries amounted to ₹ 120. Ascertain the profit made by Mr. Sumit.

3) Vinit does not keep proper books of accounts, but from the following information you are requested to find out the Profit and Loss made by him during the year ended 31st December, 2015.

| Particulars | 1.1.2015<br>₹ | 31.12.2015<br>₹ |
|---|---|---|
| Cash at Bank | 1,080 | 3,080 |
| Cash in Hand | 520 | 1,120 |
| Stock-in-Trade | 20,200 | 24,200 |
| Debtors | 30,800 | 35,600 |
| Furniture | 8,200 | 7,400 |
| Creditors | 11,400 | 9,800 |
| Bills Receivable | 22,200 | 24,800 |
| Bills Payable | 7,600 | 3,800 |

His drawings during the year 2015, amounted to ₹ 5,400. He introduced ₹ 2,600 in the business during 2014. Provide interest on capital ₹ 3,000 and charge interest on drawings ₹ 400.

4) Books of Kishore and Vilas showed the following figures :

| Particulars | 31.12.2014 ₹ | 31.12.2015 ₹ |
|---|---|---|
| Cash at Bank and in hand | 6,800 | 39,900 |
| Stock-in-Trade | 44,000 | 50,000 |
| Sundry Debtors | 60,000 | 70,000 |
| Fixtures and Fittings | 4,000 | – |
| Sundry Creditors | 46,800 | 37,000 |
| Office Car | 2,000 | – |

The Capital of Kishore on 31.12.2014 was more than that of Vilas by ₹ 40,000. On 31.12.2015, an analysis of the Cash Book for the year showed as under :

| Particulars | ₹ |
|---|---|
| Receipts from Customers | 2,70,000 |
| Receipts from Cash Sales | 32,000 |
| Discounts allowed to Customers | 2,800 |
| Further Capital brought in on 1.7.2015 | 4,000 |
| Salaries upto 30.11.2015 | 22,000 |
| Office Rent upto 30.11.2015 | 4,400 |
| Advertising | 1,800 |
| Motor Up-keep | 2,700 |
| Printing and Stationery | 1,600 |
| Drawings – Kishore | 7,200 |
| Drawings – Vilas | 6,000 |
| Payments to Trade Creditors | 2,24,000 |
| Discount allowed by them | 400 |
| Samples | 600 |
| Travelling Expenses | 1,400 |
| General Expenses | 1,200 |

There were bills outstanding for Petrol ₹ 52, Advertising ₹ 150 and Printing ₹ 90, Reserve of 5% on Debtors for Doubtful Debts is to be provided, and Motor Car and Fixtures are to be depreciated by 20% and 5% respectively. 5% Interest to be calculated on the capital of each partner.

From the above information, you have to prepare Trading and Profit and Loss Account for the year ending 31st December, 2015, and a Balance Sheet as that date.

5. Rohit maintained his accounts on Single Entry system. His balances for the year ended 31.12.2014 and 31.12.2015 were as follows :

| Particulars | As on 31.12.2014 ₹ | As on 31.12.2015 ₹ |
|---|---|---|
| Bills Receivable | 8,000 | 4,800 |
| Stock | 15,800 | 17,600 |
| Creditors | 18,800 | 16,700 |
| Cash | 7,816 | 3,926 |
| Bills Payable | 6,942 | 10,102 |
| Furniture | 4,000 | 4,000 |
| Debtors | 18,722 | 16,710 |

From his Cash Book for the year 2015, the following information was available.

**Receipts :** Bills Receivable ₹ 8,600, Sales ₹ 2,400, Received from Debtors ₹ 4,900, Miscellaneous Income ₹ 8,600.

**Payments :** Wages ₹ 60, Bills payable ₹ 6,000, Miscellaneous expenses ₹ 1,400, Payments to Creditors ₹ 1,800, Purchases ₹ 1,200, Personal expenses ₹ 1,500, Salaries ₹ 1,600, Investments ₹ 2,850.

On inquiry Rajan told that during the year 2015, discounts allowed and received were ₹ 800 and ₹ 710 respectively. During the period his bad debts amounted to ₹ 1,120 and Bills Receivable dishonoured ₹ 600.

You are required to show the Trading and Profit and Loss  Account for the year ended 31.12.2015, and Balance Sheet as on that date. Also show Total Debtors Account, Total Creditors Account, Bills Receivable Account and Bills Payable Account.

6.  P, Q and R were partners sharing profit and losses in the ratio of 2 : 1 : 1. The Balance Sheet of their firm as on 31.12.2014 was as follows :

| Liabilities | ₹ | Assets | ₹ |
|---|---|---|---|
| Bank Overdraft | 25,000 | Cash in hand | 3,300 |
| Creditors | 10,000 | Stock | 8,700 |
| Outstanding Wages | 1,200 | Debtors | 15,400 |
| Capital Accounts | | Bills Receivables | 10,100 |
| P | 20,000 | Plant and Machinery | 20,000 |
| Q | 20,000 | Land and Building | 30,000 |
| R | 10,000 | R's Current A/c | 1,200 |
| Current Accounts | | | |
| P | 1,000 | | |
| Q | 1,500 | | |
| | 88,700 | | 88,700 |

On 31.12.2015, the Assets and Liabilities were valued as follows :

| | | ₹ |
|---|---|---|
| Stock | – | 18,500 |
| Debtors | – | 20,000 |
| Bills Receivables | – | 8,000 |
| Cash in Hand | – | 5,100 |
| Plant and Machinery | – | 20,000 |
| Land and Building | – | 35,000 |
| Creditors | – | 25,000 |
| Bank Overdraft | – | 19,000 |
| Outstanding Wages | – | 2,100 |
| Investments | – | 3,000 |

Find out the profit or loss made by the firm during 2015, and the Balance Sheet on 31.12.2015, after passing the following adjustments :

i)   Provide 5% for doubtful debts on Debtors and Bills Receivables.

ii)  Provide 6% interest on Capital Accounts.

iii) Provide 2% for reserve for discount on Creditors.

iv)  Drawings of partners were as follows :

P – ₹ 900, Q – ₹ 1,000 and R – ₹ 800.

7. From the following information, prepare Total Debtors Account, Bills Receivable Account, Total Creditors Account and Bills Payable Account for the year ended 31.12.2015.

| Particulars | ₹ | Particulars | ₹ |
|---|---|---|---|
| Total Debtors on 1.1.2015 | 40,370 | Bad Debt Written off | 1,030 |
| Total Creditors on 1.1.2015 | 32,840 | Discount Allowed | 970 |
| Bills Receivable on 1.1.2015 | 10,320 | Discount Received | 540 |
| Bills Payable on 1.1.2015 | 8,430 | Returns Inwards | 1,330 |
| Cash Received from Customers | 20,760 | Returns Outwards | 1,440 |
| Cash paid to Suppliers | 15,420 | Bills Receivables encashed | 5,740 |
| Bills Receivable dishonoured | 1,490 | Bills Payable paid | 3,570 |
| Total Debtors on 31.12.2015 | 50,770 | Total Creditors on 31.12.2015 | 35,410 |
| Bills Payable on 31.12.2015 | 9,760 | Bills Receivables on 31.12.2015 | 8,930 |

✱✱✱

Chapter 8

# ANALYSIS OF FINANCIAL STATEMENTS

**SYNOPSIS**

## 8.0 INTRODUCTION

Financial Statements contain a wealth of information which, if properly analysed and interpreted, provide valuable insights into firm's performance and position. The principal tool of **Financial Statement Analysis** is ratio analysis. The concerned unit explores this tool in much detail and interprets the problems of financial statement analysis.

## 8.1 MEANING

**Financial Statement Analysis** is an analysis which highlights important relationships in the financial statements. It focuses on evaluation of past operations as revealed by the analysis of basic statements. **Financial Statement Analysis** embraces the methods used in assessing and interpreting the result of past performance and current financial position as they relate to particular factors of interest in investment decisions. It is an important means of assessing past performance and in forecasting and planning future performance.

**Definitions :**

**According to Lev,**

"**Financial Statement Analysis** is an information processing system designed to provide data for decision making models, such as the portfolio selection model, bank lending decision models, and corporate financial management models".

**"Financial Statement Analysis, according to Myers**

"is largely a study of relationship among the various financial factors in a business as disclosed by a single set of statements and a study of the trends of these factors as shown in series of statement".

**In the words of W. B. Meig,**

"Financial statements thus are organised summaries of detailed information and are thus a form of analysis. The type of statements accountants prepare, the way they arrange items on these statements and their standards of disclosure are all influenced by a desire to provide information in a convenient form".

The focus of **Financial Analysis** is on key figures contained in the Financial Statements and the significant relationship that exists between them.

**Analysis of Financial Statements, According to Metcalf and Titard,**

"is a process of evaluating the relationship between component parts of a Financial Statement to obtain a better understanding of a firm's position and performance".

**Interpretation :**

Interpretation means bringing out the meaning of the financial statements with the help of the analysis. In other words, interpretation means to present an explanation of financial data with the help of the analysis.

**Analysis :**

'**Analysis** is the simplification of the data incorporated in the financial statements, whereas '**Interpretation**' is explaining the meaning and significance of the data so simplified.

In short, the analysis is the prerequisite to "interpretation" and analysis is useless without interpretation.

Thus, **Analysis and Interpretation** both, assist the management in measuring and maintaining efficiency at various levels.

## 8.2 OBJECTIVES OF FINANCIAL STATEMENT ANALYSIS

The major **objectives of financial statement analysis** is to provide decision makers, information about a business enterprise for use in decision-making. Users of financial statement information are the decision makers concerned with evaluating the economic situation of the firm and predicting its future course. The major groups of users are management for evaluating the operational and financial efficiency of the enterprise as a whole or of sub-units (e.g. departments); investors for making investment decisions and portfolio decisions, lenders and creditors for determining the creditworthiness and solvency position; employees and labour unions for deciding economic status of the enterprise and making sound decisions in wage and salary negotiations, regulatory authorities for controlling the activities of the firm and making overall corporate policy, economists, researchers and planners for studying firm and specific data behaviour.

**Financial Statement Analysis** can be used by different users and decision makers to achieve the following **objectives and purposes** :

**i) Assessment of Past Performance and Current Position :**

Past performance is often a good indicator of future performance. Therefore, an investor or a creditor is interested in the trend of past sales, expenses, net income, cash flow and return on investment. These trends offer a means for judging management's past performance and are possible indicators of future performance. Similarly, the analysis of current position indicates where the business stands today. For instance. the current position analysis will show the types of assets owned by a business enterprise and the different liabilities due against the enterprise. It will indicate what the cash position is, how much debts the company has in relation to equity and how reasonable the inventories and receivables are.

**ii) Credit appraisal decisions by Financial Institutions and Banks :**

Financial statement analysis is used by financial institutions, loaning agencies, banks and others to make sound loan or credit decisions. In this way, they can make proper allocation of credit among the different borrowers. All lenders are primarily concerned with repayment of loan and payment of interest on the due dates. This requires comprehensive investigation and analysis of the financial statements submitted by the borrowers. Financial statement analysis helps in determining credit risk, deciding terms and conditions of loan if sanctioned, interest rate, maturity date etc.

**iii) Prediction of Net Income and Growth Prospects :**

Financial statement analysis helps in predicting the earning prospects and growth rate in the earnings which are used by investors while comparing investment alternatives and other users interested in judging the earning potential of business enterprises. Investors also consider the risk or uncertainty associated with the expected return. The decision makers are futuristic and are always concerned with the future financial statements which contain information on past performances analysed and interpreted as a basis for forecasting future rates of return and for assessing the risk. The prediction of future earnings tend to improve the financial decisions made by the investors and financial analysis.

**iv) Prediction of Bankruptcy and Failure :**

Financial statement analysis is a significant tool in predicting the bankruptcy and failure probability of business enterprises. Financial statement analysis accomplishes this through the evaluation of solvency position. After being aware of the probable failure, managers and investors both can take preventive measures to avoid or minimise losses. Corporate managements can effect changes in operating policy, reorganise financial structure or even go for voluntary liquidation to shorten the length of time losses.

In accounting and finance area, empirical studies conducted have suggested a set of financial ratios which can give early signal of corporate failure. Such a prediction model based on financial statement analysis is useful to managers, investors and creditors. Managers may use the ratios prediction model to assess the solvency position of their firms and thus can take appropriate corrective actions. Investors and shareholders can use the model to make the optimum portfolio selection and to bring changes in the investment strategy in accordance with their investment goals. Similarly, creditors can apply the prediction model while evaluating the creditworthiness of business enterprises.

## 8.3 METHODS OF FINANCIAL ANALYSIS

The classification of financial analysis can be made either on the basis of material used for the same or according to modus operandi of the analysis. The following Figure 9.1 shows the Methods of Financial Analysis :

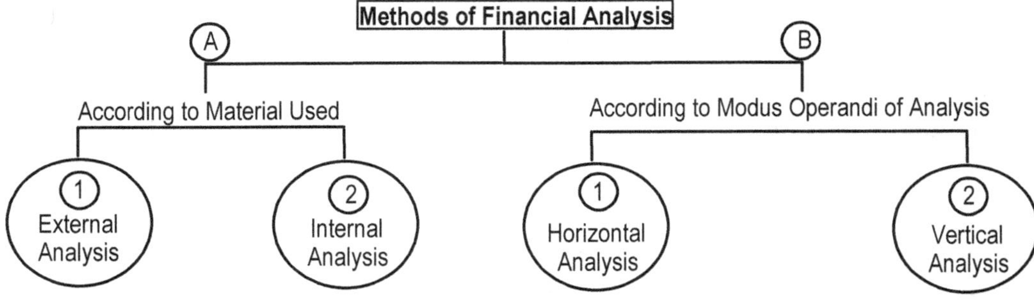


Fig. 8.1 : Methods of Financial Analysis

**A) According to Material Used :**

**1) External Analysis :**

This is effected by those who do not have access to the detailed accounting records of the concern. This group comprising investors, credit agencies, government and public, depends almost entirely on published financial statements. With the recent development in the Government regulations requiring business concern to make available detailed information to the public through audited accounts, the position of the external analysis has been considerably improved.

**2) Internal Analysis :**

This is effected by those who have access to the books of accounts and other information relating to the business concern. Any financial analysis is conducted with reference to a part or the whole unit. This type of analysis meant for managerial purpose, is conducted by executives and employees of the business concerns as well as governmental agencies which have statutory control and jurisdiction over such units.

**B) According to Modus Operandi of Analysis :**

**1) Horizontal Analysis :**

When financial statements for a certain number of years are examined and analysed, the analysis is called a 'horizontal analysis'. It is also called "Dynamic analysis". This is based on the data or information spread over a period of years rather than on one date or period of time.

**2) Vertical Analysis :**

This refers to analysis of ratios developed for one date for one accounting period. This is also known as "static analysis". But vertical analysis does not facilitate a proper analysis and interpretation of figures in perspective and also comparisons over a period of years. As such this type of analysis is not resorted to by the financial analysts.

**Techniques of Financial Statement Analysis :**

Various techniques are used in the analysis of financial data, among the more widely used of these techniques are the following :

i) Horizontal and Vertical Analysis, ii) Trend Analysis, iii) Ratio Analysis.

**i) Horizontal and Vertical Analysis :**

The percentage analysis of increase or decrease in corresponding items in comparative financial statements is called **'Horizontal Analysis'**. On the other hand, **Vertical Analysis** uses percentages to show the relationship of the different parts to the total in a single statement.

**ii) Trend Analysis :**

In **Trend Analysis**, percentage changes are calculated for several successive years instead of between two years. Trend analysis uses an index number of a period of time. Trend analysis is important because, with its longrun view it may point to basic changes in the nature of business.

**iii) Ratio Analysis :**

**Ratio Analysis** is an important means of expressing the relationship between the two numbers. In this chapter or unit, we are going to discuss how ratios are related to the liquidity and short term solvency analysis of a business.

**Steps involved in Financial Statement Analysis :**

On the basis of the above discussion, it can be said that, financial statement analysis is investigative and thought provoking process in nature. The basic objective of financial statement analysis is financial planning and forecasting on the basis of meaningful interpretation of the financial data. It is a forward look exercise. Since, decisions are going to be taken on the basis of financial statement analysis, the analyst must understand various tools and techniques of accounting and their application in the analysis and interpretation of data. In addition to this, he must be careful, precise, analytical, objective and intelligent enough to undertake the financial statement analyst in a systematic way. Not only that, he should define the end objectives of financial statement analysis. He should also divide the process into different steps which are shown below :

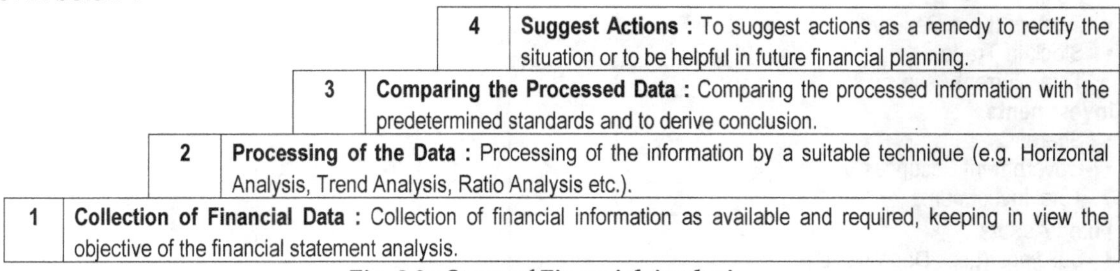

| | 4 | **Suggest Actions :** To suggest actions as a remedy to rectify the situation or to be helpful in future financial planning. |
| | 3 | **Comparing the Processed Data :** Comparing the processed information with the predetermined standards and to derive conclusion. |
| 2 | **Processing of the Data :** Processing of the information by a suitable technique (e.g. Horizontal Analysis, Trend Analysis, Ratio Analysis etc.). |
| 1 | **Collection of Financial Data :** Collection of financial information as available and required, keeping in view the objective of the financial statement analysis. |

Fig. 8.2 : Steps of Financial Analysis

**Comparative Financial Statements i.e. Horizontal Analysis :**

Joint Stock Companies are required to provide in their annual published accounts the corresponding figures for the year immediately preceeding the current financial year so as to provide a comparative picture of their business affairs. The decision-makers prefer to study the picture not only for one or two years but for few more years in the past. The Income Statement and Balance Sheet in their usual form are not much useful from the management point of view. Therefore, the analysts re-arrange the information in different groups, as the group study alongwith the individual items is more meaningful for the purpose of interpretation and decision-making. If two or more companies have to be compared (interfirm comparison), the analyst should take care that the groups are homogeneous. He should also bear in mind the size of the enterprise in terms of capital investment and turnover. A comparative financial statement may be presented in any one of the following forms :

i)       Absolute figures for the years of comparison.

ii)      Absolute figures alongwith variations (in absolute figures)

iii)     Absolute figures alongwith variation in terms of percentage or ratio.

iv)     Individual items as percentage of a base year.

Comparison may be Intra-firm Comparison or Inter-firm Comparison.

**Intra-firm or Inter-firm Comparison :**

Under this process, comparison is made of the financial statements of the same firm. In these statements figures for two or more periods are placed side by side to facilitate comparison and to ascertain the trend.

**Comparative Income Statement :**

A **Comparative Income Statement** shows the absolute figures for two or more periods, the absolute change from one period to another. The change may, if necessary, be expressed in percentages instead of in absolute figures. However, the items of incomes and expenses should be considered together while interpreting the increases or decreases.

**Comparative Balance Sheet :**

Balance sheets as on two or more different dates are compared to ascertain changes in the assets and liabilities i.e. decrease or increase in the assets and liabilities. Comparison is useful in studying the trends in an enterprise.

**Preparation of Comparative Statements :**

The comparative statements for two or more years are prepared in the horizontal form. The number of columns provided for absolute figures depend upon the number of years of comparison. After these columns of absolute figures, a column is provided to indicate increase or decrease. If the increase or decrease is decided to be expressed in percentage also, an additional column showing this percentage is provided.

**A Proforma of Comparative Balance Sheet**
**In the books of ......**
**Comparative Balance Sheet As on 31ˢᵗ March, 2015 and 2016**

| Particulars | 31st March 2015 | 31st March 2016 | Amount of increase or decrease in 2015-2016 | Percentage of increase or decrease in 2015-2016 |
|---|---|---|---|---|
| **Assets :** | | | | |
| **Current Assets :** | | | | |
| • Cash | | | | |
| • Debtors (Less Reserve) | | | | |
| • Stock-in-Trade   (+) | | | | |
| ∴ Total Current Assets | | | | |
| **Investments** | | | | |
| • Shares | | | | |
| • Government Securities   (+) | | | | |
| ∴ Total Investments | | | | |
| **Fixed Assets** | | | | |
| • Buildings (Less Depreciation) | | | | |
| • Machinery (Less Depreciation) | | | | |
| • Furniture (Less Depreciation)   (+) | | | | |
| **∴ Total Fixed Assets**   (+) | | | | |
| **∴ Total Assets** | | | | |
| **Liabilities and Capital** | | | | |
| **Current Liabilities :** | | | | |
| • Sundry Creditors | | | | |
| • Bills Payable   (+) | | | | |
| ∴ Total Current Liabilities | | | | |
| **Fixed Liabilities :** | | | | |
| • Debentures | | | | |
| • Long-Term Loans   (+) | | | | |
| **∴ Total Fixed Liabilities**   (+) | | | | |
| **∴ Total Liabilities** | | | | |

| | | | | |
|---|---|---|---|---|
| **Capital :** | | | | |
| • Equity Share Capital | | | | |
| • Preference Share Capital | | | | |
| • General Reserve | | | | |
| • Retained Earnings | | | | |
| ∴ Total Surplus | | | | |
| ∴ Total Capital | | | | |
| ∴ Total Liabilities and Capital | | | | |

**A Proforma of Comparative Income Statement**

**In the books of ......**

**Comparative Income Statement for the year ended 31ˢᵗ March, 2015 and 2016**

| Particulars | 31$^{st}$ March 2015 | 31$^{st}$ March 2016 | Amount of increase or decrease in 2015-2016 | Percentage of increase or decrease in 2015-2016 |
|---|---|---|---|---|
| Net Sales | | | | |
| **Less :** Cost of Goods Sold | | | | |
| ∴ Gross Margin (or Profit) | | | | |
| **Operating Expenses :** | | | | |
|    Administrative Expenses : | | | | |
|    • ............................. | | | | |
|    • ............................. | | | | |
|    • ............................. (+) | | | | |
| ∴ Total Administrative Expenses | | | | |
|    **Selling Expenses :** | | | | |
|    • ............................. | | | | |
|    • ............................. (+) | | | | |
| **Total Selling Expenses :** | | | | |
|    **Finance Expenses :** | | | | |
|    • ............................. | | | | |
|    • ............................. | | | | |
| ∴ Total Finance Expenses (+) | | | | |
| Total Operating Expenses | | | | |
| Operating Profit | | | | |
| **Add :** Other Incomes | | | | |
| **Less :** Other Expenses | | | | |
| Income or Net Profit before Income-Tax | | | | |
| **Less :** Income-Tax | | | | |
| Net Profit after Tax | | | | |

**Precautions before preparing Comparative Statements :**

Analysis of financial statement is a technical job which can be performed properly only by a knowledgeable and experienced financial analyst. In order to be successful in his analysis and interpretation, a financial analyst must possess thorough knowledge of accounting theory and practice. In addition to this, he must also understand the industry environment in which the unit is operating. His personal qualities such as penetrating vision and insight, tactfulness, alertness, leadership qualities, etc., help him greatly in the successful discharge of his functions as financial analyst.

Before preparing comparative statements, it is necessary to ensure that the following precautions are taken. If the following principles are not followed, the comparison cannot be made, and if it is made the results will be misleading and misinterpreting.

   i)    The financial statements should contain full disclosure of the information by way of foot-notes, schedules, annexure.

   ii)    Proper accounting procedure is to be followed every year while preparing the accounts and the financial statements.

iii) The items in the balance-sheet are to be properly classified and uniformity is to be maintained in such classification and allocation.

iv) Concept of consistency and other relevant concepts and conventions are to be followed in preparation of financial statements.

v) Personal judgements are to be properly exercised as the accuracy of the accounting statements depend to a large extent on the integrity, experience and wisdom with which judements are exercised.

vi) If two or more companies are being compared, it should be seen that their nature and size do not widely differ.

vii) If there has been any change in the depreciation policy, inventory valuation method, or any other variable affecting profit figure and assets and liabilities, the analyst should first make the data comparable by making necessary adjustments in the concerning items.

viii) Sometimes a percentage figure is misleading. Therefore, the analysis of statements submited to management should contain absolute figures alongwith their percentages.

**EXAMPLE**

On 31st March, 2016, the Profit and Loss Account and Balance Sheet of Asian Paints Ltd., Ajmer stood as under :

### Profit and Loss Account for the year ended at 31st March, 2016

| 2014-15 ₹ | Expenditure | 2015-14 ₹ | 2014-15 ₹ | Incomes | 2015-16 ₹ |
|---|---|---|---|---|---|
| 20,000 | To Opening Stock | 20,000 | 2,80,000 | By Sales | 4,00,000 |
| 1,20,000 | To Purchases | 1,50,000 | 20,000 | By Closing Stock | 50,000 |
| 10,000 | To Carriage Inward | 15,000 | | | |
| 50,000 | To Direct Wages | 90,000 | | | |
| 20,000 | To Gas, Water and Power | 50,000 | | | |
| 80,000 | To Gross Profit C/D | 1,25,000 | | | |
| **3,00,000** | | **4,50,000** | **3,00,000** | | **4,50,000** |
| 8,000 | To Salaries | 9,000 | 80,000 | By Gross Profit B/D | 1,25,000 |
| 2,500 | To Rent and Taxes | 3,000 | | | |
| 1,000 | To Printing and Stationery | 1,500 | | | |
| 800 | To Advertising | 1,000 | | | |
| 2,000 | To Interest on loans | 1,000 | | | |
| 65,700 | To Net Profit C/D | 1,09,500 | | | |
| **80,000** | | **1,25,000** | **80,000** | | **1,25,000** |

You are required to compare the performance of the company by rearranging the data suitably and give your comments on the operational performance of the enterprise.

**ANSWER**

### In the books of Asian Paints Ltd., Ajmer
### Comparative Income Statement for the year ended ......

| | Particulars | | 2014-15 ₹ | 2015-2016 ₹ | Increase / decrease (±) ₹ | Percentage of Increase / Decrease |
|---|---|---|---|---|---|---|
| | 1 | | 2 | 3 | 4 | 5 |
| 1. | Sales | | 2,80,000 | 4,00,000 | + 1,20,000 | + 43% |
| 2. | Purchases | | 1,20,000 | 1,50,000 | + 30,000 | + 25% |
| | Carriage Inward | | 10,000 | 15,000 | + 5,000 | + 50% |
| | Direct Wages | | 50,000 | 90,000 | + 40,000 | + 80% |
| | Gas, Water and Power | (+) | 20,000 | 50,000 | + 30,000 | + 150% |
| 3. | Direct Cost of Production | | 2,00,000 | 3,05,000 | 1,05,000 | 52% |
| | Opening Stock | (+) | 20,000 | 20,000 | – | – |
| | | | 2,20,000 | 3,25,000 | 1,05,000 | + 52% |
| | **Less :** Closing Stock | (–) | 20,000 | 50,000 | 30,000 | + 150% |

| | | | | |
|---|---|---|---|---|
| 4. Cost of Sales | 2,00,000 | 2,75,000 | 75,000 | + 37% |
| 5. Gross Margin | 80,000 | 1,25,000 | + 45,000 | + 56% |
| 6. **Operating Expenses :** | | | | |
| • Salaries | 8,000 | 9,000 | + 1,000 | + 12 $^1/_2$% |
| • Rent and Taxes | 2,500 | 3,000 | + 500 | + 20% |
| • Printing and Stationery | 1,000 | 1,500 | + 500 | + 50% |
| • Advertising  (+) | 800 | 1,000 | + 200 | + 25% |
| Total Operating Expenses | 12,300 | 14,500 | + 2,200 | + 18% |
| Net Operating Income | 67,700 | 1,10,500 | + 42,800 | + 63% |
| **Less :** Interest Charges  (–) | 2,000 | 1,000 | 1,000 | – 50% |
| ∴ Profit after Interest but before taxes | 65,700 | 1,09,500 | + 43,800 | + 67% |

**Interpretation :**

An analysis of the Income statement in the above form clearly shows the variations in the individual item of 2016 as compared to their corresponding figures in 2015. An increase of 43% in sales has led to an increase of 56% in Gross Margin which represents an encouraging position. The operating cost has gone up only by 18% which shows an efficient control over overhead charges.

A study of the composition of direct cost reveals that the increase in direct wages and gas water and power has been 80% and 150% respectively. Such an increase seems disproportionately high as compared to increase in the volume of sales. The increase in these items need to be further investigated in order to ascertain real causes for such an abnormal increase in these direct expenses of production. However, the overall performance of the enterprise in 2015-16 as compared to 2014-15 is quite satisfactory.

### EXAMPLE

On 31st March, 2016, the Balance Sheet of Bharat Forge Ltd., Bengaluru stood as under :

**Balance Sheet as on 31st March, 2016**

| 2014-15 ₹ | Capital and Liabilities | 2015-16 ₹ | 2014-15 ₹ | Property and Assets | 2015-16 ₹ |
|---|---|---|---|---|---|
| 4,00,000 | Share Capital | 5,00,000 | 2,50,000 | Land and Buildings | 2,95,000 |
| 60,000 | General Reserve | 80,000 | 4,50,000 | Plant and Machinery | 4,05,000 |
| 8,000 | Investment Fluctuation Fund | 10,000 | 50,000 | Furniture and Fixtures | 75,000 |
| 6,000 | Workmen's Compensation Fund | 15,000 | 1,00,000 | Investments | 1,50,000 |
| | | | 1,25,000 | Stock in trade | 2,00,000 |
| 2,00,000 | .15% Debentures | 3,00,000 | 58,000 | Sundry Debtors | 1,50,000 |
| 2,00,000 | Loans from IDBI | 1,50,000 | 30,000 | Bills Receivable | 56,000 |
| 2,00,000 | Fixed Deposit | 3,00,000 | 20,000 | Market Securities | 40,000 |
| 80,000 | Sundry Creditors | 1,00,000 | 25,000 | Cash Balances | 50,000 |
| 4,000 | Rent Outstanding | 6,000 | 50,000 | Pre-operation Expenses | 40,000 |
| **11,58,000** | | **14,61,000** | **11,58,000** | | **14,61,000** |

You are required to re-cast the above Balance Sheet so as to reflect the financial position more clearly.

ANSWER

### In the books of Bharat Forge Ltd., Bengaluru
### Comparative Balance Sheet as on ......

| | | | 2014-15 | 2015-16 | Increase / decrease | Percentage of Increase/ Decrease |
|---|---|---|---|---|---|---|
| | | | ₹ | ₹ | ₹ | |
| 1. | **Fixed Assets :** | | | | | |
| | • Land and Buildings | | 2,50,000 | 2,95,000 | + 45,000 | + 18% |
| | • Plant and Machinery | | 4,50,000 | 4,05,000 | − 45,000 | 10% |
| | • Furnitures | (+) | 50,000 | 75,000 | + 25,000 | + 50% |
| | **Total Fixed Assets** | | 7,50,000 | 7,75,000 | + 25,000 | + 33% |
| 2. | **Investment :** | | 1,00,000 | 1,50,000 | 50,000 | + 50% |
| 3. | **Current Assets :** | | | | | |
| | a) **Liquid Assets :** | | | | | |
| | • Cash balances | | 25,000 | 50,000 | + 25,000 | 100% |
| | • Debtors | | 58,000 | 1,50,000 | + 92,000 | 159% |
| | • Bills Receivable | | 30,000 | 56,000 | + 26,000 | + 87% |
| | • Marketable Securities | (+) | 20,000 | 40,000 | + 20,000 | + 100% |
| | | | 1,33,000 | 2,96,000 | + 1,63,000 | + 123% |
| | b) **Non-liquid Assets :** | | | | | |
| | • Stock in Trade | (+) | 1,25,000 | 2,00,000 | + 75,000 | + 60% |
| | ∴ **Total Current Assets** | | 2,58,000 | 4,96,000 | + 2,38,000 | + 92% |
| 4. | **Pre-Operative Expenses :** | | 50,000 | 40,000 | − 10,000 | − 20% |
| | ∴ **Total Assets** | | **11,58,000** | **14,61,000** | **+ 3,03,000** | **+ 26%** |
| 1. | **Capital and Internal Liabilities :** | | | | | |
| | • Share Capital | | 4,00,000 | 5,00,000 | + 1,00,000 | + 25% |
| | • General Reserve | | 60,000 | 80,000 | + 20,000 | + 33% |
| | • Investment Fluctuation Fund | | 8,000 | 10,000 | + 2,000 | + 25% |
| | • Workmen Compensation Fund | (+) | 6,000 | 15,000 | + 9,000 | + 15% |
| | ∴ **Total Capital** | | **4,74,000** | **6,05,000** | **+ 1,31,000** | **+ 28%** |
| 2. | **Long-Term Liabilities :** | | | | | |
| | • Debentures | | 2,00,000 | 3,00,000 | 1,00,000 | + 50% |
| | • Loans from IDBI | | 2,00,000 | 1,50,000 | − 50,000 | − 25% |
| | • Fixed Deposits | (+) | 2,00,000 | 3,00,000 | + 1,00,000 | + 50% |
| | **Total Long-term Liabilities** | | **6,00,000** | **7,50,000** | **+ 1,50,000** | **+ 25%** |
| 3. | **Current Liabilities :** | | | | | |
| | • Sundry Creditors | | 80,000 | 1,00,000 | + 20,000 | + 25% |
| | • Rent Outstanding | (+) | 4,000 | 6,000 | + 2,000 | + 50% |
| | ∴ **Total Current Liabilities** | | **84,000** | **1,06,000** | **+ 22,000** | **+ 26%** |
| | ∴ **Total Liabilities** | (+) | **11,58,000** | **14,61,000** | **3,03,000** | **+ 26%** |

**Interpretation :**

A comparative study of assets structure reveals that there has been negligible increase of 3.3% in the total fixed assets in 2016 in comparison with 2015. The investments have gone up by 50% and there has been considerable increase in liquid and non-liquid assets as they have gone up by 123% and 60% respectively. Whether such an increase in current assets (92%) truely shows the liquid position is an issue which should be decided in the light of the current liabilities of the company. The decrease in the preoperative expenses clearly shows that the company has written off such expenses to the tune of 20% during the current year.

As regards the liabilities, the shareholder's funds as represented by capital and other reserves have gone up by 28%. There has been a marked increase of 150% in the workmen compensation fund due to transfer of ₹ 9,000 in the current year, long-term liabilities and current liabilities have increased by 25% and 26% respectively. The management should further investigate the causes for marked variations in current assets and workmen's compensation fund with a view to review their credit policy and the policy for building up of the workmen compensation fund.

Long-term liabilities in terms of debentures and fixed deposits have increased by 50% each. Provisions for repayment of these liabilities are essential.

**Common Size-Statement i.e. Vertical Analysis :**

The Profit and Loss Account and Balance Sheet can also be presented in the form of Common-size statements. A statement in which individual items are expressed as a percentage of same common base is termed as a 'common size statement'. In a common size statement Profit and Loss Account, the sales figure is generally taken as base (Sale – 100) to calculate the proportion of other items figuring in the Profit and Loss Account and a common size Balance Sheet expresses individual assets and liabilities as percentage of total assets/liabilities. Common-size comparative statements provide a better historical perspective of an undertaking. Any significant departure from the normal trend needs further investigation to ascertain the reasons for unusual movement in the figures so that due care is taken in the formulation of future plans.

Thus, all the figures in the financial statements are converted into a common size i.e. percentage and related to a common base i.e. 100. These statements are called common-size statements or '100 percent' statements. Thus, the relationship of the items in the Income Statement is established with 'Sales' and that of items in the Balance Sheet with total assets or liabilities vertically. Therefore, this type of analysis is called vertical analysis. This type of statement facilitates comparisons between the amounts in the same statements and also between the amounts in the successive statements.

**EXAMPLE**

Prepare a common-size statement on the basis of data given in the Example on page number 9.8 and interpret the results.

**ANSWER**

**In the books of Asian Paints Ltd., Ajmer**
**Common-size Profit and Loss Account**

| | | 2014-2015 | | 2015-2016 | |
|---|---|---|---|---|---|
| **Particulars** | | **Amount ₹** | **% to Sales** | **Amount ₹** | **% to Sales** |
| **Sales :** | | **2,80,000** | **100** | **4,00,000** | **100** |
| i) | Cost of Production | 2,00,000 | 71.4 | 3,05,000 | 76.3 |
| ii) | Cost of Sales | 2,00,000 | 71.4 | 2,75,000 | 68.7 |
| iii) | Gross Margin | 80,000 | 28.3 | 1,25,000 | 31.2 |
| iv) | Operating Expenses | 12,300 | 4.4 | 14,500 | 3.6 |
| v) | Net Operating Profit | 65,700 | 24.2 | 1,10,500 | 27.6 |
| vi) | Profit after Interest | 65,700 | 23.4 | 1,09,500 | 24.9 |

**Interpretation :**

The cost of goods sold and other expenses have decreased over the last year. This has resulted in increasing the percentage of net income from 24.2% in 2014-2015 to 27.6% in 2015-2016 to net sales. The sales in 2015-2016 have increased by ₹ 1,20,000. Cost of production has increased from 71.4% to 76.3%. On the other hand, operating expenses have decreased from 4.4% to 3.6%.

EXAMPLE

Prepare a common size Balance Sheet on the basis of data given in Example on page number 9.9 and interpret the results.

ANSWER

**In the books of Bharat Forge Ltd., Bengaluru**
**Common Size Balance Sheet as on ......**

| Items | 2014-15 ₹ | % of Total Assets | 2015-16 ₹ | % to Total Assets |
|---|---|---|---|---|
| (A) • Land and Buildings | 2,50,000 | 21.6 | 2,95,000 | 20.2 |
| • Plant and Machinery | 4,50,000 | 38.8 | 4,05,000 | 27.7 |
| • Furniture and Fixtures | 50,000 | 4.4 | 75,000 | 5.2 |
| ∴ Fixed Assets | 7,50,000 | 64.8 | 7,75,000 | 53.1 |
| (B) Investments | 1,00,000 | 8.6 | 1,50,000 | 10.2 |
| (C) • Cash Balances | 25,000 | 2.2 | 50,000 | 3.4 |
| • Debtors | 58,000 | 5.0 | 1,50,000 | 10.4 |
| • Bills Receivable | 30,000 | 2.6 | 56,000 | 3.8 |
| • Marketable Securities | 20,000 | 1.7 | 40,000 | 2.7 |
| ∴ Liquid Assets | 1,33,000 | 11.5 | 2,96,000 | 20.3 |
| • Stock-in-Trade (Non-liquid assets) | 1,25,000 | 10.8 | 2,00,000 | 13.7 |
| ∴ **Total Current Assets** | **2,58,000** | **22.3** | **4,96,000** | **34.0** |
| (D) Pre-operating Expenses | 50,000 | 4.3 | 40,000 | 2.7 |
| **Total Assets** | **11,58,000** | **100** | **14,61,000** | **100** |
| **Capital and Liabilities :** | | | | |
| • Share Capital | 4,00,000 | 34.5 | 5,00,000 | 34.2 |
| • General Reserve | 60,000 | 5.2 | 80,000 | 5.5 |
| • Investment Fluctuation Fund | 8,000 | 0.7 | 10,000 | 0.7 |
| • Workmen's Compensation Fund | 6,000 | 0.5 | 15,000 | 1.0 |
| **Total Shareholders Fund** | **4,74,000** | **40.9** | **6,05,000** | **41.4** |
| **Long Term Liabilities :** | | | | |
| Debentures | 2,00,000 | 17.3 | 3,00,000 | 20.5 |
| Loans | 2,00,000 | 17.3 | 1,50,000 | 10.3 |
| Fixed Assets | 2,00,000 | 17.2 | 3,00,000 | 20.5 |
| ∴ **Total Long-Term liabilities** | **6,00,000** | **51.8** | **7,50,000** | **51.3** |
| **Current Liabilities :** | | | | |
| Sundry Creditors | 80,000 | 6.9 | 1,00,000 | 6.8 |
| Rent Outstanding | 4,000 | 0.4 | 6,000 | 0.4 |
| ∴ **Total Current Liabilities** | **84,000** | **7.3** | **1,06,000** | **7.2** |
| ∴ **Total Liabilities** | **11,58,000** | **100** | **14,61,000** | **100** |

**Interpretation :**

The common size Balance Sheet shows the assets and liabilities structure in relation to total assets or liabilities. As is evident from the above, the fixed assets in 2016 formed 53.1% of the total assets in the same year. The current assets accounted for 34% which consisted of liquid and non-liquid assets of 20.3% and 13.7% respectively. Pre-operative expenses were only 2.7% of the total assets. It may be understood that the asset structure of any enterprise depends upon its very nature.

In the above case the structure of assets in 2016 has substantially changed. The fixed assets which were 64.8% in 2015 had gone down to 53.1% despite additions to land, building and furniture. The decline is because of the decrease in the value of assets due to depreciation. The liquid position of the company has significantly improved from just 22.3% to 34.0% but this may be rightly interpreted in relation to corresponding current liabilities.

As regards liabilities, the shareholder's funds represented by capital and reserves accounted for 40.9% and 41.4% at the end of year 2015 and 2016 respectively. The long-term liabilities were 51.8% and 51.3% at the same point of time. Current liabilities constituted 7.3% and 7.2% at the end of the same periods. Thus, the liabilities structure in 2016 is not much different from that at the end of the year 2015. From this type of observation, one may be tempted to conclude that the company has not grown over a period of one year as the percentage constituents of different liabilities are more or less the same. This type of conclusion will be erroneous. It may be realised that the common size statements present vertical representation of facts at a point of time and the comparison in the above form may mislead the analyst. Therefore, the consideration of absolute figures of assets and liabilities alongwith their percentages is highly important before any conclusion is drawn.

**Use of Vertical Analysis :**

The common size statements do not show variations in respective items from period to period. They do not give information about the trend of individual items but they only indicate trend of their relationship to total. Observation of these trends is not very useful because there are no definite norms for the proportion of each item to total. Though these statements are not of much use for financial analysis, they are useful for studying the comparative financial position of two or more businesses, provided they follow the same accountancy procedure, conventions and concepts.

**Trend Analysis :**

For the purpose of comparative study of financial statements over a number of years trend analysis or trend percentage are very useful. The absolute figure of an activity is not much useful in decision making. Therefore, a set of figures for purposes of comparison is necessary. The accounting figure relating to sales, production, profit, overheads, working capital, etc. for the last few years expressed as a percentage of some figure in a base period give trend which throws more light on the related problem. Generally, the figures for the last 3 to 5 years should be considered for better understanding of an economic phenomenon. The trend indicates general tendency or direction of change in which management is more interested, but the fact that a trend is more influenced by the base year figure should always be borne in mind. The analysis and interpretation will not be fruitful if the base year figure is unusually high or low. Therefore, the selection of the base year should be done carefully. It should be the year of normal conditions. The trend can be rightly interpreted if the effect of inflation on different years figures of money income is neutralised. Another method of proper analysis would be to calculate the percentage of physical quantities, wherever possible, by the use of index numbers technique. The percentage of current year may be calculated as under :

$$\text{Percentage of current year} = \frac{\text{Current year figure}}{\text{Base year figure}} \times 100$$

The trend percentages are calculated only for major items and not for each item. Management is interested in knowing changes in important items only.

## EXAMPLE

The trend analysis may be understood by persuing the following financial statement based on imaginary figures for few important items of Income and Financial Statements of Castrol India Ltd., Cochin.

Statement showing trends of various items of Castrol India Ltd., Cochin for 5 years (i.e. from 2011 to 2015).

| Items | 2011 | | 2012 | | 2013 | | 2014 | | 2015 | |
|---|---|---|---|---|---|---|---|---|---|---|
| | Amount ₹ | % | Amount ₹ | % | Amount ₹ | % | Amount ₹ | % | Amount ₹ | % |
| Sales | 20,000 | 100 | 22,000 | 110 | 30,000 | 150 | 25,000 | 125 | 32,000 | 160 |
| Direct Cost | 8,000 | 100 | 10,000 | 125 | 14,000 | 175 | 11,000 | 137 | 13,000 | 163 |
| Factory Overheads | 1,000 | 100 | 1,200 | 120 | 1,400 | 140 | 1,200 | 120 | 1,500 | 150 |
| Administration Overheads | 800 | 100 | 800 | 100 | 1,000 | 125 | 1,000 | 125 | 1,000 | 125 |
| Selling Overheads | 200 | 100 | 250 | 125 | 300 | 150 | 250 | 125 | 350 | 175 |
| Gross Margin | 12,000 | 100 | 12,000 | 100 | 16,000 | 133 | 14,000 | 117 | 19,000 | 158 |
| Profit before Tax | 10,000 | 100 | 9,750 | 97 | 13,300 | 133 | 11,550 | 115 | 16,150 | 161 |
| Gross working Capital | 40,000 | 100 | 45,000 | 112 | 45,000 | 112 | 50,000 | 125 | 80,000 | 200 |
| Current Liabilities | 20,000 | 100 | 25,000 | 125 | 25,000 | 125 | 30,000 | 150 | 35,000 | 175 |

## ANSWER

**Interpretation :** The sales shows the increasing trend. The sales in 2015 have increased by 60% as compared to the base year 2011. The direct cost is also increased by 63%. In 2015, factory overheads also increased by 50%. The Gross Margin also increased by 58% in 2015. The gross margin is increasing very slowly which is not a good sign. It is necessary to exercise control over the operating expenses to check the rising tendency and to increase the net margin.

Gross working capital position is better, it increased by 100% in the year 2015. On the other hand, current liabilities position has also increased i.e. 75% in the year 2015. The current financial position seems to be very bad.

## EXAMPLE

The following are the comparative financial statements of Dabur India Ltd., Delhi for three years. You are required to analyse them and give your opinion.

### Comparative Income Statements for the year ended 31st March,

| | Particulars | | 2014 ₹ | 2015 ₹ | 2016 ₹ |
|---|---|---|---|---|---|
| | Sales | | 2,34,800 | 2,37,200 | 2,44,800 |
| **Less :** | Cost of Goods Sold | (–) | 1,21,000 | 1,22,400 | 1,24,800 |
| | Gross Margin | | 1,13,800 | 1,14,800 | 1,20,000 |
| **Less :** | Operating Expenses | (–) | 72,000 | 73,500 | 75,400 |
| | **Net Income** | | **41,800** | **41,300** | **44,600** |

### Comparative Balance Sheet as on 31st March ......

| Capital and Liabilities | 2014 ₹ | 2015 ₹ | 2016 ₹ | Assets and Properties | 2014 ₹ | 2015 ₹ | 2016 ₹ |
|---|---|---|---|---|---|---|---|
| Share Capital | 1,74,000 | 1,73,000 | 1,85,000 | **Fixed Assets :** | | | |
| **Current Liabilities :** | | | | • Furniture | 92,000 | 98,000 | 1,10,000 |
| Bank Overdraft | 2,000 | 6,000 | 9,000 | **Current Assets :** | | | |
| Creditors | 41,500 | 53,500 | 86,500 | • Cash | 20,000 | 14,000 | 44,000 |
| Accrued Expenses (+) | 4,500 | 3,000 | 1,500 | • Debtors | 42,000 | 49,000 | 27,000 |
| **Total** | **48,000** | **62,500** | **97,000** | • Inventory | 67,000 | 73,000 | 98,000 |
| | | | | • Prepaid Expenses (+) | 1,000 | 1,500 | 3,000 |
| | | | | **Total** | **1,30,000** | **1,37,500** | **1,72,000** |
| **Total Liabilities** | **2,22,000** | **2,35,500** | **2,82,000** | **Total Assets** | **2,22,000** | **2,35,500** | **2,82,000** |

(**Year** –    2014   :    1-4-2013 to 31-3-2014
            2015   :    1-4-2014 to 31-3-2015
            2016   :    1-4-2015 to 31-3-2016)

| ANSWER |

**In the books of Dabur India Ltd., Delhi**

**Trend Analysis**

| Particulars | Base Year 2014 ₹ | 2015 ₹ | 2016 ₹ |
|---|---|---|---|
| Sales | 100 | 101 | 104 |
| Cost of Sales | 100 | 101 | 103 |
| Expenses | 100 | 102 | 103 |
| Net Income | 100 | 99 | 107 |
| Current Assets | 100 | 106 | 132 |
| Current Liabilities | 100 | 130 | 202 |
| Debtors | 100 | 117 | 64 |
| Inventory | 100 | 109 | 146 |
| Fixed Assets | 100 | 107 | 120 |
| Capital | 100 | 99 | 106 |

**Interpretation :**

i)    The sales shows very slow increasing trend. The sales in 2016 have increased only by 4% as compared to the base year 2014. In 2015, the sales have increased by 1% only. As against, cost of sales is also increased in 2016. The net income in 2015 is reduced by 1%. The cost of sales and other operating expenses are showing rapid increase from year to year which is a very bad situation. It is almost necessary to exercise control over the expenses.

ii)    The current assets have increased by 6% and 32% in the year 2015 and 2016 respectively. On the other hand, the current liabilities have been increased by 30% and 102% during the same years which makes the short-term solvency position very weak. Working capital cycle is disturbing.

iii)    The Sundry Debtors have gone down to 64% in 2016 whereas the Stock position has gone up to 146% in 2016. This shows the surplus stock position in the business. Unsold stock lying in godown, not converted into sales, which indicates the current financial position seems to be very bad.

iv)    Investment in Furniture is showing a rising trend. As the long-term capital is not available for new investment made in Furniture, it means that working capital fund is utilised for furniture purchases, which is not a good situation.

In short, corrective steps are necessary to overcome the financial difficulties faced by the business. Change in policy and strict control over the cost is essential for better results.

## 8.4 RATIO ANALYSIS

**Meaning and Definition :**

**Ratio Analysis** is one of the popular tools of financial statement analysis. In simple words, ratio is the quotient formed when one magnitude is divided by another measured in the same unit. A ratio is defined as "the indicated quotient of two mathematical expressions" and as "the relationship between two or more things". **Robert Anthony** defines Ratio, "one number expressed in terms of another". Usually, the ratio is stated as a percentage i.e. distribution expenses might be stated as 20.5 percent of sales. Often, however, the ratio is expressed in units, thus sales might be expressed as 20 times inventory. Thus, the ratio is a pure quantity or number, independent of the measurement units being used. A financial ratio is defined as a relationship between two variables taken from financial statements of a concern. It is a mathematical yardstick that measures the relationship between two financial figures which are interrelated. It involves the breakdown for the examined financial report into component parts which are then evaluated in relation to each other and to exogenous standards. Financial ratio expedite the analysis by reducing the large number of items involved to a relatively small set of readily comprehended and economically meaningful indicators.

As **ratio** represents a relationship between figures therefore, number of ratios can be formed by taking any two figures from the financial statements. However, such an approach would not fulfil any purpose unless the figures chosen are significantly correlated with each other. Furthermore, many of the ratios tend to deal with aspects of the same relationship, and there is little point in calculating several ratios in order to investigate the same point. Experts have identified some ratios as significant and important since they throw considerable light on the financial position of a concern. However, given the large number of ratios available, it is difficult to discern, the inter-relationships among them required for a comprehensive understanding of the entity being analysed. What is required is a parsimonious, integrated system of financial ratios, which will incorporate the essential ratios and highlight the inter-relationships among them.

**Interpretation of Ratio :**

One of the most difficult problems confronting the analyst is the **interpretation and analysis of financial ratios**. An adequate financial analysis involves more than an understanding and interpretation of each of the individual ratios. Furthermore, the analyst requires an insight into the meaning of the inter-relationships among the ratios and financial data in the statements. Gaining such an insight and understanding requires considerable experience in the analysis and interpretation of financial statements. Moreover, even experienced analyst cannot apply their skills equally well to analyse and interpret the financial statements of different concerns. The characteristics may differ from industry to industry and from firm to firm within the same industry. A ratio that is high for one firm at one time may be low for another firm or for the same firm at a different time. Therefore, the analyst must be familiar with the characteristics of the firm of which he is interpreting the financial ratios.

The analyst must not undertake the interpretation and analysis of financial ratios in isolation from other information. The various factors must be considered while analysing the financial ratios : i) General economic condition of the firm, ii) Risk acceptance, iii) Future expectations, iv) Future opportunities, v) Analysis and interpretation system used by other firms in the industry and vi) Accounting system of the industry.

The analysis and interpretation of the financial ratios in the light of above listed factors can be useful, but the analyst must still rely on skill, insight and even intention in order to interpret the ratios and arrive at a decision. The interpretation of the ratios can be made by comparing them with –

|     |                  |   |                                              |
|-----|------------------|---|----------------------------------------------|
| a)  | Previous figures | – | i.e. Trend Analysis.                         |
| b)  | Similar firms    | – | i.e. Inter Firm Comparisons                  |
| c)  | Targets          | – | i.e. Individual ratio set to meet the objective |

**a)    Trend Analysis :**

The analyst usually uses historical standards for evaluating the performance of the firm. The historical standards represent the financial ratio/s computed over a period of time - Trend. The trend analysis provides enough clues to the analyst for proper evaluation of the financial ratios. However, the changes in firm's policies over the period must be considered while interpreting ratios from comparison over a time. Furthermore, the average of the ratios, for several years can also be used for this purpose.

**b)    Inter-firm Comparisons :**

Inter-firm comparisons may make the comparisons of similar ratios for a number of different firms in the same industry. Such an attempt would facilitate the comparative study of financial position and performance of the firm in the industry. The published ratios of trade associations or financial institutions can be of great help to the analyst in the interpretation of the financial ratio. However, the variations in accounting system and changes in the policies and procedures of the firm in comparison with the industry have to be taken care of while making use of inter-firm comparisons.

**c)    Targets :**

Under this method, the interpretation of the ratio is made by comparing it with the standard set for this purpose, such a standard ratio, based upon accepted conventions serves as a measuring scale for the evaluation of the ratios. The best example of such standard is the 1 : 1 ratio which is to be considered as a good ratio for analysing acid-test ratio.

Generally speaking the use of single standard ratio for the interpretation of the ratios is not much useful. The accounting experts usually recommended the use of the group of standard ratios for the evaluation of financial ratios.

## 8.5 OBJECTIVES OF RATIO ANALYSIS

Important objectives of Ratio Analysis are as follows :

a)    To provide the necessary basis for inter-firm comparison as well as intra-firm comparison.

**Inter-firm comparison :**
i)    Between one company and its competitor.
ii)   Between one company and the best company in the industry.
iii)  Between one company and the global average.
iv)   Between one company and the average performance in the industry.

b)    To provide the necessary basis for Inter period comparison.

**Inter period comparison :**
i)    Between two years.        ii)   Between two months.
iii)  Between two quarters.     iv)   Between 'X' month of the current year and 'X' month of previous year.

c)    To help in providing a part of information needed in the process of decision making.

d)    To focus on facts on a comparative basis and facilitate drawing of conclusions relating to the performance of a firm.

e)    To evaluate the performance of a firm in determining the important aspects of a business such as liquidity, solvency, operational efficiency, overall profitability, capital gearing etc.

f)    To throw light on the degree of efficiency in the management and the effectiveness in the utilisation of its assets.

g)    To provide the way for effective control of the enterprise in the matter of achieving the physical and monetary targets.

h)    To help the management in discharging its basic functions like forecasting, planning, co-ordination, communication, control etc.

i)    To promote co-ordination among the departments and the staff by a study of performance and efficiency of each department.

j)    To point out the financial condition of business whether it is very strong, good, questionable or poor and enables the management to take necessary steps.

k)    To act as an index of the efficiency of an enterprise.

## 8.6 NATURE OF RATIO ANALYSIS

The ratio is calculated by dividing one figure by the other figure. It may be expressed in any of the three ways – 'times', 'proportion', or 'percentage' according to the convenience or suitability.

A more meaningful financial analysis involves ratios and their comparison relating to a business concern i) over a period of years, ii) against another unit, iii) against the industry as a whole, iv) against the predetermined standards, v) for one department or division against another department or division of the same unit.

Infact, **Ratio Analysis** does not provide an end in itself, but only a means in understanding of the business concern's financial position. The nature of ratio analysis indicates that quantitative ratio analysis does not provide solutions for all the problems faced by a financial manager, unless several ratios, each of which relates to other, are compiled and analysed in a perfect perspective.

While analysis based on a single set of financial statement is helpful, it may often have to be supplemented with time series analysis which provides insight into a firm's performance and condition over a period of time. In this context, index analysis and analysis of time series of financial ratios are helpful tools.

Actually, for tackling any problem, initially, one should determine what ratios would be helpful in throwing light on the above situation and compute only such ratios.

Several ratios have some common element (Sales, for example, is used in various turnover ratios) and some items tend to move in harmony because of some common underlying factor. Though industry averages and other yardsticks are commonly used in financial ratios, it is some what difficult to judge whether a certain ratio is 'good' or 'bad'. Therefore, it is a process requiring, proper care, sophistication, experience, etc.

**Advantages of Ratio Analysis :**

**Ratio Analysis** helps management to pinpoint specific areas that reflect improvement or deterioration as well as to detect any trouble spots that may prevent the attainment of objectives. The interested parties frequently undertake examination of these three areas to evaluate managements ability to maintain a satisfactory balance among them, and to appraise the efficiency and effectiveness with which management directs the firm's operations. Thus, the purpose of ratio analysis is to help the reader of asset of accounts to understand the information shown by highlighting a number of key relationships. However, following are the **principal advantages** claimed by ratio analysis :

i)    It guides the management in formulating future financial planning and policies.
ii)    It throws light on the efficiency of the business organisation.
iii)    It permits comparisons of the firm's figures with data for similar firms, and possibly with industry-wise data. It permits the data to be measured against yardstick of performance or of sound financial conditions.
iv)    It ensures effective cost control.
v)    It provides greater clarity, perspective, or meaning to the data and it brings out information not otherwise apparent.
vi)    It measures profitability and solvency of a concern.
vii)    It permits monetary figures of many digits to be condensed into two or three digits which enhances the managerial efficiency.
viii)    It helps in investment decisions.

**Limitations of Ratio Analysis :**

In using ratios, the analyst must keep a few general limitations in mind. The **main limitations** attached to ratio analysis are :

i)    It lacks standard values for the ratio, therefore scientific analysis is not possible.
ii)    As there are no standards with which to compare, it fails to throw light on the efficiency of any activity of the business.
iii)    It gives only the relationship between different variables and the actual magnitudes are not known through ratios.
iv)    Ratios are derived from the financial statements and naturally reflect their drawbacks.
v)    It fails to indicate immediately where the mistake or error lies.
vi)    It does not take into consideration the market and other changes.

**Classification of Ratios :**

Ratios have been classified by different experts differently based on their peculiar characteristics. Some authorities **classify ratios on the basis of the financial statements** or statements from which the financial figures are selected. Accordingly the following classification of ratio can be formed **on the basis of financial statements**.

**a)    Profit and Loss Ratios :**

These ratios indicate the relationship between two such variables which have been taken from the profit and loss account. Basically, there are two types of such ratios viz.

i) Those showing the current year's figure as a percentage of last year, thus facilitating comparison of the changes in the various profit and loss items and ii) Those expressing a relationship among different items for the current year; e.g. the percentage of distribution expenses to sales.

**b)    Balance Sheet Ratios :**

Top management will probably want to view the financial structure of the company in terms of basic ratios of asset or liability categories to total assets. These ratios attempt to express the relationship between two balance sheet items, e.g. the ratio of stock to debtors, or the ratio of owner's equity to total equity.

**c)    Inter-statement Ratios or Mixed Ratios :**

The components for computation of these ratios are drawn from both balance sheet and Profit and Loss Account. These ratios deal with the relationship between operating and balance sheet items. The example of such ratios are debtors turnover ratio, fixed assets turnover ratio, working capital turnover ratio, and stock turnover ratio.

Some authorities **classify the ratios on the basis of time**. On this basis the ratios can be divided into following two major groups :

**a)    Structural Ratios :**

Structural ratios exhibit the relation between two such items which relate to the same financial period. Thus above mentioned classification of ratios i.e. Profit and Loss ratios, balance sheet ratios, and mixed ratios are covered under structural ratios if the components for the computation of these ratios are drawn from the financial statements that relate to the same period.

**b)    Trend Ratio :**

These ratios deal with the relationship between items over a period of time. Trend ratios indicate the behaviour of the ratios for the period under study and thus provide enough scope for the proper evaluation of the business.

Another classification of ratios as developed by the financial experts is **on the basis of significance** of the ratios. Some ratios are considered more important than others when ratios are evaluated in the light of the objectives of the business. Accordingly, the following two main groups of ratios are covered under this classification.

**a)    Primary Ratios :**

Every commercial concern considers profit as its prime objective and therefore, any ratio that relates to such objective is treated as a primary ratio. The ratios covered by this category are return on capital, gross margin to sale, etc.

**b)    Secondary Ratios :**

The ratios other than the primary ratio are known as secondary ratios. Such ratios are treated as supporting ratios to the primary ratio because these ratios attempt to explain the primary ratios. The ratios such as turnover ratios, expense ratios, earning per share are considered secondary ratios.

The ratios have also been **classified according to their financial characteristics** that they describe. Accordingly, the following classification of ratio is given :

a) Liquidity Ratio, b) Leverage Ratios, c) Profitability Ratios, and d) Activity Ratios.

The classification on the basis of characteristics is simple to calculate and easy to understand as compared to other classifications discussed above. Therefore, this classification is always preferred by the financial analyst to evaluate the business performance. Accordingly detailed discussion follows on the classification of the ratios based on the their financial characteristics.

## 8.7 TYPES OF RATIOS

Ratios can broadly be classified into four groups i.e. liquidity capital, structure, leverage, profitability and activity respectively.

**a) Liquidity Ratio :**

Liquidity ratios measure the ability of a firm to meet its short-term obligations, and reflect its short-term financial strength or solvency. Important Liquidity Ratios are : (i) Current Ratio and (ii) Quick or Acid-test Ratio. Current ratio is the ratio of total current assets to total current liabilities. A satisfactory current ratio would enable a firm to meet its obligations even if the value of the current assets declines. It is, however, a quantitative index of liquidity as it does not differentiate between the components of current assets, such as cash and inventory which are not equally liquid. The quick ratio or acid test ratios takes into consideration the different liquidity of the components of current assets. It represents the ratio between quick current assets, and the total current liabilities. It is a rigorous measure and superior to the current ratio. However, both these ratios should be used to analyse the liquidity of a firm.

**b) Capital structure or Leverage Ratios :**

The capital structure/leverage ratios throw light on the long-term solvency of a firm. This is reflected in its ability to assure the long-term creditors with regard to periodic payment of interest, and the repayment of a loan on maturity, or in pre-determined instalments at due date. There are two types of such ratios : (i) Debt equity or Debt assets, and (ii) Coverage. The first type is computed from the balance sheet and reflects the relative contribution/stake of owners and creditors in financing the assets of the firm. In other words, such ratios reflect the safety margin to the long-term creditors. The second category of such ratios is based on the income statement and shows the number of times the fixed obligations are covered by earnings before interest and taxes. They indicate, in other words, the extent to which a fall in operating profits is tolerable, in that the ability to repay would not be adversely affected.

**c) Profitability Ratios :**

The profitability of a firm can be measured by the profitability ratios. Such ratios can be computed either from sales or investments. The profitability ratios based on sales are : (i) Profit Margin (gross and net), and ii) Expenses or Operating ratios. They indicate the proportion of sales consumed by operating costs, and the proportion available to meet financial and other expenses. The profitability related to investments include: i) Return on assets, (ii) Return on capital employed and (iii) Return on shareholders equity, including earning per share, dividend payout ratio, earning end dividend yield. The overall profitability (earning power) is measured by the return on investment, which is computed as a combined product of net profit margin and investment turnover. It is a central measure of the earning power and operating efficiency of a firm.

**d) Activity or Turnover or Efficiency Ratio :**

The last category of ratios is the activity ratios. They are also known as the efficiency or turnover ratios. Such ratios are concerned with measuring the efficiency in assets management. The efficiency with which assets are managed/used is reflected in the speed and rapidity with which they are converted into sales. Thus, the activity ratios are a test of relationship between sales or cost of goods sold and assets. Depending upon the type of asset, activity ratios may be : i) Inventory or Stock turnover ii) Receivables or Debtors turnover, and iii) Total assets turnover. The first of these indicates the number of times inventory is replaced during the year or how quickly the goods are sold. It is a test of efficiency inventory management. The second category of turnover ratios is indicative of the efficiency of receivables management as it shows how quickly trade goods are sold. It reveals the efficiency in managing and utilising the total assets.

## 8.8 TABULAR EXPLANATION OF TYPES OF RATIOS

### I. Balance Sheet Ratios

| Name of the Ratio | Formula for calculation of Ratio | Types of Ratios According to | | Significance | Precautions |
|---|---|---|---|---|---|
| | | Nature | Function | | |
| 1 | 2 | 3 | 4 | 5 | 6 |
| 1) **Current Ratio** **OR** **Working Capital Ratio** **OR** **'2 : 1 Ratio'** | Current Assets / Current Liabilities<br><br>Current Assets includes – Cash in hand/Bank, Marketable Securities, other short-term high quality investments, bills receivable, pre-paid expenses, work-in-progress, Sundry Debtors and Inventories etc.<br>Current Liabilities includes – Sundry Creditors, Bills Payable, Outstanding and accrued expenses, Income-Tax payable, Overdraft, Proposed dividend etc. | Balance Sheet | Liquidity Short-Term Solvency | This Ratio indicates the solvency of the business i.e. ability to meet the liabilities of the business as and when they fall due. This ratio also indicates how much current assets are there as against each rupee of Current Liabilities.<br>The Current Assets are the sources from which the Current Liabilities have to be met. It is also measure of the margin of safety that management maintains in order to allow for the inevitable unevenness in the flow of funds through the Current Assets and Liabilities Accounts.<br>Certain authorities have recommended that in order to ensure solvency of a concern, Current Assets should be atleast twice the current liabilities and therefore this ratio is known as "2 : 1 Ratio". This ratio is also named as, "Working Capital Ratio" as it represents the working capital being the excess of the current assets over current liabilities.<br><br>Though 2 : 1 ratio is concerned desirable, it is not must – it depends upon the nature of the business. What is important is not the size of the current ratio but the allocation and characteristics of current assets and current liabilities and their relation to the prospective turnover. | This ratio is sensitive to a number of factors which must be taken into account for accurate results such as –<br>1. It must be ascertained whether the Current Assets and Current Liabilities are properly valued.<br>2. For proper influence the composition of Current Assets should not be over-looked. If majority of Current Assets are in the form of Inventory, even a 2 : 1 ratio will not result into favourable consideration because inventory is considered to be the least liquid assets out of all current assets of a firm.<br>3. A very high current ratio may not indicate a very favourable position because it means that excessive investments in current assets is made. This will result in decrease in profitability because of large funds blocked in working capital.<br>4. For studying the solvency of the concern from the current ratio still another factor must not be lost sight of i.e. shrinkage in value of current assets on a forced liquidation. |
| 2) **Liquid Ratio OR Quick Ratio OR Acid Test Ratio** | Quick or Liquid Assets / Quick or Liquid Liabilities<br>Quick Assets include all Current Assets except inventory (stock) and prepaid expenses. | Balance Sheet | Liquidity Short-Term Solvency | As regard to the ability to honour day today commitment, liquid ratio is a better tool.<br>It is the ratio between liquid assets and liquid liabilities.<br>An ideal liquid ratio is considered as 1 : 1 | The adequacy of this ratio depends on the industry which the firm operates.<br>**Precautions :** Same as Current Ratio.<br>Care must be exercised in placing too much reliance on 100% acid test ratio without further investigation e.g. a seasonal business which seeks to stabilise production will tend to have a weak acid test ratio during its period |

| | | | | |
|---|---|---|---|---|
| | Quick liabilities include all current liabilities except overdraft and accrued expenses. Some experts advocate that only Stock from Current Assets and Overdraft from Current Liabilities should be excluded. | | | It signifies a very short term liquidity of a business concern and is, therefore, also called liquid ratio.<br>If it is desired to apply a still stiffer and rigorous test of solvency, the application of acid-test ratio is suitable.<br>The acid-test ratio assumes that stock may not be realised immediately and therefore, this item is excluded in the computation of this ratio.<br>The logic for exclusion of bank overdraft is based on the fact that bank overdraft is generally a permanent way of financing.<br>Too low a ratio suggests not only inability to meet current claims but also inability to take advantages of cash discounts and other rewards for prompt payment. On the other hand, an excessive amount of quick assets could indicate that these assets should be put to more productive or profitable use elsewhere in the enterprise. | of slack sales, but probably a powerful one in its period of highest selling, so that earlier weak or downward position would have to be judged in relation to the market prospects for the firm's products in the latter period.<br>An acid-test ratio of 1 : 1 is usually considered an ideal and satisfactory. However, this is rule of thumb and should be applied with care. |
| **3) Proprietory Ratio OR Tangible Worth to Total Assets Ratio OR Capital to Total Assets Ratio OR Equity Ratio** | Proprietor's Fund<br>——————————<br>Total Assets/Total Capital<br>Proprietor's Fund or Owners Equity = Share Capital*, Reserves & Surplus (both preferential and equity)<br>Total Assets = Fixed & Current Assets<br>Some experts are of the opinion that total assets includes only tangible assets. It means "Goodwill" shall be excluded from the total assets. | Balance Sheet | Leverage | It is primarily, the ratio between proprietor's funds and Total Assets. It indicates the strength of the funding of the company. As a very rough measure, it may be suggested that $2/3^{rd}$ to $3/4^{th}$ of the total assets should be financed by proprietor funds. However, the optimum ratio is different in different lines of business.<br>A high proprietory ratio is however frequently indicative of over capitalisation and an excessive investment in fixed assets in relation to actual needs.<br>A ratio nearing 100% often gives low earnings per share and consequently, a low rate of dividend to shareholders.<br>On the other hand, a low proprietory ratio is a symptom of under capitalisation and an excessive use of creditors fund to finance the business.<br>This ratio is normally a test of strength of credit worthiness of the business. | This ratio should be considered alongwith the current ratio while observing the solvency of the business.<br>Recall that the owner's equity is the residual interest in the firm's assets after allowance had been made for the claims of creditors against assets. |

| | | | | | |
|---|---|---|---|---|---|
| 4) **Capital Gearing Ratio** | Equity Share Capital + Reserves and Surplus * Preference Share Capital + Loan Capital (* Fixed interest bearing securities) | Balance Sheet | Leverage | It is used to express the relationship between equity share capital and fixed interest bearing securities of a company. When fluctuation in profit of a company is followed by a disproportionately large increase or decrease in return to equity shareholders, a company is considered to be highly geared. If the proportion of preference shares and a loan capital is high or where the proportion of ordinary share capital to the total output is low, capital is said to be highly geared and reverse is the position in low gearing. Low gearing indicates that the equity share capital is not paid an adequate return because the profits are swallowed up by the high fixed charges in the form of interest and dividend. Capital gearing signifies the process of maintaining a desired and appropriate gear ratio in an enterprise. While inflationary conditions are expected, high gearing is to be employed and in the period marked by trade depression, low gearing should be employed. | As it affects the company's capacity to maintain a stable dividend distribution policy during the difficult trading periods, it must be carefully planned. |
| 5) **Debt Equity Ratio OR Total Liabilities to Proprietor's Fund Ratio** | Total Debt i.e. Long-term + Short term. Net Worth / Owners' Equity | Balance Sheet | Leverage | The ratio establishes the relationship between owner's funds and external debts or there relationship between proprietor's fund and borrowed capital. The long term solvency of the firm can be assessed from this ratio. Here, 'Debt' refers to the external or borrowed capital and the equity refers to the shareholders' fund or internal capital. This ratio reveals the claims of shareholders and creditors against the assets of the firm. The normal and safe ratio is 2 : 1. If the ratio is higher, it indicates that the firm is depending 'heavily' on creditors. If the ratio is low, it means that the firm is depending mainly on internal sources and owner's funds. The purpose of Debt to Equity Ratio is to derive an idea of the amount of capital supplied to the firm by the owners and of asset "cushion" available to the Creditors on liquidation. | The interpretation of the ratio, however, depends almost entirely on the financial and business policy of the enterprise. From this point of view, the importance of the ratio lies in highlighting the seemingly irreconcilable view points of the owners and creditors regarding the method of financing the business; the former having always the temptation of doing business with other people's fund and the latter insisting on that the owner should atleast have as large as an investment as creditors. Therefore, on the average debt to equity ratio 1 : 1 is also acceptable. Too much reliance on external equities may indicate under capitalisation whereas too much reliance on internal equity may lead to over capitalisation. |

| 6) | **Stock Working Capital Ratio OR Inventory to working capital ratio** | $\dfrac{\text{Closing Stock}}{\text{Working Capital}}$ | Balance Sheet | Liquidity Short-term solvency | The ratio is an index of the position of over-stocking. It shows what part of working capital is represented by the closing stocks. The size of Closing Stocks must bear a proper proportion of the quantum of working capital. The higher is the cover given by working capital the lower is the risk of loss by the likely fall in the value of inventories in future.<br><br>There is a need to supplement the ratio of net sales to inventory by another ratio to confirm the position shown by the Inventory and the net working capital and provides a relatively more stable basis for comparison than is supplied by the Inventory turnover ratio<br><br>Inventory Ratio should be calculated as under :<br><br>$= \dfrac{\text{Cost of goods sold}}{\text{* Average Inventory at Cost}}$<br><br>* Average Inventory =<br>$\dfrac{\text{Opening Stock + Closing Stock}}{2}$<br><br>**OR**<br><br>$= \dfrac{\text{Net Sales}}{\text{Average Inventory at selling price}}$ | The ratio should be interpreted with maximum care. It should not be treated as a conclusive proof of overstocking. This ratio should be considered alongwith stock turnover ratio to arrive at the correct decision. |

| **II. Revenue Statement Ratios** |

| 1. | **Gross Profit Ratio** | $\dfrac{\text{Gross Profit}}{\text{Net Sales}} \times 100$ | Revenue | Profitability | The Gross Profit Ratio represents the gross margin. It expresses the relationship of gross profit on sales to net sales in terms of percentage. It is the ratio which is most commonly employed by accountants for comparing the earning of business for one period with those of other or earning of one concern with those of another in the same industry.<br><br>It indicates the degree to which selling prices of goods per unit may decline without resulting in losses on operations for the firm.<br><br>A high gross profit ratio as compared with that of the other firm in the same industry implies that the firm in question produces its products at lower cost. It is a sign of good management. | Gross profit is the ultimate result of interaction between prices, sales, volume and costs. A change in the gross profit can be effected by changes in any of these factors. This gross profit indicates the limit beyond which the sale price of goods cannot be allowed to fall.<br><br>Sometimes, a high gross profit ratio may also be due to unsatisfactory basis of valuation of stock i.e. over valuation of closing stock or under valuation of opening stock. A detailed analysis of various factors alone will give a proper clue for the increased gross profit ratio. |

| | | | | | |
|---|---|---|---|---|---|
| 2) Expenses Ratios | Expenses Ratio = <br> $\dfrac{\text{Specific Operating Expenses}}{\text{Sales}}$ <br><br> 1) Fixed Expenses to Total Cost Ratio <br><br> $= \dfrac{\text{Fixed Expenses}}{\text{Total Cost}}$ <br><br> 2) Material Consumption to Sales Ratio <br><br> $\dfrac{\text{Material Consumption}}{\text{Sales}} \times 100$ <br><br> 3) Wages to Sales Ratio <br> $= \dfrac{\text{Wages}}{\text{Sales}}$ <br><br> 4) Office Administrative Expenses to Sales Ratio <br> $= \dfrac{\text{Office Adm. Expenses}}{\text{Sales}}$ <br><br> 5) Selling and Distribution Expenses to Sales Ratio = <br> $\dfrac{\text{Selling \& Distribution Expenses}}{\text{Sales}}$ | Revenue <br><br><br><br><br> Revenue | Profitability <br><br><br><br><br> Profitability | On the other hand, a low gross profit ratio may indicate unfavourable purchasing and mark up policies, the liability of management to develop sales volume, theft, damage, bad maintenance, markets reduction in selling prices not accompanied by proportionate decreases in cost of goods etc. <br><br> These supplement the information given by the revenue profit ratios. As there is a very important relationship existing between operating expenses and volume of sales, expenses ratios are calculated by dividing net sales into each individual operating expenses. (Selling, administrative and general expenses). These ratios represent a summation of changes in net sales and in the expense items. These ratios are valuable in comparing two similar businesses or operating data from year to year of the same business. <br><br> 1) Fixed Expenses to Total Cost Ratio : This Ratio shows the idle capacity in the organisation. Sometimes this ratio increases without corresponding increase in fixed expenses. In such circumstances, the matter should be properly examined. <br> 2) Material consumption to Sales Ratio : This Ratio shows as to how much material is consumed and what is its percentage share in total sales. If the share is high, the profit of the firm declines. <br> 3) Wages to Sales Ratio : This ratio indicates the percentage of wages to sales. If the ratio is higher, the profit margin will come down. <br> 4) Office and Administrative Expenses to Sales Ratio : This ratio indicates the impact of indirect expenses on sales or profit. Higher the ratio lesser will be the margin of profit. | While interpreting the expenses ratio it should be remembered that certain fixed expenses e.g. insurance premium, rates and taxes would decrease as the sales increases, but variable expenses like commission of sales would remain constant. |

| Ratio | Formula | | | Explanation | Interpretation |
|---|---|---|---|---|---|
| | | | | (5) Selling and Distribution Expenses to Sales Ratio : This ratio indicates the impact of selling expenses (particularly expenses on advertisement) on sales. Higher the ratio lesser will be the margin of profit). | |
| 3) Operating Ratio | $\dfrac{\text{Cost of goods sold plus Operating Exp.}}{\text{Net Sales}} \times 100$<br><br>Operating Expenses consists of Factory Exp Administrative Exps and Selling & Dist Exp. | Revenue | Profitability | The ratio indicates the percentage of net sales that is absorbed by the cost of goods sold and operating expenses. Naturally, higher the ratio, the less favourable it is because it would have a small margin to meet interest, dividends and other operating needs.<br><br>Naturally, the higher the operating ratio the less favourable it is, because it would leave a smaller margin to meet interest, dividends, and other corporate needs. It can also be used as a partial index of overall profitability, but cannot be used as test of financial conditions without taking into account financial and extraordinary items. | In interpreting operating ratio full recognition must be given to the possibility of variations in expenses from year to year or company to company, due to changes or differences in policies involving expenses that are subject to managerial decisions. |
| 4) Net Operating Profit Ratio OR Operating Profit Ratio | $= \dfrac{*\text{Operating Net Profit}}{\text{Net Sales}} \times 100$<br><br>*Operating net profit is the net profit minus income from external securities and others such as, interest, dividend, profit on sale of securities etc. | Revenue | Profitability | This Ratio is mainly concerned with operating profit or profit obtained from the main line of activity. Non-business income is also included in the profit and when a ratio has to be obtained from business profit this ratio has to be computed.<br>The profitability of a firm can be easily measured by this ratio. The operating efficiency of a firm is ultimately adjusted by the profits earned by it.<br><br>The Operating profit ratio is a tool in the hands of management to control the cost of production and other expenses like administrative and selling expenses. It shows the amount of profit earned for each rupee of sales. If the amount earned is more, it means that there is a low cost of operation and if the profit is low, the cost of production and other expenses are on the increase. | Non-operating incomes and expenses are strictly excluded, when this ratio is calculated. This ratio indicates the firm's capacity to withstand adverse economic conditions. |
| 5. Net Profit Ratio | $\dfrac{\text{Net Profit after Taxes}}{\text{Net Sales}} \times 100$ | Revenue | Profitability | Net Profit is that portion of Net Sales which remains to the owners or the shareholders after all costs, charges, and expenses including income-tax, have been deducted. | To get a meaningful interpretation of profitability of the firm, a financial analyst must evaluate both the Gross Profit Ratio and Net Profit Ratio jointly. |

The relationship of net profit to net sales is established by this ratio and is expressed in percentage.

This ratio shows the balance of profit left to proprietors, after all expenses are met with. This ratio normally ranges between 5% and 10%. Higher will be the ratio, higher will be the profit left to shareholders. This ratio assists the management in controlling costs and in increasing the turnover.

A firm with a high net profit ratio would be in an advantageous position to survive in the face of falling sales prices, rising costs of production or declining demand for the product. A firm with a low net profit ratio may find it difficult to withstand these adversities. A high net profit ratio can enable the firm to reap the benefits of favourable conditions, such as rising, sales prices, falling costs of production or increasing demand for the product. Such a firm can accelerate its profits at a faster rate than a firm with a low net profit ratio.

## III. Composite Ratios

| Name of the Ratio | Formula for calculation of Ratio | Types of Ratios According to | | Significance | Precautions |
|---|---|---|---|---|---|
| | | Nature | Function | | |
| 1 | 2 | 3 | 4 | 5 | 6 |
| 1) Return on Capital Employed OR Net Profit to Assets Ratio OR Return on Total Assets | $\dfrac{\text{Net Profit before tax \& Interest}}{\text{Capital Employed}} \times 100$<br>Capital Employed means – either non-current liabilities plus share-holders funds OR Working Capital plus non-current assets. (If the term capital employed is taken as Gross Capital Employed then it means Total Assets).<br>OR<br>Capital Employed = Share Capital + Reserves & Surplus + Long term loan – (Non-business Assets + Fictitious Assets) | Composite | Profitability | The Ratio shows how well the firm has used the resources of the owners. This ratio is a measure of the profitableness of an enterprise. It is also used as basis for various managerial decisions. There are difference of opinion regarding the calculation of capital employed. Some of the financial managers are of the view that the amount of capital employed must be such that it may fairly represent capital investment throughout the year and therefore, they bring the concept of average capital employed. Alternatively, it is equal to working capital plan Non-Current Assets. The term operating profit means profit before Interest and Tax. | Following points are important regarding calculation of capital employed.<br>1) Fictitious assets like preliminary expenses, accounts of deferred revenue expenditure are excluded.<br>2) Intangible assets like goodwill are generally excluded.<br>3) Though idle assets are excluded from capital employed, stand by plant and equipment essential to normal running machinery should not be excluded.<br>4) Investments made outside the business are to be excluded but those made for bonafide purposes of the business are included. |

4) Variations of the ROCE (Return on Capital Employed)

a) $\text{ROCE} = \dfrac{\text{Net Profit after Taxes}}{\text{Capital Employed}} \times 100$

b) $\text{ROCE} = \dfrac{(\text{Net Profit after Tax} + \text{Interest})}{(\text{Capital Employed})} \times 100$

c) $\text{ROCE} = \dfrac{(\text{Net Profit after Taxes} + \text{Interest})}{\text{Capital Employed} - \text{Intabgible Assets}} \times 100$

d) $\text{ROCE} = \dfrac{\text{Operating Profit}}{\text{Capital Employed}} \times 100$

Average Capital Employed =

$$\dfrac{\text{C.E. Employed at the beginning of the year} + \text{C.E. at the end of the year}}{2}$$

In fact, the starting point of business budgeting should be the determination of minimum rate of profit on capital investment which is then worked backwards for planning the details of business operations. This is the minimum return expected on capital employed and in order to attract capital to a particular business, a fair return has to be paid. There is hardly any criterion for determining the minimum return with reference to which return on capital investment may be judged. Return on capital employed is the measure which can be said to show satisfactorily, the overall performance of an undertaking from the stand point of profitability. It enables the management to show whether the funds entrusted to it have been properly used or not. Thus, it can become an integral part of budgetary control system in order that management may be able to follow the progress being made and to take corrective actions, if necessary

5) All stocks are included, valuing them on a consistent basis, generally at cost.

6) Trade debtors are included after taking into account provision for bad debts.

7) Any balance at bank in excess of the normal requirements of a business may be excluded.

| Ratio | Formula | | | Explanation | |
|---|---|---|---|---|---|
| 2) Return on Proprietor's Funds OR Return on Share-holders Investments OR Return on Total Shareholders' Equity | $\dfrac{\text{Net profit after interest \& taxes}}{\text{Shareholders fund}} \times 100$<br><br>The term of 'Net Profit' here means, Net Income after Interest and Taxes. It is different from 'Net Operating Profits'<br>The shareholders' fund will include equity share capital, preference share capital, share premium and Reserves & Surplus less accumulated losses. | Composite | Profitability | This ratio shows how well the firm has used the resources of the owners. This ratio is a measure of the profitableness of an enterprise. The realisation of satisfactory net income is the major objective of a business and the ratio shows the extent to which this objective is being achieved. This ratio should be compared with the ratio of similar companies.<br>The shareholders' equity also refers to the net worth of a firm. | Alongwith this ratio a) return on assets and b) Return on capital employed should also be useful for meaningful financial analysis. |
| 3) Return on Equity Capital OR Common Equity | $\dfrac{\text{Net Profit (after taxes \& Pref. Dividend)}}{\text{Equity Share Capital}} \times 100$<br>= Rate of Return on Equity Capital | | | The profitability from the point of view of the equity shareholders will be judged after taking into account the amount of dividend payable to the preference shareholders. | Actually this ratio is very useful to the investors. It helps the investors to take buying decisions. |

| | Composite | Profitability | |
|---|---|---|---|
| Equity shareholders fund will include paid up share capital (equity) plus share premium plus Reserve & Surplus less accumulated losses. | Composite | Profitability | This is one of the most important relationship in ratio analysis. Obtaining a satisfactory return is the most desirable objective of a business. The ratio of net profit to owners equity reflects the extent to which this objective has been accomplished. This ratio is thus, of great interest to present as well as prospective shareholders and also of great concern to management, which has the responsibility of maximising the owners' welfare.<br>The Returns on owner's equity of the company should be compared to the ratio of other similar companies and the industry average. This will indicate the relative performance and strength of the company in attracting the prospective investors. | |
| 4) Earning per equity share OR (EPS Ratio) Earning Per Share Ratio<br><br>$\dfrac{\text{Net Profit (after Tax \& Pref. Div.)}}{\text{No. of equity shares}}$ | Composite | Profitability | This ratio shows percentage of profit available to equity shareholders or how much return they earn per share. It is used to compare the performance of a company with higher rate of return will have greater demand in the market, resulting in increase in the market value. This ratio is adopted to know the return to shareholders on the capital employed. According to this, the earning net profit (after tax & pref. dividend) as numerator and number held by the shareholders as denominator. | While adopting EPS ratio, it should also be remembered that if there is any increase in EPS ratio, it should not be taken to mean an increase in the profitability of a firm, since retained earnings might have been utilised for payment of dividend.<br>Another demerit of EPS ratio is that it does not clearly disclose as to what portion of profits have been paid to the owners as a dividend and what portion has been retained in the business. This only represents how much of the profits belong to the equity shareholders rather theoretically. |
| 5) Price Earning Ratio or PER or P/E Ratio<br><br>$\dfrac{\text{Market Price Per Equity share}}{\text{Earning Per Equity Share}}$ | Composite | Profitability | The price earning ratio is widely used by the security analyst to evaluate the firm's performance as expected by the investors. It indicates investors' judgement or expectations of the firm's performance. Management is also interested in this method of market appraisal of the firm's performance and would like to find the causes if the P/E Ratio declines. As a rule, the higher the P/E ratio, the better it is for the equity shareholders. | While estimating the earnings, only normal earnings associated with the existing assets alone are considered. |

| | Formula | | | Description |
|---|---|---|---|---|
| 6) Earning Price Ratio OR E.P. Ratio OR Earning Yield Ratio | $\dfrac{\text{Earning Per Equity Share}}{\text{Market Price Per Equity Share}} \times 100$ | Composite | Profitability | This ratio is reciprocal or complementary of P/E Ratio as low percentage may reflect a high rate of growth in the past. |
| 7) Dividend Payout Ratio OR Pay Out Ratio OR D/P Ratio | $\dfrac{\text{Total Dividend paid to equity holders}}{\text{Total Net Profits belonging to Equity holders}} \times 100$<br>Alternatively, it can be found –<br>$\dfrac{\text{Dividend Per Share (DPS)}}{\text{Earning Per Share (EPS)}} \times 100$ | Composite | Profitability | This ratio is also known as pay out ratio. It measures the relationship between the earnings belonging to the equity holders and dividend actually paid to them. Precisely, the D/P ratio expresses what percentage share of net profits after taxes and preference dividend is paid out as dividend to the equity shareholders. This ratio is computed by dividing the total dividends paid to equity |
| | | Composite | Profitability | holders by the total profits belonging to them. The D/P Ratio is popular ratio. A comparison of this ratio with that of similar firms, industry average and over years, would reflect on the adequacy or otherwise of dividend paid to the equity holders. This ratio also indicates another important aspect. It throws light on the aspect of retained earning. When the dividend payout is high, the retained earning will be less and this means less internal finance. The finance decision of the companies vary.<br>The payout ratio indicates whether the dividend paid is high or low and on this basis, the firm can decide whether it has to change its dividend payout decision with a view to increasing the retained earning.<br><br>Many companies after attaining a stage would like to utilise the self generated funds or self Reliance Fund (i.e. retained earnings) for expansion by capitalising these funds. The retained earning can be built-up over a period if the company follows a conservative dividend policy. Hence, the less payout to the shareholders. |
| 8) Dividend Yield Ratio | $\dfrac{\text{Dividend Per Equity Share}}{\text{Market Price Per Equity Share}} \times 100$ | Composite | Profitability | As the market price is different from face value and paid up value of equity share, the rate of return of the investor cannot be equal to the rate of dividend declared by the company. Suppose, the company had declared 50% dividend on its Equity shares of ` 100 each and if the market price of the share is 200, the purchaser of the share will have to pay ` 200 and on ` 200 he will get dividend of ` 50. It means, he will get the dividend at rate of 25% on his investment.<br><br>Besides indicating the general level of market, dividend yield reflects the market estimates of future dividend growth and risk. Higher the dividend growth expectations for given share, the lower the current yield, the higher the market's estimate of risk, the higher the current yield. |

| | | | |
|---|---|---|---|
| 9) a) Debtors Turn-over Ratio OR Receivable Turnover Ratio OR Debtor's Velocity | $= \dfrac{\text{Accounts Receivables}}{\text{Average Daily Sales}}$ <br> OR $\dfrac{\text{No. of days} \times \text{Accounts Receivables}}{\text{Net Sales}} \times 365 \text{ (or 360)}$ <br><br> $\dfrac{\text{Net Credit Sales}}{\text{Average Accounts Receivable (OR Debtors)}}$ OR <br> $\dfrac{\text{Credit Sales (Net)}}{\text{Average Debtors}}$ <br><br> Accounts Receivables includes Trade Debtors and Bills Receivables | Composite | Activity |

The dividend yield is calculated by dividing the cash dividends per equity share by the market value per share.

Debtors constitute an important elements of current assets and therefore, the quality of debtors to a great extent determines the liquidity of a firm. Two ratios are used by financial analyst to judge the liquidity of a firm.

a) Debtors Turnover Ratio

b) Debts collection period or Average Collection period

a) Debtors Turnover ratio indicates the efficiency of the staff incharge of the collection of book debts. The higher the value of the debtors turnover, the more efficient is the management of receivables. The ratio should be compared with ratios of similar firms and industry average to get a better picture of quality of debtors. The ratio also helps in cash budgeting since the flow of cash from customers can be estimated on the basis of estimated sales.

b) This ratio indicates the number of times the debtors turn each year. It also indicates the collection period of debtors. A high turnover is considered to be good as there will be better cash flow. If the collection period is shorter, the quality of debtors will be good and this means the debtors promptly pay their dues. The scope of bad debts will be less. 40 to 60 days are usually considered as normal ratio and the quality of the debt will be good. If the turnover is low, the cash in flow will be slow and the quality of debts will not be good.

The collection period, however, has to be compared with the standard and the standard being the industry turnover. When compared to the industry turnover, if the ratio is low, it means that the firm is not collecting the debts regularly. However, hard and fast rules cannot be adopted as far as credit sales policy is concerned. The firm should strike a balance between rigidity and liberalism. Then only a normal collection period prevails.

Many other factors, such as business environment, outlook of the management, the pricing policy, the nature of the product sold etc. also decide the credit sales policy and credit sales policy decides the debtors turnover ratio.

| | | |
|---|---|---|
| b) Debts Collection Period Ratio OR Average Collection Period Ratio | i) $\dfrac{\text{Months or (Days) in a year'}}{\text{Debtors Turnover}}$ <br> ii) $\dfrac{\text{Average Accounts Receivable} \times \text{Months (or days) in a year}}{\text{Net Credit Sales for the year}}$ <br> ii) $\dfrac{\text{Accounts Receivable}}{\text{Average (Monthly or Daily) Credit Sales (Net)}}$ | |

| | | | | |
|---|---|---|---|---|
| 10) Stock Turnover Ratio OR Inventory Turnover Ratio | Note : In case, credit sales figure is not given, total sales figure can be used to compute receivable turnover<br><br>Cost of goods sold / Average Inventory at Cost<br>OR<br>Net Sales / *Average Inventory at Selling Price<br>(where cost of goods sold is not available, net Sales are taken)<br>*Average Inventory or Stock =<br>Opening Stock + Closing Stock / 2<br>(If Opening Stock is not available, Closing Stock is to be taken as Average Stock)<br>(Cost of goods sold refers to goods sold minus gross profit) | Composite | Profitability | Change in the ratio indicates change in the company's credit policy or changes in its ability to collect its receivables.<br>The main objective of the comparison implied in the debtors turnover ratio, is to learn how old the accounts are and partly to learn how fast cash will flow from their collections.<br>This Ratio relates the cost of goods sold during a given period to the average inventory. This ratio helps in determining the liquidity of a business concern in as much as it indicates the rate at which the inventory are converted into sales and into cash ultimately. This ratio also throws light on the inventory policy persued by any unit and the reasonableness of the same.<br>A high inventory turnover ratio is good from the liquidity point of view. On the other hand, a low ratio would indicate that the inventory does not move fast and remains in warehouse for a longer time. |

The relation is between variables. If both items (Net Sales and Stock) increase in the same proportion, the ratio remains unchanged and a situation may develop that may inadvertantly lead to bad financial condition. For example,

| | | | |
|---|---|---|---|
| Sale (Net) | 1,00,000 | 1,50,000 | 2,50,000 |
| Stock or | | | |
| Inventory | 10,000 | 15,000 | 25,000 |
| Ratio | 10 : 1 | 10 : 1 | 10 ;1 |
| Working Capital | 12,500 | 12,500 | 1,2500 |

A too high inventory turnover may be the result of a very low level of inventory which results frequent stock outs. The turnover will be very high if the firm replenishes its inventory in too many small lot sizes. The situations of frequent stock-outs and too many small inventory replacement are costly to the firm. Thus, too high and too low inventory ratios need to be investigate into further. The computation of inventory turnover ratios for the individual components of inventory may help the management in detecting the imbalance investments in various inventory components

An inventory turnover ratio, standing by itself, means absolutely nothing because there is no fixed norm for turnover. To give meaning to turnover figure one must compare it with other such figures so that a comparative analysis with industry or over a time is possible.

Though the ratio is constant for 3 years, inventory may prove excessive for size of business and could ultimately result in bankruptcy.

In order to discern this danger point this ratio must be supplemented by the ratio of inventory to working capital.

While employing Inventory Turnover Ratio, the following factors must be kept in mind.

(i) Seasonal conditions (ii) Supply conditions (iii) Price trends and (iv) Trend of volume of business.

| | | | | | |
|---|---|---|---|---|---|
| 11) Creditors' Turn-over Ratio | i) Creditor's Turnover Ratio $$= \frac{\text{Credit Purchases}}{\text{*Average Creditors}}$$ (* Average creditors are obtained by adding closing creditor to operating creditors and dividing the same by two) In absence of detailed information the following formula can be adopted $$= \frac{\text{Total Credit Purchases}}{\text{Closing Creditors}}$$ Alternative Method : Creditors Turnover Ratio = $$\frac{\text{Creditors}}{\text{Credit Purchases}} \times 365 \text{ OR } 360$$ | Composite | Activity | This ratio reveals the number of times the creditors turn on the average each year. This tells at what speed the creditors are paid. If the payment to creditors is delayed the firm sometimes may have to bear the burden of debt service charges. This ratio can be computed as per first method, when the information regarding credit purchases, opening and closing balance of creditors are available. In absence of the detailed information as said earlier, the alternative formula can be adopted to compute the ratio. From the stand point of liquidity and solvency if longer credit period is allowed by the creditors the firm will be in an advantageous position. The safety period is 60 to 90 days. The credit worthiness of the firm is also established by this ratio. The firm can promptly pay its creditors if the payment time is properly adjusted. The ratio will tell whether the time period is normal or not. | This ratio is a combination of several factors. The figures drawn from financial statements are subject to change as time passes. The "time value" concept will not be considered at the time of computing ratio. |
| 12) a) Fixed Assets Turnover Ratio | $$\frac{\text{Sales}}{\text{Net Fixed Assets}} = \text{No. of times}$$ | Composite | Activity | The ratio indicates the efficiency in the utilisation of fixed assets. This ratio also indicates whether the fixed assets are being fully utilised. It is an important measure of efficiency and profit earning capacity of the business. A high ratio is an index of the overtrading and low ratio suggests idle capacity and excessive investment in fixed assets. Generally, a standard ratio is taken as five times. | The analyst should be cautious in deriving conclusions from the fixed assets turnover ratio. To obtain fixed assets turnover ratio, sales are dividend by depreciated value of fixed assets. Hence, as with the fixed assets turnover ratio, the total assets turnover ratio should be cautiously used. In the denominator of this ratio assets are net of depreciation. Therefore, older assets with lower book value may create a misleading impression of high turnover. |
| b) Total Assets Turnover Ratio | $$= \frac{\text{Sales}}{\text{Total Assets *}}$$ * Some analyst exclude intangible assets, in such case Ratio should be $$= \frac{\text{Sales}}{\text{Total Tangible Assets}}$$ | Composite | Activity | Not only fixed assets are directly concerned with the generation of sales, but other assets also contribute to the production and sales activity of the firm. The firm must manage its total assets efficiently and should generate maximum sales through their proper utilisation. | |

• As per the revised syllabus the problems on Ratio Analysis are restricted to the following ratios only i.e. Gross Profit Ratio, Net Profit Ratio, Operating Ratio, Stock Turnover Ratio, Current Ratio and Liquid Ratio, etc.

## SUMMARY

- Financial Statement Analysis is a process of evaluating the relationship between component parts of a financial statement to obtain a better understanding of a firm's position and performance.

- The main objectives of a financial statement analysis is to provide decision makers, information about a business enterprise for use of decision-making.

- Interpretation means bringing out the meaning of financial statements with the help of analysis. In other words, interpretation means to present an explanation of financial data with the help of analysis.

- Classification of financial analysis : a) According to material used – i) External Analysis and (ii) Internal Analysis, b) According to modus Operendi of analysis – i) Horizontal Analysis and ii) Vertical Analysis.

- The percentage analysis of increase or decrease in corresponding items in comparative financial statements is called horizontal analysis. On the other hand, vertical analysis uses percentages to show the relationship of the different parts to the total in a single statement.

- A 'Ratio' is defined as "the indicated quotient of two mathematical expressions" and as "the relationship between two or more things".

- Steps of financial analysis : i) Collection of financial data ii) Processing of the data, iii) Comparing the processed data and iv) Suggesting actions.

- Comparison is useful in studying the trends in an enterprise.

- In order to be successful in analysis and interpretation, a financial analyst must possess thorough knowledge of accounting theory and practice.

- A statement in which individual items are expressed as a percentage of same common base is termed as common-size statement.

- For the purpose of comparative study of financial statements over a number of years "trend analysis" are very useful.

- Ratio analysis does not provide an end in itself, but only a means to understanding of business concern's financial position.

- Classification of Ratios I) a) Profit and Loss Ratios b) Balance Sheet Ratios, c) Mixed Ratios.

- Classification of Ratios – II) a) Structural Ratios b) Trend Ratios.

  Classification of Ratios III) – a) Primary Ratios and b) Secondary Ratios).

- Types of Ratios – a) Liquidity Ratios, b) Leverage Ratios, c) Profitability Ratios, and d) Activity Ratios.

- Each and every ratio has its own nature, function, formula for calculation and significance.

- Liquidity refers to the ability of the firm to meet its obligation in the short-run, usually one year. Leverage refers to use of debt finance. Profitability ratios reflect the final result of business operations.

## 8.9 ILLUSTRATIONS

### ILLUSTRATION 1

From the following Balance Sheet of Arvind Mills Ltd., Aurangabad as on 31-3-2016 calculate the following ratios :

a) Current Ratio, b) Liquid Ratio, c) Absolute Liquid Ratio, d) Current Assets to Fixed Assets Ratio, e) Debt to Equity Ratio, f) Proprietary Ratio, g) Capital Gearing Ratio and h) Fixed Assets Ratio.

**Balance Sheet as on 31st March, 2016**

| Liabilities | ₹ | Assets | ₹ |
|---|---|---|---|
| Equity Capital | 10,00,000 | Goodwill (At cost) | 5,00,000 |
| 6% Preference Capital | 5,00,000 | Plant and Machinery | 6,00,000 |
| General Reserve | 1,00,000 | Land and Buildings | 7,00,000 |
| Profit and Loss | 4,00,000 | Furniture | 1,00,000 |
| Provision for Taxation | 1,76,000 | Inventories | 6,00,000 |
| Bills Payable | 1,24,000 | Bills Receivable | 30,000 |
| Bank Overdraft | 20,000 | Sundry Debtors | 1,50,000 |
| Sundry Creditors | 80,000 | Bank | 2,00,000 |
| 12% Debentures | 5,00,000 | Investment (Short-term) | 20,000 |
| | **29,00,000** | | **29,00,000** |

### SOLUTION

a)    $\text{Current Ratio} = \dfrac{\text{Current Assets}}{\text{Current Liabilities}} = \dfrac{₹\,10,00,000}{₹\,4,00,000} = 2.5 : 1$

(**N.B.** : Current Assets include Inventories, Debtors, Bills Receivable, Bank Balance and Short-term Investments. Current Liabilities include Creditors, Bills Payable, Bank Overdraft, Taxation Provision).

b)    $\text{Liquid Ratio} = \dfrac{\text{Liquid Assets}}{\text{Liquid Liabilities}} = \dfrac{₹\,10,00,000 - ₹\,6,00,000}{₹\,4,00,000 - ₹\,20,000}$

(Liquid Assets = Current Assets – Stock and Liquid Liabilities = Current Liabilities – Bank Overdraft)

$$= \dfrac{₹\,4,00,000}{₹\,3,80,000} = 1.05 : 1$$

c)    $\text{Absolute Liquidity Ratio} = \dfrac{\text{Cash at Bank + Short-Term Investments}}{\text{Current Liabilities}} = \dfrac{₹\,2,20,000}{₹\,4,00,000}$

$$= 0.55 : 1$$

d)    $\text{Current Assets to Fixed Assets} = \dfrac{\text{Current Assets}}{\text{Fixed Assets}} = \dfrac{₹\,10,00,000}{₹\,19,00,000} = 0.526 : 1$

( **N.B.** : Fixed Assets include Goodwill, Plant and Machinery, Furniture, Land and Buildings etc.)

e)    $\text{Debt to Equity Ratio} =$ i) $\dfrac{\text{Long-Term Debt}}{\text{Shareholders Funds}}$

$$= \dfrac{₹\,5,00,000}{\underset{\substack{\text{Equity} \\ \text{Capital}}}{₹\,10,00,000} + \underset{\substack{\text{Preference} \\ \text{Capital}}}{₹\,5,00,000} + \underset{\substack{\text{General} \\ \text{Reserve}}}{₹\,1,00,000} + \underset{\substack{\text{Profit and Loss}}}{₹\,4,00,000}}$$

$$= \dfrac{₹\,5,00,000}{₹\,20,00,000} = 0.25 : 1$$

ii) $\dfrac{\text{Long-Term Debt}}{\text{Long-Term Debt + Shareholders Fund}}$

$$= \frac{₹\,5,00,000}{₹\,5,00,000 + ₹\,20,00,000} = \frac{₹\,5,00,000}{₹\,25,00,000} = 0.20 : 1$$

(f)       Proprietory Ratio $= \dfrac{\text{Shareholders Funds}}{\text{Total Assets}} = \dfrac{₹\,20,00,000}{₹\,29,00,000} = 0.69 : 1$

(g)   Capital Gearing Ratio $= \dfrac{\text{Fixed Interest bearing securities}}{\text{Equity Capital + Reserves and Surplus}}$

$$= \frac{₹\,10,00,000\ [₹\,5,00,000\ \text{Preference Capital} + ₹\,5,00,000\ \text{Debentures}]}{₹\,10,00,000 + ₹\,5,00,000}$$

$$= \frac{₹\,10,00,000}{₹\,15,00,000} = 0.66 : 1$$

(h)       Fixed Assets Ratio $= \dfrac{\text{Fixed Assets}}{\text{Capital employed}} = \dfrac{₹\,19,00,000}{₹\,25,00,000} = 0.76 : 1$

## ILLUSTRATION 2

Bharat Petro Ltd., Badalapur submits the following Profit and Loss Account for the year ended 31st March, 2016.

**Dr.**        **Profit and Loss Account for the year ended on 31-3-2016**        **Cr.**

| Particulars | ₹ | Particulars | ₹ |
|---|---|---|---|
| To Opening Stock | 52,00,000 | By Sales | 3,20,00,000 |
| To Purchase | 1,60,00,000 | By Closing Stock | 76,00,000 |
| To Wages | 48,00,000 | | |
| To Manufacturing Expenses | 32,00,000 | | |
| To Gross Profit C/D | 1,04,00,000 | | |
| | **3,96,00,000** | | **3,96,00,000** |
| To Selling Expenses | 8,00,000 | By Gross Profit B/D | 1,04,00,000 |
| To Administration Expenses | 45,60,000 | By Profit on Sale of shares | 9,60,000 |
| To Loss by Fire | 2,40,000 | | |
| To Loss on sale of Furniture | 1,60,000 | | |
| To Net Profit C/D | 56,00,000 | | |
| | **1,13,60,000** | | **1,13,60,000** |

Calculate : a) Gross Profit Ratio, b) Net Profit Ratio, c) Operating Profit Ratio, d) Operating Net Profit Ratio.

## SOLUTION

a)       Gross Profit Ratio $= \dfrac{\text{Gross Profit}}{\text{Sales}} \times 100 \quad = \dfrac{₹\,1,04,00,000}{₹\,3,20,00,000} \times 100 = 32.5\%$

b)       Net Profit Ratio $= \dfrac{\text{Net Profit}}{\text{Sales}} \times 100 \quad = \dfrac{₹\,56,00,000}{₹\,3,20,00,000} \times 100 = 17.5\%$

c)       Operating Ratio $= \dfrac{\text{Cost of goods sold + Operating expenses}}{\text{Sales}} \times 100$

$$= \frac{₹\,2,16,00,000 + ₹\,53,60,000}{₹\,3,20,00,000} \times 100 = 84.25\%$$

d)       Operating Profit Ratio $= \dfrac{\text{Operating Net Profit}}{\text{Sales}} \times 100$

$$= \frac{₹\,56,00,000 + ₹\,1,60,000 + ₹\,9,60,000}{₹\,3,20,00,000} \times 100 = 15\%$$

## ILLUSTRATION 3

The following are summarised Profit and Loss Account for the year ended 31st March 2016 and the Balance Sheet as on that date of Cipla Ltd., Cochin.

**Profit and Loss Account for the year ended 31-3-2016**

| Particulars | ₹ | Particulars | ₹ |
|---|---|---|---|
| To Opening Stock | 10,000 | By Sales | 1,00,000 |
| To Purchases | 55,000 | By Closing Stock | 15,000 |
| To Gross Profit C/D | 50,000 | | |
| | **1,15,000** | | **1,15,000** |
| To Administration Expenses | 15,000 | By Gross Profit B/D | 50,000 |
| To Interest | 3,000 | | |
| To Selling Expenses | 12,000 | | |
| To Net Profit C/D | 20,000 | | |
| | **50,000** | | **50,000** |

**Balance Sheet as on 31st March 2015**

| Liabilities | ₹ | Assets | ₹ |
|---|---|---|---|
| Share Capital | | Land and Buildings | 50,000 |
| (10,000 Shares of ₹ 10 each) | 1,00,000 | Plant and Machinery | 30,000 |
| Profit and Loss | 20,000 | Stock | 15,000 |
| Creditors | 25,000 | Debtors | 15,000 |
| Bills Payable | 15,000 | Bills Receivable | 12,500 |
| | | Cash at Bank | 17,500 |
| | | Furniture | 20,000 |
| | **1,60,000** | | **1,60,000** |

Additional Information :

Average debtors : ₹ 12,500, Credit Purchases : ₹ 40,000, Credit Sales : ₹ 80,000

Calculate,

- a) Stock Turnover Ratio,    b) Debtors Turnover Ratio,   c) Creditors Turnover Ratio
- d) Working Capital Turnover Ratio,    e) Sales to Capital Employed,
- f) Return on Shareholders Funds, g) Gross Profit Ratio,   h) Net Profit Ratio,
- i) EPS (Earnings per share), and j) Operating Ratio.

## SOLUTION

a) $\quad$ Stock Turnover Ratio $= \dfrac{\text{Cost of goods sold}}{\text{Average Stock}}$

$$= \frac{₹\,50,000\,(\text{Sales} - \text{Gross Profit})}{₹\,10,000 + ₹\,15,000/2} = \frac{₹\,50,000}{₹\,12,500} = 4 \text{ times}$$

b) $\quad$ Debtors Turnover Ratio $= \dfrac{\text{Credit Sales}}{\text{Average Debtors}} = \dfrac{₹\,80,000}{₹\,12,500} = 6.4 \text{ times}$

c) $\quad$ Creditors Turnover Ratio $= \dfrac{\text{Credit Purchases}}{\text{Average A/c's payable}} = \dfrac{₹\,40,000}{₹\,40,000\,[\text{Crs.} + \text{B/P}]} = 1 \text{ time}$

d) Working Capital Turnover $= \dfrac{\text{Sales}}{\text{Working Capital}}$

$$[\text{Current Assets} - \text{Current Liabilities}]$$

$$= \frac{₹\,1,00,000}{₹\,20,000} = 5 \text{ times}$$

e) Sales to Capital Employed $= \dfrac{\text{Sales}}{\text{Capital employed}}$

$$= \dfrac{₹\,1,00,000}{₹\,1,00,000 + ₹\,20,000} = \dfrac{₹\,1,00,000}{₹\,1,20,000} = 0.83 : 1$$

[Capital Employed = Share Capital + Profit and Loss A/c]

f) Returns on Shareholders Funds $= \dfrac{\text{Net Profit}}{\text{Shareholders funds}} \times 100$

$$= \dfrac{₹\,20,000}{₹\,1,20,000} \times 100 = 16.67\%$$

g) Gross Profit Ratio $= \dfrac{\text{Gross Profit}}{\text{Sales}} \times 100 = \dfrac{₹\,50,000}{₹\,1,00,000} \times 100 = 50\%$

h) Net Profit Ratio $= \dfrac{\text{Net Profit}}{\text{Sales}} \times 100 = \dfrac{₹\,20,000}{₹\,1,00,000} \times 100 = 20\%$

i) EPS (Earnings per share) $= \dfrac{\text{Net Profit}}{\text{Number of Equity shares}} = \dfrac{₹\,20,000}{₹\,10,000} = ₹\,2$

j) Operating Ratio $= \dfrac{\text{Cost of goods sold + Operating Expenses}}{\text{Sales}} \times 100$

$$= \dfrac{₹\,50,000 + ₹\,27,000}{₹\,1,00,000} \times 100 = 77\%$$

---

## ILLUSTRATION 4

The summarised Balance Sheet of Dabur India Ltd., Delhi. as on 31st March 2014, 2015 and 2016 is given below :

**Balance Sheet as on 31st March**      (₹ in crores) ......

| Liabilities | 2014 | 2015 | 2016 |
|---|---|---|---|
| Paid-up Capital | 194 | 194 | 194 |
| Long-Term Borrowings | | | |
| i)    from banks | 68 | 97 | 127 |
| ii)    from Others | 281 | 343 | 376 |
| Current Liabilities | 52 | 54 | 99 |
| **Total** | **595** | **688** | **796** |
| Net Block | 286 | 261 | 239 |
| Current Assets | 143 | 199 | 234 |
| Profit and Loss | 166 | 228 | 323 |
| **Total** | **595** | **688** | **796** |

Calculate the following ratios for the three years :

a)    Debt Equity Ratio, b) Current Ratio, c)  Fixed Assets Ratio, and d) Proprietory Ratio

## SOLUTION

| | 31-3-2014 | 31-3-2015 | 31-3-2016 |
|---|---|---|---|
| a) Debt Equity Ratio $= \dfrac{\text{Long-term debt}}{\text{Shareholders Equity funds}}$ | $\dfrac{₹\,349}{₹\,194 - ₹\,166}$ | Negative | Negative |
| | $= \dfrac{₹\,349}{₹\,28}$ | | |
| | $= 12.46$ | | |
| b)  Current Ratio $= \dfrac{\text{Current Assets}}{\text{Current Liabilities}}$ | $\dfrac{₹\,143}{₹\,52}$ | $\dfrac{199}{54}$ | $\dfrac{234}{99}$ |
| | $= 2.75 : 1$ | $= 3.685 : 1$ | $= 2.36 : 1$ |

|  |  |  |  |  |
|---|---|---|---|---|
| (c) Fixed Assets Ratio $= \dfrac{\text{Fixed Assets}}{*\text{Capital Employed}}$ | $\dfrac{₹\,286}{₹\,377}$ | $\dfrac{₹\,261}{₹\,406}$ | $\dfrac{₹\,239}{₹\,374}$ |
|  | $= 0.76:1$ | $= 0.64:1$ | $= 0.64:1$ |
| (d) Proprietory Ratio $= \dfrac{\text{Shareholders Fund}}{\text{Total Assets}}$ | $\dfrac{₹\,28}{₹\,429}$ | Negative | Negative |
|  | $= 0.065:1$ |  |  |

* Capital employed = Paid-up Capital + Long-term borrowings – Profit and Loss Account – Debit balance

## ILLUSTRATION 5

Abstract of financial information for Esab India Ltd., Edalabad for three years are given below.

| Particulars | 31-3-2014 | 31-3-2015 | 31-3-2016 |
|---|---|---|---|
| Gross Profit | 36% | $33\,^1/_3\%$ | 30% |
| Stock turnover | 20 times | 25 times | 14 times |
| Average Stock | ₹ 38,400 | ₹ 36,000 | ₹ 70,000 |
| Average debtors | 87,500 | 1,68,750 | 2,00,000 |
| Income Tax rate | 50% | 50% | 50% |
| Net Income after tax as % Sales | 6% | 7% | 12% |
| Maximum credit period allowed to customers | 60 days | 60 days | 30 days |

**Required :**

i) A Statement of profits in comparative form for all three years.

ii) Evaluate the position of the company regarding profitability and liquidity on the basis of the available information.

iii) What additional information will you require to evaluate the position of company on the liquidity front ?

## SOLUTION

**i) Income Statement :**

| Particulars | | 31-3-2014 ₹ | 31-3-2015 ₹ | 31-3-2016 ₹ |
|---|---|---|---|---|
| | Sales | 12,00,000 | 13,50,000 | 14,00,000 |
| Less : | Cost of goods sold | 7,68,000 | 9,00,000 | 9,80,000 |
| | **Gross Profit** | 4,32,000 | 4,50,000 | 4,20,000 |
| Less : | Operating Expenses | 2,88,000 | 2,61,000 | 84,000 |
| | **Profit before Tax** | 1,44,000 | 1,89,000 | 3,36,000 |
| Less : | Taxes | 72,000 | 94,500 | 1,68,000 |
| | **Profit After Tax** | **72,000** | **94,500** | **1,68,000** |

| Particulars | 31-3-2014 | 31-3-2015 | 31-3-2016 |
|---|---|---|---|
| **Working Note :** | | | |
| Cost of goods sold | 20 × ₹ 38,400 | 25 × ₹ 36,000 | 14 × ₹ 70,000 |
| Stock turnover × Average Stock | = ₹ 7,68,000 | = ₹ 9,00,000 | = ₹ 9,80,000 |
| Cost of goods sold as % of Sales | 64% | $66\frac{2}{3}\,\%$ | 70% |
| Sales | ₹ 12,00,000 | ₹ 13,50,000 | ₹ 14,00,000 |
| Net Income as % to Sales (given) | 6% | 7% | 12% |
| Net Income / PAT | ₹ 72,000 | ₹ 94,500 | ₹ 1,68,000 |
| Profit before tax | ₹ 1,44,000 | ₹ 1,89,000 | ₹ 3,36,000 |
| Operating Expenses | ₹ 2,88,000 | ₹ 2,61,000 | ₹ 84,000 |
| (Gross Profit – Profit before Tax) | | | |

### ii) Evaluation of the Company :

From the above statements it is quite clear that the profitability of the company is increasing consistently. From 6% in the year 2014 it has gone up to 7% in 2015 and upto 12% in 2016. However, Stock turnover ratio which was 20 times in 2014 has slumped to 14 times in 2015 after going upto 25% in 2015. This needs improvement for improving liquidity.

The debtors turnover ratio was 13.7 times in first year and 8 and 7 times respectively in the second and third year (Sales ÷ Average debtors) which has also gone down and needs to be improved. It should also be noted that debtors turnover ratio is increasing inspite of reducing credit allowed to debtors in the third year. This suggests that collection policy needs to be tightened.

### iii) Requirement of Additional Information :

In order to evaluate the position of the company on liquidity front additional information relating to current liabilities and current assets should also be made available.

---

### ILLUSTRATION 6

From the following information, prepare Balance Sheet of Fulford India Ltd., Fattepur as on 31$^{st}$ March, 2016 with as many details as possible.

a) Current Ratio = 2.5 to 1, b) Liquid Ratio = 1.5 to 1, c) Working Capital = ₹ 60,000, d) Reserves and Surplus = ₹ 20,000, e) Bank Overdraft = ₹ 10,000, f) Fixed Assets to Proprietor's funds = 0.75 and g) There are no long-term liabilities or fictitious assets.

### SOLUTION

The Balance-Sheet can be prepared with the help of the following working notes :

a)    **Working Capital :** ₹ 60,000 which is Current Assets – Current Liabilities

∴    Current Assets – Current Liabilities = ₹ 60,000

or              2.5 – 1 = ₹ 60,000

(Current Ratio is 2.5 which means Current Assets are 2.5 times the Current Liabilities)

or                 1.5 = ₹ 60,000

                    1 = ₹ 40,000

Therefore,

     Current Liabilities = ₹ 40,000   Current Assets are 2.5 × ₹ 40,000 = ₹ 1,00,000

b)   To find out **Liquid Current Assets,** the following calculations can be made :

$$\text{Liquid Ratio} = 1.5 = \frac{\text{Liquid Current Assets}}{\text{Current Liabilities – Bank Overdraft}}$$

$$1.5 = \frac{\text{LCA}}{₹\,40,000 – ₹\,10,000} \qquad ∴ \quad \text{LCA} = ₹\,45,000$$

Therefore,         Stock = ₹ 55,000 (1,00,000 – 45,000)

c)   Fixed Assets to Proprietor's funds = 0.75 which means that out of proprietors funds 75% amount is invested in fixed assets. This suggests that remaining 25% of proprietor's funds are invested in working capital.

                  25% = ₹ 60,000 (working capital)

                100% = ₹ 2,40,000 – Proprietor's funds

       Fixed Assets = 75% of Proprietors funds = ₹ 1,80,000

   Proprietor's Funds = Share Capital + Reserves

                   = ₹ 2,00,000 + ₹ 40,000 = ₹ 2,40,000

**Balance Sheet as on 31-3-2016**

| Liabilities | | ₹ | Assets | | ₹ |
|---|---|---|---|---|---|
| Share Capital | | 2,00,000 | Fixed Assets | | 1,80,000 |
| Reserves and Surplus | | 40,000 | **Current Assets :** | | |
| **Current Liabilities :** | | 40,000 | • Stock | 55,000 | |
| • Creditors | 30,000 | | • Other Current Assets | (+) 45,000 | 1,00,000 |
| • Bank Overdraft | (+) 10,000 | | | | |
| | | 2,80,000 | | | 2,80,000 |

## ILLUSTRATION 7

Using the following data relating to Garden Silk Ltd., Gaziabad, complete the Balance Sheet as shown below :

| | ₹ |
|---|---|
| Gross Profit : 20% of Sales | 60,000 |
| Shareholders Funds | 50,000 |
| Credit Sales | 80% of total sales |
| Total Assets Turnover | 3 times |
| Inventory Turnover (to cost of sales) | 8 times |
| Average collection period (360 days in a year) | 18 days |
| Current Ratio | 1.6 |
| Long-term debt to Equity | 40% |

**Balance Sheet as on ......**

| Liabilities | ₹ | Assets | ₹ |
|---|---|---|---|
| Creditors | ................ | Cash | ................ |
| Long-Term debt | ................ | Debtors | ................ |
| Shareholders Equity | ................ | Inventory | ................ |
| | | Fixed Assets | ................ |
| | ................ | | ................ |

## SOLUTION

a)      Gross Profit : 20% of Sales   =   ₹     60,000

Therefore,            Sales   =   ₹     3,00,000

Cost of Sales = ₹ 3,00,000 – ₹ 60,000   =   ₹     2,40,000

b)      Inventory Turnover Ratio   =   8 times

$$8 \ = \ \frac{\text{Cost of goods sold}}{\text{Average Inventory}} = \frac{₹\,2,40,000}{\text{Average Inventory}}$$

∴      Average Inventory   =   ₹ 30,000

Since, Opening Stock is not given therefore, ₹ 30,000 is taken as Closing Stock.

c)      Total Assets Turnover   =   3 times $= \dfrac{\text{Sales}}{\text{Total Assets}} = \dfrac{₹\,3,00,000}{\text{Total Assets}}$

∴      Total Assets   =   ₹ 1,00,000

∴      Total Liabilities   =   ₹ 1,00,000

d)      Average Collection Period   =   18 days

∴      Debtors Turnover Ratio   =   $\dfrac{360 \text{ days}}{18 \text{ days}}$ = 20 times

Debtors   =   $\dfrac{₹\,2,40,000}{20}$ = ₹ 12,000

e)    Debt-Equity Ratio (long-term) = 40% of Shareholders Funds

$$\text{Shareholders funds} = ₹\,50,000$$
$$\text{Debt 40\% of } ₹\,50,000 = ₹\,20,000$$

f)    Creditors = Total Liabilities – Equity – Long-term debt

$$= ₹\,1,00,000 - ₹\,50,000 - ₹\,20,000$$
$$= ₹\,30,000$$

g)    $\text{Current Ratio} = \dfrac{\text{Current Assets}}{\text{Current Liabilities (Crs.)}}$

$$1.6 = \dfrac{\text{C.A.}}{₹\,30,000} \qquad \therefore \quad \text{Current Assets} = ₹\,48,000$$

h)    Fixed Assets = ₹ 1,00,000 – ₹ 48,000 = ₹ 52,000

**Balance Sheet as on ................**

| Liabilities | ₹ | Assets | ₹ |
|---|---|---|---|
| Creditors | 30,000 | Cash | 6,000 |
| Long-Term Debt | 20,000 | Debtors | 12,000 |
| Shareholders equity | 50,000 | Inventory | 30,000 |
| | | Fixed Assets | 52,000 |
| | **1,00,000** | | **1,00,000** |

### ILLUSTRATION 8

The following is the Balance Sheet of Hikal Ltd., Hoshangpur as on 31st March, 2016.

**Balance Sheet as on 31st March, 2016**

| Liabilities | ₹ | Assets | ₹ |
|---|---|---|---|
| Share Capital | 2,00,000 | Land and Buildings | 1,40,000 |
| Profit and Loss | 30,000 | Plant and Machinery | 3,50,000 |
| General Reserve | 40,000 | Stock-in Trade | 2,00,000 |
| 12% Debentures | 4,20,000 | Debtors | 1,00,000 |
| Creditors | 1,00,000 | Bills Receivable | 10,000 |
| Bills Payable | 50,000 | Bank Balance | 40,000 |
| | **8,40,000** | | **8,40,000** |

Calculate :

a) Current Ratio,    b) Quick Ratio,   c) Inventory to Working Capital, d) Debt to Equity e) Proprietory Ratio, f) Capital Gearing Ratio and g) Current Assets to Fixed Assets

### SOLUTION

a)    $\text{Current Ratio} = \dfrac{\text{Current Assets}}{\text{Current Liabilities}} = \dfrac{₹\,3,50,000}{₹\,1,50,000} = 2.33:1$

**(N.B. :**    Current Assets = Stock + Debtors + Bills Receivable + Bank Balance

Current Liabilities = Creditors + Bills Payable)

b)    $\text{Quick Ratio} = \dfrac{\text{Liquid Current Assets}}{\text{Current Liabilities}} = \dfrac{₹\,1,50,000}{₹\,1,50,000} = 1:1$

**(N.B. :**

Liquid Current Assets = Debtors + Bills Receivables + Bank Balance)

c)    $\text{Inventory to Working Capital} = \dfrac{\text{Inventory}}{\text{Working Capital}} = \dfrac{₹\,2,00,000}{₹\,2,00,000} = 1:1$

**(N.B. :**

Working Capital = Current Assets – Current Liabilities)

d)    $\text{Debt to Equity Ratio} = \dfrac{\text{Long-term debt}}{\text{Shareholder funds}} = \dfrac{₹\,4,20,000}{₹\,2,70,000} = 1.55:1$

**(N.B. :**

$$\text{Long-term Debt} = \text{12\% Debentures}$$

$$\text{Shareholder's funds} = \text{Share Capital + Reserves + Profit and Loss A/c)}$$

(e) $\quad$ Proprietory Ratio $= \dfrac{\text{Proprietor's Funds}}{\text{Total Assets}} = \dfrac{₹\,2,70,000}{₹\,8,40,000} = 0.32 : 1$

**(N.B. :**

$$\text{Proprietors funds} = \text{Share Capital + Reserve + Profit and Loss A/c)}$$

(f) Capital Gearing Ratio $= \dfrac{\text{Fixed Income bearing Securities i.e. 12\% Debentures}}{\text{Share Capital}} = \dfrac{₹\,4,20,000}{₹\,2,00,000} = 2 : 1 : 1$

(g) $\quad$ Current Assets to Fixed Assets $= \dfrac{\text{Current Assets}}{\text{Fixed Assets}} = \dfrac{₹\,3,50,000}{₹\,4,90,000} = 0.71 : 1$

---

**ILLUSTRATION 9**

The following figures are extracted from the books of Indian Nippon Ltd., Nagpur as on 31$^{st}$ March 2016.

| Particulars | | Amount ₹ |
|---|---|---|
| | Sales | 24,00,000 |
| **Less :** | Operating Expenses (–) | 18,00,000 |
| | ∴ **Gross Profit** | 6,00,000 |
| **Less :** | Non-Operating Expenses (–) | 2,40,000 |
| | ∴ **Net Profit** | 3,60,000 |
| • | Current Assets | 7,60,000 |
| • | Inventories | 8,00,000 |
| • | Fixed Assets (+) | 14,40,000 |
| | ∴ **Total Assets** | **30,00,000** |
| • | Net Worth | 15,00,000 |
| • | Debt | 9,00,000 |
| • | Current Liabilities (+) | 6,00,000 |
| • | **Total Liabilities** | **30,00,000** |
| • | Working Capital | 9,60,000 |

**Calculate :**

a) Gross Profit Ratio, b) Net Profit Ratio, c) Return on Assets, d) Inventory Turnover, e) Working Capital Turnover, and f) Net worth to Debt.

**SOLUTION**

a) $\quad$ Gross Profit Ratio $= \dfrac{\text{Gross Profit}}{\text{Sales}} \times 100 = \dfrac{₹\,6,00,000}{₹\,24,00,000} \times 100 = 25\%$

b) $\quad$ Net Profit Ratio $= \dfrac{\text{Net Profit}}{\text{Sales}} \times 100 = \dfrac{₹\,3,60,000}{₹\,24,00,000} \times 100 = 15\%$

c) $\quad$ Return on Assets $= \dfrac{\text{Net Profit}}{\text{Total Assets}} \times 100 = \dfrac{₹\,3,60,000}{₹\,30,00,000} \times 100 = 12\%$

d) $\quad$ Inventory Turnover $= \dfrac{\text{Sales}}{\text{Average Inventory}} = \dfrac{₹\,24,00,000}{₹\,8,00,000} = 3 \text{ times}$

N.B. i) $\quad$ In the absence of 'Cost of goods sold', Sales are taken for calculation of this ratio.

ii) $\quad$ Opening Stock is not given in the example and therefore closing stock is taken as Average Inventory.

e) $\quad$ Working Capital Turnover $= \dfrac{\text{Sales}}{\text{Net Working Capital}} = \dfrac{₹\,24,00,000}{₹\,9,60,000} = 2.5 \text{ times}$

**(N.B. :** $\quad$ Net Working Capital $=$ Current Assets – Current Liabilities)

f) $\quad$ Net Worth to Debt $= \dfrac{\text{Net Worth}}{\text{Debt}} = \dfrac{₹\,15,00,000}{₹\,9,00,000} = 1.66 : 1$

---

## ILLUSTRATION 10

The following are the summarised Profit and Loss Account and Balance-Sheet of Jai Corporation Ltd., Jamner for the year ended 31st December, 2016.

**Dr.**      **Profit and Loss Account for the year ended on 31-3-2016**      **Cr.**

| Particulars | ₹ | Particulars | ₹ |
|---|---|---|---|
| To Opening Stock | 99,500 | By Sales | 9,50,000 |
| To Purchases | 5,45,000 | By Closing Stock | 1,50,000 |
| To Carriage Inward | 15,500 | | |
| To Gross Profit C/D | 4,40,000 | | |
| | **11,00,000** | | **11,00,000** |
| To Operating Expenses | 2,00,000 | By Gross Profit B/D | 4,40,000 |
| To Non-Operating Expenses | 40,000 | By Non-Operating Income | 60,000 |
| To Net Profit C/D | 2,60,000 | | |
| | **5,00,000** | | **5,00,000** |

**Balance Sheet as on 31-3-2015**

| Liabilities | ₹ | Assets | ₹ |
|---|---|---|---|
| Capital | 2,00,000 | Land and Buildings | 1,50,000 |
| (20,000 Equity Shares of ₹ 10 each) | | Plant and Machinery | 1,80,000 |
| Reserve | 2,00,000 | Stock-in Trade | 50,000 |
| Profit and Loss | 60,000 | Debtors | 45,000 |
| Other Current Liabilities | 90,000 | Cash and Bank | 60,000 |
| Bills Payable | 40,000 | Bills Receivable | 1,05,000 |
| | **5,90,000** | | **5,90,000** |

**Calculate :**

a) Gross Profit Ratio, b) Net Profit Ratio, c) Operating Profit Ratio, d) Operating Ratio, e) Return on Capital Employed, f) Net Profit to Fixed Assets, g) Stock Turnover Ratio, h) Debtors Turnover Ratio, i) Creditors Turnover Ratio, j) Sales to Working Capital, k) Sales to Fixed Assets, l) Sales to Capital Employed, m) Returns on Total Resources, and n) Turnover to Total Assets

## SOLUTION

a)      Gross Profit Ratio $= \dfrac{\text{Gross Profit}}{\text{Sales}} \times 100 = \dfrac{₹\,4,40,000}{₹\,9,50,000} \times 100 = 46.31\%$

b)      Net Profit Ratio $= \dfrac{\text{Net Profit}}{\text{Sales}} \times 100 = \dfrac{₹\,2,60,000}{₹\,9,50,000} \times 100 = 27.36\%$

c)      Operating Profit Ratio $= \dfrac{\text{Operating Profit}}{\text{Sales}} \times 100 = \dfrac{₹\,2,40,000}{₹\,9,50,000} \times 100 = 25.26\%$

**(N.B. :**    Operating Profit = Net Profit + Non-Operating Expenses – Non Operating Income

= ₹ 2,60,000 + ₹ 40,000 – ₹ 60,000 = ₹ 2,40,000 )

d)      Operating Ratio $= \dfrac{\text{Cost of goods sold + Operating Expenses}}{\text{Sales}} \times 100$

$= \dfrac{₹\,5,10,000 + ₹\,2,00,000}{₹\,9,50,000} \times 100 = 74.74\%$

e)      Return on Capital Employed $= \dfrac{\text{Net Profit}}{{}^{*}\text{Capital Employed}} \times 100 = \dfrac{₹\,2,60,000}{{}^{*}\,₹\,4,60,000} \times 100 = 56.52\%$

(*Capital Employed = Share Capital + Reserves + Profit and Loss A/c)

f) $\quad$ Net Profit to Fixed Assets $= \dfrac{\text{Net Profit}}{\text{Fixed Assets}} \times 100 = \dfrac{₹\,2,60,000}{₹\,3,30,000} \times 100 = 78.78\%$

g) $\quad$ Stock Turnover Ratio $= \dfrac{\text{Cost of goods sold}}{\text{Average Stock *}} = \dfrac{₹\,5,10,000}{₹\,1,24,750} = 4.088 \text{ times}$

$\quad$ (*Average Stock $= \dfrac{\text{Opening Stock + Closing Stock}}{2} = \dfrac{₹\,99,500 + ₹\,1,50,000}{2} = 1,24,750$)

h) $\quad$ Debtors Turnover Ratio $= \dfrac{\text{Credit Sales}}{\text{Average Debtors + Average Bills Receivables}}$

$$= \dfrac{₹\,9,50,000}{₹\,45,000 + ₹\,1,05,000} = 6.33$$

**N.B. :**

i) $\quad$ It is assumed that all sales are on credit.

ii) $\quad$ In the absence of information Closing Debtors and Bills Receivable are assumed to be Average Debtors and Bills Receivable.

i) $\quad$ Creditors Turnover Ratio $= \dfrac{\text{Credit Purchases}}{\text{Average Creditors + Average Bills Payable}}$

$$= \dfrac{₹\,5,45,250}{₹\,50,000 + ₹\,40,000} = 6.05 \text{ times}$$

**N.B. :**

i) $\quad$ All purchases are assumed to be on credit.

ii) $\quad$ Creditors are not given clearly in the example and therefore they are assumed to be ₹ 50,000 out of other Current Liabilities.

iii) $\quad$ Closing balances of Bills Payable and Creditors are assumed to be average balances.

j) $\quad$ Sales to Working Capital $= \dfrac{\text{Sales}}{\text{Working Capital}} = \dfrac{₹\,9,50,000}{₹\,1,25,000} = 7.6 \text{ times}$

$\quad$ Working Capital $=$ Stock + Debtors + Cash and Bank + B/R –

$\qquad\qquad\qquad\qquad$ (Other Current  Liabilities + Bills Payable)

$\qquad\qquad\quad = $ ₹ 50,000 + ₹ 45,000 + ₹ 60,000 + ₹ 1,05,000 –

$\qquad\qquad\qquad$ (₹ 90,000 + ₹ 45,000)

$\qquad\qquad\quad = $ ₹ 2,60,000 – ₹ 1,35,000

$\qquad\qquad\quad = $ ₹ 1,25,000

k) $\quad$ Sales to Fixed Assets $= \dfrac{\text{Sales}}{\text{Fixed Assets}} = \dfrac{₹\,9,50,000}{₹\,3,30,000} = 2.87 \text{ times}$

l) $\quad$ Sales to Capital Employed $= \dfrac{\text{Sales}}{\text{Capital Employed}} = \dfrac{₹\,9,50,000}{₹\,4,60,000} = 2.06 \text{ times}$

m) $\quad$ Return on Total Resources $= \dfrac{\text{Net Profit}}{\text{Total Assets}} \times 100 = \dfrac{₹\,2,60,000}{₹\,5,90,000} \times 100 = 44.06\%$

n) $\quad$ Turnover to Total Assets $= \dfrac{\text{Sales}}{\text{Total Assets}} = \dfrac{₹\,9,50,000}{₹\,5,90,000} = 1.61 \text{ times}$

ILLUSTRATION 11

The following is the condensed Balance Sheet of Kerala Steel Ltd., Kanpur for three years ended on 31st March, 2014, 31st March 2015, and 31st March, 2016.

(₹ 00,000)

| Particulars | | 31-3-2014 ₹ | 31-3-2015 ₹ | 31-3-2016 ₹ |
|---|---|---|---|---|
| **Current Assets :** | | | | |
| • Stock :   • Raw Materials | | 12 | 18 | 20 |
|       • Finished Goods | | 30 | 35 | 25 |
|       • Stores and Spares | | 3 | 4 | 5 |
| • Debtors | | 40 | 50 | 50 |
| • Cash at Bank | | 5 | 10 | 20 |
| Fixed Assets | (+) | 90 | 110 | 120 |
| ∴ **Total Assets** | | **180** | **227** | **240** |
| Current Liabilities | | 20 | 32 | 30 |
| Debenture-Secured | | 60 | 60 | 60 |
| Unsecured Loans – Bank | | 15 | 40 | 45 |
| Reserves and Surplus | | 30 | 32.5 | 38.75 |
| Profit and Loss A/c before providing for taxation and dividends | | 15 | 22.5 | 26.25 |
| Equity Shares (₹ 100/- each) | | 20 | 20 | 20 |
| 10% Preference Shares (100 Each) | (+) | 20 | 20 | 20 |
| ∴ **Total Liabilities** | | **180** | **227** | **240** |
| Sales | | 300 | 360 | 400 |
| Gross Profit | | 15% | 18% | 20% |

The company earned the net profits before providing for Income-tax @ 50%. Equity shareholders to get dividends 50% more than Preference Shareholders. Show the Appropriation Account and work out the following ratios after reworking the Balance Sheet.

i) Acid-Test Ratio, ii) Stock Turnover Ratio, iii) Earning per share, iv) Ratio of fixed assets to shareholders funds, and v) Return on capital employed

SOLUTION

### In the books of Kerala Steel Ltd., Kanpur

### Profit and Loss Appropriation Account

| Particulars | | 31-3-2014 ₹ | 31-3-2015 ₹ | 31-3-2016 ₹ |
|---|---|---|---|---|
| Profit before tax and dividend | | 15,00,000 | 22,50,000 | 26,25,000 |
| **Less :** Income-tax @ 50% | (–) | 7,50,000 | 11,25,000 | 13,12,500 |
| ∴ **Profit after Tax** | | 7,50,000 | 11,25,000 | 13,12,500 |
| **Less :** Preference Dividends (10%) | (–) | 2,00,000 | 2,00,000 | 2,00,000 |
| ∴ Earnings for Equity Shareholders | | 5,50,000 | 9,25,000 | 11,12,500 |
| **Less :** Equity dividends (15%) | (–) | 3,00,000 | 3,00,000 | 3,00,000 |
| ∴ **Balance of Profits** | | **2,50,000** | **6,25,000** | **8,12,500** |

**Balance Sheet as on ........**

| Particulars | 31-3-2014 ₹ | 31-3-2015 ₹ | 31-3-2016 ₹ |
|---|---|---|---|
| Current Liabilities | 20,00,000 | 32,00,000 | 30,00,000 |
| **Add :** Provision for Taxation    (+) | 7,50,000 | 11,25,000 | 13,12,500 |
| Total Current Liabilities | 27,50,000 | 43,25,000 | 43,12,500 |
| Current Assets * | 90,00,000 | 1,17,00,000 | 1,20,00,000 |
| Working Capital (Current Assets – Current Liabilities) | 62,50,000 | 73,75,000 | 76,87,500 |
| **Add :** Fixed Assets | 90,00,000 | 1,10,00,000 | 1,20,00,000 |
| Capital employed | 1,52,50,000 | 1,83,75,000 | 1,96,87,500 |
| Shareholder's funds – Equity | 20,00,000 | 20,00,000 | 20,00,000 |
| Share Capital – Preference | 20,00,000 | 20,00,000 | 20,00,000 |
| Reserve and Surplus | 30,00,000 | 32,50,000 | 38,75,000 |
| Profit and Loss Appropriation Account Balance | 2,50,000 | 6,25,000 | 8,12,500 |
| **Shareholder's Funds** | **72,50,000** | **78,75,000** | **86,87,500** |

* Current Assets = Total Assets – Fixed Assets

**Calculation of Ratio :**

| Particulars | 31-3-2014 | 31-3-2015 | 31-3-2016 |
|---|---|---|---|
| i)   Acid Test Ratio = $\dfrac{\text{Liquid Current Assets}}{\text{Current Liabilities}}$ | $\dfrac{₹\,45,00,000}{₹\,27,50,000}$ <br> 1.64 : 1 | $\dfrac{₹\,60,00,000}{₹\,43,25,000}$ <br> 1.39 : 1 | $\dfrac{₹\,70,00,000}{₹\,43,12,500}$ <br> 1.62 : 1 |
| ii) Stock Turnover Ratio = $\dfrac{\text{Cost of Goods sold}}{\text{Average Stock}}$ | $\dfrac{₹\,2,55,00,000}{₹\,45,00,000}$ <br> = 5.67 times | $\dfrac{₹\,2,95,00,000}{₹\,51,00,000}$ <br> = 5.78 times | $\dfrac{₹\,3,20,00,000}{53,50,000}$ <br> = 5.98 times |
| iii) Earnings per share <br> = $\dfrac{\text{Earnings for Equity shareholders}}{\text{Number of Equity shares}}$ | $\dfrac{₹\,5,50,000}{₹\,20,000}$ <br> = ₹ 27.5 | $\dfrac{₹\,9,25,000}{₹\,20,000}$ <br> = ₹ 46.25 | $\dfrac{₹\,11,12,500}{₹\,20,000}$ <br> = ₹ 55.63 |
| iv) Fixed Assets to Shareholder's Funds <br> = $\dfrac{\text{Fixed Assets}}{\text{Shareholder's Funds}}$ | $\dfrac{₹\,90,00,000}{₹\,72,50,000}$ <br> = 1.24 times | $\dfrac{₹\,1,10,00,000}{₹\,78,75,000}$ <br> = 1.4 times | $\dfrac{₹\,1,20,00,000}{₹\,86,87,500}$ <br> = 1.38 times |
| v) Return on Capital Employed <br> = $\dfrac{\text{Profit after tax}}{\text{Capital Employed}}$ | $\dfrac{₹\,7,50,000}{₹\,1,52,50,000}$ <br> × 100 <br> = 4.92% | $\dfrac{₹\,11,25,000}{₹\,1,83,75,00}$ <br> × 100 <br> = 6.12% | $\dfrac{₹\,13,12,500}{₹\,1,96,87,500}$ <br> × 100 <br> = 6.67% |

### ILLUSTRATION 12

From the following annual accounts of Lupin Chemicals Ltd., Lohgaon for the year ended on 31st March, 2015 and 31st March, 2016, you are required to calculate important ratios which will help the management in assessing overall performance of the company.

| Particulars | 31-3-2015 ₹ | 31-3-2016 ₹ |
|---|---|---|
|    Sales | 12,00,000 | 14,96,000 |
| **Less :** Cost of Sales    (−) | 9,44,000 | 11,92,000 |
| ∴    Gross Profits | 2,56,000 | 3,04,000 |
| **Less : Expenses :** | | |
|    Warehousing and Transport | 76,000 | 96,000 |

|  |  |  |  |  |
|---|---|---|---|---|
| • | Administration | | 76,000 | 76,000 |
| • | Selling | | 44,000 | 56,000 |
| • | Debenture Interest | (−) | – | 8,000 |
| ∴ | **Net Profit** | | **60,000** | **68,000** |
| | Fixed Assets : **Less** : Depreciation | | 1,20,000 | 1,60,000 |
| | Stock | | 2,40,000 | 3,76,000 |
| | Debtors | | 2,00,000 | 3,28,000 |
| | Cash | (+) | 40,000 | 28,000 |
| ∴ | **Total Assets** | | **6,00,000** | **8,92,000** |
| | Share Capital | | 3,00,000 | 3,00,000 |
| | Reserves | | 60,000 | 1,20,000 |
| | Profit and Loss | | 40,000 | 48,000 |
| | Debentures | | – | 1,20,000 |
| | Current Liabilities | (+) | 2,00,000 | 3,04,000 |
| | ∴   **Total Liabilities** | | **6,00,000** | **8,92,000** |

### SOLUTION

In order to comment on overall performance of the company, it is necessary to calculate the following ratios

**1) Profitability Ratios :**

| Particulars | 31-3-2015 | 31-3-2016 |
|---|---|---|
| a) Gross Profit $= \dfrac{\text{Gross Profit}}{\text{Sales}} \times 100$ | $= \dfrac{₹\,2,56,000}{₹\,12,00,000} \times 100$ | $= \dfrac{₹\,3,04,000}{₹\,14,96,000} \times 100$ |
| | $=$ 21.33% | $=$ 20.32% |
| b) Net Profit Ratio $= \dfrac{\text{Net Profit}}{\text{Sales}} \times 100$ | $= \dfrac{₹\,60,000}{₹\,12,00,000} \times 100$ | $= \dfrac{₹\,68,000}{₹\,14,96,000} \times 100$ |
| | $=$ 5% | $=$ 4.54% |
| c)  Operating Net Profit Ratio $=$ <br> $\dfrac{\text{Operating Net Profit}}{\text{Sales}} \times 100$ | $= \dfrac{₹\,60,000}{₹\,12,00,000} \times 100$ | $= \dfrac{₹\,68,000 + ₹\,8,000^{*}}{₹\,14,96,000}$ <br> $\times 100$ |
| | $=$ 5% | $=$ 5.08% |

      * ₹ 8,000 = Interest on Debentures

| | | |
|---|---|---|
| d) Operating Ratio $=$ <br> $\dfrac{\text{Cost of goods sold + Operating Expenses}}{\text{Sale}}$ <br> $\times 100$ | $\dfrac{₹\,9,44,000 + ₹\,1,96,000}{₹\,12,00,000}$ <br> $\times 100$ <br> $=$  95% | $\dfrac{₹\,11,92,000 + ₹\,2,28,000}{₹\,14,96,000}$ <br> $\times 100$ <br> $=$  94.92% |

**Note :** Operating expenses are the expenses excluding interest on debentures

| | | |
|---|---|---|
| e)  Return on Capital Employed $=$ <br> $\dfrac{\text{Net Profit}}{\text{Capital Employed}} \times 100$ | $= \dfrac{₹\,60,000}{₹\,4,00,000} \times 100$ <br> $=$  15% | $= \dfrac{₹\,76,000}{₹\,5,88,000} \times 100$ <br> $=$  12.93% |

(**N.B. :** Capital employed = Share Capital + Reserves + Profit and Loss A/c + Debentures)

**2) Financial Position :**

| Particulars | | 31-3-2015 | 31-3-2016 |
|---|---|---|---|
| a) Current Ratio = $\dfrac{\text{Current Assets}}{\text{Current Liabilities}}$ | = | $\dfrac{₹\,4,80,000}{₹\,2,00,000}$ | $= \dfrac{₹\,7,32,000}{₹\,3,04,000}$ |
| | = | 2.4 : 1 | = ₹ 2.41 : 1 |
| b) Quick Ratio = $\dfrac{\text{Quick Assets}}{\text{Current Liabilities}}$ | = | $\dfrac{₹\,4,80,000 - ₹\,2,40,000}{₹\,2,00,000}$ | $= \dfrac{₹\,7,32,000 - ₹\,3,76,000}{₹\,3,04,000}$ |
| * Stock | = | 1.2 : 1 | = 1.17 : 1 |
| c) Debt-Equity Ratio = $\dfrac{\text{Long-term Debt}}{\text{Propreitor's funds}}$ | | NIL | $= \dfrac{₹\,1,20,000}{₹\,4,68,000}$ |
| (Share Capital = Profit and Loss A/c + Reserves) | | | = 0.256 : 1 |
| d) Proprietory Ratio = $\dfrac{\text{Total Assets}}{\text{Proprietor's funds}}$ | = | $\dfrac{₹\,6,00,000}{₹\,4,00,000}$ | $= \dfrac{₹\,8,92,000}{₹\,4,68,000}$ |
| | = | 1.5 : 1 | = 1.90 : 1 |

**3) Turnover Ratio :**

| Particulars | | 31-3-2015 | 31-3-2016 |
|---|---|---|---|
| a) Fixed Assets Turnover = $\dfrac{\text{Sales}}{\text{Fixed Assets}}$ | = | $\dfrac{₹\,12,00,000}{₹\,1,20,000}$ | $= \dfrac{₹\,14,96,000}{₹\,1,60,000}$ |
| | = | 10 times | = 9.35 times |
| b) Working Capital Turnover $\dfrac{\text{Sales}}{*\,\text{Working Capital}}$ | = | $\dfrac{₹\,12,00,000}{₹\,2,80,000}$ | $= \dfrac{₹\,14,96,000}{₹\,4,28,000}$ |
| * Current Assets – Current Liabilities | = | 4.28 times | = 3.49 times |
| c) Debtors Turnover Ratio = $\dfrac{\text{Credit Sales}}{\text{Average Debtors}}$ | = | $\dfrac{12,00,000}{₹\,2,00,000}$ | $= \dfrac{₹\,14,96,000}{₹\,3,28,000}$ |
| (Closing Debtors) | = | 6 times | = 4.56 : 0.1 times |
| d) Stock Turnover Ratio = $\dfrac{\text{Cost of goods sold}}{\text{Average Stock}}$ | = | $\dfrac{₹\,9,44,000}{₹\,2,40,000}$ | $= \dfrac{₹\,11,92,000}{₹\,3,76,000}$ |
| | = | 3.93 times | = 3.17 times |

**Comment :**

If we have a glance at the above mentioned ratios, it is clearly seen that most of the ratios in profitability group are declining in 2015-16 as compared to 2014-15. The only exception to this is the ratio of operating net profit to sales which has increased marginally from 5% to 5.08% in the year 2014-15.

The turnover ratios are also showing a declining trend. There is an increase in fixed assets as well as working capital in the year 2014-15 but this increase has not resulted in increase in sales. As a result of this, various turnover ratios are declining in 2015-16 as compared to 2014-15.

The financial ratios are more or less stable in both the years. However, Debt-equity ratio in 2015-16 is 0.256 : 1 against a nil ratio in 2014-15 because the company has issued debentures in the year 2015-16.

In conclusion it can be said that the overall position of the company seems to be on the decline and therefore, an urgent action is required to rectify the situation.

**ILLUSTRATION 13**

From the following figures and ratios, make out the Balance Sheet of Orchid Ltd., Osmanabad as on 31st March, 2016 in the following format.

**Balance Sheet as on 31st March, 2016**

| Liabilities | ₹ | Assets | ₹ |
|---|---|---|---|
| Equity Share Capital | 3,00,000 | Fixed Assets | 6,00,000 |
| Retained Earnings | 2,00,000 | Inventory | – |
| Debentures | 1,25,000 | Debtors | – |
| Long-Term Loans | – | Cash | – |
| Accounts Payable | 1,00,000 | | |
| **Total** | | **Total** | |

Gross Profit Margin = 20%, Quick Ratio = 1.5 : 1, Stock Turnover Ratio = 12 times, Average collection period = 30 days, Total Assets Turnover = 3 times, and Other long-term debts (excluding debentures) to proprietor's funds = 0.75 : 1.

**SOLUTION**

a)    Long-term debt to Proprietor's Funds    $= \dfrac{\text{Other long-term debt}}{\text{Proprietor's funds}}$

$$0.75 = \dfrac{\text{Other Long-term debt}}{\underset{\text{Share Capital + Retained Earnings}}{₹\,3,00,000 + ₹\,2,00,000}}$$

∴    Other long-term debt $= 0.75 \times ₹\,5,00,000$

$= ₹\,3,75,000$

b)    Sales :

Total assets turnover ratio $= \dfrac{\text{Sales}}{\text{Total Assets}}$

$$3 = \dfrac{\text{Sales}}{₹\,11,00,000}$$

Sales $= ₹\,33,00,000$

(**N.B. :**    Total Assets $=$ Total Liabilities

Total Liabilities $=$ Share Capital + Retained Earnings + Debentures + Other long-term debt + Account Payable

$= ₹\,3,00,000 + ₹\,2,00,000 + ₹\,1,25,000 + ₹\,3,75,000 + ₹\,1,00,000$

$= ₹\,11,00,000)$

c)    Debtors :

Average collection period $=$ 30 days

Sales $= ₹\,33,00,000$

Debtors turnover $= \dfrac{360 \text{ days}}{30 \text{ days}} = 12$ times

Debtors turnover $= \dfrac{\text{Credit Sales}}{\text{Average Debtors (Closing balance)}}$

$$12 = \dfrac{₹\,33,00,000}{\text{Debtors}}$$

Therefore,    Debtors $= ₹\,2,75,000$

(**N.B. :**   (i)    It is assumed that there are 360 days in a year.

(ii)    All sales are assumed to be on credit in the absence of information.)

(d)   Inventory :

$$\text{Inventory turnover ratio} = \frac{\text{Cost of goods sold}}{\text{Average Inventory}}$$

$$12 = \frac{₹\,26,40,000}{\text{Average Inventory}}$$

Therefore, Average Inventory (Closing) = ₹ 2,20,000

(**N.B. :**    (i)     Cost of goods sold = Sales – Gross profit

           (ii)    In the absence of information, Closing Inventory is taken as average inventory).

|  |  | ₹ |
|---|---|---:|
| **Total Assets** |  | **11,0,000** |
| Fixed Assets |  | 6,00,000 |
| Debtors (As per c) |  | 2,75,000 |
| Inventory (As per d) |  | 2,20,000 |
| Cash (Balancing figure)* | (+) | 5,000 |
| **Total** |  | **11,00,000** |

Balance Sheet as on 31<sup>st</sup> March, 2016

| Liabilities | ₹ | Assets | ₹ |
|---|---:|---|---:|
| Equity Capital | 3,00,000 | Fixed Assets | 6,00,000 |
| Retained Earnings | 2,00,000 | Debtors | 2,75,000 |
| Debentures | 1,25,000 | Inventory | 2,20,000 |
| Long-term Loans | 3,75,000 | Cash | 5,000 |
| Accounts Payable | 1,00,000 |  |  |
| **Total** | **11,00,000** | **Total** | **11,00,000** |

### ILLUSTRATION 14

The following data represents the ratios pertaining Parakh Industries Ltd., Pune for the year ending 31<sup>st</sup> March, 2016.

|  | ₹ |
|---|---:|
| Annual Sales | 40,00,000 |
| Sales to net worth | 4 times |
| Current Liabilities to Net Worth | 50% |
| Total Debt to Net Worth | 80% |
| Current Ratio | 2.2 times |
| Sales to Inventory | 8 times |
| Average collection period | 40 days |
| Fixed Assets to Net Worth | 70% |

From the above information, prepare the Balance Sheet with as many details as possible. Assume all sales on Credit.

### SOLUTION

a)                 Sales to Net Worth   =   4 times

                            Sales   =   ₹ 40,00,000

$$\text{Therefore,}\qquad 4 = \frac{₹\,40,00,000}{\text{Net worth}}$$

                Net Worth   =   ₹ 10,00,000

b)     Current Liabilities to net worth   =   50%

        This means that Current liabilities are 50% of net worth

           Therefore, Current Liabilities   =   ₹ 5,00,000

c)         Total Debt to Net Worth   =   80%

This means that total debt is 80% of Net Worth

Therefore,         Total Debt   =   ₹ 8,00,000

d)         Current Ratio   $= \dfrac{\text{Current Assets}}{\text{Current Liabilities}} = 2.2$

Therefore,    $\dfrac{\text{Current Assets}}{₹\,5,00,000} = 2.2$

i.e. Current Assets   =   ₹ 11,00,000

e)         Sales to Inventory   =   8 times

Sales   =   ₹ 40,00,000

Inventory   $= \dfrac{₹\,40,00,000}{8} = ₹\,5,00,000$

f)         Average collection period   =   40 days

Sales   =   ₹ 40,00,000

Debtors turnover   $= \dfrac{360 \text{ days}}{40 \text{ days}} = 9 \text{ times}$

Therefore,         Debtors   $= \dfrac{₹\,40,00,000}{9} = ₹\,4,44,444$

g)         Fixed Assets to Net Worth   =   70%

Therefore,         Fixed Assets   =   70% of ₹ 10,00,000 = ₹ 7,00,000

### Balance Sheet as on 31st March, 2016

| Liabilities | ₹ | Assets | | ₹ |
|---|---|---|---|---|
| Net Worth | 10,00,000 | Fixed Assets | | 7,00,000 |
| Long-Term Debt | 3,00,000 | **Current Assets :** | | |
| Current Liabilities | 5,00,000 | •    Stock | 5,00,000 | |
| | | •    Debtors | 4,44,444 | |
| | | •    Cash | (+) 1,55,556 | 11,00,000 |
| **Total** | **18,00,000** | | **Total** | **18,00,000** |

(**Note :**

i)     Total Debt is ₹ 8,00,000/- and Current Liabilities are ₹ 5,00,000.

Therefore,     Long-term Debt   =   ₹ 3,00,000

ii)     Total Current Assets   =   ₹ 11,00,000

Out of these, Stock and Debtors together are ₹ 9,44,444. Therefore, Cash ₹ 1,55,556 is the balancing figure.)

### ILLUSTRATION 15

The standard ratios for the industry and the ratios of Ramco Ltd., Ramgad are given below. Determine the efficiency of the working of the company.

| Particulars | 31-3-2016 Standard | 31-3-2016 Company |
|---|---|---|
| Current Ratio | 2.50 | 1.90 |
| Gross Profit Ratio | 0.30 | 0.35 |
| Fixed Expenses to Sales | 0.15 | 0.20 |
| Variable Expenses to Sales | 0.10 | 0.08 |
| Sales/Capital | 3.00 | 4.00 |
| Fixed Assets/Long-term funds | 1.00 | 0.90 |
| Rate of Return on Capital | 15% | 22% |

### SOLUTION

a) The profitability of Ramco Ltd., Ramgad is better than the industry standard. The Gross Profit ratio as well as fixed and variable expenses to sales and rate of return on capital is better for the Co. than the industry standard.

b) Current ratio for the Co. is however not satisfactory as compared to industry standard. There is a scope for improvement for the Co. in this respect.

## QUESTIONS FOR SELF STUDY

**I. Theory Questions :**

1) Give a brief account of the techniques of financial statements analysis.

2) What is an accounting ratio ? Explain the significance of Accounting Ratio technique in financial analysis of a company.

3) How do you classify accounting ratios ? Which basis of classification do you consider more appropriate ?

4) The success of accounting ratio technique depends upon many things. What precautions will you take in the analysis and interpretation of financial statements ?

5) "Current ratio should always be 2 : 1 to represent adequate short period solvency". Comment on this statement.

6) How do you apply the accounting ratio technique in the measurement of profitability of a business concern ? Do you think that an increase in Gross Profit Ratio is always an enhancement of profitability ?

7) Explain the following accounting ratios :

a) Acid Test Ratio, b) Current Ratio, c) Debt Equity ratio, d) Gross Profit Ratio, e) Operating Ratio, f) Balance Sheet Ratios, g)  Combined Ratios, h) Return on Capital Employed.

**II. Practical Problems**

1) The following are the summarised Profit and Loss Account of Salora Ltd., Surat for the year ended 31-3-2016 and Balance Sheet on that date.

**Profit and Loss Account for the year ended 31-3-2016**

| Particulars | ₹ | Particulars | ₹ |
|---|---|---|---|
| To Opening Stock | 9,950 | By Sales | 85,000 |
| To Purchase | 54,525 | By Closing Stock | 14,900 |
| To Incidental Expenses | 1,425 | | |
| To Gross Profit C/D | 34,000 | | |
| | **99,900** | | **99,900** |
| To Operating Expenses | | By Gross Profit B/D | 34,000 |
| To Selling and Distribution | 3,000 | By Non-Operating Incomes | |
| To Administration | 15,000 | •   Interest    300 | |
| To Finance | 1,500 | •   Profit on sale of shares   (+) 600 | 900 |
| To Non-Operating Expenses | | | |
| To Loss on sale of Assets | 400 | | |
| To Net Profit C/D | 15,000 | | |
| | **34,900** | | **34,900** |

**Balance Sheet as on 31-3-2016**

| Liabilities | ₹ | Assets | ₹ |
|---|---|---|---|
| Issued Share Capital | | Land and Building | 15,000 |
| 2,000 Equity Shares of ₹ 10 each | 20,000 | Plant and Machinery | 8,000 |
| Reserve | 9,000 | Stock in Trade | 14,900 |
| Profit and Loss | 6,000 | Sundry Debtors | 7,100 |
| Current Liabilities | 13,000 | Cash at Bank | 3,000 |
| **Total** | **48,000** | **Total** | **48,000** |

Compute : a) Current Ratio, b) Operating Ratio, c) Stock Turnover Ratio and d) Return on total resources.

2)    With the help of the following ratios regarding Tata Ltd., Tatanagar draw the Balance-Sheet of the company for the year 2016.

Current Ratio          2.5          Net Working Capital ₹ 3,00,000

Liquid Ratio          1.5          Stock Turnover Ratio = 6 times (Cost of Sales/Closing Stock)

Gross Profit Ratio          20%          Fixed Assets Turnover Ratio (on Cost of Sales) 2 times

Debt Collection Period 2 months    Fixed Assets to Shareholders Net Worth = 0.80

Reserves and Surplus to Capital 0.50

3)    Following is the Balance Sheet of Usha Beltron Ltd., Uttamnagar as on 31-3-2016.

**Balance Sheet as on 31-3-2016**

| Liabilities | ₹ | Assets | ₹ |
|---|---|---|---|
| Equity Share Capital | 2,00,000 | Goodwill | 1,20,000 |
| Capital Reserve | 40,000 | Fixed Assets | 2,80,000 |
| 8% Loan on Mortgage | 1,60,000 | Stock | 60,000 |
| Trade Creditors | 80,000 | Debtors | 60,000 |
| Bank Overdraft | 20,000 | Investments | 20,000 |
| Taxation – Current | 20,000 | Cash in hand | 60,000 |
| **Profit and Loss** | | | |
| Profit for the year ending 2006 | | | |
| (After taxation and interest on fixed | | | |
| deposit)        1,20,000 | | | |
| **Less :** Transfer to Reserve    (–) <u>40,000</u> | 80,000 | | |
| | **6,00,000** | | **6,00,000** |

Sales amounted to ₹ 12,00,000

You are required to calculate the following ratios :

a) Current Ratio, b) Quick Ratio, c) Equity Ratio,  d) Debt to Equity Ratio, e) Net Profit Ratio

4)    From the following ratios and given additional information prepare Balance Sheet of Vikrant Industries Ltd., Vijaypur as on 31-3-2016.

(a)    Current Ratio                           :     2.5 to 1

(b)    Liquid Ratio                            :     1.5 to 1

(c)    Working Capital                      :     ₹ 60,000

(d)    Bank Overdraft                       :     ₹ 10,000

(e)    Fixed Assets to Proprietor's Fund     :     0.75

(f)    Reserve and Surplus               :     ₹ 40,000

There were no Fictitious Assets or long-term loans.

5) Following is the Balance Sheet of Warren Tea Ltd., Walchandnagar as on 31-3-2016 together with additional information as on that date.

**Balance Sheet as on 31-3-2016**

| Liabilities | ₹ | Assets | ₹ |
|---|---|---|---|
| Paid-up Capital | 2,00,000 | Goodwill | 30,000 |
| Reserve Fund | 50,000 | Building | 1,20,000 |
| Profit and Loss | 12,750 | Machinery | 29,000 |
| Bank Overdraft | 11,250 | Stock in Trade | 66,000 |
| Creditors | 36,000 | Debtors | 85,000 |
| Taxation Provision | 20,000 | | |
| | **3,30,000** | | **3,30,000** |

**Additional Information :**

Gross Profit – ₹ 2,10,000, Average Stock on hand – ₹ 63,000, Turnover for the year 2015-2016 ₹ 8,40,000.

You are required to calculate the following accounting ratios –

a) Current Ratio, b) Liquid Ratio, c) Proprietory Ratio, d) Stock Turnover Ratio, e) Gross Profit Ratio.

6) Following is the Balance Sheet of Binaca Ltd., Bangalore as on 31-3-2016.

| Liabilities | ₹ | Assets | ₹ |
|---|---|---|---|
| Paid-up Capital | 12,00,000 | Goodwill | 2,00,000 |
| Reserve | 2,00,000 | Land | 6,00,000 |
| Profit and Loss | 4,30,000 | Plant | 4,30,000 |
| Sundry Creditors | 5,00,000 | Sundry Debtors | 8,20,000 |
| Bank Overdraft | 1,00,000 | Stock of goods | 2,50,000 |
| | | Bank Balance | 1,30,000 |
| | **24,30,000** | | **24,30,000** |

**Additional Information :**

| | ₹ |
|---|---|
| Gross Profit for the year 2015-2016 | 9,00,000 |
| Sales for the year 2015-2016 | 30,00,000 |
| Stock of gods on 1-4-2015 | 2,00,000 |

From the above information calculate the following accounting ratios –

a) Current Ratio, b) Liquid Ratio, c) Gross Profit Ratio, d) Stock Turnover Ratio, e) Proprietory Ratio

7) From the following information relating to Charminar Ltd., Chalisgaon calculate the following ratios.

a) Current Ratio, b) Liquidity Ratio, c) Debt Equity Ratio, d) Proprietory Ratio, e) Fixed Assets to Proprietory fund ratio

| Assets and Liabilities | | ₹ | ₹ |
|---|---|---|---|
| Fixed Assets | | | 85,00,000 |
| Current Assets | | | 85,00,000 |
| (i) | Stock in trade | 30,00,000 | |
| (ii) | Stores and spares | 14,00,000 | |
| (iii) | Sundry Debtors | 35,00,000 | |
| (iv) | Advances and Deposits  (+) | 6,00,000 | |
| | **Total** | | **1,70,00,000** |
| Share Capital and Reserves | | | 1,00,00,000 |
| Long-term borrowings – Debentures | | | 50,00,000 |
| Bank Overdraft – Cash Credit | | | 20,00,000 |
| | **Total** | | **1,70,00,000** |

8) The following details are worked out from the financial statements of a business concern for the year ended 31-3-2016. You are required to reconstruct the Balance Sheet of the concern as on 31-3-2016.

| | |
|---|---|
| Fixed Assets | ₹ 10,50,000 |
| (after writing off 30% depreciation) | |
| Fixed Assets Turnover Ratio | 2.00 |
| Finished Goods Turnover Ratio | 6.00 |
| Gross Profit/Sales% | 25.00 |
| Net Profit (before interest) Sales% | 8.00 |
| Interest cover (Debenture Interest @ 7%) | 8.00 |
| Debt collection period (months) | 1.50 |
| Materials consumed/Sales% | 30.00 |
| Stock of Raw Materials (Months of consumption) | 3.00 |
| Current Ratio | 2.40 |
| Quick Ratio | 1.00 |
| Reserves/Capital | 0.21 |

9) From the following information relating to Zenith India Ltd., Jharkhand prepare the Balance Sheet as on 31-3-2016.

| | |
|---|---|
| Paid up Capital | ₹ 50,000 |
| Plant | ₹ 1,25,000 |
| Annual Turnover | ₹ 5,00,000 |
| Gross Profit Margin | 25% |
| Annual Credit Sales | 80% of Net Sales |
| Current Ratio | 2 |
| Inventory Turnover | 4 |
| Fixed Assets Turnover | 2 |
| Returns Inward | 20% of Sales |
| Average collection period | 73 days |
| Bank credit to trade credit | 2 |
| Cash to Inventory | 1 : 15 |
| Total debt to current liabilities | 3 |

10) Using the information and the form given below, compute the Balance Sheet items for Earth Movers Ltd., Edalabad having an annual turnover of ₹ 30 lakhs.

| | |
|---|---|
| Sales / Total Assets | 3 |
| Sales / Fixed Assets | 5 |
| Sales / Current Assets | 7.5 |
| Sales / Inventories | 20 |
| Sales / Debtors | 15 |
| Current Ratio | 2 |
| Total Assets / Net Worth | 25 |
| Debt / Equity | 1 |

**Balance Sheet as on ............**

| Liabilities | ₹ | Assets | ₹ |
|---|---|---|---|
| Net Worth | – | Fixed Assets | – |
| Long-term Deposits | – | Inventories | – |
| Current Liabilities | – | Debtors | – |
| | | Liquid Assets | – |
| | | Total Current Assets | – |

✷✷✷

# APPENDICES



### Difficult Terms and their Simple Explanations

- **Abnormal Goods :** These are the goods of irregular nature or slow moving type or damaged which are valued at cost or at a lower value as specified.

- **Acceptances, Endorsements and other obligations :** These are the bills accepted or endorsed by the Bank on behalf of the customers to get the advantage of their credit. Other obligations include letter of credit issued and guarantees given by the Bank on behalf of its customers.

- **Accounting Standard :** It is a selected set of accounting policies or broad guidelines regarding the principles and methods to be chosen of several alternatives.

- **Allocable Expenses :** These are certain expenses incurred for the benefit of more than one department but allocation of which can be made on some equitable basis.

- **Analysis :** It is the simplification of data incorporated in the financial statements.

- **Average Clause :** As the basic purpose of insurance is to compensate the loss, but not allow to earn a profit, a fire insurance policy usually includes a clause wherein the claim for the loss of stock is proportionately reduced having regard to under insurance of stock.

- **Banking :** Accepting for the purpose of lending or investment of deposits of money from the public, to be payable on demand or otherwise withdrawable by cheque, draft, order or otherwise.

- **Banking Company :** Any company which transacts the business of banking in India.

- **Bills for collection :** These are the bills received by the Bank from its clients to collect them on their due dates from the acceptors and credit the amount to their current accounts, charging certain amount of commission for these services.

- **Bills Payable :** These are the unpaid bank drafts, telegraphic transfers, mail transfers and travellers cheques issued by a bank on another bank for remitting funds from one place to another.

- **Branch :** It is a section of an enterprise, geographically separated from the rest of the business, controlled by a head office and generally carrying on the same activities as of the enterprise.

- **Broker :** The specific agent through whom the sale and purchase of securities is effected.

- **Brokerage :** It is the commission payable to the broker for effecting the sale and purchase of securities.

- **Business Segment :** It is made on the basis of products or services, which are exposed to different risks and returns.

- **Carrying Amount :** It is the amount at which the asset is shown in the Balance-sheet, hence carrying amount = Cost of Asset less Depreciation less Impairment loss.
- **Cash in Transit :** It represents such cash which has been remitted by head office to branch or vice-versa, a few days before the close of accounting period, but the same still remains in the way.
- **Construction Contract :** It is contract specifically negotiated for the construction of an asset or combination of assets closely interrelated or interdependent.
- **Cost Accounting :** It is the process of accounting for cost from the point at which expenditure is incurred or committed to the establishment of its ultimate relationship with cost centres and cost units.
- **Credit Risk :** It is the risk that one party to a financial instrument will cause financial loss for the other party by failing to discharge an obligation.
- **Cum-Interest Transactions :** These are the transactions when the right to receive interest or dividend from the insurer, passes from the seller to the buyer.
- **Currency Risk :** It is that type of market risk in which the fair value or future cash flows of a financial instrument will fluctuate because of changes in foreign exchange rates.
- **Current Ratio :** It is the ratio which indicates how much current assets and there as against each rupee of current liabilities.
- **Debtors System :** It is a synthetic method of accounting record followed by the head office in which a branch is treated as a debtor of the head office and a separate account for each branch is opened.
- **Dependent Branches :** These are the branches which depend solely on the head office for all their requirements i.e. for goods and expenses and they do not maintain a complete record of their transactions.
- **Doubtful Assets :** These are certain loan assets of a Bank which has remained as a non-performing asset for a period exceeding two years.
- **Employee Benefits :** These are all forms of considerations given by an enterprise directly to the employee or their spouses, children or other dependents or to others such as trust, insurance companies in exchange of services rendered by the employees.
- **Enterprise Revenue :** It is a revenue from sales to external customers as reported in the statement of profit or loss.
- **Equity Instrument :** Any contract that evidences a residual interest in the assets of an entity after deducting all of its liabilities.
- **Ex-Interest Transactions :** These are the transactions when the seller retains the right to receive interest or dividend.
- **External Analysis :** It is the simplification of financial data effected by those who do not have access to the detailed accounting records of the concern.
- **Farm Accounting :** It is a branch of accountancy that classifies, records, determines profit or loss and arranges data for farm management decision through analysis of farm transactions.

- **FIFO Method :** First-In-First-Out is a method of valuation of balance of investment under which it is assumed that the investments purchased first are sold first.

- **Final Accounts System :** It is a method of finding out the profit or loss of a branch at the end of a financial period by preparing Memorandum Trading Account and Profit and Loss Account, recording the items of stock at cost price and the items of branch expenses and incomes relating to that period.

- **Financial Accounting :** It is the art of recording, classifying and summarising in a significant manner and in terms of money transactions and events which are in part at least of a financial character and interpreting the results thereof.

- **Financial Instrument :** It is a document which has a monetary value such as draft, cheque, bill of exchange and promissory note.

- **Financial Ratio :** It is a relationship between two variables taken from financial statements of a concern.

- **Financial Statement Analysis :** It is a process of evaluating the relationship between component parts of a financial statement to obtain a better understanding of a firm's position and performance.

- **Fire Insurance :** It is a contract whereby the insurer in consideration of a premium undertakes to indemnify the assured against loss or damage to the property by fire during a certain period agreed upon and upto the specified amount.

- **Geographical Segment :** It is made on the basis of its operation in different geographical areas, which are exposed to different risks and returns.

- **Goods in Transit :** It represents such goods which are sent by the head office to the branch or vice-versa, a few days before the close of accounting period, but the same still remains in the way.

- **Government Grants :** These are certain assistance by the Government in the form of cash or kind to an enterprise in return for past or future compliance with certain conditions.

- **Gross Profit Ratio :** It indicates the relationship of gross profit to net sales in terms of percentage.

- **Horizontal Analysis :** It is the analysis and examination of financial statements for a number of years.

- **Impairment of Assets :** An asset is said to be impaired when carrying amount of an asset is more than its recoverable amount.

- **Indemnity Period :** It is the period during which the sales are expected to be affected due to fire, for which the loss of profit policy is taken out.

- **Insurance :** It is a co-operative device to spread the loss caused by a particular risk over a number of persons, who are exposed to it and who agree to insure themselves against the risk.

- **Insurance Claims :** These are the claims filed for compensation against the losses with the insurance company, when a business suffers a loss.

- **Insured standing charges :** These are the fixed charges which are required to be incurred irrespective of whether the business activities are suspended or not, specified in the policy which the insured desires to recover in case of an accident.

- **Inter Departmental Transfers :** These are the goods supplied by one department to another, debited to Trading Account of the receiving department and credited to Trading Account of the supplying department.

- **Interest Rate Risk :** It is that type of market risk in which the fair value or future cash flows of a financial instrument will fluctuate because of changes in market interest rates.

- **Internal Analysis :** It is the simplification of financial data effected by those who have access to the detailed accounting records of the concern.

- **Interpretation :** It means bringing out the meaning of the financial statements with the help of the analysis.

- **Investment :** It is the employment of funds with the aim of achieving additional income or growth in value.

- **Invoice Price :** It is the marked up price of goods which includes certain percentage of profit. This price is higher than the cost price.

- **Joint Venture :** It is a contractual arrangement whereby two or more parties carry on economic activity under joint control.

- **Jointly Control Operation :** It is that form of joint venture, when joint venture is not a separate entity, the ventures may carry out the joint venture activities side by side of their main business.

- **Jointly Controlled Assets :** It is that form of joint venture, in which there may be joint ownership of assets, the jointly owned assets are used for the purpose of joint venture and the venture shares economic benefits of these assets in an agreed proportion.

- **Jointly Controlled Entities :** It is that form of joint venture in which a separate jointly controlled entity is established.

- **Liquid Ratio :** It is the ratio which indicates the relation of liquid assets (i.e. all current assets except stock and prepaid expenses) with liquid liabilities (i.e. all current liabilities except bank overdraft and accrued expenses).

- **Liquidity Risk :** It is the risk that entity will encounter difficulty in meeting obligations associated with financial liabilities.

- **Loading :** It is the difference between the invoice price and cost price of goods.

- **Loss Assets :** These are certain loan assets of a Bank where the loss has been identified by the Bank, but the amount has not been written off, wholly or partly.

- **Management Accounting :** It is the presentation of accounting information in such a way as to assist management in the creation of policy and in the day-to-day operation of an undertaking.

- **Market Risk :** It is the risk that the fair value or future cash flows of a financial instrument will fluctuate because of changes in market prices.

- **Memorandum Trading Account :** It is a normal trading account temporarily prepared upto the date of fire to calculate the estimated value of stock on the date of fire.

- **Money at call and short notices :** These are the loans advanced by banks having surplus funds to another bank repayable within twenty four hours are termed as 'money at call' and repayable by a notice of seven days are termed as 'money at short notice'.

- **Net Profit Ratio :** It indicates the relationship of net profit to net sales in terms of percentage.

- **Non-Performing Assets (NPA) :** It is an asset which ceases to generate income for a Bank. It means a credit facility in respect of which the interest or installment remains past due for a period of two quarters i.e. six months.

- **Operating Ratio :** It is the ratio which indicates the percentage of net sales that is absorbed by cost of goods sold and operating expenses.

- **Policy of Insurance :** It is an instrument containing the contract to insure.

- **Rebate on Bills Discounted :** On discounting a bill by the Bank the total amount of discount is credited to discount account. But it is likely that the bill may be maturing sometime during the next year. As such proportionate amount of discount relating to the period falling in the next year becomes the income of the next year and is carried forward as a liability as discount received in advance or unexpired discount.

- **Related Party :** It is essentially a party that controls or can significantly influence the management or operating policies of the company during the reporting period.

- **Related Party Transactions :** It is transfer of resources or obligations between related parties, regardless of whether or not a price is charged.

- **Segment Expense :** It is one that is directly attributable and that can be allocated on a reasonable basis and includes transactions with other segments of the same enterprise.

- **Segment Reporting :** It is the disclosure of such information which is used to assess the risk and return of multiple products or services and its operation in different geographical areas.

- **Short Sales :** It is the difference between expected sales and actual sales during the indemnity period.

- **Single Entry System :** It is a method adopted by many small businessmen to maintain their books of accounts in which two fold aspect of transaction is ignored totally.

- **Standard Assets :** These are certain loan assets of a Bank which does not disclose any problem and which does not carry more than normal risk attached to the business.

- **Standard Turnover :** It is the turnover during the period of twelve months immediately prior to the date of damage which corresponds with the indemnity period.

- **Statement of Affair :** It is statement of assets and liabilities prepared on a particular date on the basis of some ledger accounts and estimates, to find out the balance of capital account.

- **Statutory Reserve :** It is a reserve created by every Banking Company incorporated in India, out of the balance of profit of each year, before declaration of any dividend, by transferring a sum equivalent to not less than twenty percent of such profit.

- **Stock and Debtors System :** It is an analytical method of accounting record, followed by the head office in which elaborate records are maintained by opening several accounts for each branch.
- **Stock Salvaged :** These are the items of stock saved from fire and are deducted from the stock on the date of fire to find out the correct value of stock on the date of fire.
- **Stock Turnover Ratio :** It refers to the number of times in a year inventories are sold and replaced.
- **Sub-standard Assets :** These are certain loan assets of a Bank which are classified as a non-performing asset for a period not exceeding two years.
- **Transaction Cost :** These are the costs which are incremental and are directly attributable to the acquisitions, issue or disposal of a financial asset or a liability.
- **Treasury Shares :** These are re-acquirements by an entity of their own equity instruments in the buy back process.
- **Under Insurance :** It is the case when the actual insurance cover taken is less than insurance cover required.
- **Vertical Analysis :** It is the analysis of financial ratios developed for a particular date for a particular accounting period.

**Non-Banking Assets :** A Banking Company cannot acquire certain assets, which are not required for its own use, but it can lend money against the security of such assets. The Banking Company may take possession of such assets offered as security if the borrower fails to repay the loan.

*******

## TRUE OR FALSE STATEMENTS

- **State with reasons whether the following statements are True or False :**
  1. Banking Companies in India are governed by Banking Regulation Act, 1952.
  2. The main functions of a Banking Company are to accept deposits of money from the public and to lend or invest these deposits.
  3. Non-Banking Assets must be shown in the Balance Sheet in Schedule 8.
  4. Every Banking Company incorporated in India must transfer to the Reserve Fund a sum equivalent to not less than 25% of profit of each year before declaration of dividend.
  5. Acceptances, Endorsements and other obligations are a contingent liability of a Bank.
  6. Rebate on Bills discounted is an income received in advance which is carried forward as other liability.
  7. Transfer of money from one place to another i.e. mail transfer, is an item to be excluded from Bills Payable.
  8. An asset becomes non-performing when it ceases to generate income for a Bank.
  9. Banks are to recognise their income on cash basis in respect of income on performing assets.
  10. Sub-standard asset is one which has been classified as non-performing asset for a period not exceeding three years.
  11. Insurance is a financial service for collecting the savings of the public and providing them with a risk of coverage.
  12. The Insurance Company cannot prevent the happening of risk but can provide for losses at the happening of the risk.
  13. A marine insurance policy is taken to cover the claims for loss of stock.
  14. The amount paid by an insured to insurer as a consideration is known as premium.
  15. General Insurance business in India is transacted by Life Insurance Corporation of India.
  16. A Memorandum Trading Account is to be prepared to ascertain the value of stock on the date of fire.
  17. A policy of fire insurance is intended to protect the assured against the loss caused by fire.
  18. Gross Profit must always be calculated as a percentage on purchases.
  19. Average Clause is applicable in case of under insurance.
  20. A fire policy covers loss of or damage to insured property.
  21. Stock salvaged from fire is deducted from the stock value on the date of fire to find out the stock destroyed by fire.
  22. Trading Account of the previous year is to be prepared to find out percentage of net profit to sales.
  23. The value of stock on the date of fire can be ascertained by constructing a Memorandum Trading Account for a period starting from the first day of ascertaining period and ending on the date of fire.
  24. Average Clause means the claim for the loss of stock is proportionately reduced having regard to under insurance of stock.
  25. The Gross Profit percentage gets disturbed due to existence of normal items of purchases and sales.

26. Reduction of sales during the dislocation period leads to loss of profit on reduced sales during that period.
27. Case of under insurance, attracts the application of average clause under loss of profit policy.
28. A businessman needs insurance especially to cover loss of stock destroyed by fire.
29. Abnormal items of goods are required to be separated from normal items so as to reflect the correct gross profit percentage to sales.
30. The rate of gross profit has a direct impact on the value of claim for loss of stock.
31. Investment refers to the money invested in various securities in order to earn regular and definite income.
32. A security is said to be at discount when acquired or sold at a price more than its face value.
33. When investments are very large, it becomes necessary to maintain a separate account for each type of security.
34. Debt-capital is the important external source of raising short term funds.
35. Cum-Interest transactions can be expanded as exclusive of interest.
36. Ex-Interest transactions can be expanded as exclusive of interest.
37. At the end of the accounting year, the balance of investment is to be valued on the basis of cost price or market price whichever is lower.
38. On receipt of the first amount of interest on investment, on the due date Interest Account will be debited with the whole amount of that period.
39. Interest or dividend is always calculated on the face value of investment.
40. In purchase transactions the amount of brokerage is deducted from the purchase price of investment.
41. A branch is a clearly identifiable profit centre of a business house.
42. The need for branch accounting arises as to fulfil the audit requirements under Section 282 of the Companies Act, 1956.
43. The branch which does not maintain a complete record of its transactions is said to be independent one.
44. The branch which keeps full system of accounting is said to be an independent one.
45. Synthetic method of maintaining accounts for dependent branches is more suitable for small size businesses having very few transactions.
46. Analytical method of maintaining accounts for dependent branches is usually adopted when the branches are of large size and their transactions are more.
47. After receiving the goods by the branch, goods sent to Branch Account is debited in the books of head office.
48. Commission payable to Branch Manager is always debited to Branch Account.
49. The difference between invoice price and cost price of goods is called 'Loading'.
50. Loading on goods lost by fire in transit should be charged to Branch Stock Account.
51. If goods are distributed as free samples, separate entry is made in Branch Account.
52. The basic purpose of supplying goods to branch at invoice price is to have greater control over the stock at the branch.
53. Branch Adjustment Account is prepared to ascertain the net profit of the branch.
54. In departmental accounts each department is treated as a separate profit centre.
55. Department accounting information generally provides a basis for intelligent planning and control.
56. Allocable expenses are those which are incurred for the benefit of more than one department, but allocation of which cannot be made on equitable basis.

57. Labour Welfare expenses are to be apportioned on the basis of number of employees more suitably.
58. When goods are transferred from one department to another at inflated price, there is no need to make the adjustment in respect of provision for unrealised profit.
59. In departmental accounts legal fees are to be debited to Profit and Loss Account.
60. Excess of selling price over cost price is included in the value of stock which remains unsold is termed as unrealised profit.
61. Agricultural Farm Accounting are the principles and techniques of accounting farm transactions in accordance with their typicalities.
62. Valuation of farm inventory is a very simple task.
63. Proper maintenance of farm accounts and records improve the managerial ability of the farmer.
64. Farm Accounting may be simplified by using simple cash book.
65. The increase in net worth means profit and the decrease in net worth means loss.
66. Single Entry System is the most scientific and accurate method of recording books of accounts.
67. Single entry constitutes incomplete records rather than single entry accounting.
68. Under pure single entry system only impersonal accounts are kept.
69. It is difficult to conduct the audit of single entry records.
70. Incomplete records system is used only by small traders, hawkers and pedlers.
71. If the closing capital is more than the opening capital, the difference is treated as a loss.
72. Opening balance of capital can be calculated by preparing a statement of affairs at the beginning of the accounting year.
73. Under Conversion Method, credit purchases can be found out by preparing Total Debtors Account.
74. Financial Statement Analysis is an important means of assessing past performance and in forecasting and planning future performance.
75. Analysis is the simplification of data incorporated in the financial statements.
76. Analysis and interpretation both, assist the management in measuring and maintaining efficiency at various levels.
77. Financial statement analysis can be used for assessment of past performance only.
78. Ratio analysis is an important means of expressing the relationship between two numbers.
79. Ratio analysis helps in investment decisions.
80. Liquid ratio is also known as 2 : 1 ratio.
81. Current ratio indicates the solvency position of the business.
82. An ideal liquid ratio is considered as 1 : 1.
83. The gross profit represents the net margin.
84. Operating ratio indicates the percentage of net sales that is absorbed by cost of goods sold and non-operating expenses.
85. To get a meaningful interpretation of profitability of the firm, a financial analyst must evaluate both the gross profit ratio and net profit ratio jointly.
86. Inventory turnover ratio throws light on the inventory policy pursued by the management and the reasonableness of the same.
87. Ratio analysis provides useful data for inter-firm and intra-firm comparison.
88. Reliability of ratios depend upon the reliability of financial data.
89. Acid test ratio is a measure of the extent to which liquid resources are immediately made available to meet current obligations.

90. A low inventory turnover may reflect higher investment in inventory.

91. Commercial Banks are joint stock companies dealing in money and credit.

92. Banking company can engage in any trade, or buy or sell or barter goods for others otherwise than in connection with bills of exchange.

93. The subscribed capital of Banking company must not be less than 50% of its authorised capital.

94. As per Narsimham committee recommendations, the bank should classify their loan assets into standard Assets, Sub-standard Assets, Doubtful Assets and Loss Assets.

95. Banking companies in India are Governed by Banking regulation Act, 1949, however provisions of Indian companies Act, 1956 are not applicable to them.

96. A Banking company cannot create a floating charge on its undertaking unless it gets a certificate from the Reserve Bank of India that such charge is not detrimental to the interests of the depositor of the Banking company.

97. A business unit can have a loss of profit insurance policy without a fire policy.

98. Under loss of stock policy current years Trading Account should be prepared to find out the normal rate of gross profit.

99. A memorandum Trading Account discloses only the stock of normal items of goods on the date of fire.

100. The period of actual dislocation or the period of indemnity whichever is less is the period for which expected profit that is lost shall be considered.

101. A department is a section of an enterprise, geographically separated from the rest of the business, controlled by a head office, and generally carrying on the same activities as of the enterprise.

102. A departmental office is the parent shop which controls the subsidiary establishment to earn huge amount of profits.

103. The need for branch accounting arises so as to ascertain the profitability of each branch separately at the end of the accounting period.

104. The branches which are totally dependent on head office are also termed as Agency Branches.

105. The independent branches are autonomous as they are allowed to make their own purchases from open markers and pay for their expenses.

106. Inland branches is the expansion of a business enterprise by opening different shops in other countries.

107. The method of Branch Accounting varies with the nature and the status of branch.

108. Actual petty expenses paid by branch from petty cash are to be shown separately in Branch Account.

109. Dependent branch does not keep any books of account as their entire accounting work is performed by the head office.

110. The branch official can easily find out the profit margin earned when the head office supplies goods to their branches at loaded price.

111. Departmental Accounting is a systematic technique of record keeping by which the costs and results of individual department can be ascertained accurately.

112. No depreciation is charged on agricultural land, however, it is always charged on agricultural implements.

113. In farm accounting standing crops are to be valued at cost or net realisable value whichever is more.

114. Under single entry system arithmetical accuracy of the accounting records can be checked.

115. Management Accounting is concerned with the accounting information which is useful to the administration.
116. Management Accounting goes beyond the figures provided by Financial Accounting which are mute in nature and make them self explanatory.
117. Management Accounting aims at preparing reports and supplying information to management for planning, controlling and decision making.
118. The generally accepted accounting principles are not important in financial accounting and are not used at all.
119. Management Accounting is an extension of the managerial aspects of cost accounting.
120. Management Accounting reports are subject to the statutory audit.
121. Financial statement Analysis is an important means of assessing post performance and in forecasting and planning future performance.
122. Analysis is the pre-requisite to interpretation of financial data.
123. External financial analysis is effected by those who have access to the books of accounts and other financial information relating to the business.
124. Ratio Analysis ensures effective cost control.
125. An ideal current ratio is considered as 1 : 2.
126. If the Debt Equity Ratio is higher, it indicates that the company is depending heavily on debtors.
127. Accounting as a language of business communicates the financial performance and position of an enterprise to various interested parties.
128. Standards are not designed to confine practise within rigid limits but rather to serve as guide posts to truth, honesty and fair dealing.
129. AS-7 does not apply to contractors.
130. As per AS-7 architect's services are not included in construction contract.
131. As per AS-7 Research and Development cost is to be excluded from contract cost.
132. AS-7 deals with the accounting for Government Grants.
133. Government assistance, which cannot be valued reasonably, is excluded from Government Grants.
134. As per AS-15, accumulating compensated absences can be carried forward, if the current periods entitlement is not used in full.
135. As per AS-17, segment expense does not include income tax expense.
136. As per AS-17, related party relationship and transactions between a reporting enterprise and its related parties, facts should not be disclosed.
137. As per AS-19, financial lease substantially transfers all the risk and reward to ownership of an asset to the lessee.
138. Weight of a bonus share is calculated from the last of the accounting year.
139. A parent co. should account for the investment in subsidiaries in accordance with AS-13.
140. AS-21 deals with accounting for investments in joint ventures.
141. According to AS-22, tax on income is determined on the principle of accrual concept.
142. Justification for method of calculating periodic deferred tax is based on the concept of matching of periodic expense to periodic revenue.
143. AS-24 covers discontinuing operations rather than discontinued operations.
144. The main objective of AS-27 is to disclose the information about discontinuing operations.
145. AS-25, does not indicate the frequency of interim financial report.
146. AS-25 focuses on change in accounting policy, also.
147. As per AS-28, impairment of asset means decrease in the value of asset.

148. AS-28, concentrates on impairment of discontinuing operations also.

149. An asset is impaired when carrying amount of asset is less than its recoverable amount.

150. Financial instrument is not defined in AS-31, however it is defined in AS-30.

151. As per AS-30, prepaid expenses are not financial instruments.

152. AS-30, prescribes the presentation requirements for treasury shares.

153. AS-32, prescribes the disclosure requirements for financial instruments in financial statements.

154. AS-32, does apply to insurance contracts.

## ANSWERS

**True :**

2, 5, 6, 8, 11, 12, 14, 16, 17, 19, 20, 21, 23, 24, 26, 27, 28, 29, 30, 31, 33, 36, 37, 39, 41, 44, 45, 46, 48, 49, 52, 54, 55, 57, 60, 61, 63, 65, 67, 69, 70, 72, 74, 75, 76, 78, 79, 81, 82, 85, 86, 87, 88, 89, 91, 93, 94, 96, 99, 100, 103, 104, 105, 107, 109, 111, 112, 116, 117, 119, 121, 122, 124, 127, 128, 131, 133, 134, 135, 137, 139, 141, 142, 143, 145, 146, 147, 148, 151, 153.

**False :**

1 – Banking Regulation Act, 1949, 3 – Schedule 11, 4 – not less than 20%, 7 – to be included in Bills Payable, 9 – on accrual basis, 10 – not exceeding two years, 13 – fire insurance, 15 – by General Insurance Corporation of India, 18 – gross profit on sales, 22 – percentage of gross profit to sales, 25 – abnormal items of purchases and sales, 32 – lower than its face value, 34 – long-term funds, 35 – inclusive of interest, 38 – will be credited, 40 – added to the purchase price, 42 – under Section 228, 43 – to be dependent one, 47 – is credited, 50 – charged to Branch Adjustment Account, 51 – no separate entry, 53 – gross profit of the branch, 56 – can be made on equitable basis, 58 – there is a need to make the adjustment, 59 – are to be debited to General Profit and Loss Account, 62 – difficult task, 64 – by using Analytical Columnar Cash Book, 66 – is the most unscientific and inaccurate method, 68 – only personal accounts are kept, 71 – is treated as a profit, 73 – by preparing Total Creditors Account, 77 – for assessment of past performance and current position, 80 – current ratio, 83 – gross margin, 84 – and operating expenses, 90 – lower investment in inventory, 92 – No Banking Company can engage, 95 – are also applicable to them, 97 – cannot, 98 – previous years, 101 – branch, 102 – head office, 106 – foreign branches, 108 – not to be shown, 110 – at cost price, 113 – lower. 114 – cannot, 115 – useful to management, 118 – are important in financial accounting and are used extensively, 120 – are not subject to, 123 – internal financial analysis, 125 – 2 : 1, 126 – creditors, 129 – to contracter, 130 are also included, 132 – AS-12, 136 – should be disclosed, 138 – first day, 140 – does not deal with, 144 – AS-24, 199 – is more than, 150 – not defined in AS-30, however it is defined in AS-31, 152 – AS-31, 154 – does not apply.

*** Fill in the blanks**

1. Banking companies in India are governed by ……..
2. The paid up capital of a Banking company must not be …….. than 50% of its subscribed capital.
3. Every Banking company incorporated in India shall transfer to the Reserve fund a sum equivalent to not less than …….. out of the balance of profit of each year.
4. …….. are certain bills received by the Bank from their customers to collect them on their due dates from the acceptors.
5. Every Banking company should prepare a Balance-sheet and profit and loss account as on …….. each year.
6. An asset becomes non-performing when it …….. to generate income for a Bank.
7. Banks are to recognise their income on …….. basis in respect of income on performing assets.
8. Banks are to recognise their income on …….. basis in respect of income on non-performing assets.
9. …….. assets are certain loan assets of a Bank which does not disclose any problem and which does not carry more than normal risk attached to the business.
10. Sub-standard assets are certain loan assets of a bank which are classified as …….. asset for a period not exceeding two years.
11. Doubtful assets are certain loan assets of a bank which has remained as a non-performing asset for a period exceeding …….. years.
12. According to …….. Committee, income from non-performing assets should not be recognised on accrual basis but should be booked as income only when it is actually received.
13. In case of Bank finance given for industrial projects, the payment of interest becomes due only after the …….. is over.
14. Banks should ensure that while granting loans and advances realistic repayment schedules are to be fixed on the basis of …….. flows, with the borrowers.
15. A Banking company follows the principles of …….. system while in recording their transactions in the books of accounts.
16. The banking companies in India have to follow the new format of their final account w.e.f. accounting year ending on, ……..
17. The loans advanced by the Banks to another Bank repayable within twenty four hours are termed as ……..
18. The loans advanced by the Banks to another Bank repayable by a notice of seven days are termed as ……..
19. …….. is a short-term obligation issued by the Govt. at a discount bearing no interest and repayable at par on maturity.
20. In the Balance Sheet of a Banking Company, investment in Silver is shown on the asset side under the heading ………
21. A Banking Company can pay dividend on its shares within …….. days of the date of declaration.
22. A business takes a …….. insurance policy to cover the claims for loss of stock and loss of profit.
23. The computation of loss by fire is very simple taken when a …….. asset is destroyed.
24. The value of stock on the date of fire can be ascertained more precisely by preparation of a …….. Trading Account.

25. …….. clause is applicable in case of under insurance.
26. The gross profit percentage gets disturbed due to existence of …….. item of purchases and sales.
27. A …….. policy covers loss of gross profit sustained as a consequence of business interruption.
28. The period for which a policy is taken is known as …….. period.
29. A …….. policy covers loss of stock, fixed assets, profit, expenses etc.
30. Due to the inclusion of 'average clause' in the fire insurance policy, an insured becomes a …….. in the event of under insurance.
31. The employment of funds with the aim of achieving additional income, is termed as ……..
32. Cum-interest basis means the purchase price of securities …….. interest from the last day of interest payment to the date of the transaction.
33. Ex-interest basis means the purchase price of securities …….. interest.
34. The expenses incurred on purchase of investments are to be …….. to the purchase price of investments.
35. The expenses incurred on sale of investments are to be …….. from the sale price of investments.
36. The investments on hand at the end of the period are valued at cost price or market price whichever is ……..
37. Under the …….. method of valuation of closing investment it is assumed that the investment purchased first are sold first.
38. In investment transactions income-tax, if any charged on interest is to be …….. from the amount of interest.
39. Interest and brokerage are to be calculated on the …….. of investments and not on the purchase or sales price.
40. Investment are treated as …….. Account even though they are not physical assets.
41. A …….. is a subordinate division of a central office.
42. A branch is a clearly identifiable …….. centre of a business house.
43. The expansion of a business enterprise by opening different shops in different parts of the city and indifferent cities of the country is known as …….. branches.
44. The …….. branches are not allowed to make their own purchases from open market.
45. The foreign branches enjoy highest degree of power and total …….. in their day-to-day working.
46. …….. method of branch accounting is usually adopted when the branch is of the small size.
47. The normal and abnormal stock of goods does not appear in Branch Account as the closing stock is at the …….. figure.
48. Commission payable to Branch Manager after charging such commission.

$$= \text{Net Profit before Commission} (\times) \frac{\text{Rate of Commission}}{100 \ (+) \ ……}$$

49. Stock and debtors method of branch accounting is generally used where branch turnover is substantially ……..
50. Under analytical method of branch accounting a Branch Stock Account is generally to ascertain any …….. in stock.
51. Loading on surplus in stock is ……..to Branch Adjustment Account.
52. Under stock and debtors system general income is credited to …….. account.
53. The cancellation of loading in stock at the end is credited to …….. account.

54. In Branch Accounting, the balance on Stock Reserve Account at the end of the period is shown in the Balance Sheet by way of deduction from ........
55. Goods sent by the Head Office at the end of the year but not received by Branch before the year end is known as ........
56. The closing balance of book debts account is ascertained by preparing Branch ........ Account.
57. The removal of loading from the items of branch stock is adjusted through Branch ........ Account.
58. A ........ is generally a physical part of the business established under the same roof.
59. A ........ system of departmental accounts is more convenient, where the number of departments are very small.
60. A ........ departmental accounting system is more useful for systematic planning, effective decision-making and efficient control.
61. The accounting record of goods supplied by one department to other department is recorded through ........
62. Preparation of departmental accounts is necessary to know ........ of each department.
63. The unallocable expenses under departmental accounting are to be debited to ......... Account.
64. Carriage inward can be allocated in departmental accounting on the basis of ........ of each department.
65. Inter-departmental transactions are debited to Trading Account of the ........ department.
66. In India Farm Accounting is in its ........ state.
67. Depreciation is not charged on ........ land.
68. In farm accounting the farm yard manure is valued at the estimated ........ price.
69. ........ system of Book-keeping is the only scientific method to record farming transactions.
70. Most of the farming transactions are transacted on ........ basis.
71. Single entry constitutes incomplete records rather than single entry ........
72. Under pure single entry system only ........ accounts are kept.
73. Under the ........ entry system personal accounts, cash-book and other subsidiary books are kept separately.
74. ........ entry system is a mixture of single entry, double entry and no entry.
75. Management Accounting is concerned with improvement in the efficiency of various phases of ........
76. ........ Accounting serves as a vital source of data for management planning.
77. The users of financial accounting statements are mainly ........ to the business enterprise.
78. ........ Accounting is mainly concerned with the future plans and policies.
79. Management Accounting is not based on ........ entry system.
80. ........ Accounting is not bound to use the generally accepted accounting principles.
81. The focus on ........ analysis is on key figures contained in the financial statements and the significant relationship that exists between them.
82. Analysis and interpretation of financial data, assist the management in measuring and maintaining ........ at various levels.
83. Analysis of financial data is useless without .........
84. The major objectives of financial statement analysis is to provide important financial information to decision makers for use in ........
85. ........ is a significant tool in predicting the bankruptcy and failure probably of business enterprises.

86. ........ financial analysis is effected by those who do not have access to the detailed accounting records of the concern.
87. When the financial statements for a certain number of years are examined and analysed, the analysis is called, ........ analysis.
88. ........ analysis is not usually resorted to by the financial analysts.
89. Trend Analysis uses an ........ number of a period of time.
90. ........ is the indicated quotient of two mathematical expressions.
91. Ratio analysis acts as an ........ of efficiency of an enterprise.
92. ........ ratios measure the ability of a firm to meet its short-term obligations.
93. The ........ ratios are the test of relationship between sales and assets.
94. Current ratio indicates ........ of the business.
95. An ideal liquid ratio is considered as ........
96. A high gross profit as compared with that of other firm in the same industry, is a sign of ........ management.
97. ........ ratio indicates the percentage of net sales that is absorbed by the cost of goods and operating expenses.
98. Net Profit Ratio = $\dfrac{\text{Net Profit after Taxes}}{\phantom{xxxxxxxxxxxx}} \times 100$
99. The quality of debtors determines the ........ of a firm.
100. The ........ the value of debtors turnover, the more efficient is the management of receivables.
101. The Accounting Standards Board (India) was formed by the Institute of Chartered Accountants of India in April ........
102. Accounting standards in India are issued by the ........
103. The important objective of Accounting Standards is to ........ the diverse accounting policies and practices at present in use, in India.
104. At present, ........ are regarded as a major component in the framework of accounting and reporting practices.
105. Accounting Standards are beneficial not only to the business enterprises but also to the ........ as well.
106. ........ deals with the financial statement which summarises for a given period, the sources and applications of funds of an enterprises.
107. ........ exhibits the flow of incoming and outgoing cash.
108. ........ statement is one of the important tools for assessing the liquidity and solvency position of the enterprise.
109. AS-7 deals with accounting for construction contracts in financial statements of ........
110. AS-26 deals with the treatment of costs of ........ in financial statements.
111. Investment made by Govt. as equity, in the ownership of an enterprise is known as Govt. ........
112. Govt. Grants become ........ because of non-fulfillment of the conditions attached to that grant.
113. AS-15 deals with accounting for retirement benefits in the financial statements of ........
114. Revised AS-15 : Employee Benefits, is applicable in respect of accounting periods commencing on or after 1st April, ........
115. AS ........ also focuses on profit sharing and bonus plan.
116. AS-17 : Segment reporting applies to those companies which have an annual turnover of ₹ ........ crores or more.
117. ........ reporting helps uses of financial statements to better assess the risks and returns of the enterprises.
118. As per AS-19, in ........ lease risk and reward is not transferred to the lessee.
119. In financial lease, as per AS-19, leased asset is shown in the Balance-Sheet of ........
120. AS-20, deals with the presentation and computation of ........
121. Earnings per share, is a very important financial ratio, computed for assessing the state of ........ price of share.

122. Right issue is generally made at a price lower than …….. value of shares.
123. AS …….. deals with the preparation of consolidated financial statements with aim to present financial statements of a parent and its subsidiaries as a single economic entity.
124. AS-22, prescribes the accounting treatment for taxes on ……..
125. AS …….. is not applicable when consolidated financial statement of investor is not made.
126. According to AS-24, any planned change in the product line may not be treated as …….. operation.
127. Operator of a joint venture should be accounted for any fees in accordance with AS ………
128. As per AS-28, an asset is said to be impaired, when carrying amount of an asset is …….. than its recoverable amount.
129. Impairment of Assets is nothing but ……… in the value of assets.
130. Recoverable amount of an asset is …….. of selling price and value of asset in use.
131. Impairment Loss = Recoverable Amount minus …….. amount.
132. AS-31, basically addresses the issue of …….. of financial instrument in financial statements.
133. If the entity re-acquires its own equity instruments from related parties, it should provide disclosures as per AS ……..
134. …….. will be applicable to all commercial, industrial and business entities other than small and medium sized entities.

## ANSWERS

1. Banking Regulation Act, 1949, 2. less, 3. 20%, 4. Bank for Collection, 5. 31st March, 6. Ceases, 7. accrual, 8. cash, 9. standard, 10. non-performing, 11. two, 12. Narsimham, 13. moratorium, 14. cash, 15. double entry, 16. 31st March, 1992, 17. money at call, 18. money at short notice, 19. Treasury Bills, 20. Other assets, 21. 42, 22. fire, 23, fixed, 24. memorandum, 25. average, 26. abnormal, 27. loss of profit, 28. indemnity, 29. comprehensive, 30. co-insurer, 31. investment, 32. includes, 33. excludes, 34. added, 35. deducted, 36. less, 37. FIFO, 38. deducted, 39. face value, 40. real, 41. branch, 42. profit, 43. home, 44. dependent, 45. autonomy, 46. debtors, 47. adjusted, 48. rate of commission, 49. high 50. shortage or surplus, 51. credited, 52. branch profit and loss, 53. stock reserve, 54. closing stock, 55. goods in transit, 56. debtors, 57. adjustment, 58. department, 59, manual, 60. computerised, 61. departmental transfer analysis sheet, 62. profitability, 63. general profit and loss, 64. purchases, 65. receiving, 66. infant, 67. agricultural, 68. procurements, 69. double entry, 70. cash, 71. accounting, 72. personal, 73. quasi, 74. single, 75. management, 76. management, 77. external, 78. management, 79. double, 80. management, 81. financial, 82. efficiency, 83. interpretation. 84, decision-making, 85. financial statement analysis, 86. external, 87. horizontal, 88. vertical, 89. index, 90. ratio, 91. index, 92. liquidity, 93. activity, 94. solvency, 95. 1 : 1, 96. good, 97. operating, 98. net sales, 99. liquidity, 100. higher, 101. 1977, 102. Institute of Chartered Accountants of India (ICAI), 103. harmonise, 104. accounting standards, 105. accountants and auditors, 106. AS-3, 107. Cash flow statement, 108. cash flow, 109. contractors, 110. research and development, 111. participation, 112. refundable, 113. employers, 114. 2006, 115. 15, 116. 50, 117. segment, 118. operating, 119. lessee, 120 earnings per share, 121. market, 122. fair,     123. 21, 124. income, 125. 23, 126. discontinuing, 127. 9, 128. more, 129. decrease, 130. higher, 131. carrying, 132. presentation, 133. 18, 134. AS-32.

# BIBLIOGRAPHY


1. Shukla and Grewal : Advanced Accounts

   (S. Chand & Co. Ltd., New Delhi)

2. Jain and Narang : Advanced Accounts

   (Kalyani Publishers)

3. D. S. Rawat : Students Guide to Accounting Standards

   (Taxmann, New Delhi)

4. Sanjeev Singhal : Accounting Standards

   (Bharat Law House, New Delhi)

5. Dr. S. N. Maheshwari : Corporate Accounting

   (Vikas Publishing House Pvt. Ltd., New Delhi)

6. S. K. Paul : Accounting – Volume I and II

   (New Central Book Agency, Kolkata)

7. Dr. S. N. Maheshwari : Principles of Management Accounting.

8. Ravi Kishor : Advanced Management Accounting

   (Taxmann, New Delhi)

9. Dr. Ashok Sehgal & Dr. Deepak Sehgal : Advanced Accounting

   (Taxmann, New Delhi)

10. Guidance Notes issued by ICAI.


*******

# April 2016

**Time: 3 Hours**                                                  **Max. Marks: 80**

**Instructions to the candidates:**

1.    All questions are compulsory.

2.    Figures to the right indicate full marks.

3.    Use of calculator is allowed.

**Q. 1 (a) Answer in one sentence only (Any Five) :**                      **[10]**

(i)    Accounting standard 3 stands for what?

(ii)   What are insured Standing Charges'?

(iii)  What are Non-Performing Assets'?

(iv)   What do you mean by TDS?

(v)    What is single entry system'?

(vi)   Which ratio indicates short term Solvency of the business enterprise?

(vii)  Why goods are invoiced to branch at the selling Price/Invoice Price?

**(b)   Write Short Notes on (Any Two)**                                    **[14]**

(i)    Service Tax

(ii)   AS - 15 Employee-Benefits

(iii)  Core - Banking - System

(iv)   VAT

(v)    Debt Equity Ratio

**Q. 2** Following is the Trial Balance of Rupee Bank Ltd. as on 31ˢᵗ March, 2015.       **[14]**

### Trial Balance

| Particulars | Debit ₹ | Credit ₹ |
|---|---|---|
| Fixed Deposit Accounts | – | 4,00,000 |
| Current Deposits | – | 6,30,000 |
| Savings Deposit Accounts | – | 3,10,000 |
| Share Capital : 5000 Equity Shares of ₹ 100 each | – | 5,00,000 |
| Share Premium Account | – | 10,000 |
| Investments at cost | 2,35,000 | – |
| Interim Dividend Paid | 18,000 | – |
| Dividend Equalisation Reserve | – | 32,000 |
| Profit and Loss Account (1/4/2014) | – | 40,000 |
| Statutory Reserve | – | 40,000 |

| | | |
|---|---:|---:|
| Investment Fluctuation Fund | – | 70,000 |
| Premises Less Depreciation | 4,04,000 | – |
| Furniture Less Depreciation | 40,000 | – |
| Depreciation on Banking Assets | 40,000 | – |
| Interest Paid | 75,000 | – |
| Interest and Discount Received | – | 2,40,000 |
| Director's Fees | 7,000 | – |
| Balance with RBI | 3,10,000 | – |
| Cash in Hand | 3,40,000 | – |
| Stationery and Printing | 12,000 | – |
| Rent, Taxes and insurance | 4,800 | – |
| Salaries | 72,000 | – |
| Unexpired Discount | – | 4,000 |
| Legal Expenses | 3,900 | – |
| Deposits with Other Banks | 2,05,000 | – |
| Bills Discounted and Purchased | 54,000 | – |
| Bills Receivable being bills for collections | 1,77,000 | 1,77,000 |
| Owing by Foreign Correspondents | 21,000 | – |
| Borrowings from other Banks | – | 61,000 |
| Commission and Exchange | – | 1,42,000 |
| Loans, Cash Credit and Overdraft | 6,37,300 | – |
| **Total** | **26,56,000** | **26,56,000** |

Prepare Profit and Loss Account for the year ended 31st March 2015 and the Balance sheet as on that date after considering the following adjustments.

(i) Interim dividend was declared at 4% actual.

(ii) Transfer ₹ 8,000 to Dividend Equalisation Reserve.

(iii) Audit charges are outstanding to the extent of ₹ 5,000.

(iv) Provide ₹ 38,000 for taxation. Reserve and ₹ 32,000 for doubtful. Debts.

(v) The Bank has accepted on behalf of the customers bills worth ₹1,00,000 against the securities of ₹ 1,80,000 lodged with the bank.

(vi) The directors decided to show the investments at market value of ₹ 1,90,000.

(vii) Interest on doubtful debts ₹ 7,500 is included in Interest and Discount Received Account.

**OR**

From the following Trial Balance of Urban Vikas credit co-operative society Ltd. Pune prepare Profit and Loss Account for the year ended 31st March 2015 and Balance Sheet as on that date.

### Trial Balance as on 31.3.2015

| Particulars | Debit ₹ | Credit ₹ |
|---|---:|---:|
| Salaries and Honorarium | 79,600 | |
| Interest on deposits and Loans | 3,32,000 | |
| Postage | 1,000 | |
| Printing and Stationery | 7,200 | |
| Office Expenses | 7,500 | |
| Office Rent | 6,300 | |
| Travelling Expenses | 7,600 | |
| Meeting Expenses | 1,600 | |
| Telephone Charges | 4,000 | |
| Audit fees | 1,000 | |
| Advertisements | 1,400 | |
| Commission | 120 | |
| Donation | 200 | |
| Legal Charges | 3,000 | |
| Insurance | 1,600 | |
| Motor Tax | 2,200 | |
| Sundry Expenses | 1,400 | |
| Share Capital | – | 10,00,000 |
| Interest Received | – | 5,80,900 |
| Commission Received | – | 900 |
| Dividend Received | – | 8,700 |
| Reserve Fund | – | 71,000 |
| Dividend Equalisation Reserve | – | 6,000 |
| Deposits : | | |
| Fixed | – | 9,16,000 |
| Savings | – | 1,30,000 |
| Loans and Overdrafts | – | 16,00,000 |
| Development Fund | – | 29,000 |
| Cash in Hand | 16,000 | – |
| Cash at Bank | 2,91,000 | |
| Dividend Paid | 40,000 | |
| P.D.C.C. Bank Shares | 2,00,000 | |
| Loans | 32,60,000 | – |
| Motor Car | 1,15,000 | – |
| Stock of Stationery | 30,000 | – |
| Profit for the year 2013-2014 | – | 67,220 |
| **Total** | **44,09,720** | **44,09,720** |

**Additional information:**

(a) Provide depreciation on Motor Car ₹ 16,000

(b) Outstanding expenses were - Electricity charges ₹ 300, Office Rent ₹ 500.

(c) Prepaid Insurance amounted to ₹ 200.

(d) Outstanding interest on Loans to members ₹ 5000.

(e) Dividend at 5% was declared on Share Capital of R. 9,00,000 as on 31/03/2014.

(f) Transfer 25% of the profit of 2013-14 to Reserve Fund.

**Q. 3 (a)** A fire occurred in the premises of M/S Nagarwala on 15th October 2014. From the following particulars ascertain the loss of stock and prepare a claim for insurance. **[8]**

| Particulars | ₹ |
|---|---|
| Stock on 1. L2013 | 30,600 |
| Purchases From 1.1.2013 to 31.12.2013 | 1,22,000 |
| Sales -from 1.1.2013 to 31.12.2013 | 1,80,000 |
| Stock on 31.12.2013 | 27,000 |
| Purchases from 1.1.2014 to 14.10.2014 | 1,47,000 |
| Sales from 1.1.2014 to 14.10.2014 | 1,50,000 |

The stocks were always valued at 90 per cent of cost. The stock saved was worth ₹ 18,000. The amount of the policy was ₹ 63,000. There was an average clause in the policy.

**(b)** X Ltd. Pune has a branch at Ahmednagar to which goods are supplied at cost plus 20% profit. Prepare Branch Stock Account, Branch Debtors Account, Branch Petty Cash Account, Branch Expenses Account and Branch Adjustment Account in the hooks of X Ltd Head Office for the year 2014-15. **[14]**

| Particulars | ₹ |
|---|---|
| Opening balances as on 1.4.2014 | |
| (i)   Stock of Goods | 42,000 |
| (ii)  Debtor's | 75,600 |
| (iii) Petty Cash | 1,200 |
| Goods invoiced to branch | 2;52,000 |
| Goods returned by branch | 6,000 |
| Cash Turnover | 1,05,000 |
| Sales to Credit Customers | 1,70,400 |
| Surplus in Stock | 23,400 |
| Cash received from Debtors | 1,71,000 |
| Allowances to customers | 1,200 |
| Discount allowed to Branch Debtors | 9,000 |
| Bad Debt Written off | 3,000 |
| Return from customers | 3,000 |
| Advertisement | 6,000 |
| Salaries | 20,000 |
| Rent (Including prepaid for 2015-16 ₹ 800) | 8,000 |
| Cash sent to branch for petty expenses | 2,400 |
| Commission paid | 6,000 |
| Closing balances as on 31/3/2015 | |
| (I)   Debtors | 58,800 |
| (II)  Petty Cash | 600 |

**Q. 4** From the following Profit and Loss Account and Balance sheet of a company,

Calculate following ratios with its significance:                    **[20]**

(i)   Current Ratio                    (ii)   Operating Ratio
(iii) Stock Turnover Ratio             (iv)   Debtors Turnover Ratio
(v)   Liquid Ratio                     (vi)   Gross Profit Ratio
(vii) Net Profit Ratio

### Trading and Profit and Loss Account for the year ended 31st March 2015.

Dr.                                                                              Cr.

| Particulars | ₹ | Particulars | ₹ |
|---|---|---|---|
| To Opening Stock | 10,00,000 | By Sales | 90,00,000 |
| To Purchases | 60,00,000 | By Closing Stock | 12,00,000 |
| To Carriage Inwards | 2,00,000 | | |
| To Gross Profit | 30,00,000 | | |
| | **1,02,00,000** | | **1,02,00,000** |
| To Administrative Expenses | 14,00,000 | By Gross Profit | 30,00,000 |
| To Selling and Distribution | | By Sundry Income | 1,00,000 |
| Expenses | 2,50,000 | | |
| To Non-Operating Expenses | 50,000 | | |
| To Net Profit | 14,00,000 | | |
| | **31,00,000** | | **31,00,000** |

### Balance Sheet as on 31/3/2015

| Liabilities | ₹ | Assets | ₹ |
|---|---|---|---|
| Capital | 20,00,000 | Land and Building | 10,00,000 |
| Reserve and Surplus | 17,00,000 | Plant and Machinery | 12,00,000 |
| Sundry Creditors | 10,00,000 | Stock | 12,00,000 |
| Provision for Tax | 2,00,000 | Debtors | 12,00,000 |
| Bills Payable | 3,00,000 | Cash at Bank | 6,00,000 |
| | **52,00,000** | | **52,00,000** |

### OR

Mr. X maintained his accounts on single entry system. His balances for the year ended 31st March 2014 and 31st March 2015 were as follows.

| Particulars | ₹<br>31/3/2014 | ₹<br>31/3/2015 |
|---|---|---|
| Bills Receivables | 2,000 | 1,200 |
| Stock | 3,950 | 4,400 |
| Creditors | 4,700 | 4,175 |
| Cash | 1,954 | 981 |
| Bills Payable | 1,736 | 2,525 |
| Debtors | 4,680 | 4,178 |
| Furniture | 1,000 | 1,000 |

From his Cash book for the year 2014-2015, following information is available.

| Particulars | ₹ |
|---|---:|
| Wages | 450 |
| Bills Payable | 11,500 |
| Bills Receivable | 2,150 |
| Miscellaneous Expenses | 350 |
| Salary | 400 |
| Investment Purchased | 500 |
| Sales | 600 |
| Purchases | 300 |
| Received from Debtors | 1,225 |
| Paid 'to Creditors | 712 |
| Miscellaneous Income | 15 |
| Drawings | 750 |

On enquiry you are told that in 2014-2015.

(i)    Discount Allowed ₹ 200.

(ii)    Discount Received ₹ 178.

(iii)    Bills Payable Issued ₹ 2,290.

(iv)    Bills Receivable Received ₹ 1,500.

(v)    Bad Debts written off ₹ 280.

(vi)    Bills Receivable dishonoured ₹ 150.

You are required to prepare Trading Account, Profit and. Loss Account for the year ended 31st March 2015 and the Balance sheet as on that date.

*******

# April 2017

Max. Marks: 80

**Time: 3 Hours**

**Instructions to the candidates:**

1. All questions are compulsory.
2. Figures to the right indicate full marks.
3. Use of calculator is allowed.

**Q. 1 (a) Answer in one sentence only (any five) :** [10]

    (i) What is the other name for unexpired discount?

    (ii) What is indemnity period?

    (iii) What does accounting standard 20 stands for?

    (iv) Give the formula to calculate Liquid Ratio.

    (v) Which Act governs the working of banking companies in India?

    (vi) Name any two types of five Insurance Policies.

    (vii) Which transactions are recorded in Branch Account?

**(B) Write short notes on (any two)** [14]

    (i) Accounting standard 7 - construction contracts

    (ii) Core banking solutions

    (iii) Value Added Tax

    (iv) Claim for loss of Fixed Assets

    (v) Features of co-operative societies

**Q. 2** Following is the trial balance of Sadhana Bank Ltd. as on 31st March 2016. You are required to prepare Profit and Loss Account for the year ended 31st March 2016 and Balance Sheet as on that date. [14]

Trial Balance as on 31St March 2016

| Particulars | Debit ₹ | Credit ₹ |
|---|---|---|
| Share Capital | | |
| 30,000 Equity shares of ₹100 each ₹ 50 paid up | | 15,00,000 |
| Profit and Loss Account (1st April 2015) | | 1,22,250 |
| Current Deposits Accounts | | 32,16,500 |
| Fixed Deposits Accounts | | 35,14,000 |
| Savings Bank Accounts | | 16,60,500 |
| Directors fees | 13,950 | |
| Audit fees | 13,200 | |
| Furniture | 1,28,850 | |

| Particulars | Debit ₹ | Credit ₹ |
|---|---|---|
| Interest paid | 6,00,600 | |
| Interest and Discount | | 10,56,000 |
| Commission and Exchange | | 3,04,500 |
| 6% Govt. Bonds | 15,60,000 | |
| Shares in companies | 12,00,000 | |
| Branch Adjustment Account | 3,06,000 | |
| Postage and printing | 10,350 | |
| Premises | 25,54,500 | |
| Salaries | 1,00,500 | |
| Law Charges | 7,950 | |
| Provident Fund Contribution | 16,800 | |
| Cash in Hand | 3,10,500 | |
| Bills purchased and discounted | 1,00,500 | |
| Unexpired Insurance | 4,050 | |
| Statutory Reserve Fund | | 1,27,500 |
| Loans, Cash credit and Overdrafts | 45,73,500 | |
| | **1,15,01,250** | **1,15,01,250** |

Following additional information:

(a)    Rebate on bills discounted amounted to ₹ 10,650/-

(b)    Provide ₹ 57,750 for doubtful debts.

(c)    The bank has accepted bills worth ₹ 3,75,000 on behalf of the customers against the securities of ₹ 4,65,000 lodged with the bank.

(d)    Provide depreciation on premises ₹ 1,09,500 and on furniture ₹ 8,850.

(e)    Provide for Taxation ₹ 11,250.

**OR**

Following is the trial balance of Gauri consumer's co-operative society ltd. For the year ended 31st March 2015: Prepare trading and profit and loss account for the year ended 31st March 2015 and Balance sheet as on that date.

| Particulars | Debit ₹ | Credit ₹ |
|---|---|---|
| Opening stock of Goods | 12,000 | |
| Purchases | 3,27,000 | |
| Carriage Inward | 4,000 | |

| Particulars | Debit ₹ | Credit ₹ |
|---|---:|---:|
| Sales | | 3,44,000 |
| Sale of Empty bags | | 14,000 |
| Return outward | | 5,000 |
| Salaries | 12,000 | |
| Interest on Govt. Loan | 720 | |
| General expenses | 150 | |
| Printing and Stationery | 1,420 | |
| Cash in hand | 4,840 | |
| Cash at Bank | 6,000 | |
| National Saving Certificate | 500 | |
| Electricity | 320 | |
| Advances | 850 | |
| Debtors | 5,600 | |
| Dead stock | 800 | |
| Reserve fund | | 10,000 |
| Government Loans | | 6,000 |
| Educational fund | | 1,000 |
| Building | 60,000 | |
| Share capital | | 50,000 |
| Creditors | | 6,200 |
| | **4,36,200** | **4,36,200** |

**Adjustments:**

(1) Closing stock was valued at ₹ 18,000.

(2) Audit fees payable ₹ 500.

(3) Charge depreciation @10% on dead stock and 5% on building.

(4) Make provision for bad debts ₹ 200.

(5) Authorised capital is ₹ 1,00,000 divided into shares of ₹20 each.

**Q. 3 (a)** From the following particulars, ascertain the claim to be lodged in respect of the consequential loss policy: **[8]**

(i) Fire occured on April 01, 2015 and affected sales for 3 months.

(ii) Sales for 3 months ending 30th June 2014 and 30th June 2015 were ₹ 3,00,000 and ₹ 1,00,000 respectively.

(iii) The policy was for ₹ 9,00,000 with a six months period of indemnity.

(iv)   Sales for 12 months ended 31st March 2015 were ₹ 38,00,000.

(v)   Accounts are prepared on 31st December. The net profit for 2014 amounted to ₹ 5,00,000 after debiting standing charges of ₹ 2,20,000 (all insured). Sales for 2014 were ₹ 36,00,000.

(vi)   A sum of ₹ 7,000 was spent as additional expenses to mitigate the effect of the loss.

**(b)**   M/s. Gajanan Traders, Pune has a branch at Nashik. The goods are invoiced to the branch so as to show a profit of 30% on Invoice price, under the strict instructions of selling goods only at invoice price.

Following are the particulars relating to the branch.      [14]

| Particulars | ₹ |
|---|---|
| Stock on 01-01-2016 (Invoice Price) | 12,000 |
| Debtors on 01-01-2016 | 6,200 |
| Goods sent to Branch (at Invoice Price) during the year 35,000 | 35,000 |
| Goods returned by the branch (at invoice price) | 1,000 |
| Credit sales made during the year | 21,000 |
| Cash sales made during the year | 20,000 |
| Goods returned by customers | 600 |
| Cash from debtors | 19,000 |
| Discount allowed to debtors | 300 |
| Allowances made to debtors | 200 |
| Bad debts in the year | 600 |
| Cheques sent to branch for: | |
|     Salaries       3,300 | |
|     Rent and Rates       2,000 | 5,300 |
| Shortage of Goods at the branch | 400 |

Ascertain the profit or loss made by the branch by preparing:

(1)   Branch Stock A/c        (2)   Branch Debtors A/c

(3)   Branch Expenses A/c       (4)   Branch Adjustment A/c

**Q. 4** Mr. Joshi Keeps his books on single entry system. The summary of assets and liabilities is as follows:

| Assets and Liabilities | As on 01/04/2015 | As on 31/03/2016 |
|---|---|---|
| Cash at Bank | – | 1,700 |
| Bank overdraft | 6,000 | – |
| Bills receivable | 20,000 | 21,000 |
| Creditors | 15,000 | 12,500 |

| Assets and Liabilities | As on 01/04/2015 | As on 31/03/2016 |
|---|---|---|
| Stock-in-trade | 4,500 | 6,000 |
| Bills payable | 16,500 | 14,500 |
| Debtors | 24,000 | 27,000 |
| Plant and Machinery | 30,000 | 30,000 |
| Furniture and Fixtures | 6,000 | 8,000 |

The Summary of cash transactions is as follows:

**Dr.**        **Cash book for the year ended 31/3/2016**        **Cr.**

| Receipts | ₹ | Payment | ₹ |
|---|---|---|---|
| To Debtors | 68,000 | By Balance b/d | 6,000 |
| To Commission | 1,400 | (Bank Overdraft) | |
| To Sales | 23,000 | By Creditors | 40,000 |
| To Bills Receivable | 7,800 | By Purchases | 16,000 |
| | | By Bank Interest | 500 |
| | | By Wages | 6,000 |
| | | By Salary | 2,000 |
| | | By Insurance | 2,500 |
| | | By Miscellaneous Expenses | 2,000 |
| | | By Carriage outward | 500 |
| | | By Rent | 1,000 |
| | | By Joshi's Drawings | 4,000 |
| | | By Carriage Inward | 4,000 |
| | | By Furniture and Fixtures | 2,000 |
| | | By Bills Payable | 12,000 |
| | | By balance c/d | 1,700 |
| | **1,00,200** | | **1,00,200** |

The other adjustments are as follows:

(1) Goods distributed as free samples for advertisement purposes amounted to ₹ 1,500.

(2) Of Sundry Debtors ₹ 400 were to be written off as provision for R.D.D.

(3) Interest on capital is to be allowed @5% p.a.

(4) Provide depreciation on plant and Machinery @5% and on furniture and fixtures @ 10% on opening balance.

(5) Discount allowed to debtors amounted to ₹300 whereas discount received from creditors was ₹ 300.

Prepare Trading Account and Profit and Loss Account for the year ended 31st March 2016 and Balance Sheet as on that date. **[20]**

**OR**

Ajinkya Ltd. provides the following information. Balance Sheet as on 31st December 2014

| Liabilities | ₹ | Assets | | ₹ |
|---|---|---|---|---|
| Equity Share Capital | 15,00,000 | Plant and Machinery | | 9,60,000 |
| Retained Earning | 5,52,000 | Land and Building | | 1,38,000 |
| Sundry Creditors | 1,56,000 | Cash | | 1,00,000 |
| Bills Payable | 3,00,000 | Sundry Debtors | 5,40,000 | |
| Other Current Liabilities | | (−) R.D.D. | 60,000 | 4,80,000 |
| Prepaid Expenses | 30,000 | Stock | | 7,20,000 |
| | | Prepaid Expenses | | 1,40,000 |
| | **25,38,000** | | | **25,38,000** |

Statement of profit for the year ended 31st December 2014.

| Particulars | ₹ |
|---|---|
| Sales | 60,00,000 |
| Less: Cost of goods sold | 46,20,000 |
| Gross Profit | 13,80,000 |
| Less: Operating Expenses | 10,20,000 |
| Net profit before tax | 3,60,000 |
| Less: Taxes @50% | 1,80,000 |
| Net Profit after Tax | 1,80,000 |

Sundry debtors and stock at the beginning of the year were ₹ 4,50,000 and ₹ 6,00,000 respectively. Calculate the following ratios and state their significance

(1)   Current Ratio            (2)   Acid-Test Ratio

(3)   Stock Turnover Ratio      (4)   Debtors Turnover Ratio

(5)   Gross Profit Ratio        (6)   Net Profit Ratio (after tax)

(7)   Operating Ratio

**✱✱✱**